KANE AND ABEL

'With KANE AND ABEL, Jeffrey Archer ranks in the top ten storytellers in the world'
Los Angeles Times

'A novel of outstanding power'
Evening News

'One of the most compelling novels of the season'
The Bookseller

'Jeffrey Archer is a storyteller in the class and style of Alexander Dumas'
Washington Post

'Archer is bang on target with this latest shot from his quiver. A good read with a twist in the tail that is moving indeed'
Daily Express

'A blockbuster . . . a big bestseller'
Publishers Weekly

KANE AND ABEL

'This is bestseller material, highly enjoyable and immensely readable . . . Jeffrey Archer deserves to attract many new readers'
Book Buyer

'I defy anyone not to enjoy this book which is one of the best novels I have ever read'
Otto Preminger

'Archer has a gift for a plot that can only be described as genius, and with KANE AND ABEL he is destined to join the Bible, Shakespeare, and Harold Robbins as one of the world's supersellers. This book of the month is destined to become the book of the year'
Now!

'Jeffrey Archer has a great gift for storytelling'
Susan Howatch

'Britain's number one storyteller does it again, a book that will rank alongside GONE WITH THE WIND and THE FORSYTE SAGA
Radio 2, Pete Murray

KANE AND ABEL

'KANE AND ABEL is by any standards a classic, taut, moving and rich in dialogue and descriptive power. Archer tells a tremendous story in masterly fashion, establishing himself as one of the great writers of modern times. For my money this has to be the novel of the decade'
Wolverhampton Express and Star

'The kind of book Galsworthy would have written'
Yorkshire Post

'Rattling good entertainment, full of humour and not a little sadness'
The Birmingham Post

'This book was of such compelling attraction that I read it from cover to cover in one session and I think it only fair to warn you not to read the first five pages if you've planned anything else for the weekend. It is in every sense a triumphant work of fiction, and if the Nobel Prize was awarded for storytelling, Archer could go and collect his for KANE AND ABEL'
Newcastle Evening Chronicle

KANE AND ABEL

'Archer is arguably the greatest storyteller of our age.
With KANE AND ABEL he has given us a book that will
surely survive the test of time'
Manchester Evening News

'A gripping saga of the life and times of America through
much of this century that is a quite marvellous piece of
storytelling'
Bristol Evening Post

'KANE AND ABEL marks Archer's coming of age as a
writer. It is a marvellous story, skilfully told with brilliant
clarity. And true to form, Archer keeps the real teaser until
the last few pages of this long and enormously enjoyable
book'
Grimsby Evening Telegraph

'Archer's done it again, a memorable book that puts him
into the top league of novelists'
Sheffield Star

'KANE AND ABEL is a book to be read in one sitting.
Make a free 48 hours and thoroughly enjoy yourself.
I was spellbound'
Huddersfield Daily Examiner

KANE AND ABEL

'KANE AND ABEL is a big book, another significant work by a bestselling author. It is bound to be widely read and enthusiastically acclaimed – a tour de force of fiction'
Eastern Daily Express

'Archer has emerged as one of the best storytellers of the seventies, one who grips the reader in a tight fist and doesn't let go until the last page is turned'
Dumfries and Galloway Standard

'A remarkable gift for storytelling, it is one of those rare books that are really hard to put down'
The Hull Daily Mail

'Archer's third book is quite simply magnificent. With KANE AND ABEL he is now a master storyteller'
Middlesbrough Evening Gazette

'Grips the reader from first page to last. A smash hit of the season, it has the magic word "bestseller" written all over it'
John Barkham Reviews

Jeffrey Archer is a master storyteller, the author of six novels which have all been worldwide bestsellers. NOT A PENNY MORE, NOT A PENNY LESS was his first book which achieved instant success. Next came the tense and terrifying thriller SHALL WE TELL THE PRESIDENT? followed by A QUIVER FULL OF ARROWS, a collection of short stories. After this came the triumphant bestseller KANE AND ABEL, and then the superb sequel, THE PRODIGAL DAUGHTER. This was followed by FIRST AMONG EQUALS, the story of four men's battle to control our lives. His latest book is A MATTER OF HONOUR, available now in hardback from Hodder and Stoughton, and in paperback from Coronet in June 1987.

Jeffrey Archer was born in 1940 and educated at Wellington School and Brasenose College, Oxford. He represented Oxford, Somerset, and Great Britain in the 100 metres in the early sixties, and became the youngest member of the House of Commons when he won the by-election at Louth in 1969. He wrote his first novel, NOT A PENNY MORE, NOT A PENNY LESS, in 1974. From September 1985 to October 1986 he was Deputy Chairman of the Conservative Party. Jeffrey Archer is married with two children and lives in London and Cambridge.

KANE AND ABEL

JEFFREY ARCHER

CORONET BOOKS
Hodder and Stoughton

Copyright © 1979 by Jeffrey Archer

First published in Great Britain by Hodder & Stoughton Limited

Coronet edition, September 1980
Reprinted 1980 twice
Reprinted 1981 nine times
Reprinted 1982 six times
Reprinted 1983 five times
Reprinted 1984 four times
Reprinted 1985 five times
Reprinted 1986 twice
This impression June 1987

The characters and situations in this book are entirely imaginary and bear no relation to any real person or actual happening.

This book is sold subject to the condition that it shall not, by way of trade or otherwise, be lent, re-sold, hired out or otherwise circulated without the publisher's prior consent in any form of binding or cover other than that in which it is published and without a similar condition including this condition being imposed on the subsequent purchaser.

No part of this publication may be reproduced or transmitted in any form or by any means, electronically or mechanically, including photocopying, recording or any information storage or retrieval system, without either the prior permission in writing from the publisher or a licence, permitting restricted copying, issued by the Copyright Licensing Agency, 33–34 Alfred Place, London WC1E 7DP.

British Library C.I.P.

Archer, Jeffrey
Kane and Abel
I. Title
823'9'1F   PR6051.R285K/

ISBN 0 340 25733 4

Printed and bound in Great Britain for Hodder and Stoughton Paperbacks, a division of Hodder and Stoughton Ltd., Mill Road, Dunton Green, Sevenoaks, Kent TN13 2YA.
(Editorial Office: 47 Bedford Square, London WC1B 3DP) by Cox & Wyman Ltd., Reading

To Michael and Jane

Acknowledgments

The author would like to thank the two men who made this book possible. They both wish to remain anonymous, one because he is working on his own autobiography and the other because he is still a public figure in the United States.

Book One

1

April 18th, 1906   *Slonim, Poland*

She only stopped screaming when she died. It was then that he started to scream.

The young boy who was hunting rabbits in the forest was not sure whether it had been the woman's last cry or the child's first that alerted him. He turned suddenly, sensing the possible danger, his eyes searching for an animal that was so obviously in pain. He had never known any animal to scream in quite that way before. He edged towards the noise cautiously; the scream had now turned to a whine, but it still did not sound like any animal he knew. He hoped it would be small enough to kill; at least that would make a change from rabbit for dinner.

The young boy moved stealthily towards the river, where the strange noise came from, running from tree to tree, feeling the protection of the bark against his shoulder blades, something to touch. Never stay in the open, his father had taught him. When he reached the edge of the forest, he had a clear line of vision all the way down the valley to the river, and even then it took him some time to realise that the strange cry emanated from no ordinary animal. He continued to creep towards the whining, but he was out in the open on his own now. Then suddenly he saw the woman, with her dress above her waist, her bare legs splayed wide apart. He had never seen a woman like that before. He ran quickly to her side and stared down at her belly, quite frightened to touch. There, lying between the woman's legs, was the body of a small, damp, pink animal. attached by something that looked like rope. The young hunter dropped his freshly skinned rabbits and collapsed on his knees beside the little creature.

He gazed for a long, stunned moment and then turned his eyes towards the woman, immediately regretting the decision. She was already blue with cold; her tired twenty-three-year-old face looked middle-aged to the boy; he did not need to be told that she was dead. He picked up the slippery little body – had you asked him why, and no one ever did, he would have told you that the tiny fingernails clawing the crumpled face had worried him – and then he became aware that mother and child were inseparable because of the slimy rope.

He had watched the birth of a lamb a few days earlier and he tried to remember. Yes, that's what the shepherd had done, but dare he, with a child? The whining had stopped and he sensed that a decision was now urgent. He unsheathed his knife, the one he had skinned the rabbits with, wiped it on his sleeve and hesitating only for a moment, cut the rope close to the child's body. Blood flowed freely from the severed ends. Then what had the shepherd done when the lamb was born? He had tied a knot to stop the blood. Of course, of course; he pulled some grass out of the earth beside him and hastily tied a crude knot in the cord. Then he took the child in his arms. He rose slowly from his knees, leaving behind him three dead rabbits and a dead woman who had given birth to this child. Before finally turning his back on the mother, he put her legs together, and pulled her dress down over her knees. It seemed to be the right thing to do.

'Holy God,' he said aloud, the first thing he always said when he had done something very good or very bad. He wasn't yet sure which this was.

The young hunter then ran towards the cottage where he knew his mother would be cooking supper, waiting only for his rabbits; all else would be prepared. She would be wondering how many he might have caught today; with a family of eight to feed, she needed at least three. Sometimes he managed a duck, a goose or even a pheasant that had strayed from the Baron's estate, on which his father worked. Tonight he had caught a different animal, and when he reached the cottage the young hunter dared not let go of his prize even with one hand, so he kicked at the door with his bare foot until his mother opened it. Silently, he held out his offering to her. She made no immediate move to take the creature from him but stood, one hand on her breast, gazing at the wretched sight.

'Holy God,' she said and crossed herself. The boy stared up at his mother's face for some sign of pleasure or anger. Her eyes were now showing a tenderness that the boy had never seen in them before. He knew then that the thing which he had done must be good.

'Is it a baby, Matka?'

'It's a little boy,' said his mother, nodding her head sorrowfully, 'Where did you find him?'

'Down by the river, Matka,' he said.

'And the mother?'

'Dead.'

She crossed herself again.

'Quickly, run and tell your father what has happened. He will find Urszula Wojnak on the estate and you must take them both to the mother, and then be sure they come back here.'

The young hunter handed over the little boy to his mother, happy enough not to have dropped the slippery creature. Now, free of his quarry, he rubbed his hands on his trousers and ran off to look for his father.

The mother closed the door with her shoulder and called out for her eldest child, a girl, to put the pot on the stove. She sat down on a wooden stool, unbuttoned her bodice and pushed a tired nipple towards the little puckered mouth. Sophia, her youngest daughter, only six months old, would have to go without her supper tonight; come to think of it, so would the whole family.

'And to what purpose?' the woman said out loud, tucking a shawl around her arm and the child together. 'Poor little mite, you'll be dead by morning.'

But she did not repeat those feelings to old Urszula Wojnak when the midwife washed the little body and tended to the twisted umbilical stump late that night. Her husband stood silently by observing the scene.

'When a guest comes into the house, God comes into the house,' declared the woman, quoting the old Polish proverb.

Her husband spat. 'To the cholera with him. We have enough children of our own.'

The woman pretended not to hear him as she stroked the dark, thin hairs on the baby's head.

'What shall we call him?' the woman asked, looking up at her husband.

He shrugged. 'Who cares? Let him go to his grave nameless.'

2

April 18th, 1906 *Boston, Massachusetts*

The doctor picked up the newborn child by the ankles and slapped its bottom. The infant started to cry.

In Boston, Massachusetts, there is a hospital that caters mainly for those who suffer from the diseases of the rich, and on selected occasions allows itself to deliver the new rich. At the Massachusetts General Hospital the mothers don't scream, and certainly they don't give birth fully dressed. It is not the done thing.

A young man was pacing up and down outside the delivery room; inside, two obstetricians and the family doctor were on duty. This father did not believe in taking risks with his first born. The two obstetricians would be paid a large fee merely to stand by and witness events. One of them, who wore evening clothes under his long white coat, had a dinner party to attend later, but he could not afford to absent himself from this particular birth. The three had earlier drawn straws to decide who should deliver the child, and Doctor MacKenzie, the family G.P., had won. A sound, secure name, the father considered, as he paced up and down the corridor. Not that he had any reason to be anxious. Roberts had driven his wife, Anne, to the hospital in the hansom carriage that morning, which she had calculated was the twenty-eighth day of her ninth month. She had started labour soon after breakfast, and he had been assured that delivery would not take place until his bank had closed for the day. The father was a disciplined man and saw no reason why a birth should interrupt his well-ordered life. Nevertheless, he continued to pace. Nurses and young doctors hurried past him, aware of his presence, their voices lowered when they were near him, and raised again only when they were out of his earshot. He didn't notice because everybody had always treated him that way. Most of them had never seen him in person; all of them knew who he was.

If it was a boy, a son, he would probably build the new children's wing that the hospital so badly needed. He had already built a library and a school. The expectant father tried to read the evening paper, looking over the words but not taking in their meaning. He was nervous, even worried. It would never do for them (he looked upon almost everyone as 'them') to realise that it had to be a boy, a boy who would one day take his place as president of the bank. He turned the pages of the *Evening Transcript*. The Boston Red Sox had beaten the New York Highlanders – others would be celebrating. Then he recalled the headline on the front page and returned to it. The worst-ever earthquake in the history of America. Devastation in San Francisco, at least four hundred people dead – others would be mourning. He hated that. That would take away from the birth of his son. People would remember something else had happened on that day. It never occurred to him, not even for a moment, that it might be a girl. He turned to the financial pages and checked the stock market, down sharply; that damned earthquake had taken one hundred thousand dollars off the value of his own holdings in the bank, but as his personal fortune remained comfortably over sixteen million dollars, it was going to take more than a Californian earthquake to move him. He could now live off the interest from his interest, so the sixteen million capital would always remain intact, ready for his son, still unborn. He continued to pace and pretend to read the *Transcript*.

The obstetrician in evening dress pushed through the swing doors of the delivery room to report the news. He felt he must do something for his large unearned fee and he was the most suitably dressed for the announcement. The two men stared at each other for a moment. The doctor also felt a little nervous, but he wasn't going to show it in front of the father.

'Congratulations, sir, you have a son, a fine-looking little boy.'

What silly remarks people make when a child is born, the father thought; how could he be anything but little? The news hadn't yet dawned on him – a son. He almost thanked God. The obstetrician ventured a question to break the silence.

'Have you decided what you will call him?'

The father answered without hesitation. 'William Lowell Kane.'

3

Long after the excitement of the baby's arrival had passed and the rest of the family had gone to bed, the mother remained awake with the little child in her arms. Helena Koskiewicz believed in life, and she had borne nine children to prove it. Although she had lost three in infancy, she had not let any of them go easily.

Now at thirty-five she knew that her once lusty Jasio would give her no more sons or daughters. God had given her this one; surely he was destined to live. Helena's was a simple faith, which was good, for her destiny was never to afford her more than a simple life. She was grey and thin, not through choice but through little food, hard work, and no spare money. It never occurred to her to complain but the lines on her face would have been more in keeping with a grandmother than a mother in today's world. She had never worn new clothes even once in her life.

Helena squeezed her tired breasts so hard that dull red marks appeared around the nipples. Little drops of milk squirted out. At thirty-five, halfway through life's contract, we all have some useful piece of expertise to pass on and Helena Koskiewicz's was now at a premium.

'Matka's littlest one,' she whispered tenderly to the child, and drew the milky teat across its pursed mouth. The blue eyes opened and tiny drops of sweat broke out on the baby's nose as he tried to suck. Finally the mother slumped unwillingly into a deep sleep.

Jasio Koskiewicz, a heavy, dull man with a full moustache, his only gesture of self-assertion in an otherwise servile existence, discovered his wife and the baby asleep in the rocking chair when he rose at five. He hadn't noticed her absence from their bed that night. He stared down at the bastard who had, thank God, at least stopped wailing. Was it dead? Jasio considered the easiest way out of the dilemma was to get himself to work and not interfere with the intruder; let the woman worry about life and death : his preoccupation was to be on the Baron's estate by first light. He took a few long swallows of goat's milk and wiped his luxuriant moustache on his sleeve. Then he grabbed a hunk of bread with one hand and his traps with the other, slipping noiselessly out of the cottage for fear of waking the woman and getting himself involved. He strode away towards the forest, giving no more thought to the little intruder other than to assume that he had seen him for the last time.

Florentyna, the elder daughter, was next to enter the kitchen, just before the old clock, which for many years had kept its own time, claimed that six a.m. had arrived. It was of no more than ancillary assistance to those who wished to know if it was the hour to get up or go to bed. Among Florentyna's daily duties was the preparation of the breakfast, in itself a minor task involving the simple division of a skin of goat's milk and a lump of rye bread among a family of eight. Nevertheless, it required the wisdom of Solomon to carry out the task in such a way that no one complained about another's portion.

Florentyna struck those who saw her for the first time as a pretty, frail, shabby little thing. It was unfair that for the last three years she had had only one dress to wear, but those who could separate their opinion of the child from that of her surroundings understood why Jasio had fallen in love with her mother. Florentyna's long fair hair shone while her hazel eyes sparkled in defiance against the influence of her birth and diet.

She tiptoed up to the rocking chair and stared down at her mother and the little boy whom she had adored at first sight. She had never in her eight years owned a doll. Actually she had only seen one once, when the family had been invited to a celebration of the feast of St. Nicholas at the Baron's castle. Even then she had not actually touched the beautiful object, but now she felt an inexplicable urge to hold this baby in her arms. She bent down and eased the child away from her mother and, staring down into the little blue eyes – such blue eyes – she began to hum. The change of temperature from the warmth of the mother's breast to the cold of the little girl's hands made the baby indignant. He immediately started crying which woke the mother, whose only reaction was of guilt for ever having fallen asleep.

'Holy God, he's still alive,' she said to Florentyna. 'You prepare breakfast for the boys while I try to feed him again.'

Florentyna reluctantly handed the infant back and watched her mother once again pump her aching breasts. The little girl was mesmerised.

'Hurry up, Florcia,' chided her mother, 'the rest of the family must eat as well.'

Florentyna obeyed, and as her brothers arrived from the loft where they all slept, they kissed their mother's hands in greeting and stared at the newcomer in awe. All they knew was that this one had not come from Mother's stomach. Florentyna was too excited to eat her breakfast that morning, so the boys divided her portion among them without a second thought and left their mother's share on the table. No one noticed, as they went about their daily tasks, that their mother hadn't eaten anything since the baby's arrival.

Helena Koskiewicz was pleased that her children had learned so early in life to fend for themselves. They could feed the animals, milk the goats and cows, tend the vegetable garden, and go about their daily tasks without her help or prodding. When Jasio returned home in the evening she suddenly realised that she had not prepared supper for him, but that Florentyna had taken the rabbits from Franck, her brother the hunter, and had already started to cook them. Florentyna was proud to be in charge of the evening meal, a responsibility she was entrusted with only when her mother was unwell, and Helena Koskiewicz rarely allowed herself that luxury. The young hunter had brought home four rabbits and the father six mushrooms and three potatoes: tonight would be a veritable feast.

After dinner, Jasio Koskiewicz sat in his chair by the fire and studied the child properly for the first time. Holding the little baby under the armpits, with his two thumbs supporting the helpless neck, he cast a trapper's eye over the infant. Wrinkled and toothless, the face was redeemed only by the fine, blue, unfocusing eyes. Directing his gaze towards the thin body, something immediately attracted his attention. He scowled and rubbed the delicate chest with his thumbs.

'Have you noticed this, Helena?' said the trapper prodding the baby's ribs. 'The ugly little bastard has only one nipple.'

His wife frowned as she in turn rubbed the skin with her thumb, as though the action would supply the missing organ. Her husband was right: the minute and colourless left nipple was there, but where its mirror image should have appeared on the right-hand side the shallow breast was completely smooth and uniformly pink.

The woman's superstitious tendencies were immediately aroused. 'He has been given to me by God,' she exclaimed. 'See His mark upon him.'

The man thrust the child angrily at her. 'You're a fool, Helena. The child was given to its mother by a man with bad blood.' He spat into the fire, the more precisely to express his opinion of the child's parentage. 'Anyway, I wouldn't bet a potato on the little bastard's survival.'

Jasio Koskiewicz cared even less than a potato that the child should survive. He was not by nature a callous man but the boy was not his, and one more mouth to feed could only compound his problems. But if it was so to be, it was not for him to question the Almighty, and with no more thought of the boy, he fell into a deep sleep by the fire.

As the days passed by, even Jasio Koskiewicz began to believe the child might survive and, had he been a betting man, he would have lost a potato. The eldest son, the hunter, with the help of his younger brothers, made the child a cot out of wood which they had collected from the Baron's forest. Florentyna made his clothes by cutting little pieces off her own dresses and then sewing them together. They would have called him Harlequin if they had known what it meant. In truth, naming him caused more disagreement in the household than any other single problem had done for months; only the father had no opinion to offer. Finally, they agreed on Wladek; the following Sunday, in the chapel on the Baron's great estate, the child was christened Wladek Koskiewicz, the mother thanking God for sparing his life, the father resigning himself to whatever must be.

That evening there was a small feast to celebrate the christening, augmented by the gift of a goose from the Baron's estate. They all ate heartily.

From that day on, Florentyna learned to divide by nine.

4

Anne Kane had slept peacefully through the night. When her son William returned after breakfast in the arms of one of the hospital's nurses, she could not wait to hold him again.

'Now then, Mrs. Kane,' said the white-uniformed nurse briskly, 'shall we give baby his breakfast too?'

She sat Anne, who was abruptly aware of her swollen breasts, up in bed and guided the two novices through the procedure. Anne, conscious that to appear embarrassed would be considered unmaternal, gazed fixedly into William's blue eyes, more blue even than his father's, and assimilated her new position, with which it would have been illogical to be other than pleased. At twenty-one, she was not conscious that she lacked anything. Born a Cabot, married into a branch of the Lowell family, and now a first born son to carry on the tradition summarised so succinctly in the card sent to her by an old school friend:

> Here's to the city of Boston,
> Land of the bean and the cod,
> Where Cabots talk only to Lowells,
> And Lowells talk only to God.

Anne spent half an hour talking to William but obtained little response. He was then retired for a sleep in the same manner by which he had arrived. Anne nobly resisted the fruit and candy piled by her bedside. She was determined to get back into all her dresses by the summer season and reassume her rightful place in all the fashionable magazines. Had not the Prince de Garonne said that she was the only beautiful object in Boston? Her long golden hair, fine delicate features, and slim figure had attracted excited admiration in cities she had never even visited. She checked in the mirror: no telltale lines on her face; people would hardly believe that she was the mother of a bouncing boy. Thank God it had been a bouncing boy, thought Anne.

She enjoyed a light lunch and prepared herself for the visitors who would appear during the afternoon, already screened by her private secretary. Those allowed to see her on the first days had to be family or from the very best families; others would be told she was not yet ready to receive them. But as Boston was the last city remaining in America where each knew their place to the finest degree of social prominence, there was unlikely to be any unexpected intruder.

The room which she alone occupied could have easily taken another five beds had it not already been smothered in flowers. A casual passer-by could have been forgiven for mistaking it for a minor horticultural show, if it had not been for the presence of the young mother sitting upright in bed. Anne switched on the electric light, still a novelty for her; Richard and she had waited for the Cabots to have them fitted, which all of Boston had interpreted as an oracular sign that electromagnetic induction was as of that moment socially acceptable.

The first visitor was Anne's mother-in-law, Mrs. Thomas Lowell Kane, the head of the family since her husband had died the previous year. In elegant late middle-age, she had perfected the technique of sweeping into a room to her own total satisfaction and to its occupants' undoubted discomfiture. She wore a long chemise dress, which made it impossible to view her ankles; the only man who had ever seen her ankles was now dead. She had always been lean. In her opinion, fat women meant bad food and even worse breeding. She was now the oldest Lowell alive; the oldest Kane, come to that. She therefore expected and was expected to be the first to arrive to view her new grandson. After all, had it not been she who had arranged the meeting between Anne and Richard? Love had seemed of little consequence to Mrs. Kane. Wealth, position and prestige she could always come to terms with. Love was all very well, but it rarely proved to be a lasting commodity; the other three were. She kissed her daughter-in-law approvingly on the forehead. Anne touched a button on the wall, and a quiet buzz could be heard. The noise took Mrs. Kane by surprise; she could not believe electricity would ever catch on. The nurse reappeared with the heir. Mrs. Kane inspected him, sniffed her satisfaction and waved him away.

'Well done, Anne,' the old lady said, as if her daughter-in-law had won a minor gymkhana prize. 'All of us are very proud of you.'

Anne's own mother, Mrs. Edward Cabot, arrived a few minutes later. She, like Mrs. Kane, had been widowed within recent years and differed so little from her in appearance that those who observed them only from afar tended to get them muddled up. But to do her justice, she took considerably more interest in her new grandson and in her daughter. The inspection moved to the flowers.

'How kind of the Jacksons to remember,' murmured Mrs. Cabot.

Mrs. Kane adopted a more cursory procedure. Her eyes skimmed over the delicate blooms then settled on the donors' cards. She whispered the soothing names to herself: Adamses, Lawrences, Lodges, Higginsons. Neither grandmother commented on the names they didn't know; they were both past the age of wanting to learn of anything or anyone new. They left together, well pleased: an heir had been born and appeared, on first sight, to be adequate. They both considered that their final family obligation had been successfully, albeit vicariously, performed and that they themselves might now progress to the role of chorus.

They were both wrong.

Anne and Richard's close friends poured in during the afternoon with gifts and good wishes, the former of gold or silver, the latter in high-pitched Brahmin accents.

When her husband arrived after the close of business, Anne was somewhat overtired. Richard had drunk champagne at lunch for the first time in his life – old Amos Kerbes had insisted and, with the whole Somerset Club looking on, Richard could hardly have refused. He seemed to his wife to be a little less stiff than usual. Solid in his long black frock coat and pinstripe trousers, he stood fully six feet one; his dark hair with its centre parting gleamed in the light of the large electric bulb. Few would have guessed his age correctly as only thirty-three : youth had never been important to him; substance was the only thing that mattered. Once again William Lowell Kane was called for and inspected, as if the father were checking the balance at the end of the banking day. All seemed to be in order. The boy had two legs, two arms, ten fingers, ten toes and Richard could see nothing that might later embarrass him, so William was sent away.

'I wired the headmaster of St. Paul's last night. William has been admitted for September, 1918.'

Anne said nothing. Richard had so obviously started planning William's career.

'Well, my dear, are you fully recovered today?' he went on to inquire, never having spent a day in hospital during his thirty-three years.

'Yes – no – I think so,' responded his wife timidly, suppressing a rising tearfulness that she knew would only displease her husband. The answer was not of the sort that Richard could hope to understand. He kissed his wife on the cheek and returned in the hansom carriage to the Red House on Louisburg Square, their family home. With staff, servants, the new baby and his nurse, there would now be nine mouths to feed. Richard did not give the problem a second thought.

William Lowell Kane received the Church's blessing and the names his father had apportioned him before birth at the Protestant Episcopal Church of St. Paul's, in the presence of everybody in Boston who mattered and a few who didn't. Ancient Bishop Lawrence officiated, J. P. Morgan and Alan Lloyd, bankers of impeccable standing, along with Milly Preston, Anne's closest friend, were the chosen godparents. His Grace sprinkled the Holy Water on William's head; the boy didn't murmur. He was already learning the Brahmin approach to life. Anne thanked God for the safe birth of her son and Richard thanked God, whom he regarded as an external bookkeeper whose function was to record the deeds of the Kane family from generation to generation, that he had a son to whom he could leave his fortune. Still, he thought, perhaps he had better be certain and have a second boy. From his kneeling position he glanced sideways at his wife, well pleased with her.

Book Two

5

Wladek Koskiewicz grew slowly. It became apparent to his foster mother that the boy's health would always be a problem. He caught all the illnesses and diseases that growing children normally catch and many that they don't, and he passed them on indiscriminately to the rest of the Koskiewicz family. Helena treated him as any other of her brood and always vigorously defended him when Jasio began to blame the devil rather than God for Wladek's presence in their tiny cottage. Florentyna, on the other hand, took care of Wladek as if he were her own child. She loved him from the first moment she had set eyes on him with an intensity that grew from a fear that no one would ever want to marry her, the penniless daughter of a trapper. She must, therefore, be childless. Wladek was her child.

The eldest brother, the hunter, who had found Wladek, treated him like a plaything but was too afraid of his father to admit that he liked the frail infant who was growing into a sturdy toddler. In any case, next January the hunter was to leave school and start work on the Baron's estate, and children were a woman's problem, so his father had told him. The three younger brothers, Stefan, Josef and Jan, showed little interest in Wladek and the remaining member of the family, Sophia, was happy enough just to cuddle him.

What neither parent had been prepared for was a character and mind so different from those of their own children. No one could dismiss the physical or intellectual difference. The Koskiewiczes were all tall, large-boned with fair hair and grey eyes. Wladek was short and round, with dark hair and intensely blue eyes. The Koskiewiczes had minimal pretensions to scholarship and were removed from the village school as soon as age or discretion allowed. Wladek, on the other hand, though he was late in walking, spoke at eighteen months. Read at three, but was still unable to dress himself. Wrote at five, but continued to wet his bed. He became the despair of his father and the pride of his mother. His first four years on this earth were memorable only as a continual physical attempt through illness to try to depart from it, and for the sustained efforts of Helena and Florentyna to insure that he did not succeed. He ran around the little wooden cottage barefoot, dressed in his harlequin outfit, a yard or so behind his mother. When Florentyna returned from school, he would transfer his allegiance, never leaving her side until she put him to bed. In her division of the food by nine, Florentyna often sacrificed half of her own share to Wladek or, if he were ill, the entire portion. Wladek wore the clothes she made for him, sang the songs she taught him and shared with her the few toys and presents she had been given.

Because Florentyna was away at school most of the day, Wladek wanted from a young age to go with her. As soon as he was allowed to (holding firmly on to Florentyna's hand until they reached the village school), he walked the eighteen wiorsta, some nine miles, through the woods of moss-covered birches and cypresses and the orchards of lime and cherry to Slonim to begin his education.

Wladek liked school from the first day; it was an escape from the tiny cottage which had until then been his whole world. School also confronted him for the first time in life with the savage implications of the Russian occupation of eastern Poland. He learned that his native Polish was to be spoken only in the privacy of the cottage and that while at school, only Russian was to be used. He sensed in the other children around him a fierce pride in the oppressed mother tongue and culture. He, too, felt that same pride. To his surprise, Wladek found that he was not belittled by Mr. Kotowski, his schoolteacher, the way he was at home by his father. Although still the youngest, as at home, it was not long before he rose above all his classmates in everything except height. His tiny stature misled them into continual underestimation of his real abilities: children always imagine biggest is best. By the age of five, Wladek was first in every subject taken by his class except ironwork.

At night, back at the little wooden cottage, while the other children would tend the violets and poplars that bloomed so fragrantly in their spring-time garden, pick berries, chop wood, catch rabbits or make dresses, Wladek read and read, until he was reading the unopened books of his eldest brother and then those of his elder sister. It began to dawn slowly on Helena Koskiewicz that she had taken on more than she had bargained for when the young hunter had brought home the little animal in place of three rabbits; already Wladek was asking questions she could not answer. She knew soon that she would be quite unable to cope, and she wasn't sure what to do about it. She had an unswerving belief in destiny and so was not surprised when the decision was taken out of her hands.

One evening in the autumn of 1911 came the first turning point in Wladek's life. The family had all finished their plain supper of beetroot soup and meatballs, Jasio Koskiewicz was seated snoring by the fire, Helena was sewing, and the other children were playing. Wladek was sitting at the feet of his mother, reading, when above the noise of Stefan and Josef squabbling over the possession of some newly painted pine cones, they heard a loud knock on the door. They all were silent. A knock was always a surprise to the Koskiewicz family, for the little cottage was eighteen wiorsta from Slonim and over six from the Baron's estate. Visitors were almost unknown, and could be offered only a drink of berry juice and the company of noisy children. The whole family looked towards the door apprehensively. As if it had not happened, they waited for the knock to come again. It did, if anything a little louder. Jasio rose sleepily from his chair, walked to the door and opened it cautiously. When they saw the man standing there, everyone bowed their heads except Wladek, who stared up at the broad, handsome, aristocratic figure in the heavy bearskin coat, whose presence dominated the tiny room and brought fear into the father's eyes. A cordial smile allayed that fear, and the trapper invited the Baron Rosnovski into his home. Nobody spoke. The Baron had never visited them in the past and no one was sure what to say.

Wladek put down his book, rose, and walked towards the stranger, thrusting out his hand before his father could stop him.

'Good evening, sir,' said Wladek.

The Baron took his hand and they stared into each other's eyes. As the Baron released him, Wladek's eyes fell on a magnificent silver band around his wrist with an inscription on it that he could not quite make out.

'You must be Wladek.'

'Yes, sir,' said the boy, neither sounding nor showing surprise that the Baron knew his name.

'It is about you that I have come to see your father,' said the Baron.

Wladek remained before the Baron, staring up at him. The trapper signified to his children by a wave of the arm that they should leave him alone with his master, so two of them curtsied, four bowed and all six retreated silently into the loft. Wladek remained, and no one suggested he should do otherwise.

'Koskiewicz,' began the Baron, still standing, as no one had invited him to sit. The trapper had not offered him a chair for two reasons: first, because he was too shy and second, because he assumed the Baron was there to issue a reprimand. 'I have come to ask a favour.'

'Anything, sir, anything,' said the father, wondering what he could give the Baron that he did not already have a hundred-fold.

The Baron continued. 'My son, Leon, is now six and is being taught privately at the castle by two tutors, one from our native Poland and the other from Germany. They tell me he is a clever boy, but that he lacks competition as he has only himself to beat. Mr. Kotowski, the teacher of the village school at Slonim, tells me that Wladek is the only boy capable of providing the competition that Leon so badly needs. I wonder therefore if you would allow your son to leave the village school and to join Leon and his tutors at the castle.'

Wladek continued to stand before the Baron, gazing, while before him there opened a wondrous vision of food and drink, books and teachers wiser by far than Mr. Kotowski. He glanced towards his mother. She, too, was gazing at the Baron, her face filled with wonder and sorrow. His father turned to his mother, and the instant of silent communication between them seemed an eternity to the child.

The trapper gruffly addressed the Baron's feet. 'We would be honoured, sir.'

The Baron looked interrogatively at Helena Koskiewicz.

'The Blessed Virgin forbid that I should ever stand in my child's way,' she said softly, 'though She alone knows how much it will cost me.'

'But, Madam Koskiewicz, your son can return home regularly to see you.'

'Yes, sir. I expect he will do so, at first.' She was about to add some plea but decided against it.

The Baron smiled. 'Good. It's settled then. Please bring the boy to the castle tomorrow morning by seven o'clock. During the school term Wladek will live with us, and when Christmas comes, he can return to you.'

Wladek burst into tears.

'Quiet, boy,' said the trapper.

'I will not go,' said Wladek firmly, wanting to go.

'Quiet, boy,' said the trapper, this time a little louder.

'Why not?' asked the Baron, with compassion in his voice.

'I will never leave Florcia – never.'

'Florcia?' queried the Baron.

'My eldest daughter, sir,' interjected the trapper. 'Don't concern yourself with her, sir. The boy will do as he is told.'

No one spoke. The Baron considered for a moment. Wladek continued to cry controlled tears.

'How old is the girl?' asked the Baron.

'Fourteen,' replied the trapper.

'Could she work in the kitchens?' asked the Baron, relieved to observe that Helena Koskiewicz was not going to burst into tears, as well.

'Oh yes, Baron,' she replied, 'Florcia can cook and she can sew and she can...'

'Good, good, then she can come as well. I shall expect to see them both tomorrow morning at seven.'

The Baron walked to the door and looked back and smiled at Wladek, who returned the smile. Wladek had won his first bargain, and accepted his mother's tight embrace while he stared at the closed door and heard her whisper, 'Ah, Matka's littlest one, what will become of you now?'

Wladek couldn't wait to find out.

Helena Koskiewicz packed for Wladek and Florentyna during the night, not that it would have taken long to pack the entire family's possessions. In the morning, the remainder of the family stood in front of the door to watch them both depart for the castle each holding a paper parcel under one arm. Florentyna tall and graceful, kept looking back, crying and waving; but Wladek, short and ungainly, never once looked back. Florentyna held firmly to Wladek's hand for the entire journey to the Baron's castle. Their roles were now reversed; from that day on she was to depend on him.

They were clearly expected by the magnificent man in the embroidered suit of green livery who was summoned by their timid knock on the great oak door. Both children had gazed in admiration at the grey uniforms of the soldiers in the town who guarded the nearby Russian-Polish border, but they had never seen anything so resplendent as this liveried servant, towering above them and evidently of overwhelming importance. There was a thick carpet in the hall and Wladek stared at the green and red patterning, amazed by its beauty, wondering if he should take his shoes off and surprised when he walked across it, his footsteps made no sound. The dazzling being conducted them to their bedrooms in the west wing. Separate bedrooms – would they ever get to sleep? At least there was a connecting door, so they needed never to be too far apart, and in fact for many nights they slept together in one bed.

When they had both unpacked, Florentyna was taken to the kitchen, and Wladek to a playroom in the south wing of the castle to meet the Baron's son, Leon. He was a tall, good-looking boy who was so immediately charming and welcoming to Wladek that he abandoned his prepared pugnacious posture with surprise and relief. Leon had been a lonely child, with no one to play with except his niania, the devoted Lithuanian woman who had breast-fed him and attended to his every need since the premature death of his mother. The stocky boy who had come out of the forest promised companionship. At least in one matter they both knew they had been deemed equals.

Leon immediately offered to show Wladek around the castle, and the tour took the rest of the morning. Wladek remained astounded by its size, the richness of the furniture and fabric, and those carpets in every room. To Leon he admitted only to being agreeably impressed: after all, he had won his place in the castle on merit. The main part of the building is early Gothic, explained the Baron's son, as if Wladek were sure to know what Gothic meant. Wladek nodded. Next Leon took his new friend down into the immense cellars, with line upon line of wine bottles covered in dust and cobwebs. Wladek's favourite room was the vast dining hall, with its massive pillared vaulting and stone-flagged floor. There were animals' heads all around the walls. Leon told him they were bison, bear, elk, boar and wolverine. At the end of the room, resplendent, was the Baron's coat of arms below stag's antlers. The Rosnovski family motto read 'Fortune favours the brave'. After a lunch, which Wladek ate so little of because he couldn't master a knife and fork, he met his two tutors who did not give him the same warm welcome, and in the evening he climbed up on to the longest bed he had ever seen and told Florentyna about his adventures. Her excited eyes never once left his face, nor did she even close her mouth, agape with wonder, especially when she heard about the knife and fork, which Wladek described with the fingers of his right hand held out tight together, those of his left splayed wide apart.

The tutoring started at seven sharp, before breakfast, and continued throughout the day with only short breaks for meals. Initially, Leon was clearly ahead of Wladek, but Wladek wrestled determinedly with his books so that as the weeks passed the gap began to narrow, while friendship and rivalry between the two boys developed simultaneously. The German and Polish tutors found it hard to treat their two pupils, the son of a baron, and the son of a trapper, as equals, although they reluctantly conceded to the Baron when he enquired that Mr. Kotowski had made the right academic choice. The tutors' attitude towards Wladek never worried him because by Leon he was always treated as an equal.

The Baron let it be known that he was pleased with the progress the two boys were making and from time to time he would reward Wladek with clothes and toys. Wladek's initial distant and detached admiration for the Baron developed into respect and, when the time came for the boy to return to the little cottage in the forest to rejoin his father and mother for Christmas, he became distressed at the thought of leaving Leon.

His distress was well-founded. Despite the initial happiness he felt at seeing his mother, the short space of three months that he had spent in the Baron's castle had revealed to him deficiencies in his own home of which he had previously been quite unaware. The holiday dragged on. Wladek felt himself stifled by the little cottage with its one room and loft, and dissatisfied by the food dished out in such meagre amounts and then eaten by hand: no one had divided by nine at the castle. After two weeks Wladek longed to return to Leon and the Baron. Every afternoon he would walk the six wiorsta to the castle and sit and stare at the great walls that surrounded the estate. Florentyna, who had lived only among the kitchen servants, took to returning more easily and could not understand that the cottage would never be home again for Wladek. The trapper was not sure how to treat the boy, who was now well-dressed, well-spoken, and talked of things at six that the man did not begin to understand, nor did he want to. The boy seemed to do nothing but waste the entire day reading. Whatever would become of him, the trapper wondered. If he could not swing an axe or trap a hare, how could he ever hope to earn an honest living? He too prayed that the holiday would pass quickly.

Helena was proud of Wladek, and at first avoided admitting to herself that a wedge had been driven between him and the rest of the children. But in the end it could not be avoided. Playing at soldiers one evening, both Stefan and Franck, generals on opposing sides, refused to have Wladek in their armies.

'Why must I always be left out?' cried Wladek. 'I want to learn to fight too.'

'Because you are not one of us,' declared Stefan. 'You are not really our brother.'

There was a long silence before Franck continued. 'Ojciec never wanted you in the first place; only Matka was on your side.'

Wladek stood motionless and cast his eye around the circle of children, searching for Florentyna.

'What does Franck mean, I am not your brother?' he demanded.

Thus Wladek came to hear of the manner of his birth and to understand why he had been always set apart from his brothers and sisters. Though his mother's distress at his now total self-containment became oppressive, Wladek was secretly pleased to discover that he came from unknown stock, untouched by the meanness of the trapper's blood, containing with it the germ of spirit that would now make all things seem possible.

When the unhappy holiday eventually came to an end, Wladek returned to the castle with joy. Leon welcomed him back with open arms; for him, as isolated by the wealth of his father as Wladek was by the poverty of the trapper, it had also been a Christmas with little to celebrate. From then on the two boys grew even closer and soon became inseparable. When the summer holidays came around, Leon begged his father to allow Wladek to remain at the castle. The Baron agreed for he too had grown to love Wladek. Wladek was overjoyed and only entered the trapper's cottage once again in his life.

When Wladek and Leon had finished their classroom work, they would spend the remaining hours playing games. Their favourite was chowanego, a sort of hide and seek; as the castle had seventy-two rooms, the chance of repetition was small. Wladek's favourite hiding place was in the dungeons under the castle, in which the only light by which one could be discovered came through a small stone grille set high in the wall and even then one needed a candle to find one's way around. Wladek was not sure what purpose the dungeons served, and none of the servants ever made mention of them, as they had never been used in anyone's memory.

Wladek was conscious that he was Leon's equal only in the classroom, and was no competition for his friend when they played any game, other than chess. The river Strchara that bordered the estate became an extension to their playground. In spring they fished, in summer they swam, and in winter, when the river was frozen over, they would put on their wooden skates and chase each other across the ice, while Florentyna sat on the river bank anxiously warning them where the surface was thin. But Wladek never heeded her and was always the one who fell in. Leon grew quickly and strong; he ran well, swam well and never seemed to tire or be ill. Wladek became aware for the first time what good-looking and well-built meant, and he knew when he swam, ran, and skated he could never hope to keep up with Leon. Much worse, what Leon called the belly button was, on him, almost unnoticeable, while Wladek's was stumpy and ugly and protruded rudely from the middle of his plump body. Wladek would spend long hours in the quiet of his own room, studying his physique in a mirror, always asking why, and in particular why only one nipple for him when all the boys he had ever seen barechested had the two that the symmetry of the human body appeared to require. Sometimes as he lay in bed unable to sleep, he would finger his naked chest and tears of self-pity would flood on to the pillow. He would finally fall asleep praying that when he awoke in the morning, things would be different. His prayers were not answered.

Wladek put aside each night a time to do physical exercises that could not be witnessed by anyone, not even Florentyna. Through sheer determination he learned to hold himself so that he looked taller. He built up his arms and his legs and hung by the tips of his fingers from a beam in the bedroom in the hope that it would make him grow, but Leon grew taller even while he slept. Wladek was forced to accept the fact that he would always be a head shorter than the Baron's son, and that nothing, nothing was ever going to produce the missing nipple. Wladek's dislike of his own body was unprompted, for Leon never commented on his friend's appearance; his knowledge of other children stopped short at Wladek, whom he adored uncritically.

Baron Rosnovski became increasingly fond of the fierce dark-haired boy who had replaced the younger brother for Leon, so tragically lost when his wife had died in childbirth.

The two boys would dine with him in the great stone-walled hall each evening, while the flickering candles cast ominous shadows from the stuffed animal heads on the wall and the servants came and went noiselessly with the great silver trays and golden plates, bearing geese, hams, crayfish, fine wine and fruits, and sometimes the mazureks that had become Wladek's particular favourites. Afterwards as the darkness fell ever more thickly around the table, the Baron dismissed the waiting servants and would tell the boys stories of Polish history and allowed them a sip of Danzig vodka, in which the tiny gold leaves sparkled bravely in the candlelight. Wladek begged as often as he dared for the story of Tadeusz Kosciuszko.

'A great patriot and hero,' the Baron would reply. 'The

very symbol of our struggle for independence, trained in France...'

'Whose people we admire and love as we have learned to hate all Russians and Austrians,' supplied Wladek, whose pleasure in the tale was enhanced by his word-perfect knowledge of it.

'Who is telling whom the story, Wladek?' The Baron laughed. '... And then fought with George Washington in America for liberty and democracy. In 1792 he led the Poles in battle at Dubienka. When our wretched king, Stanislas Augustus, deserted us to join the Russians, Kosciuszko returned to the homeland he loved to throw off the yoke of Tsardom. He won the battle of where, Leon?'

'Raclawice, sir, and then he freed Warsaw.'

'Good, my child. Then, alas, the Russians mustered a great force at Maciejowice and he was finally defeated and taken prisoner. My great-great-great-grandfather fought with Kosciuszko on that day, and later with Dabrowski's legions for the mighty Emperor Napoleon Bonaparte.'

'And for his service to Poland was created the Baron Rosnovski, a title your family will ever bear in remembrance of those great days,' said Wladek, as stoutly as if the title would one day pass to him.

'Those great days will come again,' said the Baron quietly. 'I only pray that I may live to see them.'

At Christmas time, the peasants on the estate would bring their families to the castle for the celebration of the blessed vigil. Throughout Christmas Eve they fasted and the children would look out of the windows for the first star, which was the sign the feast might begin. The Baron would say grace in his fine deep voice: *'Benedicte nobis, Domine Deus, et his donis quae ex liberalitate tua sumpturi sumus,'* and once they had sat down Wladek would be embarrassed by the huge capacity of Jasio Koskiewicz, who addressed himself squarely to every one of the thirteen courses from the barsasz soup through to the cakes and plums, and would as in previous years be sick in the forest on the way home.

After the feast Wladek enjoyed distributing the gifts from the Christmas tree, laden with candles and fruit, to the awestruck peasant children – a doll for Sophia, a forest knife for Josef, a new dress for Florentyna, the first gift Wladek had ever requested of the Baron.

'It's true,' said Josef to his mother when he received his gift from Wladek, 'he is not our brother, Matka.'

'No,' she replied, 'but he will always be my son.'

Through the winter and spring of 1914 Wladek grew in strength and learning. Then suddenly, in July, the German tutor left the castle without even saying farewell; neither boy was sure why. They never thought to connect his departure with the assassination in Sarajevo of the Archduke Francis Ferdinand by a student anarchist, described to them by their other tutor in unaccountably solemn tones. The Baron became withdrawn; neither boy was sure why. The younger servants, the children's favourites, began to disappear one by one; neither boy was sure why. As the year passed Leon grew taller, Wladek grew stronger, and both boys became wiser.

One morning in the summer of 1915, a time of fine, lazy days, the Baron set off on the long journey to Warsaw to put, as he described it, his affairs in order. He was away for three and a half weeks, twenty-five days which Wladek marked off each morning on a calendar in his bedroom; it seemed to him a lifetime. On the day he was due to return, the two boys went down to the railway station at Slonim to await the weekly train with its one carriage and greet the Baron on his arrival. The three of them travelled home in silence.

Wladek thought the great man looked tired and older, another unaccountable circumstance, and during the following week the Baron often conducted with the chief servants a rapid and anxious dialogue, broken off whenever Leon or Wladek entered the room, an uncharacteristic surreptitiousness that made the two boys uneasy and fearful that they were the unwitting cause of it. Wladek despaired that the

Baron might send him back to the trapper's cottage – always aware he was a stranger in a stranger's home.

One evening a few days after the Baron had returned he called for the two boys to join him in the great hall. They crept in, fearful of him. Without explanation he told them that they were about to make a long journey. The little conversation, insubstantial as it seemed to Wladek at the time, remained with him for the rest of his life.

'My dear children,' began the Baron in a low, faltering tone, 'the warmongers of Germany and the Austro-Hungarian empire are at the throat of Warsaw and will soon be upon us.'

Wladek recalled an inexplicable phrase flung out by the Polish tutor at the German tutor during their last tense days together. 'Does that mean that the hour of the submerged peoples of Europe is at last upon us?' he asked.

The Baron regarded Wladek's innocent face tenderly. 'Our national spirit has not perished in one hundred and fifty years of attrition and repression,' he replied. 'It may be that the fate of Poland is as much at stake as that of Serbia, but we are powerless to influence history. We are at the mercy of the three mighty empires that surround us.'

'We are strong, we can fight,' said Leon. 'We have wooden swords and shields. We are not afraid of Germans or Russians.'

'My son, you have only played at war. This battle will not be between children. We will now find a quiet place to live until history has decided our fate and we must leave as soon as possible. I can only pray that this is not the end of your childhood.'

Leon and Wladek were both mystified and irritated by the Baron's words. War sounded like an exciting adventure which they would be sure to miss if they had to leave the castle. The servants took several days to pack the Baron's possessions and Wladek and Leon were informed that they would be departing for their small summer home in the north of Grodno on the following Monday. The two boys continued, largely unsupervised, with their work and play but they could now find no one in the castle with the inclination or time to answer their myriad questions.

On Saturdays, lessons were held only in the morning. They were translating Adam Mickiewicz's *Pan Tadeusz* into Latin when they heard the guns. At first, Wladek thought the familiar sounds meant only that another trapper was out shooting on the estate; the boys returned to the poetry. A second volley of shots, much closer, made them look up and then they heard the screaming coming from downstairs. They stared at each other in bewilderment; they feared nothing as they had never experienced anything in their short lives that should have made them fearful. The tutor fled leaving them alone, and then came another shot, this time in the corridor outside their room. The two boys sat motionless, terrified and unbreathing.

Suddenly the door crashed open and a man no older than their tutor, in a grey soldier's uniform and steel helmet, stood towering over them. Leon clung on to Wladek, while Wladek stared at the intruder. The soldier shouted at them in German, demanding to know who they were, but neither boy replied, despite the fact that they had mastered the language, and could speak it as well as their mother tongue. Another soldier appeared behind his companion as the first advanced on the two boys, grabbed them by the necks, not unlike chickens, and pulled them out into the corridor, down the hall to the front of the castle and then into the gardens, where they found Florentyna screaming hysterically as she stared at the grass in front of her. Leon could not bear to look, and buried his head in Wladek's shoulder. Wladek gazed as much in surprise as in horror at a row of dead bodies, mostly servants, being placed face downwards. He was mesmerised by the sight of a moustache in profile against a pool of blood. It was the trapper. Wladek felt nothing as Florentyna continued screaming.

'Is Papa there?' asked Leon. 'Is Papa there?'

Wladek scanned the line of bodies once again. He

thanked God that there was no sign of the Baron Rosnovski. He was about to tell Leon the good news when a soldier came up to them.

'*Wer hat gesprochen?*' he demanded fiercely.

'*Ich*,' said Wladek defiantly.

The soldier raised his rifle and brought the butt crashing down on Wladek's head. He sank to the ground, blood spurting over his face. Where was the Baron, what was happening, why were they being treated like this in their own home? Leon quickly jumped on top of Wladek, trying to protect him from the second blow which the soldier had intended for Wladek's stomach, but as the rifle came crashing down the full force caught the back of Leon's head.

Both boys lay motionless, Wladek because he was still dazed by the blow and the sudden weight of Leon's body on top of him, and Leon because he was dead.

Wladek could hear another soldier berating their tormentor for the action he had taken. They picked up Leon, but Wladek clung on to him. It took two soldiers to prise his friend's body away and dump it unceremoniously with the others, face down on the grass. Wladek's eyes never left the motionless body of his dearest friend until he was finally marched back inside the castle, and, with a handful of dazed survivors, led to the dungeons. Nobody spoke for fear of joining the line of bodies on the grass, until the dungeon doors were bolted and the last murmur of the soldiers had vanished in the distance. Then Wladek said, 'Holy God.' For there in a corner, slumped against the wall, sat the Baron, uninjured but stunned, staring into space, alive only because the conquerors needed someone to be responsible for the prisoners. Wladek went over to him, while the others sat as far away from their master as possible. The two gazed at each other, as they had on the first day they had met. Wladek put his hand out, and as on the first day the Baron took it. Wladek watched the tears course down the Baron's proud face. Neither spoke. They had both lost the one person they had loved most in the world.

6

William Kane grew very quickly, and was considered an adorable child by all who came in contact with him; in the early years of his life these were generally besotted relatives and doting servants.

The top floor of the Kanes' eighteenth-century house in Louisburg Square on Beacon Hill had been converted into nursery quarters, crammed with toys. A further bedroom and a sitting room were made available for the newly acquired nurse. The floor was far enough away from Richard Kane for him to be unaware of problems such as teething, wet nappies and the irregular and undisciplined cries for more food. First sound, first tooth, first step and first word were all recorded in a family book by William's mother along with the progress in his height and weight. Anne was surprised to find that these statistics differed very little from those of any other child with whom she came into contact on Beacon Hill.

The nurse, an import from England, brought the boy up on a regimen that would have gladdened the heart of a Prussian cavalry officer. William's father would visit him each evening at six o'clock. As he refused to address the child in baby language, he ended up not speaking to him at all; the two merely stared at each other. William would grip his father's index finger, the one with which balance sheets were checked, and hold on to it tightly. Richard would allow himself a smile. At the end of the first year the routine was slightly modified and the boy was allowed to come downstairs to see his father. Richard would sit in his highbacked, maroon leather chair watching his first-born weave his way on all fours in and out of the legs of the furniture reappearing when least expected, which led Richard to observe that the child would undoubtedly become a senator.

William took his first steps at thirteen months while clinging on to the tails of his father's topcoat. His first word was 'Dada', which pleased everyone, including Grandmother Kane and Grandmother Cabot, who were regular visitors. They did not actually push the vehicle in which William was perambulated around Boston, but they did deign to walk a pace behind the nurse in the park on Thursday afternoons, glaring at infants with a less disciplined retinue. While other children fed the ducks in the public gardens, William succeeded in charming the swans in the lagoon of Mr. Jack Gardner's extravagant Venetian Palace.

When two years had passed, the grandmothers intimated by hint and innuendo that it was high time for another prodigy, an appropriate sibling for William. Anne obliged them by becoming pregnant and was distressed to find herself feeling and looking progressively off colour as she entered her fourth month.

Doctor MacKenzie ceased to smile as he checked the growing stomach and hopeful mother, and when Anne miscarried at sixteen weeks he was not altogether surprised, but did not allow her to indulge her grief. In his notes he wrote 'pre-eclampsia?' and then told her, 'Anne, my dear, the reason you have not been feeling so well is that your blood pressure was too high, and would probably have become much higher as your pregnancy progressed. I fear doctors haven't found the answer to blood pressure yet, in fact we know very little other than it's a dangerous condition for anyone, particularly for a pregnant woman.'

Anne held back her tears while considering the implications of a future without more children.

'Surely it won't happen in my next pregnancy?' she asked, phrasing her question to dispose the doctor to a favourable answer.

'I should be very surprised if it did not, my dear. I am sorry to have to say this to you, but I would strongly advise you against becoming pregnant again.'

'But I don't mind feeling off-colour for a few months if it means...'

'I am not talking about feeling off-colour, Anne. I am talking about not taking any unnecessary risks with your life.'

It was a terrible blow for Richard and Anne, who themselves had both been only children, largely as a result of their respective fathers' premature deaths. They had both assumed that they would produce a family appropriate to the commanding size of their house and their responsibilities to the next generation. 'What else is there for a young woman to do?' enquired Grandmother Cabot of Grandmother Kane. No one cared to mention the subject again, and William became the centre of everyone's attention.

Richard, who had taken over as the president of Kane and Cabot Bank and Trust Company when his father had died in 1904, had always immersed himself in the work of the bank. The bank, which stood on State Street, a bastion of architectural and fiscal solidity, had offices in New York, London and San Francisco. The last had presented a problem to Richard soon after William's birth when, along with Crocker National Bank, Wells Fargo, and the California Bank, it collapsed to the ground, not financially, but literally, in the great earthquake of 1906. Richard, by nature a cautious man, was comprehensively insured with Lloyd's of London. Gentlemen all, they had paid up to the penny, enabling Richard to rebuild. Nevertheless, Richard spent an uncomfortable year jolting across America on the four-day train journey between Boston and San Francisco, supervising the rebuilding. He opened the new office in Union Square in October 1907, barely in time to turn his attention to other problems arising on the Eastern seaboard. There was a minor run on the New York banks, and many of the smaller establishments were unable to cope with large withdrawals and started going to the wall. J. P. Morgan, the legendary chairman of the mighty bank bearing his name, invited Richard to join a consortium to hold firm during the crisis. Richard agreed, the courageous stand worked, and the problem began to dissipate, but not before Richard had had a few sleepless nights.

William, on the other hand, slept soundly, unaware of earthquakes and collapsing banks. After all, there were swans that must be fed and endless trips to and from Milton, Brookline and Beverly to be shown to his distinguished relatives.

Early in the spring of the following year Richard acquired a new toy in return for a cautious investment of capital in a man called Henry Ford, who was claiming he could produce a motor car for the people. The bank entertained Mr. Ford at luncheon, and Richard was coaxed into the acquisition of a Model T for the princely sum of eight hundred and fifty dollars. Henry Ford assured Richard that if only the bank would back him, the cost could eventually fall to three hundred and fifty dollars within a few years and everyone would be buying his cars, thus ensuring a large profit for his backers. Richard did back him, and it was the first time he had placed good money behind someone who wished his product to halve in price.

Richard was initially apprehensive that his motor car, sombrely black though it was, might not be regarded as a serious mode of transport for the chairman of a bank, but he was reassured by the admiring glances from the pavements which the machine attracted. At ten miles an hour it was noisier than a horse but it did have the virtue of leaving no mess in the middle of Mount Vernon Street. His only quarrel with Mr. Ford was that the man would not listen to the suggestion that a Model T should be made available in a variety of colours. Mr. Ford insisted that every car should be black in order to keep the price down. Anne, more sensitive than her husband to the approbation of polite society, would not drive in the vehicle until the Cabots had acquired one.

William, on the other hand, adored the 'automobile', as the press called it, and immediately assumed that the vehicle had been bought for him to replace his now redundant and unmechanised pram. He also preferred the chauffeur – with his goggles and flat hat – to his nurse. Grandmother Kane and Grandmother Cabot claimed that they would never travel in the dreadful machine and never did, although it should be pointed out that Grandmother Kane travelled to her funeral in a motor car, but was never informed.

During the next two years the bank grew in strength and size, as did William. Americans were once again investing for expansion, and large sums of money found their way to Kane and Cabot's to be reinvested in such projects as the expanding Lowell leather factory in Lowell, Massachusetts. Richard watched the growth of his bank and his son with unsurprised satisfaction. On William's fifth birthday, he took the child out of womens' hands by engaging at four hundred and fifty dollars per annum a private tutor, a Mr. Munro, personally selected by Richard from a list of eight applicants who had earlier been screened by his private secretary. Mr. Munro was charged to ensure that William was ready to enter St. Paul's by the age of twelve. William immediately took to Mr. Munro, whom he thought to be very old and very clever. He was, in fact, twenty-three and the possessor of a second-class honours degree in English from the University of Edinburgh.

William quickly learned to read and write with facility but saved his real enthusiasm for figures. His only complaint was that, of the eight lessons taught every weekday, only one was arithmetic. William was quick to point out to his father that one-eighth of the working day was a small investment of time for someone who would one day be the president of a bank.

To compensate for his tutor's lack of foresight, William dogged the footsteps of his accessible relatives with demands for sums to be executed in his head. Grandmother Cabot, who had never been persuaded that the division of an integer by four would necessarily produce the same answer as its multiplication by one quarter, and indeed in her hands the two operations often did result in two different numbers, found herself speedily outclassed by her grandson, but Grandmother Kane, with some small leaning to cleverness, grappled manfully with vulgar fractions, compound interest and the division of eight cakes among nine children.

'Grandmother,' said William, kindly but firmly, when she had failed to find the answer to his latest conundrum, 'you can buy me a slide-rule; then I won't have to bother you.'

She was astonished at her grandson's precocity, but she bought him one just the same, wondering if he really knew how to use the gadget. It was the first time in her life that Grandmother Kane had been known to take the easy way out of any problem.

Richard's problems began to gravitate eastwards. The chairman of his London branch died at his desk and Richard felt himself required in Lombard Street. He suggested to Anne that she and William should accompany him to Europe, feeling that the education would not do the boy any harm: he could visit all the places about which Mr. Munro had so often talked. Anne, who had never been to Europe, was excited by the prospect, and filled three steamer trunks with elegant and expensive new clothes in which to confront the Old World. William considered it unfair of his mother not to allow him to take that equally essential aid to travel, his bicycle.

The Kanes travelled to New York by train to join the *Aquitania* bound for her voyage to Southampton. Anne was appalled by the sight of the immigrant street peddlers pushing their wares, and she was glad to be safely on board and resting in her cabin. William, on the other hand, was amazed by the size of New York; he had, until that moment, always imagined that his father's bank was the biggest building in America, if not the world. He wanted to buy a pink and yellow ice cream from a man all dressed in white and wearing a boater, but his father would not hear of it; in any case, Richard never carried small change.

William adored the great vessel on sight and quickly became friendly with the captain, who showed him all the secrets of the Cunard Steamships' prima donna. Richard and Anne, who naturally sat at the captain's table, felt it necessary, before the ship had long left America, to apologise for the amount of the crew's time that their son was occupying.

'Not at all,' replied the white-bearded skipper. 'William and I are already good friends. I only wish I could answer all his questions about time, speed and distance. I have to be coached each night by the first engineer in the hope of first anticipating and then surviving the next day.'

The *Aquitania* sailed into the Solent to dock at Southampton after a six-day journey. William was reluctant to leave her, and tears would have been unavoidable had it not been for the magnificent sight of the Rolls-Royce Silver Ghost, waiting at the quayside complete with a chauffeur, ready to whisk them off to London. Richard decided on the spur of the moment that he would have the car transported back to New York at the end of the trip, which was the most out-of-character decision he made during the rest of his life. He informed Anne, rather unconvincingly, that he wanted to show the vehicle to Henry Ford.

The Kane family always stayed at the Ritz in Piccadilly when they were in London, which was convenient for Richard's office in the City. Anne used the time while Richard was occupied at the bank to show William the Tower of London, Buckingham Palace and the Changing of the Guard. William thought everything was 'great' except the English accent which he had difficulty in understanding.

'Why don't they talk like us, Mommy?' he demanded, and was surprised to be told that the question was more often put the other way around, as 'they' came first. William's favourite pastime was to watch the soldiers in their bright red uniforms with large shiny brass buttons who kept guard duty outside Buckingham Palace. He tried to engage them in conversation but they stared past him into space and never even blinked.

'Can we take one home?' he asked his mother.

'No, darling, they have to stay here and guard the King.'

'But he's got so many of them, can't I have just one?'

As a 'special treat' – Anne's words – Richard allowed himself an afternoon off to take his wife and son to the West End to see a traditional English pantomime called *Jack and the Beanstalk* playing at the London Hippodrome.

William loved Jack and immediately wanted to cut down every tree he laid his eyes on, imagining them all to be sheltering a monster. They had tea after the show at Fortnum and Mason in Piccadilly, and Anne let William have two cream buns and a new-fangled thing called a doughnut. Daily thereafter William had to be escorted back to the tearoom at Fortnum's to consume another 'doughbun', as he called them.

The holiday passed by all too quickly for William and his mother, whereas Richard, satisfied with his progress in Lombard Street and pleased with his newly appointed chairman, began to look forward to the day of their departure. Cables were daily arriving from Boston that made him anxious to be back in his own boardroom. Finally, when one such missive informed him that twenty-five thousand workers at a cotton mill with which his bank had a heavy investment in Lawrence, Massachusetts, had gone out on strike, he was relieved that his planned date of sailing was now only three days away.

William was looking forward to returning and telling Mr. Munro all the exciting things he had done in England and to being reunited with his two grandmothers again. He felt sure they had never done anything so exciting as visiting a real live theatre with the general public. Anne was also happy to be going home, although she had enjoyed the trip almost as much as William, for her clothes and beauty had been much admired by the normally undemonstrative North Sea Islanders. As a final treat for William the day before they were due to sail, Anne took him to a tea party in Eaton Square given by the wife of the newly appointed chairman of Richard's London branch. She, too, had a son, Stuart, who was eight – and William had, in the two weeks in which they had been playing together, grown to regard him as an indispensable grown-up friend. The party, however, was rather subdued because Stuart felt unwell and William, in sympathy with his new chum, announced to his mother that he was going to be ill too. Anne and William returned to the Ritz Hotel earlier than they had planned.

She was not greatly put out as it gave her a little more time to supervise the packing of the large steamer trunks, although she was convinced William was only putting on an act to please Stuart. When she tucked William up in bed that night, she found that he had been as good as his word and was running a slight fever. She remarked on it to Richard over dinner.

'Probably all the excitement at the thought of going home,' he offered, sounding unconcerned.

'I hope so,' replied Anne. 'I don't want him to be sick on a six-day sea voyage.'

'He'll be just fine by tomorrow,' said Richard, issuing an unheeded directive, but when Anne went to wake William the next morning, she found him covered in little red spots and running a temperature of one hundred and three. The hotel doctor diagnosed measles and was politely insistent that William should on no account be sent on a sea journey, not only for his own good but for the sake of the other passengers. There was nothing for it but to leave him in bed with his stone hot water bottle and wait for the departure of the next ship. Richard was unable to countenance the three-week delay and decided to sail as planned. Reluctantly, Anne allowed the hurried changes of booking to be made. William begged his father to let him accompany him: the twenty-one days before the *Aquitania* was due back in Southampton seemed like an eternity to the child. Richard was adamant, and hired a nurse to attend William and convince him of his poor state of health.

Anne travelled down to Southampton with Richard in the new Rolls-Royce.

'I shall be lonely in London without you, Richard,' she ventured diffidently in their parting moment, risking his disapproval of emotional women.

'Well, my dear, I dare say that I shall be somewhat lonely in Boston without you,' he said, his mind on the striking cotton workers.

Anne returned to London on the train, wondering how she would occupy herself for the next three weeks. William had a better night and in the morning the spots looked less ferocious. Doctor and nurse were unanimous however in their insistence that he should remain in bed. Anne used the extra time to write long letters to the family, while William remained in bed, protesting, but on Thursday morning he got himself up early and went into his mother's room, very much back to his normal self. He climbed into bed next to her and his cold hands immediately woke her up. Anne was relieved to see him so obviously fully recovered. She rang to order breakfast in bed for both of them, an indulgence William's father would never have countenanced.

There was a quiet knock on the door and a man in gold and red livery entered with a large, silver breakfast tray. Eggs, bacon, tomato, toast and marmalade – a veritable feast. William looked at the food ravenously as if he could not remember when he had last eaten a full meal. Anne casually glanced at the morning paper. Richard always read *The Times* when he stayed in London so the management assumed she would require it as well.

'Oh, look,' said William, staring at the photograph on an inside page, 'a picture of Daddy's ship. What's a CA-LA-MITY, Mommy?'

All across the width of the newspaper was a picture of the *Titanic*.

Anne, unmindful of behaving as should a Lowell or a Cabot, burst into frenzied tears, clinging on to her only son. They sat in bed for several minutes, holding on to each other, William wasn't sure why. Anne realised that they had both lost the one person whom they had loved most in the world.

Sir Piers Campbell, young Stuart's father, arrived almost immediately at Suite 107 of the Ritz Hotel. He waited in the lounge while the widow put on a suit, the only dark piece of clothing she possessed. William dressed himself, still not certain what a 'calamity' was. Anne asked Sir Piers to explain the full implications of the news to her son, who only said, 'I wanted to be on the ship with him, but they wouldn't let me go.' He didn't cry because he refused to believe anything could kill his father. He would be among the survivors.

In all Sir Piers' career as a politician, diplomat and now chairman of Kane and Cabot, London, he had never seen such self-containment in one so young. Presence is given to very few, he was heard to remark some years later. It had been given to Richard Kane and had been passed on to his only son.

The lists of survivors, arriving spasmodically from America, were checked and double-checked by Anne. Each confirmed that Richard Lowell Kane was still missing at sea, presumed drowned. After a further week even William almost abandoned hope of his father's survival.

Anne found it hard to board the *Aquitania*, but William was strangely eager to put to sea. Hour after hour, he would sit on the observation deck, scanning the featureless water.

'Tomorrow I will find him,' he promised his mother, at first confidently, and then in a voice that barely disclaimed his own disbelief.

'William, no one can survive for three weeks in the Atlantic.'

'Not even my father?'

'Not even your father.'

When Anne returned to Boston, both grandmothers were waiting for her at the Red House, mindful of the duty that had been thrust upon them.

The responsibility had been passed back to the grandmothers. Anne passively accepted their proprietory role. Life for her now had little purpose left other than William, whose destiny they now seemed determined to control. William was polite but uncooperative. During the day he sat silently in his lesson with Mr. Munro and at night wept into the lap of his mother.

'What he needs is the company of other children,' declared the grandmothers briskly, and they dismissed Mr. Munro and the nurse and sent William off to Sayre Academy in the hope that an introduction to the real world and the constant company of other children might bring him back to his old self.

Richard had left the bulk of his estate to William, to remain in the family trust until his twenty-first birthday. There was a codicil added to the will. Richard expected his son to become chairman of Kane and Cabot on merit. It was the only part of his father's testament that inspired William, for the rest was his by birthright. Anne received a capital sum of five hundred thousand dollars and an income for life of one hundred thousand dollars a year after taxes which would cease, if she remarried. She also received the house on Beacon Hill, the summer mansion on the North Shore, the home in Maine, and a small island off Cape Cod, all of which were to pass to William on his mother's death. Both grandmothers received two hundred and fifty thousand dollars, and letters leaving them in no doubt about their responsibility if Richard died before them. The family trust was to be handled by the bank, with William's godparents acting as co-trustees. The income from the trust was to be reinvested each year in conservative enterprises.

It was a full year before the grandmothers came out of mourning, and although Anne was still only twenty-eight, she looked her age for the first time in her life.

The grandmothers, unlike Anne, concealed their grief from William until he finally reproached them for it.

'Don't you miss my father?' he asked, gazing at Grandmother Kane with the blue eyes that brought back memories of her own son.

'Yes, my child, but he would not have wished us to sit around and feel sorry for ourselves.'

'But I want us to always remember him – always,' said William, his voice cracking.

'William, I am going to speak to you for the first time as though you were quite grown up. We will always keep his memory hallowed between us, and you shall play your own part by living up to what your father would have expected of you. You are the head of the family now and the heir to a large fortune. You must, therefore, prepare yourself through work to be fit for that inheritance in the same spirit in which your father worked to increase the inheritance for you.'

William made no reply. He was thus provided with the motive for life which he had lacked before, and he acted upon his grandmother's advice. He learned to live with his sorrow without complaining and from that moment on he threw himself steadfastly into his work at school, satisfied only if Grandmother Kane seemed impressed. At no subject did he fail to excel, and in mathematics he was not only top of his class but far ahead of his years. Anything his father had achieved, he was determined to better. He grew even closer to his mother and became suspicious of anyone who was not family, so that he was often thought of as a solitary child, a loner and, unfairly, as a snob.

The grandmothers decided on William's seventh birthday that the time had come to instruct the boy in the value of money. They therefore allowed him pocket money of one dollar a week, but insisted that he keep an inventory accounting for every cent he had spent. With this in mind, they presented him with a green leather-bound ledger book, at a cost of ninety-five cents, which they deducted from his first week's allowance of one dollar. From the second week the grandmothers divided the dollar every Saturday morning. William invested fifty cents, spent twenty cents, gave ten cents to any charity of his choice, and kept twenty cents in reserve. At the end of each quarter the grandmothers would inspect the ledger and his written report on any transactions. When the first three months had passed, William was well ready to account for himself. He had given one dollar twenty cents to the newly founded Boy Scouts of America, and saved four dollars, which he had asked Grandmother Kane to invest in a savings account at the bank of his godfather, J. P. Morgan. He had spent a further three dollars eight cents for which he did not have to account and had kept a dollar in reserve. The ledger was a source of great satisfaction to the grandmothers: there was no doubt William was the son of Richard Kane.

At school, William made few friends, partly because he was shy of mixing with anyone other than Cabots, Lowells or children from families wealthier than his own. This restricted his choice severely, so he became a somewhat broody child, which worried his mother, who wanted William to lead a more normal existence, and did not in her heart approve of the ledgers or the investment programme. Anne would have preferred William to have a lot of young friends rather than old advisors, to get himself dirty and bruised rather than remain spotless, to collect toads and turtles rather than stocks and company reports; in short to be like any other little boy. But she never had the courage to tell the grandmothers about her misgivings and in any case the grandmothers were not interested in any other little boy.

On his ninth birthday William presented the ledger to his grandmothers for the second annual inspection. The green leather book showed a saving during the two years of more than fifty dollars. He was particularly proud to point out an entry marked B6 to the grandmothers, showing that he had taken his money out of J. P. Morgan's Bank immediately on hearing of the death of the great financier, because he had noted that his own father's bank shares had fallen in value after his death had been announced. He had reinvested the same amount three months later before the public realised the company was bigger than any one man.

The grandmothers were suitably impressed and allowed William to trade in his old bicycle and purchase a new one, after which he still had a capital sum of over one hundred dollars, which his grandmother had invested for him with the Standard Oil Company of New Jersey. Oil, said William knowingly, can only get more expensive. He kept the ledger meticulously up-to-date until his twenty-first birthday. Had the grandmothers still been alive then, they would have been proud of the final entry in the right hand column marked 'assets'.

7

Wladek was the only one of those left alive who knew the dungeons well. In his days of hide and seek with Leon he had spent many happy hours in the freedom of the small stone rooms, carefree in the knowledge that he could return to the castle whenever it suited him.

There were in all four dungeons, on two levels. Two of the rooms, a larger and a smaller one, were at ground level. The smaller one was adjacent to the castle wall, which afforded a thin filter of light through a grille set high in the stones. Down five steps there were two more stone rooms in perpetual darkness and with little air. Wladek led the Baron into the small upper dungeon where he remained sitting in a corner, silent and motionless, staring fixedly into space; he then appointed Florentyna to be his personal servant.

As Wladek was the only person who dared to remain in the same room as the Baron, the servants never questioned his authority. Thus, at the age of nine, he took charge of the day-to-day responsibility of his fellow prisoners. And in the dungeon he became their master. He split the remaining twenty-four servants into three groups of eight, trying to keep families together wherever possible. He moved them regularly in a shift system, the first eight hours in the upper dungeons for light, air, food and exercise; the second and most popular shift of eight hours working in the castle for their captors; and the final eight hours given to sleep in one of the lower dungeons. No one except the Baron and Florentyna could be quite sure when Wladek slept, as he was always there at the end of every shift to supervise the servants moving on. Food was distributed every twelve hours. The guards would hand over a skin of goats' milk, black bread, millet and occasionally some nuts which Wladek would divide by twenty-eight, always giving two portions to the

Baron without ever letting him know. The new occupants of the dungeons, their placidity rendered into miserable stupefaction by incarceration, found nothing strange in a situation that had put a nine-year-old in control of their lives.

Once Wladek had each shift organised, he would return to the Baron in the smaller dungeon. Initially he expected guidance from him, but the fixed gaze of his master was as implacable and comfortless in its own way as were the eyes of the constant succession of German guards. The Baron had never once spoken from the moment he had been subjected to captivity in his own castle. His beard had grown long and matted on his chest and his strong frame was beginning to dwindle into frailty. The once proud look had been replaced with one of resignation. Wladek could scarcely remember the well-loved voice of his patron, and accustomed himself to the thought that he would never hear it again. After a while, he complied with the Baron's unspoken wishes by remaining silent in his presence.

When he had lived in the safety of the castle, Wladek had never thought of the previous day with so much occupying him from hour to hour. Now he was unable to remember even the previous hour, because nothing ever changed. Hopeless minutes turned into hours, hours into days, and then months that he soon lost track of. Only the arrival of food, darkness or light indicated that another twelve hours had passed, while the intensity of that light, and its eventual giving way to storms, and then ice forming on the dungeon walls, melting only when a new sun appeared, heralded each season in a manner that Wladek could never have learned from a nature study lesson. During the long nights Wladek became even more aware of the stench of death that permeated even the farthest corners of the four dungeons, alleviated occasionally by the morning sunshine, a cool breeze, or the most blessed relief of all, the return of rain.

At the end of one day of unremitting storms, Wladek and Florentyna took advantage of the rain by washing themselves in a puddle of water which formed on the stone floor of the upper dungeon. Neither of them noticed that the Baron's eyes were following Wladek with interest as he removed his tattered shirt and rolled over like a dog in the relatively clean water, continuing to rub himself until white streaks appeared on his body. Suddenly, the Baron spoke.

'Wladek' – the word was barely audible – 'I cannot see you clearly,' he said, the voice cracking. 'Come here.'

Wladek was stupefied by the sound of his patron's voice after so long a silence and didn't even look in his direction. He was immediately sure that it heralded the incipience of the madness which already held two of the older servants in its grip.

'Come here, boy.'

Wladek obeyed fearfully, and stood before the Baron, who narrowed his enfeebled eyes in a gesture of intense concentration as he groped towards the boy. He ran his finger over Wladek's chest and then peered at him incredulously.

'Wladek, can you explain this small deformity?'

'No, sir,' said Wladek, feeling embarrassed. 'It has been with me since birth. My foster-mother used to say it was the mark of God the Father upon me.'

'Stupid woman. It is the mark of your own father,' the Baron said softly, and lapsed into silence for some minutes.

Wladek remained standing in front of him, not moving a muscle.

When at last the Baron spoke again, his voice was brisk. 'Sit down, boy.'

Wladek obeyed immediately. As he sat down, he noticed once again the heavy band of silver, now hanging loosely round the Baron's wrist. A shaft of light through a crack in the wall made the magnificent engraving of the Rosnovski coat of arms glitter in the darkness of the dungeon.

'I do not know how long the Germans intend to keep us locked up here. I thought at first that this war would be over in a matter of weeks. I was wrong, and we must now consider the possibility that it will continue for a very long time. With that thought in mind, we must use our time more constructively as I know my life is nearing an end.'

'No, no,' Wladek began to protest, but the Baron continued as if he had not heard him.

'Yours, my child, has yet to begin. I will, therefore, undertake the continuation of your education.'

The Baron did not speak again that day. It was as if he were considering the implications of his pronouncement. Thus Wladek gained his new tutor and as they neither possessed reading nor writing material he was made to repeat everything the Baron said. He was taught great tracts from the poems of Adam Mickiewicz and Jan Kochanowski and long passages from the *Aeneid*. In that austere classroom Wladek learned geography, mathematics and four languages: Russian, German, French and English. But his happiest moments were once again when he was taught history. The history of his nation through a hundred years of partition, the disappointed hopes for a united Poland, the further anguish of the Poles at Napoleon's crushing loss to Russia in 1812. He learnt of the brave tales of earlier and happier times, when King Jan Casimir had dedicated Poland to the Blessed Virgin after repulsing the Swedes at Czestochowa, and how the mighty Prince Radziwill, great landowner and lover of hunting, had held his court in the great castle near Warsaw. Wladek's final lesson each day was on the family history of the Rosnovskis. Again and again, he was told – never tiring of the tale – how the Baron's illustrious ancestor who had served in 1794 under General Dabrowski and then in 1809 under Napoleon himself had been rewarded by the great Emperor with land and a barony. He also learned how the Baron's grandfather had sat on the council of Warsaw and his father had played his own part in building the new Poland. Wladek found such happiness when the Baron turned his little dungeon into a classroom.

The guards at the dungeon door were changed every four hours and conversation between them and the prisoners was '*strengst verboten*'. In snatches and fragments Wladek learned of the progress of the war, of the actions of Hindenburg and Ludendorff, of the rise of revolution in Russia and of her subsequent withdrawal from the war by the Treaty of Brest-Litovsk.

Wladek began to believe that the only escape from the dungeons for the inmates was death. The doors opened nine times during the next two years and Wladek started to wonder if he was destined to spend the rest of his days in that filthy hell-hole, fighting a vain battle against despair, while equipping himself with a mind of useless knowledge that would never know freedom.

The Baron continued to tutor him despite his progressively failing sight and hearing. Wladek had to sit closer and closer to him each day.

Florentyna – his sister, mother and closest friend – engaged in a more physcial struggle against the rankness of their prison. Occasionally the guards would provide her with a fresh bucket of sand or straw to cover the soiled floor, and the stench became a little less oppressive for the next few days. Vermin scuttled around in the darkness for any dropped scraps of bread or potato and brought with them disease and still more filth. The sour smell of decomposed human and animal urine and excrement assaulted their nostrils and regularly brought Wladek to a state of sickness and nausea. He longed above all to be clean again, and would sit for hours gazing at the dungeon ceiling, recalling the steaming tubs of hot water and the good, rough soap with which the niania had, so short a distance away and so long a time ago, washed the accretion of a mere day's fun from Leon and himself, with many a muttering and tut-tut for muddy knees or a dirty fingernail.

By the spring of 1918, only fifteen of the twenty-six captives who had been incarcerated with Wladek in the dungeons were still alive. The Baron was always treated by everyone as the master, while Wladek had become his acknowledged steward. Wladek felt saddest for his beloved Florentyna, now twenty. She had long since despaired of life and was convinced that she was going to spend her remaining days in the dungeons. Wladek never admitted in her presence to giving up hope, but although he was only twelve, he too was beginning to wonder if he dared believe in any future.

One evening, early in the autumn, Florentyna came to Wladek's side in the larger dungeon.

'The Baron is calling for you.'

Wladek rose quickly, leaving the allocation of food to a senior servant, and went to the old man. The Baron was in severe pain, and Wladek saw with terribly clarity and – as though for the first time – how illness had eroded whole areas of the Baron's flesh, leaving the green-mottled skin covering a now skeletal face. The Baron asked for water and Florentyna brought it from the half-full mug that balanced from a stick outside the stone grille. When the great man had finished drinking, he spoke slowly and with considerable difficulty.

'You have seen so much of death, Wladek, that one more will make little difference to you. I confess that I no longer fear escaping this world.'

'No, no, it can't be,' cried Wladek, clinging on to the old man for the first time in his life. 'We have so nearly triumphed. Don't give up, Baron. The guards have assured me that the war is coming to an end and then we will soon be released.'

'They have been promising us that for months, Wladek. We cannot believe them any longer, and in any case I fear I have no desire to live in the new world they are creating.' He paused as he listened to the boy crying. The Baron's only thought was to collect the tears as drinking water, and then he remembered that tears were saline and he laughed to himself.

'Call for my butler and first footman, Wladek.'

Wladek obeyed immediately, not knowing why they should be required.

The two servants, woken from a deep sleep, came and stood in front of the Baron. After three years captivity sleep was the easiest commodity to come by. They still wore their embroidered uniforms, but one could no longer tell that they had once been the proud Rosnovski colours of green and gold. They stood silently waiting for their master to speak.

'Are they there, Wladek?' asked the Baron.

'Yes, sir. Can you not see them?' Wladek realised for the first time that the Baron was now completely blind.

'Bring them forward so that I might touch them.'

Wladek brought the two men to him and the Baron touched their faces.

'Sit down,' he commanded. 'Can you both hear me, Ludwik, Alfons?'

'Yes, sir.'

'My name is Baron Rosnovski.'

'We know, sir,' replied the butler innocently.

'Do not interrupt me,' said the Baron. 'I am about to die.'

Death had become so common that the two men made no protest.

'I am unable to make a new will as I have no paper, quill, or ink. Therefore I make my will in your presence and you can act as my two witnesses as recognised by the ancient law of Poland. Do you understand what I am saying?'

'Yes, sir,' the two men replied in unison.

'My first born son, Leon, is dead.' The Baron paused. 'And so I leave my entire estate and possessions to the boy known as Wladek Koskiewicz.'

Wladek had not heard his surname for many years and did not immediately comprehend the significance of the Baron's words.

'And as proof of my resolve,' the Baron continued, 'I give him the family band.'

The old man slowly raised his right arm, removed from his wrist the silver band and held it forward to a speechless Wladek, whom he clasped on to firmly, running his fingers over the boy's chest as if to be sure that it was he. 'My son,' he said, as he placed the silver band on the boy's wrist.

Wladek wept, and lay in the arms of the Baron all night until he could no longer hear his heart, and could feel the fingers stiffening around him. In the morning the Baron's body was removed by the guards and they allowed Wladek to bury him by the side of his son, Leon, in the family churchyard, up against the chapel. As the body was lowered into its shallow grave, dug by Wladek's bare hands, the Baron's tattered shirt fell open. Wladek stared at the dead man's chest.

He had only one nipple.

Thus Wladek Koskiewicz, aged twelve, inherited sixty thousand acres of land, one castle, two manor houses, twenty-seven cottages, and a valuable collection of paintings, furniture and jewelry, while he lived in a small stone room under the earth. From that day on, the captives took him as their rightful master and his empire was four dungeons, his retinue thirteen broken servants and his only love Florentyna.

He returned to what he felt was now an endless routine until long into the winter of 1918. On a mild, dry day there burst upon the prisoners' ears a volley of shots and the sound of a brief struggle. Wladek was sure that the Polish army had come to rescue him and that he would now be able to lay claim to his rightful inheritance. When the German guards deserted the iron door of the dungeons, the inmates remained in terrified silence huddled in the lower rooms. Wladek stood alone at the entrance, twisting the silver band around his wrist, triumphant, waiting for his liberators. Eventually those who had defeated the Germans arrived and spoke in the coarse Slavic tongue, familiar from school days, which he had learned to fear even more than German. Wladek was dragged unceremoniously out into the passage with his retinue. The prisoners waited, then were cursorily inspected and thrown back into the dungeons. The new conquerors were unaware that this twelve-year-old boy was the master of all their eyes beheld. They did not speak his tongue. Their orders were clear and not to be questioned : kill the enemy if they resist the agreement of Brest-Litovsk, which made this section of Poland theirs and send those who do not resist to camp 201 for the rest of their days. The Germans had left meekly to retreat behind their new border while Wladek and his followers waited, hopeful of a new life, ignorant of their impending fate.

After spending two more nights in the dungeons, Wladek resigned himself to believing that they were to be incarcerated for another long spell. The new guards did not speak to him at all, a reminder to him of what life had been like three years before; he began to realise that discipline had at least become lax under the Germans but once again was tight.

On the morning of the third day, much to Wladek's surprise, they were all dragged out on to the grass in front of the castle, fifteen thin filthy bodies. Two of the servants collapsed in the unaccustomed sunlight. Wladek himself found the intense brightness his biggest problem and kept having to shield his eyes from it. The prisoners stood in silence on the grass and waited for the soldiers' next move. The guards made them all strip and ordered them down to the river to wash. Wladek hid the silver band in his clothes and ran down to the water's edge, his legs feeling weak even before he reached the river. He jumped in, gasping for breath at the coldness of the water, although it felt glorious on his skin. The rest of the prisoners followed him, and tried vainly to remove three years of filth.

When Wladek came out of the river exhausted, he noticed that some of the guards were looking strangely at Florentyna as she washed herself in the water. They were laughing and pointing at her. The other women did not seem to arouse the same degree of interest. One of the guards, a large ugly man whose eyes had never left Florentyna for a moment, grabbed her arm as she passed him on her way back up the river bank, and threw her to the ground. He then started to take his clothes off quickly, hungrily, while at the same time folding them neatly on the grass. Wladek stared in disbelief at the man's swollen erect penis and flew at the soldier, who was now holding Florentyna down on the ground, and hit him in the middle of his stomach with his head with all the force he could muster. The man reeled back, and a second soldier jumped up and held Wladek helpless with his hands pinned behind his back. The commotion attracted the attention of the other guards, and they strolled over to watch. Wladek's captor was now laughing, a loud belly laugh with no humour in it. The other soldiers' words only added to Wladek's anguish

'Enter the great protector,' said the first.

'Come to defend his nation's honour.' The second one.

'Let's at least allow him a ringside view.' The one who was holding him.

More laughter interspersed the remarks that Wladek couldn't always comprehend. He watched the naked soldier advance his hard, well-fed body slowly towards Florentyna, who started screaming. Once again Wladek struggled, trying desperately to free himself from the vice-like grip, but he was helpless in the arms of his guard. The naked man fell clumsily on top of Florentyna and started kissing her and slapping her when she tried to fight or turn away; finally he lunged into her. She let out a scream such as Wladek had never heard before. The guards continued talking and laughing among themselves, some not even watching.

'Goddamn virgin,' said the first soldier as he withdrew himself from her.

They all laughed.

'You've just made it a little easier for me,' said the second guard.

More laughter. As Florentyna stared into Wladek's eyes, he began to retch. The soldier holding on to him showed little interest, other than to be sure that none of the boy's vomit soiled his uniform or boots. The first soldier, his penis now covered in blood, ran down to the stream, yelling as he hit the water. The second man undressed, while yet another held Florentyna down. The second guard took a little longer over his pleasure, and seemed to gain considerable satisfaction from hitting Florentyna; when he finally entered her, she screamed again but not quite as loud.

'Come on, Valdi, you've had long enough.'

With that the man came out of her suddenly and joined his companion-at-arms in the stream. Wladek made himself look at Florentyna. She was bruised and bleeding between the legs. The soldier holding him spoke again.

'Come and hold the little bastard, Boris, it's my turn.'

The first soldier came out of the river and took hold of Wladek firmly. Again he tried to hit out, and this made them laugh even louder.

'Now we know the full might of the Polish army.'

The unbearable laughter continued as yet another guard started undressing to take his turn with Florentyna, who now lay indifferent to his charms. When he had finished, and had gone down to the river, the second soldier returned and started putting on his clothes.

'I think she's beginning to enjoy it,' he said, as he sat in the sun watching his companion. The fourth soldier began to advance on Florentyna. When he reached her, he turned her over, forced her legs as wide apart as possible, his large hands moving rapidly over her frail body. The scream when he entered her had now turned into a groan. Wladek counted sixteen soldiers who raped his sister. When the last soldier had finished with her, he swore and then added, 'I think I've made love to a dead woman,' and left her motionless on the grass.

They all laughed even more loudly, as the disgruntled soldier walked down to the river. At last Wladek's guard released him. He ran to Florentyna's side, while the soldiers lay on the grass drinking wine and vodka taken from the Baron's cellar, and eating the bread from the kitchens.

With the help of two of the servants, Wladek carried Florentyna's light body to the edge of the river, weeping as he tried to wash away her blood and bruises. It was useless, for she was black and red all over, insensible to help and unable to speak. When Wladek had done the best he could he covered her body with his jacket and held her in his arms. He kissed her gently on the mouth, the first woman he had ever kissed. She lay in his arms, but he knew she did not recognise him, and as the tears ran down his face on to her bruised body, he felt her go limp. He wept as he carried her dead body up the bank. The guards went silent as they watched him walk towards the chapel. He laid her down on the grass beside the Baron's grave and started digging with his bare hands. When the sinking sun had caused the castle to cast its long shadow over the graveyard, he had finished digging. He buried Florentyna next to Leon and made a little cross with two sticks which he placed at her head. Wladek collapsed on the ground between Leon and Florentyna, and fell asleep, caring not if he ever woke again.

8

William returned to Sayre Academy in September and immediately began to look for competition among those older than himself. Whatever he took up, he was never satisfied unless he excelled in it, and his contemporaries almost always proved too weak an opposition. William began to realise that most of those from backgrounds as privileged as his own lacked any incentive to compete, and that fiercer rivalry was to be found from boys who had, compared with himself, relatively little.

In 1915, a craze for collecting match-box labels hit Sayre Academy. William observed this frenzy for a week with great interest but did not join in. Within a few days, common labels were changing hands at a dime, while rarities commanded as much as fifty cents. William considered the situation and decided to become not a collector, but a dealer.

On the following Saturday, he went to Leavitt and Pearce, one of the largest tobacconists in Boston, and spent the afternoon taking down the names and addresses of all the major match-box manufacturers throughout the world, making a special note of those who were not at war. He invested five dollars in notepaper, envelopes and stamps, and wrote to the chairman or president of every company he had listed. His letter was simple despite having been rewritten seven times.

> Dear Mr. Chairman or Mr. President,
> I am a dedicated collector of match-box labels, but I cannot afford to buy all the matches. My pocket money is only one dollar a week, but I enclose a three-cent stamp for postage to prove that I am serious about my hobby. I am sorry to bother you personally, but yours was the only name I could find to write to.
> Your friend,
> William Kane (aged 9)
> P.S. Yours are one of my favourites.

Within three weeks, William had a fifty-five per cent reply which yielded one hundred and seventy-eight different labels. Nearly all his correspondents also returned the three-cent stamp, as William had anticipated they would.

During the next seven days, William set up a market in labels within the school, always checking what he could sell at even before he had made a purchase. He noticed that some boys showed no interest in the rarity of the match-box label, only in its looks, and with them he made quick exchanges to obtain rare trophies for the more discerning collectors. After a further two weeks of buying and selling he sensed that the market was reaching its zenith and that if he were not careful, with the holidays fast approaching, interest might begin to die off. With much trumpeted advance publicity in the form of a printed handout which cost him a further half cent a sheet, placed on every boy's desk, William announced that he would be holding an auction of his match-box labels, all two hundred and eleven of them. The auction took place in the school washroom during the lunch hour and was better attended than most school hockey games.

The result was that William netted fifty-seven dollars thirty-two cents, a profit of fifty-two dollars thirty-two cents on his original investment. William put twenty-five dollars on deposit with the bank at two and a half per cent, bought himself a camera for eleven dollars, gave five dollars to the Young Men's Christian Association, who had broadened their activities to help the new flood of immigrants, bought his mother some flowers, and put the remaining few dollars into his pocket. The market in match-box labels collapsed even before the school term ended. It was to be the first of many such occasions that William got out at the top of the market. The grandmothers would have been proud of him; it was not unlike the way their husbands had made their fortunes in the panic of 1873.

When the holidays came, William could not resist finding out if it was possible to obtain a better return on his invested capital than the two and a half per cent yielded by his savings account. For the next three months he invested – again through Grandmother Kane – in stocks highly recommended by the *Wall Street Journal*. During the next term at school he lost over half of the money he had made on the match-box labels. It was the only time in his life that he relied on the expertise of the *Wall Street Journal*, or on information available at any street corner.

Angry with his loss of over twenty dollars William decided that it must be recouped during the Easter holidays. On arriving home he worked out which parties and functions his mother would expect him to attend, and found he was left with only fourteen free days, just enough time for his new venture. He sold all his remaining *Wall Street Journal* shares, which netted him only twelve dollars. With this money he bought himself a flat piece of wood, two sets of wheels, axles and a piece of rope, at a cost, after some bargaining, of five dollars. He then put on a flat cloth cap and an old suit he had outgrown and went off to the local railroad station. He stood outside the exit, looking hungry and tired, informing selected travellers that the main hotels in Boston were near the railroad station, so that there was no need to take a taxi or the occasional surviving hansom carriage as he, William, could carry their luggage on his moving board for twenty per cent of what the taxis charged; he added that the walk would also do them good. By working six hours a day, he found he could make roughly four dollars.

Five days before the new school term was due to start, he had made back all his original losses and a further ten dollars profit. He then hit a problem. The taxi drivers were starting to get annoyed with him. William assured them that he would retire, aged nine, if each one of them would give him fifty cents to cover the cost of his home-made trolley – they agreed, and he made another eight dollars fifty cents. On the way home to Beacon Hill, William sold his trolley for five dollars to a school friend two years his senior, who was soon to discover that the market had passed its peak; moreover, it rained for every day of the following week.

On the last day of the holidays, William put his money back on deposit in the bank, at two and a half per cent. During the following term this decision caused him no anxiety as he watched his savings rise steadily. The sinking of the *Lusitania* and Wilson's declaration of war against Germany in April of 1917 didn't concern William. Nothing and no one could ever beat America, he assured his mother. William even invested ten dollars in Liberty Bonds to back his judgment.

By William's eleventh birthday the credit column of his ledger book showed a profit of four hundred and twelve dollars. He had given his mother a fountain pen and his two grandmothers brooches from a local jewellery shop. The fountain pen was a Parker and the jewellery arrived at his grandmothers' homes in Shreve, Crump and Low boxes, which he had found after much searching in the dustbins behind the famous store. To do the boy justice, he had not wanted to cheat his grandmothers, but he had already learned from his match-box label experience that good packaging sells products. The grandmothers, who noted the missing Shreve, Crump and Low hallmark still wore their brooches with considerable pride.

The two old ladies continued to follow William's every move and had decided that when he reached the age of twelve, he should proceed as planned to St. Paul's School in Concord, New Hampshire. For good measure the boy rewarded them with the top mathematics scholarship, unnecessarily saving the family some three hundred dollars a year. William accepted the scholarship and the grandmothers returned the money for, as they expressed it, 'a less fortunate child'. Anne hated the thought of William leaving her to go away to boarding school, but the grandmothers insisted and, more importantly, she knew it was what Richard would have wanted. She sewed on William's name tapes, marked his boots, checked his clothes, and finally packed his trunk refusing any help from the servants. When the time came for William to go his mother asked him how much pocket money he would like for the new term ahead of him.

'None,' he replied without further comment.

William kissed his mother on the cheek; he had no idea how much she was going to miss him. He marched off down the path, in his first pair of long trousers, his hair cut very short, carrying a small suitcase towards Roberts, the chauffeur. He climbed into the back of the Rolls-Royce and it drove him away. He didn't look back. His mother waved and waved, and later cried. William wanted to cry too, but he knew his father would not have approved.

The first thing that struck William Kane as strange about his new prep school was that the other boys did not care who he was. The looks of admiration, the silent acknowledgment of his presence were no longer there. One older boy actually asked his name, and what was worse, when told, was not manifestly impressed. Some even called him Bill which he soon corrected with the explanation that no one had ever referred to his father as Dick.

William's new domain was a small room with wooden book-shelves, two tables, two chairs, two beds and a comfortably shabby leather settee. The other chair, table and bed were occupied by a boy from New York called Matthew Lester, whose father was also in banking.

William soon became used to the school routine. Up at

seven thirty, wash, breakfast in the main dining room, with the whole school – two hundred and twenty boys munching their way through eggs, bacon and porridge. After breakfast, chapel, three fifty-minute classes before lunch and two after it, followed by a music lesson which William detested because he could not sing a note in tune and he had even less desire to learn to play any musical instrument. Football in the autumn, hockey and squash in the winter, and rowing and tennis in the spring left him with very little free time. As a mathematics scholar, William had special tutorials in the subject three times a week from his housemaster, G. Raglan, Esquire, known to the boys as Grumpy.

During his first year, William proved to be well worthy of his scholarship, among the top few boys in almost every subject, and in a class of his own in mathematics. Only his new friend, Matthew Lester, was any real competition for him, and that was almost certainly because they shared the same room. While establishing himself academically William also acquired a reputation as a financier. Although his first investment in the market had proved disastrous, he did not abandon his belief that to make a significant amount of money, sizeable capital gains on the stock market were essential. He kept a wary eye on the *Wall Street Journal*, company reports and, at the age of twelve, started to experiment with a ghost portfolio of investments. He recorded every one of his ghost purchases and sales, the good and the not-so-good in a newly acquired, different coloured ledger book, and compared his performance at the end of each month against the rest of the market. He did not bother with any of the leading listed stocks, concentrating instead on the more obscure companies, some of which traded only over the counter, so that it was impossible to buy more than a few shares in them at any one time. William expected four things from his investments: a low multiple of earnings, a high growth rate, strong asset backing and a favourable trading outlook. He found few shares which fulfilled all these rigorous criteria, but when he did, they almost invariably showed him a profit.

The moment he found that he was regularly beating the Dow-Jones Index with his ghost investment programme, William knew he was ready to invest his own money once again. He started with one hundred dollars and never stopped refining his method. He would always follow profits and cut losses. Once a stock had doubled, he would sell half his holding but keep the remaining half intact, trading the stock he still held as a bonus. Some of his early finds, such as Eastman Kodak and I.B.M., went on to become national leaders. He also backed the first mail order company, convinced it was a trend that would catch on.

By the end of his first year he was advising half the school staff and some of the parents. William Kane was happy at school.

Anne Kane had been unhappy and lonely at home with William away at St. Paul's and a family circle consisting only of the two grandmothers, now approaching old age. She was miserably conscious that she was past thirty, and that her smooth and youthful prettiness had disappeared without leaving much in its place. She started picking up the threads, severed by Richard's death, with some of her old friends. John and Milly Preston, William's godmother, whom she had known all her life, began inviting her to dinners and the theatre, always including an extra man, trying to make a match for Anne. The Preston's choices were almost always atrocious, and Anne used privately to laugh at Milly's attempts at match-making until one day in January 1919, just after William had returned to school for the winter term, Anne was invited to yet another dinner for four. Milly confessed she had never met her other guest, Henry Osborne, but that they thought he had been at Harvard at the same time as John.

'Actually,' confessed Milly over the phone, 'John doesn't know much about him, darling, except that he is rather good-looking.'

On that score, John's opinion was verified by Anne and Milly. Henry Osborne was warming himself by the fire when

Anne arrived and he rose immediately to allow Milly to introduce them. A shade over six feet, with dark eyes, almost black, and straight black hair, he was slim and athletic looking. Anne felt a quick flash of pleasure that she was paired for the evening with this energetic and youthful man, while Milly had to content herself with a husband, who was showing signs of middle-age by comparison with his dashing college contemporary. Henry Osborne's arm was in a sling, almost completely covering his Harvard tie.

'A war wound?' asked Anne sympathetically.

'No, I fell down the stairs the week after I got back from the Western Front,' he said, laughing.

It was one of those dinners, lately so rare for Anne, at which the time at the table slipped by happily and unaccountably. Henry Osborne answered all Anne's inquisitive questions. After leaving Harvard, he had worked for a real estate management firm in Chicago, his home town, but when the war came he couldn't resist having a go at the Germans. He had a fund of splendid stories about Europe and the life he had led there as a young lieutenant preserving the honour of America on the Marne. Milly and John had not seen Anne laugh so much since Richard's death and smiled at one another knowingly when Henry asked if he might drive her home.

'What are you going to do now that you've come back to a land fit for heroes?' asked Anne, as Henry Osborne eased his Stutz out on to Charles Street.

'Haven't really decided,' he replied. 'Luckily, I have a little money of my own, so I don't have to rush into anything. Might even start my own real estate firm right here in Boston. I've always felt at home in the city since my days at Harvard.'

'You won't be returning to Chicago, then?'

'No, there's nothing to take me back there. My parents are both dead, and I was an only child, so I can start afresh anywhere I choose. Where do I turn?

'Oh, first on the right,' said Anne.

'You live on Beacon Hill?'

'Yes, About a hundred and fifty yards on the right hand side up Chestnut and it's the red house on the corner of Louisburg Square.'

Henry Osborne parked the car and accompanied Anne to the front door of her home. After saying goodnight, he was gone almost before she had time to thank him. She watched his car glide slowly back down Beacon Hill knowing that she wanted to see him again. She was delighted, though not entirely surprised, when he telephoned her the following morning.

'Boston Symphony Orchestra, Mozart, and that flamboyant new fellow, Mahler, next Monday – can I persuade you?'

Anne was a little taken aback by the extent to which she looked forward to Monday. It seemed so long since a man whom she found attractive had pursued her. Henry Osborne arrived punctually for the outing, they shook hands rather awkwardly, and he accepted a Scotch highball.

'It must be pleasant to live on Louisburg Square. You're a lucky girl.'

'Yes, I suppose so, I've never really given it much thought. I was born and raised on Commonwealth Avenue. If anything, I find this slightly cramped.'

'I think I might buy a house on the Hill myself if I do decide to settle in Boston.'

'They don't come on the market all that often,' said Anne, 'but you may be lucky. Hadn't we better be going? I hate being late for a concert and having to tread on other people's toes to reach my seat.'

Henry glanced at his watch. 'Yes I agree, wouldn't do to miss the conductor's entrance, but you don't have to worry about anyone's feet except mine. We're on the aisle.'

The cascades of sumptuous music made it natural for Henry to take Anne's arm as they walked to the Ritz. The only other person who had done that since Richard's death had been William, and only after considerable persuasion as he considered it sissy. Once again the hours slipped by for

Anne: was it the excellent food, or was it Henry's company? This time he made her laugh with his stories of Harvard and cry with recollections of the war. Although she was well aware that he looked younger than herself, he had done so much with his life that she always felt deliciously youthful and inexperienced in his company. She told him about her husband's death, and cried a little more. He took her hand and she spoke of her son with glowing pride and affection. He said he had always wanted a son. Henry scarcely mentioned Chicago or his own home life but Anne felt sure that he must miss his family. When he took her home that night, he stayed for a quick drink and kissed her gently on the cheek as he left. Anne went back over the evening minute by minute before she fell asleep.

They went to the theatre on Tuesday, visited Anne's cottage on Cape Cod on Wednesday, gyrated to the Grizzly Bear and the Temptation Rag on Thursday, shopped for antiques on Friday, and made love on Saturday. After Sunday, they were rarely apart. Milly and John Preston were 'absolutely delighted' that their match-making had at last proved so successful. Milly went around Boston telling everyone that she had been responsible for putting the two of them together.

The announcement during that summer of the engagement came as no surprise to anyone except William. He had disliked Henry intensely from the day that Anne, with a well-founded sense of misgiving, introduced them to each other. Their first conversation took the form of long questions from Henry, trying to prove he wanted to be a friend, and monosyllabic answers from William, showing that he didn't. And he never changed his mind. Anne ascribed her son's resentment to an understandable feeling of jealousy; William had been the centre of her life since Richard's death. Moreover, it was perfectly proper that in William's estimation, no one could possibly take the place of his own father. Anne convinced Henry that given time William would get over his sense of outrage.

Anne Kane became Mrs. Henry Osborne in October of

that year at the Old North Church just as the golden and red leaves were beginning to fall, a little over ten months after they had met. William feigned illness in order not to attend the wedding and remained firmly at school. The grandmothers did attend, but were unable to hide their disapproval of Anne's remarriage, particularly to someone who appeared to be so much younger than herself. 'It can only end in disaster,' said Grandmother Kane.

The newlyweds sailed for Greece the following day, and did not return to the Red House on the Hill till the second week of December, just in time to welcome William home for the Christmas holidays. William was shocked to find the house had been redecorated, leaving almost no trace of his father. Over Christmas, William's attitude to his step-father showed no sign of softening despite the present as Henry saw it – bribe as William construed it – of a new bicycle. Henry Osborne accepted this rebuff with surly resignation. It saddened Anne that her splendid new husband made so little effort to win over her son's affection.

William felt ill at ease in his invaded home and would often disappear for long periods during the day. Whenever Anne inquired where he was going, she received little or no response : it certainly was not to the grandmothers. When the Christmas holidays came to an end, William was only too happy to return to school and Henry was not sad to see him go. Only Anne was uneasy about both the men in her life.

9

'Up, boy. Up, boy.'

One of the soldiers was digging his rifle butt into Wladek's ribs. He sat up with a start and looked at the grave of his sister and those of Leon and of the Baron, and he did not shed a single tear as he turned towards the soldier.

'I will live, you will not kill me,' he said in Polish. 'This is my home, and you are on my land.'

The soldier spat on Wladek and pushed him back to the lawn where the servants were waiting, all dressed in what looked like grey pyjamas with numbers on their backs. Wladek was horrified at the sight of them, realising what was about to happen to him. He was taken by the soldier to the north side of the castle and made to kneel on the ground. He felt a knife scrape across his head as his thick black hair fell on to the grass. With ten bloody strokes, like the shearing of a sheep, the job was completed. Shaven-headed, he was ordered to put on his new uniform, a grey rubaskew shirt and trousers. Wladek managed to keep the silver band well hidden and rejoined his servants at the front of the castle.

While they all stood waiting on the grass – numbers now, not names – Wladek became conscious of a noise in the distance that he had never heard before. His eyes turned towards the menacing sound. Through the great iron gates came a vehicle moving on four wheels, but not drawn by horses or oxen. All the prisoners stared at the moving object in disbelief. When it had come to a halt, the soldiers dragged the reluctant prisoners towards it and made them climb aboard. Then the horseless wagon turned round, moved back down the path and through the iron gates. Nobody dared to speak. Wladek sat at the rear of the truck and stared at his castle until he could no longer see the Gothic turrets.

The horseless wagon somehow drove itself towards Slonim. Wladek would have worried about how the vehicle worked if he had not been even more worried about where it was taking them. He began to recognise the roads from his days at school, but his memory had been dulled by three years in the dungeons, and he could not recall where the road finally led. After only a few miles, the truck came to a stop and they were all pushed out. It was the local railway station. Wladek had only seen it once before in his life, when he and Leon had gone there to welcome the Baron home from his trip to Warsaw. He remembered the guard had saluted them when they first walked on to the platform; this time no guard saluted them. The prisoners were fed on goats' milk, cabbage soup and black bread, Wladek again taking charge, dividing the portions carefully among the remaining fourteen. He sat on a wooden bench, assuming that they were waiting for a train. That night they slept on the ground below the stars, paradise compared with the dungeons. He thanked God for the mild winter.

Morning came and still they waited. Wladek made the servants take some exercise but most collapsed after only a few minutes. He began to make a mental note of the names of those who had survived thus far. Eleven of the men and two of the women, spared from the original twenty-seven in the dungeons. Spared for what? he thought. They spent the rest of the day waiting for a train that never came. Once, a train did arrive, from which more soldiers disembarked, speaking their hateful tongue, but it departed without Wladek's pitiful army. They slept yet another night on the platform.

Wladek lay awake below the stars considering how he might escape, but during the night one of his thirteen made a run for it across the railway track and was shot down by a guard even before he had reached the other side. Wladek gazed at the spot where his compatriot had fallen, frightened to go to his aid for fear he would meet the same fate. The guards left the body on the track in the morning, as a warning to those who might consider a similar course of action.

No one spoke of the incident the next day, although Wladek's eyes rarely left the body of the dead man. It was the Baron's butler, Ludwik – one of the witnesses to the Baron's will, and his heritage – dead.

On the evening of the third day another train chugged into the station, a great steam locomotive pulling open freight cars, the floors strewn with straw and the word 'cattle' painted on the sides. Several cars were already full, full of humans, but from where Wladek could not judge, so hideously did their appearance resemble his own. He and his band were thrown together into one of the cars to begin the journey. After a wait of several more hours the train started to move out of the station, in a direction which Wladek judged, from the setting sun, to be eastward.

To every three carriages there was a guard sitting cross-legged on a roofed car. Throughout the interminable journey an occasional flurry of bullet shots from above demonstrated to Wladek the futility of any further thoughts of escape.

When the train stopped at Minsk, they were given their first proper meal: black bread, water, nuts, and more millet, and then the journey continued. Sometimes they went for three days without seeing another station. Many of the reluctant travellers died of starvation and were thrown overboard from the moving train. And when the train did stop they would often wait for two days to allow another train going west use of the track. These trains which delayed their progress were inevitably full of soldiers, and it became obvious to Wladek that the troop trains had priority over all other transport. Escape was always uppermost in Wladek's mind, but three things prevented him from advancing that ambition. First, no one had yet succeeded; second, there was nothing but miles of wilderness on both sides of the track; and third, those who had survived the dungeons were now totally dependent on him to protect them. It was Wladek who organised their food and drink, and tried to give them all the will to live. He was the youngest and the last one still to believe in life.

At night, it became bitterly cold, often thirty degrees below zero, and they would all lie up against each other in a line on the carriage floor so that each body would keep the person next to him warm. Wladek would recite the *Aeneid* to himself while he tried to snatch some sleep. It was impossible to turn over unless everyone agreed, so Wladek would lie at the end and each hour, as near as he could judge by the changing of the guards, he would slap the side of the carriage, and they would all roll over and face the other way. One after the other, the bodies would turn like falling dominoes. Sometimes a body did not move – because it no longer could – and Wladek would be informed. He in turn would inform the guard and four of them would pick up the body and throw it over the side of the moving train. The guards would pump bullets into the head to be sure it was not someone hoping to escape.

Two hundred miles beyond Minsk, they arrived in the small town of Smolensk, where they received warm cabbage soup and black bread. Wladek was joined in his car by some new prisoners who spoke the same tongue as the guards. Their leader seemed to be about the same age as Wladek. Wladek and his ten remaining companions, nine men and one woman, were immediately suspicious of the new arrivals, and they divided the carriage in half, with the two groups remaining apart for several days.

One night, while Wladek lay awake staring at the stars, trying to get warm, he watched the leader of the Smolenskis crawl towards the end man of his own line with a small piece of rope in his hand. He watched him slip it round the neck of Alfons, the Baron's first footman, who was sleeping. Wladek knew if he moved too quickly, the boy would hear him and escape back to his own half of the carriage and the protection of his comrades, so he crawled slowly on his belly down the line of Polish bodies. Eyes stared at him as he passed, but nobody spoke. When he reached the end of the line, he leaped forward upon the aggressor, immediately waking everyone in the truck. Each faction shrank back to its own end of the carriage, with the exception of Alfons, who lay motionless in front of them.

The Smolenski leader was taller and more agile than Wladek, but it made little difference while the two were fighting on the floor. The struggle lasted for several minutes, with the guards laughing and taking bets as they watched the two gladiators. One guard, who was getting bored by the lack of blood, threw a bayonet into the middle of the car. Both boys scrambled for the shining blade with the Smolenski leader grabbing it first. The Smolenski band cheered their hero as he thrust the bayonet into the side of Wladek's leg, pulled the blood-covered steel back out and lunged again. On the second thrust the blade lodged firmly in the wooden floor of the jolting car next to Wladek's ear. As the Smolenski leader tried to wrench it free, Wladek kicked him in the groin with every ounce of energy he had left, and in throwing his adversary backwards released the bayonet. With a leap, Wladek grabbed the handle and jumped on top of the Smolenski, running the blade right into his mouth. The man gave out a shriek of agony that awoke the entire train. Wladek pulled the blade out, twisting it as he did so, and thrust it back into the Smolenski again and again, long after he had ceased to move. Wladek knelt over him, breathing heavily, and then picked up the body and threw it out of the carriage. He heard the thud as it hit the bank, and the shots that the guards pointlessly aimed after it.

Wladek limped towards Alfons, still lying motionless on the wooden boards, and knelt by his side shaking his lifeless body: his second witness dead. Who would now believe that he, Wladek, was the chosen heir to the Baron's fortune? Was there any purpose left in life? He collapsed to his knees. He picked up the bayonet with both hands, pointing the blade towards his stomach. Immediately a guard jumped down and wrested the weapon away from him.

'Oh no, you don't,' he grunted. 'We need the lively ones like you for the camps. You can't expect us to do all the work.'

Wladek buried his head in his hands, aware for the first time of an aching pain in his bayoneted leg. He had lost his inheritance and traded it to become the leader of a band of penniless Smolenskis.

The whole truck once again became his domain and he now had twenty prisoners to care for. He immediately split them up so that a Pole would always sleep next to a Smolenski, making it impossible for there to be any further warfare between the two groups.

Wladek spent a considerable part of his time learning their strange tongue, not realising for several days that it was actually Russian, so greatly did it differ from the classical Russian language taught him by the Baron, and then the real significance of the discovery dawned on him for the first time when he realised where the train was heading.

During the day Wladek used to take on two Smolenskis at a time to tutor him, and as soon as they were tired, he would take on two more, and so on until they were all exhausted.

Gradually he became able to converse easily with his new dependents. Some of them were Russian soldiers, exiled after repatriation for the crime of having been captured by the Germans. The rest were White Russians, farmers, miners, labourers, all bitterly hostile to the Revolution.

The train jolted on past terrain more barren than Wladek had ever seen before, and through towns of which he had never heard – Omsk, Novo Sibirsk, Krasnoyarsk – the names rang ominously in his ears. Finally, after three months and more than three thousand miles, they reached Irkutsk, where the railway track came to an abrupt end.

They were hustled off the train, fed, and issued with felt boots, jackets and heavy coats and although fights broke out for the warmest clothing, they still provided little protection from the ever intensifying cold.

Horseless wagons appeared, not unlike the one which had borne Wladek away from his castle, and long chains were thrown out. Then, to Wladek's disbelief and horror, the prisoners were cuffed to the chain by one hand, twenty-five pairs side by side on each chain. The trucks pulled the mass of prisoners along while the guards rode on the back. They marched like that for twelve hours, before being given a two-hour rest, and then they marched again. After three days, Wladek thought he would die of cold and exhaustion, but once clear of populated areas they travelled only during the day and rested at night. A mobile field kitchen run by prisoners from the camp supplied turnip soup and bread at first light and then again at night. Wladek learned from these prisoners that conditions at the camp were even worse.

For the first week they were never unshackled from those chains, but later when there could be no thought of escape they were released at night to sleep, digging holes in the snow for warmth. Sometimes on good days they found a forest in which to bed down : luxury began to take strange forms. On and on they marched, past enormous lakes and across frozen rivers, ever northwards, into the face of viciously cold winds and deeper falls of snow. Wladek's injured leg gave him a constant dull pain, soon surpassed in intensity by the agony of frostbitten fingers and ears. There was no sign of life or food in all the expanse of whiteness, and Wladek knew that to attempt an escape at night could only mean slow death by starvation. The old and the sick were starting to die, quietly at night, if they were lucky. The unlucky ones, unable to keep up the pace, were uncuffed from the chains and cast off to be left alone in the endless snow. Those who survived walked on, on, on, always towards the north, until Wladek lost all sense of time and was simply conscious of the inexorable tug of the chain, not even sure when he dug his hole in the snow to sleep at night that he would wake the next morning: those that didn't had dug their own grave.

After a trek of nine hundred miles, those who had survived were met by Ostyaks, nomads of the Russian steppes, in reindeer-drawn sleds. The trucks discharged their cargo and turned back. The prisoners, now chained to the sleds, were led on. A great blizzard forced them to halt for the greater part of two days and Wladek seized the opportunity to communicate with the young Ostyak to whose sled he was chained. Using classical Russian, with a Polish accent, he was understood only very imperfectly but he did discover that the Ostyaks hated the Russians of the south, who treated them almost as badly as they treated their captives. The Ostyaks were not unsympathetic to the sad prisoners with no future, the 'unfortunates' as they called them.

Nine days later, in the half light of the early Arctic winter night, they reached camp 201. Wladek would never have believed he could have been glad to see such a place: row upon row of wooden huts in the stark open space. The huts, like the prisoners were numbered. Wladek's hut was 33. There was a small black stove in the middle of the room, and, projecting from the walls, tiered wooden bunks on which were hard straw mattresses and one thin blanket. Few of them managed to sleep at all that first night, and the groans and cries that came from hut 33 were often louder than the howls of the wolves outside.

The next morning before the sun rose, they were woken by the sound of a hammer against an iron triangle. There was thick frost on both sides of the window and Wladek thought that he must surely die of the cold. Breakfast in a freezing communal hall lasted for ten minutes and consisted of a bowl of lukewarm gruel, with pieces of rotten fish and a leaf of cabbage floating in it. The newcomers spat the fish bones out on the table while the more seasoned prisoners ate the bones and even the fishes' eyes.

After breakfast, they were allocated tasks. Wladek became a wood chopper. He was taken seven miles through the featureless steppes into a forest and ordered to cut a certain number of trees each day. The guard would leave him and his little group of six to themselves with their food ration, tasteless yellow magara porridge and bread. The guards had no fear of the prisoners attempting to escape, for it was over a thousand miles to the nearest town, even if you knew in which direction to head.

At the end of each day, the guard would return and count the number of logs of wood they had chopped; he informed the prisoners that if they failed to reach the required number, he would stop the group's food for the following day. But when he came back at seven in the evening to collect the reluctant woodsmen, it was already dark, and he could not always see exactly how many new logs they had cut. Wladek taught the others in his team to spend the last part of the afternoon clearing the snow off the wood cut the previous day and lining it up with what they had chopped that day. It was a plan that always worked, and Wladek's group never lost a day's food. Sometimes they managed to return to the camp with a small piece of wood, tied to the inside of their legs, to put in the coal stove at night. Caution was required, for at least one of them was searched every time they left and entered the camp, often having to remove one or both boots, and to stand there in the numbing snow. If they were caught with anything on them it meant three days without food.

As the weeks went by, Wladek's leg started to become very stiff and painful. He longed for the coldest days, when the temperature went down to forty below zero, and outside work was called off, even though the lost day would have to be made up on a free Sunday when they were normally allowed to lie on their bunks all day.

One evening when Wladek had been hauling logs across the waste, his leg began to throb unmercifully. When he looked at the scar caused by the Smolenski, he found that it had become puffy and shiny. That night, he showed the wound to a guard, who ordered him to report to the camp doctor before first light in the morning. Wladek sat up all night with his leg nearly touching the stove, surrounded by wet boots, but the heat was so feeble that it couldn't ease the pain.

The next morning Wladek rose an hour earlier than usual. If you had not seen the doctor before work was due to start, then you missed him until the next day. Wladek couldn't face another day of such intense pain. He reported to the doctor, giving his name and number. Pierre Dubien was a sympathetic old man, bald-headed, with a pronounced stoop, and Wladek thought he looked even older than the Baron. He inspected Wladek's leg without speaking.

'Will the wound be all right, doctor?' asked Wladek.

'You speak Russian?'

'Yes, sir.'

'Although you will always limp, young man, your leg will be good again. But good for what? A life here dragging wood.'

'No, doctor, I intend to escape and get back to Poland,' said Wladek.

The doctor looked sharply at him. 'Keep your voice down, stupid boy. You must realise by now that escape is impossible. I have been in captivity fifteen years, and not a day has passed that I have not thought of escape. There is no way; no one has ever escaped and lived, and even to talk of it means ten days in the punishment cell, and there they feed you every third day and light the stove only to melt the ice off the walls.

If you come out of that place alive, you can consider yourself lucky.'

'I will escape, I will, I will,' said Wladek, staring at the old man.

The doctor looked into Wladek's eyes and smiled. 'My friend, never mention escape again or they may kill you. Go back to work, keep your leg exercised and report to me first thing every morning.'

Wladek returned to the forest and to the chopping of wood, but found that he could not drag the logs more than a few feet, and that the pain was so intense he believed his leg might fall off. When he returned the next morning, the doctor examined the leg more carefully.

'Worse, if anything,' he said. 'How old are you, boy?'

'I think I am thirteen,' said Wladek. 'What year is it?'

'Nineteen hundred and nineteen,' replied the doctor.

'Yes, thirteen. How old are you?' asked Wladek.

The old man looked down into the young boy's blue eyes, surprised by the question.

'Thirty-eight,' he said quietly.

'God help me,' said Wladek.

'You will look like this when you have been a prisoner for fifteen years, my boy,' said the doctor matter of factly.

'Why are you here at all?' said Wladek. 'Why haven't they let you go after all this time?'

'I was taken prisoner in Moscow in 1904, soon after I had qualified as a doctor and I was working in the French Embassy. They said I was a spy and put me in a Moscow jail. I thought that was bad until after the Revolution when they sent me to this hell-hole. Even the French have now forgotten that I exist. Few have been known to complete their sentence at camp Two-O-One so I must die here, like everyone else, and it can't be too soon.'

'No, you must not give up hope, doctor.'

'Hope? I gave up hope for myself a long time ago, perhaps I shall not give it up for you, but always remember never to mention that hope to anyone; there are prisoners here who trade in loose tongues, when their reward can be nothing more than an extra piece of bread or perhaps a blanket. Now Wladek, I am going to put you on kitchen duty for a month and you must continue to report to me every morning. It is the only chance that you have of not losing that leg, and I do not relish being the man who has to cut it off. We don't exactly have the latest surgical instruments here,' he added, staring at a large carving knife.

Wladek shuddered.

Doctor Dubien wrote out Wladek's name on a slip of paper. Next morning, Wladek reported to the kitchens, where he cleaned the plates in freezing water and helped to prepare food that required no refrigeration. After carrying logs all day, he found it a welcome change: extra fish soup, thick black bread with shredded nettles, and the chance to stay inside and keep warm. On one occasion he even shared half an egg with the cook, although neither of them could be sure what fowl had laid it. Wladek's leg mended slowly, leaving him with a pronounced limp. There was little Doctor Dubien could do in the absence of any real medical supplies except keep an eye on his progress. As the days went by, the doctor began to befriend Wladek and even to believe in his youthful hope for the future. They would converse in a different language each morning, but the old man most enjoyed speaking in French, his native tongue.

'In seven days time, Wladek, you will have to return to forest duty; the guards will inspect your leg and I will not be able to keep you in the kitchens any longer. So listen carefully, for I have decided upon a plan for your escape.'

'Together, doctor,' said Wladek. 'Together.'

'No, only you. I am too old for such a long journey, and although I have dreamed about escape for over fifteen years, I would only hold you up. It will be enough for me to know someone else has achieved it, and you are the first person I've ever met who has convinced me that he might succeed.'

Wladek sat on the floor in silence listening to the doctor's plan.

'I have, over the last fifteen years, saved two hundred

rubles – you don't exactly get overtime as a Russian prisoner.' Wladek tried to laugh at the camp's oldest joke. 'I keep the money hidden in a drug bottle, four fifty-ruble notes. When the time comes for you to leave, the money must be sewn into your clothes. I will have already done this for you.'

'What clothes?' asked Wladek.

'I have a suit and a shirt I bribed from a guard twelve years ago when I still believed in escape. Not exactly the latest fashion, but they will serve your purpose.'

Fifteen years to scrape together two hundred rubles, a shirt and a suit, and the doctor was willing to sacrifice them to Wladek in a moment. Wladek never again in his life experienced such an act of selflessness.

'Next Thursday will be your only chance,' the doctor continued. 'New prisoners arrive by train at Irkutsk, and the guards always take four people from the kitchen to organise the food truck for the new arrivals. I have already arranged with the senior cook' – he laughed at the word – 'that in exchange for some drugs you will find yourself on the kitchen truck. It was not too hard. No one exactly wants to make the trip there and back – but you will only be making the journey there.'

Wladek was still listening intently.

'When you reach the station, wait until the prisoners' train arrives. Once they are all on the platform, cross the line and get yourself on to the train going to Moscow, which cannot leave until the prisoners' train comes in, as there is only one track outside the station. You must pray that with hundreds of new prisoners milling around the guards will not notice you disappear. From then on you're on your own. Remember if they do spot you, they will shoot you on sight without a second thought. There is only one last thing I can do for you. Fifteen years ago when I was brought here, I drew a map from memory of the route from Moscow to Turkey. It may not be totally accurate any longer, but it should be adequate for your purpose. Be sure to check that the Russians haven't taken over Turkey as well. God knows what they have been up to recently. They may even control France for all I know.'

The doctor walked over to the drug cabinet and took out a large bottle which looked as if it was full of a brown substance. He unscrewed the top and took out an old piece of parchment. The black ink had faded over the years. It was marked October 1904. It showed a route from Moscow to Odessa, and from Odessa to Turkey, seventeen hundred miles to freedom.

'Come to me every morning this week, and we will go over the plan again and again. If you fail, it must not be from lack of preparation.'

Wladek stayed awake each night, gazing at the wolves' sun through the window, rehearsing what he would do in any given situation, preparing himself for every eventuality. In the morning he would go over the plan again and again with the doctor. On the Wednesday evening before Wladek was to try the escape, the doctor folded the map into eight, placed it with the four fifty-ruble notes in a small package and sewed the package into a sleeve of the suit. Wladek took off his clothes, put on the suit and then replaced the prison uniform on top of it. As he put on the uniform again, the doctor's eye caught the Baron's band of silver which Wladek, ever since he had been issued his prison uniform, had always kept above his elbow for fear the guards would spot his only treasure and steal it.

'What's that?' he asked. 'It's quite magnificent.'

'A gift from my father,' said Wladek. 'May I give it to you to show my thanks?' He slipped the band off his wrist and handed it to the doctor.

The doctor stared at the silver band for several moments and bowed his head. 'Never,' he said. 'This can only belong to one person.' He stared silently at the boy. 'Your father must have been a great man.'

The doctor placed the band back on Wladek's wrist and shook him warmly by the hand.

'Good luck, Wladek. I hope we never meet again.'

They embraced and Wladek parted for what he prayed was his last night in the prison hut. He was unable to sleep at all that night for fear one of the guards would discover the suit under his prison clothes. When the morning bell sounded, he was already dressed and he made sure that he was not late reporting to the kitchen. The senior prisoner in the kitchen pushed Wladek forward when the guards came for the truck detail. The team chosen were four in all and Wladek was by far the youngest.

'Why this one?' asked the guard, pointing to Wladek. 'He has been at the camp for less than a year.'

Wladek's heart stopped and he went cold all over. The doctor's plan was going to fail; and there would not be another batch of prisoners coming to the camp for at least three months. By then he would no longer be in the kitchens.

'He's an excellent cook,' said the senior prisoner. 'Trained in the castle of a baron. Only the best for the guards.'

'Ah,' said the guard, greed overcoming suspicion. 'Hurry up, then.'

The four of them ran to the truck, and the convoy started.

The journey was again slow and arduous, but at least he was not walking this time, nor, being summer, was it unbearably cold. Wladek worked hard on preparing the food and, as he had no desire to be noticed, hardly spoke to anyone for the entire journey other than Stanislaw, the chief cook.

When they eventually reached Irkutsk, the drive had taken nearly sixteen days. The train waiting to go to Moscow was already standing in the station. It had been there for several hours, but was unable to continue its journey until the train bringing the new prisoners had arrived. Wladek sat on the side of the platform with the others from the field kitchen, three of them with no interest or purpose in anything around them, dulled by the experience, but one of them intent on every move, studying the train on the other side of the platform carefully. There were several open entrances and Wladek quickly selected the one he would use when his moment came.

'Are you going to try an escape?' asked Stanislaw suddenly.

Wladek began to sweat but did not answer.

Stanislaw stared at him. 'You *are*?'

Still Wladek said nothing.

The old cook stared at the thirteen-year-old boy. He nodded his head up and down in agreement. If he had had a tail, it would have wagged.

'Good luck. I'll make sure they don't realise you're missing for at least two days.'

Stanislaw touched his arm and Wladek caught sight of the prisoners' train in the distance, slowly inching its way towards them. He tensed in anticipation, his heart pounding, his eyes following the movement of every soldier. He waited for the incoming train to come to a halt and watched the tired prisoners pile out on to the platform, hundreds of them, anonymous men with only a past. When the station was a chaos of people and the guards were fully occupied, Wladek ran under the carriage and jumped on to the other train. No one showed any interest as he went into a lavatory at the end of the carriage. He locked himself in and waited and prayed, every moment expecting someone to knock on the door. It seemed a lifetime to Wladek before the train began to move out of the station. It was, in fact, seventeen minutes.

'At last, at last,' he said out loud. He looked through the little window and watched the station growing smaller and smaller in the distance, a mass of new prisoners being hitched up to the chains, ready for the journey to camp 201, the guards laughing as they locked them in. How many would reach the camp alive? How many would be fed to the wolves? How long before they missed him?

Wladek sat in the lavatory for several more minutes, terrified to move, not sure what he ought to do next. Suddenly there was a banging on the door. Wladek thought quickly – the guard, the ticket collector, a soldier – a succession of images flashed through his mind, each one more frightening than the last. He needed to use the lavatory for the first time. The banging persisted.

'Come on, come on,' said a man in coarse Russian.

Wladek had little choice. If it was a soldier, there was no way out, a dwarf could not have squeezed through the little window. If it wasn't a soldier, he would only draw attention to himself by staying there. He took off his prison clothes, made them into as small a bundle as possible, and threw them out of the window. Then he removed a soft hat from the pocket of his suit to cover his shaved head, and opened the door. An agitated man rushed in, pulling down his trousers even before Wladek had left.

Once in the corridor, Wladek felt isolated and terrifyingly conspicuous in his out-of-date suit, an apple placed on a pile of oranges. He immediately went in search of another lavatory. When he found one that was unoccupied, he locked himself in and quickly undid the stitches in his suit, extracting one of the four fifty-ruble notes. He replaced the other three and returned to the corridor. He looked for the most crowded carriage he could find and hid himself in a corner. Some men were playing pitch-and-toss in the middle of the carriage for a few rubles to while away the time. Wladek had always beaten Leon when they had played in the castle, and he would have liked to have joined the contestants, but he feared winning and drawing attention to himself. The game went on for a long time and Wladek began to remember the stratagems. The temptation to risk his two hundred rubles was almost irresistible.

One of the gamblers, who had parted with a considerable amount of his money, retired in disgust and sat down by Wladek, swearing.

'The luck wasn't with you,' said Wladek, wanting to hear the sound of his own voice.

'Ah, it's not luck,' the gambler replied. 'Most days I could beat that lot of peasants, but I have run out of rubles.'

'Do you want to sell your coat?' asked Wladek.

The gambler was one of the few passengers in the carriage wearing a good, old, thick bearskin coat. He stared at the youth.

'Looking at that suit I'd say you couldn't afford it, boy.' Wladek could tell from the man's voice that he hoped he could. 'I would want seventy-five rubles.'

'I'll give you forty,' said Wladek.

'Sixty,' said the gambler.

'Fifty,' said Wladek.

'No. Sixty is the least I'd let it go for; it cost over a hundred,' said the gambler.

'A long time ago,' said Wladek, as he considered the implications of taking extra money from inside the lining of his coat in order to secure the full amount needed. He decided against doing so as it would only draw further attention to himself; he would have to wait for another opportunity. Wladek was not willing to show he could not afford the coat, and he touched the collar of the garment and said, with considerable disdain, 'You paid too much for it, my friend; fifty rubles, not a kopeck more.' Wladek rose as if to leave.

'Wait, wait,' said the gambler. 'I'll let you have it for fifty.'

Wladek took the fifty rubles out of his pocket and the gambler took off his coat and exchanged it for the grimy red note. The coat was far too big for Wladek, nearly touching the ground, but it was exactly what he needed to cover his conspicuous suit. For a few moments, he watched the gambler, back in the game, once again losing. From his new tutor he had learned two things : never to gamble unless the odds are tipped in your favour by superior knowledge or skill, and always to be willing to walk away from a deal when you have reached your limit.

Wladek left the carriage, feeling a little safer under his new-old coat. He started to examine the layout of the train with a little more confidence. The carriages seemed to be in two classes; general ones where passengers stood or sat on the wooden boards and special ones where they could sit on upholstered seats. Wladek found that all the carriages were packed, with but one exception, a sitting carriage with a solitary woman in it. She was middle-aged, as far as Wladek could tell, and dressed a little more smartly with a little more flesh on her bones than most of the other passengers on the train. She wore a dark blue dress and a scarf over her head. She smiled at Wladek as he stood staring at her, and this gesture gave him the confidence to enter the carriage.

'May I sit down?'

'Please do,' said the woman, looking at him carefully.

Wladek did not speak again, but studied the woman and the contents of the carriage. She had a sallow skin covered with tired lines, a little overweight – the little bit you could be on Russian food. Her short black hair and brown eyes suggested that she once might have been quite attractive. She had two large cloth bags on the rack and a small valise by her side. Despite the danger of his position Wladek was suddenly aware of feeling desperately tired. He was wondering if he dared to sleep when the woman spoke.

'Where are you travelling?'

The question took Wladek by surprise and he tried to think quickly. 'Moscow,' he said, holding his breath.

'So am I,' she replied.

Wladek was already regretting the isolation of the carriage and the information he had given. Don't talk to anyone, the doctor had warned him; remember, trust nobody.

To his relief the woman asked no more questions. As he began to regain his lost confidence, the ticket collector arrived. Wladek started to sweat, despite the temperature being minus twenty degrees. The collector took the woman's ticket, tore it, gave it back to her, and then turned to Wladek.

'Ticket, comrade,' was all he said in a slow, monotonous tone.

Wladek was speechless, and started thumbing around in his coat pocket.

'He's my son,' said the woman firmly.

The ticket collector looked back at the woman, once more at Wladek, and then he bowed to the woman and left the carriage without another word.

Wladek stared at her. 'Thank you,' he breathed, not quite sure what else he could say.

'I watched you come from under the prisoners' train,' the woman remarked quietly. Wladek felt sick. 'But I shall not give you away. I have a young cousin in one of those terrible camps, and all of us fear that one day we might end up there. What do you have on under your coat?'

Wladek weighed the relative merits of dashing out of the carriage and unfastening his coat. If he dashed out of the carriage there was no escape. He unfastened his coat.

'Not as bad as I had feared,' she said. 'What did you do with your prison uniform?'

'Threw it out of the window.'

'Let's hope they don't find it before you reach Moscow.'

Wladek said nothing.

'Do you have anywhere to stay in Moscow?'

He thought again of the doctor's advice to trust nobody, but he had to trust her.

'I have nowhere to go.'

'Then you can stay with me until you find somewhere to live. My husband,' she explained, 'is the station master in Moscow, and this carriage is for government officials only. If you ever make that mistake again, you will be taking the train back to Irkutsk.'

Wladek swallowed. 'Should I leave now?'

'No, not now that the ticket collector has seen you. You will be safe with me for the time being. Do you have any identity papers?'

'No. What are they?'

'Since the Revolution every Russian citizen must have identity papers to show who he is, where he lives and where he works, otherwise he ends up in jail until he can produce them, and as he can never produce them once in jail, he stays there for ever,' she added matter of factly. 'You will have to stick by me once we reach Moscow, and be sure you don't open your mouth.'

'You are being very kind to me,' said Wladek suspiciously.

'Now the Tsar is dead, none of us is safe. I was lucky to be married to the right man,' she added, 'but there is not a citizen in Russia, including government officials, who does not live in constant fear of arrest and the camps. What is your name?'

'Wladek.'

'Good, now you sleep, Wladek, because you look exhausted, the journey is long and you are not safe yet.'

Wladek slept.

When he woke, several hours had passed, and it was now

dark outside. He stared at his protectress, and she smiled. Wladek returned her smile, praying that she could be trusted not to tell the officials who he was – or had she already done so? She produced some food from one of her bundles and Wladek ate the offering silently. When they reached the next station, nearly all the passengers got out, some of them permanently, but most to seek what little refreshment was available or to stretch their stiff limbs.

The middle-aged woman rose, looked at Wladek. 'Follow me,' she said.

He stood up and followed her on to the platform. Was he about to be given up? She put out her hand, and he took it as any thirteen-year-old child accompanying his mother would do. She walked towards a lavatory marked for women only. Wladek hesitated. She insisted, and once inside she told Wladek to take off his clothes. He obeyed her unquestioningly as he hadn't anyone since the death of the Baron. While he undressed she turned on the solitary tap, which with reluctance yielded a trickle of cold brownish water. She was disgusted. But to Wladek, it was a vast improvement on the camp water. The woman started to bathe his wounds with a wet rag and attempted hopelessly to wash him. She winced when she saw the scar on his leg. Wladek didn't murmur from the pain that came with each touch, gentle as she tried to be.

'When we get you home, I'll make a better job of those wounds,' she said, 'but that will have to do for now.'

Then she saw the silver band, studied the inscription and looked carefully at Wladek. 'Is that yours?' she asked. 'Who did you steal it from?'

Wladek looked offended. 'I didn't steal it. My father gave it to me before he died.'

She stared at him again, and a different look came into her eyes. Was it fear or respect? She bowed her head. 'Be careful, Wladek, men would kill for such a valuable prize.'

He nodded his agreement and started to dress quickly. They returned to their carriage. A delay of an hour at a station was not unusual and when the train started lurching forward, Wladek was glad to feel the wheels clattering underneath him again. The train took twelve and a half days to reach Moscow. Whenever a new ticket collector appeared, they went through the same routine, Wladek unconvincingly trying to look innocent and young. The woman a convincing mother. The ticket collectors always bowed respectfully to the middle-aged lady, and Wladek began to think that station masters must be very important in Russia.

By the time they completed the one-thousand-mile journey to Moscow, Wladek had put his trust completely in the middle-aged lady and was looking forward to seeing her house. It was early afternoon when the train came to its final halt and despite everything Wladek had been through, he had never visited a big city, let alone the capital of all the Russias. He was terrified, once again tasting the fear of the unknown. So many people all rushing around in different directions. The middle-aged lady sensed his apprehension.

'Follow me, do not speak, and whatever you do don't take your cap off.'

Wladek took her bags down from the rack, pulled his cap over his head – now covered in a black stubble – down to his ears and followed her out on to the platform. A throng of people at the barrier were waiting to go through a tiny exit, which caused a holdup as everyone had to show their identification papers to the guard. As they approached the barrier, Wladek could hear his heart beating like a soldier's drum, but when their turn came the fear was over in a moment. The guard only glanced at the woman's documents.

'Comrade,' he said, and saluted. He looked at Wladek.

'My son,' she explained.

'Of course, comrade.' He saluted again.

Wladek was in Moscow.

Despite the trust he had placed in his new-found companion, his first instinct was to run but as one hundred and fifty rubles was hardly enough to live on, he decided for the time being to stay put. He could always run at some later time. A horse and cart was waiting at the station and took the woman and her new son home. The station master was not there when they arrived, so the woman immediately set about making up the spare bed for Wladek. Then she poured water, heated on a stove, into a large tin tub and told him to get in. It was the first bath he had had in over four years, unless he counted the dip in the stream. She heated some more water and reintroduced him to soap, scrubbing his back, the only part of his body with unbroken skin. The water began to change colour and after twenty minutes, it was black. Once Wladek was dry, the woman put some ointment on his arms and legs, and bandaged the parts of his body that looked particularly fierce. She stared at his one nipple. He dressed quickly and then joined her in the kitchen. She had already prepared a bowl of hot soup and some beans. Wladek ate the veritable feast hungrily. Neither of them spoke. When he had finished the meal, she suggested that it might be wise for him to go to bed and rest.

'I do not want my husband to see you before I have told him why you are here,' she explained. 'Would you like to stay with us, Wladek, if my husband agrees?'

Wladek nodded thankfully.

'Then off you go to bed,' she said.

Wladek obeyed and prayed that her husband would allow him to live with them. He undressed slowly and climbed on to the bed. He was too clean, the sheets were too clean, the mattress was too soft, and he threw the pillow on the floor, but he was so tired that he slept despite the comfort of the bed. He was woken from his deep sleep some hours later by the sound of raised voices coming from the kitchen. He could not tell how long he had slept. It was already dark outside as he crept off the bed, walked to the door, eased it open and listened to the conversation taking place in the kitchen below.

'You stupid woman.' Wladek heard a piping voice. 'Do you not understand what would have happened if you had been caught? It would have been you who would have been sent to the camps.'

'But if you had seen him, Piotr, like a hunted animal.'

'So you decided to turn us into hunted animals,' said the male voice. 'Has anyone else seen him?'

'No,' said the woman, 'I don't think so.'

'Thank God for that. He must go immediately before anyone knows he's here, it's our only hope.'

'But go where, Piotr? He is lost, and has no one,' Wladek's protectress pleaded. 'And I have always wanted a son.'

'I do not care what you want or where he goes, he is not our responsibility and we must be quickly rid of him.'

'But Piotr, I think he is royal, I think his father was a Baron. He wears a silver band around his wrist and inscribed on it are the words...'

'That only makes it worse. You know what our new leaders have decreed. No tsars, no royalty, no privileges. We would not even have to bother to go to the camp, the authorities would just shoot us.'

'We have always wanted a son, Piotr. Can we not take this one risk in our lives?'

'With your life, perhaps, but not mine. I say he must go and go now.'

Wladek did not need to listen to any more of their conversation. Deciding that the only way he could help his benefactress would be to disappear without trace into the night, he dressed quickly and stared at the slept-in bed, hoping it would not be four more years before he saw another one. He was unlatching the window when the door was flung open and into the room came the station master, a tiny man, no taller than Wladek, with a large stomach and an almost bald head covered in long strands of grey hair. He wore rimless spectacles, which had produced little red semicircles under each eye. The man carried a paraffin lamp. He stood, staring at Wladek. Wladek stared defiantly back.

'Come downstairs,' he commanded.

Wladek followed him reluctantly to the kitchen. The woman was sitting at the table crying.

'Now listen, boy,' he said.

'His name is Wladek,' the woman interjected.

'Now listen, boy,' he repeated. 'You are trouble, and I

want you out of here and as far away as possible. I'll tell you what I am going to do to help you.'

Help? Wladek gazed at him stonily.

'I am going to give you a train ticket. Where do you want to go?'

'Odessa,' said Wladek, ignorant of where it was or how much it would cost, knowing only that it was the next city on the doctor's map to freedom.

'Odessa, the mother of crime – an appropriate destination,' sneered the station master. 'You can only be among your own kind and come to harm there.'

'Then let him stay with us, Piotr. I will take care of him, I will ...'

'No, never. I would rather pay the bastard.'

'But how can he hope to get past the authorities?' the woman pleaded.

'I will have to issue him a working pass for Odessa.' He turned his head towards Wladek. 'Once you are on that train, boy, if I see or hear of you again in Moscow, I will have you arrested on sight and thrown into the nearest jail. You will then be back in that prison camp as fast as the train can get you there if they don't shoot you first.'

He stared at the clock on the kitchen mantlepiece: five after eleven. He turned to his wife. 'There is a train that leaves for Odessa at midnight. I will take him to the station myself. I want to be sure he leaves Moscow. Have you any baggage, boy?'

Wladek was about to say no, when the woman said, 'Yes, I will go and fetch it.'

Wladek and the station master stood, staring at each other with mutual contempt. The woman was away for a long time. The grandfather clock struck once in her absence. Still neither spoke, and the station master's eyes never left Wladek. When his wife returned, she was carrying a large brown paper parcel wrapped up with string. Wladek stared at it and began to protest, but as their eyes met, he saw such fear in hers that he only just got out the words, 'Thank you.'

'Eat this,' she said, thrusting her bowl of cold soup towards him.

He obeyed, although his shrunken stomach was now overfull, gulping down the soup as quickly as possible, not wanting her to be in any more trouble.

'Animal,' the man said.

Wladek looked at him, hatred in his eyes. He felt pity for the woman, bound to such a man for life.

'Come, boy, it's time to leave,' the station master said. 'We don't want you to miss your train, do we?'

Wladek followed the man out of the kitchen. He hesitated as he passed the woman and touched her hand, feeling the response. Nothing was said; no words would have been adequate. The station master and the refugee crept through the streets of Moscow, hiding in the shadows, until they reached the station. The station master obtained a one-way ticket to Odessa and gave the little red slip of paper to Wladek.

'My pass?' said Wladek defiantly.

From his inside pocket the man drew out an official looking form, signed it hurriedly, and handed it over furtively to Wladek. The station master's eyes kept looking all around him for any possible danger. Wladek had seen those eyes so many times during the past four years: the eyes of a coward.

'Never let me see or hear of you again,' he said, the voice of a bully.

Wladek had also heard that voice many times before in the last four years. He looked up, wanting to say something, but the station master had already retreated into the shadows of the night where he belonged. He looked at the eyes of the people who hurried past him. The same eyes, the same fear; was anyone in the world free? Wladek gathered the brown paper parcel under his arm, checked his hat, and walked towards the barrier. This time he felt more confident, showing his pass to the guard; he was ushered through without comment. He climbed on board the train. It had been a short visit to Moscow, and he would never see the city again in his life, though he would always remember the kindness of the woman, the station master's wife, Comrade ... He didn't even know her name.

Wladek stayed in the general class standing carriages for his journey. Odessa looked less distant from Moscow than Irkutsk, about a thumb's length on the doctor's sketch, eight hundred and fifty miles in reality. While Wladek was studying his rudimentary map, he became distracted by another game of pitch-and-toss which was taking place in the carriage. He folded the parchment, replaced it safely in the lining of his suit and began taking a closer interest in the game. He noticed that one of the gamblers was winning consistently, even when the odds were stacked against him. Wladek watched the man more carefully and soon realised that he was cheating.

He moved to the other side of the carriage to make sure he could still spot the man cheating when facing him, but he couldn't. He edged forward and made a place for himself in the circle of gamblers. Every time the cheat had lost twice in a row, Wladek backed him with one ruble, doubling his stake until he won. The cheat was either flattered or considered he would be wise to remain silent about Wladek's luck, because he never once even glanced in his direction. By the time they reached the next station, Wladek had won fourteen rubles, two of which he used to buy himself an apple and a cup of hot soup. He had won enough to last the entire journey to Odessa and, pleased with the thought that he could win even more rubles with his new safe system, he silently thanked the unknown gambler and climbed back on to the train ready to resume the strategy. As his foot touched the top step, he was knocked flying into a corner. His arm was jerked painfully behind his back and his face was pushed hard against the carriage wall. His nose began to bleed and he could feel the point of a knife touching the lobe of his ear.

'Do you hear me, boy?'

'Yes,' said Wladek, petrified.

'If you go back to my carriage again, I take this ear right off, then you won't be able to hear me, will you?'

'No, sir,' said Wladek.

Wladek felt the point of the knife breaking the surface of the skin behind his ear and blood began trickling down his neck.

'Let that be a warning to you, boy.'

A knee suddenly came up into his kidneys with as much force as the gambler could muster. Wladek collapsed to the ground. A hand rummaged into his coat pockets and the recently acquired rubles were removed.

'Mine, I think,' the voice said.

Blood was now coming out of Wladek's nose and from behind his ear. When he summoned up the courage to look up from the corner of the corridor, it was empty, and there was no sign of the gambler. Wladek tried to get to his feet, but his body refused to obey the order from his brain, so he remained slumped in the corner for several minutes. Eventually when he was able to rise, he walked slowly to the other end of the train, as far away from the gambler's carriage as possible, his limp grotesquely exaggerated. He hid in a carriage occupied mostly by women and children, and fell into a deep sleep.

At the next stop, Wladek didn't leave the train. He undid his little parcel and started to investigate. Apples, bread, nuts, two shirts, a pair of trousers and even shoes were contained in that brown-papered treasure trove. What a woman, what a husband.

He ate, he slept, he dreamed. And finally, after six nights and five days, the train chugged into the terminal at Odessa. The same check at the ticket barrier, but the guard hardly gave Wladek a second look. This time his papers were all in order, but now he was on his own. He still had one hundred and fifty rubles in the lining of his suit, and no intention of wasting any of them.

Wladek spent the rest of the day walking around the town trying to familiarise himself with its geography, but he found he was continually distracted by sights he had never seen before: big town houses, shops with windows, hawkers selling their colourful trinkets on the street, gaslights, and even a monkey on a stick. Wladek walked on until he reached the harbour and stopped to stare at the open sea beyond it. Yes, there it was – what the Baron had called an ocean. He gazed into the blue expanse longingly: that way was freedom and escape from Russia. The city must have seen its fair share of fighting: burnt-out houses and squalor were all too evident, grotesque in the mild, flower-scented sea air. Wladek wondered whether the city was still at war. There was no one he could ask. As the sun disappeared behind the high buildings, he began to look for somewhere to spent the night. Wladek took a side road and kept walking. He must have looked a strange sight with his skin coat dragging along the ground and the brown paper parcel under his arm. Nothing looked safe to him until he came across a railway siding in which a solitary old carriage stood in isolation. He stared into it cautiously; darkness and silence: no one was there. He threw his paper parcel into the carriage, raised his tired body up on to the boards, crawled into a corner and lay down to sleep. As his head touched the wooden floor, a body leaped on top of him and two hands were quickly around his throat. He could barely breathe.

'Who are you?' hissed a boy who, in the darkness, sounded no older than himself.

'Wladek Koskiewicz.'

'Where do you come from?'

'Moscow.' Slonim had been on the tip of Wladek's tongue.

'Well, you're not sleeping in my carriage, Muscovite,' said the voice.

'Sorry,' said Wladek. 'I didn't know.'

'Got any money?' His thumbs pressed into Wladek's throat.

'A little,' said Wladek.

'How much?'

'Seven rubles.'

'Hand it over.'

Wladek rummaged in the pocket of his overcoat, while

the boy also pushed one hand firmly into it, releasing the pressure on Wladek's throat.

In one movement, Wladek brought up his knee with every ounce of force he could muster into the boy's crotch. His attacker flew back in agony, clutching his testicles. Wladek leaped on him, hitting him in places the boy would never have thought of. The rules had suddenly changed. He was no competition for Wladek; sleeping in a derelict carriage was five-star luxury compared to the dungeons and a Russian labour camp.

Wladek stopped only when his adversary was pinned to the carriage floor, helpless. The boy pleaded with Wladek.

'Go to the far end of the carriage and stay there,' said Wladek. 'If you so much as move a muscle, I'll kill you.'

'Yes, yes,' said the boy, scrambling away.

Wladek heard him hit the far end of the carriage. He sat still and listened for a few moments – no movement – then he lowered his head once more on to the floor, and in moments he was sleeping soundly.

When he awoke, the sun was already shining through the slits between the boards of the carriage. He turned over slowly and studied his adversary of the previous night for the first time. He was lying in a foetal position, still asleep at the other end of the carriage.

'Come here,' commanded Wladek.

The boy woke slowly.

'Come here,' repeated Wladek, a little more loudly.

The boy obeyed immediately. It was the first chance Wladek had had to look at him properly. They were about the same age, but the boy was a clear foot taller with a younger-looking face and scruffy fair hair. His general appearance suggested that talk of soap and water would have been treated as an insult.

'First things first,' said Wladek. 'How does one get something to eat here?'

'Follow me,' said the boy, leaping out of the carriage. Wladek limped after him and followed the boy up the hill into the town where the morning market was being set up.

He had not seen so much wholesome food since those magnificent dinners with the Baron. Row upon row of stalls with fruit, vegetables, greens, and even his favourite nuts. The boy could see Wladek was overwhelmed by the sight.

'Now I'll tell you what we do,' the boy said, sounding confident for the first time. 'I will go over to the corner stall and steal an orange, and then make a run for it. You will shout at the top of your voice, 'Stop thief'. The stallkeeper will chase me and when he does, you move in and fill your pockets. Don't be greedy; enough for one meal. Then you return here. Got it?'

'Yes, I think so,' said Wladek.

'Lets see if you're up to it, Moscovite.' The boy looked at him, snarled, and was gone. Wladek watched him in admiration as he swaggered to the corner of the first market stall, removed an orange from the top of a pyramid, made some short unheard remark to the stallkeeper and started to run slowly. He glanced back at Wladek, who had entirely forgotten to shout 'Stop thief', but the stall owner looked up and immediately began to chase the boy. While everyone's eyes were on Wladek's accomplice, he moved in quickly and managed to take three oranges, an apple and a potato, and put them in the large pockets of his overcoat. When the stallkeeper looked as if he were about to catch his accomplice, the boy lobbed the orange back at him. The man stopped to pick it up and swore at him, waving his fist, complaining vociferously to the other merchants as he returned to his stall.

Wladek was shaking with mirth as he took in the scene when a hand was placed firmly on his shoulder. He turned round in the horror of having been caught.

'Did you get anything, Moscovite, or are you only here as a sightseer?'

Wladek burst out laughing with relief and produced the three oranges, apple and potato. The boy joined in the laughter.

'What's your name?' said Wladek.

'Stefan.'

'Let's do it again, Stefan.'

'Hold on, Muscovite, don't you start getting too clever. If we do *my* scheme again, we'll have to go to the other end of the market and wait for at least an hour. You're working with a professional now, but don't imagine you won't get caught occasionally.'

The two boys went quietly through to the other end of the market, Stefan walking with a swagger for which Wladek would have traded the three oranges, apple, potato and his one hundred and fifty rubles. They mingled with the morning shoppers and when Stefan decided the time was right, they repeated the trick twice. Satisfied with the results, they returned to the railway carriage to enjoy their captured spoils; six oranges, five apples, three potatoes, a pear, several varieties of nuts, and the special prize, a melon. In the past, Stefan had never had pockets big enough to hold one. Wladek's greatcoat took care of that.

'Not bad,' said Wladek, as he dug his teeth into a potato.

'Do you eat the skins as well?' asked Stefan, horrified.

'I've been places where the skins are a luxury,' replied Wladek.

Stefan looked at him with admiration.

'Next problem is how do we get some money?' said Wladek.

'You want everything in one day, don't you, o master?' said Stefan. 'Chain gang on the waterfront is the best bet, if you think you're up to some real work, Muscovite.'

'Show me,' said Wladek.

After they had eaten half the fruit and hidden the rest under the straw in the corner of the carriage, Stefan took Wladek down the steps to the harbour and showed him all the ships. Wladek couldn't believe his eyes. He had been told by the Baron of the great ships that crossed the high seas delivering their cargoes to foreign lands, but these were so much bigger than he had ever imagined, and they stood in a line as far as the eye could see.

Stefan interrupted his thoughts. 'See that one over there, the big green one; well, what you have to do is pick up a basket at the bottom of the gangplank, fill it with grain, climb up the ladder and then drop your load in the hold. You get a ruble for every four trips you make. Be sure you can count, Muscovite, because the bastard in charge of the gang will swindle you as soon as look at you and pocket the money for himself.'

Stefan and Wladek spent the rest of the afternoon carrying grain up the ladder. They made twenty-six rubles between them. After a dinner of stolen nuts, bread, and an onion they hadn't intended to take, they slept happily in their carriage.

Wladek was the first to wake the next morning and Stefan found him studying his map.

'What's that?' asked Stefan.

'This is a route showing me how to get out of Russia.'

'What do you want to leave Russia for when you can stay here and team up with me?' said Stefan. 'We could be partners.'

'No, I must get to Turkey; there I will be a free man for the first time. Why don't you come with me, Stefan?'

'I could never leave Odessa. This is my home, the railway is where I live and these are the people I have known all my life. It's not good, but it might be worse in the place you call Turkey. But if that's what you want, I will help you to escape because I know how to find out where every ship has come from.'

'How do I discover which ship is going to Turkey?' asked Wladek.

'Easy. We'll get the information from One Tooth Joe at the end of the pier. You'll have to give him a ruble.'

'I'll bet he splits the money with you.'

'Fifty-fifty,' said Stefan. 'You're learning fast, Muscovite.' And with that he leaped out of the carriage.

Wladek followed him as he ran swiftly between the carriages, again conscious of how easily other boys moved, and how he limped. When they reached the end of the pier, Stefan took him into a small room full of dust-covered books and old timetables. Waldek couldn't see anyone there, but then he heard a voice from behind a large pile of books saying, 'What do you want, urchin? I don't have time to waste on you.'

'Some information for my travelling companion, Joe. When is the next luxury cruise to Turkey?'

'Money up front,' said an old man whose head appeared from behind the books, a lined weatherbeaten face wearing a seaman's cap. His black eyes were taking in Wladek.

'Used to be a great sea dog,' said Stefan in a whisper loud enough for Joe to hear.

'None of your cheek, boy. Where is the ruble?'

'My friend carries my purse,' said Stefan. 'Show him the ruble, Wladek.'

Wladek pulled out a coin. Joe bit it with his one remaining tooth, shuffled over to the bookcase and pulled out a large green timetable. Dust flew everywhere. He started coughing as he thumbed through the dirty pages, moving his short, stubby, rope-worn finger down the long columns of names.

'Next Thursday the *Renaska* is coming in to pick up coal, probably will leave on Saturday. If the ship can load quickly enough, she may sail on the Friday night and save the berthing tariffs. She'll dock on berth seventeen.'

'Thanks, One Tooth,' said Stefan. 'I'll see if I can bring along any more of my wealthy associates in the future.'

One Tooth Joe raised his fist cursing, as Stefan and Wladek ran out on to the wharf.

For the next three days the two boys stole food, loaded grain and slept. By the time the Turkish ship arrived on the following Thursday, Stefan had almost convinced Wladek that he should remain in Odessa. But Wladek's fear of the Russians outweighed the attraction of his new life with Stefan.

They stood on the quayside, staring at the new arrival docking at berth 17.

'How will I ever get on the ship?' asked Wladek.

'Simple,' said Stefan. 'We can join the chain gang tomorrow morning. I'll take the place behind you, and when the coal hold is nearly full, you can jump in and hide while I pick up your basket and walk on down the other side.'

'And collect my share of the money, no doubt,' said Wladek.

'Naturally,' said Stefan. 'There must be some financial reward for my superior intelligence or how could a man hope to sustain his belief in free enterprise?'

They joined the chain gang first thing the next morning and hauled coal up and down the gangplank until they were both ready to drop, but it still wasn't enough. The hold wasn't half full by nightfall. The two black boys slept soundly that night. The following morning, they started again and by mid-afternoon, when the hold was nearly full, Stefan kicked Wladek's ankle.

'Next time, Muscovite,' he said.

When they reached the top of the gangway, Wladek threw his coal in, dropped the basket on the deck, jumped over the side of the hold and landed on the coal, while Stefan picked up his basket and continued down the other side of the gangplank whistling.

'Goodbye, my friend,' he said, 'and good luck with the infidel Turks.'

Wladek pressed himself against a corner of the hold and watched the coal come pouring in beside him. The dust was everywhere, in his nose and mouth, in his lungs and eyes. With painful effort he avoided coughing for fear of being heard by one of the ship's crew. Just as he thought that he could no longer bear the air of the hold, and would have to return to Stefan and think of some other way of escape, he saw the doors slide shut above him. He coughed luxuriously.

After a few moments he felt something take a bite at his ankle. His blood went cold, realising what it had to be. He looked down, trying to work out where it had come from. No sooner had he thrown a piece of coal at the monster and sent him scurrying away than another one came at him, then another and another. The braver ones went for his legs. They seemed to appear from nowhere. Black, large, and hungry. It was the first time in his life that Wladek realised that rats had red eyes. He clambered to the top of the pile of coal and pulled open the hatch. The sunlight came flooding through and the rats disappeared back into their tunnels in the coal. He started to climb out, but the ship was already well clear of the quayside. He fell back into the hold, terrified. If the ship were forced to return and hand Wladek over, he knew it would mean a one-way journey back to camp 201 and the White Russians. He chose to stay with the black rats. As soon as Wladek closed the hatch, they came at him again. As fast as he could throw lumps of coal at the verminous creatures, a new one would appear from another angle. Every few moments Wladek had to open the hatch to let some light in, for light seemed to be the only ally that would frighten the black rodents away.

For two days and three nights Wladek waged a running battle with the rats without ever catching a moment of quiet sleep. When the ship finally reached the port of Constantinople and a deck-hand opened the hold, Wladek was black from his head to his knees with dirt, and red from his knees to his toes with blood. The deck-hand dragged him out. Wladek tried to stand up but collapsed in a heap on the deck.

When Wladek came to – he knew not where or how much later – he found himself on a bed in a small room with three men in long white coats who were studying him carefully, speaking a tongue he did not know. How many languages were there in the world? He looked at himself, still red and black, and when he tried to sit up, one of the white-coated men, the oldest of the three, with a thin, lined face and a goatee, pushed him back down. He addressed Wladek in the strange tongue. Wladek shook his head. He then tried Russian. Wladek again shook his head – that would be the quickest way back to where he had come. The next language the doctor tried was German, and Wladek realised that his command of that language was greater than his inquisitor's.

'You speak German?'

'Yes.'

'Ah, so you're not Russian, then?'

'No.'

'What were you doing in Russia?'

'Trying to escape.'

'Ah.' He then turned to his companions and seemed to report the conversation in his own tongue. They left the room.

A nurse came in and scrubbed him clean, taking little notice of his cries of anguish. She covered his legs in a thick, brown ointment and left him to sleep again. When Wladek awoke for the second time, he was quite alone. He lay staring at the white ceiling, considering his next move.

Still not sure of which country he was in, he climbed on to the window sill and stared out of the window. He could see a market place, not unlike the one in Odessa, except that the men wore long white robes and had darker skins. They also wore colourful hats that looked like small flower pots upside down, and sandals on their feet. The women were all in black and had even their faces covered except for their black eyes. Wladek watched the strange race in the market place bargaining for their daily food; that was one thing at least that seemed to be international.

He watched the scene for several minutes before he noticed that running down by the side of the building was a red iron ladder stretching all the way to the ground, not unlike the fire escape in his castle in Slonim. His castle. Who would believe him now? He climbed down from the window sill, walked cautiously to the door, opened it and peered into the corridor. Men and women were walking up and down, but none of them showed any interest in him. He closed the door gently, found his belongings in a cupboard in the corner of his room and dressed quickly. His clothes were still black with coal dust and felt gritty on his clean skin. Back to the window sill. The window opened easily. He gripped the fire escape, swung out of the window and started to climb down towards freedom. The first thing that hit him was the heat. He wished he was no longer wearing the heavy overcoat.

Once he touched the ground Wladek tried to run, but his legs were so weak and painful that he could only walk slowly. How he wished he could rid himself of that limp. He did not look back at the hospital until he was lost in the throng of the crowd in the market place.

Wladek stared at the tempting food on the stalls and decided to buy an orange and some nuts. He went to the lining in his suit; surely the money had been under his right arm? Yes it had, but it was no longer there, and far worse, the silver band had also gone. The men in the white coats had stolen his possessions. He considered going back to the hospital to retrieve the lost heirloom and decided against returning until he had had something to eat. Perhaps there was still some money in his pockets. He searched around in the large overcoat pocket and immediately found the three notes and some coins. They were all together with the doctor's map and the silver band. Wladek was overjoyed at the discovery. He slipped the silver band on, and pushed it above his elbow.

Wladek chose the largest orange he could see and a handful of nuts. The stallkeeper said something to him that he could not understand. Wladek felt the easiest way out of the language barrier was to hand over a fifty ruble note. The stallkeeper looked at it, laughed, and threw his arms in the sky.

'Allah,' he cried, snatching back the nuts and the orange from Wladek and waving him away with his forefinger. Wladek walked off in despair; a different language meant different money, he supposed. In Russia he had been poor; here he was penniless. He would have to steal an orange; if he were caught, he would throw it back to the stallkeeper. Wladek walked to the other end of the market place in the same way as Stefan had done, but he couldn't imitate the swagger, and he didn't feel the same confidence. He chose the end stall and when he was sure no one was watching, he picked up an orange and started to run. Suddenly there was uproar. It seemed as if half the city were chasing him.

A big man jumped on the limping Wladek and threw him to the ground. Six or seven people seized hold of different parts of his body while a larger group thronged around as he was dragged back to the stall. A policeman awaited them. Notes were taken, and there was a shouted exchange between the stall owner and the policeman, each man's voice rising with each new statement. The policeman then turned to Wladek and shouted at him too, but Wladek could not understand a word. The policeman shrugged his shoulders and marched Wladek off by the ear. People continued to bawl at him. Some of them spat on him. When Wladek reached the police station, he was taken underground and thrown into a tiny cell, already occupied by twenty or thirty criminals; thugs, thieves or he knew not what. Wladek did not speak to them, and they showed no desire to talk to him. He remained with his back to a wall, cowering, quiet, terrified. For at least a day and a night, he was left there with no food or light. The smell of excreta made him vomit until there was nothing left in him. He never thought the day would come when the dungeons in Slonim would seem uncrowded and peaceful.

The next morning Wladek was dragged from the basement by two guards and marched to a hall where he was lined up with several other prisoners. They were all roped to each other around the waist and led from the jail in a long line down into the street. Another large crowd had gathered outside and their loud cheer of welcome made Wladek feel that they had been waiting some time for the prisoners to appear. The crowd followed them all the way to the market place – screaming, clapping and shouting – for what reason Wladek feared even to contemplate. The line came to a halt when they reached the market square. The first prisoner was unleashed from his rope and taken into the centre of the square, which was already crammed with hundreds of people, all shouting at the top of their voices.

Wladek watched the scene in disbelief. When the first

prisoner reached the middle of the square, he was knocked to his knees by the guard and then his right hand was strapped to a wooden block by a giant of a man who raised a large sword above his head and brought it down with terrible force, aiming at the prisoner's wrist. He only managed to catch the tips of the fingers. The prisoner screamed with pain as the sword was raised again. This time the sword hit the wrist but still did not finish the job properly and the wrist dangled from the prisoner's arm, blood pouring out on to the sand. The sword was raised for a third time, and for the third time it came down. The prisoner's hand at last fell to the ground. The crowd roared its approval. The prisoner was at last released, and he slumped in a heap, unconscious. He was dragged off by a disinterested guard and left on the edge of the crowd. A weeping woman, his wife, Wladek presumed, hurriedly tied a tourniquet of dirty cloth around the bloody stump. The second prisoner died of shock before the fourth blow was struck. The giant executioner was not interested in death so he continued his task; he was paid to remove hands.

Wladek looked around in terror and would have vomited if there had been anything left in his stomach to bring up. He searched in every direction for help or some means of escape; no one had told him that under Islamic law the punishment for trying to escape would be the loss of a foot. His eyes darted around the mass of faces until he saw a man in the crowd dressed like a European, wearing a dark suit. The man was standing about twenty yards away from Wladek and was watching the spectacle with obvious disgust. But he did not once look in Wladek's direction, nor could he hear his shouts for help in the uproar arising from the crowd every time the sword was brought down. Was he French, German, English or even Polish? Wladek could not tell, but for some reason he was there to witness this macabre spectacle. Wladek stared at him, willing him to look his way. But he did not. Wladek waved his free arm but still could not gain the European's attention. They untied the man two in front of Wladek and dragged him along the ground towards the block. When the sword went up again the crowd cheered, the man in the dark suit turned his eyes away in disgust and Wladek waved frantically at him again.

The man stared at Wladek and then turned to talk to a companion, whom Wladek had not noticed. The guard was now struggling with the prisoner immediately in front of Wladek. He placed the prisoner's hand under the strap; the sword went up and removed the hand in one blow. The crowd seemed disappointed. Wladek stared again at the Europeans. They were now both looking at him. He willed them to move, but they only continued to stare.

The guard came over, threw Wladek's fifty-ruble overcoat to the ground, undid his shirt and rolled up his sleeve. Wladek struggled futilely as he was dragged across the square. He was no match for the guard. When he reached the block, he was kicked in the back of his knees and collapsed to the ground. The strap was fastened over his right wrist, and there was nothing left for him to do but close his eyes as the sword was raised above the executioner's head. He waited in agony for the terrible blow, and then there was a sudden hush in the crowd as the Baron's silver band fell from Wladek's elbow down to his wrist and on to the block. An eerie silence came over the crowd as the heirloom shone brightly in the sunlight. The executioner stopped and put down his sword and studied the silver band. Wladek opened his eyes. He tried to pull it over Wladek's wrist, but he couldn't get it past the leather strap. A man in uniform ran quickly forward and joined the executioner. He too, studied the band and the inscription and then ran to another man, who must have been of higher authority, because he walked more slowly towards Wladek. The sword was resting on the ground and the crowd were now beginning to jear and hoot. The second officer also tried to pull the silver band off, but could not get it over the block either and he seemed unwilling to undo the strap. He shouted words at Wladek, who did not understand what he was saying and replied in Polish, 'I do not speak your language.'

The officer looked surprised and threw his hands in the

air shouting, 'Allah.' That must be the same as 'Holy God' thought Wladek. The officer walked slowly towards the two men in the crowd wearing western suits, arms going in every direction like a disorganised windmill. Wladek prayed to God; in such situations any man prays to any god, be it Allah or the Ave Maria. The Europeans were still staring at Wladek, and Wladek nodded his head up and down frantically. One of the men in the dark suits joined the Turkish officer as he walked back towards the block. The former knelt down by Wladek's side, studied the silver band and then looked carefully at him. Wladek waited. He could converse in five languages and prayed that the gentleman would speak one of them. His heart sank when the European turned to the officer and addressed him in his own tongue. The crowd was now hissing and throwing rotten fruit at the block. The officer was nodding his agreement, while the gentleman stared intently at Wladek.

'Do you speak English?'

Wladek heaved a sigh of relief. 'Yes, sir, not bad. I am Polish citizen.'

'How did you come into possession of that silver band?'

'It belong my father, sir. He die in prison by the Germans in Poland, and I captured and sent to a prison camp in Russia. I escape and come here by ship. I have no eat for days. When stallkeeper no accept my rubles for orange, I take one because I much, much hungry.'

The Englishman rose slowly from his knees, turned to the officer and spoke to him very firmly. The latter, in turn, addressed the executioner who looked doubtful, but when the officer repeated the order a little louder, he bent down and reluctantly undid the leather strap. This time Wladek did vomit.

'Come with me,' said the Englishman. 'And quickly, before they change their minds.'

Still in a daze, Wladek grabbed his coat and followed him. The crowd booed and jeered, throwing things at him as he departed, and the swordsman quickly put the next prisoner's hand on the block and with his first blow only managed to remove a thumb. This seemed to pacify the mob.

The Englishman moved swifty through the hustling crowd out of the square where he was joined by his companion.

'What's happening, Edward?'

'The boy says he is a Pole and that he escaped from Russia. I told the official in charge that he was English, so now he is our responsibility. Let's get him to the embassy and find out if the boy's story bears any resemblance to the truth.'

Wladek ran between the two men as they hurried on through the bazaar and into the Street of Seven Kings. He could still faintly hear the mob behind him screaming their approval every time the executioner brought down his sword.

The two Englishmen walked over a pebbled courtyard towards a large grey building and beckoned Wladek to follow them. On the door were the welcoming words, British Embassy. Once inside the building Wladek began to feel safe for the first time. He walked a pace behind the two men down a long hall with walls filled with paintings of strangely clad soldiers and sailors. At the far end was a magnificent portrait of an old man in a blue naval uniform liberally adorned with medals. His fine beard reminded Wladek of the Baron. A soldier appeared from nowhere and saluted.

'Take this boy, Corporal Smithers, and see that he gets a bath. Then feed him in the kitchens. When he has eaten and smells a little less like a walking pigsty, bring him to my office.'

'Yes, sir,' said the corporal and saluted.

'Come with me, my lad.' The soldier marched away. Wladek followed him obediently, having to run to keep up with his walking pace. He was taken to the basement of the embassy and left in a little room; this time it had a window. The corporal told him to get undressed and then left him on his own. He returned a few minutes later to find Wladek still sitting on the edge of the bed fully dressed, dazedly twisting the silver band around and around his wrist.

'Hurry up, lad; you're not on a rest cure.'

'Sorry, sir,' Wladek said.

'Don't call me sir, lad. I am Corporal Smithers. You call me corporal.'

'I am Wladek Koskiewicz. You call me Wladek.'

'Don't be funny with me, lad. We've got enough funny people in the British army without you wishing to join their ranks.'

Wladek did not understand what the soldier meant. He undressed quickly.

'Follow me at the double.'

Another marvellous bath with hot water and soap. Wladek thought of his Russian protectress, and of the son he might have become to her but for her husband. A new set of clothes, strange but clean and fresh-smelling. Whose son had they belonged to? The soldier was back at the door.

Corporal Smithers took Wladek to the kitchen and left him with a fat, pink-faced cook, with the warmest face he had seen since leaving Poland. She reminded him of niania. Wladek could not help wondering what would happen to her waistline after a few weeks in camp 201.

'Hello,' she said with a beaming smile. 'What's your name, then?'

Wladek told her.

'Well, laddie, it looks as though you could do with a good British meal inside of you — none of this Turkish muck will suffice. We'll start with some hot soup and beef. You'll need something substantial if you're to face Mr. Prendergast.' She laughed. 'Just remember, his bite's not as bad as his bark. Although he is an Englishman, his heart's in the right place.'

'You are not an English, Mrs. Cook?' asked Wladek, surprised.

'Good Lord no, laddie, I'm Scottish. There's a world of difference. We hate the English more than the Germans do,' she said, laughing. She set a dish of steaming soup, thick with meat and vegetables, in front of Wladek. He had entirely forgotten that food could smell and taste so appetising. He ate the meal slowly for fear it might not happen again for a very long time.

The corporal reappeared. 'Have you had enough to eat, my lad?'

'Yes, thank you, Mr. Corporal.'

The corporal gave Wladek a suspicious look, but he saw no trace of cheek in the boy's expression. 'Good, then let's be moving. Can't be late on parade for Mr. Prendergast.'

The corporal disappeared through the kitchen door, and Wladek stared at the cook. He hated always having to say goodbye to someone he'd just met, especially when they had been so kind.

'Off you go, laddie, if you know what's good for you.'

'Thank you, Mrs. Cook,' said Wladek. 'Your food is best I can ever remember.'

The cook smiled at him. He again had to limp hard to catch up with the corporal, whose marching pace still kept Wladek trotting. The soldier came to a brisk halt outside a door that Wladek nearly ran into.

'Look where you're going, my lad, look where you're going.'

The corporal gave a short rap-rap on the door.

'Come,' said a voice.

The corporal opened the door and saluted. 'The Polish boy, sir, as you requested, scrubbed and fed.'

'Thank you, Corporal. Perhaps you would be kind enough to ask Mr. Grant to join us.'

Edward Prendergast looked up from his desk. He waved Wladek to a seat without speaking and continued to work at some papers. Wladek sat looking at him and then at the portraits on the wall. More generals and admirals and that old, bearded gentleman again, this time in khaki army uniform. A few minutes later the other Englishman he remembered from the market square came in.

'Thank you for joining us, Harry. Do have a seat, old boy.'

Mr. Prendergast turned to Wladek. 'Now, my lad, let's

hear your story from the beginning, with no exaggerations, only the truth. Do you understand?'

'Yes, sir.'

Wladek started his story with his days in Poland. It took him some time to find the right English words. It was apparent from the looks on the faces of the two Englishmen that they were at first incredulous. They occasionally stopped him and asked questions, nodding to each other at his answers. After an hour of talking Wladek's life history had reached the office of His Britannic Majesty's second consul to Turkey.

'I think, Harry,' said the second consul, 'it is our duty to inform the Polish Delegation immediately and then hand young Koskiewicz over to them as I feel in the circumstances he is undoubtedly their responsibility.'

'Agreed,' said the man called Harry. 'You know, my boy, you had a narrow escape in the market today. The Sher – that is the old Islamic religious law – which provides for cutting off a hand for the theft was officially abandoned in theory years ago. In fact it is a crime under the Ottoman Penal Code to inflict such a punishment. Nevertheless, in practice the barbarians still continue to carry it out.' He shrugged.

'Why not my hand?' asked Wladek, holding on to his wrist.

'I told them they could cut off all the Moslem hands they wanted, but not an Englishman's,' Edward Prendergast interjected.

'Thank God,' said Wladek faintly.

'Edward Prendergast, actually,' he said, smiling for the first time. The second consul continued. 'You can spend the night here, and we will take you to your own delegation tomorrow. The Poles do not actually have an embassy in Constantinople,' he said, slightly disdainfully, 'but my opposite number is a good fellow considering he's a foreigner.' He pressed a button and the corporal reappeared immediately.

'Sir.'

127

'Corporal, take young Koskiewicz to his room, and in the morning see he is given breakfast and is brought to me at nine sharp.'

'Sir. This way, boy, at the double.'

Wladek was led away by the corporal. He was not even given enough time to thank the two Englishmen who had saved his hand – and perhaps his life. Back in the clean little room, with its clean little bed neatly turned down as if he were an honoured guest, he undressed, threw his pillow on the floor and slept soundly until the morning light shone through the tiny window.

'Rise and shine, lad, sharpish.'

It was the corporal, his uniform immaculately smart and knife-edge pressed, looking as though he had never been to bed. For an instant Wladek, surfacing from sleep, thought himself back in camp 201, as the corporal's banging on the end of the bed frame with his cane resembled the noise he had grown so accustomed to. He fell out of bed and reached for his clothes.

'Wash first, my lad, wash first. We don't want your horrible smells worrying Mr. Prendergast so early in the morning, do we?'

Wladek was unsure which part of himself to wash, so unusually clean did he feel himself to be. The corporal was staring at him.

'What's wrong with your leg, lad?'

'Nothing, nothing,' said Wladek, turning himself away from the staring eyes.

'Right. I'll be back in three minutes. Three minutes, do you hear, my lad, be sure you're ready.'

Wladek washed his hands and face quickly and then dressed. He was waiting at the end of the bed in his long bearskin coat when the corporal returned to take him to the second consul. Mr. Prendergast welcomed him and seemed to have softened considerably since their first meeting.

'Good morning, Koskiewicz.'

'Good morning, sir.'

'Did you enjoy your breakfast?'

'I no had breakfast, sir.'

'Why not?' said the second consul, looking towards the corporal.

'Overslept, I'm afraid, sir. He would have been late for you.'

'Well, we must see what we can do about that. Corporal, will you ask Mrs. Henderson to try and rustle up an apple or something?'

'Yes, sir.'

Wladek and the Second Consul walked slowly along the corridor towards the embassy front door, and across the pebbled courtyard to a waiting car, an Austin, one of the few engine driven vehicles in Turkey and Wladek's first journey in one. He was sorry to be leaving the British embassy. It was the first place in which he had felt safe for years. He wondered if he was ever going to sleep more than one night in the same bed for the rest of his life. The corporal ran down the steps and took the driver's seat. He passed Wladek an apple and some fresh warm bread.

'See there are no crumbs left in the car, lad. The cook sends her compliments.'

The drive through the hot busy streets was conducted at walking pace as the Turks did not believe anything could go faster than a camel, and made no attempt to clear a path for the little Austin. Even with all the windows open Wladek was sweating from the oppressive heat while Mr. Prendergast remained quite cool and unperturbed. Wladek hid himself in the back of the car for fear that someone who had witnessed the previous day's events might recognise him and stir the mob to anger again. When the little black Austin came to a halt outside a small decaying building marked 'Konsulat Polski', Wladek felt a twinge of excitement mingled with disappointment.

The three of them climbed out.

'Where's the apple core, boy?' demanded the corporal.

'I eat him.'

The corporal laughed and knocked on the door. A friendly-looking little man with dark hair and firm jaw opened the door to them. He was in shirt sleeves and deeply tanned, obviously by the Turkish sun. He addressed them in Polish. His words were the first Wladek had heard in his native tongue since leaving the labour camp. Wladek answered quickly, explaining his presence. His fellow countryman turned to the British second consul.

'This way, Mr. Prendergast,' he said in perfect English. 'It was good of you to bring the boy over personally.'

A few diplomatic niceties were exchanged before Prendergast and the corporal took their leave. Wladek gazed at them, fumbling for an English expression more adequate than 'Thank you.'

Prendergast patted Wladek on the head as he might a cocker spaniel. The corporal closed the door, and winked at Wladek. 'Good luck, my lad; God knows you deserve it.'

The Polish consul introduced himself to Wladek as Pawel Zaleski. Again Wladek was required to recount the story of his life, finding it easier in Polish than he had in English. Pawel Zaleski heard him out in silence, shaking his head sorrowfully.

'My poor child,' he said heavily. 'You have borne more than your share of our country's suffering for one so young. And now what are we to do with you?'

'I must return to Poland and reclaim my castle,' said Wladek.

'Poland,' said Pawel Zaleski. 'Where's that? The area of land where you lived remains in dispute and there is still heavy fighting going on between the Poles and the Russians. General Piludski is doing all he can to protect the territorial integrity of our fatherland. But it would be foolish for any of us to be optimistic. There is little left for you now in Poland. No, your best plan would be to start a new life in England or America.'

'But I don't want to go to England or America. I am Polish.'

'You will always be Polish, Wladek, no one can take that away from you wherever you decided to settle, but you must be realistic about your life – which hasn't even begun.'

Wladek lowered his head in despair. Had he gone through all this only to be told he could never return to his native land? He fought back the tears.

Pawel Zaleski put his arm round the boy's shoulders. 'Never forget that you are one of the lucky ones who escaped and came out of the holocaust alive. You only have to remember your friend, Doctor Dubien, to be aware of what life might have been like.'

Wladek didn't speak.

'Now, you must put all thoughts of the past behind you and think only for the future, Wladek, and perhaps in your lifetime you will see Poland rise again, which is more than I dare hope for.'

Wladek remained silent.

'Well, there's no need to make an immediate decision,' said the consul kindly. 'You can stay here for as long as it takes you to decide on your future.'

10

The future was something that was worrying Anne. The first few months of her marriage were happy, marred only by her anxiety over William's increasing dislike of Henry, and her new husband's seeming inability to start working. Henry was a little touchy on the point, explaining to Anne that he was still disorientated by the war and that he wasn't willing to rush into something he might well have to stick with for the rest of his life. She found this hard to swallow and finally it brought on their first row.

'I don't understand why you haven't opened that real estate business you used to be so keen on, Henry.'

'I can't. The time isn't quite right. The real estate market's not looking that promising at the moment.'

'You've been saying that now for nearly a year; I wonder if it will ever be promising enough for you.'

'Sure it will; truth is, I need a little more capital to help myself set up. Now if you would loan me some of your money, I could get cracking tomorrow.'

'That's impossible, Henry. You know the terms of Richard's will; my allowance was stopped the day we were married, and now I have only the capital left.'

'A little of that would help me on my way, and don't forget that precious boy of yours has well over twenty million in the family trust.'

'You seem to know a lot about William's trust,' said Anne suspiciously.

'Oh, come on, Anne, give me a chance to be your husband. Don't make me feel like a guest in my own home.'

'What's happened to your money, Henry? You always led me to believe that you had enough to start your own business.'

'You've always known I was not in Richard's class financially, and there was a time, Anne, when you claimed it didn't matter. I'd marry you Henry, if you were penniless,' he mocked.

Anne burst into tears, and Henry tried to console her. She spent the rest of the evening in his arms talking the problem over. Anne managed to convince herself she was being unwifely and ungenerous. She had more money than she could possibly need: couldn't she trust a little of it to the man to whom she was so willing to entrust the rest of her life?

Acting upon these thoughts, she agreed to let Henry have one hundred thousand dollars to set up his own real estate firm in Boston. Within a month Henry had found a smart new office in a fashionable part of town, appointed staff, and started work. Soon he was mixing with all the city politicians and real estate men of Boston. They talked of the boom in farm land, and they flattered Henry. Anne didn't care very much for them as social company, but Henry was happy and appeared to be successful at his work.

William, now fourteen, was in this third year at St. Paul's, sixth in his class overall and first in mathematics. He had also become a rising figure in the Debating Society. He wrote to his mother once a week, reporting his progress, always addressing his letters to Mrs. Richard Kane, refusing to acknowledge that Henry Osborne even existed. Anne wasn't sure whether she should talk to him about it, and each Monday she would carefully extract William's letter from the box to be certain that Henry never saw the envelope. She continued to hope that in time William would come around to liking Henry, but it became clear that that hope was unrealistic when, in one particular letter to his mother, he sought her permission to stay with his friend, Matthew Lester, for the summer holidays. The request came as a painful blow to Anne, but she took the easy way out and fell in with William's plans, which Henry also seemed to favour.

William hated Henry Osborne and nursed the hatred passionately, not sure what he could actually do about it. He was relieved that Henry never visited him at school; he could not have tolerated the other boys seeing his mother with that man. It was bad enough that he had to live with him in Boston.

For the first time since his mother's marriage, William was anxious for the holidays to come.

The Lesters' Packard chauffeured William and Matthew noiselessly to the summer camp in Vermont. On the journey, Matthew casually asked William what he intended to do when the time came for him to leave St. Paul's.

'When I leave I will be top of the class, Class President, and have won the Hamilton Memorial Mathematics Scholarship to Harvard,' replied William without hesitation.

'Why is all that so important?' asked Matthew innocently.

'My father did all three.'

'When you've finished beating your father, I will introduce you to mine.'

William smiled.

The two boys had an energetic and enjoyable four weeks in Vermont playing every game from chess to American football. When the month came to an end they travelled to New York to spend the last part of the holiday with the

Lester family. They were greeted at the door by a butler who addressed Matthew as sir and a twelve-year-old girl covered in freckles who called him Fatty. It made William laugh because his friend was so thin and it was she who was fat. The little girl smiled and revealed teeth almost totally hidden behind braces.

'You would never believe Susan was my sister, would you?' asked Matthew disdainfully.

'No, I suppose not,' said William, smiling at Susan. 'She's so much better looking than you.'

She adored William from that moment on.

William adored Matthew's father the moment they met; he reminded him in so many ways of his own father and he begged Charles Lester to let him see the great bank of which he was chairman. Charles Lester thought carefully about the request. No child had been allowed to enter the orderly precincts of 17 Broad Street before, not even his own son. He compromised, as bankers often do, and showed the boy around the Wall Street building on a Sunday afternoon.

William was fascinated to see the different offices, the vaults, the foreign exchange dealing room, the board room and the chairman's office. Compared with Kane and Cabot, the Lester bank was considerably more extensive, and William knew from his own small personal investment account, which provided him with a copy of the annual general report, that they had a far larger capital base than Kane and Cabot. William was silent, pensive, as they were driven home in the car.

'Well, William, did you enjoy your visit to my bank?' asked Charles Lester genially.

'Oh, yes, sir,' replied William. 'I certainly did enjoy it.' William paused for a moment and then added, 'I intend to be chairman of your bank one day, Mr. Lester.'

Charles Lester laughed, and dined out on the story of how young William Kane had reacted to Lester and Co., which in turn made those who heard it laugh too.

Only William had not meant the remark as a joke.

Anne was shocked when Henry came back to her for more money.

'It's as safe as a house,' he assured her. 'Ask Alan Lloyd. As chairman of the bank he can only have your best interests at heart.'

'But two hundred and fifty thousand?' Anne queried.

'A superb opportunity, my dear. Look upon it as an investment that will be worth double that amount within two years.'

After another more prolonged row, Anne gave in once again and life returned to the same smooth routine. When she checked her investment portfolio with the bank, Anne found she was down to one hundred and forty thousand dollars, but Henry seemed to be seeing all the right people and clinching all the right deals. She considered discussing the whole problem with Alan Lloyd at Kane and Cabot, but in the end dismissed the idea; it would have meant displaying distrust in the husband whom she wished the world to respect, and surely Henry would not have made the suggestion at all had he not been sure that the loan would have met with Alan's approval.

Anne also started seeing Doctor MacKenzie again to find out if there was any hope of her having another baby, but he still advised against the idea. With the high blood pressure that had caused her earlier miscarriage, Andrew MacKenzie did not consider thirty-five a good age for Anne to start thinking about being a mother again. Anne raised the idea with the grandmothers, but they agreed wholeheartedly with the views of the good doctor. Neither of them cared for Henry very much, and they cared even less for the thought of an Osborne offspring making claims on the Kane family fortune after they were gone. Anne began to resign herself to the fact that William was going to be her only child. Henry became very angry about what he described as her betrayal, and told Anne that if Richard were still alive, she would have tried again. How different the two men were, she thought, and couldn't account for why she had loved them both. She tried to soothe Henry, praying that his business projects would work out well and keep him fully occupied. He certainly had taken to working very late at the office.

It was on a Monday in October, the weekend after they had celebrated their second wedding anniversary, that Anne started receiving the letters from an unsigned 'friend', informing her that Henry could be seen escorting other women around Boston, and one lady in particular whom the writer didn't care to name. To begin with Anne burned the letters immediately and although they worried her, she never discussed them with Henry, praying that each letter would be the last. She couldn't even summon up the courage to raise the matter with Henry when he asked her for the last hundred and fifty thousand dollars.

'I am going to lose the whole deal if I don't have that money right now, Anne.'

'But it's all I have, Henry. If I give you that amount, I'll be left with nothing.'

'This house alone must be worth over two hundred thousand. You could mortgage it tomorrow.'

'The house belongs to William.'

'William, William, William. It's always William who gets in the way of my success,' shouted Henry as he stormed out.

He returned home after midnight, contrite, and told her he would rather she kept her money and that he went under, for at least they would still have each other. Anne was comforted by his words and later they made love. She signed a cheque for one hundred and fifty thousand dollars the next morning, trying to forget that it would leave her penniless until Henry pulled off the deal he was pursuing. She couldn't help wondering if it was more than a coincidence that Henry had asked for the exact amount that remained of her inheritance.

The next month Anne missed her period.

Doctor MacKenzie was anxious but tried not to show it; the grandmothers were horrified and did; while Henry was delighted and assured Anne that it was the most wonderful thing that had ever happened to him in his whole life, and even agreed to building a new children's wing for the hospital that Richard had planned before he died.

When William heard the news by letter from his mother, he sat deep in thought all evening unable to tell even Matthew what was preoccupying him. The following Saturday morning, having been granted special permission by his housemaster, Grumpy Raglan, he boarded a train to Boston and on arrival withdrew one hundred dollars from his savings account. He then proceeded to the law offices of Cohen, Cohen and Yablons in Jefferson Street. Mr. Thomas Cohen, the senior partner, a tall angular man with a dark jowl was somewhat surprised when William was ushered into his office.

'I have never been retained by a sixteen-year-old before,' Mr. Cohen began. 'It will be quite a novelty for me—' he hesitated '—Mr. Kane.' He found Mr. Kane did not run easily off the tongue. 'Especially as your father was not exactly – how shall I put it? – known for his sympathy for my co-religionists.'

'My father,' replied William, 'was a great admirer of the achievements of the Hebrew race and in particular had considerable respect for your firm when you acted on behalf of rivals. I heard him mention your name on several occasions. That's why I have chosen you, Mr. Cohen, not you me. That should be reassurance enough.'

Mr. Cohen quickly put aside the fact that William was only sixteen. 'Indeed, indeed. I feel I can make an exception for the son of Richard Kane. Now, what can we do for you?'

'I wish you to answer three questions for me, Mr. Cohen. One, I want to know if my mother, Mrs. Henry Osborne, were to give birth to a child, son or daughter, whether that child would have any legal rights to the Kane family trust. Two, do I have any legal obligations to Mr. Henry Osborne because he is married to my mother, and three, at what age can I insist that Mr. Henry Osborne leave my house on Louisburg Square in Boston?'

Thomas Cohen's quill pen sped furiously across the paper

in front of him, spattering little blue spots on an already ink-stained desk top.

William placed one hundred dollars on the desk. The lawyer looked taken aback but picked the notes up and counted them.

'Use the money prudently, Mr. Cohen. I will need a good lawyer when I leave Harvard.'

'You have already been accepted at Harvard, Mr. Kane? My congratulations. I am hoping my son will go there too.'

'No, I have not, but I shall have done so in two years' time. I will return to Boston to see you in one week, Mr. Cohen. If I ever hear in my lifetime from anyone other than yourself on this subject, you may consider our relationship at an end. Good day, sir.'

Thomas Cohen would have also said good day, if he could have spluttered the words out before William closed the door behind him.

William returned to the offices of Cohen, Cohen and Yablons seven days later.

'Ah, Mr. Kane,' said Thomas Cohen, 'how nice to see you again. Would you care for some coffee?'

'No, thank you.'

'Shall I send someone out for a Coca-Cola?'

William's face was expressionless.

'To business, to business,' said Mr. Cohen, slightly embarrassed. 'We have dug around a little on your behalf, Mr. Kane, with the help of a very respectable firm of private investigators to assist us with the questions you asked that were not purely academic. I think I can safely say we have the answers to all your questions. You asked if Mr. Osborne's offspring by your mother, were there to be any, would have a claim on the Kane estate, or in particular on the trust left to you by your father. No is the simple answer, but of course Mrs. Osborne can leave any part of the five hundred thousand dollars bequeathed to her by your father to whom she pleases.'

Mr. Cohen looked up.

'However, it may interest you to know, Mr. Kane, that your mother has drawn out the entire five hundred thousand from her private account at Kane and Cabot during the last eighteen months, but we have been unable to trace how the money has been used. It is possible she may have decided to deposit the amount in another bank.'

William looked shocked, the first sign of any lack of the self-control that Thomas Cohen had noted.

'There would be no reason for her to do that,' William said. 'The money can only have gone to one person.'

The lawyer remained silent, expecting to hear more, but William steadied himself and added nothing, so Mr. Cohen continued.

'The answer to your second question is that you have no personal or legal obligations to Mr. Henry Osborne at all. Under the terms of your father's will, your mother is a trustee of the estate along with a Mr. Alan Lloyd and a Mrs. John Preston, your surviving godparents, until you come of age at twenty-one.'

Thomas Cohen looked up again. William's face showed no expression at all. Cohen had already learned that that meant he should continue.

'And thirdly, Mr. Kane, you can never remove Mr. Osborne from Beacon Hill as long as he remains married to your mother and continues to reside with her. The property comes into your possession by natural right on her death. Were he still alive then, you could require him to leave. I think you will find that covers all your questions, Mr. Kane.'

'Thank you, Mr. Cohen,' said William. 'I am obliged for your efficiency and discretion in this matter. Now perhaps you could let me know your professional charges?'

'One hundred dollars doesn't quite cover the work, Mr. Kane, but we have faith in your future and . . .'

'I do not wish to be beholden to anyone, Mr. Cohen. You must treat me as someone with whom you might never deal again. With that in mind, how much do I owe you?'

Mr. Cohen considered the matter for a moment. 'In those

circumstances we would have charged you two hundred and twenty dollars, Mr. Kane.'

William took six twenty-dollar notes from his inside pocket and handed them over to Cohen. This time, the lawyer did not count them.

'I am grateful to you for your assistance, Mr. Cohen, I am sure we shall meet again. Good day, sir.'

'Good day, Mr. Kane. May I be permitted to say that I never had the privilege of meeting your distinguished father but having dealt with you, I wish that I had.'

William smiled and softened. 'Thank you, sir.'

Preparing for the baby kept Anne fully occupied; she found herself easily tired and resting a good deal. Whenever she enquired of Henry how business was going, he always had some plausible answer to hand, enough to reassure her that all was well without supplying her with any actual details.

Then one morning the anonymous letters started coming again. This time they gave more details, the names of the women involved and the places they could be seen with Henry. Anne burned them even before she could commit the names or places to memory. She didn't want to believe that her husband could be unfaithful while she was carrying his child. Someone was jealous and had it in for Henry, and he or she had to be lying.

The letters kept coming, sometimes with new names. Anne continued to destroy them, but now they were beginning to prey on her mind. She wanted to discuss the whole problem with someone, but couldn't think of anybody in whom she could confide. The grandmothers would have been appalled and were, in any case, already prejudiced against Henry. Alan Lloyd at the bank could not be expected to understand as he had never married, and William was far too young. No one seemed suitable. Anne considered consulting a psychiatrist after listening to a lecture given by Sigmund Freud, but a Lowell could never discuss a family problem with a complete stranger.

The matter finally came to a head in a way that even

Anne had not been prepared for. One Monday morning, she received three letters, the usual one from William addressed to Mrs. Richard Kane, asking if he could once again spend his summer holidays with his friend Matthew Lester in New York. Another anonymous letter alleging that Henry was having an affair with, with ... Milly Preston, and the third from Alan Lloyd, as chairman of the bank, asking if she would be kind enough to telephone and make an appointment to see him. Anne sat down heavily, feeling breathless and unwell, and forced herself to re-read all three letters. William's letter stung her by its detachment. She hated knowing that he preferred to spend his holidays with Matthew Lester. They had been growing continually further apart since her marriage to Henry. The anonymous letter suggesting that Henry was having an affair with her closest friend was impossible to ignore. Anne couldn't help remembering that it had been Milly who had introduced her to Henry in the first place, and that she was William's godmother. The third letter from Alan Lloyd somehow filled her with even more apprehension. The only other letter she had ever received from Alan was one of condolence on the death of Richard. She feared another could only mean more bad news.

She called the bank. The operator put her straight through.

'Alan, you wanted to see me?'

'Yes, my dear, I would like to have a chat sometime. When would suit you?'

'Is it bad news?' asked Anne.

'Not exactly, but I would rather not say anything over the phone, but there's nothing for you to worry about. Are you free for lunch, by any chance?'

'Yes I am, Alan.'

'Well, let's meet at the Ritz at one o'clock. I look forward to seeing you then, Anne.'

One o'clock, only three hours away. Her mind switched from Alan to William to Henry, but settled on Milly Preston. Could it be true? Anne decided to take a long warm bath and put on a new dress. It didn't help. She felt, and was beginning to look, bloated. Her ankles and calves, which had always been so elegant and so slim, were becoming mottled and puffy. It was a little frightening to conjecture how much worse things might become before the baby was born. She sighed at herself in the mirror and did the best she could with her outward appearance.

'You look very smart, Anne. If I weren't an old bachelor considered well past it, I'd flirt with you shamelessly,' said the silver haired banker, greeting her with a kiss on both cheeks as though he were a French general.

He guided her to his table. It was an unspoken tradition that the table in the corner was always occupied by the chairman of Kane and Cabot, if he were not lunching at the bank. Richard had done so and now it was the turn of Alan Lloyd. It was the first occasion that Anne had sat at that table with anyone. Waiters fluttered around them like starlings, seeming to know exactly when to disappear and reappear without interrupting a private conversation.

'When's the baby due, Anne?'

'Oh, not for another three months.'

'No complications, I hope. I seem to remember...'

'Well,' admitted Anne, 'the doctor sees me once a week and pulls long faces about my blood pressure, but I'm not too worried.'

'I'm so glad, my dear,' he said and touched her hand gently as an uncle might. 'You do look rather tired, I hope you're not overdoing things.'

Alan Lloyd raised his hand slightly. A waiter materialised at his side, and they both ordered.

'Anne, I want to seek some advice from you.'

Anne was painfully aware of Alan Lloyd's gift for diplomacy. He wasn't having lunch with her for advice. There was no doubt in her mind that he had come to dispense it – kindly.

'Do you have any idea how well Henry's real estate projects are going?'

'No, I don't,' said Anne. 'I never involve myself with Henry's business activities. You'll remember I didn't with Richard's either. Why? Is there any cause for concern?'

'No, no, none of which we at the bank are aware. On the contrary, we know Henry is bidding for a large city contract to build the new hospital complex. I was only enquiring, because he has come to the bank for a loan of five hundred thousand dollars.'

Anne was stunned.

'I see that surprises you,' he said. 'Now, we know from your stock account that you have a little under twenty thousand dollars in reserve, while running a small overdraft of seventeen thousand dollars on your personal account.'

Anne put down her soup spoon, horrified. She had not realised that she was so badly overdrawn. Alan could see her distress.

'That's not what this lunch is about, Anne,' he added quickly. 'The bank is quite happy to lose money on the personal account for the rest of your life. William is making over a million dollars a year on the interest from his trust, so your overdraft is hardly significant, nor indeed is the five hundred thousand Henry is requesting, if it were to receive your backing as William's legal guardian.'

'I didn't realise that I had any authority over William's trust money,' said Anne.

'You don't on the capital sum, but legally the interest earned from his trust can be invested in any project thought to benefit William, and is under the guardianship of yourself, myself and Milly Preston as godparents until William is twenty-one. Now as chairman of William's trust I can put up that five hundred thousand with your backing. Milly has already informed me that she would be quite happy to give her approval so that would give you two votes and my opinion would therefore be invalid.'

'Milly Preston has already given her approval, Alan?'

'Yes. Hasn't she mentioned the matter to you?'

Anne did not reply immediately. 'What is *your* opinion?' she asked finally.

'Well, I haven't seen Henry's accounts, because he only started his company eighteen months ago and he doesn't bank with us, so I have no idea what expenditure is over income for the current year and what return he is predicting for 1923.'

'You realise that during the last eighteen months I've given Henry five hundred thousand of my own money?' said Anne.

'My chief teller informs me any time a large amount of cash is withdrawn from any account. I didn't know that was what you were using the money for, and it was none of my business, Anne. That money was left to you by Richard and is yours to spend as you see fit.

'Now, in the case of the interest from the family trust, that is a different matter. If you decide to withdraw five hundred thousand dollars to invest in Henry's firm, then the bank will have to inspect Henry's books, because the money would be considered as another investment for William's portfolio. Richard did not give the trustees the authority to make loans, only to invest on William's behalf. I have already explained this situation to Henry, and if we were to go ahead and make this investment, the trustees would have to decide what percentage of Henry's company would be an appropriate exchange for the five hundred thousand. William, of course, is always aware what we are doing with his trust income, because we saw no reason not to comply with his request that he receive a quarterly investment programme statement from the bank in the same way as all the trustees do. I have no doubt in my own mind that he will have his own ideas on the subject which he will be fully aware of after he receives the next quarterly report.

'It may amuse you to know, that since William's sixteenth birthday he has been sending me back his own opinions on every investment we make. To begin with I looked on them with the passing interest of a benevolent guardian. Of late, I have been studying them with considerable respect. When William takes his place on the board of Kane and Cabot, this bank may well turn out to be too small for him.

'I've never been asked for advice on Williams' trust before,' said Anne forlornly.

'Well, my dear, you do see the reports that the bank sends you on the first day of every quarter, and it has always been in your power as a trustee to query any of the investments we make on William's behalf.'

Alan Lloyd took a slip of paper from his pocket, and remained silent until the sommelier had finished pouring the Nuits Saint Georges. Once he was out of earshot, Alan continued.

'William has over twenty-one million invested in the bank at four and a half per cent until his twenty-first birthday. We reinvest the interest for him each quarter in stocks and shares. We have never in the past invested in a private company. It may surprise you to hear, Anne, that we now carry out this reinvestment on a fifty-fifty basis: fifty per cent following the bank's advice and fifty per cent following the suggestions put forward by William. At the moment we are a little ahead of him, much to the satisfaction of Tony Simmons, our investment director, whom William has promised a Rolls-Royce in any year that he can beat the boy by over ten per cent.'

'But where would William get hold of the ten thousand dollars for a Rolls-Royce if he lost the bet – when he's not allowed to touch the money in his trust until he is twenty-one?'

'I do not know the answer to that, Anne. What I do know is he would be far too proud to come to us direct and I am certain he would not have made the wager if he could not honour it. Have you by any chance seen his famous ledger book lately?'

'The one given to him by his grandmothers?'

Alan Lloyd nodded.

'No, I haven't seen it since he went away to school. I didn't know it still existed.'

'It still exists and I would,' said the banker, 'give a month's wages to know what the credit column in that ledger book now stands at. I suppose you are aware that he banks that money with Lester's in New York, and not with us? They don't take on private accounts at under ten thousand dollars. I'm also fairly certain they wouldn't make an exception, even for the son of Richard Kane.'

'The son of Richard Kane,' said Anne.

'I'm sorry, I didn't mean to sound rude, Anne.'

'No, no, there is no doubt he is the son of Richard Kane. Do you know he has never asked me for a penny since his twelfth birthday?' She paused. 'I think I should warn you, Alan, that he won't take kindly to being told he has to invest five hundred thousand dollars of his trust money in Henry's company.'

'They don't get on well?' enquired Alan, his eyebrows rising.

'I'm afraid not,' said Anne.

'I'm sorry to hear that. It certainly would make the transaction more complicated if William really stood out against the whole scheme. Although he has no authority over the trust until he is twenty-one, we have already discovered through sources of our own that he is not beyond going to an independent lawyer to find out his legal position.'

'Good God,' said Anne, 'you can't be serious.'

'Oh, yes, quite serious, but there's nothing for you to worry about. To be frank, we at the bank were all rather impressed and once we realised where the enquiry was coming from, we released information we would normally have kept very much to ourselves. For some private reason he obviously didn't want to approach us directly.'

'Good heavens,' said Anne, 'what will he be like when he's thirty?'

'That will depend,' said Alan, 'on whether he is lucky enough to fall in love with someone as lovely as you. That was always Richard's strength.'

'You are an old flatterer, Alan. Can we leave the problem of the five hundred thousand until I have had a chance to discuss it with Henry?'

'Of course, my dear. I told you I had come to seek your advice.'

Alan ordered coffee and took Anne's hand gently in his. 'And do remember to take care of yourself, Anne. You're far more important than the fate of a few thousand dollars.

When Anne returned home from lunch she immediately started to worry about the other two letters she had received that morning. Of one thing she was now certain, after all she had learned about her own son from Alan Lloyd; she would be wise to give in gracefully and let William spend the forthcoming holidays with his friend, Matthew Lester.

Henry and Milly's relationship raised a problem to which she was unable to compose so simple a solution. She sat in the maroon leather chair, Richard's favourite, looking out through the bay window on to a beautiful bed of red and white roses, seeing nothing, only thinking. Anne always took a long time to make a decision, but once she had, she seldom went back on it.

Henry came home earlier than usual that evening, and she couldn't help wondering why. She soon found out.

'I hear you had lunch with Alan Lloyd today,' he said as he entered the room.

'Who told you that, Henry?'

'I have spies everywhere,' he said, laughing.

'Yes, Alan invited me to lunch. He wanted to know how I felt about the bank investing five hundred thousand dollars of William's trust money in your company.'

'What did you say?' asked Henry, trying not to sound anxious.

'I told him I wanted to discuss the matter with you first, but why in heaven's name didn't you let me know earlier that you had approached the bank, Henry? I felt such a fool hearing the whole thing from Alan for the first time.'

'I didn't think you took any interest in business, my dear, and I only found out by sheer accident that you, Alan Lloyd and Milly Preston are all trustees, and each have a vote on William's investment income.'

'How did you find out,' asked Anne, 'when I wasn't aware of the situation myself?'

'You don't read the small print, my darling. As a matter of fact, I didn't myself until just recently. Quite by chance Milly Preston told me the details of the trust, and as William's godmother, it seems she is also a trustee. It came as quite a surprise. Now let's see if we can turn the position to our advantage. Milly says she will back me, if you agree.'

The mere sound of Milly's name made Anne feel uneasy.

'I don't think we ought to touch William's money,' she said. 'I've never looked upon the trust as having anything to do with me. I would be much happier leaving well enough alone and just continue letting the bank reinvest the interest as it has always done in the past.'

'Why be satisfied with the bank's investment programme when I am on to such a good thing with this city hospital contract? William would make a lot of money out of my company. Surely Alan went along with that?'

'I'm not certain how he felt. He was his usual discreet self though he certainly said the contract would be an excellent one to win and that you had a good chance of being awarded it.'

'Exactly.'

'But he did want to see your books before he came to any firm conclusions, and he also wondered what had happened to my five hundred thousand.'

'Our five hundred thousand, my darling, is doing very well as you will soon discover. I'll send the books around to Alan tomorrow morning so that he can inspect them for himself. I can assure you that he will be very impressed.'

'I hope so, Henry, for both our sakes,' said Anne. 'Now let's wait and see what opinion he forms; you know how much I have always trusted Alan.'

'But not me,' said Henry.

'Oh, no, Henry, I didn't mean . . .'

'I was only teasing. I assumed you would trust your own husband.'

Anne felt the tearfulness that she had always suppressed in front of Richard welling up. For Henry she didn't even try to hold it back.

'I hope I can. I've never had to worry about money before, and it's all too much to cope with just now. The baby always makes me feel so tired and depressed.'

Henry's manner changed quickly to one of solicitude. 'I know, my darling. I don't want you ever to have to bother your head with business matters; I can always handle that side of things. Look, why don't you go to bed early and I'll bring you up some supper on a tray? That will give me a chance to go back to the office and pick up those files I need to show Alan in the morning.'

Anne complied, but once Henry had left, she made no attempt to sleep, tired as she was, but sat up in bed reading Sinclair Lewis. She knew it would take Henry about fifteen minutes to reach his office, so she waited a full twenty and then called his number. The ringing tone continued for almost a minute.

Anne tried a second time twenty minutes later; still no one answered the phone. She kept trying every twenty minutes, but no one ever came on the line. Henry's remark about trust began to echo bitterly in her head.

When Henry eventually returned home after midnight, he appeared apprehensive at finding Anne sitting up in bed. She was still reading Sinclair Lewis.

'You shouldn't have stayed awake for me.'

He gave her a warm kiss. Anne thought she could smell perfume – or was she becoming overly suspicious?

'I had to stay on a little later than I had expected since I couldn't immediately find all the papers Alan would require. Damn silly secretary filed some of them under the wrong headings.'

'It must be lonely sitting there in the office all on your own in the middle of the night,' said Anne.

'Oh, it's not that bad if you have a worthwhile job to do,' said Henry, climbing into bed and settling against Anne's back. 'At least there's one thing to be said for it, you can get a lot more done when the phone isn't continually interrupting you.'

He was asleep in minutes. Anne lay awake, now resolved to carry through the plan she had made that afternoon.

When Henry had left for work after breakfast the next morning – not that Anne was sure where Henry went to work any more – she studied the *Boston Globe* and did a little research among the small advertisements. Then she picked up the phone and made an appointment which took her to the south side of Boston, a few minutes before midday. Anne was shocked by the dinginess of the buildings. She had never previously visited the southern district of the city, and in normal circumstances she could have gone through her entire life without even knowing such places existed.

A small wooden staircase littered with matches, cigarette ends and rubbish created its own paper chase to a door with a frosted glass window on which appeared in large black letters, 'Glen Ricardo', and underneath 'Private Detective (Registered in the Commonwealth of Massachusetts)'. Anne knocked quietly.

'Come right in, the door's open,' shouted a deep, hoarse voice.

Anne entered. The man seated behind the desk, his legs stretched over its surface, glanced up from what might have been a girly magazine. His cigar stub nearly fell out of his mouth when he caught sight of Anne. It was the first time a mink coat had ever walked into his office.

'Good morning' he said, rising quickly. 'My name is Glen Ricardo.' He leant across the desk and offered a hairy, nicotine-stained hand to Anne. She took it, glad that she was wearing gloves. 'Do you have an appointment?' Ricardo asked, not that he cared whether she did or not. He was always available for a consultation with a mink coat.

'Yes, I do.'

'Ah, then you must be Mrs. Osborne. Can I take your coat?'

'I prefer to keep it on,' said Anne, unable to see anywhere Ricardo could hang it except on the floor.

'Of course, of course.'

Anne eyed Ricardo covertly as he sat back in his seat and lit a new cigar. She did not care for his light green suit, the motley-coloured tie, or his thickly greased hair. It was only the fact that she doubted if it would be better anywhere else that kept her seated.

'Now what's the problem?' said Ricardo, who was sharpening an already short pencil with a blunt knife. The wooden shavings dropped everywhere except into the wastepaper basket. 'Have you lost your dog, your jewellery, or your husband?'

'First, Mr. Ricardo, I want to be assured of your complete discretion,' Anne began.

'Of course, of course, it goes without saying,' replied Ricardo, not looking up from his disappearing pencil.

'Nevertheless, I am saying it,' said Anne.

'Of course, of course.'

Anne thought that if the man said 'of course' once more, she would scream. She drew a deep breath. 'I have been receiving anonymous letters which allege that my husband has been having an affair with a close friend. I want to know who is sending the letters, and if there is any truth in the accusations.'

Anne felt an immense sense of relief at having voiced her fears out loud for the first time. Ricardo looked at her impassively, as if it were not the first time he had heard such fears expressed. He put his hand through his long black hair which, Anne noticed for the first time, matched his finger nails.

'Right,' he began. 'The husband will be easy. Who's responsible for sending the letters will be a lot harder. You've kept the letters, of course?'

'Only the last one,' said Anne.

Glen Ricardo sighed and stretched his hand across the table wearily. Anne reluctantly took the letter out of her bag and then hesitated for a moment.

'I know how you feel, Mrs. Osborne, but I can't do the job with one hand tied behind my back.'

'Of course, Mr. Ricardo, I'm sorry.'

Anne couldn't believe she had said 'of course'.

Ricardo read the letter through two or three times before speaking. 'Have they all been typed on this sort of paper and sent in this sort of envelope?'

'Yes, I think so,' said Anne. 'As far as I can remember.'

'Well, when the next one comes be sure to—'

'Can you be so certain there will be another one?' interrupted Anne.

'Of course, so be sure to keep it. Now give me all the details about your husband. Do you have a photograph?'

'Yes.' Once again she hesitated.

'I only want to look at the face. Don't want to waste my time chasing the wrong man, do I?' said Ricardo.

Anne opened her bag again and passed him a worn-edged photograph of Henry in a lieutenant's uniform.

'Good-looking man, Mr. Osborne,' said the detective. 'When was this photograph taken?'

'About five years ago, I think,' said Anne. 'I didn't know him when he was in the army.'

Ricardo questioned Anne for several minutes on Henry's daily movements. She was surprised to find how little she really knew of Henry's habits, or past.

'Not a lot to go on, Mrs. Osborne, but I'll do the best I can. Now, my charges are ten dollars a day plus expenses. I will make a written report for you once a week. Two weeks' payment in advance, please.' His hand came across the desk again, this time more eagerly.

Anne opened her handbag once more and took out two crisp new one hundred-dollar notes and passed them over to Ricardo. He studied the notes carefully as if he wasn't certain which distinguished American should be engraved on them. Benjamin Franklin gazed imperturbably at Ricardo, who obviously had not seen him for some time. Ricardo handed Anne sixty dollars in grubby fives.

'I see you work on Sundays, Mr. Ricardo,' said Anne, pleased with her mental arithmetic.

'Of course,' he said. 'Will the same time next week suit you, Mrs. Osborne?'

'Of course,' said Anne and left quickly to avoid having to shake hands with the man behind the desk.

When William read in his quarterly trust report from Kane and Cabot that Henry Osborne – Henry Osborne, he repeated the name out loud to be sure he could believe it – was requesting five hundred thousand dollars for a personal investment, he had a bad day. For the first time in four years at St. Paul's he came second in a maths test. Matthew Lester, who beat him, asked if he was feeling well.

That evening, William rang Alan Lloyd at home. The chairman of Kane and Cabot was not altogether surprised to hear from him after Anne's disclosure of the unhappy relationship between her son and Henry.

'William, dear boy, how are you and how are things at St. Paul's?'

'All is well this end, thank you, sir, but that's not why I telephoned.'

The tact of an advancing Mack truck, thought Alan. 'No, I didn't imagine it was,' he replied drily. 'What can I do for you?'

'I'd like to see you tomorrow afternoon.'

'On a Sunday, William?'

'Yes, as it's the only day I can get away from school, I'll come to you any time any place.' William made the statement sound as though it were a concession on his part. 'And under no condition is my mother to know of our meeting.'

'Well, William...' Alan Lloyd began.

William's voice grew firmer. 'I don't have to remind you, sir, that the investment of trust money in my step-father's personal venture, while not actually illegal, could undoubtedly be considered as unethical.'

Alan Lloyd was silent for a few moments, wondering if he

should try and placate the boy over the telephone. The boy. He also thought about remonstrating with him, but the time for that had now passed.

'Fine, William. Why don't you join me for a spot of lunch at the Hunt Club, say one o'clock?'

'I'll look forward to seeing you then, sir.' The telephone clicked.

At least the confrontation is to be on my home ground, thought Alan Lloyd with some relief as he replaced the mouthpiece, cursing Mr. Bell for inventing the damn machine.

Alan had chosen the Hunt Club because he did not want the meeting to be too private. The first thing William asked when he arrived at the clubhouse was that he should be allowed a round of golf after lunch.

'Delighted, my boy,' said Alan, and reserved the first tee for three o'clock.

He was surprised when William did not discuss Henry Osborne's proposal at all during lunch. Far from it, the boy talked knowledgeably about President Harding's views on tariff reform and the incompetence of Charles G. Dawes as the President's fiscal adviser. Alan began to wonder whether William, having slept on it, had now changed his mind about discussing Henry Osborne's loan, but was going through with the meeting not wishing to admit a change of heart. Well, if that's the way the boy wants to play it, thought Alan, that's fine by me. He looked forward to a quiet afternoon of golf. After an agreeable lunch, and the better part of a bottle of wine – William limited himself to one glass – they changed in the clubhouse and walked to the first tee.

'Do you still have a nine handicap, sir?' asked William.

'Thereabouts, my boy. Why?'

'Will ten dollars a hole suit you?'

Alan Lloyd hesitated, remembering that golf was the one game that William played competently. 'Yes, fine.'

Nothing was said at the first hole, which Alan managed in four while William took a five. Alan also won the second and the third quite comfortably, and began to relax a little, rather pleased with his game. By the time they reached the fourth, they were over half a mile from the clubhouse. William waited for Alan to raise his club.

'There are no conditions under which you will loan five hundred thousand dollars of my trust money to any company or person associated with Henry Osborne.'

Alan hit a bad tee shot which went wildly into the rough. Its only virtue was that it put him far enough away from William, who had made a good drive, to give him a few minutes to think about how to address both William and the ball. After Alan Lloyd had played three more shots, they eventually met on the green. Alan conceded the hole.

'William, you know I only have one vote out of three as a trustee and you must also be aware that you have no authority over trust decisions, as you will not control the money in your own right until your twenty-first birthday. You must also realise that we ought not to be discussing this subject at all.'

'I am fully aware of the legal implications, sir, but as both the other trustees are sleeping with Henry Osborne...'

Alan Lloyd looked shocked.

'Don't tell me you are the only person in Boston who doesn't know that Milly Preston is having an affair with my step-father?'

Alan Lloyd said nothing.

William continued. 'I want to be certain that I have your vote, and that you intend to do everything in your power to influence my mother against this loan, even if it means going to the extreme of telling her the truth about Milly Preston.'

Alan hit an even worse tee shot. William's went right down the middle of the fairway. Alan chopped the next shot into a bush he had never even realised existed before and swore out loud for the first time in forty-three years. He had got a hiding on that occasion as well.

'That's asking a little too much,' said Alan, as he joined up with William on the fifth green.

'It's nothing compared with what I'd do if I couldn't be sure of your support, sir.'

'I don't think your father would have approved of threats, William,' said Alan as he watched William's ball sink from fourteen feet.

'The only thing of which my father would not have approved is Osborne,' retorted William. Alan Lloyd two-putted four feet from the hole.

'In any case, sir, you must be well aware that my father had a clause inserted in the deed that money invested by the trust was a private affair, and the benefactor should never know that the Kane family was personally involved. It was a rule he never broke in his life as a banker. That way he could always be certain there was no conflict of interest between the bank's investments and those of the family trust.'

'Well, your mother obviously feels that the rule can be broken for a member of the family.'

'Henry Osborne is not a member of my family, and when I control the trust it is a rule I, like my father, would never break.'

'You may live to regret taking such a rigid stance, William.'

'I think not, sir.'

'Well, try and consider for a moment the affect such actions might have on your mother,' added Alan.

'My mother has already lost five hundred thousand dollars of her own money, sir. Isn't that enough for one husband? Why do I have to lose five hundred thousand of mine as well?'

'We don't know that to be the case, William. The investment may still yield an excellent return; I haven't had a chance yet to look carefully into Henry's books.'

William winced when Alan Lloyd called his step-father Henry.

'I can assure you, sir, he's blown nearly every penny of my mother's money. To be exact, he has thirty-three thousand, four hundred and twelve dollars of the original sum left. I suggest you take very little notice of Osborne's books and check more thoroughly into his background, past business record and associates. Not to mention the fact that he gambles – heavily.'

From the eighth tee Alan hit his ball into a lake directly in front of them, a lake even novice players managed to clear. He conceded the hole.

'How did you come by your information on Henry?' asked Alan, fairly certain it had been through Thomas Cohen's office.

'I prefer not to say, sir.'

Alan kept his own counsel; he thought he might need that particular ace up his sleeve to play a little later in William's life.

'If all you claim turned out to be accurate, William, naturally I would have to advise your mother against any investment in Henry's firm, and it would be my duty to have the whole thing out in the open with Henry as well.'

'So be it, sir.'

Alan hit a better shot, but felt he wasn't winning.

William continued. 'It may also interest you to know that Osborne needs the five hundred thousand from my trust not for the hospital contract but to clear a long-standing debt in Chicago. I take it that you were not aware of that, sir?'

Alan said nothing; he certainly had not been aware. William won the hole.

When they reached the eighteenth, Alan was eight holes down and was about to complete the worst round he cared to remember. He had a five-foot putt that would at least enable him to halve the final hole with William.

'Do you have any more bombshells for me?' asked Alan.

'Before or after your putt, sir?'

Alan laughed and decided to call his bluff. 'Before the putt, William,' he said, leaning on his club.

'Osborne will not be awarded the hospital contract. It is thought by those who matter that he's been bribing junior officials in the city government. Nothing will be brought out into the open, but to be sure of no repercussions later his company has been removed from the final list. The contract will actually be awarded to Kirkbride and Carter. The last piece of information, sir, is confidential. Even Kirkbride and Carter will not be informed until a week from

Thursday, so I'd be obliged if you would keep it to yourself.'

Alan missed his putt. William holed his, walked over to the chairman and shook him warmly by the hand.

'Thank you for the game, sir. I think you'll find you owe me ninety dollars.'

Alan took out his wallet and handed over a hundred-dollar note. 'William, I think the time has come for you to stop calling me "sir". My name, as you well know, is Alan.'

'Thank you, Alan.' William handed him ten dollars.

Alan Lloyd arrived at the bank on Monday morning with a little more to do than he had originally anticipated before the weekend. He put five departmental managers to work immediately on checking out the accuracy of William's allegations. He feared that he already knew what their enquiries would reveal and, because of Anne's position at the bank, he made certain that no one department was aware of what the others were up to. His instructions to each manager were clear: all reports were to be strictly confidential and for the chairman's eyes only. By Wednesday of the same week he had five preliminary reports on his desk. They all seemed to be in agreement with William's judgment although each manager had asked for more time to verify some of the details. Alan decided against worrying Anne until he had some more concrete evidence to go on. The best he felt he could do for the time being was to take advantage of a buffet supper the Osbornes were giving that evening to advise Anne against any immediate decision on the loan.

When Alan arrived at the party, he was shocked to see how tired and drawn Anne looked, which predisposed him to soften his approach even more. When he managed to catch her alone, they only had a few moments together. If only she were not having a baby just at the time all this was happening, he thought.

Anne turned and smiled at him. 'How kind of you to come Alan, when you must be so busy at the bank.'

'I couldn't afford to miss out on one of your parties, my dear, they're still the toast of Boston.'

She smiled. 'I wonder if you ever say the wrong thing.'

'All too frequently. Anne, have you had time to give any more thought to the loan?' He tried to sound casual.

'No, I am afraid I haven't. I've been up to my eyes with other things, Alan. How did Henry's accounts look?'

'Fine, but we only have one year's figures to go on, so I think we ought to bring in our own accountants to check them over. It's normal banking policy to do that with anyone who has been operating for less than three years. I am sure Henry would understand our position and agree.'

'Anne, darling, lovely party,' said a loud voice over Alan's shoulder. He did not recognise the face; presumably one of Henry's politician friends. 'How's the little mother-to-be?' continued the effusive voice.

Alan slipped away, hoping that he had bought some time for the bank. There were a lot of politicians at the party, from City Hall and even a couple from Congress, which made him wonder if William would turn out to be wrong about the big contract. Not that he needed the bank to investigate that: the official announcement from City Hall was due the following week. He said goodbye to his host and hostess, picked up his black overcoat from the cloakroom and left.

'This time next week,' he said aloud, as if to reassure himself as he walked back down Chestnut Street to his own house.

During the party Anne found time to watch Henry whenever he was near Milly Preston. There was certainly no outward sign of anything between them; in fact, Henry spent more of his time with John Preston. Anne began to wonder if she had not misjudged her husband and thought about cancelling her appointment with Glen Ricardo the next day. The party came to an end two hours later than Anne had anticipated; she hoped it meant that everybody had enjoyed themselves.

'Great party, Anne, thanks for inviting us.' It was the loud voice again, leaving last. Anne couldn't remember his name, something to do with City Hall. He disappeared down the drive.

Anne stumbled upstairs, undoing her dress even before she had reached the bedroom, promising herself that she would give no more parties before having the baby in ten weeks' time.

Henry was already undressing. 'Did you get a chance to have a word with Alan, darling?'

'Yes, I did,' replied Anne. 'He said the books look fine, but as the company can only show one year's figures, he must bring his own accountants in to double check; apparently that's normal banking policy.'

'Normal banking policy be damned. Can't you sense William's presence behind all this? He's trying to hold up the loan, Anne.'

'How can you say that? Alan said nothing about William.'

'Didn't he?' said Henry, his voice rising. 'He didn't bother to mention to you that William had lunch with him on Sunday at the golf club while we sat here at home alone?'

'What?' said Anne. 'I don't believe it. William would never come to Boston without seeing me. You must be mistaken, Henry.'

'My dear, half of the city was there, and I don't imagine that William travelled some fifty miles just for a round of golf with Alan Lloyd. Listen, Anne, I need that loan or I'm going to fail to qualify as a bidder for the city contract. Some time – and very soon now – you are going to have to decide whether you trust William or me. I must have the money by a week from tomorrow, only eight days from now, because if I can't show City Hall I'm good for that amount, I'll be disqualified. Disqualified because William didn't approve of your wanting to marry me. Please Anne, will you call Alan tomorrow and tell him to transfer the money?'

His angry voice boomed in Anne's head, making her feel faint and dizzy.

'No, not tomorrow, Henry. Can it wait until Friday? I have a heavy day tomorrow.'

Henry collected himself with an effort and came over to her as she stood naked looking at herself in the mirror. He ran his hand over her bulging stomach. 'I want this little fellow to be given as good a chance as William.'

The next day Anne told herself a hundred times that she would not go to see Glen Ricardo, but a little before noon she found herself hailing a cab. She climbed the creaky wooden stairs, apprehensive of what she might learn. She could still turn back. She hesitated, then knocked quietly on the door.

'Come in.'

She opened the door.

'Ah, Mrs. Osborne, how nice to see you again. Do have a seat.'

Anne sat and they stared at each other.

'The news, I am afraid, is not good,' said Glen Ricardo, pushing his hand through his long dark hair.

Anne's heart sank. She felt sick.

'Mr. Osborne has not been seen with Mrs. Preston or any other woman during the past seven days.'

'But you said the news wasn't good,' said Anne.

'Of course, Mrs. Osborne, I assumed you were looking for grounds for divorce. Angry wives don't normally come to me hoping I'll prove their husbands are innocent.'

'No, no,' said Anne, suffused with relief. 'It's the best piece of news I've had in weeks.'

'Oh, good,' said Mr. Ricardo, slightly taken aback. 'Let us hope the second week reveals nothing as well.'

'Oh, you can stop the investigation now, Mr. Ricardo. I am sure you'll not find anything of any consequence next week.'

'I don't think that would be wise, Mrs. Osborne. To make a final judgment on only one week's observation would be, to say the least, premature.'

'All right, if you believe it will prove the point, but I still feel confident that you won't uncover anything new next week.'

'In any case,' continued Glen Ricardo, puffing away at his cigar, which looked bigger and smelled better to Anne than it had the previous week, 'you have already paid for the two weeks.'

'What about the letters?' asked Anne, suddenly remembering them. 'I suppose they must have come from someone jealous of my husband's achievements.'

'Well, as I pointed out to you last week, Mrs. Osborne, tracing the sender of anonymous letters is never easy. However, we have been able to locate the shop where the stationary was bought, as the brand was fairly unusual, but for the moment I have nothing further to report on that front. Again, I may have a lead by this time next week. Have you received any more letters in the past few days?'

'No, I haven't.'

'Good, then it all seems to be working out for the best. Let us hope, for your sake, that next week's meeting will be our last.'

'Yes,' said Anne happily, 'let us hope so. Can I settle your expenses next Thursday?'

'Of course, of course.'

Anne had nearly forgotten the phrase, but this time it made her laugh. She decided as she was driven home that Henry must have the five hundred thousand loan and the chance to prove William and Alan wrong. She had still not recovered from the knowledge that William had come to Boston without letting her know; perhaps Henry had been right in his suggestion that William was trying to work behind their backs.

Henry was delighted when Anne told him that night of her decision on the loan, and he produced the legal documents the following morning for her signature. Anne couldn't help thinking that he must have had the papers prepared for some time, especially as Milly Preston's signature was already on them, or was she being overly suspicious again? She dismissed the thought and signed quickly.

She was fully prepared for Alan Lloyd when he telephoned the following Monday morning.

'Anne, let me at least hold things over until Thursday. Then we'll know who has been awarded the hospital contract.'

'No, Alan, the decision can't wait. Henry needs the money now. He has to prove to City Hall that he's financially strong enough to fulfil the contract and you already have the signatures of two trustees so the responsibility is no longer yours.'

'The bank could always guarantee Henry's position without actually passing over the money. I'm sure City Hall would find that acceptable. In any case, I haven't had enough time to check over his company's accounts.'

'But you did find enough time to have lunch with William a week ago Sunday, without informing me.'

There was a momentary silence from the other end of the line.

'Anne, I . . .'

'Don't say you didn't have the opportunity. You came to our party on Wednesday, and you could easily have mentioned it to me then. You chose not to, but you did find the time to advise me to postpone judgment on the loan to Henry.'

'Anne, I am sorry. I can understand how that might look and why you are upset, but there really was a reason, believe me. May I come around and explain everything to you?'

'No, Alan, you can't. You're all ganging up against my husband. None of you wants to give him a chance to prove himself. Well, I am going to give him that chance.'

Anne put the telephone down, pleased with herself, feeling she had been loyal to Henry in a way that fully atoned for her ever having doubted him in the first place.

Alan Lloyd rang back, but Anne instructed the maid to say she was out for the rest of the day. When Henry returned home that night, he was delighted to hear how Anne had dealt with Alan.

'It will all turn out for the best, my love, you'll see. On Thursday morning I will be awarded the contract, and you can kiss and make up with Alan; still, you had better keep out of his way until then. In fact, if you like we can have a celebration lunch on Thursday at the Ritz and wave at him from the other side of the room.'

Anne smiled and agreed. She could not help remembering that she was meant to be seeing Ricardo for the last time at twelve o'clock that day. Still, that would be early enough for her to be at the Ritz by one and she could celebrate both triumphs at once.

Alan tried repeatedly to reach Anne, but the maid always had a ready excuse. Since the document had been signed by two trustees, he could not hold up the payment for more than twenty-four hours. The wording was typical of a legal agreement drawn up by Richard Kane; there were no loop-holes to crawl out of. When the cheque for five hundred thousand dollars left the bank by special messenger on Tuesday afternoon, Alan sat down and wrote a long letter to William setting out the events that had culminated in the transfer of the money, withholding only the unconfirmed findings of his departmental reports. He sent a copy of the letter to each director of the bank, conscious that although he had behaved with the utmost propriety, he had laid himself open to accusations of concealment.

William received Alan Lloyd's letter at St. Paul's on the Thursday morning while having breakfast with Matthew.

Breakfast on Thursday morning at Beacon Hill was the usual eggs and bacon, hot toast, cold oatmeal, and a pot of steaming coffee. Henry was simultaneously tense and jaunty, snapping at the maid, joking with a junior city official who telephoned to say the name of the company who had been awarded the hospital contract would be posted on the notice board at City Hall around ten o'clock. Anne was almost looking forward to her last meeting with Glen Ricardo. She flicked through *Vogue*, trying not to notice that Henry's hands, clutching the *Boston Globe*, were trembling.

'What are you going to do this morning?' Henry asked, trying to make conversation.

'Oh, nothing much before we have our celebration lunch.

Will you be able to build the children's wing in memory of Richard?' Anne asked.

'Not in memory of Richard, my darling. This will be my achievement, so let it be in your honour – "The Mrs. Henry Osborne Wing",' he added grandly.

'What a good idea,' Anne said, as she put her magazine down and smiled at him. 'But you mustn't let me drink too much champagne at lunch as I have a full check-up with Doctor MacKenzie this afternoon, and I don't think he would approve of me being drunk only nine weeks before the baby is due. When will you know for certain that the contract is yours?'

'I know now,' Henry said. 'The clerk I just spoke to was a hundred per cent confident, but it will be official at ten o'clock.'

'The first thing you must do then, Henry, is to phone Alan and tell him the good news. I'm beginning to feel quite guilty about the way I treated him last week.'

'No need for you to feel any guilt; he didn't bother to keep you informed of William's actions.'

'No, but he tried to explain later, Henry, and I didn't give him a chance to tell me his side of the story.'

'All right, all right, anything you say. If it'll make you happy, I'll phone him at five past ten, and then you can tell William I've made him another million.'

He looked at his watch. 'I'd better be going. Wish me luck.'

'I thought you didn't need any luck,' said Anne.

'I don't, I don't. It's only an expression. See you at the Ritz at one o'clock.' He kissed her on the forehead. 'By tonight, you'll be able to laugh about Alan, William, contracts, and treat them all as problems of the past, believe me. Goodbye, darling.'

'I hope so, Henry.'

An uneaten breakfast was laid out in front of Alan Lloyd. He was reading the financial pages of the *Boston Globe*, noting a small paragraph in the right hand column reporting that the city would be announcing at ten o'clock that morning which company had been awarded the five-million-dollar hospital contract.

Alan Lloyd had already decided what course of action he must take if Henry failed to secure the contract and everything that William had claimed turned out to be accurate. He would do exactly what Richard would have done faced with the same predicament, and act only in the best interests of the bank. The latest departmental reports on Henry's personal finances disturbed Alan Lloyd greatly. Osborne was indeed a heavy gambler and no trace could be found of the trust's five hundred thousand dollars having gone into Henry's company. Alan Lloyd sipped his orange juice and left the rest of his breakfast untouched, apologised to his housekeeper and walked to the bank. It was a pleasant day.

'William, are you up to a game of tennis this afternoon?'

Matthew Lester was standing over William as he read the letter from Alan Lloyd for a second time.

'What did you say?'

'Are you going deaf or just becoming a senile adolescent? Do you want me to beat you black and blue on the tennis court this afternoon?'

'No, I won't be here this afternoon, Matthew. I have more important things to attend to.'

'Naturally, old buddy, I forgot that you're off on another of your mysterious trips to the White House. I know President Harding is looking for someone to be his new fiscal advisor, and you're exactly the right man to take the place of that posturing fool, Charles G. Dawes. Tell him you'll accept, subject to his inviting Matthew Lester to be the Administration's next Attorney General.'

There was still no response from William.

'I know the joke was pretty weak, but I thought it worthy of some comment,' said Matthew as he sat down beside William and looked more carefully at his friend. 'It's the eggs, isn't it? Taste as though they've come out of a Russian prisoner-of-war camp.'

'Matthew, I need your help,' said William, as he put Alan's letter back into its envelope.

'You've had a letter from my sister and she thinks you'll do as a temporary replacement for Rudolf Valentino.'

William stood up. 'Quit kidding, Matthew. If your father's bank was being robbed, would you sit around making jokes about it?'

The expression on William's face was unmistakably serious. Matthew's tone changed. 'No, I wouldn't.'

'Right, then let's get out of here, and I'll explain everything.'

Anne left Beacon Hill a little after ten to do some shopping before going on to her final meeting with Glen Ricardo. The telephone started to ring as she disappeared down Chestnut Street. The maid answered it, looked out the window and decided that her mistress was too far away to be pursued. If Anne had returned to take the call she would have been informed of City Hall's decision on the hospital contract, whereas instead she selected some silk stockings and tried out a new perfume. She arrived at Glen Ricardo's office a little after twelve, hoping her new perfume might counter the smell of cigar smoke.

'I hope I'm not late, Mr. Ricardo,' she began briskly.

'Have a seat, Mrs. Osborne.' Ricardo did not look particularly cheerful, but, thought Anne to herself, he never does. Then she noticed that he was not smoking his usual cigar.

Glen Ricardo opened a smart brown file, the only new thing Anne could see in the office, and unclipped some papers.

'Let's start with the anonymous letters, shall we, Mrs. Osborne?'

Anne did not like the tone of his voice at all or the word start. 'Yes, all right,' she managed to get out.

'They are being sent by a Mrs. Ruby Flowers.'

'Who? Why?' said Anne, impatient for an answer she did not want to hear.

'I suspect one of the reasons must be that Mrs. Flowers is at present suing your husband.'

'Well, that explains the whole mystery,' said Anne. 'She must want revenge. How much does she claim Henry owes her?'

'She is not suggesting debt, Mrs. Osborne.'

'Well, what is she suggesting then?'

Glen Ricardo pushed himself up from the chair, as if the movement required the full strength of both his arms to raise his tired frame. He walked to the window and looked out over the crowded Boston harbour.

'She is suing for a breach of promise, Mrs. Osborne.'

'Oh, no,' said Anne.

'It appears that they were engaged to be married at the time that Mr. Osborne met you, when the engagement was suddenly terminated for no apparent reason.'

'Gold digger; she must have wanted Henry's money.'

'No, I don't think so. You see, Mrs. Flowers is already well off. Not in your class, of course, but well off all the same. Her late husband owned a soft drink bottling company, and had left her financially secure.'

'Her late husband – how old is she?'

The detective walked back to the table and flicked over a page or two of his file before his thumb started moving down the page. The black nail came to a halt.

'She'll be fifty-three on her next birthday.'

'Oh, my God,' said Anne. 'The poor woman. She must hate me.'

'I dare say she does, Mrs. Osborne, but that will not help us. Now I must turn to your husband's other activities.'

The nicotine-stained finger turned over some more pages.

Anne began to feel sick. Why had she come, why hadn't she left well alone last week? She didn't have to know. She didn't want to know. Why didn't she get up and walk away? How she wished Richard was by her side. He would have known exactly how to deal with the whole situation. She found herself unable to move, transfixed by Glen Ricardo and the contents of his smart new file.

'On two occasions last week Mr. Osborne spent over three hours alone with Mrs. Preston.'

'But that doesn't prove anything,' began Anne desperately, 'I know they were discussing a very important financial document.'

'In a small hotel on La Salle Street.'

Anne didn't interrupt the detective again.

'On both occasions they were seen walking into the hotel holding hands, whispering and laughing. It's not conclusive of course, but we have photographs of them together entering and leaving the hotel.'

'Destroy them,' said Anne quietly.

Glen Ricardo blinked. 'As you wish, Mrs. Osborne. I'm afraid there is more. Further enquiries show that Mr. Osborne was never at Harvard nor was he an officer in the American armed forces. There was a Henry Osborne at Harvard who was five-foot-five, sandy-haired and came from Alabama. He was killed on the Maine in 1917. We also know that your husband is considerably younger than he claims to be and that his real name is Vittorio Togna, and he has served—'

'I don't want to hear any more,' said Anne, tears flooding down her cheeks. 'I don't want to hear any more.'

'Of course, Mrs. Osborne, I understand. I am only sorry that my news is so distressing. In my job sometimes . . .'

Anne fought for a measure of self-control. 'Thank you, Mr. Ricardo. I appreciate all you have done. How much do I owe you?'

'Well, you have already paid for the two weeks in advance, and my expenses came to seventy-three dollars.'

Anne passed him a hundred-dollar note and rose from her chair.

'Don't forget your change, Mrs. Osborne.'

She shook her head and waved a disinterested hand.

'Are you feeling all right, Mrs. Osborne? You look a little pale to me. Can I get you a glass of water or something?'

'I'm fine,' lied Anne.

'Perhaps you would allow me to drive you home?'

'No, thank you, Mr. Ricardo, I'll be able to get myself home.' She turned and smiled at him. 'It was kind of you to offer.'

Glen Ricardo closed the door quietly behind his client, walked slowly to the window, bit the end off his last big cigar, spat it out and cursed his job.

Anne paused at the top of the stairs, clinging to the banister, almost fainting. The baby kicked inside her, making her feel nauseous. She found a cab on the corner of the block and, huddled in the back, was unable to stop herself sobbing or to think what to do next. As soon as she was dropped at the Red House, she went to her bedroom before any of the staff could see her crying. The telephone was ringing as she entered the room, and she picked it up, more from habit than from any curiosity to know who it might be.

'Could I speak to Mrs. Kane, please?'

She recognised Alan's clipped tone at once. Another tired, unhappy voice.

'Hello, Alan. This *is* Anne.'

'Anne, my dear, I was so sorry to learn about this morning's news.'

'How do you know about it, Alan, how can you possibly know? Who told you?'

'City Hall phoned me and gave me the details soon after ten this morning. I tried to call you then, but your maid said that you had already left to do some shopping.'

'Oh, my God,' said Anne. 'I had quite forgotten about the contract.' She sat down heavily, unable to breathe freely.

'Are you all right, Anne?'

'Yes, I'm just fine,' she said, trying unsuccessfully to hide the sobbing in her voice. 'What did City Hall have to say?'

'The hospital contract was awarded to a firm called Kirkbride and Carter. Apparently Henry wasn't even placed in the top three. I've been trying to reach him all morning, but it seems he left his office soon after ten and he hasn't been back since. I don't suppose you know where he is, Anne?'

'No, I haven't any idea.'

'Do you want me to come around, my dear?' he said. 'I could be with you in a few minutes.'

'No, thank you, Alan.' Anne paused to draw a shaky breath. 'Please forgive me for the way I have been treating you these past few days. If Richard were still alive, he would never have forgiven me.'

'Don't be silly, Anne, our friendship has lasted for far too many years for a silly little incident like that to be of any significance.'

The kindness of his voice triggered off a fresh burst of weeping. Anne staggered to her feet.

'I must go, Alan. I can hear someone at the front door; it might be Henry.'

'Take care, Anne, and don't worry about today. As long as I'm chairman, the bank will always support you. Don't hesitate to call if you need me.'

Anne put the telephone down, the noise thudding in her ears. The effort of breathing was stupendous. She sank to the floor and as she did so, the long-forgotten sensation of a vigorous contraction overwhelmed her.

A few moments later the maid knocked quietly on the door. She looked in; William was at her shoulder. He had not entered his mother's bedroom since her marriage to Henry Osborne. The two rushed to Anne's side. She was shaking convulsively, unaware of their presence. Little flecks of foam spattered her upper lip. In a few seconds the attack passed, and she lay moaning quietly.

'Mother,' said William urgently. 'What's the matter?'

Anne opened her eyes and stared wildly at her son. 'Richard. Thank God you've come. I need you.'

'It's William, Mother.'

Her gaze faltered. 'I have no more strength left, Richard. I must pay for my mistakes. Forgive . . .'

Her voice trailed off to a groan as another powerful contraction started.

'What's happening?' said William helplessly.

'I think it must be the baby coming,' the maid said, 'although it isn't due for several weeks.'

'Get Dr. MacKenzie on the phone immediately,' William said to the maid as he ran to the bedroom door. 'Matthew,' he shouted, 'come up quickly.'

Matthew bounded up the stairs and joined William in the bedroom.

'Help me get my mother down to the car,' he said.

Matthew knelt down. The two boys picked Anne up and carried her gently downstairs and out to the car. She was panting and groaning, and obviously still in immense pain. William ran back to the house and grabbed the phone from the maid while Matthew waited in the car.

'Doctor MacKenzie.'

'Yes, who's this?'

'My name is William Kane; you won't know me, sir.'

'Don't know you, young man? I delivered you. What can I do for you now?'

'I think my mother is in labour. I'll bring her to the hospital immediately. I should be there in a few minutes' time.'

Doctor MacKenzie's tone changed. 'All right, William, don't worry. I'll be here waiting for you and everything will be under control by the time you arrive.'

'Thank you, sir.' William hesitated. 'She seemed to have some sort of a fit. Is that normal?'

William's words chilled the doctor. He too hesitated.

'Well, not quite normal. But she'll be all right once she has had the baby. Get here as quickly as you can.'

William put down the phone, ran out of the house and jumped into the Rolls Royce.

He drove the car in fits and starts, never once getting out of first gear and never stopping for anything until they had reached the doctor at the hospital. The two boys carried Anne, and a nurse with a stretcher guided them through to the maternity section. Doctor MacKenzie was standing at the entrance of an operating room, waiting. He took over and asked them both to remain outside.

The two boys sat in silence on the small bench and waited. Frightening cries and screams, unlike any sound they had ever heard anyone make, came from the delivery room; to be succeeded by an even more frightening silence. For the first time in his life William felt totally helpless. The two of them sat there for over an hour, without a word passing between them. Eventually a tired Doctor MacKenzie emerged. The two boys rose, and the doctor looked at Matthew Lester.

'William?' he asked.

'No, sir, I am Matthew Lester; this is William.'

The doctor turned to William and put a hand on his shoulder. 'William, I'm so sorry, your mother died a few minutes ago ... and the child, a little girl, was stillborn.' William's legs gave way and he sank on to the bench. 'We did everything in our power to save them, but it was hopeless.' He shook his head wearily. 'She wouldn't listen to me, she insisted on having the baby. It should never have happened.'

William sat silently, stunned by the whiplash sound of the doctor's words.

'How *could* she die?' he whispered. 'How could you *let* her die?'

The doctor sat down on the bench between the boys. 'She wouldn't listen,' he repeated slowly. 'I warned her repeatedly after her miscarriage not to have another child, but when she married again, she and your step-father never took my warnings seriously. She had high blood pressure during her last pregnancy. It was worrying me during this one, although it was never near danger level. But when you brought her in today, for no apparent reason it had soared up to the level where eclampsia ensues.'

'Eclampsia?'

'Convulsions. Sometimes patients can survive several attacks. Sometimes they simply – stop breathing.'

William drew a shuddering breath and placed his head in his hands. Matthew Lester guided his friend gently along the corridor. The doctor followed them. When they reached the door, he looked at William.

'Her blood pressure went up so suddenly. It's very unusual, and she didn't put up a real fight, almost as if she didn't care. Strange, had something been troubling her lately?'

William raised his tear-streaked face. 'Not some*thing*,' he said with hatred. 'Some*one*.'

Alan Lloyd was sitting in a corner of the drawing room when the two boys arrived back at the Red House. He rose as they entered.

'William,' he said immediately. 'I blame myself for allowing the loan.'

William stared at him, not taking in what he was saying.

Matthew Lester stepped into the silence. 'I don't think that's important any longer, sir,' he said quietly. 'William's mother has just died in childbirth.'

Alan Lloyd turned ashen, steadied himself by grasping the mantelpiece, and turned away. It was the first time that either of them had seen a grown man weep.

'It's my fault,' said the banker. 'I'll never forgive myself. I didn't tell her everything I knew. I loved her so much that I never wanted her to be distressed.'

His anguish enabled William to be calm.

'It certainly was not your fault, Alan,' he said firmly. 'You did everything you could, I know that, and now it's I who am going to need your help.'

Alan Lloyd braced himself. 'Has Osborne been informed about your mother's death?'

'I neither know nor care.'

'I've been trying to reach him all day about the investment. He left his office soon after ten this morning, and he hasn't been seen since.'

'He'll turn up here sooner or later,' said William grimly.

After Alan Lloyd left, William and Matthew sat alone in the front room most of the night, dozing off and on. At four o'clock in the morning, William counted the chimes of the grandfather clock and thought that he heard a noise in the street. Matthew was staring out of the window down the drive. William walked stiffly over to join him. They both watched Henry Osborne stagger across Louisburg Square with a half-full bottle in his hand. He fumbled with some keys for some time and finally appeared in the doorway, blinking dazedly at the two boys.

'I want Anne, not you. Why aren't you at school? I don't want you,' he said, his voice thick and slurred, trying to push William aside. 'Where's Anne?'

'My mother is dead,' said William quietly.

Henry Osborne looked at him stupidly for a few seconds. The incomprehension of his gaze snapped William's self-control.

'Where were you when she needed a husband?' he shouted.

Still Osborne stood, swaying slightly. 'What about the baby?'

'Stillborn, a little girl.'

Henry Osborne slumped into a chair, drunken tears starting to run down his face. 'She lost my little baby?'

William was nearly incoherent with rage and grief. 'Your baby? Stop thinking about yourself for once,' he shouted. 'You know Doctor MacKenzie advised her against becoming pregnant again.'

'Expert in that as well, are we, like everything else? If you had minded your own fucking business, I could have taken care of my own wife without your interference.'

'And her money, it seems.'

'Money. You tight-fisted little bastard, I bet losing that hurts you more than anything else.'

'Get up,' William said between his teeth.

Henry Osborne pushed himself up, and smashed the bottle across the corner of the chair. Whisky splashed all over the carpet. He swayed towards William with the broken bottle in his raised hand. William stood his ground while Matthew came between them and easily removed the bottle from the drunken man's grasp.

William pushed his friend aside and advanced until his face was only inches away from Henry Osborne's.

'Now, you listen to me and listen carefully. I want you out of this house in one hour. If I ever hear from you again in my life, I shall instigate a full legal investigation into what has happened to my mother's half million dollar investment in your firm, and I shall re-open my research into who you really are and your past life in Chicago. If, on the other hand, I do not hear from you again, ever, I shall consider the ledger balanced and the matter closed. Now get out before I kill you.'

The two boys watched him leave, sobbing, incoherent and furious.

The next morning William paid a visit to the bank. He was immediately shown into the chairman's office. Alan Lloyd was packing some documents into a briefcase. He looked up, and handed a piece of paper to William without speaking. It was a short letter to all board members tendering his resignation as chairman of the bank.

'Could you ask your secretary to come in?' said William quietly.

'As you wish.'

Alan Lloyd pressed a button on the side of his desk, and a middle-aged, conservatively dressed lady entered the room from a side door.

'Good morning, Mr. Kane,' she said when she saw William. 'I was so sorry to learn about your mother.'

'Thank you,' said William. 'Has anyone else seen this letter?'

'No, sir,' said the secretary. 'I was about to type twelve copies for Mr. Lloyd to sign.'

'Well, don't type them, and please forget that this draft ever existed. Never mention its existence to anyone, do you understand?'

She stared into those blue eyes of the sixteen-year-old boy. So like his father, she thought. 'Yes, Mr. Kane.' She left quietly closing the door. Alan Lloyd looked up.

'Kane and Cabot doesn't need a new chairman at the moment, Alan. You did nothing my father would not have done in the same circumstances.'

'It's not as easy as that,' Alan said.

'It's as easy as that,' said William. 'We can discuss this again when I am twenty-one and not before. Until then I would be obliged if you would run my bank in your usual diplomatic and conservative manner. I want nothing of what has happened to be discussed outside this office. You will destroy any information you have on Henry Osborne and consider the matter closed.'

William tore up the letter of resignation and dropped the pieces of paper into the fire. He put his arm around Alan's shoulders.

'I have no family now, Alan, only you. For God's sake don't desert me.'

William was driven back to Beacon Hill. On his arrival the butler informed him that Mrs. Kane and Mrs. Cabot were waiting for him in the drawing room. They both rose as he entered the room. It was the first time that William realised that he was now the head of the Kane family.

The funeral took place quietly two days later at the Old North Church on Beacon Hill. None but the family and close friends were invited, and the only notable absentee was Henry Osborne. As the mourners departed, they paid their respects to William. The grandmothers stood one pace behind him, like sentinels, watching, approving the calm and dignified way in which he conducted himself. When everyone had left, William accompanied Alan Lloyd to his car.

The chairman was delighted by William's one request of him.

'As you know, Alan, my mother had always intended to build a children's wing to the new hospital, in memory of my father. I would like her wishes carried out.'

11

Wladek stayed at the Polish Delegation in Constantinople for eighteen months, working day and night for Pawel Zaleski, becoming an indispensable aide and close friend. Nothing was too much trouble for him and Zaleski soon began to wonder how he managed before Wladek arrived. He visited the British embassy once a week to eat in the kitchen with Mrs. Henderson, the Scottish cook, and, on one occasion, with His Britannic Majesty's second consul himself.

Around them the old Islamic way of life was dissolving, and the Ottoman Empire was beginning to totter. Mustafa Kemal was the name on everyone's lips. The sense of impending change made Wladek restless. His mind returned incessantly to the Baron and all whom he had loved in the castle. The necessity to survive from day to day in Russia had kept them from his mind's eye, but in Turkey they rose up before him, a silent and slow procession. Sometimes, he could see them strong and happy, Leon swimming in the river, Florentyna playing cat's cradle in his bedroom, the Baron's face strong and proud in the evening candlelight, but always each well-remembered, well-loved face would waver and, try as Wladek did to hold them firm, they would change horribly to that last dreadful aspect, Leon dead on top of him, Florentyna bleeding in agony, and the Baron almost blind and broken.

Wladek began to face the fact that he could never return to a land peopled by such ghosts, until he had made something worthwhile of his life. With that single thought in mind he set his heart on going to America, as his countryman Tadeusz Kosciuszko, of whom the Baron had told so many enthralling tales, had done so long before him. The United States, described by Pawel Zaleski as the 'New World'. The very name inspired Wladek with a hope for the future and a chance to return to Poland in triumph. It was Pawel Zaleski who put up the money to purchase an immigrant passage for him to the United States. They were difficult to come by, for they were always booked at least a year in advance. It seemed to Wladek as though the whole of Eastern Europe was trying to escape and start afresh in the New World.

In the spring of 1921, Wladek Koskiewicz finally left Constantinople and boarded the S.S. *Black Arrow*, bound for Ellis Island, New York. He possessed one suitcase, containing all his belongings, and a set of papers issued by Pawel Zaleski.

The Polish consul accompanied him to the wharf, and embraced him affectionately. 'Go with God, my boy.'

The traditional Polish response came naturally from the depths of Wladek's early childhood. 'Remain with God,' he replied.

As he reached the top of the gangplank, Wladek recalled his terrifying journey from Odessa to Constantinople. This time there was no coal in sight, only people, people everywhere, Poles, Lithuanians, Estonians, Ukrainians and others of many racial types unfamiliar to Wladek. He clutched his few belongings and waited in the line, the first of many long waits with which he later associated his entry into the United States.

His papers were sternly scrutinised by a deck officer who was clearly predisposed to the suspicion that Wladek was trying to avoid military service in Turkey, but Pawel Zaleski's documents were impeccable; Wladek invoked a silent blessing on his fellow countryman's head as he watched others being turned back.

Next came a vaccination and a cursory medical examination which, had he not had eighteen months of good food and the chance to recover his health in Constantinople, Wladek would certainly have failed. At last with all the checks over he was allowed below deck into the steerage quarters. There were separate compartments for males, females and married couples. Wladek quickly made his way to the male quarters and found the Polish group occupying a large block of iron berths, each containing four two-tiered bunk beds. Each bunk had a thin straw mattress, a light blanket and no pillow. Having no pillow did not worry Wladek who had never been able to sleep on one since leaving Russia.

Wladek selected a bunk below a boy of roughly his own age and introduced himself.

'I'm Wladek Koskiewicz.'

'I'm Jerzy Nowak from Warsaw,' volunteered the boy in his native Polish, 'and I'm going to make my fortune in America.'

The boy thrust forward his hand.

Wladek and Jerzy spent the time before the ship sailed telling each other of their experiences, both pleased to have someone to share their loneliness with, neither willing to admit their total ignorance of America. Jerzy, it turned out, had lost his parents in the war but had few other claims to attention. He was entranced by Wladek's stories: the son of a baron, brought up in a trapper's cottage, imprisoned by the Germans and the Russians, escaped from Siberia and then from a Turkish executioner thanks to the heavy silver band which Jerzy couldn't take his eyes off. Wladek had packed more in to his fifteen years than Jerzy thought he would manage in a lifetime. Wladek talked all night of the past while Jerzy listened intently, neither wanting to sleep and neither wanting to admit their apprehension of the future.

The following morning the *Black Arrow* sailed. Wladek and Jerzy stood at the rail and watched Constantinople slip away in the blue distance of the Bosphorus. After the calm of the Sea of Marmara the choppiness of the Aegean afflicted them and most of the other passengers with a horrible abruptness. The two washrooms for steerage passengers, with ten basins apiece, six toilets and cold salt water taps were rapidly inundated. After a couple of days the stench of their quarters was nauseating.

Food was served in a large filthy dining hall on long tables; warm soup, potatoes, fish, boiled beef and cabbage, brown or black bread. Wladek had tasted worse food but not since Russia and was glad of the provisions he had brought along with him: sausages, nuts and a little brandy. He and Jerzy shared them huddled in the corner of their berth. It was an unspoken understanding. They ate together, explored the ship together and at night, slept one above the other.

On the third day at sea Jerzy brought a Polish girl to their table for supper. Her name, he informed Wladek casually, was Zaphia. It was the first time in his life that Wladek had ever looked at a woman twice, but he couldn't stop looking at Zaphia. She rekindled memories of Florentyna. The warm grey eyes, the long fair hair that fell on to her shoulders and the soft voice. Wladek found he wanted to touch her. The girl occasionally smiled across at Wladek, who was miserably aware how much better looking Jerzy was than he. He tagged along as Jerzy escorted Zaphia back to the women's quarters.

Jerzy turned to him afterwards, mildly irritated. 'Can't you find a girl of your own? This one's mine.'

Wladek was not prepared to admit that he had no idea how to set about finding a girl of his own.

'There will be enough time for girls when we reach America,' he said scornfully.

'Why wait for America? I intend to have as many on this ship as possible.'

'How will you go about that?' asked Wladek, intent on the acquisition of knowledge without admitting to his own ignorance.

'We have twelve more days in this awful tub, and I am going to have twelve women,' boasted Jerzy.

'What can you do with twelve women?' asked Wladek.

'Fuck them, what else?'

Wladek looked perplexed.

'Good God,' said Jerzy. 'Don't tell me the man who survived the Germans and escaped from the Russians, killed a man at the age of twelve and narrowly missed having his hand chopped off by a bunch of savage Turks has never had a woman?'

He laughed, and a multilingual chorus from the surrounding bunks told him to 'shut up'.

'Well,' Jerzy continued in a whisper, 'the time has come to broaden your education, because at last I have found something I can teach you.' He peered over the side of his bunk even though he could not see Wladek's face in the dark. 'Zaphia's an understanding girl. I dare say she could be persuaded to expand your education a little. I shall arrange it.'

Wladek didn't reply.

No more was said on the subject, but the next day Zaphia started to pay attention to Wladek. She sat next to him at meals, and they talked for hours of their experiences and hopes. She was an orphan from Poznan, on her way to join her cousins in Chicago. Wladek told Zaphia that he was going to New York and would probably live with Jerzy.

'I hope New York is very near Chicago,' said Zaphia.

'Then you can come and see me when I am the mayor,' said Jerzy expansively.

She sniffed disparagingly. 'You're too Polish, Jerzy. You can't even speak nice English like Wladek.'

'I'll learn,' said Jerzy confidently, 'and I'll start by making my name American. From today I shall be George Novak. Then I'll have no trouble at all. Everyone in the United States will think I'm American. What about you, Wladek Koskiewicz? Nothing much you can do with that name, is there?'

Wladek looked at the newly christened George in silent resentment of his own name. Unable to adopt the title to which he felt himself the rightful heir, he hated Koskiewicz and the continual reminder of his illegitimacy.

'I'll manage,' he said. 'I'll even help you with your English if you like.'

'And I'll help you find a girl.'

Zaphia giggled. 'You needn't bother, he's found one.'

Jerzy, or George, as he now insisted they should call him, retreated after supper each night into one of the tarpaulin-covered lifeboats with a different girl. Wladek longed to know what he did there, even though some of the ladies of George's choice were not merely filthy, as they all were, but would clearly have been unattractive even when scrubbed clean.

One night after supper, when George had disappeared again, Wladek and Zaphia sat out on deck, she put her arms around him and asked him to kiss her. He pressed his mouth stiffly against hers until their teeth touched; he felt horribly unfamiliar with what he was meant to be doing. To his surprise and embarrassment, her tongue parted his lips. After a few moments of apprehension, Wladek found her open mouth intensely exciting and was alarmed to find his penis stiffening. He tried to draw away from her, ashamed, but she did not seem to mind in the least. On the contrary, she began to press her body gently and rhythmically against him and drew his hands down to her buttocks. His swollen penis throbbed against her, giving him almost unbearable pleasure. She disengaged her mouth and whispered in his ear.

'Do you want me to take my clothes off, Wladek?'

He could not bring himself to reply.

She detached herself from him, laughing. 'Well, maybe tomorrow,' she said, getting up from the deck and leaving him.

He stumbled back to his bunk in a daze, determined that the next day he would finish the job Zaphia had started. No sooner had he settled in his berth thinking of how he would go about the task than a large hand grabbed him by the hair and pulled him down from his bunk onto the floor. In an instant his sexual excitement vanished. Two men whom he had never seen before were towering above him. They dragged him to a far corner and threw him up against the wall. A large hand was now clamped firmly on Wladek's mouth while a knife touched his throat.

'Don't breathe,' whispered the man holding the knife, pushing the blade against the skin. 'All we want is the silver band around your wrist.'

The sudden realisation that his treasure might be stolen

from him was almost as horrifying to Wladek as had been the thought of losing his hand. Before he could think of anything to do, one of the men jerked the band off his wrist. He couldn't see their faces in the dark, and he feared he must have lost the band for ever, when someone leaped on to the back of the man holding the knife. This action gave Wladek the chance to punch the one who was holding him pinned to the ground. The sleepy immigrants around them began to wake and take an interest in what was happening. The two men escaped as quickly as they could, but not before George had managed to stick the knife in the side of one of the assailants.

'Go to the cholera,' shouted Wladek at his retreating back.

'It looks as if I got here just in time,' said George. 'I don't think they'll be back in a hurry.' He stared down at the silver band, lying in the trampled sawdust on the floor. 'It's magnificent,' he said, almost solemnly. 'There will always be men who want to steal such a prize from you.'

Wladek picked the band up and slipped it back on to his wrist.

'Well, you nearly lost the damn thing for good that time,' said George. 'Lucky for you I was a little late getting back tonight.'

'Why were you a little late getting back?' asked Waldek.

'My reputation,' said George boastfully, 'now goes before me. In fact, I found some other idiot in my lifeboat tonight, already with his pants down. I soon got rid of him, though, when I told him he was with a girl I would have had last week but I couldn't be sure she hadn't got the pox. I've never seen anyone get dressed so quickly.'

'What do you do in the boat?' asked Wladek.

'Fuck them silly, you ass, what do you think?' and with that he rolled over and went to sleep.

Wladek stared at the ceiling and, touching the silver band, thought about what George had said, wondering what it would be like to 'fuck' Zaphia.

The next morning they hit a storm, and all the passengers were confined below decks. The stench, intensified by the ship's steam heating system, seemed to permeate Wladek's very marrow.

'And the worst of it is,' groaned George, 'I won't make a round dozen now.'

When the storm abated, nearly all the passengers escaped to the deck. Wladek and George fought their way around the crowded gangways, thankful for the fresh air. Many of the girls smiled at George, but it seemed to Wladek that they didn't notice him at all. He would have thought they couldn't miss him in his fifty-ruble coat. A dark-haired girl, her cheeks made pink by the wind, passed George and smiled at him. He turned to Wladek.

'I'll have her tonight.'

Wladek stared at the girl and studied the way she looked at George.

'Tonight,' said George, as she passed within earshot. She pretended not to hear him and walked away, a little too quickly.

'Turn round, Wladek, and see if she is looking back at me.'

Wladek turned around. 'Yes, she is,' he said, surprised.

'She's mine tonight,' said George. 'Have you had Zaphia yet?'

'No,' said Wladek. 'Tonight.'

'About time, isn't it? You'll never see the girl again once we've reached New York.'

Sure enough, George arrived at supper that night with the dark-haired girl. Without a word being said, Wladek and Zaphia left them, arms round each other's waists, and went on to the deck and strolled around the ship several times. Wladek looked sideways at her pretty young profile. It was going to be now or never, he decided. He led her to a shadowy corner and started to kiss her as she had kissed him, open-mouthed. She moved backwards a little until her shoulders were resting against a bulwark, and Wladek moved with her. She drew his hands slowly down to her breasts. He touched them tentatively, surprised by their softness. She undid a couple of buttons on her blouse and slipped his hand inside. The first feel of the naked flesh was delicious.

'Christ, your hand is cold,' Zaphia said.

Wladek crushed himself against her, his mouth dry, his breath heavy. She parted her legs a little and Wladek thrust clumsily against her through several intervening layers of cloth. She moved in sympathy with him for a couple of minutes and then pushed him away.

'Not here on the deck,' she said. 'Let's find a boat.'

The first three they looked into were occupied, but they finally found an empty one and wriggled under the tarpaulin. In the constricted darkness Zaphia made some adjustments to her clothing that Wladek could not figure out, and pulled him gently on top of her. It took her very little time to bring Wladek to his earlier pitch of excitement through the few remaining layers of cloth between them. He thrust his penis into the yielding softness between her legs and was on the point of orgasm when she again drew her mouth away.

'Undo your trousers,' she whispered.

He felt an idiot but hurriedly undid them, and thrust again, coming immediately, feeling the sticky wetness running down the inside of her thigh. He lay dazed, amazed by the abruptness of the act, suddenly aware that the wooden notches of the boat were digging uncomfortably into his elbows and knees.

'Was that the first time you've made love to a girl?' asked Zaphia, wishing he would move over.

'No, of course not,' said Wladek.

'Do you love me, Wladek?'

'Yes, I do,' he said, 'and as soon as I've settled in New York, I'll come and find you in Chicago.'

'I'd like that, Wladek,' she said as she buttoned up her dress. 'I love you, too.'

'Did you fuck her?' was George's immediate question on Wladek's return.

'Yes.'

'Was it good?'

'Yes,' said Wladek, uncertainly, and then fell asleep.

In the morning, they were woken by a room full of excited passengers, happy in the knowledge that this was their last day on board the *Black Arrow*. Some of them had been up on deck before sunrise, hoping to catch the first sign of land. Wladek packed his few belongings in his new suitcase, put on his only suit, and his cap and then joined Zaphia and George on deck. The three of them stared into the mist that hung over the sea, waiting in silence for their first sight of the United States of America.

'There it is,' shouted a passenger on a deck above them, and cheering went up at the sight of the grey strip of Long Island approaching through the spring morning.

Little tugs bustled up to the side of the *Black Arrow* and guided her between Brooklyn and Staten Island into New York Harbour. The colossal Statue of Liberty regarded them austerely as they gazed in awe at the emerging skyline of Manhattan, great long arms stretching high into the autumn sky.

Finally they moored near the turreted and spired red brick buildings of Ellis Island. The passengers who had private cabins left the ship first. Wladek hadn't noticed them until that day. They must have been on a separate deck with their own dining hall. Their bags were carried for them by porters, and they were greeted by smiling faces at the quayside. Wladek knew that wasn't going to happen to him.

After the favoured few had disembarked, the captain announced over the loudspeaker to the rest of the passengers that they would not be leaving the ship for several hours. A groan of disappointment went up, and Zaphia sat on the deck and burst into tears. Wladek tried to comfort her. Eventually an official came around with coffee, a second with numbered labels which were hung around their necks. Wladek's was B.127; it reminded him of the last time he was a number. What had he let himself in for? Was America like the Russian camps?

In the middle of the afternoon, having been given no food or further information, they were ferried by slow moving barges from the dockside to Ellis Island. There the men were separated from the women and sent off to different sheds. Wladek kissed Zaphia and wouldn't let her go, which held up the line. A nearby official parted them.

'All right, let's get moving,' he said. 'Keep that up and we'll have you two married in no time.'

Wladek lost sight of Zaphia as he was pushed forwards with George. They spent the night in an old, damp shed, unable to sleep as interpreters moved among the crowded rows of bunks, offering curt, but not unkind, assistance to the bewildered immigrants.

In the morning they were sent for medical examinations. The first hurdle was the hardest: Wladek was told to climb a steep flight of stairs. The blue-uniformed doctor made him do it twice, watching his gait carefully. Wladek tried very hard to minimise his limp, and finally the doctor was satisfied. Wladek was made to remove his hat and stiff collar so that his face, eyes, hair, hands and neck could be examined carefully. The man directly behind Wladek had a hare lip; the doctor stopped him immediately, put a chalk cross on his shoulder and sent him to the other end of the shed. After the physical was over, Wladek joined up with George again in another long line outside the Public Examination room where each person seemed to be taking about five minutes. Three hours later when George was ushered into the room Wladek began to wonder what they would ask him.

When George came out, he grinned at Wladek and said, 'Easy, you'll walk right through it.' Wladek could feel the palms of his hands sweating as he stepped forward.

He followed the official into a small, undecorated room. There were two examiners seated and writing furiously on what looked like official papers.

'Do you speak English?' asked the first.

'Yes, sir, I do quite good,' replied Wladek, wishing he had spoken more English on the voyage.

'What is your name?'

'Wladek Koskiewicz, sir.'

The men passed him a big black book. 'Do you know what that is?'

'Yes, sir, the Bible.'

'Do you believe in God?'

'Yes, sir, I do.'

'Put your hand on the Bible, and swear that you will answer our questions truthfully.'

Wladek took the Bible in his left hand, placed his right hand on it and said, 'I promise I tell the truth.'

'What is your nationality?'

'Polish.'

'Who paid for your passage here?'

'I paid from my money that I earn in Polish Consulate in Constantinople.'

One of the officials studied Wladek's papers, nodded and then asked, 'Do you have a home to go to?'

'Yes, sir. I go stay at Mister Peter Novak. He my friend's uncle. He live in New York.'

'Good. Do you have work to go to?'

'Yes, sir. I go work in bakery of Mister Novak.'

'Have you ever been arrested?'

Russia flashed through Wladek's mind. It couldn't count. Turkey – he wasn't going to mention that.

'No, sir, never.'

'Are you an anarchist?'

'No, sir. I hate Communists, they kill my sister.'

'Are you willing to abide by the laws of the United States of America?'

'Yes, sir.'

'Have you any money?'

'Yes, sir.'

'May we see it?'

'Yes, sir.' Wladek placed on the table a bundle of notes and a few coins.

'Thank you,' said the examiner, 'you may put the money back in your pocket.'

The second examiner looked at him. 'What is twenty-one plus twenty-four?'

'Forty-five,' said Wladek, without hesitation.

'How many legs does a cow have?'

Wladek could not believe his ears. 'Four, sir,' he said, wondering if the question was a trick.

'And a horse?'

'Four, sir,' said Wladek still in disbelief.

'Which would you throw overboard if you were out at sea in a small boat which needed to be lightened, bread or money?'

'The money, sir,' said Wladek.

'Good.' The examiner picked up a card marked 'Admitted' and handed it over to Wladek. 'After you have changed your money, show this card to the immigration officer. Tell him your full name and he will give you a registration card. You will then be given an entry certificate. If you do not commit a crime for five years and pass a simple reading and writing examination at the end of that time, you will be permitted to apply for full United States citizenship. Good luck, Wladek.'

'Thank you, sir.'

At the money exchange counter Wladek handed in eighteen months of Turkish savings and the three fifty-ruble notes. He was handed forty-seven dollars twenty cents in exchange for the Turkish money but was told the rubles were worthless. He could only think of Doctor Dubien and his fifteen years of diligent saving.

The final stop was the immigration officer, who was seated behind a counter at the exit barrier directly under a picture of President Harding. Wladek and George went over to him.

'Full name?' the officer said to George.

'George Novak,' replied Jerzy firmly. The officer wrote the name on a card.

'And your address?' he asked.

'286 Broome Street, New York, New York.'

The officer passed George the card. 'This is your Immigration Certificate, 21871-George Novak. Welcome to the United States, George. I'm Polish too. You'll like it here. Many congratulations and good luck.'

George smiled and shook hands with the officer, stood to one side and waited for Wladek. The officer stared at Wladek in his long bearskin coat. Wladek passed him the card marked 'Admitted'.

'Full name?' asked the officer.

Wladek hesitated.

'What's your name?' repeated the man, a little louder, slightly impatient, wondering if he couldn't speak English.

Wladek couldn't get the words out. How he hated that peasant name.

'For the last time, what's your name?'

George was staring at Wladek. So were others who had joined the queue for the immigration officer. Wladek still didn't speak. The officer suddenly grabbed his wrist, stared closely at the inscription on the silver band, wrote on a card and passed it to Wladek.

'21872-Baron Abel Rosnovski. Welcome to the United States. Many congratulations and good luck, Abel.'

12

William returned to start his last year at St. Paul's in September, 1923, and was elected president of the Senior Class, exactly thirty-three years after his father had held the same office. William did not win the election in the usual fashion, by virtue of being the finest athlete or the most popular boy in the school. Matthew Lester, his closest friend, would undoubtedly have won any contest based on those criteria. It was simply that William was the most impressive boy in the school, and for that reason Matthew Lester could not be prevailed upon to run against him. St. Paul's entered William's name as their candidate for the Hamilton Memorial Mathematics Scholarship at Harvard, and William worked singlemindedly towards that goal during the autumn term.

When William returned to Beacon Hill for Christmas, he

was looking forward to an uninterrupted period in which to get to grips with *Principia Mathematica*. But it was not to be, for there were several invitations to parties and balls awaiting his arrival. To most of them he felt able to return a tactful regret, but one was absolutely inescapable. The grandmothers had arranged a ball, to be held at the Red House on Louisburg Square. William wondered at what age he would find it possible to defend his home against invasion by the two great ladies and decided the time had not yet come. He had few close friends in Boston, but this did not inhibit the grandmothers in their compilation of a formidable guest list.

To mark the occasion they presented William with his first dinner jacket in the latest double-breasted style; he received the gift with some pretence at indifference but later swaggered around his bedroom in the suit, often stopping to stare at himself in the mirror. The next day he put through a long distance call to New York and asked Matthew Lester to join him for the fateful weekend. Matthew's sister wanted to come as well but her mother didn't think it would be suitable.

William was there to meet him off the train.

'Come to think of it,' said Matthew, as the chauffeur drove them back to Beacon Hill, 'isn't it time you got yourself laid, William? There must be some girls in Boston with absolutely no taste.'

'Why, have you had a girl, Matthew?'

'Sure, last winter in New York.'

'What was I doing at the time?'

'Probably touching up on Bertrand Russell.'

'You never told me about it.'

'Nothing much to tell. In any case, you seemed more involved in my father's bank than my budding love life. It all happened at a staff party my father gave to celebrate Washington's birthday. Another first for old wooden teeth. Actually, to put the incident in its proper perspective, I was raped by one of the director's secretaries, a large lady called Cynthia with even larger breasts that wobbled when...'

'Did you enjoy it?'

'Yes, but I can't believe for one moment that Cynthia did. She was far too drunk to realise I was there at the time. Still, you have to begin somewhere and she was willing to give the boss's son a helping hand.'

The vision of Alan Lloyd's prim, middle-aged secretary flashed across William's mind.

'I don't think my chances of initiation by the chairman's secretary are very good,' he mused.

'You'd be surprised,' said Matthew knowingly. 'The ones that go around with their legs so firmly together are often the ones who can't wait to get them apart. I now accept most invitations, formal or informal, not that dress matters much on these occasions.'

The chauffeur put the car in the garage while the two young men ran up the steps into William's house.

'You've certainly made some changes since I was last here,' said Matthew, admiring the modern cane furniture and new paisley wallpapers. Only the crimson leather chair remained firmly rooted in its usual spot.

'The place needed brightening up a little,' William offered. 'It was like living in the Stone Age. Besides, I didn't want to be reminded of ... Come on, this is no time to hang around discussing interior decoration.'

'When is everybody arriving for this party?'

'Ball, Matthew, the grandmothers insist on calling the event a ball.'

'There is only one thing that can be described as a ball on these occasions.'

'Matthew, one director's secretary does not entitle you to consider yourself a national authority on sex education.'

'Oh, such jealousy, and from one's dearest friend', Matthew sighed mockingly.

William laughed and looked at his watch. 'The first guest should arrive in a couple of hours. Time for a shower and to change. Did you remember to bring a dinner jacket?'

'Yes, but if I didn't I can always wear my pyjamas. I usually leave one or the other behind, but I've never yet managed to forget both. In fact, it might start a whole new craze if I arrived at the ball in my pyjamas.'

'I can't see my grandmothers enjoying the joke,' said William.

The caterers arrived at six o'clock, twenty-three of them in all, and the grandmothers at seven, regal in long black lace that swept along the floor. William and Matthew joined them in the front room a few minutes before eight.

William was about to remove an inviting red cherry from the top of a magnificent iced cake when he heard Grandmother Kane's voice from behind him.

'Don't touch the food, William, it's not for you.'

He swung round. 'Then who is it for?' he asked, as he kissed her on the cheek.

'Don't be fresh, William, just because you're over six feet doesn't mean I wouldn't spank you.'

Matthew Lester laughed.

'Grandmother, may I introduce my closest friend, Matthew Lester?'

Grandmother Kane subjected him to a careful appraisal through her pince-nez before venturing: 'How do you do, young man?'

'It's an honour to meet you, Mrs. Kane. I believe you knew my grandfather.'

'Knew your grandfather? Caleb Longworth Lester? He proposed marriage to me once, over fifty years ago. I turned him down. I told him he drank too much, and that it would lead him to an early grave. I was right, so don't you drink, either of you; remember, alcohol dulls the brain.'

'We hardly get much chance with Prohibition,' remarked Matthew innocently.

'That will end soon enough, I'm afraid,' said Grandmother Kane, sniffing. 'President Coolidge is forgetting his upbringing. He would never have become President if that idiot Harding hadn't foolishly died.'

William laughed. 'Really, Grandmother, your memory is getting selective. You wouldn't hear a word against him during the police strike.'

Mrs. Kane did not reply.

The guests began to appear, many of them complete strangers to their host, who was delighted to see Alan Lloyd among the early arrivals.

'You're looking well, my boy,' he said, finding himself looking up at William for the first time in his life.

'You too, Alan. It was kind of you to come.'

'Kind? Have you forgotten that the invitation came from your grandmothers? I am possibly brave enough to refuse one of them, but both . . .'

'You too, Alan?' William laughed. 'Can you spare a moment for a private word?' He guided his guest towards a quiet corner. 'I want to change my investment plans slightly and start buying Lester's bank stock whenever it comes on to the market. I'd like to be holding about five per cent of their stock by the time I'm twenty-one.'

'It's not that easy,' said Alan. 'Lester's shares don't come on the market all that often as they are all in private hands, but I'll see what can be done. What is going on in that mind of yours, William?'

'Well, my real aim is . . .'

'William.' Grandmother Cabot was bearing down on them at speed. 'Here you are conspiring in a corner with Mr. Lloyd and I haven't seen you dance with one young lady yet. What do you imagine we organised this ball for?'

'Quite right,' said Alan Lloyd, rising. 'You come and sit down with me, Mrs. Cabot, and I'll kick the boy out into the world. We can rest, watch him dance, and listen to the music.'

'Music? That's not music, Alan. It's nothing more than a loud cacophony of sound with no suggestion of melody.'

'My dear grandmother,' said William, 'that is "Yes, We Have No Bananas", the latest hit song.'

'Then the time has come for me to depart this world,' said Grandmother Cabot, wincing.

'Never,' Alan Lloyd said gallantly.

William danced with a couple of girls whom he had a vague recollection of knowing, but he had to be reminded of their names, and when he spotted Matthew sitting in a corner, he was glad of the excuse to escape the dance floor. He had not noticed the girl sitting next to Matthew until he was right on top of them. When she looked up into William's eyes, he felt his knees give way.

'Do you know Abby Blount?' asked Matthew casually.

'No,' said William, barely restraining himself from straightening his tie.

'This is your host, Mr. William Lowell Kane.'

The young lady cast her eyes demurely downwards as he took the seat on the other side of her. Matthew had noted the look William gave Abby and went off in search of some punch.

'How is it I've lived in Boston all my life, and we've never met?' William said.

'We did meet once before. On that occasion, you pushed me into the pond on the Common; we were both three at the time. It's taken me fourteen years to recover.'

'I am sorry,' said William, after a pause during which he searched in vain for more telling repartee.

'What a lovely house you have, William.'

There was a second busy pause. 'Thank you,' said William weakly. He glanced sideways at Abby, trying to look as though he were not studying her. She was slim – oh, so slim – with huge brown eyes, long eyelashes and a profile that captivated William. Abby had bobbed her auburn hair in the style William had hated until that moment.

'Matthew tells me you are going to Harvard next year,' she tried again.

'Yes, I am. I mean, would you like to dance?'

'Thank you,' she said.

The steps that had come to him so easily a few minutes before seemed now to forsake him. He trod on her toes and continually propelled her into other dancers. He apologised, she smiled. He held her a little more closely, and they danced on.

'Do we know that young lady who seems to have been

monopolising William for the last hour?' said Grandmother Cabot suspiciously.

Grandmother Kane picked up her pince-nez and studied the girl accompanying William as he strolled through the open bay windows out on to the lawn.

'Abby Blount,' Grandmother Kane declared.

'Admiral Blount's daughter?' enquired Grandmother Cabot.

'Yes.'

Grandmother Cabot nodded a degree of approval.

William guided Abby Blount towards the far end of the garden and stopped by a large chestnut tree which he had used in the past only for climbing.

'Do you always try to kiss a girl the first time you meet her?' asked Abby.

'To be honest,' said William, 'I've never kissed a girl before.'

Abby laughed. 'I'm very flattered.'

She offered first her pink cheek and then her rosy, pursed lips and then insisted upon returning indoors. The grandmothers observed their early re-entry with some relief.

Later, in William's bedroom, the two boys discussed the evening.

'Not a bad party,' said Matthew. 'Almost worth the trip from New York out here to the provinces, despite your stealing my girl.'

'Do you think she'll help me lose my virginity?' asked William, ignoring Matthew's mock accusation.

'Well, you have three weeks to find out, but I fear you'll discover she hasn't lost hers yet,' said Matthew. 'Such is my expertise in these matters that I'm willing to bet you five dollars she doesn't succumb even to the charms of William Lowell Kane.'

William planned a careful strategem. Virginity was one thing, but losing five dollars to Matthew was quite another. He saw Abby Blount nearly every day after that, taking advantage for the first time of owning his own house and car at seventeen. He began to feel he would do better without the discreet but persistent chaperonage of Abby's parents who seemed always to be in the middle distance and he was not perceptibly nearer his goal when the last day of the holidays dawned.

Determined to win his five dollars, William sent Abby a dozen roses early in the day, took her out to an expensive dinner at Joseph's that evening and finally succeeded in coaxing her back into his front room.

'How did you get hold of a bottle of whisky while Prohibition is on?' asked Abby.

'Oh, it's not so hard,' William boasted.

The truth was that he had hidden a bottle of Henry Osborne's bourbon in his bedroom soon after he had left, and was now glad he had not poured it down the drain as had been his original intention.

William poured drinks that made him gasp and brought tears to Abby's eyes.

He sat down beside her and put his arm confidently around her shoulder. She settled in to it.

'Abby, I think you're terribly pretty,' he murmured in a preliminary way at her auburn curls.

She gazed at him earnestly, her brown eyes wide. 'Oh, William,' she breathed. 'And I think you're just wonderful.'

Her doll-like face was irresistible. She allowed herself to be kissed. Thus emboldened, William slipped a tentative hand from her wrist on to her breast, and left it there like a traffic cop halting an advancing stream of automobiles. She became pinkly indignant and pushed his arm down to allow the traffic to move on.

'William, you musn't do that.'

'Why not?' said William, struggling vainly to retain his grasp of her.

'Because you can't tell where it might end.'

'I've got a fair idea.'

Before he could renew his advances, Abby pushed him away and rose hastily, smoothing her dress.

'I think I ought to be getting home now, William.'

'But you've only just arrived.'

'Mother will want to know what I've been doing.'

'You'll be able to tell her – nothing.'

'And I think it's best it stays that way,' she added.

'But I'm going back tomorrow.' He avoided saying, 'to school'.

'Well, you can write to me, William.'

Unlike Valentino, William knew when he was beaten. He rose, straightened his tie, took Abby by the hand and drove her home.

The following day, back at school, Matthew Lester accepted the proffered five-dollar note with eyebrows raised in mock astonishment.

'Just say one word, Matthew, and I'll chase you right around St. Paul's with a baseball bat.'

'I can't think of any words that would truly express my deep feeling of sympathy.'

'Matthew, right around St. Paul's.'

William began to be aware of his housemaster's wife during his last two terms at St. Paul's. She was a good-looking woman, a little slack around the stomach and hips perhaps, but she carried her splendid bosom well and the luxuriant dark hair piled on top of her head was no more streaked with grey than was becoming. One Saturday when William had sprained his wrist on the hockey rink, Mrs. Raglan bandaged it for him in a cool compress, standing a little closer than was necessary, allowing William's arm to brush against her breast. He enjoyed the sensation. Then on another occasion when he had a fever and was confined to the infirmary for a few days, she brought him all his meals herself and sat on his bed, her body touching his legs through the thin covering, while he ate. He enjoyed that too.

She was rumoured to be Grumpy Raglan's second wife. No one in the house could imagine how Grumpy had managed to secure even one spouse. Mrs. Raglan occasionally indicated by the subtlest of sighs and silences that she shared something of their incredulity at her fate.

As part of his duties as house captain, William was required to report to Grumpy Raglan every night at ten thirty when he had completed the lights-out round and was about to go to bed himself. One Monday evening, when he knocked on Grumpy's door as usual, he was surprised to hear Mrs. Raglan's voice bidding him to enter. She was lying on the chaise-longue dressed in a loose silk robe of faintly Japanese appearance.

William kept a firm grasp on the cold door knob. 'All the lights are out and I've locked the front door, Mrs. Raglan. Good night.'

She swung her legs on to the ground, a pale flash of thigh appearing momentarily from under the draped silk.

'You're always in such a hurry, William. You can't wait for your life to start, can you?' She walked over to a side table. 'Why don't you stay and have some hot chocolate? Silly me, I made enough for two, I quite forgot that Mister Raglan won't be back until Saturday.'

There was a definite emphasis on the word 'Saturday'. She carried a steaming cup over to William and looked up at him to see whether the significance of her remarks had registered on him. Satisfied, she passed him the cup, letting her hand touch his. He stirred the hot chocolate assiduously.

'Gerald has gone to a conference,' she continued explaining. It was the first time he had ever heard Grumpy Raglan's first name. 'Do shut the door, William, and come and sit down.'

William hesitated; he shut the door, but he did not want to take Grumpy's chair nor did he want to sit next to Mrs. Raglan. He decided Grumpy's chair was the lesser of two evils and moved towards it.

'No, no,' she said, as she patted the seat next to her.

William shuffled over and sat down nervously by her side, staring into his cup for inspiration. Finding none, he gulped the contents down, burning his tongue. He was relieved to see Mrs. Raglan getting up. She refilled his cup, ignoring his murmured refusal, and then moved silently across the room, wound up the Victrola and placed the needle on the record.

'Nice and easy does it' were the first words that William heard. He was still looking at the floor, when she returned.

'You wouldn't let a lady dance by herself, would you, William?'

He looked up. Mrs. Raglan was swaying slightly in time to the music. 'We're on the road to romance, that's clear to say,' crooned Rudy Vallee. William stood up and put his arm formally round Mrs. Raglan. Grumpy could have fitted in between them without any trouble. After a few bars she moved closer to William, and he stared over her right shoulder fixedly to indicate to her that he had not noticed that her left hand had slipped from his shoulder to the small of his back. When the record stopped, William thought it would give him a chance to return to the safety of his hot chocolate, but she turned the record over and was back in his arms before he could move.

'Mrs. Raglan, I think I ought to . . .'

'Relax a little, William.'

At last he found the courage to look her in the eyes. He tried to reply, but he couldn't speak. Her hand was now exploring his back, and he felt her thigh move gently into his groin. He tightened his hold around her waist.

'That's better,' she said.

They circled slowly around the room, closely entwined, slower and slower, keeping time with the music as the record gently ran down. When she slipped away and turned out the light, William wanted her to return quickly. He stood there in the dark, not moving, hearing the rustle of silk, and able only to see a silhouette discarding clothes.

The crooner had completed his song, and the needle was scratching at the end of the record by the time she had helped William out of all his clothes and led him back to the chaise-longue. He groped for her in the dark, and his shy novice's fingers encounted several parts of her body that did not feel at all as he had imagined they would. He withdrew them hastily to the comparatively familiar territory of her breast. Her fingers exhibited no such reticence, and he began to feel sensations he would never have dreamed possible. He wanted to moan out loud, but stopped himself, fearing it would sound stupid. Her hands were on his back, pulling him gently on top of her.

William moved around wondering how he would ever enter her without showing his total lack of experience. It was not as easy as he had expected, and he began to get more desperate by the second. Then, once again, her fingers moved across his stomach and guided him expertly. With her help he entered her easily and had an immediate orgasm.

'I'm sorry,' said William, not sure what to do next. He lay silently on top of her for some time before she spoke.

'It will be better tomorrow.'

The sound of the scratching record returned to his ears.

Mrs. Raglan remained in William's mind all that endless Tuesday. That night, she sighed. On Wednesday, she panted. On Thursday, she moaned. On Friday she cried out.

On Saturday Grumpy Raglan returned from his conference, by which time William's education was complete.

During the Easter holidays, on Ascension Day to be exact, Abby Blount finally succumbed to William's charms. It cost Matthew five dollars and Abby her virginity. She was, after Mrs. Raglan, something of an anti-climax. It was the only event of note that happened during the entire holiday, because Abby went off to Palm Beach with her parents, and William spent most of his time shut away indoors with his books, at home to no one other than the grandmothers and Alan Lloyd. His final examinations were now only a matter of weeks away, and as Grumpy Raglan went to no further conferences, William had no other outside activities.

During their last term, he and Matthew would sit in their study at St. Paul's for hours, never speaking unless Matthew had some mathematical problem he was quite unable to solve. When the long awaited examinations finally came, they lasted for only one brutal week. The moment they were over, both boys were sanguine about their results, but as the days went by, and they waited and waited, their confidence began to diminish. The Hamilton Memorial Scholarship to Harvard for mathematics was awarded on a strictly competitive basis and it was open to every schoolboy in America. William had no way of judging how tough his opposition might be. As more time went by and still he heard nothing, William began to assume the worst.

When the telegram arrived, he was out playing baseball with some other sixth formers, killing the last few days of the term before leaving school, those warm summer days when boys are most likely to be expelled for drunkenness, breaking windows or trying to get into bed with one of the master's daughters, if not their wives.

William was declaring in a loud voice to those who cared to listen that he was about to hit his first home run ever. The Babe Ruth of St. Paul's, declared Matthew. Much laughter greeted this exaggerated claim. When the telegram was handed to him, home runs were suddenly forgotten. He dropped his bat and tore open the little yellow envelope. The pitcher waited, impatient, ball in hand, and so did the outfielders as he read the communication slowly.

'They want you to turn professional,' someone shouted from first base, the arrival of a telegram being an uncommon occurrence during a baseball game. Matthew walked in from the outfield to join William, trying to make out from his friend's face if the news were good or bad. Without changing his expression, William passed the telegram to Matthew, who read it, leaped high into the air with delight, and dropped the piece of paper to the ground to accompany William, racing around the bases on the way to the first home run ever scored without anyone actually hitting the ball. The pitcher watched them, picked the telegram up and read the missive himself and then he threw his ball into the bleachers with gusto. The little piece of yellow paper was then passed eagerly from player to player around the field. The last person to read the message was the second former who, having caused so much happiness but received no thanks, decided the least he deserved was to know the cause of so much excitement.

The telegram was addressed to Mr. William Lowell Kane, whom the boy assumed to be the incompetent hitter. It read: 'Congratulations on winning the Hamilton Memorial Mathematics Scholarship to Harvard, full details to follow. Abbot Lawrence Lowell, President.' William never did get his home run as he was sat heavily upon by several fielders before he reached home plate.

Matthew looked on with delight at the success of his closest friend, but he was sad to think that it meant they might now be parted. William felt it too, but said nothing; the two boys had to wait another nine days to learn that Matthew had also been accepted to Harvard.

Yet another telegram arrived, this one from Charles Lester, congratulating his son and inviting the boys to tea at the Plaza Hotel in New York. Both grandmothers sent congratulations to William, but as Grandmother Kane informed Alan Lloyd, somewhat testily, 'the boy has done no less than was expected of him and no more than his father did before him.'

The two young men sauntered down Fifth Avenue on the appointed day with considerable pride. Girls' eyes were drawn to the handsome pair, who affected not to notice. They removed their straw boaters as they entered the front door of the Plaza at three fifty-nine, strolled nonchalantly through the lounge and observed the family group awaiting them in the Palm Court. There, upright in the comfortable chairs sat both grandmothers, Kane and Cabot, flanking another old lady who, William assumed, was the Lester family's equivalent of Grandmother Kane. Mr. and Mrs. Charles Lester, their daughter Susan (whose eyes never left William), and Alan Lloyd completed the circle leaving two vacant chairs for William and Matthew.

Grandmother Kane summoned the nearest waiter with an

imperious eyebrow. 'A fresh pot of tea and some more cakes, please.'

The waiter made haste to the kitchens. 'Pot of tea and some more cakes for table twenty-three,' he shouted above the clatter.

'Coming up,' said a voice from the steamy obscurity.

'A pot of tea and some cream cakes, madam,' the waiter said on his return.

'Your father would have been proud of you today, William,' the older man was saying to the taller of the two youths.

The waiter wondered what it was that the good-looking young man had achieved to elicit such a comment.

William would not have noticed the waiter at all but for the silver band around his wrist. The piece so easily might have come from Tiffany's; the incongruity of it puzzled him.

'William,' said Grandmother Kane. 'Two cakes are quite sufficient; this is not your last meal before you go to Harvard.'

He looked at the old lady with affection and quite forgot the silver band.

13

That night as Abel lay awake in his small room at the Plaza Hotel, thinking about the boy, William, whose father would have been proud of him, he realised for the first time in his life exactly what he wanted to achieve. He wanted to be thought of as an equal by the Williams of this world.

Abel had had quite a struggle on his arrival in New York. He occupied a room that contained only two beds which he was obliged to share with George and two of his cousins. As a result, Abel slept only when one of the beds was free. George's uncle was unable to offer him a job, and after a few anxious weeks during which most of his savings had to be spent on staying alive, Abel searched from Brooklyn to Queens before finding work in a butcher's shop which paid nine dollars for a six and a half day week, and allowed him to sleep above the premises. The shop was in the heart of an almost self-sufficient little Polish community on the lower East Side, and Abel rapidly became impatient with the insularity of his fellow countrymen, many of whom made no effort to learn to speak English.

Abel still saw George and his constant succession of girl friends regularly at weekends, but he spent most of his free evenings during the week at night school learning how to read and write English. He was not ashamed of his slow progress, for he had had very little opportunity to write at all since the age of eight, but within two years he had made himself fluent in his new tongue, showing only the slightest trace of an accent. He now felt ready to move out of the butcher's shop – but to what, and how? Then, while dressing a leg of lamb one morning, he overheard one of the shop's biggest customers, the catering manager of the Plaza Hotel, grumbling to the butcher that he had had to fire a junior waiter for petty theft.

'How can I find a replacement at such short notice?' the manager remonstrated.

The butcher had no solution to offer. Abel did. He put on his only suit, walked forty-seven blocks, and got the job.

Once he had settled in at the Plaza, he enrolled for a night course in English at Columbia University. He worked steadily every night, dictionary open in one hand, pen scratching away in the other; during the mornings, between serving breakfast and setting up the tables for lunch, he would copy out the editorial from the *New York Times*, looking up any word he was uncertain of in his secondhand Webster's.

For the next three years, Abel worked his way through the ranks of the Plaza until he was promoted and became a waiter in the Oak Room, making about twenty-five dollars a week with tips. In his own world, he lacked for nothing.

Abel's instructor at Columbia was so impressed by his diligent progress in English that he advised Abel to enrol in a further night course, which was to be his first step towards a Bachelor of Arts degree. He switched his spare-time reading from English to economics and started copying out the editorials in the *Wall Street Journal* instead of those in the *New York Times*. His new world totally absorbed him, and with the exception of George he lost touch with his Polish friends of the early days.

When Abel served at table in the Oak Room, he would always study the famous among the guests carefully – the Bakers, Loebs, Whitneys, Morgans and Phelps – and try to work out why it was that the rich were different. He read H. L. Mencken, *The American Mercury*, Scott Fitzgerald, Sinclair Lewis and Theodore Dreiser in an endless quest for knowledge. He studied the *New York Times* while the other waiters flipped through the *Mirror*, and he read the *Wall Street Journal* in his hour's break while they dozed. He was not sure where his newly acquired knowledge would lead him, but he never doubted the Baron's maxim that there was no true substitute for a good education.

One Thursday in August 1926 – he remembered the occasion well, because it was the day that Rudolph Valentino died, and many of the ladies shopping on Fifth Avenue wore black – Abel was serving as usual at one of the corner tables. The corner tables were always reserved for top business men who wished to eat in privacy without fear of being overheard by prying ears. He enjoyed serving at that particular table, for it was the era of expanding business, and he often picked up some inside information from the titbits of conversation. After the meal was over, if the host had been from a bank or large holding company, Abel would look up the financial record of the company of the guests at the lunch, and if he felt the meeting had gone particularly well, he would invest one hundred dollars in the smaller company, hoping it would be in line for a takeover or expansion with the help of the larger company. If the host had ordered cigars at the end of the meal, Abel would increase his investment to two hundred dollars. Seven times out of ten, the value of the stock he had selected in this way doubled within six months, the period Abel would allow himself to hold on to the shares. Using this system he lost money only three times during the four years he worked at the Plaza.

What made waiting on the corner table unusual on that particular day was that the guests had ordered cigars even before the meal had started. Later they were joined by more guests who ordered more cigars. Abel looked up the name of the host in the *maître d*'s reservation book. Woolworth. He had seen the name in the financial columns quite recently but he could not immediately place it. The other guest was Charles Lester, a regular patron of the Plaza, whom Abel knew to be a distinguished New York banker. He listened to as much of the conversation as he could while serving the meal. The guests showed absolutely no interest in the attentive waiter. Abel could not discover any specific details of importance, but he gathered that some sort of deal had been closed that morning and would be announced to an unsuspecting public later in the day. Then he remembered. He had seen the name in the *Wall Street Journal*. Woolworth was the man who was going to start the first American five-and-ten-cent stores. Abel was determined to get his five cents worth. While the guests were enjoying their dessert course – most of them chose the strawberry cheese cake (Abel's recommendation) – he took the opportunity to leave the dining room for a few moments to call his broker in Wall Street.

'What are Woolworth's trading at?' he asked.

There was a pause from the other end of the line. 'Two and one-eighth. Quite a lot of movement lately; don't know why though,' came the reply.

'Buy up to the limit of my account until you hear an announcement from the company later today.'

'What will the announcement say?' asked the puzzled broker.

'I am not at liberty to reveal that sort of information over the telephone,' said Abel.

The broker was suitably impressed; Abel's record in the past had led him not to inquire too closely into the source of his client's information.

Abel hurried back to the Oak Room in time to serve the guests coffee. They lingered over it for some time, and Abel returned to the table only as they were preparing to leave. The man who picked up the bill thanked Abel for his attentive service, and turning so that his friends could hear him, said 'Do you want a tip, young man?'

'Thank you, sir,' said Abel.

'Buy Woolworth's shares.'

The guests all laughed. Abel laughed as well, took five dollars from the man and thanked him. He took a further two thousand four hundred and twelve dollars profit on Woolworth's shares during the next six months.

When Abel was granted full citizenship of the United States, a few days after his twenty-first birthday, he decided the occasion ought to be celebrated. He invited George and Monika, George's latest love, and a girl called Clara, an ex-love of George's, to the cinema to see John Barrymore in *Don Juan* and then on to Bigo's for dinner. George was still an apprentice in his uncle's bakery at eight dollars a week, and although Abel still looked upon him as his closest friend, he was aware of the growing difference between the penniless George and himself, who now had over eight thousand dollars in the bank and was in his last year at Columbia University studying for his B.A. in economics. Abel knew where he was going, whereas George had stopped telling everyone he would be the mayor of New York.

The four of them had a memorable evening, mainly because Abel knew exactly what to expect from a good restaurant. His three guests all had a great deal too much to eat, and when the bill was presented, George was aghast to see that it came to more than he earned in a month. Abel paid the bill without a second glance. If you have to pay a bill, make it look as if the amount is of no consequence. If it is, don't go to the restaurant again, but whatever you do, don't comment or look surprised – something else the rich had taught him.

When the party broke up at about two in the morning, George and Monika returned to the lower East Side, while Abel felt he had earned Clara. He smuggled her through the service entrance of the Plaza and up to his room in a laundry lift. She did not require much enticement to end up in bed, and Abel set about her with haste, mindful that he had some serious sleeping to do before reporting for breakfast duty. To his satisfaction, he had completed his task by two-thirty and sank into an uninterrupted sleep until his alarm rang at six a.m. It left him just time enough to have Clara once again before he had to get dressed.

Clara sat up in his bed and regarded Abel sullenly as he tied his white bow tie, and kissed her a perfunctory goodbye.

'Be sure you leave the way you came, or you'll get me into a load of trouble,' said Abel. 'When will I see you again?'

'You won't,' said Clara stonily.

'Why not?' asked Abel, surprised. 'Something I did?'

'No, something you didn't do.' She jumped out of bed and started to dress hastily.

'What didn't I do?' said Abel, aggrieved. 'You wanted to go to bed with me, didn't you?'

She turned around and faced him. 'I thought I did until I realised you have only one thing in common with Valentino – you're both dead. You may be the greatest thing the Plaza has seen in a bad year, but in bed I can tell you, you are nothing.' Fully dressed now, she paused with her hand on the door handle, composing her parting thrust. 'Tell me, have you ever persuaded any girl to go to bed with you more than once?'

Stunned, Abel stared at the slammed door and spent the rest of the day worrying about Clara's words. He could think of no one with whom he could discuss the problem. George would only laugh at him, and the staff at the Plaza all thought he knew everything. He decided that this problem, like all the others he had encountered in his life, must be one he could surmount with knowledge or experience.

After lunch, on his half day, he went to Scribner's bookshop on Fifth Avenue. They had solved all his economic and linguistic problems, but he couldn't find anything there that looked as if it might even begin to help his sexual ones. Their special book on etiquette was useless and *The Nature of Morals* by W. F. Colbert turned out to be utterly inappropriate.

Abel left the bookshop without making a purchase and spent the rest of the afternoon in a dingy Broadway cinema, not watching the film, but thinking only about what Clara had said. The film, a love story with Greta Garbo that did not reach the kissing stage until the last reel, provided no more assistance than Scribner's had.

When Abel left the cinema, the sky was already dark and there was a cool breeze blowing down Broadway. It still surprised Abel that any city could be as noisy and light by night as it was by day. He started walking uptown towards Fifty-ninth Street, hoping the fresh air would clear his mind. He stopped on the corner of Fifty-second to buy an evening paper.

'Looking for a girl?' said a voice from behind the newsstand.

Abel stared at the voice. She was about thirty-five and heavily made up, wearing the new, fashionable lipstick. Her white silk blouse had a button undone, and she wore a long black skirt with black stockings and black shoes.

'Only five dollars, worth every penny,' she said, pushing her hip out at an angle, allowing the slit in her skirt to part and reveal the top of her stockings.

'Where?' said Abel.

'I have a little place of my own in the next block.'

She turned her head, indicating to Abel which direction she meant, and he could, for the first time, see her face clearly under the street light. She was not unattractive. Abel nodded his agreement, and she took his arm and started walking.

'If the police stop us,' she said, 'you're an old friend and my name's Joyce.'

They walked to the next block and into a squalid little apartment building. Abel was horrified by the dingy room she lived in, with its single bare light bulb, one chair, a wash basin and a crumpled double bed, which had obviously already been used several times that day.

'You live here?' he said incredulously.

'Good God, no, I only use this place for my work.'

'Why do you do this?' asked Abel, wondering if he now wanted to go through with his plan.

'I have two children to bring up and no husband. Can you think of a better reason? Now, do you want me or not.'

'Yes, but not the way you think' said Abel.

She eyed him warily. 'Not another of those whacky ones, a follower of the Marquis de Sade, are you?'

'Certainly not,' said Abel.

'You're not gonna burn me with cigarettes, then?'

'No, nothing like that,' said Abel, startled. 'I want to be taught properly. I want lessons.'

'Lessons, are you joking? What do you think this is darling, a fucking night school?'

'Something like that,' said Abel and he sat down on the corner of the bed and explained to her how Clara had reacted the night before. 'Do you think you can help?'

The lady of the night studied Abel carefully, wondering if it was April the First.

'Sure,' she said finally, 'but it's going to cost you five dollars a time for a thirty-minute session.'

'More expensive than a B.A. from Columbia,' said Abel. 'How many lessons will I need?'

'Depends how quick a learner you are, doesn't it?' she said.

'Well let's start right now,' said Abel, taking five dollars out of his inside pocket and handing the money over to her. She put the note in the top of her stocking, a sure sign she never took them off.

'Clothes off, darling,' she said. 'You won't learn much fully dressed.'

When he was stripped, she looked at him critically.

'You're not exactly Douglas Fairbanks, are you? Don't worry about it, it doesn't matter what you look like once the lights are out; it only matters what you can do.'

Abel sat on the edge of the bed while she started telling him about how to treat a lady. She was surprised that Abel really did not want her and was even more surprised when he continued to turn up every day for the next two weeks.

'When will I know I've made it?' Abel inquired.

'You'll know, baby,' replied Joyce. 'If you can make me come, you can make an Egyptian mummy come.'

She taught him first where the sensitive parts of a woman's body were, and then to be patient in his love-making and the signs by which he might know that what he was doing was pleasing. How to use his tongue and lips on every place other than a woman's mouth.

Abel listened carefully to all she said and followed her instructions scrupulously and to begin with, a little bit too mechanically. Despite her assurance that he was improving out of all recognition, he had no real idea if she was telling the truth, until about three weeks and one hundred and ten dollars later, when to his surprise and delight, Joyce suddenly came alive in his arms for the first time. She held his head close to her as he gently licked her nipples. As he stroked her gently between the legs, he found she was wet — for the first time — and after he had entered her she moaned, a sound Abel had never heard before, and found intensely pleasing. She clawed at his back, commanding him not to stop. The moaning continued, sometimes loud, sometimes soft. Finally she cried out sharply, and the hands that had clutched him to her so fiercely relaxed.

When she had caught her breath, she said. 'Baby, you just graduated top of the class.'

Abel hadn't even come.

Abel celebrated the awarding of both his degrees by paying scalpers' price for ringside seats and taking George, Monika and a reluctant Clara to watch Gene Tunney fight Jack Dempsey for the heavyweight championship of the world. That night after the fight, Clara felt it was nothing less than her duty to go to bed with Abel as he had spent so much money on her. By the morning, she was begging him not to leave her.

Abel never asked her out again.

After he had graduated from Columbia, Abel became dissatisfied with his life at the Plaza Hotel, but could not figure out how to secure further advancement. Although he was surrounded by some of the most wealthy and successful men in America, he was unable to approach any of the customers directly, knowing that if he did so, it might well cost him his job and in any case, the customers could not take seriously the aspirations of a waiter. Abel had long ago decided that he wanted to be a head waiter.

One day, Mr. and Mrs. Ellsworth Statler came to lunch at the Plaza's Edwardian Room, where Abel had been on relief duty for a week. He thought his chance had come. He did everything he could think of to impress the famous hotelier, and the meal went splendidly. As he left, Statler thanked Abel warmly and gave him ten dollars, but that was the end of their association. Abel watched him disappear through the revolving doors of the Plaza, wondering if he was ever going to get a break.

Sammy, the head waiter tapped him on the shoulder:
'What did you get from Mr. Statler?'

'Nothing,' said Abel.

'He didn't tip you?' asked Sammy in a disbelieving tone.

'Oh, yes, sure,' said Abel. 'Ten dollars.' He handed the money over to Sammy.

'That's more like it,' said Sammy. 'I was beginning to think you was double-dealing me, Abel. Ten dollars, that's good even for Mr. Statler. You must have impressed him.'

'No, I didn't.'

'What do you mean?' asked Sammy.

'It doesn't matter,' said Abel, as he started walking away.

'Wait a moment, Abel, I have a note here for you. The gentleman at table seventeen, a Mr. Leroy, wants to speak to you personally.'

'What about, Sammy?'

'How should I know? Probably liked your blue eyes.'

Abel glanced over to number seventeen, strictly for the meek and the unknown, because the table was so badly placed near a swing door into the kitchen. Abel usually tried to avoid serving any of the tables at that end of the room.

'Who is he?' asked Abel. 'What does he want?'

'I don't know,' said Sammy, not bothering to look up. 'I'm not in touch with the life history of every customer the way you are. Give them a good meal, make sure you get yourself a big tip and hope they come again. You may feel it's a simple philosophy but it's sure good enough for me. Maybe they forgot to teach you the basics at Columbia. Now get your butt over there, Abel, and if its a tip be certain you bring the money straight back to me.'

Abel smiled at Sammy's bald head and went over to seventeen. There were two people seated at the table, a man in a colourful checked jacket, of which Abel did not approve, and an attractive young woman with a mop of blonde, curly hair, which momentarily distracted Abel, who uncharitably assumed she was the checked jacket's New York girlfriend. Abel put on his 'sorry smile', betting himself a silver dollar that the man was going to make a big fuss about the swing doors and try to get his table changed to impress the stunning blonde. No one liked being near the smell of the kitchens and the continual banging of waiters through the doors, but it was impossible to avoid using the table, when the hotel was already packed with residents and many New Yorkers who used the restaurant as their local eating place, and looked upon visitors as little less than intruders. Why did Sammy always leave the tricky customers for him to deal with? Abel approached the checked jacket cautiously.

'You asked to speak to me, sir?'

'Sure did,' said a Southern accent. 'My name is Davis Leroy, and this is my daughter Melanie.'

Abel's eyes left Mr. Leroy momentarily and encountered a pair of eyes as green as any he had ever seen.

'I have been watching you, Abel, for the last five days,' Mr. Leroy was saying in his Southern drawl.

If pushed, Abel would have had to admit that he had not noticed Mr. Leroy until the last five minutes.

'I have been very impressed by what I've seen, Abel, because you got class, real class, and I am always on the lookout for that. Ellsworth Statler was a fool not to pick you up right away.'

Abel began to take a closer look at Mr. Leroy. His purple cheeks and double chin left Abel in no doubt that he had not been told about Prohibition, and the empty plates in front of him accounted for his basketball belly, but neither the name nor the face meant anything to him. At a normal lunchtime, Abel was familiar with the background of anyone sitting at thirty-seven of the thirty-nine tables in the Edwardian Room. That day Mr. Leroy was one of the unknown two.

The Southerner was still talking. 'Now, I'm not one of those multi-millionaires who have to sit at your corner table when they stay at the Plaza.'

Abel was impressed. The average customer wasn't supposed to appreciate the relative merits of the various tables.

'But I'm not doing so badly for myself. In fact, my best hotel may well grow to be as impressive as this one some day, Abel.'

'I am sure it will be, sir,' said Abel, playing for time.

Leroy, Leroy, Leroy. The name didn't mean a thing.

'Lemme git to the point, son. The number one hotel in my group needs a new assistant manager, in charge of the restaurants. If you're interested, join me in my room when you come off duty.'

He handed Abel a large embossed card.

'Thank you, sir,' said Abel, looking at it: Davis Leroy. The Richmond Group of Hotels, Dallas. Underneath was inscribed the motto: 'One day a hotel in every state.' The name still meant nothing to Abel.

'I look forward to seeing you,' said the friendly, check-jacketed Texan.

'Thank you, sir,' said Abel. He smiled at Melanie, whose eyes were as coolly green as before and returned to Sammy, still head down, counting his takings.

'Ever heard of the Richmond Group of Hotels, Sammy?'

'Yes, sure, my brother was a junior waiter in one once. Must be about eight or nine of them, all over the South, run by a mad Texan, but I can't remember the guy's name. Why you asking?' said Sammy, looking up suspiciously.

'No particular reason,' said Abel.

'There's always a reason with you. Now what did table seventeen want?' said Sammy.

'Grumbling about the noise from the kitchen. Can't say I blame him.'

'What does he expect me to do, put him out on the veranda? Who does the guy think he is, John D. Rockefeller?'

Abel left Sammy to his counting and grumbling and cleared his own tables as quickly as possible. Then he went to his room and started to check out the Richmond Group. A few calls and he'd learned enough to satisfy his curiosity. The group turned out to be a private company, with eleven hotels in all, the most impressive one a three hundred and forty-two bedroom de luxe establishment in Chicago, the Richmond Continental. Abel decided he had nothing to lose by paying a call on Mr. Leroy and Melanie. He checked Mr. Leroy's room number – 85 – one of the better smaller rooms. He arrived a little before four o'clock and was disappointed to discover Melanie was no longer with her father.

'Glad you could drop by, Abel. Take a seat.'

It was the first time Abel had sat down as a guest in the more than four years he had worked at the Plaza.

'What are you paid?' said Mr. Leroy.

The suddenness of the question took Abel by surprise. 'I take in around twenty-five dollars a week with tips.'

'I'll start you at thirty-five a week.'

'Which hotel are you referring to?' asked Abel.

'If I'm a judge of character, Abel, you got off table duty

about three-thirty and took the next thirty minutes finding out which hotel. Am I right?'

Abel was beginning to like the man. 'The Richmond Continental in Chicago?' he ventured.

Davis Leroy laughed. 'I was right, and right about you.'

Abel's mind was working fast. 'How many people are there over the assistant manager on the hotel staff?'

'Only the manager and me. The manager is slow, gentle, and near retirement, and as I have ten other hotels to worry about, I don't think you'll have too much trouble – although I must confess Chicago is my favourite, my first hotel in the North, and with Melanie at school there, I find I spend more time in the Windy City than I ought to. Don't ever make the mistake New Yorkers do of underestimating Chicago. They think Chicago is only a postage stamp on a very large envelope, and they are the envelope.'

Abel smiled.

'The hotel is a little run down at the moment,' Mr. Leroy continued, 'and the last assistant manager walked out on me suddenly without an explanation, so I need a good man to take his place and to realise its full potential. Now listen, Abel, I've watched you carefully for the last five days and I know you're that man. Do you think you would be interested in coming to Chicago?'

'Forty dollars and ten per cent of any increased profits, and I'll take the job.'

'What?' said Davis Leroy, flabbergasted. 'None of my managers are paid on a profit basis. The others would raise hell if they ever found out.'

'I'm not going to tell them if you don't,' said Abel.

'Now I know I chose the right man, even if he bargains a damn sight better than a Yankee with six daughters.' He slapped the side of his chair. 'I agree to your terms, Abel.'

'Will you be requiring references, Mr. Leroy?'

'References. I know your background and history since you left Europe right through to you getting a degree in economics at Columbia. What do you think I've been doing the last few days? I wouldn't put someone who needed references in as number two in my best hotel. When can you start?'

'A month from today.'

'Good. I look forward to seeing you then, Abel.'

Abel rose from the hotel chair; he felt happier standing. He shook hands with Mr. Davis Leroy, the man from table seventeen – the one that was strictly for unknowns.

Leaving New York and the Plaza Hotel, his first real home since the castle near Slonim, turned out to be more of a wrench than Abel had anticipated. Goodbyes to George, Monika, and his few Columbia friends were unexpectedly hard. Sammy and the waiters threw a farewell party for him.

'We haven't heard the last of you, Abel Rosnovski,' Sammy said, and they all agreed.

The Richmond Continental in Chicago was well-placed on Michigan Avenue, in the heart of the fastest growing city in America. That pleased Abel, who was only too familiar with Ellsworth Statler's maxim that just three things about a hotel really mattered: position, position and position. Abel soon discovered that position was about the only good thing that the Richmond had. Davis Leroy had understated the case when he had said that the hotel was a little run down. Desmond Pacey, the manager, wasn't slow and gentle as Davis Leroy had described him; he was plain lazy and didn't endear himself to Abel by allocating him a tiny room in the staff annex across the road and leaving him out of the main hotel. A quick check on the Richmond's books revealed that the daily occupancy rate was running at less than forty per cent, and that the restaurant was never more than half full, not least of all because the food was so appalling. The staff spoke three or four languages among them, none of which seemed to be English, and there were certainly not any signs of welcome for the stupid Polack from New York. It was not hard to see why the last assistant manager had left in such a hurry. If the Richmond was

Davis Leroy's favourite hotel, Abel feared for the other ten in the group, even though his new employer seemed to have a bottomless pot of gold at the end of his Texas rainbow.

The best news that Abel learned during his first days in Chicago was that Melanie Leroy was an only child.

14

William and Matthew started their freshmen year at Harvard in the fall of 1924. Despite his grandmothers' disapproval William accepted the Hamilton Memorial Scholarship and at a cost of two hundred and ninety dollars, treated himself to 'Daisy', the latest Model T Ford, and first real love of his life. He painted Daisy bright yellow, which halved her value and doubled the number of his girlfriends. Calvin Coolidge won a landslide election to return to the White House and the volume on the New York Stock Exchange reached a five-year record of two million, three hundred and thirty-six thousand, one hundred and sixty shares.

Both young men (we can no longer refer to them as children, pronounced Grandmother Cabot) had been looking forward to college. After an energetic summer of tennis and golf, they were ready to get down to more serious pursuits. William started work on the day he arrived in their new room on the 'Gold Coast', a considerable improvement on their small study at St. Paul's, while Matthew went in search of the university rowing club. Matthew was elected to captain the freshmen crew, and William left his books every Sunday afternoon to watch his friend from the banks of the Charles River. He covertly enjoyed Matthew's success but was outwardly scathing.

'Life is not about eight big men pulling unwieldy pieces of misshapen wood through choppy water while one smaller man shouts at them,' declared William haughtily.

'Tell Yale that,' said Matthew.

William, meanwhile, quickly demonstrated to his mathematics professors that he was in his studies what Matthew was in sport – a mile ahead of the field. He also became chairman of the Freshmen Debating Society and talked his great-uncle, President Lowell, into the first university insurance plan, whereby students leaving Harvard would take out a life policy for one thousand dollars each, naming the university as the beneficiary. William estimated that the cost to each participant would be less than a dollar per week and that if forty per cent of the alumni joined the scheme, Harvard would have a guaranteed income of about three million dollars a year from 1950 onwards. The president was impressed and gave the scheme his full support, and a year later he invited William to join the board of the University Fund Raising Committee. William accepted with pride without realising the appointment was for life. President Lowell informed Grandmother Kane that he had captured one of the best financial brains of his generation, free of charge. Grandmother Kane testily replied to her cousin that, 'everything has its purpose and this will teach William to read the fine print.'

Almost as soon as the sophomore year began, it became time to choose (or to be chosen for) one of the Finals Clubs that dominated the social landscape of the well-to-do at Harvard. William was 'punched' for the Porcellian, the oldest, richest, most exclusive and least ostentatious of such clubs. In the clubhouse on Massachusetts Avenue, which was incongruously situated over a cheap Hayes-Bickford cafeteria, he would sit in a comfortable armchair, considering the four-colour map problem, discussing the repercussions of the Loeb-Leopold trial, and idly watching the street below through the conveniently angled mirror while listening to the large new-fangled radio.

During the Christmas holidays, he was persuaded to ski with Matthew in Vermont, and spent a week panting uphill in the footsteps of his fitter friend.

'Tell me, Matthew, what is the point of spending one hour

climbing up a hill only to come back down the same hill in a few seconds at considerable risk to life and limb?'

Matthew grunted. 'Sure gives me a bigger kick than graph theory, William. Why don't you admit you're not very good either at the going up or the coming down?'

They both did enough work in their sophomore year to get by, although their interpretations of 'getting by' were wildly different. For the first two months of the summer holidays, they worked as junior management assistants in Charles Lester's bank in New York, Matthew's father having long since given up the battle of trying to keep William away. When the dog days of August arrived, they spent most of their time dashing about the New England countryside in 'Daisy', sailing on the Charles River with as many different girls as possible and attending any house party to which they could get themselves invited. In no time, they were among the accredited personalities of the university, known to the cognoscenti as the Scholar and the Sweat. It was perfectly understood in Boston society that the girl who married William Kane or Matthew Lester would have no fears for her future, but as fast as hopeful mothers appeared with their fresh-faced daughters, Grandmother Kane and Grandmother Cabot despatched them unceremoniously.

On April 18, 1927, William celebrated his twenty-first birthday by attending the final meeting of the trustees to his estate. Alan Lloyd and Tony Simmons had prepared all the documents for signature.

'Well, William dear,' said Milly Preston as if a great responsibility had been lifted from her shoulders, 'I'm sure you'll be able to do every bit as well as we did.'

'I hope so, Mrs. Preston, but if ever I need to lose half a million overnight, I'll know just whom to call.'

Milly Preston went bright red but made no attempt to reply.

The trust now stood at over twenty-eight million dollars, and William had definite plans for the nurture of that money, but he had also set himself the task of making a million dollars in his own right before he left Harvard. It was not a large sum compared with the amount in his trust, but his inherited wealth meant far less to him than the balance in his account at Lester's.

That summer, the grandmothers, fearing a fresh outbreak of predatory girls, despatched William and Matthew on the grand tour of Europe, which turned out to be a great success for both of them. Matthew, surmounting all language barriers, found a beautiful girl in every major European capital – love, he assured William, was an international commodity. William secured introductions to a director of most of the major European banks – money, he assured Matthew, was also an international commodity. From London to Berlin to Rome, the two young men left a trail of broken hearts and suitably impressed bankers. When they returned to Harvard in September, they were both ready to hit the books for their final year.

In the bitter winter of 1927, Grandmother Kane died, aged eighty-five, and William wept for the first time since his mother's death.

'Come on,' said Matthew, after bearing with William's depression for several days. 'She had a good run and waited a long time to find out whether God was a Cabot or a Lowell.'

William missed the shrewd words he had so little appreciated in his grandmother's lifetime, and he arranged a funeral which she would have been proud to attend. Although the great lady arrived at the cemetery in a black Packard hearse ('One of those new-fangled contraptions – over my dead body', but, as it turned out, under it), this unsound mode of transport would have been her only criticism of William's orchestration of her departure. Her death drove William to work with ever more purpose during that final year at Harvard. He dedicated himself to winning the top mathematics prize in her memory. Grandmother Cabot died some six months later, probably, said William, because there was no one left for her to talk to.

In February 1928, William received a visit from the captain of the Debating Team. There was to be a full-dress debate the following month on the motion 'Socialism or Capitalism for America's Future', and William was naturally asked to represent capitalism.

'And what if I told you I was only willing to speak on behalf of the downtrodden masses?' William inquired of the surprised captain, slightly nettled by the thought that his intellectual views were simply assumed by outsiders because he had inherited a famous name and a prosperous bank.

'Well, I must say, William, we did imagine your own preference would be for, er...'

'It is, I accept your invitation. I take it that I am at liberty to select my partner?'

'Naturally.'

'Good, then I choose Matthew Lester. May I know who our opponents will be?'

'You will not be informed until the day before, when the posters go up in the Yard.'

For the next month Matthew and William turned their breakfast critiques of the newspapers of the left and right, and their nightly discussions about the meaning of life, into strategy sessions for what the campus was beginning to call 'The Great Debate'. William decided that Matthew should lead off.

As the fateful day approached, it became clear that most of the politically aware students, professors, and even some Boston and Cambridge notables would be attending. On the morning before the debate they walked over to the Yard to discover who their opposition would be.

'Leland Crosby and Thaddeus Cohen. Either name ring a bell with you, William? Crosby must be one of the Philadelphia Crosby's, I suppose.'

'Of course he is. "The Red Maniac of Rittenhouse

Square", as his own aunt once described him so accurately. He's the most convincing revolutionary on campus. He's loaded, and he spends all his money on the popular radical causes. I can hear his opening now.'

William parodied Crosby's grating tone. 'I know at first hand the rapacity and the utter lack of social conscience of the American monied class.' If everyone in the audience hasn't heard that fifty times already, I'd say he'll make a formidable opponent.'

'And Thaddeus Cohen?'

'Never heard of him.'

The following evening, refusing to admit to stage fright, they made their way through the snow and cold wind, heavy overcoats flapping behind them, past the gleaming columns of the recently completed Widener Library – like William's father, the donor's son had gone down on the *Titanic* – to Boylston Hall.

'With weather like this, at least if we take a beating there won't be many to tell the tale,' said Matthew hopefully.

But as they rounded the side of the library, they could see a steady stream of stamping, huffing figures ascending the stairs and filing into the hall. Inside, they were shown to chairs on the podium. William sat still but his eyes picked out the people he knew in the audience: President Lowell, sitting discreetly in the middle row; ancient old Newbury St. John, Professor of Botany; a pair of Brattle Street bluestockings he recognised from Red House parties; and to his right, a group of Bohemian-looking young men and women, some not even wearing ties, who turned and started to clap as their spokesmen – Crosby and Cohen – walked on to the stage.

Crosby was the more striking of the two, tall and thin almost to the point of caricature, dressed absent-mindedly – or very carefully – in a shaggy tweed suit, but with a stiffly pressed shirt, and dangling a pipe with no apparent connection to his body except at his lower lip. Thaddeus Cohen was shorter and wore rimless glasses and an almost too perfectly-cut, dark worsted suit.

The four speakers shook hands cautiously as the last minute arrangements were made. The bells of Memorial Church, only a hundred feet away, sounded vague and distant as they rang out seven times.

'Mr. Leland Crosby, Junior,' said the captain.

Crosby's speech gave William cause for self-congratulation. He had anticipated everything, the strident tone Crosby would take, the overstressed, nearly hysterical points he would make. He recited the incantations of American radicalism – Haymarket, Money Trust, Standard Oil, even Cross of Gold. William didn't think he had made more than an exhibition of himself although he garnered the expected applause from his claque on William's right. When Crosby sat down, he had clearly won no new supporters, and it looked as though he might have lost a few old ones. The comparison with William and Matthew – equally rich, equally socially distinguished, but selfishly refusing martyrdom for the cause of the advancement of social justice – just might be devastating.

Mathew spoke well and to the point, soothing his listeners, the incarnation of liberal toleration. William pumped his friend's hand warmly when he returned to his chair to loud applause.

'It's all over bar the shouting, I think,' he whispered.

But Thaddeus Cohen surprised virtually everyone. He had a pleasant, diffident manner and a sympathetic style. His references and quotations were catholic, pointed and illuminating. Without conveying to the audience the feeling that it was being deliberately impressed, he exuded a moral earnestness which made anything less seem a failure to a rational human being. He was willing to admit the excesses of his own side and the inadequacy of its leaders, but he left the impression that, in spite of its dangers, there was no alternative to socialism if the lot of mankind were ever to be improved.

William was flustered. A surgically logical attack on the political platform of his adversaries would be useless against Cohen's gentle and persuasive presentation. Yet to outdo him as a spokesman of hope and faith in the human spirit would be impossible. William concentrated first on refuting some of Crosby's charges and then countered Cohen's arguments with a declaration of his own faith in the ability of the American system to produce the best results through competition, intellectual and economic. He felt he had played a good defensive game, but no more, and sat down supposing that he had been well beaten by Cohen.

Crosby was his opponents' rebuttal speaker. He began ferociously, sounding as if he now needed to beat Cohen as much as William and Matthew, asking the audience if they could identify an 'enemy of the people' amongst themselves that night. He glared around the room for several long seconds, as members of the audience squirmed in embarrassed silence and his dedicated supporters studied their shoes. Then he leaned forward and roared.

'He stands before you. He has just spoken in your midst. His name is William Lowell Kane.' Gesturing with one hand towards where William sat without looking at him, he thundered: 'His bank owns mines in which the workers die to give its owners an extra million a year in dividends. His bank supports the bloody, corrupt dictatorships of Latin America. Through his bank, the American Congress is bribed into crushing the small farmer. His bank ...'

The tirade went on for several minutes. William sat in stony silence, occasionally jotting down a comment on his yellow legal pad. A few members of the audience had begun shouting 'No.' Crosby's supporters shouted loyally back. The officials began to look nervous.

Crosby's allotted time was nearly up. He raised his fist and said, 'Gentlemen, I submit that not more than two hundred yards from this very room we have the answer to the plight of America. There stands the Widener Library, the greatest private library in the world. Here poor and immigrant scholars come, along with the best educated Americans, to increase the knowledge and prosperity of the world. Why does it exist? Because one rich playboy had the misfortune to set sail sixteen years ago on a pleasure boat called the *Titanic*. I suggest, ladies and gentlemen, that not until the people of America hand each and every member of the ruling class a ticket for his own private cabin on the *Titanic* of capitalism, will the hoarded wealth of this great continent be freed and devoted to the service of liberty, equality and progress.'

As Matthew listened to Crosby's speech, his sentiments changed from exultation that, by this blunder, the victory had been secured for his side, through embarrassment at the behaviour of his adversary, to rage at the reference to the *Titanic*. He had no idea how William would respond to such provocation.

When some measure of silence had been restored, the captain walked to the lectern and said: 'Mr. William Lowell Kane.'

William strode to the platform and looked out over the audience. An expectant hush filled the room.

'It is my opinion that the views expressed by Mr. Crosby do not merit a response.'

He sat down. There was a moment of surprise silence – and then loud applause.

The captain returned to the platform, but appeared uncertain what to do. A voice from behind him broke the tension.

'If I may, Mr. Chairman, I would like to ask Mr. Kane if I might use his rebuttal time.' It was Thaddeus Cohen.

William nodded his agreement to the captain.

Cohen walked to the lectern and blinked at the audience disarmingly. 'It has long been true,' he began, 'that the greatest obstacle to the successful democratic socialism in the United States has been the extremism of some of its allies. Nothing could have exemplified this unfortunate fact more clearly than my colleague's speech tonight. The propensity to damage the progressive cause by calling for the physical extermination of those who oppose it might be understandable in a battle-hardened immigrant, a veteran of foreign struggles fiercer than our own. In America it is pathetic and inexcusable. Speaking for myself, I extend my sincere apologies to Mr. Kane.'

This time the applause was instantaneous. Virtually the entire audience rose to its feet and clapped continuously.

William walked over to shake hands with Thaddeus Cohen. It was no surprise to either of them that William and Matthew won the vote by a margin of more than one hundred and fifty votes. The evening was over, and the audience filed out into the silent, snow-covered paths, walking in the middle of the street, talking animatedly at the tops of their voices.

William insisted that Thaddeus Cohen should join him and Matthew for a drink. They set off together across Massachusetts Avenue, barely able to see where they were going in the drifting snow, and came to a halt outside a big black door almost directly opposite Boylston Hall. William opened it with his key and the three entered the vestibule.

Before the door shut behind him, Thaddeus Cohen spoke. 'I'm afraid I won't be welcome here.'

William looked startled for a second. 'Nonsense. You're with me.'

Matthew gave his friend a cautionary glance but saw that William was determined.

They went up the stairs and into a large room, comfortably but not luxuriously furnished, in which there were about a dozen young men sitting in armchairs or standing in small knots of two and three. As soon as William appeared in the doorway, the congratulations started.

'You were marvellous, William. That's exactly the way to treat those sort of people.'

'Enter in triumph, Bolski slayer.'

Thaddeus Cohen hung back, still half-shadowed by the doorway, but William had not forgotten him.

'And, gentlemen, may I present my worthy adversary, Mr. Thaddeus Cohen.'

Cohen stepped forward hesitantly.

All noise ceased. A number of heads were averted, as if

they were looking at the elm trees in the yard, their branches weighed down with new snow.

Finally, there was the crack of a floorboard as one young man left the room by another door. Then there was another departure. Without haste, without apparent agreement, the entire group filed out. The last to leave gave William a long look before he, too, turned on his heel and disappeared.

Matthew gazed at his companions in dismay. Thaddeus Cohen had turned a dull red and stood with his head bowed. William's lips were drawn together in the same tight cold fury that had been apparent when Crosby had made his reference to the *Titanic*.

Matthew touched his friend's arm. 'We'd better go.'

The three trudged off to William's rooms and silently drank some indifferent brandy.

When William woke in the morning, there was an envelope under his door. Inside there was a short note, from the chairman of the Porcellian Club informing him that 'he hoped there would never be a recurrence of last night's, best forgotten, incident.'

By lunchtime the chairman had received two letters of resignation.

After months of long, studious days, William and Matthew were almost ready – no one ever thinks he is quite ready – for their final examinations. For six days they answered questions and filled up sheets and sheets of the little books, and then they waited, not in vain for they both graduated as expected from Harvard in June of 1928.

A week later it was announced that William was the winner of the President's Mathematics Prize. He wished his father had been alive to witness the presentation ceremony. Matthew managed an honest 'C', which came as a relief to him and no great surprise to anyone else. Neither had any interest in further education, both having elected to join the real world as quickly as possible.

William's bank account in New York edged over the million dollar mark eight days before he left Harvard. It was then that he discussed in greater detail with Matthew his long term plan to gain control of Lester's Bank by merging it with Kane and Cabot.

Matthew was enthusiastic about the idea and confessed, 'That's about the only way I'll ever improve on what my old man will undoubtedly leave me when he dies.'

On graduation day, Alan Lloyd, now in his sixtieth year, came to Harvard. After the graduation ceremony, William took his guest for tea on the square. Alan eyed the tall young man affectionately.

'And what do you intend to do now that you have put Harvard behind you?'

'I'm going to join Charles Lester's bank in New York and gain some experience before I come to Kane and Cabot in a few years' time.'

'But you've been living in Lester's bank since you were twelve years old, William. Why don't you come straight to us now? We would appoint you as a director immediately.'

William said nothing. Alan Lloyd's offer came as a total surprise. With all his ambition, it had never occurred to him, even for a moment, that he might be invited to be a director of the bank before he was twenty-five, the age at which his father had achieved that distinction.

Alan Lloyd waited for his reply. It was not forthcoming. 'Well, I must say, William, it's most unlike you to be rendered speechless by anything.'

'But I never imagined you would invite me to join the board before my twenty-fifth birthday, when my father . . .'

'It's true your father was elected when he was twenty-five. However, that's no reason to prohibit you from joining the board before then if the other directors support the idea, and I know that they do. In any case, there are personal reasons why I should like to see you a director as soon as possible. When I retire from the bank in five years' time, we must be sure of electing the right chairman. You will be in a stronger position to influence that decision if you have been working for Kane and Cabot during those five years rather than as a grand functionary at Lester's. Well, my boy, will you join the board?'

It was the second time that day that William wished his father were still alive.

'I should be delighted to accept, sir,' he said.

Alan looked up at William. 'That's the first time you've called me "sir" since we played golf together. I shall have to watch you very carefully.'

William smiled.

'Good,' said Alan Lloyd, 'that's settled then. You'll be a junior director in charge of investments, working directly under Tony Simmons.'

'Can I appoint my own assistant?' asked William.

Alan Lloyd looked at him quizzically. 'Matthew Lester, no doubt?'

'Yes.'

'No. I don't want him doing in our bank what you intended to do in theirs. Thomas Cohen should have taught you that.'

William said nothing but never underestimated Alan again.

Charles Lester laughed when William repeated the conversation word for word to him.

'I'm sorry to hear you won't be coming to us, even as a spy,' he said genially, 'but I have no doubt you'll end up here some day – in one capacity or another.'

Book Three

15

When William started work as a junior director of Kane and Cabot in September 1928, he felt for the first time in his life that he was doing something really worthwhile. He began his career in a small oak-panelled office next to Tony Simmons, the bank's director of finance. From the week that William arrived, he knew without a word being spoken that Tony Simmons was hoping to succeed Alan Lloyd as chairman of the bank.

The bank's entire investment programme was Simmons' responsibility. He quickly delegated to William some aspects of his work; in particular, private investment in small businesses, land, and any other outside entrepreneurial activities in which the bank became involved. Among William's official duties was to make a monthly report on the investments he wished to recommend, at a full meeting of the board. The fourteen board members met once a month in a larger oak-panelled room, dominated at both ends by portraits, one of William's father, the other of his grandfather. William had never known his grandfather, but had always considered he must have been a 'hell of a man' to have married Grandmother Kane. There was ample room left on the walls for his own portrait.

William conducted himself during those early months at the bank with caution, and his fellow board members soon came to respect his judgment and follow his recommendations with rare exceptions. As it turned out, the advice they rejected was among the best that William ever gave. On the first occasion, a Mr. Mayer sought a loan from the bank to invest in 'talking pictures' but the board refused to see that

235

the notion had any merit or future. Another time, a Mr. Paley came to William with an ambitious plan for United, the radio network. Alan Lloyd, who had about as much respect for telegraphy as for telepathy, would have nothing to do with the scheme. The board supported Alan's views, and Louis B. Mayer later headed M.G.M. and William Paley the company that was to become C.B.S. William believed in his own judgment and backed both men with money from his trust and, like his father, never informed the recipients of his support.

One of the more unpleasant aspects of William's day-to-day work was the handling of the liquidations and bankruptcies of clients who had borrowed large sums from the bank and had subsequently found themselves unable to repay their loans. William was not by nature a soft person, as Henry Osborne had learned to his cost, but insisting that old and respected clients liquidate their stocks and even sell their homes did not make for easy sleeping at nights. William soon learned that these clients fell into two distinct categories; those who looked upon bankruptcy as a part of everyday business and those who were appalled by the very word and who would spend the rest of their lives trying to repay every penny they had borrowed. William found it natural to be tough with the first category but was almost always far more lenient with the second, with the grudging approval of Tony Simmons.

It was during such a case that William broke one of the bank's golden rules and became personally involved with a client. Her name was Katherine Brookes, and her husband, Max Brookes, had borrowed over a million dollars from Kane and Cabot to invest in the Florida land boom of 1925, an investment William would never had backed had he then been working at the bank. Max Brookes had, however, been something of a hero in Massachusetts as one of the new intrepid breed of balloonists and flyers, and a close friend of Charles Lindbergh into the bargain. Brookes' tragic death when the small plane he was piloting, at a height of all of ten feet above the ground, hit a tree only a hundred yards after take-off was reported in the press across the length and breadth of America as a national loss.

William, acting for the bank, immediately took over the Brookes estate, which was already insolvent, dissolved it and tried to cut the bank's losses by selling all the land held in Florida except for two acres on which the family home stood. The bank's loss was still over three hundred thousand dollars. Some directors were slightly critical of William's snap decision to sell off the land, a decision with which Tony Simmons had not agreed. William had Simmons' disapproval of his actions entered on the minutes and was in a position to point out some months later, that if they had held on to the land, the bank would have lost most of its original investment of one million. This demonstration of foresight did not endear him to Tony Simmons although it made the rest of the board conscious of William's uncommon perspicacity.

When William had liquidated everything the bank held in Max Brookes' name, he turned his attention to Mrs. Brookes, who was under a personal guarantee for her late husband's debts. Although William always tried to secure such a guarantee on any loans granted by the bank, the undertaking of such an obligation was not a course that he ever recommended to friends, however confident they might feel about the venture on which they were about to embark, as failure almost invariably caused great distress to the guarantor.

William wrote a formal letter to Mrs. Brookes, suggesting that she make an appointment to discuss the position. He had read the Brookes file conscientiously and knew that she was only twenty-two years old, a daughter of Andrew Higginson, the head of an old and distinguished Boston family, and that she had substantial assets of her own. He did not relish the thought of requiring her to make them over to the bank, but he and Tony Simmons were, for once, in agreement on the line to be taken, so he steeled himself for an unpleasant encounter.

What William had not bargained for was Katherine Brookes herself. In later life, he could always recall in great detail the events of that morning. He had had some harsh words with Tony Simmons about a substantial investment in copper and tin, which he wished to recommend to the board. Industrial demand for the two metals was rising steadily, and William was confident that a world shortage was certain to follow. Tony Simmons could not agree with him, insisting they should invest more cash in the stock market, and the matter was still uppermost in William's mind when his secretary ushered Mrs. Brookes into his office. With one tentative smile, she removed copper, tin and all other world shortages from his mind. Before she could sit down, he was around on the other side of his desk, settling her into a chair, simply to assure himself that she would not vanish, like a mirage, on closer inspection. Never had William encountered a woman he considered half as lovely as Katherine Brookes. Her long fair hair fell in loose and wayward curls to her shoulders, and little wisps escaped enchantingly from her hat and clung around her temples. The fact that she was in mourning in no way detracted from the beauty of her slim figure. The fine bone structure ensured that she was a woman who was going to look lovely at every age. Her brown eyes were enormous. They were also, unmistakably, apprehensive of him and what he was about to say.

William strove for his business tone of voice. 'Mrs. Brookes, may I say how sorry I was to learn of your husband's death and how much I regret the necessity of asking you to come here today.'

Two lies in a single sentence that would have been the truth five minutes before. He waited to hear her speak.

'Thank you, Mr. Kane.' Her voice was soft and had a gentle, low pitch. 'I am aware of my obligations to your bank and I assure you that I will do everything in my power to meet them.'

William said nothing, hoping she would go on speaking. She did not, so he outlined how he had disposed of Max Brookes' estate. She listened with downcast eyes.

'Now, Mrs. Brookes, you acted as guarantor for your husband's loan and that brings us to the question of your personal assets.' He consulted his file. 'You have some eighty thousand dollars in investments – your own family money, I believe – and seventeen thousand four hundred and fifty-six dollars in your personal account.'

She looked up. 'Your grasp of my financial position is commendable, Mr. Kane. You should add, however, Buckhurst Park, our house in Florida, which was in Max's name, and some quite valuable jewellery of my own. I estimate that all together I am worth the three hundred thousand dollars you still require, and I have made arrangements to realise the full amount as soon as possible.'

There was only the slightest tremor in her voice; William gazed at her in admiration.

'Mrs. Brookes, the bank has no intention of relieving you of your every last possession. With your agreement we would like to sell your stocks and bonds. Everything else you mentioned, including the house, we consider should remain in your possession.'

She hesitated. 'I appreciate your generosity, Mr. Kane. However, I have no wish to remain under any obligation to your bank or to leave my husband's name under a cloud.' The little tremor again, but quickly suppressed. 'Anyway, I have decided to sell the house in Florida and return to my parents' home as soon as possible.'

William's pulse quickened to hear that she would be coming back to Boston. 'In that case, perhaps we can reach some agreement about the proceeds of the sale,' he said.

'We can do that now,' she said flatly. 'You must have the entire amount.'

William played for another meeting. 'Don't let's make too hasty a decision. I think it might be wise to consult my colleagues and discuss this with you again at a later date.'

She shrugged slightly. 'As you wish. I don't really care about the money either way, and I wouldn't want to put you to any inconvenience.'

William blinked. 'Mrs. Brookes, I must confess to have been surprised by your magnanimous attitude. At least allow me the pleasure of taking you to lunch.'

She smiled for the first time, revealing an unsuspected dimple in her right cheek. William gazed at it in delight and did his utmost to provoke its reappearance over a long lunch at the Ritz. By the time he returned to his desk, it was well past three o'clock.

'Long lunch, William,' commented Tony Simmons.

'Yes, the Brookes problem turned out to be trickier than I had expected.'

'It looked fairly straightforward to me when I went over the papers,' said Simmons. 'She isn't complaining about our offer, is she? I thought we were being rather generous in the circumstances.'

'Yes, she thought so too. I had to talk her out of divesting herself of her last dollar to swell our reserves.'

Tony Simmons stared. 'That doesn't sound like the William Kane we all know and love so well. Still, there has never been a better time for the bank to be magnanimous.'

William grimaced. Since the day of his arrival, he and Tony Simmons had been in growing disagreement about where the stock market was heading. The Dow Jones had been moving steadily upward since Herbert Hoover's election to the White House in November 1928. In fact, only ten days later, the New York stock exchange had a record of over six million shares volume in one day. But William was convinced that the upward trend, fuelled by the large influx of money from the automobile industry, would result in prices inflating to the point of instability. Tony Simmons, on the other hand, was confident that the boom would continue so that when William advocated caution at board meetings he was invariably overruled. However, with his trust money, he was free to follow his own intuition, and started investing heavily in land, gold, commodities and even in some carefully selected Impressionist paintings, leaving only fifty per cent of his cash in stocks.

When the Federal Reserve Bank of New York put out an edict declaring that they would not re-discount loans to those banks which were releasing money to their customers for the sole purpose of speculation, William considered that the first

240

nail had been driven into the speculator's coffin. He immediately reviewed the bank's lending programme and estimated that Kane and Cabot had over twenty-six million dollars out on such loans. He begged Tony Simmons to call in these amounts, certain that, with such a government regulation in operation, stock prices would inevitably fall in the long term. They nearly had a stand-up fight at the monthly board meeting, and William was voted down by twelve to two.

On 21 March, 1929, Blair and Company announced its consolidation with the Bank of America, the third in a series of bank mergers which seemed to point to a brighter tomorrow, and on 25 March, Tony Simmons sent William a note pointing out to him that the market had broken through to yet another all time record, and proceeded to put more of the bank's money into stocks. By then, William had rearranged his capital so that only twenty-five per cent was in the stock market, a move that had already cost him over two million dollars – and a troubled reprimand from Alan Lloyd.

'I hope to goodness you know what you're doing, William.'

'Alan, I've been beating the stock market since I was fourteen, and I've always done it by bucking the trend.'

But as the market continued to climb through the summer of 1929, even William stopped selling, wondering if Tony Simmons' judgment was, in fact, correct.

As the time for Alan Lloyd's retirement drew nearer, Tony Simmons' clear intent to succeed him as chairman began to take on the look of a *fait accompli*. The prospect troubled William, who considered Simmons' thinking was far too conventional. He was always a yard behind the rest of the market, which is fine during boom years when things are going well, but can be dangerous for a bank in leaner, more competitive times. A shrewd investor, in William's eyes, did not invariably run with the herd, thundering or otherwise, but worked out in advance in which direction the herd would be turning next. William had already decided that future investment in the stock market still looked risky while Tony Simmons was convinced that America was entering a golden era.

William's other problem was simply that Tony Simmons was only thirty-nine years old and that meant that William could not hope to become chairman of Kane and Cabot for at least another twenty-six years. That hardly fitted into what they had called at Harvard 'one's career pattern'.

Meanwhile, the image of Katherine Brookes remained clearly in his mind. He wrote to her as often as he could about the sale of her stocks and bonds: formal, typewritten letters which elicited no more than formal handwritten responses. She must have thought he was the most conscientious banker in the world. Had she realised her file was becoming as large as any under William's control she might have thought about it – or at least him – more carefully. Early in the autumn she wrote to say she had found a firm buyer for the Florida estate. William wrote to request that she allow him to negotiate the terms of the sale on the bank's behalf, and she agreed.

He travelled down to Florida in early September 1929. Mrs. Brookes met him at the station and he was overwhelmed by how much more beautiful she appeared in person than in his memory. The slight wind blew her black dress against her body as she stood waiting on the platform, leaving a profile that ensured that every man except William would look at her a second time. William's eyes never left her.

She was still in mourning and her manner towards him was so reserved and correct that William initially despaired of making any impression on her. He spun out the negotiations with the farmer who was purchasing Buckhurst Park for as long as he could and persuaded Katherine Brookes to accept one-third of the agreed sale price while the bank took two-thirds. Finally, after the legal papers were signed, he could find no more excuses for not returning to Boston. He invited her to dinner at his hotel, resolved to reveal something of his feelings for her. Not for the first time, she took him by surprise. Before he had broached the subject, she asked him, twirling her glass to avoid looking at him, if he would like to stay over at Buckhurst Park for a few days.

'A sort of holiday for us both.' She blushed; William remained silent.

Finally she found the courage to continue. 'I know this might sound mad, but you must realise I've been very lonely. The extraordinary thing is that I seem to have enjoyed the last week with you more than any time I can remember.' She blushed again. 'I've expressed that badly, and you'll think the worst of me.'

William's pulse leaped. 'Kate, I have wanted to say something at least as bad as that for the last nine months.'

'Then you'll stay for a few days, William?'

'Yes, Kate, I will.'

That night she installed him in the main guest bedroom at Buckhurst Park. In later life William always looked back on these few days as a golden interlude in his life. He rode with Kate, and she outjumped him. He swam with her, and she outdistanced him. He walked with her and always turned back first and so finally he resorted to playing poker with her and won three and a half million dollars in as many hours of playing.

'Will you take a cheque?' she said grandly.

'You forget I know what you're worth, Mrs. Brookes, but I'll make a deal with you. We'll go on playing until you've won it back.'

'It may take a few years,' said Kate.

'I'll wait,' said William.

He found himself telling her of long-buried incidents in his past, things he had barely discussed even with Matthew, his respect for his father, his love for his mother, his blind hatred of Henry Osborne, his ambitions for Kane and Cabot. She, in turn, told him of her childhood in Boston, her schooldays in Virginia, and of her early marriage to Max Brookes.

Five days later when she said goodbye to him at the station, he kissed her for the first time.

'Kate, I'm going to say something very presumptuous. I hope one day you'll feel more for me than you felt for Max.'

'I'm beginning to feel that way already,' she said quietly.

William looked at her steadily. 'Don't stay out of my life for another nine months.'

'I can't – you've sold my house.'

On the way back to Boston, feeling more settled and happy than at any time since before his father's death, William drafted a report on the sale of Buckhurst Park, his mind returning continually to Kate and the past five days. Just before the train drew into the South Station, he scribbled a quick note in his neat but illegible handwriting.

Kate, I find I am missing you already. And it's only a few hours. Please write and let me know when you will be coming to Boston. Meanwhile I shall be getting back to the bank's business and find I can put you out of my mind for quite long periods (i.e. 10 ± 5 minutes) at a stretch consecutively.

Love
William

He had just dropped the envelope into the mail box on Charles Street when all thoughts of Kate were driven from his mind by the cry of a newsboy.

'Wall Street collapse.'

William seized a copy of the paper and scanned the lead story rapidly. The market had plummeted overnight; some financiers viewed it as nothing more than a readjustment; William saw it as the beginning of the landslide that he had been predicting for months. He hurried to the bank and went straight to the chairman's office.

'I'm sure the market will steady up in the long run,' said Alan Lloyd soothingly.

'Never,' said William. 'The market is overloaded. Overloaded with small investors who thought they were in for a quick profit and are certain to run for their lives now. Don't you see the balloon is about to burst? I'm going to sell everything. By the end of the year, the bottom will have dropped out of this market, and I did warn you in February, Alan.'

'I still don't agree with you, William, but I'll call a full board meeting for tomorrow, so that we can discuss your views in more detail.'

'Thank you,' said William. He returned to his office and picked up the inter-office phone.

'Alan, I forgot to tell you. I've met the girl I'm going to marry.'

'Does she know yet?' asked Alan.

'No,' said William.

'I see,' said Alan. 'Then your marriage will closely resemble your banking career, William. Anyone directly involved will be informed only after you've made your decision.'

William laughed, picked up the other phone, and immediately placed his own major stock holdings on the market and went into cash. Tony Simmons had just come in, and stood at the open door watching William, thinking he had gone quite mad.

'You could lose your shirt overnight dumping all those shares with the market in its present state.'

'I'll lose a lot more if I hold on to them,' replied William.

The loss he was to make in the following week, over one million dollars, would have staggered a less confident man.

At the board meeting the next day he also lost, by eight votes to six, his proposal to liquidate the bank's stocks; Tony Simmons convinced the board that it would be irresponsible not to hold out for a little longer. The only small victory William notched up was to persuade his fellow directors that the bank should no longer be a buyer.

The market rose a little that day, which gave William the opportunity to sell some more of his own stock. By the end of the week, when the index had risen steadily for four days in a row, William began to wonder if he had been over-reacting, but all his past training and instinct told him that he had made the right decision. Alan Lloyd said nothing; the money William was losing was not his, and he was looking forward to a quiet retirement.

On 22 October the market suffered more heavy losses and William again begged Alan Lloyd to get out while there was still a chance. This time Alan listened and allowed William to place a sell order on some of the bank's major stocks. The following day, the market fell again in an avalanche of selling, and it mattered little what holdings the bank tried to dispose of because there were no longer any buyers. The dumping of stock turned into a stampede, as every small investor in America put in a sell bid to try to get out from under. Such was the panic that the ticker tape could not keep pace with the transactions. Only when the Exchange opened in the morning, after the clerks had worked all night, did traders know for a fact how much they had lost the day before.

Alan Lloyd had a phone conversation with J. P. Morgan, and agreed that Kane and Cabot should join a group of banks who would try to shore up the national collapse in major stocks. William did not disapprove of this policy, on the grounds that if there had to be a group effort, Kane and Cabot should be responsibly involved in the action. And, of course, if it worked, all the banks would be better off. Richard Whitney, the vice-president of the New York Stock Exchange and the representative of the group Morgan had put together, went on the floor of the New York Stock Exchange and purchased thirty million dollars worth of blue-chip stocks the next day. The market began to hold. Twelve million, eight hundred and ninety-four thousand, six hundred and fifty shares were traded that day, and for the next two days the market held steady. Everyone, from President Hoover to the runners in the brokerage houses, believed that the worst was behind them.

William had sold nearly all of his private stock and his personal loss was proportionately far smaller than the bank's, which had dropped over three million dollars in four days; even Tony Simmons had taken to following all of William's suggestions. On 29 October, Black Tuesday as the day came to be known, the market fell again. Sixteen million, six hundred and ten thousand and thirty shares were traded. Banks all over the country knew that the truth was that they were now insolvent. If every one of their customers demanded cash – or if they in turn tried to call in all their loans – the whole banking system would collapse around their ears.

A board meeting held on 9 November opened with one minute's silence in memory of John J. Riordan, president of the County Trust, and a director of Kane and Cabot, who had shot himself to death in his own home. It was the eleventh suicide in Boston banking circles in two weeks; the dead man had been a close personal friend of Alan Lloyd's. The chairman went on to announce that Kane and Cabot had themselves lost nearly four million dollars, the Morgan Group had failed in its effort to unite, and it was now expected that every bank should act in its own best interests. Nearly all the bank's small investors had gone under, and most of the larger ones were having impossible cash problems. Angry mobs had already gathered outside banks in New York and the elderly guards had had to be supplemented with Pinkertons. Another week like this, said Alan, and every one of us will be wiped out. He offered his resignation, but the directors would not hear of it. His position was no different from that of any other chairman of a major bank in America. Tony Simmons also offered his resignation, but once again his fellow directors would not consider it. Tony was no longer destined to take Alan Lloyd's place so William kept a magnanimous silence. As a compromise, Simmons was sent to London to take charge of overseas investments. Out of harm's way, thought William, who now found himself appointed Director of Finance, in charge of all the bank's investments. Immediately he invited Matthew Lester to join him as his number two. This time Alan Lloyd didn't even raise an eyebrow.

Matthew agreed to join William early in the New Year, which was as soon as his father could release him. They hadn't been without their own problems. William, therefore, ran the investment department on his own, until Matthew's arrival. The winter of 1929 turned out to be a depressing period for William, as he watched small firms and large firms alike, run by friends he had known all his life, go under. For some time he even wondered if the bank itself could survive.

At Christmas William spent a glorious week in Florida

with Kate, helping her pack her belongings in tea chests ready for returning to Boston. 'The ones Kane and Cabot let me keep,' she teased.

William's Christmas presents filled another tea chest and Kate felt quite guilty about his generosity. 'What can a penniless widow hope to give you in return?' she mocked. William responded by bundling her into the remaining tea chest and labelling it 'William's present'.

He returned to Boston in high spirits, and hoped his stay with Kate augured the start of a better year. He settled down into Tony Simmons' old office to read the morning mail, knowing he would have to preside over the usual two or three liquidation meetings scheduled for that week. He asked his secretary whom he was to see first.

'I'm afraid it's another bankruptcy, Mr. Kane.'

'Oh, yes, I remember the case,' said William. The name had meant nothing to him. 'I read over the file last night. A most unfortunate affair. What time is he due?'

'At ten o'clock, but the gentleman is already in the lobby waiting for you, sir.'

'Right, said William, 'please send him in. Let's get it over with.'

William opened his file again to remind himself quickly of the salient facts. There was a line drawn through the name of the original client, a Mr. Davis Leroy. It had been replaced by that of the morning's visitor, Mr. Abel Rosnovski.

William vividly remembered the last conversation he had had with Mr. Rosnovski, and was already regretting it.

16

It took Abel about three months to appreciate the full extent of the problems facing the Richmond Continental and why the hotel went on losing so much money. The simple conclusion he came to after twelve weeks of keeping his eyes wide open, while at the same time allowing the rest of the staff to believe that he was half asleep, was that the hotel's profits were being stolen. The Richmond staff was working a collusive system on a scale which even Abel had not previously come across. The system did not, however, take into account a new assistant manager who had, in the past, had to steal bread from the Russians to stay alive. Abel's first problem was not to let anybody know the extent of his discoveries until he had a chance to look into every part of the hotel. It didn't take him long to figure out that each department had perfected its own system for stealing.

Deception started at the front desk where the clerks were registering only eight out of every ten guests and pocketing the cash payments from the remaining two for themselves. The routine they were using was a simple one; anyone who had tried it at the Plaza in New York would have been discovered in a few minutes and fired. The head desk clerk would choose an elderly couple, who had booked in from another state for only one night. He would then discreetly make sure they had no business connections in the city, and simply fail to register them. If they paid cash the following morning, the money was pocketed and, provided they had not signed the register, there was no record of the guests ever having been in the hotel. Abel had long thought that all hotels should automatically have to register every guest. They were already doing so at the Plaza.

In the dining room, the system had been refined. Of course, the cash payments of any casual guest for lunch or dinner were already being taken. Abel had expected that, but it took him a little longer to check through the restaurant bills and establish that the front desk was working with the dining room staff to ensure that there were no restaurant bills for those guests whom they had already chosen not to register. Over and above that there was a steady trail of fictitious breakages and repairs, missing equipment, disappearing food, lost bed linen, and even an occasional mattress had gone astray. After checking every department thoroughly and keeping his ears and eyes open, Abel concluded that over half of the Richmond's staff were involved in the conspiracy, and that no one department had a completely clean record.

When he had first come to the Richmond, Abel had wondered why the manager, Desmond Pacey, hadn't noticed what had been going on under his nose a long time before. He wrongly assumed the reason was that the man was lazy and could not be bothered to follow up complaints. Even Abel was slow to catch on to the fact that the lazy manager was the mastermind behind the entire operation, and the reason it worked so well. Pacey had worked for the Richmond group for over thirty years. There was not a single hotel in the group in which he had not held a senior position at one time or another, which made Abel fearful for the solvency of the other hotels. Moreover, Desmond Pacey was a personal friend of the hotels' owner, Davis Leroy. The Chicago Richmond was losing over thirty thousand dollars a year, a situation Abel knew could be redeemed overnight by firing half the staff, starting with Desmond Pacey. That posed a problem, because Davis Leroy had rarely fired anyone in thirty years. He simply tolerated the problems, hoping that in time they would go away. As far as Abel could see, the Richmond hotel staff went on stealing the hotel blind until they reluctantly retired.

Abel knew that the only way he could reverse the hotel's fortunes was to have a show-down with Davis Leroy, and to that end, early in 1928, he boarded the express train from Illinois Central to St. Louis and the Missouri Pacific to Dallas. Under his arm was a two-hundred page report which he had taken three months to compile in his small room in the hotel annex. By the time he had finished reading through the mass of evidence, Davis Leroy sat staring at him in dismay.

'These people are my friends,' were his first words as he closed the dossier. 'Some of them have been with me for thirty years. Hell, there's always been a little fiddling around in this business, but now you tell me they've been robbing me blind behind my back?'

'Some of them, I should think, for all of those thirty years,' said Abel.

'What in hell's name am I going to do about it?' said Leroy.

'I can stop the rot if you remove Desmond Pacey and give me *carte blanche* to sack anyone who has been involved in the thefts, starting tomorrow.'

'Well now, Abel, I wish the problem was as simple as that.'

'The problem is just that simple,' said Abel. 'And if you won't let me deal with the culprits, you can have my resignation as of this minute, because I have no interest in being a part of the most corruptly run hotel in America.'

'Couldn't we just demote Desmond Pacey to assistant manager? Then I could make you manager and the problem would come under your control.'

'Never,' replied Abel. 'Pacey has over two years to go and has a firm hold over the entire Richmond staff, so that by the time I get him in line you'll be dead or bankrupt, or both, as I suspect all of your other hotels are being run in the same cavalier fashion. If you want the trend reversed in Chicago, you'll have to make a firm decision about Pacey right now, or you can go to the wall on your own. Take it or leave it.'

'Us Texans have a reputation for speaking our mind, Abel but we're sure not in your class. Okay, okay, I'll give you the authority. As of this minute congratulations. You're the new manager of the Chicago Richmond. Wait till Al Capone hears you've arrived in Chicago; he'll join me down here in the peace and quiet of the great South-west. Abel, my boy,' continued Leroy, standing up and slapping his new manager on the shoulder, 'don't think I'm ungrateful. You've done a great job in Chicago, and from now on I shall look upon you as my right-hand man. To be honest with you Abel, I have been doing so well on the Stock Exchange I haven't even noticed the losses, so thank God I have one honest friend. Why don't you stay overnight and have a bite to eat?'

'I'd be delighted to join you, Mr. Leroy, but I want to spend the night at the Dallas Richmond for personal reasons.'

'You're not going to let anyone off the hook, are you, Abel?'

'Not if I can help it.'

That evening Davis Leroy gave Abel a sumptuous meal and a little too much whisky which he insisted was no more than Southern hospitality. He also admitted to Abel that he was looking for someone to run the Richmond Group so that he could take things a little easier.

'Are you sure you want a dumb Polack?' slurred Abel after one too many drinks.

'Abel, it's me who's been dumb. If you hadn't proved to be so reliable in smoking out those thieves, I might have gone under. But now that I know the truth, we'll lick them together, and I'm going to give you the chance to put the Richmond Group back on the map.'

Abel shakily raised his glass. 'I'll drink to that – and to a long and successful partnership.'

'Go get 'em, boy.'

Abel spent the night at the Dallas Richmond, giving a false name and pointedly telling the desk clerk that he would only be staying one night. In the morning when he observed the hotel's only copy of the receipt for his cash payment disappearing into the wastepaper basket, Abel had his suspicions confirmed. The problem was not Chicago's alone. He decided he would have to get Chicago straightened out first; the rest of the group's finaglings would have to wait until later. He made one call to Davis Leroy to warn him that the disease had spread to the whole group.

Abel travelled back the way he had come. The Mississippi valley lay sullenly alongside the train window, devastated by the floods of the previous year. Abel thought about the devastation he was going to cause when he returned to the Chicago Richmond.

When he arrived, there was no night porter on duty and only one clerk could be found. He decided to let them all have a good night's rest before he bade them farewell. A young bellboy opened the front door for him as he made his way back to the annex.

'Have a good trip, Mr. Rosnovski?' he asked.

'Yes, thank you. How have things been here?'

'Oh, very quiet.'

You may find it even quieter this time tomorrow, thought Abel, when you're the only member of the staff left.

Abel unpacked and called room service to order a light meal, which took over an hour to arrive. When he had finished his coffee, he undressed and stood in a cold shower, going over his plan for the following day. He had picked a good time of year for his massacre. It was early February and the hotel had only about a twenty-five per cent occupancy, and Abel was confident that he could run the Richmond with about half its present staff. He climbed into bed, threw the pillow on the floor and slept, like his unsuspecting staff, soundly.

Desmond Pacey, known to every one at the Richmond as Lazy Pacey, was sixty-two years old. He was considerably overweight and it made him rather slow of movement on his short legs. Desmond Pacey had seen seven, or was it eight, assistant managers come and go in the Richmond. Some got greedy and wanted more of his take; some just couldn't understand how it worked. The Polack, he decided, wasn't turning out to be any brighter than the others. He hummed to himself as he walked slowly towards Abel's office for their daily ten o'clock meeting. It was seventeen minutes past ten.

'Sorry to have kept you waiting,' said the manager, not sounding sorry at all.

Abel made no comment.

'I was held up with something at reception, you know how it is.'

Abel knew exactly how it was at reception.

He slowly opened the drawer of the desk in front of him and laid out forty crumpled hotel bills, some of them in four or five pieces, bills that he had recovered from wastepaper baskets and ashtrays, bills for those guests who had paid cash and who had never been registered. He watched the fat little manager trying to work out what they were, upside down.

Desmond Pacey couldn't quite fathom it. Not that he cared that much. Nothing for him to worry about. If the stupid Polack had caught on to the system, he could either take his cut or leave. Pacey was wondering what percentage he would have to give him. Perhaps a nice room in the hotel would keep him quiet for the time being.

'You're fired, Mr. Pacey, and I want you off the premises within the hour.'

Desmond Pacey didn't actually take in the words, because he couldn't believe them.

'What was that you said? I don't think I heard you right.'

'You did,' said Abel. 'You're fired.'

'You can't fire me. I'm the manager and I've been with the Richmond Group for over thirty years. If there's any firing to be done, I'll do it. Who in God's name do you think you are?'

'I am the new manager.'

'You're *what*?'

'The new manager,' Abel repeated. 'Mr. Leroy appointed me yesterday and I have just fired you, Mr. Pacey.'

'What for?'

'For larceny on a grand scale.'

Abel turned the bills around so that the bespectacled man could see them all properly.

'Every one of these guests paid their bill, but not one penny of the money reached the Richmond account, and they all have one thing in common – your signature is on them.'

'You couldn't prove anything in a hundred years.'

'I know,' said Abel. 'You've been running a good system. Well, you can go and run that system somewhere else because your luck's run out here. There is an old Polish saying, Mr. Pacey: the pitcher carries water only until the handle breaks. The handle has just broken and you're fired.'

'You don't have the authority to fire me,' said Pacey. Sweat peppered out on his forehead despite the coldness of the February day. 'Davis Leroy is a close personal friend of mine. He's the only man who can fire me. You only came out from New York three months ago. He wouldn't even listen to you once I had spoken to him. I could get you thrown out of this hotel with one phone call.'

'Go ahead,' said Abel.

He picked up the telephone and asked the operator to get Davis Leroy in Dallas. The two men waited, staring at each other. The sweat had now trickled down to the tip of Pacey's nose. For a second Abel wondered if his new employer would hold firm.

'Good morning, Mr. Leroy. It's Abel Rosnovski calling from Chicago. I've just fired Desmond Pacey, and he wants a word with you.'

Shakily, Pacey took the telephone. He listened for only a few moments.

'But, Davis, I . . . What could I do . . . ? I swear to you it isn't true . . . There must be some mistake.'

Abel heard the line click.

'One hour, Mr. Pacey,' said Abel, 'or I'll hand over these bills to the Chicago Police Department.'

'Now wait a moment,' Pacey said. 'Don't act so hasty.' His tone and attitude had changed abruptly. 'We could bring you in on the whole operation, you could make a very steady little income if we ran this hotel together, and no one would be any the wiser. The money would be far more than you're making as assistant manager and we all know Davis can afford the losses . . .'

'I'm not the assistant manager any longer, Mr. Pacey. I'm the manager so get out before I throw you out.'

'You fucking Polack,' said the ex-manager, realising he had played his last card and lost. 'You'd better keep your eyes open because you're going to be brought down to size.'

Pacey left. By lunch he had been joined on the street by the head waiter, head chef, senior housekeeper, chief desk clerk, head porter, and seventeen other members of the Richmond staff whom Abel felt were past redemption. In the afternoon, he called a meeting of the remainder of the employees, explained to them in detail why what he had done had been necessary, and assured them that their jobs were not in any danger.

'But if I can find *one*,' said Abel, 'I repeat, *one* dollar misplaced, the person involved will be sacked without references there and then. Am I understood?'

No one spoke.

Several other members of the staff left the Richmond during the next few weeks when they realised that Abel did not intend to continue Desmond Pacey's system on his own behalf, and they were quickly replaced.

By the end of March, Abel had invited four employees from the Plaza to join him at the Richmond. They had three things in common: they were young, ambitious and honest. Within six months, only thirty-seven of the original staff of one hundred and ten were still employed at the Richmond. At the end of the first year, Abel cracked a large bottle of champagne with Davis Leroy to celebrate the year's figures for the Chicago Richmond. They had shown a profit of three thousand, four hundred and eighty-six dollars. Small, but the first profit the hotel had shown in the thirty years of its existence. Abel was projecting a profit of over twenty-five thousand dollars in 1929.

Davis Leroy was mightily impressed. He visited Chicago once a month and began to rely heavily on Abel's judgment. He even came round to the point of admitting that what had been true of the Chicago Richmond might well be true of the other hotels in the group. Abel wanted to see the Chicago hotel running smoothly on its new lines before he considered tackling the others; Leroy agreed but talked of a partnership for Abel if he could do for the others what he had done with Chicago.

They started going to baseball and the races together whenever Davis was in Chicago. On one occasion, when Davis had lost seven hundred dollars without getting close in any of the six races, he threw up his arms in disgust and said, 'Why do I bother with horses, Abel? You're the best bet I've ever made.'

Melanie Leroy always dined with her father on these visits. Cool, pretty, with a slim figure and long legs which attracted many a stare from the hotel guests, she treated Abel with a slight degree of hauteur which gave him no encouragement for the aspirations he had begun to formulate for her, nor did she invite him to substitute 'Melanie' for 'Miss Leroy' until she discovered he was the holder of an economics degree from Columbia and knew more about discounted cash flow than she did herself. After that, she softened a little and came from time to time to dine with Abel alone in the hotel and seek assistance with the work she was doing for her liberal arts degree at the University of Chicago. Emboldened, he occasionally escorted her to concerts and the theatre, and began to feel a proprietorial jealousy whenever she brought other men to dine at the hotel, though she never came with the same escort twice.

So greatly had the hotel cuisine improved under Abel's iron fist that people who had lived in Chicago for thirty years and never realised the place existed were making gastronomic outings every Saturday evening. Abel redecorated the whole hotel for the first time in twenty years and put the staff into smart new green and gold uniforms. One guest, who had stayed at the Richmond for a week every year, actually retreated back out of the front door on arrival, because he thought he had walked into the wrong establishment. When Al Capone booked a dinner party for sixteen in a private room to celebrate his thirtieth birthday, Abel knew he had arrived.

Abel's personal wealth grew during this period, while the stock market flourished. Having left the Plaza with eight thousand dollars, eighteen months before, his brokerage account now stood at over thirty thousand. He was confident that the market would continue to rise, and so he always reinvested his profits. His personal requirements were still fairly modest. He had acquired two new suits and his first pair of brown shoes. He still had his rooms and food provided by the hotel and few out-of-pocket expenses. There seemed to be nothing but a bright future ahead of him. The Continental Trust had handled the Richmond account for over thirty years, so Abel had transferred his own account to them when he first came to Chicago. Every day he would go to the bank and deposit the hotel's previous day's receipts. He was taken by surprise one Friday morning by a message that the manager was asking to see him. He knew his personal account was never overdrawn, so he presumed the meeting must have something to do with the Richmond. The bank could hardly be about to complain that the hotel's account was solvent for the first time in thirty years. A junior clerk guided Abel through a tangle of corridors until he reached a handsome wooden door. A gentle knock and he was ushered in to meet the manager.

'My name is Curtis Fenton,' said the man behind the desk, offering Abel his hand before motioning him into a green leather button seat. He was a neat, rotund man who wore half-moon spectacles and an impeccable white collar and black tie to go with his three piece banker's suit.

'Thank you,' said Abel nervously.

The circumstances brought back to him memories of the past, memories he associated only with the fear of being uncertain what was going to happen next.

'I would have invited you to lunch, Mr. Rosnovski—'

Abel's heartbeat steadied a little. He was only too aware that bank managers do not dispense free meals when they have unpleasant messages to deliver.

'—but something has arisen that requires immediate action, and so I hope you won't mind if I discuss the problem with you without delay. I'll come straight to the point, Mr. Rosnovski. One of my most respected customers, an elderly lady, Miss Amy Leroy,' – the name made Abel sit up instantly – 'is in possession of twenty-five per cent of the Richmond Group stock. She has offered this holding to her brother, Mr. Davis Leroy, several times in the past but he has shown absolutely no interest in purchasing Miss Amy's shares. I can understand Mr. Leroy's reasoning. He already owns seventy-five per cent of the company, and I dare say he feels he has no need to worry about the other twenty-five per cent, which incidentally, was a legacy from their late father. However, Miss Amy Leroy is still keen to dispose of her stock as it has never paid a dividend.'

Abel was not surprised to hear that.

'Mr. Leroy has indicated that he has no objection to her

selling the stock, and she feels that at her age she would rather have a little cash to spend now than wait in the hope that the group may one day prove profitable. With that in mind, Mr. Rosnovski, I thought I would apprise you of the situation in case you might know of someone with an interest in the hotel trade and, therefore, in the purchase of my client's shares.'

'How much is Miss Leroy hoping to realise for her stock?' asked Abel.

'Oh, I feel she'd be happy to let them go for as little as sixty-five thousand dollars.'

'Sixty-five thousand dollars is a rather high price for a stock that has never paid a dividend,' said Abel, 'and has no hope of doing so for some years to come.'

'Ah,' said Curtis Fenton, 'but you must remember that the value of the eleven hotels should also be taken into consideration.'

'But control of the company would still remain in the hands of Mr. Leroy, which makes Miss Leroy's twenty-five per cent holding nothing but pieces of paper.'

'Come, come, Mr. Rosnovski, twenty-five per cent of eleven hotels would be a very valuable holding for only sixty-five thousand dollars.'

'Not while Davis Leroy has overall control. Offer Miss Leroy forty thousand dollars, Mr. Fenton, and I may be able to find you someone who is interested.'

'You don't think that person might go a little higher, do you?' Mr. Fenton's eyebrows raised on the word 'higher'.

'Not a penny more, Mr. Fenton.'

The bank manager brought his fingertips delicately together, pleased with his appraisal of Abel.

'In the circumstances, I can only ask Miss Amy what her attitude would be to such an offer. I will contact you again as soon as she has instructed me.'

After leaving Curtis Fenton's office, Abel's heart was beating as fast as when he had entered. He hurried back to the hotel to double check on his own personal holdings. His brokerage account stood at thirty-three thousand one hundred and twelve dollars, and his personal account at three thousand and eight dollars. Abel then tried to carry out a normal day's work. He found it hard to concentrate for wondering how Miss Amy Leroy would react to the bid and daydreaming about what he would do if he held a twenty-five per cent interest in the Richmond Group.

He hesitated before informing Davis Leroy of his bid, fearful that the genial Texan might view his ambitions as a threat. But after a couple of days during which he considered the matter carefully, he decided the fairest thing to do would be to call Davis Leroy and acquaint him with his intentions.

'I want you to know why I am doing this, Mr. Leroy. I believe the Richmond Group has a great future, and you can be sure that I shall work all the harder for you if I know my own money is also involved.' He paused. 'But if you want to take up that twenty-five per cent yourself, I shall naturally understand.'

To his surprise, the escape ladder was not grasped.

'Well, see here, Abel, if you have that much confidence in the group, go ahead, son, and buy Amy out. I'd be proud to have you for a partner. You've earned it. By the way, I'll be up next week for the Red Cubs game. See you then.'

Abel was jubilant. 'Thank you, Davis, you'll never have cause to regret your decision.'

'I'm sure I won't, pardner.'

Abel returned to the bank a week later. This time, it was he who asked to see the manager. Once again he sat in the green leather button chair, and waited for Mr. Fenton to speak.

'I am surprised to find,' began Curtis Fenton not looking at all surprised, 'that Miss Leroy will accept the bid of forty thousand dollars for her twenty-five per cent holding in the Richmond Group.' He paused before looking up at Abel. 'As I have now secured her agreement, I must ask if you are in a position to disclose your buyer?'

'Yes,' said Abel confidently. 'I will be the principal.'

'I see, Mr. Rosnovski,' again not showing any surprise. 'May I ask how you propose to find the forty thousand dollars?'

'I shall liquidate my stock holdings and release the spare

cash in my personal account, which will leave me short of about four thousand dollars. I hoped that you would be willing to loan me that sum, as you are so confident that the Richmond Group stock is undervalued. In any case, the four thousand dollars probably represents nothing more than the bank's commission on the deal.'

Curtis Fenton blinked and frowned. Gentlemen did not make that sort of remark in his office : it stung all the more because Abel had the sum exactly right. 'Will you give me a little more time to consider your proposal, Mr. Rosnovski, and then I will come back to you?'

'If you wait long enough, I won't need your loan,' said Abel. 'My other investments will soon be worth the full forty thousand, the way the market is moving at the moment.'

Abel had to wait a further week to be told that Continental Trust was willing to back him. He immediately cleared both his accounts and borrowed a little under four thousand dollars to make up the shortfall on the forty thousand.

Within six months, Abel had paid off his four thousand loan by careful buying and selling of stock from March to August 1929, some of the best days the stock market was ever to know.

By September, both his accounts were slightly ahead again – he even had enough to buy a new Buick – while he was now the owner of twenty-five per cent of the Richmond Group of hotels. Abel was pleased to have acquired such a firm holding in Davis Leroy's empire. It gave him the confidence to pursue his daughter and the other seventy-five per cent.

Early in October, he invited Melanie to a programme of Mozart at the Chicago Symphony Hall. Donning his smartest suit, which only emphasised he was gaining some weight, and wearing his first silk tie, he felt confident as he glanced in the mirror that the evening was to be a success. After the concert was over Abel avoided the Richmond, excellent though its food had become, and took Melanie to The Loop for dinner. He was particularly careful to talk only of economics and politics, two subjects about which he knew she was obliged to accept he was greatly the more knowledgeable. Finally, he asked her back for a drink in his rooms. It was the first time she had seen them, and she was both piqued and surprised by their smartness.

Abel poured the Coca-Cola which she requested, dropped two cubes of ice into the bubbly liquid and gained confidence from the smile he was rewarded with as he passed her the glass. He couldn't help staring at her slim, crossed legs for more than a polite second. He poured himself a bourbon.

'Thank you, Abel, for a wonderful evening.'

He sat down beside her and swirled the drink in his glass reflectively. 'For many years, I heard no music. When I did, Mozart spoke to my heart as no other composer has done.'

'How very middle-European you sound sometimes, Abel.' She pulled the edge of her silk dress, which Abel was sitting on, free. 'Who would have thought a hotel manager would give a damn for Mozart?'

'One of my ancestors, the first Baron Rosnovski,' said Abel, 'once met the maestro, and he became a close friend of the family so I have always felt he was part of my life.'

Melanie's smile was unfathomable. Abel leaned sideways and kissed her cheek just above the ear, where her fair hair was drawn back from her face. She continued the conversation without giving the slightest indication that she had even been aware of his action.

'Frederick Stock captured the mood of the third movement to perfection, wouldn't you say?'

Abel tried the kiss again. This time she turned her face towards him and allowed herself to be kissed on the lips. Then she drew away.

'I think I ought to be getting back to the university.'

'But you've only just arrived,' said Abel, dismayed.

'Yes, I know, but I have to be up early in the morning. I have a heavy day ahead of me.'

Abel kissed her again. She fell back on the couch and Abel tried to move his hand on to her breast. She broke quickly from the kiss and pushed him away.

'I must be going, Abel,' she insisted.

'Oh, come on,' he said, 'you don't have to go yet,' and once again he tried to kiss her.

This time she stopped him by pushing him away more firmly.

'Abel, what do you think you are doing? Because you give me the occasional meal and take me to a concert, doesn't mean you have the right to maul me.'

'But we've been going out together for months,' said Abel. 'I didn't think you would mind.'

'We have not been going out together for months, Abel. I eat with you occasionally in my father's dining room, but you should not construe that to mean we have been going out together for months.'

'I'm sorry,' said Abel. 'The last thing I wanted you to think was that I was mauling you. I only wanted to touch you.'

'I would never allow a man to touch me,' she said, 'unless I was going to marry him.'

'But I want to marry you,' said Abel quietly.

Melanie burst out laughing.

'What's so funny about that?' Abel asked, reddening.

'Don't be silly, Abel, I could never marry you.'

'Why not?' demanded Abel, shocked by the vehemence in her voice.

'It would never do for a Southern lady to marry a first generation Polish immigrant,' she replied, sitting up very straight and pushing her silk dress back into place.

'But I am a Baron,' said Abel, a little haughtily.

Melanie burst out laughing again. 'You don't think anybody believes that, do you Abel? Don't you realise the whole staff laughs behind your back whenever you mention your title?'

He was stunned, and felt sick, his face draining of its red embarrassment. 'They all laugh at me behind my back?' His slight accent sounded more pronounced.

'Yes,' she said. 'Surely you know what your nickname in the hotel is? The Chicago Baron.'

Abel was speechless.

'Now don't be silly and get all self-conscious about it. I think you've done a wonderful job for Daddy, and I know he admires you, but I could never marry you.'

Abel sat quietly. '*I could never marry you*,' he repeated.

'Of course not. Daddy likes you, but he would never agree to having you as a son-in-law.'

'I'm sorry to have offended you,' said Abel.

'You haven't, Abel. I'm flattered. Now let's forget you ever mentioned the subject. Perhaps you would be kind enough to take me home?'

She rose and strode towards the door, while Abel remained seated, still stunned. Somehow he managed to push himself up slowly and help Melanie on with her cloak. He became conscious of his limp as they walked along the corridor together. They went down in the lift and he took her home in a cab: neither spoke. While the taxi waited, he accompanied her to the front gate of her dormitory. He kissed her hand.

'I do hope this doesn't mean we can't still be friends,' said Melanie.

'Of course not.'

'Thank you for taking me to the concert, Abel. I'm sure you'll have no trouble in finding a nice Polish girl to marry you. Good night.'

'Goodbye,' said Abel.

Abel did not think there would be any real trouble on the New York Stock market until one of his guests asked if he might settle his hotel bill with stock. Abel held only a small amount of stock himself since nearly all his money was tied up in the Richmond Group, but he took his broker's advice and sold off his remaining shares at a small loss, relieved that the bulk of his savings was secure in bricks and mortar. He had not taken as close an interest in the day-to-day movement of the Dow-Jones as he would have if all his capital had still been in the market.

The hotel did well in the first part of the year, and Abel considered he was set fair to achieve his profit forecast of over twenty-five thousand dollars for 1929, and kept Davis

Leroy in constant touch with the way things were turning out. But when the crash came in October the hotel was half empty. Abel placed a call through to Davis Leroy on Black Tuesday. The Texan sounded depressed and preoccupied and would not be drawn into making decisions about the laying off of hotel staff which Abel now considered urgent.

'Stick with it, Abel,' he said. 'I'll come up next week and we'll sort it out together then – or we'll try to.'

Abel did not like the ring of the last phrase. 'What's the problem, Davis? Is it anything I can help with?'

'Not for the time being.'

Abel remained puzzled. 'Why don't you just give me the authority to get on with it, and I can brief you when you come up next week?'

'It's not quite as easy as that, Abel. I didn't want to discuss my problems over the phone, but the bank is giving me a little trouble over my losses in the stock market, and they are threatening to make me sell the hotels if I can't raise enough money to cover my debts.'

Abel went cold.

'Nothing for you to worry about, my boy,' continued Davis, sounding unconvincing. 'I will fill you in on all the details when I come up to Chicago next week. I am sure I can fix up something by then.'

Abel heard the phone click and could feel his whole body sweating. His first reaction was to wonder how he could assist Davis. He put a call through to Curtis Fenton and prised out of him the name of the banker who controlled the Richmond Group, feeling that if he could see him it might make things easier for his friend.

Abel called Davis several times during the next few days to tell him that things were going from bad to worse and that decisions must be made, but he sounded more and more preoccupied and was still unwilling to make any decision. When matters started getting out of control, Abel made a decision. He asked his secretary to get the banker who controlled the Richmond Group on the phone.

'Who are you calling, Mr. Rosnovski?' asked a prim-sounding lady.

Abel looked down at the name on the piece of paper in front of him and said it firmly.

'I'll put you through.'

'Good morning,' said an authoritative voice. 'May I help you?'

'I hope so. My name is Abel Rosnovski,' began Abel nervously. 'I am the manager of the Richmond Chicago and wanted to make an appointment to see you and discuss the future of the Richmond Group.'

'I have no authority to deal with anyone except Mr. Davis Leroy,' said the clipped accent.

'But I own twenty-five per cent of the Richmond Group,' said Abel.

'Then no doubt someone will explain to you that until you own fifty-one per cent you are in no position to deal with the bank unles you have the authority of Mr. Davis Leroy.'

'But he's a close personal friend . . .'

'I don't doubt that, Mr. Rosnovski.'

'. . . and I'm trying to help.'

'Has Mr. Leroy given you the authority to represent him?'

'No, but . . .'

'Then I am sorry. It would be most unprofessional of me to continue this conversation.'

'You couldn't be less helpful, could you?' asked Abel, immediately regretting his words.

'That is no doubt how you see it, Mr. Rosnovski. Good day, sir.'

Oh, to hell with you, thought Abel, slamming down the phone, even more worried about what he could do next to help Davis. He didn't have long to find out.

The next evening Abel spotted Melanie in the restaurant, not displaying her usual well-groomed confidence but looking tired and anxious, and he nearly asked her if everything was all right. He decided against approaching her and, as he left the dining room to go to his office, he found Davis Leroy standing alone in the front hall. He had on the checked jacket that he was wearing the first day he had approached Abel at the Plaza.

'Is Melanie in the dining room?'

'Yes,' said Abel. 'I didn't know you were coming into town today, Davis. I'll get the Presidential Suite ready for you immediately.'

'Only for one night, Abel, and I'd like to see you in private later.'

'Certainly.'

Abel didn't like the sound of 'in private'. Had Melanie been complaining to her father; was that why he had not found it possible to get a decision out of Davis during the last few days?

Davis Leroy hurried past him into the dining room while Abel went over to the reception desk to check on whether the suite on floor twelve was available. Half the rooms in the hotel were unoccupied and it came as no surprise that the Presidential Suite was free. Abel booked his employer in and then waited by the reception desk for over an hour. He saw Melanie leave, her face blotched as if she had been crying. Her father followed her out of the dining room a few minutes later.

'Get yourself a bottle of bourbon, Abel – don't tell me we don't have one – and then join me in my suite.'

Abel picked up two bottles of bourbon from his safe and joined Leroy in the Presidential Suite on the twelfth floor, still wondering if Melanie had said anything to her father.

'Open the bottle and pour yourself a very large one, Abel,' Davis Leroy instructed.

Once again Abel felt the fear of the unknown. The palms of his hands began to sweat. Surely he was not going to be fired for wanting to marry the boss's daughter? He and Leroy had been friends for over a year now, close friends. He did not have to wait long to find out what the unknown was.

'Finish your bourbon.'

Abel put the drink down in one gulp, and Davis Leroy swallowed his.

'Abel, I'm wiped out.' He paused, and poured both of them another drink. 'So is half America, come to think of it.'

Abel did not speak, partly because he could not think of what to say. They sat staring at each other for several minutes, then after another glass of bourbon, he managed, 'But you still own eleven hotels.'

'Used to own,' said Davis Leroy. 'Have to put it in the past tense now, Abel. I no longer own any of them; the bank took possession of the freeholds last Thursday.'

'But they belong to you, they have been in your family for two generations,' said Abel.

'They were. They aren't any longer. Now they belong to a bank. There's no reason why you shouldn't know the whole truth, Abel; the same thing's happening to almost everyone in America right now, big or small. About ten years ago I borrowed two million dollars using the hotels as collateral and invested the money right across the board in stocks and bonds, fairly conservatively and in well-established companies. I built the capital up to nearly five million, which was one of the reasons the hotel losses never bothered me too much – they were always tax deductible against the profit I was making in the market. Today I couldn't give those shares away. We may as well use them as toilet paper in the eleven hotels. For the last three weeks I've been selling as fast as I can, but there are no buyers left. The bank foreclosed on my loan last Thursday.' Abel couldn't help remembering that it was on a Thursday when he spoke to the banker. 'Most people who are affected by the crash have only pieces of paper to cover their loans, but in my case the bank who backed me has the deeds on the eleven hotels as security against their original loan. So when the bottom dropped out, they immediately took possession of them. The bastards have let me know that they intend to sell the group as quickly as possible.'

'That's madness. They'll get nothing for them right now, and if they supported us through this period, together we could show them a good return on their investment.'

'I know *you* could, Abel, but they have my past record to

throw back in my face. I went up to their main office to suggest just that. I explained about you and told them I would put all my time into the group if they would give us their backing, but they weren't interested. They fobbed me off with some smooth young puppy who had all the text book answers about cash flows, no capital base and credit restrictions. By God, if I ever get back, I'll screw him personally and then his bank. Right now the best thing we can do is get ourselves uproariously drunk, because I am finished, penniless, bankrupt.'

'Then so am I,' said Abel quietly.

'No, you have a great future ahead of you, son. Anyone who takes over this group couldn't make a move without you.'

'You forget that I own twenty-five per cent of the group.'

Davis Leroy stared at him. It was obvious that that fact had slipped his mind.

'Oh my God, Abel, I hope you didn't put all your money into me.' His voice was becoming thick.

'Every last cent,' said Abel. 'But I don't regret it, Davis. Better to lose with a wise man than win with a fool.' He poured himself another bourbon.

The tears were standing in the corners of Davis Leroy's eyes. 'You know, Abel, you're the best friend a man could ask for. You knock this hotel into shape, you invest your own money, I make you penniless, and you don't even complain, and then for good measure my daughter refuses to marry you.'

'You didn't mind me asking her?' said Abel, less incredulous than he would have been without the bourbon.

'Silly little bitch, doesn't know a good thing when she sees one. She wants to marry some horse-breeding gentleman from the South with three Confederate generals in his family tree or if she does marry a Northerner, his great grandfather has to have come over on *The Mayflower*. If everyone who claims they had a relative on that boat were ever on board together, the whole damn thing would have sunk a thousand times before it reach America. Too bad I don't have another daughter for you, Abel. No one has served me more loyally than you have. I sure would have been proud to have you as a member of the family. You and I would have made a great team, but I still reckon you can beat them all by yourself. You're young, you still have everything ahead of you.'

At twenty-three Abel suddenly felt very old.

'Thank you for your confidence, Davis,' he said, 'and who gives a damn for the stock market anyway? You know, you're the best friend I ever had.' The drink was beginning to talk.

Abel poured himself yet another bourbon and threw it down. Between them they had finished both bottles by early morning. When Davis fell asleep in his chair, Abel managed to stagger down to the tenth floor, undress and collapse on to his own bed. He was awakened from a heavy sleep by a loud banging on the door. His head was going round and round, but the banging went on and on, louder and louder. Somehow he managed to get himself off the bed and grope his way to the door. It was a bellboy.

'Come quickly, Mr. Abel, come quickly,' he said as he ran down the hall.

Abel threw on a dressing gown and slippers and staggered down the corridor to join the bellboy, who was holding back the lift door for him.

'Quickly, Mr. Abel,' he repeated.

'What's the hurry?' demanded Abel, his head still going around as the lift moved slowly down. Then he recalled the evening's talk. Maybe the bank had come to take possession.

'Someone has jumped out the window.'

Abel sobered up immediately. 'A guest?'

'Yes, I think so,' said the bellboy, 'but I'm not sure.'

The lift came to a stop at the ground floor. Abel thrust back the iron gates and ran out into the street. The police were already there. He wouldn't have recognised the body if it had not been for the checked jacket. A policeman was taking down details. A man in plainclothes came over to Abel.

'You the manager?'

'Yes, I am.'

'Do you have any idea who this man might be?'

'Yes,' said Abel, slurring the word. 'His name is Davis Leroy.'

'Do you know where he's from or how we contact his next of kin?'

Abel averted his eyes away from the broken body and answered automatically.

'He's from Dallas and a Miss Melanie Leroy, his daughter, is his next of kin. She's a student living out on the Chicago University campus.'

'Right, we'll get someone right over to her.'

'No, don't do that. I'll go and see her myself,' said Abel.

'Thank you. It's always better if they don't hear the news from a stranger.'

'What a terrible, unnecessary thing to do,' said Abel, his eyes drawn back to the body of his friend.

'It's the seventh in Chicago today,' said the officer flatly as he closed his little black notebook and strolled over towards the ambulance.

Abel watched the stretcher bearers remove Davis Leroy's body from the pavement. He felt cold, sank to his knees and was violently sick in the gutter. Once again he had lost his closest friend. Maybe if he had drunk less and thought more, he might have saved him. He picked himself up and returned to his room, took a long, cold shower and somehow managed to get himself dressed. He ordered some black coffee and then, reluctantly, went up to the Presidential Suite and unlocked the door. Other than a couple of empty bourbon bottles, there seemed to be no sign of the drama that had been enacted a few minutes earlier. Then he saw the letters on the side table by a bed which had not been slept in. The first was addressed to Melanie, the second to a lawyer in Dallas and the third to Abel. He tore his open but could barely read Davis Leroy's last words.

Dear Abel,

I'm taking the only way out after the bank's decision. There is nothing left for me to live for; I am far too old to start over. I want you to know I believe you're the one person who might make something good come out of this terrible mess.

I have made a new will in which I have left you the other seventy-five per cent of the shares in the Richmond Group. I realise they are worthless, but the stock will secure your position as the legal owner of the group. As you had the guts to buy twenty-five per cent with your own money, you deserve the right to see if you can make some deal with the bank. I've left everything else I own, including the house, to Melanie. Please be the one who tells her. Don't let it be the police. I would have been proud to have you as a son-in-law, partner.

Your friend,
Davis

Abel read the letter again and again and then folded it neatly and put it into his wallet.

He went over to the university campus later that morning and broke the news as gently as he could to Melanie. He sat nervously on the couch, unsure what he could add to the bland statement of death. She took it surprisingly well, almost as if she had known what was going to happen. No tears in front of Abel – perhaps later when he wasn't there. He felt sorry for her for the first time in his life.

Abel returned to the hotel and decided not to have any lunch and asked a waiter to bring him a tomato juice while he went over his mail. There was a letter from Curtis Fenton at the Continental Trust Bank. It was obviously going to be a day for letters. Fenton had received the advice that a Boston bank called Kane and Cabot had taken over the financial responsibility of the Richmond Group. For the time being, business was to continue as usual, until meetings had been arranged with Mr. Davis Leroy to discuss the disposal of all the hotels in the group. Abel sat staring at the words, and after a second tomato juice, he drafted a letter to the chairman of Kane and Cabot, a Mr. Alan Lloyd. He received a reply some five days later asking Abel to attend a meeting in

Boston on 4 January to discuss the liquidation of the group with the director in charge of bankruptcies. The interval would give the bank enough time to sort out the implications of Mr. Leroy's sudden and tragic death.

Sudden and tragic death? 'And who caused that death?' said Abel aloud in a fury, suddenly remembering Davis Leroy's own words. 'They fobbed me off with some smooth young puppy ... By God, if I ever get back, I'll screw him personally and then his bank.'

'Don't worry, Davis, I'll finish the job for you,' Abel said out loud.

Abel ran the Richmond hotel during the last weeks of that year with rigid control of his staff and prices and only just managed to keep his head above water. He couldn't help wondering what was happening to the other ten hotels in the group, but he didn't have the time to find out and it was no longer his responsibility anyway.

17

On 4 January 1930 Abel Rosnovski arrived in Boston. He took a taxi from the station to Kane and Cabot and was a few minutes early. He sat in the reception room, which was larger and more ornate than any bedroom in the Chicago Richmond. He started reading the *Wall Street Journal*. 1930 was going to be a better year, the paper was trying to assure him. He doubted it. A prim, middle-aged woman entered the room.

'Mr. Kane will see you now, Mr. Rosnovski.'

Abel rose and followed her down a long corridor into a small oak-panelled room with a large leather-topped desk, behind which sat a tall, good-looking man who must, Abel thought, have been about the same age as himself. His eyes were as blue as Abel's. There was a picture on the wall behind him of an older man, whom the young man behind the desk greatly resembled. I'll bet that's Dad, thought Abel bitterly. You can be sure he'll survive the collapse; banks always seem to win both ways.

'My name is William Kane,' said the young man, rising and extending his hand. 'Please have a seat, Mr. Rosnovski.'

'Thank you,' said Abel.

William stared at the little man in his ill-fitting suit, but also noted the determined eyes.

'Perhaps you will allow me to apprise you of the latest situation as I see it,' continued the blue-eyed young man.

'Of course.'

'Mr. Leroy's tragic and premature death ...' William began, hating the pomposity of his words.

Caused by your callousness, thought Abel.

'... seems to have left you with the immediate responsibility of running the group until the bank is in a position to find a buyer for the hotels. Although one hundred per cent of the shares of the group are now in your name, the property, in the form of eleven hotels, which was held as collateral for the late Mr. Leroy's loan of two million dollars, is legally in our possession. This leaves you with no responsibility at all, and if you wish to disassociate yourself from the entire operation, we will naturally understand.'

An insulting thing to suggest, thought William, but it has to be said.

The sort of thing a banker would expect a man to do, walk away from something the moment any problem arose, thought Abel.

William Kane continued. 'Until the two million debt to the bank is cleared I fear we must consider the estate of the late Mr. Leroy insolvent. We at the bank appreciate your personal involvement with the group, and we have done nothing about disposing of the hotels until we had the opportunity to speak to you in person. We thought it possible you might know of a party interested in the purchase of the property, as the buildings, the land and the business are obviously a valuable asset.'

'But not valuable enough for you to back me,' said Abel.

He ran his hand wearily through his thick, dark hair. 'How long will you give me to find a buyer?'

William hesitated for a moment when he saw the silver band around Abel Rosnovski's wrist. He had seen that band somewhere before, but he couldn't think where. 'Thirty days. You must understand that the bank is carrying the day-to-day losses on ten of the eleven hotels. Only the Chicago Richmond is making a small profit.'

'If you would give me the time and backing, Mr. Kane, I could turn all the hotels into profitable concerns. I know I could,' said Abel. 'Just give me the chance to prove I can do it, sir.' Abel found the last word sticking in his throat.

'So Mr. Leroy assured the bank when he came to see us last autumn,' said William. 'But these are hard times. There's no telling if the hotel trade will pick up, and we are not hoteliers, Mr. Rosnovski; we are bankers.'

Abel was beginning to lose his temper with the smoothly dressed banker – 'young': Davis had been right. 'They'll be hard times all right for the hotel staff,' he said. 'What will they do if you sell off the roofs from over their heads? What do you imagine will happen to them?'

'I am afraid they are not our responsibility, Mr. Rosnovski. I must act in the bank's best interests.'

'In *your* own best interests, don't you mean, Mr. Kane?' said Abel hotly.

The young man flushed. 'That is an unjust remark, Mr. Rosnovski, and I would greatly resent it if I did not understand what you are going through.'

'Too bad you didn't wheel out your understanding in time for Davis Leroy,' said Abel. 'He could have used it. You killed him, Mr. Kane, just as surely as if you had pushed him out of that window yourself, you and your simon-pure colleagues, sitting here on your backsides while we sweat our guts out to be sure you can take a rake-off when times are good and tread on people when times are bad.'

William, too, was becoming angry. Unlike Abel Rosnovski, he did not show it. 'This line of discussion is getting us nowhere, Mr. Rosnovski. I must warn you that if you are unable to find a purchaser for the group within thirty days, I shall have no choice but to put the hotels up for auction on the open market.'

'You'll be advising me to ask another bank for a loan next,' said Abel sarcastically. 'You *know* my record, and you won't back me, so where the hell do you expect me to go from here?'

'I'm afraid I have no idea,' replied William. 'That's entirely up to you. My board's instructions are simply to wind up the account as quickly as possible, and that is what I intend to do. Perhaps you would be kind enough to contact me no later than 4 February, and let me know whether you have had any success in finding a buyer. Good day, Mr. Rosnovski.'

William rose from behind the desk, and again offered his hand. This time Abel ignored it and went to the door.

'I thought after our phone conversation, Mr. Kane, you might feel embarrassed enough to offer a helping hand. I was wrong. You're just a bastard through and through, so when you go to bed at night, Mr. Kane, be sure to think about me. When you wake up in the morning, think about me again, because I'll never cease thinking about my plans for you.'

William stood frowning at the closed door. The silver band still bothered him – where had he seen it before?

His secretary returned. 'What a dreadful little man,' she said.

'No, not really,' replied William. 'He thinks we killed his business partner, and now we are disbanding his company without any thought for his employees, not to mention himself, when he had actually proved to be very capable. Mr. Rosnovski was remarkably polite in the circumstances, and I must confess I was almost sorry the board felt unable to back him.' He looked up at his secretary.

'Get me Mr. Cohen on the phone.'

18

Abel arrived back in Chicago on the morning of the following day, still preoccupied and furious with his treatment at the hands of William Kane. He didn't catch exactly what the boy was shouting at the corner news-stand as he hailed a cab and climbed into the back seat.

'The Richmond Hotel, please.'

'Are you from the newspapers?' asked the cab driver as he moved out on to State Street.

'No, what made you ask that?' said Abel.

'Oh, only because you asked for the Richmond. All the reporters are there today.'

Abel couldn't remember any functions scheduled for the Richmond that would attract the press.

The cab driver continued. 'If you're not a newspaper man, maybe I should take you to another hotel.'

'Why?' asked Abel, even more puzzled.

'Well, you won't have a very good night's sleep if you're booked in there. The Richmond has been burned to the ground.'

As the cab turned the corner of the block, Abel was faced head on with the smouldering shell of the Richmond Hotel. Police cars, fire engines, charred wood and water flooding the street. He stepped out of the cab and stared at the scorched remains of the flagship of Davis Leroy's group.

The Pole is wise when the damage is done, thought Abel, as he clenched his fist and started banging on his lame leg. He felt no pain – there was nothing left to feel.

'You bastards,' he shouted aloud. 'I've been lower than this before, and I'll still beat every one of you. Germans, Russians, Turks, that bastard Kane, and now this. Everyone. I'll beat you all. Nobody kills Abel Rosnovski.'

The assistant manager saw Abel gesticulating by the cab

and ran over to him. Abel forced himself to be calm.

'Did all the staff and guests get out of the hotel safely?' he asked.

'Yes, thank God. The hotel was nearly empty, so getting everyone out was no great problem. There were one or two minor injuries and burns, and they are being dealt with at the hospital, but there's nothing for you to worry about.'

'Good, at least that's a relief. Thank God the hotel was well insured, over a million if I remember. We may yet be able to turn this disaster to our advantage.'

'Not if what they are suggesting in the late papers is true.'

'What do you mean?' asked Abel.

'I'd rather you read it for yourself, boss,' the assistant manager replied.

Abel walked over to the news-stand and paid the boy two cents for the latest edition of the *Chicago Tribune*. The banner headline told it all.

RICHMOND HOTEL BLAZE – ARSON SUSPECTED

Abel shook his head incredulously and re-read the headline.

'Can anything else happen?' he muttered.

'Got yourself a problem?' the newsboy asked.

'A little one,' said Abel and returned to his assistant manager.

'Who's in charge of the police enquiry?'

'That officer over there leaning on the police car,' said the assistant manager, pointing to a tall, spare man who was going prematurely bald. 'His name is Lieutenant O'Malley.'

'It would be,' said Abel. 'Now you get the staff into the annex, and I'll see them all there at ten o'clock tomorrow morning. If anybody wants me before then, I'll be staying at the Stevens until I get this thing sorted out.'

'Will do, boss.'

Abel walked over to Lieutenant O'Malley and introduced himself.

The tall, thin policeman stooped slightly to shake hands with Abel.

'Ah, the long lost ex-manager has returned to his charred remains.'

'I don't find that funny, officer,' said Abel.

'I'm sorry,' he said. 'It isn't funny. It's been a long night. Let's go and have a drink.'

The policeman took Abel by the elbow and guided him across Michigan Avenue to a café on the corner. Lieutenant O'Malley ordered two milk shakes.

Abel laughed when the white, frothy mixture was put in front of him. Since he had never had a youth, it was his first milk shake.

'I know. It's funny, everybody in this city breaks the law drinking bourbon and beer,' said the detective, 'so someone has to play the game straight. In any case, Prohibition isn't going to last for ever, and then my troubles will begin, because the gangsters are going to discover I really do like milk shakes.'

Abel laughed for a second time.

'Now to your problems, Mr. Rosnovski. First I have to tell you, I don't think you have a snowball's chance in hell of picking up the insurance on that hotel. The fire experts have been going over the remains of the building with a fine tooth-comb and they found the place was soaked in kerosene. No attempt to even disguise it. There were traces of the stuff all over the basement. One match and the building must have gone up like a Roman candle.'

'Do you have any idea who is responsible?' asked Abel.

'Let me ask the questions. Do you have any idea who might bear a grudge against the hotel or you personally?'

Abel grunted. 'About fifty people, Lieutenant. I cleared out a real can of worms when I first arrived here. I can give you a list, if you think it might help.'

'I think it might, but the way people are talking out there, I may not need it,' said the lieutenant. 'But if you pick up any definite information, let me know, Mr. Rosnovski. You let me know, because I warn you, you have enemies out there.' He pointed into the milling street.

'What do you mean?' asked Abel.

'Someone is saying you did it, because you lost everything in the crash and needed the insurance money.'

Abel leaped off his stool.

'Calm down, calm down. I know you were in Boston all day and, more important, you have a reputation in Chicago for building hotels up, not burning them down. But someone did burn the Richmond down, and you can bet your ass I'm going to find out who. So let's leave it at that for the moment.' He swivelled off his own stool. 'The milk shake's on me, Mr. Rosnovski. I'll expect a favour from you sometime in the future.'

He smiled at the girl at the cash desk, admiring her ankles and cursing the new fashion for long skirts. He handed her fifty cents. 'Keep the change, honey.'

'A big thank you,' the girl replied.

'Nobody appreciates me,' said the lieutenant.

Abel laughed for a third time, which he would not have thought possible an hour before.

'By the way,' the lieutenant continued as they reached the door, 'the insurance people are looking for you. I can't remember the name of the guy, but I guess he'll find you. Don't hit him. If he feels you were involved, who can blame him? Keep in touch, Mr. Rosnovski. I'll be wanting to talk to you again.'

Abel watched the lieutenant vanish into the crowd of spectators and then walked slowly over to the Stevens Hotel and booked himself in for the night. The desk clerk, who had already checked most of the Richmond's guests in, couldn't suppress a smile at the idea of booking the manager in, too. Once in his room, Abel sat down and wrote a formal letter to Mr. William Kane, giving him whatever details of the fire he could supply, and telling him that he intended to use his unexpected freedom to make a round of the other hotels in the group. Abel could see no point in hanging around in Chicago warming himself in the Richmond embers, in the vain hope that someone would come along and bail him out.

After a first class breakfast at the Stevens the next morning – it always made Abel feel good to be in a well-run hotel

– he walked over to see Curtis Fenton at the Continental Trust Bank and apprise him of Kane and Cabot's attitude – or to be more accurate of William Kane's attitude. Although Abel thought the request was pointless, he added that he was looking for a buyer for the Richmond Group at two million dollars.

'That fire isn't going to help us, but I'll see what I can do,' said Fenton, sounding far more positive than Abel had expected. 'At the time you bought twenty-five per cent of the group's shares from Miss Leroy I told you that I thought the hotels were a valuable asset and that you'd make a good deal. Despite the crash I see no reason to change my mind about that, Mr. Rosnovski. I've watched you running your own hotel for nearly two years now, and I'd back you if the decision were left to me personally, but I fear my bank would never agree to support the Richmond Group. We've seen the financial results for far too long to have any faith in the group's future, and that fire was the last straw, if you'll pardon the expression. Nevertheless, I do have some outside contacts and I'll see if they can do anything to help. You probably have more admirers in this city than you realise, Mr. Rosnovski.'

After Lieutenant O'Malley's comments Abel had wondered if he had any friends left in Chicago at all. He thanked Curtis Fenton, returned to the front desk of the bank and asked a teller for five thousand dollars in cash from the hotel account. He spent the rest of the morning in the Richmond annex. He gave every member of his staff two week's wages and told them they could stay on at the annex for at least a month or until they had found new jobs. He then returned to the Stevens, packed the new clothes he'd had to buy as a result of the fire and prepared for a tour of the rest of the Richmond hotels.

He drove the Buick he'd bought just before the stock market crash down south first and started with the St. Louis Richmond. The trip around all the hotels in the group took nearly a month and although they were run down and, without exception, losing money, none of them was, in Abel's view, a hopeless case. They all had good locations; some were even the best-placed in the city. Old man Leroy must have been a shrewder man than his son, thought Abel. He checked every hotel insurance policy carefully; no problems there. When he finally reached the Dallas Richmond, he was certain of only one thing : that anyone who managed to buy the group for two million would be making himself a good deal. He wished that he could be given the chance, as he knew exactly what had to be done to make the group profitable.

On his return to Chicago, nearly four weeks later, he checked into the Stevens, where there were several messages awaiting him. Lieutenant O'Malley wished to contact him, so did William Kane, Curtis Fenton, and a Mr. Henry Osborne.

Abel started with the law, and after a short phone conversation with O'Malley, agreed to meet him at the café on Michigan Avenue. Abel sat on a high stool, with his back to the counter, staring at the charred shell of the Richmond Hotel, while he waited for the lieutenant. O'Malley was a few minutes late, but he did not bother to apologise as he took the next stool and swivelled around to face Abel.

'Why do we keep meeting like this?' asked Abel.

'You owe me a favour,' said the lieutenant, 'and nobody in Chicago gets away with owing O'Malley a milk shake.'

Abel ordered two, one giant, one regular.

'What did you find out?' asked Abel as he passed the detective two red and white striped straws.

'The boys from the fire department were right, it was arson okay. We've arrested a guy called Desmond Pacey, who turns out to be the old manager at the Richmond. That was in your time, right?'

'I'm afraid it was,' said Abel.

'Why do you say that?' asked the lieutenant.

'I had Pacey fired for embezzling the hotel's receipts. He said he'd get even with me if it was the last thing he did. I didn't pay any attention. I've had too many threats in my life, Lieutenant, to take any one of them that seriously, especially from a creature like Pacey.'

'Well, I have to tell you that we've taken him seriously, and so have the insurance people, because I'm told they're not paying out one penny until it's proved there was no collusion between you and Pacey over the fire.'

'That's all I need at the moment,' said Abel. 'How can you be so certain it's Pacey?'

'We traced him to the casualty ward at the local hospital, the same day as the fire. A routine check asking the hospital to let us know if anyone had come in that day with severe burns. By chance – which is so often the case in police work since we're not all born to be Sherlock Holmes – a sergeant's wife who had been a waitress at the Richmond told us that he used to be the manager. Even I can put those two and two's together. The guy came clean pretty quick, didn't seem that interested in being caught, only in pulling off what he called his own St. Valentine's Day Massacre. Until a few moments ago I wasn't sure what the object of that revenge was, but I sure know now; though I'm not too surprised. So that just about wraps the case up, Mr. Rosnovski.'

The lieutenant sucked on his straw until the gurgling sound convinced him he had drained the last drop.

'Have another milk shake?'

'No, I'll give this one a miss. I've got a heavy day ahead of me.' He got down from the stool. 'Good luck, Mr. Rosnovski. If you can prove to the insurance boys you had no involvement with Pacey, you'll get your money. I'll do everything I can to help when the case reaches court. Keep in touch.'

Abel watched him disappear through the door. He gave the waitress a dollar and walked out on to the pavement staring into space, a space where the Richmond Hotel had been less than a month ago. Then he turned and strolled back to the Stevens deep in thought.

There was another message from Henry Osborne, still leaving no clue as to who he was. There was only one way to find out. Abel called Osborne, who turned out to be a claims inspector with the Great Western Casualty Insurance Company with whom the hotel had their policy. Abel made an appointment to see the man at noon. He then called William Kane in Boston and gave him a report on the hotels he had visited in the group.

'And may I say again, Mr. Kane, that I could turn those hotels' losses into profits if your bank would give me the time and the backing. What I did in Chicago I know I can do for the rest of the group.'

'Possibly you could, Mr. Rosnovski, but I fear it will not be with Kane and Cabot's money. May I remind you that you have only five days left in which to find a backer. Good day, sir.'

'Ivy League snob,' said Abel into the deaf telephone. 'I'm not classy enough for your money, am I? Some day, you bastard...'

The next item on Abel's agenda was the insurance man. Henry Osborne turned out to be a tall good-looking man with dark eyes and a mop of dark hair just turning grey. Abel found his easy manner congenial. Osborne had little to add to Lieutenant O'Malley's story. The Great Western Casualty Insurance Company had no intention of paying any part of the claim, while the police were pressing for a charge of arson against Desmond Pacey, and until it was proved that Abel himself was in no way involved. Henry Osborne seemed to be very understanding about the whole problem.

'Has the Richmond group enough money to rebuild the hotel?' asked Osborne.

'Not a red cent,' said Abel. 'The rest of the group is mortgaged up to the hilt, and the bank is pressing me to sell.'

'Why you?' said Osborne.

Abel explained how he had come to own the group's shares without actually owning the hotels. Henry Osborne was somewhat surprised.

'Surely the bank can see for themselves how well you ran that hotel? Every businessman in Chicago is aware you were the first manager ever to make a profit for Davis Leroy. I know the banks are going through hard times, but even they ought to know when to make an exception for their own good.'

'Not this bank.'

'Continental Trust?' said Osborne. 'I've always found old Curtis Fenton a bit starchy but amenable enough.'

'It's not Continental. The hotels are owned by a Boston bank called Kane and Cabot.'

Henry Osborne went white and sat down.

'Are you all right?' asked Abel.

'Yes, I'm fine.'

'You don't by any chance know Kane and Cabot?'

'Off the record?' said Henry Osborne.

'Sure.'

'Yes, my company had to deal with them once before in the past.' He seemed to be hesitating. 'And we ended up having to take them to court.'

'Why?'

'I can't reveal the details. A messy business. Let's just say one of the directors was not totally honest and open with us.'

'Which one?' asked Abel.

'Which one did you have to deal with?' Osborne enquired.

'A man named William Kane.'

Osborne seemed to hesitate again. 'Be careful,' he said. 'He's the world's meanest son of a bitch. I can give you all the low-down on him if you want it, but that would be strictly between us.'

'I certainly owe him no favours,' said Abel. 'I may well be in touch with you, Mr. Osborne. I have a score to settle with young Mr. Kane for his treatment of Davis Leroy.'

'Well, you can count on me to help in any way I can if William Kane is involved,' said Henry Osborne, rising from behind his desk. 'But that is strictly between us. And if the court shows that Desmond Pacey burnt the Richmond and no one else was involved, the company will pay up the same day. Then perhaps we can do some more business with all your other hotels.'

'Perhaps,' said Abel.

He walked back to the Stevens and decided to have lunch and find out for himself how well they ran their main dining room. There was another message at the desk for him. A Mr. David Maxton wondered if Abel was free to join him for lunch at one.

'David Maxton,' Abel said out loud, and the receptionist looked up. 'Why do I know that name?' he asked the staring girl.

'He owns this hotel, Mr. Rosnovski.'

'Ah, yes. Please let Mr. Maxton know that I shall be delighted to have lunch with him.' Abel glanced at his watch. 'And would you tell him that I may be a few minutes late?'

'Certainly, sir,' said the girl.

Abel went quickly up to his room and changed into a new white shirt, wondering what David Maxton could possibly want.

The dining room was already packed when Abel arrived. The head waiter showed him to a private table in an alcove where the owner of the Stevens was sitting alone. He rose to greet Abel.

'Abel Rosnovski, sir.'

'Yes, I know you,' said Maxton, 'or, to be more accurate, I know you by reputation. Do sit down and let's order lunch.'

Abel was compelled to admire the Stevens. The food and the service were every bit as good as those at the Plaza. If he were to have the best hotel in Chicago, he knew it would have to be better than this one.

The head waiter reappeared with the menus. Abel studied his carefully, politely declined a first course and selected the beef, the quickest way to tell if a restaurant is dealing with the right butcher. David Maxton did not look at his menu and simply ordered the salmon. The head waiter scurried away.

'You must be wondering why I invited you to join me for lunch, Mr. Rosnovski.'

'I assumed,' said Abel, laughing, 'you were going to ask me to take over the Stevens for you.'

'You're absolutely right, Mr. Rosnovski.'

It was Maxton's turn to laugh. Abel was speechless. Even the arrival of their waiter wheeling a trolley of the finest beef did not help. The carver waited. Maxton squeezed some lemon over his salmon and continued.

'My manager is due to retire in five months' time after twenty-two years of loyal service and the assistant manager is also due for retirement very soon afterwards, so I'm looking for a new broom.'

'Place looks pretty clean to me,' said Abel.

'I'm always willing to improve, Mr. Rosnovski. Never be satisfied with standing still,' said Maxton. 'I've been watching your activities carefully. It wasn't until you took the Richmond over that it could even be classified as a hotel. It was a huge flop house before that. In another two or three years, you would have been a rival to the Stevens if some fool hadn't burned the place down before you were given the chance.'

'Potatoes, sir?'

Abel looked up at a very attractive junior waitress. She smiled at him.

'No, thank you,' he said to her. 'Well, I'm very flattered, Mr. Maxton, both by your comments and the offer.'

'I think you'd be happy here, Mr. Rosnovski. The Stevens is a well-run hotel, and I would be willing to start you off at fifty dollars a week and two per cent of the profits. You could start as soon as you like.'

'I'll need a few days to think over your generous offer, Mr. Maxton,' said Abel, 'but I confess I am very tempted. Nevertheless, I still have a few problems left over from the Richmond.'

'String beans, sir?' The same waitress, and the same smile.

The face looked familiar. Abel felt sure he had seen her somewhere before. Perhaps she had once worked at the Richmond.

'Yes, please.'

He watched her walk away. There was something about her.

'Why don't you stay on at the hotel as my guest for a few days,' Maxton asked, 'and see how we run the place? It may help you make your decision.'

'That won't be necessary, Mr. Maxton. After only one day as a guest here I knew how well the hotel is run. My problem is that I own the Richmond Group.'

David Maxton's face registered surprise. 'I had no idea,' he said. 'I assumed old Davis Leroy's daughter would now be the owner.'

'It's a long story,' said Abel, and he explained to Maxton how he had come into the ownership of the group's stock.

'The problem is a simple one, Mr. Maxton. What I really want to do is find the two million dollars myself and build that group up into something worthwhile. Something that would even give you a good run for your money.'

'I see,' said Maxton, looking quizzically at his empty plate. A waiter removed it.

'Would you like some coffee?' The same waitress. The same familiar look. It was beginning to worry Abel.

'And you say Curtis Fenton of Continental Trust is looking for a buyer on your behalf?'

'Yes, he has been for nearly a month,' said Abel. 'In fact, I shall know later this afternoon if they've had any success, but I'm not optimistic.'

'Well, that's most interesting. I had no idea the Richmond Group was looking for a buyer. Will you please keep me informed either way?'

'Certainly,' said Abel.

'How much more time is the Boston bank giving you to find the two million?'

'Only a few more days, so it won't be long before I can let you know my decision.'

'Thank you,' said Maxton. 'It's been a pleasure to meet you, Mr. Rosnovski. I feel sure I'd enjoy working with you.' He shook Abel warmly by the hand.

'Thank you, sir,' said Abel.

The waitress smiled at him again as he passed her on his way out of the dining room. When Abel reached the head waiter, he stopped and enquired what her name was.

'I'm sorry, sir, we're not allowed to give the names of any

of our staff to the customers; it's strictly against company policy. If you have a complaint, perhaps you'd be kind enough to make it to me, sir.'

'No complaint,' said Abel. 'On the contrary, an excellent lunch.'

With a job offer under his belt, Abel felt more confident about facing Curtis Fenton. He was certain the banker would not have found a buyer, but none the less, he strolled over to the Continental Trust with a spring in his heels. He liked the idea of being the manager of the best hotel in Chicago. Perhaps he could make it the best hotel in America. As soon as he arrived at the bank, he was ushered directly into Curtis Fenton's office. The tall, thin banker – did he wear the same suit every day or did he have three identical ones? – offered Abel a seat, and a large smile appeared across his usually solemn face.

'Mr. Rosnovski, how good to see you again. If you had come this morning, I would have had no news to give you, but only a few moments ago I received a call from an interested party.'

Abel's heart leaped with surprise and pleasure. He was silent for a few moments and then he said, 'Can you tell me who it is?'

'I'm afraid not. The party concerned has given me strict instructions that he must remain anonymous, as the transaction would be a private investment in some potential conflict with his own business.'

'David Maxton,' Abel murmured under his breath. 'God bless him.'

Curtis Fenton did not respond and continued. 'Well, as I said, Mr. Rosnovski, I'm not in a position . . .'

'Quite, quite,' said Abel. 'How long do you think it will be before you are in a position to let me know the gentleman's decision one way or the other?'

'I can't be sure at the moment, but I may have more news for you by Monday, so if you happen to be passing by . . .'

'Happen to be passing by?' said Abel. 'You're discussing my whole life.'

'Then perhaps we should make a firm appointment for Monday morning.'

As Abel walked down Michigan Avenue on his way back to the Stevens it started to drizzle. He found himself humming 'Singing in the Rain'. He took the lift up to his room and called William Kane to ask for an extension until the following Monday, telling him he hoped to have found a buyer. Kane seemed reluctant but eventually agreed.

'Bastard,' Abel repeated several times as he put the phone back on the hook. 'Just give me a little time, Kane. You'll live to regret killing Davis Leroy.'

Abel sat on the end of his bed, his fingers tapping on the rail, wondering how he could pass the time waiting for Monday. He wandered down into the hotel lobby. There she was again, the waitress who had served him at lunch, now on tea duty in the Tropical Garden. Abel's curiosity got the better of him, and he went over and took a seat at the far side of the room. She came up.

'Good afternoon, sir,' she said. 'Would you like some tea?' The same familiar smile again.

'We know each other, don't we?' said Abel.

'Yes, we do, Wladek.'

Abel cringed at the sound of the name and reddened slightly, remembering how the short fair hair had been long and smooth and the veiled eyes had been so inviting. 'Zaphia, we came to America on the same ship. Of course, you went to Chicago. What are you doing here?'

'I work here, as you can see. Would you like some tea, sir?' Her Polish accent warmed Abel.

'Have dinner with me tonight,' he said.

'I can't, Wladek. We're not allowed to go out with the customers. If we do, we automatically lose our jobs.'

'I'm not a customer,' said Abel. 'I'm an old friend.'

'Who was going to come and visit me in Chicago as soon as he had settled down, and when you did come you didn't even remember I was here,' said Zaphia.

'I know, I know. Forgive me. Zaphia, have dinner with me tonight. Just this once,' said Abel.

'Just this once,' she repeated.

'Meet me at Brundage's at seven o'clock. Would that suit you?'

Zaphia flushed at the name. It was probably the most expensive restaurant in Chicago, and she would have been nervous to be there as a waitress, let alone as a customer.

'No, let's go somewhere less grand, Wladek.'

'Where?' said Abel.

'Do you know The Sausage on the corner of Forty-third?'

'No, I don't,' he admitted, 'but I'll find it. Seven o'clock.'

'Seven o'clock, Wladek. That will be lovely. By the way, do you want any tea?'

'No, I think I'll skip it,' said Abel.

She smiled and walked away. He sat watching her serve tea for several minutes. She was much prettier than he had remembered her being. Perhaps killing time until Monday wasn't going to be so bad after all.

The Sausage brought back all of Abel's worst memories of his first days in America. He sipped a cold ginger beer while he waited for Zaphia and watched with professional disapproval as the waiters slapped the food around. He was unable to decide which looked worse: the service or the food. Zaphia was nearly twenty minutes late by the time she appeared in the doorway, as smart as a band-box in a crisp yellow dress that looked as if it had been recently taken up a few inches to conform with the latest fashion, but still revealed how appealing her formerly slight body had become. Her grey eyes searched the tables for Wladek, and her pink cheeks reddened as she became conscious of other men's eyes upon her.

'Good evening, Wladek,' she said in Polish.

Abel rose and offered her his chair near the fire. 'I am so glad you could make it,' he replied in English.

She looked perplexed for a moment, then, in English, she said, 'I'm sorry I'm late.'

'Oh, I hadn't noticed. Would you like something to drink, Zaphia?'

'No, thank you.'

Neither of them spoke for a moment, and then they both tried to talk at once.

'I'd forgotten how pretty...' said Abel.

'How have you...' said Zaphia.

She smiled shyly, and Abel wanted to touch her. He remembered so well experiencing the same reaction the first time he had ever seen her, over eight years before.

'How's George?' she asked.

'I haven't seen him for over two years,' replied Abel, suddenly feeling guilty. 'I've been stuck working in a hotel here in Chicago, and then...'

'I know,' said Zaphia. 'Somebody burnt the place down.'

'Why didn't you ever come over and say hello?' asked Abel.

'I didn't think you'd remember, Wladek, and I was right.'

'Then how did you ever recognise me?' said Abel. 'I've put on so much weight.'

'The silver band,' she said simply.

Abel looked down at his wrist and laughed. 'I have a lot to thank my band for, and now I can add that it has brought us back together.'

She avoided his eyes. 'What are you doing now that you no longer have a hotel to run?'

'I'm looking for a job,' said Abel, not wanting to intimidate her with the fact that he'd been offered the chance to manage the Stevens.

'There's a big job coming up at the Stevens. My boyfriend told me.'

'Your boyfriend told you?' said Abel, repeating each painful word.

'Yes,' she said, 'the hotel will soon be looking for a new assistant manager. Why don't you apply for the job? I'm sure you'd have a good chance of getting it, Wladek. I always knew you would be a success in America.'

'I might well apply,' Abel said. 'It was kind of you to think of me. Why doesn't your boyfriend apply?'

'Oh, no, he's far too junior to be considered; he's only a waiter in the dining room with me.'

Suddenly Abel wanted to change places with him.

'Shall we have dinner?' he said.

'I'm not used to eating out,' Zaphia said. She gazed at the menu in indecision. Abel, suddenly aware she still could not read English, ordered for them both.

She ate with relish and was full of praise for the indifferent food. Abel found her uncritical enthusiasm a tonic after the bored sophistication of Melanie. They exchanged the history of their lives in America. Zaphia had started in domestic service and progressed to being a waitress at the Stevens where she had stayed put for six years. Abel told her of all his experiences until finally she glanced at his watch.

'Look at the time, Wladek,' she said, 'it's past eleven and I'm on first breakfast call at six tomorrow.'

Abel had not noticed the four hours pass. He would have happily sat there talking to her for the rest of the night, soothed by her admiration which she confessed so artlessly.

'May I see you again, Zaphia?' he asked, as they walked back to the Stevens arm-in-arm.

'If you want to, Wladek.'

They stopped at the servants' entrance at the back of the hotel.

'This is where I go in,' she said. 'If you were to become the assistant manager, Wladek, you'd be allowed to go in by the front entrance.'

'Would you mind calling me Abel?' he asked her.

'Abel?' she said, as if she were trying the name on like a new glove. 'But your name is Wladek.'

'It was, but it isn't any longer. My name is Abel Rosnovski.'

'Abel's a funny name, but it suits you,' she said. 'Thank you for dinner, Abel. It was lovely to see you again. Good night.'

'Good night, Zaphia,' he said, and she was gone.

He watched her disappear through the servants' entrance, then he walked slowly around the block and into the hotel by the front entrance. Suddenly – and not for the first time in his life – he felt very lonely.

Abel spent the weekend thinking about Zaphia and the images associated with her – the stench of the steerage quarters, the confused queues of immigrants on Ellis Island and, above all, their brief but passionate encounter in the lifeboat. He took all his meals in the hotel restaurant to be near her and to study the boyfriend. He came to the conclusion that he must be the young, pimply one. He thought he had pimples, he hoped he had pimples, yes, he did have pimples. He was, regrettably, the best-looking boy among the waiters, pimples notwithstanding.

Abel wanted to take Zaphia out on Saturday, but she was working all day. Nevertheless, he managed to accompany her to church on Sunday morning and listened with mingled nostalgia and exasperation to the Polish priest intoning the unforgotten words of the Mass. It was the first time Abel had been in a church since his days at the castle in Poland. At that time he had yet to see or endure the cruelty which now made it impossible for him to believe in any benevolent deity. His reward for attending church came when Zaphia allowed him to hold her hand as they walked back to the hotel together.

'Have you thought any more about the position at the Stevens?' she enquired.

'I'll know first thing tomorrow morning what their final decision is.'

'Oh, I'm so glad, Abel. I'm sure you would make a very good assistant manager.'

'Thank you,' said Abel, realising they had been talking at cross purposes.

'Would you like to have supper with my cousins tonight?' Zaphia asked. 'I always spend Sunday evening with them.'

'Yes, I'd like that very much.'

Zaphia's cousins lived right near The Sausage itself, in the heart of the city. They were very impressed when she arrived with a Polish friend who drove a new Buick. The family, as Zaphia called them, consisted of two sisters, Katya and Janina, and Katya's husband, Janek. Abel presented the sisters with a bunch of roses and then sat down and answered, in fluent Polish, all their questions about his future prospects. Zaphia was obviously embarrassed, but Abel knew the same would be required of any new boyfriend in any Polish-American household. He made an effort to play down his progress since his early days in the butcher shop as he was conscious of Janek's envious eyes never leaving him. Katya served a simple Polish meal of pierogi and bigos which Abel would have eaten with a good deal more relish fifteen years earlier. He gave Janek up as a bad job and concentrated on making the sisters approve of him. It looked as though they did. Perhaps they also approved of the pimply youth. No, they couldn't; he wasn't even Polish – or maybe he was – Abel didn't even know his name and had never heard him speak.

On the way back to the Stevens, Zaphia asked, with a flash of coquettishness he remembered, if it was considered safe to drive a motor car and hold a lady's hand at the same time. Abel laughed and put his hand back on the steering wheel for the rest of the drive back to the hotel.

'Will you have time to see me tomorrow?' he asked.

'I hope so, Abel,' she said. 'Perhaps by then you'll be my boss. Good luck anyway.'

He smiled to himself as he watched her go through the back door, wondering how she would feel if she knew the real consequences of tomorrow's decision. He did not move until she disappeared through the service entrance.

'Assistant manager,' he said, laughing out loud as he climbed into bed, wondering what Curtis Fenton's news would bring in the morning, trying to put Zaphia out of his mind as he threw his pillow on the floor.

He woke a few minutes before five the next day. The room was still dark when he called for the early edition of the *Tribune*, and went through the motions of reading the financial section. He was dressed and ready for breakfast when the restaurant opened at seven o'clock. Zaphia was not serving in the main dining room that morning, but the pimply boyfriend was, which Abel took to be a bad omen. After breakfast he returned to his room; had he but known, only five minutes before Zaphia came on duty. He checked his tie in the mirror for the twentieth time and once again looked at his watch. He estimated that if he walked very slowly, he would arrive at the bank as the doors were opening. In fact, he arrived five minutes early and walked once around the block, staring aimlessly into store windows at expensive jewellery and new radios and hand-tailored suits. Would he ever be able to afford clothes like that? he wondered. He arrived back at the bank at four minutes past nine.

'Mr. Fenton is not free at the moment. Can you come back in half an hour or would you prefer to wait?' the secretary asked.

'I'll come back,' said Abel, not wishing to appear overanxious.

It was the longest thirty minutes he could remember since he'd been in Chicago. He had studied every shop window on La Salle Street, even the women's clothes, which made him think happily of Zaphia.

On his return to Continental Trust the secretary informed him, 'Mr. Fenton will see you now.'

Abel walked into the bank manager's office, feeling his hands sweating.

'Good morning, Mr. Rosnovski. Do have a seat.'

Curtis Fenton took a file out of his desk which Abel could see had 'Confidential' written across the cover.

'Now,' he began, 'I hope you will find my news is to your liking. The principal concerned is willing to go ahead with the purchase of the hotels on what I can only describe as favourable terms.'

'God Almighty,' said Abel.

Curtis Fenton pretended not to hear him and continued. 'In fact, most favourable terms. He will be responsible for putting up the full two million required to clear Mr. Leroy's debt while at the same time he will form a new company with you in which the shares will be split sixty per cent to him and forty per cent to you. Your forty per cent is therefore valued at eight hundred thousand dollars, which will be treated as a loan to you by the new company, a loan which will be made for a term not to exceed ten years, at four per cent, which can be paid off from the company profits at the same rate. That is to say, if the company were to make in any one year a profit of one hundred thousand dollars, forty thousand of that profit would be set against your eight hundred thousand debt, plus the four per cent interest. If you clear the loan of eight hundred thousand in under ten years you will be given the one-time option to buy the remaining sixty per cent of the company for a further three million dollars. This would give my client a first-class return on his investment and you the opportunity to own the Richmond Group outright.

'In addition to this, you will receive a salary of three thousand dollars per annum, and your position as president of the group will give you complete day-to-day control of the hotels. You will be asked to refer back to me only on matters concerning finance. I have been entrusted with the task of reporting direct to your principal, and he has asked me to represent his interests on the board of the new Richmond Group. I have been happy to comply with this stipulation. My client does not wish to be involved personally. As I have said before, there might be a conflict of professional interests for him in this transaction, which I am sure you will thoroughly understand. He also insists that you will at no time make any attempt to discover his identity. He will give you fourteen days to consider his terms, on which there can be no negotiation, as he considers, and I must agree with him, that he is striking a more than fair bargain.'

Abel could not speak.

'Pray do say something, Mr. Rosnovski.'

'I don't need fourteen days to make a decision,' said Abel finally. 'I accept your client's terms. Please thank him and tell him I will certainly respect his request for anonymity.'

'That's splendid,' said Curtis Fenton, permitting himself a wry smile. 'Now, a few small points. The accounts for all the hotels in the group will be placed with Continental Trust affiliates, and the main account will be here in this office under my direct control. I will, in turn, receive one thousand dollars a year as a director of the new company.'

'I'm glad you're going to get something out of the deal,' said Abel.

'I beg your pardon?' said the banker.

'I'll be pleased to be working with you, Mr. Fenton.'

'Your principal has also placed two hundred and fifty thousand dollars on deposit with the bank to be used as the day-to-day finance for the running of the hotels during the next few months. This will also be regarded as a loan at four per cent. You are to advise me if this amount turns out to be insufficient for your needs. I consider it would enhance your reputation with my client if you found the two hundred and fifty thousand to be sufficient.'

'I shall bear that in mind,' said Abel, solemnly trying to imitate the banker's locution.

Curtis Fenton opened a desk drawer and produced a large Cuban cigar.

'Do you smoke?'

'Yes,' said Abel, who had never smoked a cigar before in his life.

He coughed himself down La Salle Street all the way back to the Stevens. David Maxton was standing proprietorially in the foyer of the hotel as Abel arrived. Abel stubbed out his half-finished cigar with some relief and walked over to him.

'Mr. Rosnovski, you look a happy man this morning.'

'I am, sir, and I am only sorry that I will not be working for you as the manager of this hotel.'

'Then so am I, Mr. Rosnovski, but frankly the news doesn't surprise me.'

'Thank you for everything,' said Abel, injecting as much feeling as he could into the little phrase and the look with which he accompanied it.

He left David Maxton and went into the dining room in search of Zaphia, but she had already gone off duty. Abel took the lift to his room, re-lit the cigar, took a cautious puff, and called Kane and Cabot. A secretary put him through to William Kane.

'Mr. Kane, I have found it possible to raise the money required for me to take over ownership of the Richmond Group. A Mr. Curtis Fenton of Continental Trust will be in touch with you later today to provide you with the details. There will therefore be no necessity to place the hotels for sale on the open market.'

There was a short pause. Abel thought with satisfaction how galling his news must be to William Kane.

'Thank you for keeping me informed, Mr. Rosnovski. May I say how delighted I am that you found someone to back you? I wish you every success for the future.'

'Which is more than I wish you, Mr. Kane.'

Abel put the phone down, lay on his bed and thought about that future.

'One day,' he promised the ceiling, 'I am going to buy your goddam bank and make you want to jump out of a hotel bedroom on the twelfth floor.' He picked up the phone again and asked the girl on the switchboard to get him Mr. Henry Osborne at Great Western Casualty.

19

William put the telephone back on the hook, more amused than annoyed by Abel Rosnovski's pugnacious approach. He was sorry that he had been unable to persuade the bank to support the little Pole who believed so strongly that he could pull the Richmond Group through. He fulfilled his remaining responsibilities by informing the financial committee that Abel Rosnovski had found a backer, preparing the legal documents for the take-over of the hotels, and then finally closing the bank's file on the Richmond Group.

William was delighted when Matthew arrived in Boston a few days later to take up his position as manager of the bank's investment department. Charles Lester made no secret of the fact that any professional expertise gained in a rival establishment could do the boy no harm in his long-term preparation to be chairman of Lester's. William's work load was instantly halved but his time became even more fully occupied. He found himself dragged, protesting in mock horror, on to tennis courts and into swimming pools at every available free moment; only Matthew's suggestion of a ski trip to Vermont brought a determined 'No' from William, but the sudden activity at least served to somewhat alleviate his loneliness and impatience to be with Kate.

Matthew was frankly incredulous. 'I must meet the woman who can make William Kane daydream at a board meeting which is discussing whether the bank should buy more gold.'

'Wait till you see her, Matthew. I think you'll agree she's a better investment than gold.'

'I believe you. I just don't want to be the one to tell Susan. She still thinks you're the only man in the world.'

William laughed. It had never crossed his mind.

The little pile of letters from Kate, which had been growing weekly, lay in the locked drawer of William's bureau in the Red House. He read them over again and again and soon knew them all virtually by heart. At last the one he had been waiting for came, appropriately dated.

> Buckhurst Park
> 14 February 1930

Dearest William,

Finally I have packed up, sold off, given away or otherwise disposed of everything left here and I shall be coming up to Boston in a tea chest on the nineteenth. I am almost frightened at the thought of seeing you again. What if this whole marvellous enchantment bursts like a bubble in the cold of a winter on the Eastern seaboard? Dear God, I hope not. I can't be sure how I would have gotten through these lonely months but for you.

> With love,
> Kate

The night before Kate was due to arrive, William promised himself that he would not rush her into anything that either of them might later regret. It was impossible for him to assess to what extent her feelings had developed in a transient state of mind engendered by her husband's death, as he told Matthew.

'Stop being so pathetic,' said Matthew. 'You're in love, and you may as well face the fact.'

When he first spotted Kate at the station, William almost abandoned his cautious intentions there and then in the joy of watching that simple smile light up her face. He pushed towards her through the throng of travellers and clasped her so firmly in his arms that she could barely breathe.

'Welcome home, Kate.'

William was about to kiss her when she drew away. He was a little surprised.

'William, I don't think you've met my parents.'

That night William dined with Kate's family and then saw her every day that he could escape from the bank's problems and Matthew's tennis racquet, even if only for a couple of hours. After Matthew had met Kate for the first time, he offered William all his gold shares in exchange for one Kate.

'I never undersell,' replied William.

'Then I insist you tell me,' demanded Matthew, 'where you find someone as valuable as Kate?'

'In the liquidation department, where else?' replied William.

'Turn her into an asset, William, quickly, because if you don't, you can be sure I will.'

Kane and Cabot's net loss from the 1929 crash came out at over seven million dollars, which turned out to be about average for a bank their size. Many not much smaller banks had gone under, and William found himself conducting a sustained holding operation through 1930 which kept him under constant pressure.

When Franklin D. Roosevelt was elected President of the

United States on a ticket of relief, recovery and reform, William feared that the New Deal would have little to offer Kane and Cabot. Business picked up very slowly, and William found himself planning only tentatively for expansion.

Meanwhile Tony Simmons, still running the London office, had broadened the scope of its activities and made a respectable profit for Kane and Cabot during his first two years. His results looked all the better against those of William, who had barely been able to break even during the same period.

Late in 1932, Alan Lloyd recalled Tony Simmons to Boston to make a full report to the board on the bank's activities in London. No sooner had Simmons reappeared than he announced his intention of running for the chairmanship when Alan Lloyd retired in fifteen months' time. William was completely taken by surprise, for he had dismissed Simmons' chances when he had disappeared to London under a small cloud. It seemed to William unfair that that cloud had been dispelled, not by Simmons' acuity, but simply by dint of the fact that the English economy had some bright spots and was a little less paralysed than American business during the same period.

Tony Simmons returned to London for a further successful year and addressed the first board meeting, after his return, in a blaze of glory, with the announcement that the final third year's figures for the London office would show a profit of over a million dollars, a new record. William had to announce a considerably smaller profit for the same period. The abruptness of Tony Simmons' return to favour left William with only a few months in which to persuade the board that they should support him before his opponent's momentum became unstoppable.

Kate listened for hours to William's problems, occasionally offering an understanding comment, a sympathetic reply or chastising him for being over dramatic. Matthew, acting as William's eyes and ears, reported that the voting would fall, as far as was ascertainable, fifty-fifty, split between those who considered that William was too young to hold such a responsible post and those who still held Tony Simmons to blame for the extent of the bank's losses in 1929. It seemed that most of the non-executive members of the board, who had not worked directly with William, would be more influenced by the age difference between the two contenders than any of the single factors. Again and again Matthew heard: 'William's time will come.' Once, tentatively, he played the role of Satan the tempter to William: 'With your holdings in the bank, William, you could remove the entire board, replace them with men of your own choosing and get yourself elected chairman.'

William was only too aware of that route to the top, but he had already dismissed such tactics without needing seriously to consider them; he wished to become chairman solely on his own merits. That was after all, the way his father had achieved the position and it was nothing less than Kate would expect of him.

On 2 January 1934 Alan Lloyd circulated to every member the notice of a board meeting that would be held on his sixty-fifth birthday, its sole purpose being to elect his successor. As the day for the crucial vote drew nearer, Matthew found himself carrying the investment department almost single-handed, and Kate found herself feeding them both while they went over the latest state of his campaign again and again. Matthew did not complain once about the extra work load that was placed on him while William spent hours planning his bid to capture the chair. William, conscious that Matthew had nothing to gain by his success, as he would one day take over his father's bank in New York – a far bigger proposition than Kane and Cabot – hoped a time might come when he could offer Matthew the same unselfish support.

It was to come sooner than he imagined.

When Alan Lloyd's sixty-fifth birthday was celebrated, all seventeen members of the board were present. The meeting was opened by the chairman, who made a farewell speech of only fourteen minutes, which William thought would never come to an end. Tony Simmons was nervously tapping the yellow legal pad in front of him with his pen, occasionally looking up at William. Neither was listening to Alan's speech. At last Alan sat down, to loud applause, or as loud as is appropriate to sixteen Boston bankers. When the clapping died away, Alan Lloyd rose for the last time as chairman of Kane and Cabot.

'And now, gentlemen, we must elect my successor. The board is presented with two outstanding candidates, the director of our overseas division, Mr. Anthony Simmons, and the director of the American investment department, Mr. William Kane. They are both well known to you, gentlemen, and I have no intention of speaking in detail on their respective merits. Instead I have asked each candidate to address the board on how he would see the future of Kane and Cabot were he to be elected chairman.'

William rose first, as had been agreed between the two contestants the night before on the toss of a coin, and addressed the board for twenty minutes, explaining in detail that it would be his ambition to move into new fields where the bank had not previously ventured. In particular he wanted to broaden the bank's base and to get out of a depressed New England, moving close to the centre of banking which he believed was now in New York. He even mentioned the possibility of opening a holding company which might specialise in commercial banking, at which the heads of some of the older board members shook in disbelief. He wanted the bank to consider more expansion, to challenge the new generation of financiers now leading America, and to see Kane and Cabot enter the second half of the twentieth century as one of the largest financial institutions in the United States. When he sat down, he was satisfied by the murmurs of approbation; his speech had, on the whole, been well received by the board.

When Tony Simmons rose he took a far more conservative line: the bank should consolidate its position for the next few years, moving only into carefully selected areas and sticking to the traditional modes of banking that had given Kane and Cabot the reputation they currently enjoyed. He had learnt his lesson during the crash and his main concern, he added – to laughter – was to be certain that Kane and Cabot did enter the second half of the twentieth century at all. Tony spoke prudently and with an authority that William was aware he was too young to match. When Tony sat down, William had no way of knowing in whose favour the board might swing, though he still believed that the majority would be more inclined to opt for expansion rather than standing still.

Alan Lloyd informed the other directors that neither he nor the two contestants intended to vote. The fourteen voting members received their little ballots, which they duly filled in and passed back to Alan who, acting as teller, began to count slowly. William found he could not look up from his doodle-covered pad which also bore the imprint of his sweating hand firmly upon it. When Alan had completed the task of counting, a hush came over the room and he announced six votes for Kane, six votes for Simmons, with two abstentions. Whispered conversation broke out among the board members, and Alan called for order. William took a deep and audible breath in the silence that followed.

Alan Lloyd paused and then said, 'I feel that the appropirate course of action in the circumstances is to have a second vote. If any member who abstained on the first ballot finds himself able to support a candidate on this occasion, that might give one of the contestants an overall majority.'

The little slips were passed out again. William could not bear even to watch the process this time. While members wrote their choices, he listened to the steel-nibbed pens scratching across the voting papers. Once again the ballots were returned to Alan Lloyd. Once again he opened them slowly one by one, and this time he called out the names as he read them.

William Kane.
Anthony Simmons, Anthony Simmons, Anthony Simmons.
Three votes to one for Tony Simmons.
William Kane, William Kane.
Anthony Simmons.

William Kane, William Kane, William Kane. Six to four for William.

Anthony Simmons, Anthony Simmons.

William Kane.

Seven votes to six in favour of William.

It seemed to William, holding his breath, to take Alan Lloyd a lifetime to open the final voting slip.

'Anthony Simmons,' he declared. 'The vote is seven all, gentlemen.'

William knew that Alan Lloyd would now be obliged to cast the deciding vote, and although he had never told anyone whom he supported for the chair, William had always assumed that if the vote came to a deadlock, Alan would back him against Tony Simmons.

'As the voting has twice resulted in a dead heat, and since I assume that no member of the board is likely to change his mind, I must cast my vote for the candidate whom I feel should succeed me as chairman of Kane and Cabot. I know none of you will envy my position, but I have no alternative except to stand by my own judgment and back the man I feel should be the next chairman of the bank.

'That man is Tony Simmons.'

William could not believe the words he heard and Tony Simmons looked almost as shocked. He rose from his seat opposite William to a round of applause, changed places with Alan Lloyd at the head of the table and addressed Kane and Cabot for the first time as the bank's new chairman. He thanked the board for its support and praised William for never having used his strong financial and familial position to try and influence the vote. He invited William to be vice-chairman of the board and suggested that Matthew Lester should replace Alan Lloyd as a director; both suggestions received unanimous support.

William sat staring at the portrait of his father, acutely conscious of having failed him.

20

Abel stubbed out the Corona for a second time and swore that he would not light another cigar until he had cleared the two million dollars that he needed for complete control of the Richmond Group. This was no time for big cigars, with the Dow-Jones index at its lowest point in history and long soup lines in every major city in America. He gazed at the ceiling and considered his priorities. First, he needed to salvage the best of the staff from the Richmond Chicago.

He climbed off the bed, put on his jacket and went over to the hotel annex, where most of those who had not found employment since the fire were still living. Abel re-employed everyone whom he trusted, giving all those who were willing to leave Chicago work in one of the remaining ten hotels. He made his position very clear that in a period of record unemployment their jobs were secure only as long as the hotels started to show a profit. He believed all the other hotels in the group were being run as dishonestly as the old Chicago Richmond had been; he wanted that changed – and changed quickly. His three assistant managers were each put in charge of one hotel each, the Dallas Richmond, the Cincinnati Richmond and the St. Louis Richmond. He appointed new assistant managers for the remaining seven hotels in Houston, Mobile, Charleston, Atlanta, Memphis, New Orleans and Louisville. The original Leroy hotels had all been situated in the South and Mid-West including the Chicago Richmond, the only one Davis Leroy had been responsible for building himself. It took Abel another three weeks to get the old Chicago staff settled into their new hotels.

Abel decided to set up his own headquarters in the Richmond annex and to open a small restaurant on the ground floor. It made sense to be near his backer and his banker rather than to settle in one of the hotels in the South. Moreover, Zaphia was in Chicago, and Abel felt with certainty that given a little time she would drop the pimply youth and fall in love with him. She was the only woman he had ever known with whom he felt self-assured. When Abel was about to leave for New York to recruit more specialised staff, he exacted a promise from her that she would no longer see the pimply boyfriend.

'Still pimply,' said Abel to himself, 'but no longer the boyfriend.'

The night before his departure they slept together for the first time. She was soft, plump, giggly and delicious.

Abel's attentive care and gentle expertise took Zaphia by surprise.

'How many girls have there been since the *Black Arrow*?' she teased.

'None that I really cared about,' he replied.

'Enough of them to forget *me*,' she added.

'I never forgot you,' he said untruthfully, leaning over to kiss her, convinced it was the only way to stop the conversation.

When Abel arrived in New York, the first thing he did was to look up George, whom he found out of work in a garret on East Third Street. He had forgotten what those houses could be like when shared by twenty families. The smell of stale food in every room, toilets that didn't flush and beds that were slept in by three different people every twenty-four hours. The bakery, it seemed, had been closed down, and George's uncle had had to find employment at a large mill on the outskirts of New York which could not take on George as well. George leaped at the chance to join Abel and the Richmond Group – in any capacity.

Abel recruited three new employees: a pastry chef, a comptroller and a head waiter before he and George travelled back to Chicago to set up base in the Richmond annex. Abel was pleased with the outcome of his trip. Most hotels on the East coast had cut their staff to a bare minimum which had made it easy to pick up experienced people, one of them from the Plaza itself.

In early March Abel and George set out for a tour of the remaining hotels in the group. Abel asked Zaphia to join them on the trip, even offering her the chance to work in any of the hotels she chose, but she would not budge from Chicago, the only American territory familiar to her. As a compromise she went to live in Abel's rooms at the Richmond annex while he was away. George, who had acquired middle-class morals along with his American citizenship and Catholic upbringing, urged the advantages of matrimony on Abel, who, lonely in one impersonal hotel room after another, was a ready listener.

It came as no surprise to Abel to find that the other hotels were still being badly, and in some cases dishonestly run, but high national unemployment encouraged most of the staff to welcome his arrival as the saviour of the group's fortunes. Abel did not find it necessary to fire staff in the grand manner he adopted when he had first arrived in Chicago. Most of those who knew of his reputation and feared his methods had already left. Some heads had to fall and they inevitably were attached to the necks of those people who had worked with the Richmond Group for a considerable time and were unable to change their unorthodox ways merely because Davis Leroy was dead. In several cases, Abel found a move of personnel from one hotel to another engendered a new attitude. By the end of his first year as chairman, the Richmond Group was operating with only half the staff they had employed in the past and showed a net loss of only a little over one hundred thousand dollars. The turnover among the senior staff was very low; Abel's confidence in the future of the group was infectious.

Abel set himself the target of breaking even in 1932. He felt the only way he could achieve such a rapid improvement in profitability was to let every manager in the group take the responsibility for his own hotel with a share in the profits, much in the way that Davis Leroy had treated him when he had first come to the Chicago Richmond.

Abel moved from hotel to hotel, never letting up, and never staying in one particular place for more than three weeks at a time. He did not allow anyone, other than the faithful George, his surrogate eyes and ears in Chicago, to know at which hotel he might arrive next. For months he broke this exhausting routine only to visit Zaphia or Curtis Fenton.

After a full assessment of the group's financial position Abel had to make some more unpleasant decisions. The most drastic was to close temporarily the two hotels, in Mobile and Charleston, which were losing so much money that he felt they would become a hopeless drain on the rest of the finances. The staff at the other hotels watched the axe fall and worked even harder. Every time he arrived back at his little office in the Richmond annex in Chicago there would be a clutch of memos demanding immediate attention – burst pipes in washrooms, cockroaches in kitchens, flashes of temperament in dining rooms, and the inevitable dissatisfied customer who was threatening a law suit.

Henry Osborne re-entered Abel's life with a welcome offer of a settlement of $750,000 from Great Western Casualty, who could find no evidence to implicate Abel with Desmond Pacey in the fire at the Chicago Richmond. Lieutenant O'Malley's evidence had proved very helpful on that point. Abel realised he owed him more than a milk shake. Abel was happy to settle at what he considered was a fair price but Osborne suggested to him that he should hold out for a larger amount and give him a percentage of the difference. Abel, whose shortcomings had never included peculation, regarded him somewhat warily after that: if Osborne could so readily be disloyal to his own company, there was little doubt that he would have no qualms about ditching Abel when it suited him.

In the spring of 1932 Abel was somewhat surprised to receive a friendly letter from Melanie Leroy, more welcoming in tone than she had ever been in person. He was flattered, even excited, and called her to make a date for dinner at the

Stevens, a decision he regretted the moment they entered the dining room for there, looking unsophisticated, tired and vulnerable, was Zaphia. Melanie, in contrast, looked ravishing in a long mint green dress which indicated quite clearly what her body would be like if the mint were removed. Her eyes, perhaps taking courage from the dress, seemed greener and more captivating than ever.

'It's wonderful to see you looking so well, Abel,' she remarked as she took her seat in the centre of the dining room, 'and of course, everybody knows how well you are doing with the Richmond Group.'

'The Baron Group,' said Abel.

She flushed slightly. 'I didn't realise you had changed the name.'

'Yes, I changed it last year,' lied Abel. He had in fact decided at that very moment that every hotel in the group would be known as a Baron hotel. He wondered why he had never thought of it before.

'An appropriate name,' said Melanie, smiling.

Zaphia set the mushroom soup in front of Melanie with a little thud that spoke volumes to Abel. Some of the soup nearly ended up on the mint green dress.

'You're not working?' asked Abel, scribbling the words 'Baron Group' on the back of his menu.

'No, not at the moment, but things are looking up a little. A woman with a liberal arts degree in this city has to sit around and wait for every man to be employed before she can hope to find a job.'

'If you ever want to work for the Baron Group,' said Abel, emphasising the name slightly, 'you only have to let me know.'

'No, no,' said Melanie. 'I'm just fine.'

She quickly changed the subject to music and the theatre. Talking to her was an unaccustomed and pleasant challenge for Abel; she teased him, but with intelligence. She made him feel more confident in her company than he had ever been in the past. The dinner went on until well after eleven, and when everyone had left the dining room, including

Zaphia, ominously red-eyed, he drove Melanie home to her flat, and this time she did invite him in for a drink. He sat on the end of a sofa while she poured him a prohibited whisky and put a record on the phonograph.

'I can't stay long,' Abel said. 'Busy day tomorrow.'

'That's what *I'm* supposed to say, Abel. Don't rush away, this evening has been such fun, just like old times.'

She sat down beside him, her dress rising above her knees. Not quite like old times, he thought. Incredible legs. He made no attempt to resist when she edged towards him. In moments he found he was kissing her – or was she kissing him? His hands wandered on to those legs and then to her breasts, and this time she seemed to respond willingly. It was she who eventually led him by the hand to her bedroom, folded back the coverlet neatly, turned around and asked him to unzip her. Abel obliged in nervous disbelief and switched out the light before he undressed. After that it was easy for him to put Joyce's careful tuition into practice. Melanie certainly was not lacking in experience herself; Abel had never enjoyed the act of making love more and fell into a deep contented sleep.

In the morning Melanie made him breakfast and attended to his every need, right up to the moment he had to leave.

'I shall watch the Baron Group with renewed interest,' she told him, 'not that anyone doubts that it's going to be a huge success.'

'Thank you,' said Abel, 'for breakfast and a memorable night.'

'I was hoping we'd be seeing each other again sometime soon,' Melanie added.

'I'd like that,' said Abel.

She kissed him on the cheek as a wife might who was seeing her husband off to work.

'I wonder what kind of woman you'll end up marrying,' she asked innocently as she helped Abel on with his overcoat.

He looked at her and smiled sweetly. 'When I make that

decision, Melanie, you can be certain I shall only be influenced by your views.'

'What do you mean?' asked Melanie, coyly.

'Simply that I shall heed your advice,' replied Abel, as he reached the front door, 'and be sure to find myself a nice Polish girl who will marry me.'

Abel and Zaphia were married a month later. Zaphia's cousin, Janek, gave her away and George was the best man. The reception was held at the Stevens and the drinking and dancing went on far into the night. By tradition, each man paid a token sum to dance with Zaphia, and George perspired as he battled round the room, photographing the guests in every possible permutation and combination. After a midnight supper of barszcz, pierogi and bigos downed with wine, brandy and Danzig vodka, Abel and Zaphia were allowed to retire to the bridal suite, with many a wink from the men and tears from the women.

Abel was pleasantly surprised to be told by Curtis Fenton the next morning that the bill for his reception at the Stevens had been covered by Mr. Maxton and was to be treated as a wedding gift. He used the money he had saved for the reception as a down payment on a little house on Rigg Street.

For the first time in his life he possessed a home of his own.

21

In February of 1934 William decided to take a month's holiday in England before making any firm decision about his future; he even considered resigning from the board, but Matthew convinced him that that was not the course of action his father would have taken in the same circumstances. Matthew appeared to take his friend's defeat even harder than William himself. Twice in the following week he came into the bank with the obvious signs of a hangover and left important work unfinished. William decided to let these incidents pass without comment and invited Matthew to join him and Kate for dinner that night. Matthew declined, claiming that he had a backload of work on which to catch up. William would not have given the refusal a second thought if Matthew had not been dining at the Ritz Carlton that night with an attractive woman who William could have sworn was married to one of Kane and Cabot's departmental managers. Kate said nothing, except that Matthew did not look very well.

William, preoccupied with his impending departure for Europe, took less notice of his friend's strange behaviour than he might otherwise have done. At the last moment William couldn't face a month in England alone and asked Kate to accompany him. To his surprise and delight she agreed.

William and Kate sailed to England on the *Mauretania* in separate cabins. Once they had settled into the Ritz, in separate rooms, even on separate floors, William reported to the London branch of Kane and Cabot in Lombard Street and fulfilled the ostensible purpose of his trip to England by reviewing the bank's European activities. Morale was high and Tony Simmons had evidently been a well-liked manager; there was little for William to do but murmur his approval.

He and Kate spent a glorious two weeks together in London, Hampshire and Lincolnshire, looking at some land William had acquired a few months previously, over twelve thousand acres in all. The financial return from farming land is never high but, as William explained to Kate, 'It will always be there if things ever go sour again in America.'

A few days before they were due to travel back to the United States, Kate decided she wanted to see Oxford, and William agreed to drive her down early the next morning. He hired a new Morris, a car he had never driven before. In the university city, they spent the day wandering around the colleges: Magdalen, superb against the river; Christchurch, grandiose but cloisterless; and Merton where they just sat on the grass and dreamed.

'Can't sit on the grass, sir,' said the voice of a college porter.

They laughed and walked hand-in-hand like undergraduates by the side of the Cherwell watching eight Matthews straining to push a boat along as fast as possible. William could no longer imagine a life separated in any part from Kate.

They started back for London in mid-afternoon, and when they reached Henley-on-Thames, they stopped to have tea at the Bell Inn overlooking the river. After scones and a large pot of strong English tea (Kate was adventuresome and drank it with only milk, but William added hot water to dilute it), Kate suggested that they should start back before it was too dark to see the countryside, but when William had re-inserted the crank into the Morris, despite strenuous effort he could not get the engine to turn over. Finally he gave up, and since it was getting late, decided that they would have to spend the night in Henley. He returned to the front desk of the Bell Inn and requested two rooms.

'Sorry, sir, I have only one double room left,' said the receptionist.

William hesitated for a moment and then said, 'We'll take it.'

Kate looked somewhat surprised but said nothing; the receptionist looked suspiciously at her.

'Mr. and Mrs. . . . er . . . ?'

'Mr. and Mrs. William Kane,' said William firmly. 'We'll be back later.'

'Shall I put your cases in the room, sir?' the hall porter asked.

'We don't have any,' William replied, smiling.

'I see, sir.'

A bewildered Kate followed William up Henley High Street until he came to a halt in front of the parish church.

'May I ask what we're doing, William?' she asked.

'Something I should have done a long time ago, my darling.'

Kate asked no more questions. When they entered the

315

vestry. William found a verger piling up some hymn books.

'Where can I find the vicar?' demanded William.

The verger straightened himself to his full height and regarded him pityingly.

'In the vicarage, I dare say.'

'Where's the vicarage?' asked William, trying again.

'You're an American gentleman, aren't you, sir.'

'Yes,' said William, becoming impatient.

'The vicarage will be next door to the church, won't it?' said the verger.

'I suppose it will,' said William. 'Can you stay here for the next ten minutes?'

'Why should I want to do that, sir?'

William extracted a large, white, five-pound note from his inside pocket and unfolded it. 'Make it fifteen minutes to be on the safe side, please.'

The verger studied the five pounds carefully and said: 'Americans. Yes, sir.'

William left the man with his five-pound note and hurried Kate out of the church. As they passed the main notice board in the porch, he read: 'The Vicar of this Parish is The Reverend Simon Tukesbury, M.A. (Cantab),' and next to that pronouncement, hanging by one nail, was an appeal notice concerning a new roof for the church. Every penny towards the necessary five hundred pounds will help, declared the notice, not very boldly. William hastened up the path to the vicarage with Kate a few yards behind, and a smiling, pink-cheeked, plump lady answered his sharp knock on the door.

'Mrs. Tukesbury?' enquired William.

'Yes.' She smiled.

'May I speak to your husband?'

'He's having his tea at the moment. Would it be possible for you to come back a little later?'

'I'm afraid it's rather urgent,' William insisted.

Kate had caught up with him but said nothing.

'Well, in that case I suppose you'd better come in.'

The vicarage was early sixteenth century and the small stone front room was warmed by a welcoming log fire. The vicar, a tall spare man who was eating wafer-thin cucumber sandwiches, rose to greet them.

'Good afternoon, Mr. . . . ?'

'Kane, sir, William Kane.'

'What can I do for you, Mr. Kane?'

'Kate and I,' said William, 'want to get married.'

'Oh, how nice,' said Mrs. Tukesbury.

'Yes indeed,' said the vicar. 'Are you a member of this parish? I don't seem to remember . . .'

No, sir, I'm an American. I worship at St. Paul's in Boston.'

'Massachusetts, I presume, not Lincolnshire,' said the Reverend Simon Tukesbury.

'Yes,' said William, forgetting for a moment that there was a Boston in England.

'Splendid,' said the vicar, his hands raised as if he were about to give a blessing. 'And what date did you have in mind for this union of souls?'

'Now, sir.'

'Now, sir?' said the startled vicar. 'I am not aware of the traditions in the United States that surround the solemn, holy and binding institution of marriage, Mr. Kane, though one reads of some very strange incidents involving some of your compatriots from California. I do, however, consider it nothing less than my duty to inform you that those customs have not yet become acceptable in Henley-on-Thames. In England, sir, you must reside for a full calendar month in any parish before you can be married and the banns must be posted on three separate occasions, unless there are very special and extenuating circumstances. Even did such circumstances exist, I would have to seek the bishop's dispensation, and I couldn't do that in under three days,' Mr. Tukesbury added, his hands now firmly at his side.

Kate spoke for the first time. 'How much do you still need for the church's new roof?'

'Ah, the roof. Now there is a sad story, but I won't

embark upon its history at this moment, early eleventh century you know...'

'How much do you need?' asked William, tightening his grasp on Kate's hand.

'We are hoping to raise five hundred pounds. We've done commendably well so far; we've reached twenty-seven pounds four shillings and four pence in only seven weeks.'

'No, no dear,' said Mrs. Tukesbury. 'You haven't counted the one pound eleven shillings and two pence I made from my "Bring and Buy" sale last week.'

'Indeed I haven't, my dear. How inconsiderate of me to overlook your personal contribution. That will make altogether...' began Mr. Tukesbury as he tried to add the figures in his head, raising his eyes towards heaven for inspiration.

William took his wallet from his inside pocket, wrote out a cheque for five hundred pounds and silently proffered it to Mr. Tukesbury.

'I...ah, I see there are special circumstances, Mr. Kane,' said the surprised vicar. The tone changed. 'Has either of you ever been married before?'

'Yes,' said Kate. 'My husband was killed in a plane crash over four years ago.'

'Oh, how terrible,' said Mrs. Tukesbury. 'I am so sorry, I didn't...'

'Shush, my dear,' said the man of God, now more interested in the church roof than in his wife's sentiments. 'And you, sir?'

'I have never been married before,' said William.

'I shall have to telephone the bishop.' Clutching William's cheque, the Reverend disappeared into the next room.

Mrs. Tukesbury invited them to sit down and offered them the plate of cucumber sandwiches. She chatted on, but William and Kate did not hear her words as they sat gazing at each other.

The vicar returned three cucumber sandwiches later.

'It's highly irregular, highly irregular, but the bishop has agreed, on the condition, Mr. Kane, that you will confirm everything at the American Embassy tomorrow morning and then with your own bishop at St. Paul's in Boston . . . Massachusetts immediately you return home.'

He was still clutching the five-hundred-pound cheque.

'All we need now is two witnesses,' he continued. 'My wife can act as one, and we must hope that the verger is still around, so that he can be the other.'

'He is still around, I assure you,' said William.

'How can you be so certain, Mr. Kane?'

'He cost me one per cent.'

'One per cent?' said Mr. Tukesbury, baffled.

'One per cent of your church roof,' said William.

The vicar ushered William, Kate and his wife down the little path back to the church and blinked at the waiting verger.

'Indeed, I perceive that Mr. Sprogget has remained on duty . . . He has never done so for me; you obviously have a way with you, Mr. Kane.'

Simon Tukesbury put on his vestments and a surplice while the verger stared at the scene in disbelief.

William turned to Kate and kissed her gently. 'I know it's a damn silly question in the circumstances, but will you marry me?'

'Good God,' said Mr. Tukesbury, who had never blasphemed in the fifty-seven years of his mortal existence. 'You mean you haven't even asked her?'

Fifteen minutes later, Mr. and Mrs. William Kane left the parish church of Henley-on-Thames, Oxfordshire. Mrs. Tukesbury had had to supply the ring at the last moment, which she twitched from a curtain in the vestry. It was a perfect fit. The Reverend Simon Tukesbury had a new roof, and Mr. Sprogget a yarn to tell them down at The Green Man where he spent most of his five pounds.

Outside the church the vicar handed William a piece of paper. 'Two shillings and sixpence, please.'

'What for?' asked William.

'Your marriage certificate, Mr. Kane.'

'You should have taken up banking, sir,' said William, handing Mr. Tukesbury half a crown.

He walked his bride in blissful silence back down the High Street to the Bell Inn. They had a quiet dinner in the fifteenth-century oak-beamed dining room, and went to bed at a few minutes past nine. As they disappeared up the old wooden staircase to their room, the chief receptionist turned to the hall porter and winked. 'If they're married, I'm the King of England.'

William started to hum 'God Save the King.'

The next morning Mr. and Mrs. Kane had a leisurely breakfast while the car was fixed. (His father would have told him all it needed was a new fan belt.) A young waiter poured them both a coffee.

'Do you like it black or shall I add some milk?' asked William innocently.

An elderly couple smiled benignly at them.

'With milk, please,' said Kate as she reached across and touched William's hand gently.

He smiled back at her, suddenly aware the whole room was now staring at them.

They returned to London in the cool early spring air, travelling through Henley, over the Thames, and then on up through Berkshire and Middlesex into London.

'Did you notice the look the porter gave you this morning, darling?' asked William.

'Yes, I think perhaps we should have shown him our marriage certificate.'

'No, no, you'd have spoilt his whole image of the wanton American woman. The last thing he wants to tell his wife when he returns home tonight is that we were really married.'

When they arrived back at the Ritz in time for lunch, the desk manager was surprised to find William cancelling Kate's room. He was heard to comment later: 'Young Mr. Kane appeared to be such a gentleman. His late and distinguished father would never have behaved in such a way.'

William and Kate took the *Aquitania* back to New York,

having first called at the American embassy in Grosvenor Gardens to inform a consul of their new marital status. The consul gave them a long official form to fill out, charged them one pound, and kept them waiting for well over an hour. The American embassy, it seemed, was not in need of a new roof. William wanted to go to Cartier's in Bond Street and buy a gold wedding ring, but Kate would not hear of it – nothing was going to part her from the precious curtain ring.

William found it difficult to settle down in Boston under his new chairman. The precepts of the New Deal were passing into law with unprecedented rapidity, and William and Tony Simmons found it impossible to agree on whether the implications for investment would be good or bad. Expansion – on one front at least – became unstoppable when Kate announced soon after their return from England that she was pregnant, news which gave her parents and husband great joy. William tried to modify his working hours to suit his new role as a married man but found himself at his desk increasingly often throughout the hot summer evenings. Kate, cool and happy in her flowered maternity smock, methodically supervised the decoration of the nursery of the Red House. William found for the first time in his life that he could leave his work desk and look forward to going home. If he had work left over he just picked up the papers and took them back to the Red House, a pattern to which he adhered throughout their married life.

While Kate and the baby that was due about Christmas time brought William great happiness at home, Matthew was making him increasingly uneasy at work. He had taken to drinking and coming to the office late with no explanations. As the months passed, William found he could no longer rely on his friend's judgment. At first, he said nothing, hoping it was little more than an odd out-of-character reaction – which might quickly pass – to the repeal of Prohibition. But it wasn't, and the problem went from bad to worse. The last straw came one November morning when

Matthew arrived two hours late, obviously suffering from a hangover, and made a simple, unnecessary mistake, selling off an important investment which resulted in a small loss for a client who should have made a handsome profit. William knew the time had come for an unpleasant but necessary head-on confrontation. Matthew admitted his error and apologised regretfully. William was thankful to have the row out of the way and was about to suggest they go to lunch together when his secretary uncharacteristically rushed into his office.

'It's your wife, sir, she's been taken to the hospital.'

'Why?' asked William, puzzled.

'The baby,' said his secretary.

'But it's not due for at least another six weeks,' said William incredulously.

'I know, sir, but Doctor MacKenzie sounded rather anxious, and wanted you to come to the hospital as quickly as possible.'

Matthew, who a moment before had seemed a broken reed, took over and drove William to the hospital. Memories of William's mother's death and her still-born daughter came flooding back to both of them.

'Pray God not Kate,' said Matthew as he drew into the hospital car park.

William did not need to be guided to the Anne Kane Maternity Wing which Kate had officially opened only six months before. He found a nurse standing outside the delivery room who informed him that Doctor MacKenzie was with his wife, and that she had lost a lot of blood. William paced up and down the corridor helplessly, numbly waiting, exactly as he had done years before. The scene was all too familiar. How unimportant being chairman of the bank was compared with losing Kate. When had he last said to her 'I love you'? Matthew sat with William, paced with William, stood with William, but said nothing. There was nothing to be said. William checked his watch each time a nurse ran in or out of the delivery room. Seconds turned into minutes and minutes into hours. Finally Doctor MacKenzie appeared, his forehead shining with little beads of sweat, a surgical mask covering his nose and mouth. William could see no expression on the doctor's face until he removed the white mask, revealing a large smile.

'Congratulations, William, you have a boy, and Kate is just fine.'

'Thank God,' breathed William, clinging on to Matthew.

'Much as I respect the Almighty,' said Doctor MacKenzie, 'I feel I had a little to do with this birth myself.'

William laughed. 'Can I see Kate?'

'No, not right now. I've given her a sedative and she's fallen asleep. She lost rather more blood than was good for her, but she'll be fine by morning. A little weak, perhaps, but well ready to see you. But there's nothing to stop you seeing your son. But don't be surprised by his size; remember he's quite premature.'

The doctor guided William and Matthew down the corridor to a room in which they stared through a pane of glass at a row of six little pink heads in cribs.

'That one,' said Doctor MacKenzie, pointing to the infant that had just arrived.

William stared dubiously at the ugly little face, his vision of a fine, upstanding son receding rapidly.

'Well, I'll say one thing for the little devil,' said Doctor MacKenzie cheerfully, 'he's better looking than you were at that age, and you haven't turned out too badly.'

William laughed out of relief.

'What are you going to call him?'

'Richard Higginson Kane.'

The doctor patted the new father affectionately on the shoulder. 'I hope I live long enough to deliver Richard's first-born.'

William immediately wired the rector of St. Paul's, who put the boy down for a place in 1943, and then the new father and Matthew got thoroughly drunk and were both late arriving at the hospital the next morning to see Kate. William took Matthew for another look at young Richard.

'Ugly little bastard,' said Matthew, 'not at all like his beautiful mother.'

'That's what I thought,' said William.

'Spitting image of you, though.'

William returned to Kate's flower-filled room.

'Do you like your son?' Kate asked her husband. 'He's so like you.'

'I'll hit the next person who says that,' William said. 'He's the ugliest little thing I've ever seen.'

'Oh, no,' said Kate in mock indignation, 'he's beautiful.'

'A face only a mother could love,' said William and hugged his wife.

She clung to him, happy in his happiness.

'What would Grandmother Kane have said about our first-born entering the world after less than eight months of marriage? "I don't wish to appear uncharitable, but anyone born in under fifteen months must be considered of dubious parentage; under nine months definitely unacceptable,"' William mimicked. 'By the way, Kate, I forgot to tell you something before they rushed you into the hospital.'

'What was that?'

'I love you.'

Kate and young Richard had to stay in the hospital for nearly three weeks. Not until after Christmas did Kate fully recover her vitality. Richard, on the other hand, grew like an uncontrolled weed, no one having informed him that he was a Kane, and one was not supposed to do that sort of thing. William became the first male Kane to change a nappy and push a perambulator. Kate was very proud of him, and somewhat surprised. William told Matthew that it was high time he found himself a good woman and settled down.

Matthew laughed defensively. 'You're getting positively middle-aged. I shall be looking for grey hairs next.'

One or two had already appeared during the chairmanship battle. Matthew hadn't noticed.

William was not able to put a finger on exactly when his relationship with Tony Simmons began to deteriorate badly.

Tony would continually veto one policy suggestion after another, and his negative attitude made William seriously consider resignation again. Matthew was not helping matters by returning to his old drinking habits. The period of reform had not lasted more than a few months, and, if anything, he was now drinking more heavily than before and arriving at the bank a few minutes later each morning. William wasn't quite sure how to handle the new situation and found himself continually covering Matthew's work. At the end of each day, William would double-check Matthew's mail and return his unanswered calls.

By the spring of 1936, as investors gained more confidence and depositors returned, William decided the time had come to go tentatively back into the stock market, but Tony vetoed the suggestion in an off-hand, inter-office memorandum to the financial committee. William stormed into Tony's office to ask if his resignation would be welcome.

'Certainly not, William. I merely want you to recognise that it has always been my policy to run this bank in a conservative manner, and that I am not willing to charge headlong back into the market with our investors' money.'

'But we're losing business hand-over-fist to other banks while we sit on the sidelines watching them take advantage of the present situation. Banks which we wouldn't even have considered as rivals ten years ago will soon be overtaking us.'

'Overtaking us in what, William? Not in reputation. Quick profits perhaps, but not reputation.'

'But I'm interested in profits,' said William. 'I consider it a bank's duty to make good returns for its investors, not to mark time in a gentlemanly fashion.'

'I would rather stand still than lose the reputation that this bank built up under your grandfather and father over the better part of half a century.'

'Yes, but both of them were always looking for new opportunities to expand the bank's activities.'

'In good times,' said Tony.

'And in bad,' said William.

'Why are you so upset, William? You still have a free hand in the running of your own department.'

'Like hell I do. You block anything that even suggests enterprise.'

'Let's start being honest with each other, William. One of the reasons I have had to be particularly cautious lately is that Matthew's judgment is no longer reliable.'

'Leave Matthew out of this. It's me you're blocking; I am head of the department.'

'I can't leave Matthew out of it. I wish I could. The final overall responsibility to the board for anyone's actions is mine, and he is the number two man in the bank's most important department.'

'Yes, and therefore my responsibility, because I am the number one man in that department.'

'No, William, it cannot remain your responsibility alone when Matthew comes into the office drunk at eleven o'clock in the morning, no matter how long and close your friendship has been.'

'Don't exaggerate.'

'I am not exaggerating, William. For over a year now this bank has been carrying Matthew Lester, and the only thing that has stopped me mentioning my worries to you before is your close personal relationship with him and his family. I wouldn't be sorry to see him hand in his resignation. A bigger man would have done so long ago, and his friends would have told him so.'

'Never,' said William. 'If he goes, I go.'

'So be it, William,' said Tony. 'My first responsibility is to our investors, not to your old school chums.'

'You'll live to regret that statement, Tony,' said William, as he stormed out of the chairman's office and returned to his own room in a furious temper.

'Where is Mr. Lester?' William demanded as he passed his secretary.

'He's not in yet, sir.'

William looked at his watch, exasperated.

'Tell him I'd like to see him the moment he arrives.'

'Yes, sir.'

William paced up and down his office, cursing. Everything Tony Simmons had said about Matthew was accurate, which only made matters worse. He began to think back to when it had all begun, searching for a simple explanation. His thoughts were interrupted by his secretary.

'Mr. Lester has just arrived, sir.'

Matthew entered the room looking rather sheepish, displaying all the signs of another hangover. He had aged badly in the past year, and his skin had lost its fine, athletic glow. William hardly recognised him as the man who had been his closest friend for nearly twenty years.

'Matthew, where the hell have you been?'

'I overslept,' Matthew replied, uncharacteristically scratching at his face. 'Rather a late night, I'm afraid.'

'You mean you drank too much.'

'No, I didn't have that much. It was a new girlfriend who kept me awake all night. She was insatiable.'

'When will you stop, Matthew? You've slept with nearly every single woman in Boston.'

'Don't exaggerate, William. There must be one or two left; at least I hope so. And then don't forget all the thousands of married ones.'

'It's not funny, Matthew.'

'Oh, come on, William. Give me a break.'

'Give you a break? I've just had Tony Simmons on my back because of you, and what's more I know he's right. You'll jump into bed with anything wearing a skirt, and worse, you're drinking yourself to death. Your judgment has gone to pieces. Why, Matthew? Tell me why. There must be some simple explanation. Up until a year ago you were one of the most reliable men I have ever met in my life. What is it, Matthew? What am I supposed to say to Tony Simmons?'

'Tell Simmons to go to hell and mind his own business.'

'Matthew, be fair, it *is* his business. We are running a bank, not a bordello, and you came here as a director on my personal recommendation.'

'And now I'm not measuring up to your standards, is that what you're saying?'

'No, I'm not saying that.'

'Then what the hell are you saying?'

'Buckle down and do some work for a few weeks. In no time everyone will have forgotten all about it.'

'Is that all you want?'

'Yes,' said William.

'I shall do as you command, O Master,' said Matthew, and he clicked his heels and walked out of the door.

'Oh, hell,' said William.

That afternoon William wanted to go over a client's portfolio with Matthew but nobody seemed to be able to find him. He had not returned to the office after lunch and was not seen again that day. Even the pleasure of putting young Richard to bed in the evening could not distract William from his worries about Matthew. Richard could already say two and William was trying to make him say three, but he insisted on saying 'tree'.

'If you can't say three, Richard, how can you ever hope to be a banker?' William demanded of his son as Kate entered the nursery.

'Perhaps he'll end up doing something worthwhile,' said Kate.

'What's more worthwhile than banking?' William enquired.

'Well, he might be a musician, or a baseball player, or even President of the United States.'

'Of those three I'd prefer him to be a ball player – it's the only one of your suggestions that pays a decent salary,' said William as he tucked Richard into bed.

Richard's last words before sleeping were, 'Tree, Daddy.' William gave in. It wasn't his day.

'You look exhausted, darling. I hope you haven't forgotten that we're having drinks later with Andrew MacKenzie?'

'Hell, Andrew's party had totally slipped my mind. What time is he expecting us?'

'In about an hour.'

'Well, first I'm going to take a long, hot bath.'

'I thought that was a woman's privilege,' said Kate.

'Tonight I need a little pampering. I've had a nerve-racking day.'

'Tony bothering you again?'

'Yes, but I am afraid this time he's in the right. He's been complaining about Matthew's drinking habits. I was only thankful he didn't mention the womanising. It's become impossible to take Matthew to any party nowadays without the eldest daughter, not to mention the occasional wife, having to be locked away for their own safety. Will you run my bath?'

William sat in the tub for more than half an hour, and Kate had to drag him out before he fell asleep. Despite her prompting they arrived at the MacKenzie's twenty-five minutes late, only to find that Matthew, already well on the way to being inebriated, was trying to pick up a congressman's wife. William wanted to intervene, but Kate prevented him from doing so.

'Don't say anything,' she whispered.

'I can't stand here and watch him going to pieces in front of my eyes,' said William. 'He's my closest friend. I have to do something.'

But in the end he took Kate's advice and spent an unhappy evening watching Matthew become progressively drunk. Tony Simmons, from the other side of the room, was glancing pointedly at William, who was relieved at Matthew's early departure, even though it was in the company of the only unattached woman left at the party. Once Matthew had gone William started to relax for the first time that day.

'How is little Richard?' Andrew MacKenzie asked.

'He can't say "three",' said William.

'Might turn out to do something civilised after all,' said Doctor MacKenzie.

'Exactly what I thought,' said Kate. 'What a good idea William: he can be a doctor.'

'Pretty safe,' said Andrew. 'Don't know many doctors who can count past two.'

'Except when they send their bills,' said William.

Andrew laughed. 'Will you have another drink, Kate?'

'No thank you, Andrew. It's high time we went home. If we stay any longer, only Tony Simmons and William will be left, and they can both count past two so we would all have to talk banking the rest of the night.'

'Agreed,' said William. 'Thank you for a lovely party, Andrew. By the way, I must apologise for Matthew's behaviour.'

'Why?' said Doctor MacKenzie.

'Oh, come on, Andrew. Not only was he drunk, but there wasn't a woman in the room who felt safe left alone with him.'

'I might well do the same if I were in his predicament,' said Andrew MacKenzie.

'What makes you say that?' said William. 'You can't approve of his habits just because he's single.'

'No, I don't, but I try to understand them and realise I might be a little irresponsible faced with the same problem.'

'What do you mean?' asked Kate.

'My God,' said Doctor MacKenzie. 'He's your closest friend, and he hasn't told you?'

'Told us what?' they said together.

Dr. MacKenzie stared at them both, a look of disbelief on his face.

'Come into my study.'

William and Kate followed the doctor into a small room, lined almost wall-to-wall with medical books, interspersed only with occasional, sometimes unframed, photographs of student days at Cornell.

'Please have a seat, Kate,' he said. 'William I make no apology for what I am about to say, because I assumed you knew that Matthew was gravely ill, dying, in fact, of Hodgkin's disease. He has known about his condition for over a year.'

William fell back in his chair, for a moment unable to speak. 'Hodgkin's disease?'

'An almost invariably fatal inflammation and enlargement of the lymph nodes,' said the doctor rather formally.

William shook his head incredulously. 'Why didn't he tell me?'

'You've known each other since you were at school together. My guess is he's far too proud to burden anyone else with his problems. He'd rather die in his own way than let anyone realise what he's going through. I have begged him for the last six months to tell his father, and I have certainly broken my professional promise to him by letting you know, but I can't let you go on blaming him for something over which he has absolutely no control.'

'Thank you, Andrew,' said William. 'How can I have been so blind and so stupid?'

'Don't blame yourself,' said Doctor MacKenzie. 'There's no way you could have known.'

'Is there really no hope?' asked William. 'Are there no clinics, no specialists? Money would be no problem...'

'Money can't buy everything, William, and I have consulted the three best men in America, and one in Switzerland. I am afraid they are all in agreement with my diagnosis, and medical science hasn't yet discovered a cure for Hodgkin's disease.'

'How long has he got to live?' asked Kate in a whisper.

'Six months at the outside, more likely three.'

'And I thought I had problems,' said William. He held tightly on to Kate's hand as if it were a lifeline. 'We must be going, Andrew. Thank you for telling us.'

'Help him in any way you can,' said the doctor, 'but for God's sake, be understanding. Let him do what he wants to do. It's Matthew's last few months, not yours. And don't ever let him know I told you.'

William drove Kate home in silence. As soon as they reached the Red House, William called the girl Matthew had left the party with.

'Would it be possible to speak to Matthew Lester?'

'He's not here,' said a rather irritable voice. 'He dragged me off to the In and Out Club, but he was already drunk by the time we got there, and I refused to go in that place with him.' Then she hung up.

The In and Out Club. William had a hazy recollection of having seen the sign swinging from an iron bar but he couldn't remember exactly where the place was. He looked it up in the phone book, drove over to the north side of town and eventually, after questioning a passer-by, he found the club. William knocked on the door. A hatch slid back.

'Are you a member?'

'No,' said William firmly, and passed a ten-dollar note through the grill.

The hatch slid closed, and the door opened. William walked on to the middle of the dance floor, looking slightly incongruous in his three-piece banker's suit. The dancers, twined around each other, swayed incuriously away from him. William's eyes searched the smoke-filled room for Matthew, but he wasn't there. Finally he thought he recognised one of Matthew's many recent casual girlfriends, whom he felt certain he'd seen coming out of his friend's flat early one morning. She was sitting cross-legged in a corner with a sailor. William went over to her.

'Excuse me, miss,' he said.

She looked up but obviously didn't recognise William.

'The lady's with me, so beat it,' said the sailor.

'Have you seen Matthew Lester?'

'Matthew?' said the girl. 'Matthew who?'

'I told you to get lost,' said the sailor, rising to his feet.

'One more word out of you, and I'll knock your block off,' said William.

The sailor had seen anger like that in a man's eyes once before in his life and had nearly lost an eye for his trouble. He sat back down.

'Where is Matthew?'

'I don't know a Matthew, darling.' Now she, too, was frightened.

'Six-feet-two, blond hair, dressed like me, and probably drunk.'

'Oh, you mean Martin. He calls himself Martin here, darling, not Matthew.' She began to relax. 'Now let me see, who did he go off with tonight?' She turned her head towards the bar and shouted at the bartender. 'Terry, who did Martin go out with?'

The bartender removed a dead cigarette butt from the corner of his mouth. 'Jenny,' he said, and put the unlit cigarette back in place.

'Jenny, that's right,' said the girl. 'Now let me see, she's short sessions. Never lets a man stay for more than half an hour, so they should be back soon.'

'Thank you,' said William.

He waited for almost an hour at the bar sipping a scotch with a lot of water, feeling more and more out of place by the minute. Finally, the bartender, the unlit cigarette still in his mouth, gestured to a girl who was coming through the door.

'That's Jenny,' he said. Matthew was not with her.

The bartender waved for Jenny to join them. A slim, short, dark, not unattractive girl, she winked at William and walked towards him swinging her hips.

'Looking for me, darling? Well, I am available, but I charge ten dollars for half an hour.'

'No, I don't want you,' said William.

'Charming,' said Jenny.

'I'm looking for the man who's been with you, Matthew – I mean Martin.'

'Martin, he was too drunk even to get it up with the help of a crane, darling, but he paid his ten dollars, he always does. A real gentleman.'

'Where is he now?' asked William impatiently.

'I don't know, he gave it up as a bad job and started walking home.'

William ran into the street. The cold air hit him, not that he needed to be awakened. He drove his car slowly away from the club, following the route towards Matthew's flat, looking carefully at each person he passed. Some hurried on when they saw his watchful eyes; others tried to engage him in conversation. When he was passing an all-night café, he caught sight of Matthew through the steamy window, weaving his way through the tables with a cup in his hand. William parked the car, went in and sat down beside him. Matthew had slumped on to the table next to a cup of untouched spilt coffee. He was so drunk that he didn't even recognise William.

'Matthew, it's me,' said William, looking at the crumpled man. The tears started to run down his cheeks.

Matthew looked up and spilled some more of his coffee. 'You're crying, old fellow. Lost your girl, have you?'

'No, my closest friend,' said William.

'Ah, they're much harder to come by.'

'I know,' said William.

'I have a good friend,' said Matthew, slurring his words. 'He's always stood by me until we quarrelled for the first time today. My fault though. You see I've let him down rather badly.'

'No you haven't,' said William.

'How can you know?' said Matthew angrily. 'You're not even fit to know him.'

'Let's go home, Matthew.'

'My name is Martin,' said Matthew.

'I'm sorry, Martin, let's go home.'

'No, I want to stay here. There's this girl who may come by later. I think I'm ready for her now.'

'I have some fine old malt whisky at my house,' said William. 'Why don't you join me?'

'Any women at your place?'

'Yes, plenty of them.'

'You're on, I'll come.'

William hoisted Matthew up and put his arm under his shoulder, guiding him slowly through the café towards the door. It was the first time he'd ever realised how heavy Matthew was. As they passed two policemen sitting at the corner of the counter, William heard one say to the other, 'Goddamn fairies.'

He helped Matthew into the car and drove him back to Beacon Hill. Kate was waiting up for them.

'You should have gone to bed, darling.'

'I couldn't sleep,' she replied.

'I'm afraid he's nearly incoherent.'

'Is this the girl you promised me?' said Matthew.

'Yes, she'll take care of you,' said William, and he and Kate helped him up to the guest room and put him on the bed. Kate started to undress him.

'You must undress as well, darling,' he said. 'I've already paid my ten dollars.'

'When you're in bed,' said Kate lightly.

'Why are you looking so sad, beautiful lady?' said Matthew.

'Because I love you,' said Kate, tears beginning to form in her eyes.

'Don't cry,' said Matthew, 'there's nothing to cry about. I'll manage it this time, you'll see.'

When they had undressed Matthew, William covered him with a sheet and a blanket. Kate turned the light out.

'You promised you'd come to bed with me,' said Matthew, drowsily.

She closed the door quietly.

William slept on a chair outside Matthew's room for fear he might wake up in the night and try to leave. Kate woke him in the morning before taking some breakfast into Matthew.

'What am I doing here, Kate?' were Matthew's first words.

'You came back with us after Andrew MacKenzie's party last night,' replied Kate rather feebly.

'No, I didn't. I went to the In and Out with that awful girl, Patricia something or other, who refused to come in with me. God, I feel lousy. Can I have a tomato juice? I don't want to be unsociable, but the last thing I need is breakfast.'

'Of course, Matthew.'

William came in. Matthew looked up at him. They stared at each other in silence.

'You know, don't you?' said Matthew finally.

'Yes,' said William, 'and I've been a fool and I hope you'll forgive me.'

'Don't cry, William. I haven't seen you do that since you were twelve, when Covington was beating you up and I had to drag him off you. Remember? I wonder what Covington is up to now? Probably running a brothel in Tijuana; it's about all he was fit for. Mind you, if Covington is running it, the place will be damned efficient, so lead me to it. Don't cry, William. Grown men don't cry. Nothing can be done. I've seen all the specialists from New York to Los Angeles to Zurich, and there is nothing they can do. Do you mind if I skip the office this morning? I still feel bloody awful. Wake me if I stay too long or if I'm any more trouble, and I'll find my own way home.'

'This is your home,' said William.

Matthew's face changed. 'Will you tell my father, William? I can't face him. You're an only son, too; you understand the problem.'

'Yes, I will,' said William. 'I'll go down to New York tomorrow and tell him if you'll promise to stay with Kate and me. I won't stop you from getting drunk if that's what you wish to do, or from having as many women as you want, but you must stay here.'

'Best offer I've had in weeks, William. Now I think I'll sleep some more. I get so tired nowadays.'

William watched Matthew fall into a deep sleep and removed the half empty glass from his hand. A tomato stain was forming on the sheets.

'Don't die,' he said quietly. 'Please don't die, Matthew. Have you forgotten that you and I are going to run the biggest bank in America?'

William went to New York the following morning to see Charles Lester. The great man aged visibly at William's news and seemed to shrink into his seat.

'Thank you for coming, William, and telling me personally. I knew something must be wrong when Matthew stopped his monthly visits to see me. I'll come up every weekend. He will want to be with you and Kate, and I'll try not to make it too obvious how hard I took the news. God knows what he's done to deserve this. Since my wife died, I built everything for Matthew, and now there is no one to leave it to. Susan has no interest in the bank.'

'Come to Boston when ever you want to, sir. You'll always be most welcome.'

'Thank you, William, for everything you're doing for Matthew.'

The old man looked up at him. 'I wish your father were alive to see how worthy his son is of the name Kane. If only I could change places with Matthew, and let him live ...'

'I ought to be getting back to him soon, sir.'

'Yes, of course. Tell him I took the news stoically. Don't tell him anything different.'

'Yes, sir.'

William travelled back to Boston that night to find that Matthew had stayed at home with Kate and started reading America's latest best seller, *Gone With The Wind*, as he sat out on the veranda. He looked up as William came through the French windows.

'How did the old man take it?'

'He cried,' said William.

'The chairman of Lester's bank cried?' said Matthew. 'Never let the shareholders know that.'

Matthew stopped drinking and worked as hard as he could until the last few days. William was amazed by his determination and had continually to make him slow down. He was always on top of his work and would tease William by checking his mail at the end of each day. In the evenings before a large dinner, Matthew would play tennis with William or row against him on the river. 'I'll know I'm dead when I can't beat you,' he mocked. Matthew never entered the hospital, preferring to stay on at the Red House. The weeks went so slowly and yet so quickly for William, waking each morning wondering if Matthew would still be alive.

Matthew died on a Thursday, forty pages still to read of *Gone With The Wind*.

The funeral was held in New York, and William and Kate stayed with Charles Lester. In six months, he had become an old man, and as he stood by the graves of his wife and only son, he told William that he no longer saw any purpose in this life. William said nothing; no words of his could help the grieving father. William and Kate returned to Boston the next day. The Red House seemed strangely empty without Matthew. The past few months had been at once the happiest and unhappiest period in William's life. Death had brought him a closeness, both to Matthew and to Kate, that normal life would never have allowed.

When William returned to the bank after Matthew's death, he found it hard to get back into any sort of normal routine. He would get up and start to head towards Matthew's office for advice or a laugh, or merely to be assured of his existence, but he was no longer there. It was weeks before William could prevent himself from doing this.

Tony Simmons was very understanding, but it didn't help. William lost all interest in banking, even in Kane and Cabot itself, as he went through months of remorse over Matthew's death. He had always taken it for granted that he and Matthew would grow old together and share a common destiny. No one commented that William's work was not up to its usual high standard. Even Kate grew worried by the hours William would spend alone.

Then one morning she awoke to find him sitting on the edge of the bed staring down at her. She blinked up at him. 'Is something wrong, darling?'

'No, I'm just looking at my greatest asset and making sure I don't take it for granted.'

22

By the end of 1932, with America still in the grip of a depression, Abel was becoming a little apprehensive about the future of the Baron Group. Two thousand banks had been closed during the past two years, and more were shutting their doors every week. Nine million people were still unemployed, which had as its only virtue the assurance that Abel could maintain a highly professional staff in his hotels. Still, the Baron Group lost seventy-two thousand dollars during a year in which he had predicted that they would break even, and he began to wonder whether his backer's purse and patience would hold out long enough to allow him the chance to turn things around.

Abel had begun to take an active interest in American politics during Anton Cermak's successful campaign to become mayor of Chicago. Cermak talked Abel into joining the Democratic Party, which had launched a virulent campaign against Prohibition; Abel threw himself wholeheartedly behind Cermak, as Prohibition had proved very damaging to the hotel trade. The fact that Cermak was himself an immigrant, from Czechoslovakia, created an immediate bond between the two men, and Abel was delighted to be chosen as a delegate representative at the Democratic Convention held in Chicago that year where Cermak brought a packed audience to its feet with the words: 'It's true I didn't come over on the *Mayflower*, but I came as soon as I could.'

At the convention Cermak introduced Abel to Franklin D. Roosevelt, who made a lasting impression on him. F.D.R. went on to win the Presidential election easily and he swept Democratic candidates into office all over the country. One of the newly elected aldermen at Chicago City Hall was Henry Osborne. When Anton Cermak was killed a few weeks later in Miami by an assassin's bullet intended for F.D.R., Abel decided to contribute a considerable amount of time and money to the cause of the Polish Democrats in Chicago.

During 1933 the group lost only twenty-three thousand dollars, and one of the hotels, the St. Louis Baron, actually showed a profit. When President Roosevelt had delivered his first fireside chat on 12 March, exhorting his countrymen 'to once again believe in America', Abel's confidence soared and he decided to re-open the two hotels that he had closed the previous year.

Zaphia grew querulous at his long absences in Charleston and Mobile, while he took the two hotels out of mothballs. She had never wanted Abel to be more than the deputy manager of the Stevens, a level at which she felt she could keep pace. The pace was quickening as every month passed, and she became conscious of falling behind Abel's ambitions and feared he was beginning to lose interest in her.

She was also becoming anxious about her childlessness, and started to see doctors who reassured her that there was nothing to prevent her from becoming pregnant. One offered the suggestion that Abel should also be examined, but Zaphia demurred, knowing he would regard the very mention of the subject as a slur on his manhood. Finally, after the subject had become so charged that it was difficult for them to discuss it at all, Zaphia missed her period. She waited hopefully for another month before saying anything to Abel or even seeing the doctor again. He confirmed that she was at last pregnant. To Abel's delight, Zaphia gave birth to a daughter, on New Year's Day, 1934. They named her Florentyna, after Abel's sister. Abel was besotted the moment he set eyes on the child and Zaphia knew from that moment she could no longer be the first love of his life. George and Zaphia's cousin were the child's Kums, and Abel gave a traditional ten-course Polish dinner on the evening of the christening. Many gifts were presented to the child, including a beautiful antique ring from Abel's backer. He returned the gift in kind when the Baron Group made a profit of sixty-three thousand dollars at the end of the year. Only the Mobile Baron was still losing money.

After Florentyna's birth Abel found he was spending much more of his time in Chicago which prompted him to decide that the time had come to build a Baron there. Hotels in the city were booming in the aftermath of the World's Fair. Abel intended to make his new hotel the flagship of the group in memory of Davis Leroy. The company still owned the site of the old Richmond Hotel on Michigan Avenue, and although Abel had had several offers for the land, he had always held out, hoping that one day he would be in a strong enough financial position to rebuild the hotel. The project required capital and Abel decided to use the seven hundred and fifty thousand dollars he had eventually received from Great Western Casualty for the old Chicago Richmond to start construction. As soon as his plans were formulated, he told Curtis Fenton of his intention, with the sole reservation that if David Maxton did not want a rival to the Stevens, Abel was willing to drop the whole project; he felt it was the least he could do in the circumstances. A few days later, Curtis Fenton advised him that his backer was delighted by the idea of 'The Chicago Baron'.

It took Abel twelve months to build the new Baron with a large helping hand from Alderman Henry Osborne, who hurried through the permits required from City Hall in the shortest possible time. The building was opened in 1936 by the mayor of the city, Edward J. Kelly, who, after the death of Anton Cermak, had become the prime organiser of the Democratic machine. In memory of Davis Leroy, the hotel had no twelfth floor – a tradition Abel continued in every new Baron he built.

Both Illinois senators were also in attendance to address the two thousand assembled guests. The Chicago Baron was superb both in design and construction. Abel had wound up spending well over a million dollars on the hotel, and it looked as though every penny had been put to good use. The public rooms were large and sumptuous with high stucco ceilings and decorations in pastel shades of green, pleasant and relaxing; the carpets were thick. The dark green embossed 'B' was discreet but ubiquitous, adorning everything from the flag that fluttered on the top of the forty-two storey building to the neat lapel of the most junior bellhop.

'This hotel already bears the hallmark of success,' said J. Hamilton Lewis, the senior senator from Illinois, 'because, my friends, it is the man, not the building, who will always be known as "The Chicago Baron".' Abel beamed with undisguised pleasure as the two thousand guests roared their approval.

Abel's reply of acknowledgment was well turned and confidently delivered, and it earned him a standing ovation. He was beginning to feel very much at home among big businessmen and senior politicians. Zaphia hovered uncertainly in the background during the lavish celebration: the occasion was a little too much for her. She neither understood nor cared for success on Abel's scale; and even though she could now afford the most expensive clothes, she still looked unfashionable and out-of-place, and she was only too aware that it annoyed Abel. She stood by while Abel chatted with Henry Osborne.

'This must be the high point of your life,' Henry was saying, slapping Abel on the back.

'High point – I've just turned thirty,' said Abel. A camera flashed as he placed an arm round Henry's shoulder. Abel beamed, realising for the first time how pleasant it was to be treated as a public figure. 'I'm going to put Baron hotels right across the globe,' he said, just loud enough for the reporter to hear. 'I intend to be to America what César Ritz was to Europe. Stick with me, Henry, and you'll enjoy the ride.'

23

At breakfast the next morning, Kate pointed to a small item on page seventeen of the *Globe*, reporting the opening of the Chicago Baron.

William smiled as he read the article. Kane and Cabot had been foolish not to listen when he had advised them to support the Richmond Group. It pleased him that his own judgment on Rosnovski had turned out to be right even though the bank had lost out on the deal. His smile broadened as he read the nickname 'The Chicago Baron'. Then, suddenly, he felt sick. He examined the accompanying photograph more closely, but there was no mistake, and the caption confirmed his first impression: 'Abel Rosnovski, the chairman of the Baron Group talking with Mieczyslaw Szymczak, a governor of the Federal Reserve Board, and Alderman Henry Osborne.'

William dropped the paper on to the breakfast table and thought for a moment. As soon as he arrived at his office, he called Thomas Cohen at Cohen, Cohen and Yablons.

'It's been a long time, Mr. Kane,' were Thomas Cohen's first words. 'I was very sorry to learn of the death of your friend, Matthew Lester. How are your wife and your son – Richard – isn't that his name?'

William always admired Thomas Cohen's instant recall of names and relationships.

'Yes, it is. They're both well, thank you, Mr. Cohen.'

'Well, what can I do for you this time, Mr. Kane?' Thomas also remembered that William could only manage about one sentence of small talk.

'I want to employ, through you, the services of a reliable investigator. I do not wish my name to be associated with this enquiry, but I need another run-down on Henry Osborne. Everything he's done since he left Boston, and in particular whether there is any connection between him and Abel Rosnovski of the Baron Group.'

There was a pause before the lawyer said, 'Yes.'

'Can you report to me in one week?'

'Two please, Mr. Kane, two,' said Mr. Cohen.

'Full report on my desk at the bank in two weeks, Mr. Cohen?'

'Two weeks, Mr. Kane.'

Thomas Cohen was as reliable as ever, and a full report was on William's desk on the fifteenth morning. William read the dossier with care. There appeared to be no formal business connections between Abel Rosnovski and Henry Osborne. Rosnovski, it seemed, found Osborne useful as a political contact, but nothing more. Osborne himself had bounced from job to job since leaving Boston, ending up in the main office of the Great Western Casualty Insurance Company. In all probability, that was how Osborne had come in contact with Abel Rosnovski, as the old Chicago Richmond had always been insured by Great Western. When the hotel burned down, the insurance company had originally refused to pay the claim. A certain Desmond Pacey, the manager, had been sent to prison for ten years, after pleading guilty to arson, and there was some suspicion that Abel Rosnovski might himself have been involved. Nothing was proved, and the insurance company settled later for three-quarters of a million dollars. Osborne, the report went on, is now an alderman and full-time politician at City Hall, and it is common knowledge that he hopes to become a congressman for Chicago. He has recently married a Miss Marie Axton, the daughter of a wealthy drug manufacturer, and as yet they have no children.

William went over the report again to be sure that he had not missed anything, however inconsequential. Although there did not seem to be a great deal to connect the two men, he couldn't help feeling that the association between Abel Rosnovski and Henry Osborne, both of whom hated him, for totally disparate reasons, was potentially dangerous to him. He mailed a cheque to Thomas Cohen and requested that he update the file every quarter, but as the months passed, and the quarterly reports revealed nothing new, he began to stop worrying, thinking perhaps he had overreacted to the photograph in the *Boston Globe*.

Kate presented her husband with a daughter in the spring of 1937, whom they christened Virginia. William started changing nappies again, and such was his fascination for 'the little lady' that Kate had to rescue the child each night for fear she would never get any sleep. Richard, now two and a half, didn't care too much for the new arrival to begin with, but time and a new wooden soldier on a horse, combined to allay his jealousy.

By the end of the year, William's department at Kane and Cabot had made a handsome profit for the bank. He had emerged from the lethargy that had overcome him on Matthew's death and was fast regaining his reputation as a shrewd investor in the stock market, not least when 'sell 'em short' Smith admitted he had only perfected a technique developed by William Kane of Boston. Even Tony Simmons' direction had become less irksome. Nevertheless, William was secretly worried by the prospect that he could not become chairman of Kane and Cabot until Simmons retired in seventeen years' time, and he began to consider looking around for employment in another bank.

William and Kate had taken to visiting Charles Lester in New York about once a month at weekends. The great man had grown very old over the three years since Matthew's death, and rumours in financial circles were that he had lost all interest in his work and was rarely seen at the bank. William was beginning to wonder how much longer the old man would live, and then a few weeks later he died. William travelled down to the funeral in New York. Everyone seemed to be there including the Vice-President of the United States, John Nance Garner. After the funeral, William and Kate took the train back to Boston, numbly conscious that they had lost their last link with the Lester family.

It was some six months later that William received a

communication from Sullivan and Cromwell, the distinguished New York lawyers, asking him if he would be kind enough to attend the reading of the will of the late Charles Lester at their offices in Wall Street. William went to the reading, more from loyalty to the Lester family than from any curiosity to know what Charles Lester had left him. He hoped for a small memento that would remind him of Matthew and join the 'Harvard Oar' that still hung on the wall of the guest room of the Red House. He also looked forward to the opportunity of renewing his acquaintance with many members of the Lester family whom he had come to know in school and college holidays spent with Matthew.

William drove down to New York in his newly acquired Daimler the night before the reading and stayed at the Harvard Club. The will was to be read at ten o'clock the following morning, and William was surprised to find on his arrival in the offices of Sullivan and Cromwell that over fifty people were already present. Many of them glanced up at William as he entered the room, and he greeted several of Matthew's cousins and aunts, looking rather older than he remembered them; he could only conclude that they must be thinking the same about him. His eyes searched for Matthew's sister Susan, but he couldn't see her. At ten o'clock precisely Mr. Arthur Cromwell entered the room, accompanied by an assistant carrying a brown leather folder. Everyone fell silent in hopeful expectation. The lawyer began by explaining to the assembled would-be beneficiaries that the contents of the will had not been disclosed until six months after Charles Lester's death at Mr. Lester's specific instruction : having no son to whom to leave his fortune he had wanted the dust to settle after his death before his final intentions were made clear.

William looked around the room at the intent faces which were hanging on every syllable issuing from the lawyer's mouth. Arthur Cromwell took nearly an hour to read the will. After reciting the usual bequests to family retainers, charities and Harvard University, Cromwell went on to reveal that Charles Lester had divided his personal fortune among all his relatives, treating them more or less according to their degree of kinship. His daughter, Susan, received the largest share of the estate while the five nephews and three neices each received an equal portion of the rest. All their money and shares were to be held in trust by the bank until they were thirty. Several other cousins, aunts and distant relations were given immediate cash payments.

William was surprised when Mr. Cromwell annouced: 'That disposes of all the known assets of the late Charles Lester.'

People began to shuffle around in their seats, as a murmur of nervous conversation broke out. No one wanted to admit that the unfortunate death had made them fortunate.

'That is not, however, the end of Mr. Charles Lester's last will and testament,' said the imperturbable lawyer, and everyone sat still again, fearful of some late and unwelcome thunderbolt.

Mr. Cromwell went on. 'I shall now continue in Mr. Charles Lester's own words: "I have always considered that a bank and its reputation are only as good as the people who serve it. It was well known that I had hoped my son Matthew would succeed me as chairman of Lester's, but his tragic and untimely death has intervened. Until now, I have never divulged my choice of successor for Lester's bank. I therefore wish it to be known that I desire William Lowell Kane, son of one of my dearest friends, the late Richard Lowell Kane, and at present the vice-chairman of Kane and Cabot, be appointed chairman of Lester's Bank and Trust Company following the next full board meeting."'

There was an immediate uproar. Everyone looked around the room for the mysterious Mr. William Lowell Kane of whom few but the immediate Lester family had ever heard.

'I have not yet finished,' said Arthur Cromwell quietly.

Silence fell once more, as the members of the audience, anticipating another bombshell, exchanged fearful glances.

The lawyer continued. 'All the above grants and division of shares in Lester's and Company are expressly conditional upon the beneficiaries voting for Mr. Kane at the next annual board meeting, and continuing to do so for at least the following five years, unless Mr. Kane himself indicates that he does not wish to accept the chairmanship.'

Uproar broke out again. William wished he was a million miles away, not sure whether to be deliriously happy or to concede that he must be the most detested person in that room.

'That concludes the last will and testament of the late Charles Lester,' said Mr. Cromwell, but only the front row heard him.

William looked up. Susan Lester was walking towards him. The puppy fat had disappeared while the attractive freckles remained. He smiled, but she walked straight past him without even acknowledging his presence. William frowned.

Ignoring the babble, a tall, grey-haired man wearing a pin-striped suit and a silver tie moved quickly towards William.

'You are William Kane, are you not, sir?'

'Yes, I am,' said William nervously.

'My name is Peter Parfitt,' said the stranger.

'The bank's vice-chairman,' said William.

'Correct, sir,' he said. 'I do not know you, but I do know something of your reputation, and I count myself lucky to have been acquainted with your distinguished father. If Charles Lester thought you were the right man to be chairman of his bank, that's good enough for me.'

William had never been so relieved in his life.

'Where are you staying in New York?' continued Peter Parfitt before William could reply.

'At the Harvard Club.'

'Splendid. May I ask if you are free for dinner tonight by any chance?'

'I had intended to return to Boston this evening,' said William, 'but I expect I shall now have to stay in New York for a few days.'

'Good. Why don't you come to my house for dinner, say about eight o'clock?'

The banker handed William his card with an address embossed in copperplate script. 'I shall enjoy the opportunity of chatting with you in more convivial surroundings.'

'Thank you, sir,' said William, pocketing the card as others began crowding around him. Some stared at him in hostility; others waited to express their congratulations.

When William eventually managed to make his escape and returned to the Harvard Club, the first thing he did was to call Kate and tell her the news.

She said very quietly, 'How happy Matthew would be for you, darling.'

'I know,' said William.

'When are you coming home?'

'God knows. I'm dining tonight with a Mr. Peter Parfitt who is a vice-chairman of Lester's. He's being most helpful over the whole affair, which is making life much easier. I'll spend the night here at the club, and then call you sometime tomorrow to let you know how things are working out.'

'All right, darling.'

'All quiet on the Eastern seaboard?'

'Well, Virginia has cut a tooth and seems to think she deserves special attention, Richard was sent to bed early for being rude to Nanny, and we all miss you.'

William laughed. 'I'll call you tomorrow.'

'Yes, please do. By the way, many congratulations. I approve of Charles Lester's judgment even if I'm going to hate living in New York.'

It was the first time William had thought about living in New York.

William arrived at Peter Parfitt's home on East Sixty-fourth Street at eight o'clock that night and was taken by surprise to find his host had dressed for dinner. William felt slightly embarrased and ill at east in his dark banker's suit. He quickly explained to his hostess that he had originally anticipated returning to Boston that evening. Diana Parfitt, who turned out to be Peter's second wife, could not have been more charming to her guest, and she seemed delighted that

William was to be the next chairman of Lester's. During an excellent dinner William could not resist asking Peter Parfitt how he thought the rest of the board would react to Charles Lester's wishes.

'They'll all fall in line,' said Parfitt. 'I've spoken to most of them already. There's a full board meeting on Monday morning to confirm your appointment and I can only see one small cloud on the horizon.'

'What's that?' said William, trying not to sound anxious.

'Well, between you and me, the other vice-chairman, Ted Leach, was rather expecting to be appointed chairman himself. In fact, I think I would go as far as saying that he anticipated it. We had all been informed that no nomination could be made until after the will had been read, but Charles Lester's wishes must have come as rather a shock to Ted.'

'Will he put up a fight?' asked William.

'I'm afraid he might, but there's nothing for you to worry about.'

'I don't mind admitting,' said Diana Parfitt, as she studied the rather flat soufflé in front of her, 'that he has never been my favourite man.'

'Now, dear,' said Parfitt reprovingly, 'we mustn't say anything behind Ted's back before Mr. Kane has had a chance to judge for himself. There is no doubt in my mind that the board will confirm Mr. Kane's appointment at the meeting on Monday, and there's even the possibility that Ted Leach will resign.'

'I don't want anyone to feel they have to resign because of me,' said William.

'A very creditable sentiment,' said Parfitt. 'But don't bother yourself about a puff of wind. I'm confident that the whole matter is well under control. You go quietly back to Boston tomorrow, and I'll keep you informed on the lay of the land.'

'Perhaps it might be wise if I dropped in at the bank in the morning. Won't your fellow officers find it a little curious if I make no attempt to meet any of them?'

'No, I don't think that would be advisable given the circumstances. In fact, I feel it might be wiser for you to stay out of their way until the Monday board meeting is over. They won't want to seem any less independent than necessary, and they may already feel like glorified rubber stamps. Take my advice, Bill, you go back to Boston, and I'll call you with the good news before noon on Monday.'

William reluctantly agreed to Peter Parfitt's suggestion and went on to spend a pleasant evening discussing with both of them where he and Kate might stay in New York while they were looking for a permanent home. William was somewhat surprised to find that Peter Parfitt seemed to have no desire to discuss his own views on banking, and he assumed the reason was because of Diana Parfitt's presence. An excellent evening ended with a little too much brandy, and William did not arrive back at the Harvard Club until after one o'clock.

Once William had returned to Boston he made an immediate report to Tony Simmons of what had transpired in New York as he did not want him to hear about the appointment from anyone else. Tony turned out to be surprisingly sanguine about the news.

'I'm sorry to learn that you will be leaving us, William. Lester's may well be two or three times the size of Kane and Cabot, but I shall be unable to replace you, and I hope you'll consider very carefully before accepting the appointment.'

William was surprised and couldn't help showing it. 'Frankly, Tony, I would have thought you'd have been only too glad to see the back of me.'

'William, when will you ever believe that my first interest has always been the bank, and there has never been any doubt in my mind that you are one of the shrewdest investment advisers in America today? If you leave Kane and Cabot now, many of the bank's most important clients will naturally want to follow you.'

'I would never transfer my own money to Lester's,' said William, 'any more than I would expect any of the bank's clients to move with me.'

'Of course you wouldn't solicit them to join you, William,

but some of them will want you to continue managing their portfolios. Like your father and Charles Lester, they believe quite rightly that banking is about people and reputations.'

William and Kate spent a tense weekend waiting for Monday and the result of the board meeting in New York. William sat nervously in his office the whole of Monday morning, answering every telephone call personally, but he heard nothing as the morning dragged into the afternoon. He didn't even leave the office for lunch, and Peter Parfitt finally called a little after six.

'I'm afraid there's been some unexpected trouble, Bill,' were his opening words.

William's heart sank.

'Nothing for you to worry about since I still feel I have the situation well under control, but the board wants the right to oppose your nomination with their own candidate. Some of them have produced legal opinions that go as far as saying the relevant clause of the will has no real validity. I've been given the unpleasant task of asking if you would be willing to fight an election against the board's candidate.'

'Who would be the board's candidate?' asked William.

'No names have been mentioned by anyone yet, but I imagine their choice will be Ted Leach. No one else has shown the slightest interest in running against you.'

'I'd like a little time to think about it,' William replied. 'When will the next board meeting be?'

'A week from today,' said Parfitt. 'But don't you go and get yourself all worked up about Ted Leach; I'm still confident that you will win easily, and I'll keep you informed of any further developments as the week goes by.'

'Do you want me to come down to New York, Peter?'

'No, not for the moment. I don't think that would help matters.'

William thanked him and put the phone down. He packed his old leather briefcase and left the office, feeling more than a little depressed. Tony Simmons, carrying a suitcase, caught up with him in the private parking lot.

'I didn't know you were going out of town, Tony.'

'It's only the monthly bankers' dinner in New York. I'll be back by tomorrow afternoon. I think I can safely leave Kane and Cabot for twenty-four hours in the capable hands of the next chairman of Lester's.'

William laughed. 'I may already be the ex-chairman,' he said and explained the latest development. Once again, William was surprised by Tony Simmons' reaction.

'It's true that Ted Leach has always expected to be the next chairman of Lester's,' he mused. 'That's common knowledge in financial circles. But he's a loyal servant of the bank, and I can't believe he would oppose Charles Lester's express wishes.'

'I didn't realise you even knew him,' said William.

'I don't know him all that well,' said Tony. 'He was a class ahead of me at Yale, and now I see him from time to time at these damned bankers' dinners that you'll have to attend when you're a chairman. He's bound to be there tonight. I'll have a word with him if you like.'

'Yes, please do, but be very careful, won't you?' said William.

'My dear William, you've spent nearly ten years of your life telling me I'm far too careful.'

'I'm sorry, Tony. Funny how one's judgment is impaired when one is worrying about one's own problems, however sound the same judgment might be considered when dealing with other peoples'. I'll put myself in your hands and do whatever you advise.'

'Good then, you leave it to me. I'll see what Leach has to say for himself and call you first thing in the morning.'

Tony called from New York a few minutes after midnight and woke William from a deep sleep.

'Have I woken you, William?'

'Yes, who is it?'

'Tony Simmons.'

William switched on the light by his side of the bed and looked at his alarm clock. Ten minutes past twelve.

'Well, you did say you would call first thing in the morning.'

Tony laughed. 'I'm afraid what I have to tell you won't seem quite so funny. The man who is opposing you for chairman of Lester's Bank is Peter Parfitt.'

'*What?*' said William, suddenly awake.

'He's been trying to push the board into supporting him behind your back. Ted Leach, as I expected, is in favour of your appointment as chairman, but the board is now split down the middle.'

'Hell. First, thank you, Tony, and second, what do I do now?'

'If you want to be the next chairman of Lester's, you'd better get down here fast before the members of the board wonder why you're hiding away in Boston.'

'Hiding away?'

'That's what Parfitt has been telling the directors for the past few days.'

'The bastard.'

'Now that you mention the subject, I am unable to vouch for his parentage,' said Tony.

William laughed.

'Come and stay at the Yale Club. Then we can talk the whole thing out first thing in the morning.'

'I'll be there as quickly as I can,' said William.

'I may be asleep when you arrive. It'll be your turn to wake me.'

William put the phone down and looked over at Kate, blissfully oblivious to his new problems. She had slept right through the entire conversation. How he wished he could manage that. A curtain had only to flutter in the breeze, and he was awake. She would probably sleep right through the Second Coming. He scribbled a few lines of explanation to her and put the note on her bedside table, dressed, packed – this time including a dinner jacket – and set off for New York.

The roads were clear and the run in the new Daimler took him only five hours. He drove into New York with cleaners, mailmen, newsboys, and the morning sun, and checked in at the Yale Club as the hall clock chimed once. It was six-fifteen. He unpacked and decided to rest for an hour before waking Tony. The next thing he heard was an insistent tapping on his door. Sleepily, he got up to open it only to find Tony Simmons standing outside.

'Nice dressing gown, William,' said Tony, grinning. He was fully dressed.

'I must have fallen asleep. If you wait a minute, I'll be right with you,' said William.

'No, no, I have to catch a train back to Boston. You take a shower and get yourself dressed while we talk.'

William went into the bathroom and left the door open.

'Now your main problem . . .' started Tony.

William put his head around the bathroom door. 'I can't hear you while the water's running.'

Tony waited for it to stop. 'Peter Parfitt is your main problem. He assumed he was going to be the next chairman, and that his would be the name that was read out in Charles Lester's will. He's been manoeuvring the directors against you and playing board-room politics ever since. Ted Leach can fill you in on the finer details and would like you to join him for lunch today at the Metropolitan Club. He may bring two or three other board members with him on whom you can rely. The board, by the way, still seems to be split right down the middle.'

William nicked himself with his razor. 'Damn. Which club?'

'Metropolitan, just off Fifth Avenue on East Sixtieth Street.

'Why there and not somewhere down in Wall Street?'

'William, when you're dealing with the Peter Parfitts of this world, you don't telegraph your intentions. Keep your wits about you, and play the whole thing very coolly. From what Leach tells me, I believe you can still win.'

William came back into the bedroom with a towel round his waist. 'I'll try,' he said, 'to be cool, that is.'

Tony smiled. 'Now, I must get back to Boston. My train leaves Grand Central in ten minutes.' He looked at his watch. 'Damn, six minutes.'

Tony paused at the bedroom door. 'You know, your father never trusted Peter Parfitt. Too smooth, he always used to say. Never anything more, just a little too smooth.' He picked up his suitcase. 'Good luck, William.'

'How can I begin to thank you, Tony?'

'You can't. Just put it down to my trying to atone for the lousy way I treated Matthew.'

William watched the door close as he put in his collar stud and then straightened his tie, reflecting on how curious it was that he had spent years working closely with Tony Simmons without ever really getting to know him but that now, in only a few days of personal crisis, he found himself instantly liking and trusting a man he had never before really seen. He went down to the dining room and had a typical club breakfast: a cold boiled egg, one piece of hard toast, butter and English marmalade from someone else's table. The porter handed him a copy of the *Wall Street Journal*, which hinted on an inside page that everything was not running smoothly at Lester's following the nomination of William Kane as their next chairman. At least, the *Journal* did not seem to have any inside information.

William returned to his room and asked the operator for a number in Boston. He was kept waiting for a few minutes before he was put through.

'I do apologise, Mr. Kane. I had no idea that you were on the line. May I congratulate you on your appointment as chairman of Lester's. I hope this means that our New York office will be seeing a lot more of you in the future.'

'That may well depend on you, Mr. Cohen.'

'I don't think I quite understand,' the lawyer replied.

William explained what had happened over the past few days and read out the relevant section of Charles Lester's will.

Thomas Cohen spent some time taking down each word and then going over his notes carefully.

'Do you think his wishes would stand up in court?' asked William.

'Who knows? I can't think of a precedent for such a situation. A nineteenth-century Member of Parliament once bequeathed his constituency in a will, and no one objected, and the beneficiary went on to become Prime Minister. But that was over a hundred years ago – and in England. Now in this case, if the board decided to contest Mr. Lester's will, and you took their decision to court, I wouldn't care to predict which way the judge might jump. Lord Melbourne didn't have to contend with a surrogate of New York County. Nevertheless, a nice legal conundrum, Mr. Kane.'

'What do you advise?' said William.

'I am a Jew, Mr. Kane. I came to this country on a ship from Germany at the turn of the century, and I have always had to fight hard for anything I've wanted. Do you want to be chairman of Lester's that badly?'

'Yes, Mr. Cohen, I do.'

'Then you must listen to an old man who has, over the years, come to view you with great respect, and if I may say so, with some affection, and I'll tell you exactly what I'd do if I were faced with your predicament.'

An hour later William put the phone down, and having some time to kill, he strolled up Park Avenue. Along the way, he passed a site on which a huge building was well into construction. A large, neat billboard announced 'The next Baron Hotel will be in New York. When the Baron has been your host, you'll never want to stay anywhere else.' William smiled for the first time that morning and walked with a lighter step towards the Metropolitan Club.

Ted Leach, a short dapper man with dark brown hair and a lighter moustache, was standing in the foyer of the club, waiting for him. He ushered William into the bar. William admired the Renaissance style of the club, built by Otto Kuhn and Standford White in 1894. J. P. Morgan had founded the club when one of his closest friends was blackballed at the Union League.

'A fairly extravagant gesture even for a very close friend,' Ted Leach suggested, trying to make conversation. 'What will you have to drink, Mr. Kane?'

'A dry sherry, please,' said William.

A boy in a smart blue uniform returned a few moments later with a dry sherry and a scotch and water; he hadn't needed to ask Mr. Leach for his order.

'To the next chairman of Lester's,' said Ted Leach, raising his glass.

William hesitated.

'Don't drink, Mr. Kane. As you know, you should never drink to yourself.'

William laughed, unsure how to reply.

A few minutes later two older men were walking towards them, both tall and confident in the bankers' uniform of grey three-piece suits, stiff collars and dark unpatterned ties. Had they been strolling down Wall Street, William would not have given them a second glance. In the Metropolitan Club he studied them carefully.

'Mr. Alfred Rodgers and Mr. Winthrop Davies,' said Ted Leach as he introduced them.

William smiled reservedly, still unsure whose side anyone was on. The two newcomers were studying him equally carefully. No one spoke for a moment.

'Where do we start?' said the one called Rodgers, a monocle falling from his eye as he spoke.

'By going on up to lunch,' said Ted Leach.

The three of them turned around, obviously knowing exactly where they were going. William followed. The dining room on the second floor was vast, with another magnificent high ceiling. The *maître d'* placed them in the window seat, overlooking Central Park, were no one could overhear their conversation.

'Let's order and then talk,' said Ted Leach.

Through the window William could see the Plaza Hotel. Memories of his graduation celebration with the grandmothers and Matthew came flooding back to him – and there was something else he was trying to recall about that tea at the Plaza . . .

'Mr. Kane, let's put our cards on the table,' said Ted Leach. 'Charles Lester's decision to appoint you as chairman of the bank came as a surprise, not to put too fine a point on it. But if the board ignores his wishes, the bank could be plunged into chaos and that is an outcome none of us needs. He was a shrewd old man, and he will have had his reasons for wanting you as the bank's next chairman, and that's good enough for me.'

William had heard those words before – from Peter Parfitt.

'All three of us,' said Winthrop Davies, taking over, 'owe everything we have to Charles Lester, and we will carry out his wishes if it's the last thing we do as members of the board.'

'It may turn out to be just that,' said Ted Leach, 'if Peter Parfitt does succeed in becoming chairman.'

'I'm sorry, gentlemen,' said William, 'to have caused so much consternation. If my appointment as chairman came as a surprise to you, I can assure you it was nothing less than a bolt from the blue for me. I imagined I would receive some minor personal memento of Matthew's from Charles Lester's will, not the responsibility of running the entire bank.'

'We understand the position you've been placed in, Mr. Kane,' said Ted Leach, 'and you must trust us when we say we are here to help you. We are aware that you will find that difficult to believe after the treatment that has been meted out to you by Peter Parfitt and the tactics he has been using behind your back to try and secure the chair for himself.'

'I have to believe you, Mr. Leach, because I have no choice but to place myself in your hands and seek your advice as to how you view the current situation.'

'Thank you,' said Leach. 'That situation is clear to me. Peter Parfitt's campaign is well organised, and he now feels he is acting from a position of strength. We, therefore, Mr. Kane, must be entirely open with each other if we are to have any chance of beating him. I am assuming, of course, that you have the stomach for such a fight.'

'I wouldn't be here if I didn't, Mr. Leach. And now that you have put the position so succinctly, perhaps you will allow me to suggest how we should go about defeating Mr. Parfitt.'

'Certainly,' said Ted Leach.

All three men listened intently.

'You are undoubtedly right in saying that Parfitt feels he is now in a strong position because to date he has always been the one on the attack, always knowing what is going to happen next. Might I suggest that the time has come for us to reverse that trend and take up the attack ourselves where and when he least expects it – in his own board room.'

'How do you propose we go about that, Mr. Kane?' enquired Winthrop Davies, looking somewhat surprised.

'I'll tell you if you will first permit me to ask you some questions. How many full-time executive directors are there with a vote on the board?'

'Sixteen,' said Ted Leach instantly.

'And with whom does their allegiance lie at this moment?' William asked.

'Not the easiest question to answer, Mr. Kane,' Winthrop Davies chipped in. He took a crumpled envelope from his inside pocket and studied the back of it before he continued. 'I think we can count on six sure votes, and Peter Parfitt can be certain of five. It came as a shock for me to discover this morning that Rupert Cork-Smith, who was Charles Lester's closest friend, is unwilling to support you, Mr. Kane. Really strange, because I know he doesn't care for Parfitt. I think that may make the voting six apiece.'

'That gives us until Thursday,' added Ted Leach, 'to find out how the other four board members are likely to react to your appointment.'

'Why Thursday?' asked William.

'Day of the next board meeting,' answered, Leach stroking his moustache, which William had noticed he always did when he started to speak. 'And more important, Item One on the agenda is the election of a new chairman.'

'I was told the next meeting would not take place until Monday,' said William in astonishment.

'By whom?' Davies asked.

'Peter Parfitt,' said William.

'His tactics,' Ted Leach commented, 'have not been altogether those of a gentleman.'

'I've learned enough about that gentleman,' William said, placing an ironic stress on the words, 'to make me realise that I shall have to take the battle to him.'

'Easier said than done, Mr. Kane. He is very much in the driver's seat at this moment,' said Winthrop Davies, 'and I'm not sure how we go about removing him from it.'

'Switch the traffic lights to red,' replied William. 'Who has the authority to call a board meeting?'

'While the board is without a chairman, either vice-chairman,' said Ted Leach. 'Which in reality means Peter Parfitt or myself.'

'How many board members form a quorum?'

'Nine,' said Davies.

'And if you are one of the two vice-chairmen, Mr. Leach, who is the company secretary?'

'I am,' said Alfred Rodgers, who until then had hardly opened his mouth, the exact quality William always looked for in a company secretary.

'How much notice do you have to give to call an emergency board meeting, Mr. Rodgers?'

'Every director must be informed at least twenty-four hours beforehand although that has never actually happened except during the crash of twenty-nine. Charles Lester always tried to give at least three days notice.'

'But the bank's rules do allow for an emergency meeting to be held on twenty-four hours notice?' asked William.

'They do, Mr. Kane,' Alfred Rodgers affirmed, his monocle now firmly in place and focused on William.

'Excellent, then let's call our own board meeting.'

The three bankers stared at William as if they had not quite heard him clearly.

'Think about it, gentlemen,' William continued. 'Mr. Leach, as vice-chairman, calls the board meeting and Mr. Rodgers, as company secretary, informs all the directors.'

'When would you want this board meeting to take place?' asked Ted Leach.

'Tomorrow afternoon.' William looked at his watch. 'Three o'clock.'

'Good God, that's cutting it a bit fine,' said Alfred Rodgers. 'I'm not sure...'

'Cutting it very fine for Peter Parfitt, wouldn't you say?' said William.

'That's true,' said Ted Leach, 'if you know precisely what you have planned for the meeting?'

'You leave the meeting to me. Just be sure that it's correctly convened and that every director is properly informed.'

'I wonder how Peter Parfitt is going to react,' said Ted Leach.

'Don't worry about Parfitt,' said William. 'That's the mistake we've made all along. Let him start to worry about us for a change. As long as he is given the full twenty-four hours notice and he's the last director informed, we have nothing to fear. We don't want him to have any more time than necessary to stage a counter-attack. And gentlemen, do not be surprised by anything I do or say tomorrow. Trust my judgment, and be there to support me.'

'You don't feel we ought to know exactly what you have in mind?'

'No, Mr. Leach, you must appear at the meeting as disinterested directors doing no more than carrying out your duty.'

It was beginning to dawn on Ted Leach and his two colleagues why Charles Lester had chosen William Kane to be their next chairman. They left the Metropolitan Club a good deal more confident than when they had arived, despite their being totally in the dark as to what would actually happen at the board meeting they were about to instigate. William, on the other hand, having carried out the first part of Thomas Cohen's instructions, was now looking forward to pulling off the harder second part.

He spent most of the afternoon and evening in his room at the Yale Club, meticulously considering his tactics for the next day's meeting and taking only a short break to call Kate.

'Where are you, darling?' she said. 'Stealing away in the middle of the night to I know not where.'

'To my mistress in New York,' said William.

'Poor girl,' said Kate. 'She probably doesn't know the half of it. What's her advice on the devious Mr. Parfitt?'

'Haven't had time to ask her, we've been so busy doing other things. While I have you on the phone, what's your advice?'

'Do nothing Charles Lester or your father wouldn't have done in the same circumstances,' said Kate, suddenly serious.

'They're probably playing golf together on the eighteenth cloud and taking a side bet watching us the whole time.'

'Whatever you do, William, you won't go far wrong if you do remember they are watching you.'

When dawn broke, William was already awake, having only managed to sleep for short, fitful intervals. He rose a little after six, had a cold shower, went for a long walk through Central Park to clear his head, and returned to the Yale Club for a light breakfast. There was a message waiting for him in the front hall – from his wife. William laughed when he read it for a second time at the line, 'If you're not too busy could you remember to buy Richard a baseball glove.' William picked up the *Wall Street Journal* which was still running the story of trouble in the Lester's board room over the selection of a new chairman. It now had Peter Parfitt's version of the story, hinting that his appointment as chairman would probably be confirmed at Thursday's meeting. William wondered whose version would be reported in tomorrow's paper. Oh, for a look at tomorrow's *Journal* now. He spent the morning double checking the articles of incorporation and by-laws of Lester's Bank. He had no lunch but did find time to visit Schwalts and buy a baseball glove for his son.

At two-thirty William took a cab to the bank on Wall Street and arrived a few minutes before three. The young doorman asked him if he had an appointment to see anyone.

'I'm William Kane.'

'Yes, sir; you'll want the board room.'

Good God, thought William, I can't even remember where it is.

The doorman observed his embarrassment. 'You take the corridor on the left, sir, and then it's the second door on the right.'

'Thank you,' said William, and walked as confidently as he could down the corridor. He had always thought the expression a stomach full of butterflies a stupid one until that moment. He felt his heartbeat was louder than the clock in the front hall; he would not have been surprised to hear himself chiming three o'clock.

Ted Leach was standing alone at the entrance to the board room. 'There's going to be trouble,' were his opening words.

'Good,' said William. 'That's the way Charles Lester would have liked it, and he would have faced the trouble head on.'

William strode into the impressive oak-panelled room and did not need to count heads to be sure that every director was present. This was not going to be one of those board meetings a director could occasionally afford to skip. The conversation stopped the moment William entered the room, and there was an awkward silence as they all stood around and stared at him. William quickly took the chairman's seat at the head of the long mahogany table before Peter Parfitt could realise what was happening.

'Gentlemen, please be seated,' said William, hoping his voice sounded firm.

Ted Leach and some of the other directors took their seats immediately; others were more reluctant. Murmuring started.

William could see that two directors whom he didn't know were about to rise and interrupt him.

'Before anyone else says anything I would, if you will allow me, like to make an opening statement, and then you can decide how you wish to proceed from there. I feel that is the least we can do to comply with the wishes of the late Charles Lester.'

The two men sat down.

'Thank you, gentlemen. To start with, I would like to make it clear to all those present that I have absolutely no desire to be the chairman of this bank—' William paused for effect '—unless it be the wish of the majority of its directors.'

Every eye in the room was now fixed on William.

'I am, gentlemen, at present vice-chairman of Kane and Cabot, and I own fifty-one per cent of their stock. Kane and Cabot was founded by my grandfather, and I think it compares favourably in reputation, though not in size, with Lester's. Were I required to leave Boston and move to New York to become the next chairman of Lester's, in compliance with Charles Lester's wishes, I cannot pretend the move would be an easy one for myself or for my family. However, as it was Charles Lester's wish that I should do just that – and he was not a man to make such a proposition lightly – I am, gentlemen, bound to take his wishes seriously myself. I would also like to add that his son, Matthew Lester, was my closest friend for over fifteen years, and I consider it a tragedy that it is I, and not he, who is addressing you today as your nominated chairman.'

Some of the directors were nodding their approval.

'Gentlemen, if I am fortunate enough to secure your support today, I will sacrifice everything I have in Boston in order to serve you. I hope it is unnecessary for me to give you a detailed account of my banking experience. I shall assume that any director present who has read Charles Lester's will must have taken the trouble to find out why he considered that I was the right man to succeed him. My own chairman, Anthony Simmons, whom many of you will know, has asked me to stay on at Kane and Cabot.

'I had intended to inform Mr. Parfitt yesterday of my final decision, had he taken the trouble to call me and seek out that information. I had the pleasure of dining with Mr. and Mrs. Parfitt last Friday evening at their home, and on that occasion Mr. Parfitt informed me that he had no interest in becoming the next chairman of this bank. My only rival, in his opinion, was Mr. Edward Leach, your other vice-chairman. I have since consulted with Mr. Leach himself, and he informs me that I have always had his support for the chair. I assumed, therefore, that both vice-chairmen were backing me. After reading the *Wall Street Journal* this morning, not that I have ever trusted their forecasting since the age of eight' – a little laughter – 'I felt I should attend today's meeting to assure myself that I had not lost the support of the two vice-chairmen, and that the *Journal*'s account was inaccurate. Mr. Leach called this board meeting, and I must ask him at this juncture if he still supports me to succeed Charles Lester as the bank's next chairman.'

William looked towards Ted Leach, whose head was bowed. The wait for his verdict was palpable. A thumbs-down from him would mean the Parfittians could eat the Christian.

Ted Leach raised his head slowly and said, 'I support Mr. Kane unreservedly.'

William looked directly at Peter Parfitt for the first time that day. He was sweating profusely, and when he spoke, he did not take his eyes off the yellow pad in front of him.

'Well, some members of the board,' he began, 'felt I should throw my hat in the ring ...'

'So you have changed your mind about supporting me and complying with Charles Lester's wishes?' interrupted William, allowing a small note of surprise to enter his voice.

Peter Parfitt raised his head a little. 'The problem is not quite that easy, Mr. Kane.'

'Yes or no, Mr. Parfitt?'

'Yes, I shall stand against you,' said Peter Parfitt suddenly, forcefully.

'Despite telling me last Friday you had no interest in being chairman yourself?'

'I would like to be able to state my own position,' said Parfitt, 'before you assume too much. This is not your board room yet, Mr. Kane.'

'Certainly, Mr. Parfitt.'

So far, the meeting had gone exactly as William had

planned. His own speech had been carefully prepared and delivered, and Peter Parfitt now laboured under the disadvantage of having lost the initiative, to say nothing of having been publicly called a liar.

'Gentlemen,' he began, as if searching for words. 'Well,' he said.

The eyes had turned their gaze from William and now fixed on Parfitt. It gave William the chance to relax and study the faces of the other directors.

'Several members of the board approached me privately after I had dinner with Mr. Kane, and I felt that it was no more than my duty to consider their wishes and offer myself for election. I have never at any time wanted to oppose the wishes of Mr. Charles Lester, whom I always admired and respected. Naturally, I would have informed Mr. Kane of my intention before tomorrow's scheduled board meeting, but I confess to have been taken somewhat by surprise by today's events.'

He drew a deep breath and started again. 'I have served Lester's for twenty-two years, six of them as your vice-chairman. I feel, therefore, that I have the right to be considered for the chair. I would be delighted if Mr. Kane were to join the board, but I now find myself unable to back his appointment as chairman. I hope my fellow-directors will find it possible to support someone who has worked for this bank for over twenty years rather than elect an unknown outsider on the whim of a man distraught by the death of his only son. Thank you, gentlemen.'

He sat down.

In the circumstances, William was rather impressed by the speech, but Parfitt did not have the benefit of Mr. Cohen's advice on the power of the last word in a close contest. William rose again.

'Gentlemen, Mr. Parfitt has pointed out that I am personally unknown to you. I, therefore, want none of you to be in any doubt as to the type of man I am. I am, as I said, the grandson and the son of bankers. I've been a banker all my life and it would be less than honest of me to pretend I would not be delighted to serve as the next chairman of Lester's. If, on the other hand, after all you have heard today, you decide to back Mr. Parfitt as chairman, so be it. I shall return to Boston and serve my own bank quite happily. I will, moreover, announce publicly that I have no wish to be the chairman of Lester's, and that will insure you against any claims that you have been derelict in fulfilling the provisions of Charles Lester's will.

'There are, however, no conditions on which I would be willing to serve on your board under Mr. Parfitt. I have no intention of being less than frank with you on that point. I come before you, gentlemen, at the grave disadvantage of being, in Mr. Parfitt's words, "an unknown outsider". I have however, the advantage of being supported by a man who cannot be present today. A man whom all of you respected and admired, a man not known for yielding to whims or making hasty decisions. I therefore suggest this board wastes no more of its valuable time in deciding whom they wish to serve as the next chairman of Lester's. If any of you have any doubts in your mind about my ability to run this bank, then I can only suggest you vote for Mr. Parfitt. I shall not vote in this election myself, gentlemen, and I assume Mr. Parfitt will not do so either.'

'You *cannot* vote,' said Peter Parfitt, angrily. 'You are not a member of this board yet. I am, and I shall vote.'

'So be it, Mr. Parfitt. No one will ever be able to say you did not have the opportunity to gain every possible vote.'

William waited for the effect of his words to sink in, and as a director who was a stranger to William was about to interrupt, he continued, 'I will ask Mr. Rodgers as company secretary to carry out the electoral procedure, and when you have completed your vote, gentlemen, perhaps you could pass the ballot papers back to him.'

Alfred Rodgers' monocle had been popping out periodically during the entire meeting. Nervously, he passed voting slips around to each director. When each had written down the name of the candidate whom he supported, the slips were returned to him.

'Perhaps it might be prudent under the circumstances, Mr. Rodgers, if the votes were counted aloud, thus making sure no inadvertent error is made that might lead the directors to require a second ballot.'

'Certainly, Mr. Kane.'

'Does that meet with your approval, Mr. Parfitt?'

Peter Parfitt nodded his agreement without looking up.

'Thank you. Perhaps you would be kind enough to read the votes out to the board, Mr. Rodgers.'

The company secretary opened the first voting slip.

'Parfitt.'

And then the second.

'Parfitt,' he repeated.

The game was now out of William's hands. All the years of waiting for the prize he had told Charles Lester so long ago would be his would be over in the next few seconds.

'Kane. Parfitt. Kane.'

Three votes to two against him; was he going to meet the same fate as he had in his contest with Tony Simmons?

'Kane. Kane. Parfitt.'

Four votes all. He could see that Parfitt was sweating profusely at the other side of the table and he didn't exactly feel relaxed himself.

'Parfitt.'

No expression crossed William's face. Parfitt allowed himself a smile.

Five votes to four.

'Kane. Kane. Kane.'

The smile disappeared.

Just two more, two more, pleaded William, nearly out loud.

'Parfitt. Parfitt.'

The company secretary took a long time opening a voting slip which someone had folded and refolded several times.

'Kane.' Eight votes to seven in William's favour.

The last piece of paper was now being opened. William watched Alfred Rodgers' lips. The company secretary looked up; for that one moment he was the most important man in the room.

'Kane.' Parfitt's head sank into his hands.

'Gentlemen, the tally is nine votes for Mr. William Kane, seven votes for Mr. Peter Parfitt. I therefore declare Mr. William Kane to be the duly elected chairman of Lester's Bank.'

A respectful silence fell over the room and every head except Peter Parfitt's turned towards William and waited for the new chairman's first move.

William exhaled a great rush of air and stood once again, this time to face his board.

'Thank you, gentlemen, for the confidence you have placed in me. It was Charles Lester's wish that I should be your next chairman and I am delighted you have confirmed that wish with your vote. I now intend to serve this bank to the best of my ability, which I shall be unable to do without the wholehearted support of the board. If Mr. Parfitt would be kind enough ...'

Peter Parfitt looked up hopefully.

'... to join me in the chairman's office in a few minutes time, I would be much obliged. After I have seen Mr. Parfitt, I would like to see Mr. Leach. I hope, gentlemen, that tomorrow I shall have the opportunity of meeting all of you individually. The next board meeting will be the monthly one. This meeting is now adjourned.'

The directors began to rise and talk among themselves. William walked quickly into the corridor, avoiding Peter Parfitt's stare. Ted Leach caught up with him and directed him to the chairman's office.

'That was a great risk you took,' said Ted Leach, 'and you only just pulled it off. What would you have done if you'd lost the vote?'

'Gone back to Boston,' said William, sounding unperturbed.

Ted Leach opened the door to the chairman's office for William. The room was almost exactly as he remembered it; perhaps it had seemed a little larger when, as a prep-school boy, he had told Charles Lester that he would one day run the bank. He stared at the portrait of the great man behind his desk and winked at the late chairman. Then he sat down in the big red leather chair, and put his elbows on the mahogany desk. As he took a small, leather-bound book out of his jacket pocket and placed it on the desk in front of him, there was a knock on the door. An old man entered, leaning heavily on a black stick with a silver handle. Ted Leach left them alone.

'My name is Rupert Cork-Smith,' he said, with a hint of an English accent.

William rose to greet him. He was the oldest member of the board. His grey hair, long sideburns and heavy gold watch all came from a past era, but his reputation for probity was legendary in banking circles. No man needed to sign a contract with Rupert Cork-Smith : his word had always been his bond. He looked William firmly in the eye.

'I voted against you, sir, and naturally you can expect my resignation to be on your desk within the hour.'

'Will you have a seat, sir?' said William gently.

'Thank you, sir,' he replied.

'I think you knew my father and grandfather.'

'I had that privilege. Your grandfather and I were at Harvard together, and I still remember with regret your father's tragic death.'

'And Charles Lester?' said William.

'Was my closest friend. The provisions in his will have preyed upon my conscience. It was no secret that my choice would not have been Peter Parfitt. I would have had Ted Leach for chairman, but as I have never abstained from anything in my life, I felt I had to support the candidate who stood against you, as I found myself unable to vote for a man I had never even met.'

'I admire your honesty, Mr. Cork-Smith, but now I have a bank to run. I need you at this moment far more than you need me so I, as a younger man, beg you not to resign.'

The old man raised his head and stared into William's eyes. 'I'm not sure it would work, young man. I can't change my attitudes overnight,' said Cork-Smith, both hands resting on his stick.

'Give me six months, sir, and if you still feel the same way I won't put up a fight.'

They both sat in silence before Cork-Smith spoke again. 'Charles Lester was right: you are the son of Richard Kane.'

'Will you continue to serve this bank, sir?'

'I will, young man. There's no fool like an old fool, don't you know.'

Rupert Cork-Smith rose slowly with the aid of his stick. William moved to help him but was waved away.

'Good luck, my boy. You can rely on my total support.'

'Thank you, sir,' said William.

When he opened the door, William saw Peter Parfitt waiting in the corridor. As Rupert Cork-Smith left, the two men did not speak.

Peter Parfitt blustered in. 'Well, I tried and I lost. A man can't do more,' he said laughing. 'No hard feelings, Bill?' He extended his hand.

'There are no hard feelings, Mr. Parfitt. As you so rightly say, you tried and you lost, and now you will resign from your post at this bank.'

'I'll do what?' said Parfitt.

'Resign,' said William.

'That's a bit rough, isn't it, Bill? My action wasn't at all personal, I simply felt . . .'

'I don't want you in my bank, Mr. Parfitt. You'll leave by tonight and never return.'

'And if I say I won't go? I own a good many shares in the bank, and I still have a lot of support on the board, you know, and what's more I could take you to court.'

'Then I would recommend that you read the bank's by-laws, Mr. Parfitt, which I spent some considerable time studying only this morning.'

William picked up the small, leather-bound book which was still lying on the desk in front of him and turned a few pages over. Having found a paragraph he had marked that morning, he read aloud: 'The chairman has the right to remove any office holder in whom he has lost confidence.' He looked up. 'I have lost confidence in you, Mr. Parfitt, and you will therefore resign, receiving two years' pay. If, on the other hand, you force me to remove you, I shall see that you leave the bank with nothing other than your stock. The choice is yours.'

'Won't you give me a chance?'

'I gave you a chance last Friday night, and you lied and cheated. Not traits I am looking for in my next vice-chairman. Will it be resignation or do I throw you out, Mr. Parfitt?'

'Damn you, Kane, I'll resign.'

'Good. Sit down and write the letter now.'

'No, I'll let you have it in the morning in my own good time.' He started walking towards the door.

'Now – or I fire you,' said William.

Peter Parfitt hesitated and then came back and sank heavily into a chair by the side of William's desk. William handed him a piece of the bank's stationery and proffered him a pen. Parfitt took out his own pen and started writing. When he had finished, William picked up the letter and read it through carefully.

'Good day, Mr. Parfitt.'

Peter Parfitt left without speaking. Ted Leach came in a few moments later.

'You wanted to see me, Mr. Chairman?'

'Yes,' said William. 'I want to appoint you as the bank's overall vice-chairman. Mr. Parfitt felt he had to resign.'

'Oh, I'm surprised to hear that, I would have thought...'

William passed him the letter. Ted Leach read it and then looked at William.

'I shall be delighted to be overall vice-chairman. Thank you for your confidence in me.'

'Good. I will be obliged if you will arrange for me to meet every director during the next two days. I shall start work at eight o'clock tomorrow morning.'

'Yes, Mr. Kane.'

'Perhaps you will also be kind enough to give Mr. Parfitt's letter of resignation to the company secretary?'

'As you wish, Mr. Chairman.'

'My name is William, another mistake Mr. Parfitt made.'

Ted Leach smiled tentatively. 'I'll see you tomorrow morning—' he hesitated '—William.'

When he had left, William sat in Charles Lester's chair and whirled himself around in an uncharacteristic burst of sheer glee till he was dizzy. Then he looked out of the window on to Wall Street, elated by the bustling crowds, enjoying the view of the other great banks and brokerage houses of America. He was part of all that now.

'And who, pray, are you?' said a female voice from behind him.

William swivelled round, and there standing in front of him was a middle-aged woman, primly dressed, looking very irate.

'Perhaps I may ask you the same question,' said William.

'I am the chairman's secretary,' said the woman stiffly.

'And I,' said William, 'am the chairman.'

During the next few weeks William moved his family to New York where they found a house on East Sixty-eighth Street. Settling in took longer than they had originally anticipated possible. For the first three months William wished, as he tried to extricate himself from Boston in order to carry out his job in New York, that every day had forty-eight hours in it, and he found the umbilical cord was hard to sever completely. Tony Simmons was most helpful, and William began to appreciate why Alan Lloyd had backed him to be chairman of Kane and Cabot, and for the first time was willing to admit Alan had been right.

Kate's life in New York was soon fully occupied. Virginia could already crawl across a room and get into William's study before Kate could turn her head, and Richard wanted a new windbreaker, like every other boy in New York. As the wife of the chairman of a New York bank she regularly had to give cocktail parties and dinners, subtly making sure certain directors and major clients were always given the chance to catch the private ear of William to seek his advice or voice their own opinions. Kate handled all situations with great charm, and William was eternally grateful to the liquidation department of Kane and Cabot for supplying his greatest asset. When she informed William that she was going to have another baby, all he could ask was 'When did I find the time?' Virginia was thrilled by the news, not fully understanding why Mummy was getting so fat, and Richard refused to discuss it.

Within six months the clash with Peter Parfitt was a thing of the past, and William had become the undisputed chairman of Lester's bank and a figure to be reckoned with in New York financial circles. Not many more months had passed before he began to wonder in which direction he should start to set himself a new goal. He had achieved his life's ambition by becoming chairman of Lester's at the age of thirty-three although, unlike Alexander, he felt there were more worlds still to conquer, and he had neither the time nor the inclination to sit down and weep.

Kate gave birth to their third child at the end of William's first year as chairman of Lester's, a second girl, whom they named Lucy. William taught Virginia, who was now walking, how to rock Lucy's cradle; while Richard, now almost five years old and due to enter kindergarten at The Buckley School, used the new arrival as the opportunity to talk his father into a new baseball bat.

In William's first year as chairman of Lester's the bank's profits were slightly up and he was forecasting a considerable improvement in his second year.

Then on 1 September 1939 Hitler marched into Poland.

One of William's first reactions was to think of Abel Rosnovski and his new Baron on Park Avenue, already becoming the toast of New York. Quarterly reports from Thomas Cohen showed that Rosnovski went from strength to strength although his latest ideas for expansion to Europe looked as if they might be in for a slight delay. Cohen continued to find no direct association between Henry Osborne and Abel

Rosnovski, but he admitted that it was becoming increasingly difficult to ascertain all the facts he required.

William never thought that America would involve herself in a European war, but nevertheless he kept the London branch of Lester's open to show clearly which side he was on and not for one moment did he consider selling his twelve thousand acres in Hampshire and Lincolnshire. Tony Simmons in Boston, on the other hand, informed William that he intended to close Kane and Cabot's London branch. William used the problems created in London by the war as an excuse to visit his beloved Boston and have a meeting with Tony.

The two chairmen now met on extremely easy and friendly terms since they no longer had any reason to see themselves as rivals. In fact, each had come to use the other as a springboard for new ideas. As Tony had predicted, Kane and Cabot had lost some of its more important clients when William became the chairman of Lester's, but William always kept Tony fully informed whenever an old client expressed a desire to move his account and he never solicited a single one. When they sat down at the corner table of Locke-Ober's for lunch, Tony Simmons lost little time in repeating his intent to close the London branch of Kane and Cabot.

'My first reason is simple,' he said as he sipped the imported burgundy, apparently not giving a moment's thought to the strong likelihood that German boots were about to trample on the grapes in most of the vineyards in France. 'I think the bank will lose money if we don't cut our losses and get out of England.'

'Of course, you will lose a little money,' said William, 'but we must support the British.'

'Why?' asked Tony. 'We're a bank, not a supporters' club.'

'Britain's not a baseball team, Tony; it's a nation of people to whom we owe our entire heritage...'

'You should take up politics,' said Tony. 'I'm beginning to think your talents are wasted in banking. Nevertheless, I feel there's a far more important reason why we should close the branch. If Hitler marches into Britain the way he has into

Poland and France – and I'm sure that is exactly what he intends to do – the bank will be taken over, and we would lose every penny we have in London.'

'Over my dead body,' said William. 'If Hitler puts so much as a foot on British soil, America will enter the war the same day.'

'Never,' said Tony. 'F.D.R. has said, "all aid short of war". And the America Firsters would raise an almighty hue and cry.'

'Never listen to a politician,' said William. 'Especially Roosevelt. When he says "never", that only means not today, or at least not this morning. You only have to remember what Wilson told us in 1916.'

Tony laughed. 'When are you going to run for the Senate, William?'

'Now there is a question to which I can safely answer never.'

'I respect your feelings, William, but I want out.'

'You're the chairman,' replied William. 'If the board backs you, you can close the London branch tomorrow, and I would never use my position to act against a majority decision.'

'Until you join the two banks together, and it becomes your decision.'

'I told you once, Tony, that I would never attempt to do that while you were chairman. It's a promise I intend to honour.'

'But I think we *ought* to merge.'

'What?' said William, spilling his burgundy on the tablecloth, unable to believe what he had just heard. 'Good heavens, Tony, I'll say one thing for you, you're never predictable.'

'I have the best interests of the bank at heart, as always, William. Think about the present situation for a moment. New York is now, more than ever, the centre of U.S. finance, and when England goes under to Hitler, it will be the centre of world finance, so that's where Kane and Cabot needs to be. Moreover, if we merged, we would create a more comprehensive institution because our specialities are complementary. Kane and Cabot has always done a great deal of ship and heavy industry financing while Lester's does very little. Conversely, you do a lot of underwriting, and we hardly touch it. Not to mention the fact that in many cities we have unnecessary duplicating offices.'

'Tony, I agree with everything you've said, but I would still want to stay in Britain.'

'Exactly proving my point, William. Kane and Cabot's London branch would be closed, but we would still keep Lester's. Then, if London goes through a rough passage, it won't matter as much because we would be consolidated and therefore stronger.'

'But how would you feel if I said that while Roosevelt's restrictions on merchant banks will only allow us to work out of one state, a merger could succeed only if we ran the entire operation from New York treating Boston as nothing more than a holding office?'

'I'd back you,' said Tony and added, 'You might even consider going into commercial banking and dropping the straight investment work.'

'No, Tony. F.D.R. has made it impossible for an honest man to do both, and in any case my father believed that you could either serve a small group of rich people or a large group of poor people so Lester's will always remain in traditional merchant banking as long as I'm chairman. But if we did decide to merge the two banks don't you foresee major problems?'

'Very few we couldn't surmount given goodwill on both sides. However, you will have to consider the implications carefully, William, as you would undoubtedly lose overall control of the new bank as a minority shareholder which would always make you vulnerable to a takeover bid.'

'I'd risk that to be chairman of one of the largest financial institutions in America.'

William returned to New York that evening, elated by his discussion and called a board meeting of Lester's to outline

Tony Simmons' proposal. When he found that the board approved of a merger in principle, he instructed each manager in the bank to consider the whole plan in greater detail.

The departmental heads took three months before they reported back to the board, and to a man they came to the same conclusion: a merger was no more than common sense, as the two banks were complementary in so many ways. With different offices all over America and branches in Europe, they had a great deal to offer each other. Moreover, the chairman of Lester's had continued to own fifty-one per cent of Kane and Cabot, making the merger simply a marriage of convenience. Some of the directors on Lester's board could not understand why William hadn't thought of the idea before. Ted Leach was of the opinion that Charles Lester must have had it in his mind when he nominated William as his successor.

The details of the merger took nearly a year to negotiate and lawyers were kept at work into the small hours to complete the necessary paper work. In the exchange of shares, William ended up as the largest stockholder with eight per cent of the new company and was appointed the new bank's president and chairman. Tony Simmons remained in Boston as one vice-chairman and Ted Leach in New York as the other. The new merchant bank was renamed Lester, Kane and Company, but was still to be referred to as Lester's.

William decided to hold a press conference in New York to announce the successful merger of the two banks and he chose Monday, 8 December 1941 to inform the financial business world at large. The press conference had to be cancelled, because the morning before the Japanese had launched an attack on Pearl Harbor.

The prepared press release had already been mailed to the newspapers some days before, but the Tuesday morning financial pages understandably allocated the announcement of the merger only a small amount of space. This lack of coverage was no longer foremost in William's mind.

He couldn't quite work out how or when he was going to tell Kate that he intended to enlist. When Kate heard the news she was horrified and immediately tried to talk him out of the decision.

'What do you imagine you can do that a million others can't?' she demanded.

'I'm not sure,' William replied, 'But all I can be certain of is that I must do what my father or grandfather would have done given the same circumstances.'

'They would have undoubtedly done what was in the best interest of the bank.'

'No,' replied William quickly. 'They would have done what was in the best interest of America.'

Book Four

24

Abel studied the news item on Lester, Kane and Company in the financial section of the *Chicago Tribune*. With all the space devoted to the implications of the Japanese attack on Pearl Harbor, he would have missed the brief article had it not been accompanied by a small out-of-date photograph of William Kane, so out-of-date that Kane looked much as he had when Abel had visited him in Boston over ten years before. Certainly Kane appeared too young in that photograph to live up to the journal's description of him as the brilliant chairman of the newly formed Lester, Kane and Company. The article went on to predict: 'The new bank, a joining of Lester's of New York and Kane and Cabot of Boston, could well become one of the most important financial institutions in America after Mr. Kane's decision to merge the two distinguished family banks. As far as the *Trib* could ascertain the shares would be in the hands of about twenty people related to, or closely associated with the two families.'

Abel was delighted by that particular piece of information, realising that Kane must have lost overall control. He read the news item again. William Kane had obviously risen in the world since they had crossed swords, but then so had he, and he still had an old score to settle with the newly appointed chairman of Lester's.

So handsomely had the Baron Group's fortunes prospered over the decade that Abel had paid back all the loans to his backer and honoured to the letter the original agreement with his backer and had secured one hundred per cent ownership of the company within the required ten-year period.

By the last quarter of 1939, not only had Abel paid off the loan, but the profits for 1940 passed the half million mark. This milestone coincided with the opening of two new Barons, one in Washington, the other in San Francisco.

Though Abel had become a less devoted husband during this period, he could not have been a more doting father. Zaphia, longing for a second child, finally goaded him into seeing his doctor. When he learned that, because of a low sperm count, probably caused by sickness and malnutrition in his days under the Germans and Russians, Florentyna would almost certainly be his only child, he gave up all hope for a son and proceeded to lavish everything on her.

Abel's fame was now spreading across America and even the press had taken to referring to him as 'The Chicago Baron'. He no longer cared about the jokes behind his back. Wladek Koskiewicz had arrived and, more importantly, he was here to stay. By 1941 the profits from his thirteen hotels were just short of one million and, with his new surplus of capital, he decided the time had come for even further expansion.

Then the Japanese attacked Pearl Harbor.

Abel had already been sending considerable sums of money to the British Red Cross for the relief of his countrymen since that dreadful day in September 1939 on which the Nazis had marched into Poland, later to meet the Russians at Brest Litovsk and once again divide his homeland between them. He had waged a fierce battle, both within the Democratic Party and in the press, to push an unwilling America into the war even if now it had to be on the side of the Russians. His efforts so far had been fruitless, but on that December Sunday, with every radio station across the country blaring out the details to an incredulous nation, Abel knew that America must now be committed to the war. On 11 December he listened to President Roosevelt tell the nation that Germany and Italy had officially declared war on the United States. Abel had every intention of joining in, but first he had a private declaration of war he wished to make, and to that end he placed a call to Curtis Fenton at the Continental Trust Bank. Over the years Abel had grown to trust Fenton's judgment and had kept him on the board of the Baron Group when he gained overall control in order to keep a close link between the group and Continental Trust.

Curtis Fenton came on the line, his usual formal and always polite self.

'How much spare cash am I holding in the group's reserve account?' asked Abel.

Curtis Fenton picked out the file marked 'Number 6 Account', remembering the days when he could put all Mr. Rosnovski's affairs into one file. He scanned some figures.

'A little under two million dollars,' he said.

'Good,' said Abel. 'I want you to look into a newly formed bank called Lester, Kane and Company. Find out the name of every shareholder, what percentage they control and if there are any conditions under which they would be willing to sell. All this must be done without the knowledge of the bank's chairman, Mr. William Kane and without my name ever being mentioned.'

Curtis Fenton held his breath and said nothing. He was glad that Abel Rosnovski could not see his surprised face. Why did Abel Rosnovski want to put money into anything to do with William Kane? Fenton had also read in the *Wall Street Journal* about the merging of the two famous family banks. What with Pearl Harbor and his wife's headache, he too had nearly missed the item. Rosnovski's request jogged his memory – he must send a congratulatory wire to William Kane. He pencilled a note on the bottom of the Baron Group file while listening to Abel's instructions.

'When you have a full rundown I want to be briefed in person, nothing on paper.'

'Yes, Mr. Rosnovski.'

I suppose someone knows what's going on between those two, Curtis Fenton added silently to himself, but I'm damned if I do.

Abel continued. 'I'd also like to know in your quarterly reports the details of every official statement issued by Lester's and which companies they are involved with.'

'Certainly, Mr. Rosnovski.'

'Thank you, Mr. Fenton. By the way, my market research team is advising me to open a new Baron in Montreal.'

'The war doesn't worry you, Mr. Rosnovski?'

'Good God, no. If the Germans reach Montreal we can all close down, Continental Trust included. In any case, we beat the bastards last time, and we'll beat them again. The only difference is that this time I'll be able to join the action. Good day, Mr. Fenton.'

Will I ever understand what goes on in the mind of Abel Rosnovski, Curtis Fenton wondered, as he hung up the phone. His thoughts switched back to Abel's other request, for the details of Lester's shares. That worried him even more. Although William Kane no longer had any connection with Rosnovski, he feared where this might all end if his client obtained a substantial holding in Lester's. He decided against giving his views to Rosnovski for the time being, supposing the day would come when one of them would explain what they were both up to.

Abel also wondered if he should tell Curtis Fenton why he wanted to buy stock in Lester's but came to the conclusion that the fewer the number of people who knew of his plan, the better.

He put William Kane temporarily out of his mind and asked his secretary to find George, who was now a vice-president of the Baron Group. He had grown along with Abel and was now his most trusted lieutenant. Sitting in his office on the forty-second floor of the Chicago Baron, Abel looked down at Lake Michigan, on what was known as the Gold Coast, but his own thoughts returned to Poland. He wondered if he would ever live to see his castle again, now well inside the Russian borders under Stalin's control. Abel knew he would never settle in Poland, but he still wanted his castle restored to him. The idea of the Germans or Russians occupying his magnificent home once again made him want to ... His thoughts were interrupted by George.

'You wanted to see me, Abel?'

George was the only member of the group who still called the Chicago Baron by his first name.

'Yes, George. Do you think you could keep the hotels ticking along for a few months if I were to take a leave of absence?'

'Sure I can,' said George. 'Why, are you finally going to take that vacation you promised yourself?'

'No,' replied Abel. 'I'm going to war.'

'What?' said George. 'What?' he repeated.

'I'm going to New York tomorrow morning to enlist in the army.'

'You're crazy, you could get yourself killed.'

'That isn't what I had in mind,' replied Abel. 'Killing some Germans is what I plan to do. The bastards didn't get me the first time around and I have no intention of letting them get me now.'

George continued to protest that America could win the war without Abel. Zaphia protested too; she hated the very thought of war and little Florentyna, just turned eight years old, burst into tears. She did not quite know what war meant, but she did understand that Daddy would have to go away for a very long time.

Despite their protests, Abel took his first plane flight to New York the next day. All of America seemed to be going in different directions and he found the city full of young men in khaki saying their farewells to parents, sweethearts and wives, all assuring each other that the war would be over in a few weeks but none of them believing it.

Abel arrived at the New York Baron in time for dinner. The dining room was packed with young people, girls clinging desperately to soldiers, sailors and airmen, while Frank Sinatra crooned to the rhythms of Tommy Dorsey's big band. As Abel watched the young people on the dance floor, he wondered how many of them would ever have a chance to enjoy an evening like this again. He couldn't help remembering Sammy explaining how he had become *maître d'* at the Plaza. The three men senior to him had returned from the Western Front with one leg between them. None of the young people dancing could begin to know what war was really like. He didn't join in the celebration – if that's what it was. He went to his room instead.

In the morning, he dressed in a plain dark suit and went down to the recruiting office in Times Square. He had chosen to enlist in New York because he feared someone might recognise him in Chicago and all he could hope to end up with would be a swivel chair. The office was even more crowded than the dance floor had been the night before, but here no one was clinging on to anyone else. Abel hung around the entire morning in order to fill out one form that would have taken him three minutes in his own office. He couldn't help noticing that all the other recruits looked fitter than he. He then stood in line for two more hours waiting to be interviewed by a recruiting sergeant who asked him what he did for a living.

'Hotel management,' said Abel, and went on to tell the officer of his experiences in the first war. The sergeant stared silently at the five foot seven, one hundred and ninety pound man with an expression of incredulity. If Abel had told him he was the Chicago Baron, the officer would not have doubted his stories of imprisonment and escape, but he chose to keep this information to himself and be treated like any of his fellow countrymen.

'You'll have to take a full physical tomorrow morning,' was all the recruiting sergeant said at the end of Abel's monologue, adding, as though he felt the comment was no less than his duty, 'Thank you for volunteering.'

The next day Abel had to wait several more hours for his physical examination. The doctor in charge was fairly blunt about Abel's general condition. He had been protected from such comments for several years by his position and success. It came as a rude awakening when the doctor classified him 4F.

'You're overweight, your eyes are not too good, your heart is weak, and you limp. Frankly, Rosnovski, you're plain unfit. We can't take soldiers into battle who are likely to have a heart attack even before they find the enemy. That doesn't mean we can't use your talents; there's a lot of paperwork to be done in this war if you are interested.'

Abel wanted to hit him, but he knew that wouldn't help get him into uniform.

'No, thank you ... sir,' he said. 'I want to fight the Germans, not send letters to them.'

He returned to the hotel that evening despondent, but Abel decided that he wasn't licked yet. The next day he tried again, going to another recruiting office, but he came back to the Baron with the same result. Admittedly, the second doctor had been a little more polite, but he was every bit as firm about his condition, and once again Abel had ended up with a 4F. It was obvious to Abel that he was not going to be allowed to fight anybody in his present state of health.

The next morning, he found a gymnasium on West Fifty-seventh Street and paid a private instructor to do something about his physical condition. For three months he worked every day on his weight and general fitness. He boxed, wrestled, ran, jumped, skipped, pressed weights and starved. When he was down to one hundred and fifty-five pounds, the instructor assured him he was never going to be much fitter or thinner. Abel returned to the first recruiting office and filled in the same form under the name of Wladek Koskiewicz. Another recruiting sergeant was a lot more hopeful this time, and the medical officer who gave him several tests finally accepted him as a reserve, waiting to be called up.

'But I want to go to war now,' said Abel. 'I want to fight the bastards.'

'We'll be in touch with you, Mr. Koskiewicz,' said the sergeant. 'Please keep yourself fit and prepared. You can never be sure when we will need you.'

Abel left, furious as he watched younger, leaner Americans being readily accepted for active service, and as he barged through the door, not sure what his next ploy should be, he walked straight into a tall, gangling man wearing a uniform adorned with stars on the shoulders.

'I'm sorry, sir,' said Abel, looking up and backing away.

'Young man,' said the general.

Abel walked on, not thinking that the officer was addressing him, as no one had called him young man for ... he didn't want to think for how long, despite the fact that he was still only thirty-five.

The general tried again. 'Young man,' he said a little more loudly.

This time Abel turned around. 'Me, sir?' he asked.

'Yes, you, sir.'

Abel walked over to the general.

'Will you come to my office please, Mr. Rosnovski?'

Damn, thought Abel, this man knows who I am, and now nobody's going to let me fight in this war. The general's temporary office turned out to be at the back of the building, a small room with a desk, two wooden chairs, peeling green paint and an open door. Abel would not have allowed a junior member of his staff at a Baron to work in such surroundings.

'Mr. Rosnovski,' the general began, exuding energy, 'my name is Mark Clark and I command the U.S. Fifth Army. I'm over from Governors Island for the day on an inspection tour, so literally bumping into you is a pleasant surprise. I have for a long time been an admirer. Your story is one to gladden the heart of any American. Now tell me what you are doing in this recruiting office.'

'What do you think?' said Abel, not thinking. 'I'm sorry, sir,' he corrected himself quickly. 'I didn't mean to be rude, it's only that no one will let me get into this damn war.'

'What do you want to do in this damn war?' asked the general.

'Sign up,' said Abel, 'and fight the Germans.'

'As a foot soldier?' enquired the incredulous general.

'Yes,' said Abel, 'don't you need every man you can get?'

'Naturally,' said the general, 'but I can put your particular talents to a far better use than as a foot soldier.'

'I'll do anything,' said Abel, 'anything.'

'Will you now?' said the general, 'and if I asked you to place your New York hotel at my disposal as army headquarters here, how would you react to that? Because frankly, Mr. Rosnovski, that would be of far more use to me than if you managed to kill a dozen Germans personally.'

'The Baron is yours,' said Abel. 'Now will you let me go to war?'

'You know you're mad, don't you?' said General Clark.

'I'm Polish,' said Abel. They both laughed. 'You must understand,' he continued in a more serious tone. 'I was born near Slonim. I saw my home taken over by the Germans, my sister raped by the Russians. I later escaped from a Russian labour camp and was lucky enough to reach America. I'm not mad. This is the only country in the world where you can arrive with nothing and become a millionaire through damned hard work regardless of your background. Now those same bastards want another war. I'm not mad, General. I'm human.'

'Well, if you're so eager to join up, Mr. Rosnovski, I could use you, but not in the way you imagine. General Denvers needs someone to take over responsibility as quartermaster for the Fifth Army while they are fighting in the front lines. If you believe Napoleon was right when he said an army marches on its stomach, you could play a vital role. The job carries the rank of major. That is one way in which you could unquestionably help America to win this war. What do you say?'

'I'll do it, General.'

'Thank you, Mr. Rosnovski.'

The general pressed a buzzer on his desk and a very young lieutenant came in and saluted smartly.

'Lieutenant, will you take Major Rosnovski to personnel and then bring him back to me?'

'Yes, sir.' The lieutenant turned to Abel. 'Will you come this way, please, Major?'

Abel followed him, turning as he reached the door. 'Thank you, General,' he said.

He spent the weekend in Chicago with Zaphia and Florentyna. Zaphia asked him what he wanted her to do with his fifteen suits.

'Hold on to them,' he replied, wondering what she meant. 'I'm not going to get myself killed in this war.'

'I'm sure you're not, Abel,' she replied. 'That wasn't what was worrying me. It's just that now they're all three sizes too large for you.'

Abel laughed and took the suits to the Polish refugee centre. He then returned to New York, went to the Baron, cancelled the advance guest list, and twelve days later handed the building over to the American Fifth Army. The press hailed Abel's decision as a 'selfless gesture', worthy of a man who had been a refugee of the First World War.

It was another three months before Abel was called to active duty, during which time he organised the smooth running of the New York Baron for General Clark and then reported to Fort Benning, to complete an officers' training programme. When he finally did receive his orders to join General Denvers and the Fifth Army, his destination turned out to be somewhere in North Africa. He began to wonder if he would ever get to Germany.

The day before Abel left, he drew up a will, instructing his executors to offer the Baron Group to David Maxton on favourable terms, and dividing the rest of his estate between Zaphia and Florentyna. It was the first time in nearly twenty years that he had contemplated death, not that he was sure how he could get himself killed in the regimental canteen.

As his troop ship sailed out of New York harbour, Abel stared back at the Statue of Liberty. He could well remember how he had felt on seeing the statue for the first time nearly twenty years before. Once the ship had passed the Lady, he did not look at her again, but said out loud, 'Next time I look at you, you French bitch, America will have won this war.'

Abel crossed the Atlantic, taking with him two of his top chefs and five kitchen staff. The ship docked at Algiers on 17 February 1943. He spent almost a year in the heat and the dust and the sand of the desert, making sure that every member of the division was as well fed as possible.

'We eat badly, but we eat a damn sight better than anyone else,' was General Clark's comment.

Abel commandeered the only good hotel in Algiers and turned the building into a headquarters for General Clark. Although Abel could see he was playing a valuable role in the war, he itched to get into a real fight, but majors in charge of catering are rarely sent into the front line.

He wrote to Zaphia and George and watched his beloved daughter Florentyna grow up by photograph. He even received an occasional letter from Curtis Fenton, reporting that the Baron Group was making an even larger profit because every hotel in America was packed because of the continual movement of troops and civilians. Abel was sad not to have been at the opening of the new hotel in Montreal, where George had represented him. It was the first time that he had not been present at the opening of a Baron, but George wrote at reassuring length of the new hotel's great success. Abel began to realise how much he had built up in America and how much he wanted to return to the land he now felt was his home.

He soon became bored with Africa and its mess kits, baked beans, blankets and fly swatters. There had been one or two spirited skirmishes out there in the western desert, or so the men returning from the front assured him, but he never saw any real action, although often when he took the food to the front he would hear the firing, and it made him even angrier. One day to his excitement, General Clark's Fifth Army was ordered to invade Southern Europe.

The Fifth Army landed on the Italian coast in amphibious craft while American aircraft gave them tactical cover. They met considerable resistance, first at Anzio and then at Monte Cassino but the action never involved Abel and he dreaded the end of a war in which he had seen no combat.

But he could never devise a plan which would get him into the front lines. His chances were not improved when he was promoted to Lieutenant Colonel and sent to London to await further orders.

With D-Day, the great thrust into Europe began. The Allies marched into France and liberated Paris on 25 August 1944. As Abel paraded with the American and Free French soldiers down the Champs Elysées behind General de Gaulle to a hero's welcome, he studied the still magnificent city and once again decided exactly where he was going to build his first Baron hotel in France.

The Allies moved on through northern France and across the German border in a final drive towards Berlin. Abel was posted to the First Army under General Bradley. Food was coming mainly from England: local supplies were almost non-existent, as each succeeding town at which they arrived had already been ravaged by the retreating German army. When Abel arrived in a new city, it would take him only a few hours to commandeer the entire remaining food supply before other American quartermasters had worked out exactly where to look. British and American officers were always happy to dine with the Ninth Armoured Division and would leave wondering how they had managed to requisition such excellent supplies. On one occasion when General George S. Patton joined General Bradley for dinner, Abel was introduced to the famous general who always led his troops into battle brandishing an ivory-handled revolver.

'The best meal I've had in the whole damn war,' said Patton.

By February 1945, Abel had been in uniform for nearly three years and he knew the war would be over in a matter of months. General Bradley kept sending him congratulatory notes and meaningless decorations to adorn his ever-expanding uniform, but they didn't help. Abel begged the general to let him fight in just one battle, but Bradley wouldn't hear of it.

Although it was the duty of a junior officer to drive the food trucks up to the front lines and then supervise the meals for the troops, Abel often carried out the responsibility himself. And, as in the running of his hotels, he would never let any of his staff know when or where he next intended to pounce.

It was the continual flow of blanket-covered stretchers into the camp that damp St. Patrick's Day that made Abel want to go up to the Front and take a look for himself. When it reached a point where he could no longer bear a one-way traffic of bodies, Abel rounded up his men and personally organised the fourteen food trucks. He took with him one lieutenant, one sergeant, two corporals, and twenty-eight privates.

The drive to the Front, although only twenty miles, was tiresomely slow that morning. Abel took the wheel of the first truck – it made him feel a little like General Patton – through heavy rain and thick mud; he had to pull off the road several times to allow ambulance details the right of way in their return from the Front. Wounded bodies took precedence over empty stomachs. Abel wished that most of them were no more than wounded, but only the occasional nod or wave suggested any sign of life. It became obvious to Abel with each mud-tracked mile that something big was going on near Remagen, and he could feel the beat of his heart quicken. Somehow, he knew this time he was going to be involved.

When he finally reached the command post he could hear the enemy fire in the distance, and he started pounding his leg in anger as he watched stretchers bringing back yet more dead and wounded comrades from he knew not where. Abel was sick of learning nothing about the real war until it was part of history. He suspected that any reader of the *New York Times* was better informed than he was.

Abel brought his convoy to a halt by the side of the field kitchen and jumped out of the truck shielding himself from the heavy rain, feeling ashamed that others only a few miles away were shielding themselves from bullets. He began to supervise the unloading of one hundred gallons of soup, a ton of corned beef, two hundred chickens, half a ton of butter, three tons of potatoes and one hundred and ten pound cans of baked beans – plus the inevitable K rations – in readiness for those going to, or returning from, the front. When Abel arrived in the mess tent he found it full of long tables and empty benches. He left his two chefs to prepare the meal and the orderlies to start peeling one thousand potatoes while he went off in search of the duty officer.

Abel headed straight for Brigadier-General John Leonard's tent to find out what was going on, continually passing stretchers of dead and – worse – nearly dead soldiers, the sight of whom would have made any ordinary man sick but at Remagen had the air of being commonplace. As Abel was about to enter the tent, General Leonard, accompanied by his aide, was rushing out. He conducted a conversation with Abel while continuing to walk.

'What can I do for you, Colonel?'

'I have started preparing the food for your battalion as requested in overnight orders, sir. What . . .?'

'You needn't bother with the food for now, Colonel. At first light this morning Lieutenant Burrows of the Ninth discovered an undamaged railroad bridge north of Remagen, and I gave orders that it should be crossed immediately and every effort made to establish a bridge head on the east bank of the river. Up to now, the Germans have been successful in blowing up every bridge across the Rhine long before we reached it so we can't hang around waiting for lunch before they demolish this one.'

'Did the Ninth succeed in getting across?' asked a puffing Abel.

'Sure did,' replied the general, 'but they encountered heavy resistance when they reached the forest on the far side of the river. The first platoons were ambushed and God knows how many men we lost. So you had better eat the food yourself, Colonel, because my only interest is getting as many of my men back alive as possible.'

'Is there anything I can do?' asked Abel.

The fighting commander stopped running for a moment

and studied the fat colonel. 'How many men have you under your direct command?'

'One lieutenant, one sergeant, two corporals, and twenty-eight privates; thirty-three in all including myself, sir.'

'Good. Report to the field hospital with your men and make yourself useful out there by bringing back as many dead and wounded as you can find.'

'Yes, sir,' said Abel and ran all the way back to the field kitchen where he found his own men sitting in a corner smoking. None of them noticed when he entered the tent.

'Get up, you bunch of lazy bastards. We've got real work to do for a change.'

Thirty-two men snapped to attention.

'Follow me,' shouted Abel, 'on the double.'

He turned and started running again, this time towards the field hospital. A young doctor was briefing sixteen medical corpsmen when Abel and his out of breath, unfit men appeared at the entrance to the tent.

'Can I help you, sir?' asked the doctor.

'No, I hope I can help you,' replied Abel. 'I have thirty-two men here who have been detailed by General Leonard to join your group' – it was the first time they had heard of it.

The doctor stared in amazement at the colonel. 'Yes, sir.'

'Don't call me sir,' said Abel. 'We're here to find out how we can assist *you*.'

'Yes, sir,' the doctor said again.

He handed Abel a carton of Red Cross armbands which the chefs, kitchen orderlies and potato peeler proceeded to put on as they listened to the doctor continue his briefing, giving details of the action in the forest on the far side of the Ludendorff bridge.

'The Ninth has sustained heavy casualties,' he continued. 'Those soldiers with medical expertise will remain in the battle zone, while the rest of you will bring back as many of the wounded as possible to this field hospital.'

Abel was delighted at the opportunity to do something positive for a change. The doctor, now in command of a team of forty-nine men, passed out eighteen stretchers, and each soldier received a full medical pack. He then led his motley band towards the Ludendorff bridge. Abel was only a yard behind him. They started singing as they marched through the mud and rain; they stopped singing when they reached the bridge and were greeted by stretcher after stretcher showing clearly the outline of a body covered only in blankets. They marched silently across the bridge in single file by the side of the railroad track where they could see the results of the German explosion that had failed to destroy its foundations. On up towards the forest and the sound of fire, Abel found he was excited by the thought of being so near the enemy, and horrified by the realisation of what that enemy was capable of inflicting on his fellow countrymen. Everywhere he turned he saw, or worse, heard cries of anguish coming from his comrades. Comrades who until that day had wistfully thought the end of the war was near – but not that near.

He watched the young doctor stop again and again and do the best he could for each man. Sometimes he would mercifully kill a man quickly when there was not the slightest hope of trying to patch him up. Abel ran from soldier to soldier organising the stretchers of those unable to help themselves and guiding the wounded who could still walk back towards the Ludendorff bridge. By the time their group reached the edge of the forest only the doctor, one of the potato peelers and himself were left of the original party; all the others were carrying the dead and wounded back to the camp.

As the three of them marched into the forest they could hear the enemy guns close by. Abel could see the outline of a big gun, hidden in undergrowth and still pointing towards the bridge, but now damaged beyond repair. Then he heard a volley of bullets that sounded so loud that he realised for the first time that the enemy were only a few hundred yards ahead of him. He quickly crouched down on one knee, expectant, his senses heightened to screaming pitch. Suddenly there was another burst of fire in front of him. He jumped up and ran forward, reluctantly followed by the doctor and the potato peeler. They ran on for another hundred yards, when they came across a beautiful stretch of lush green grass in a hollow covered in a bed of white crocuses, littered with the bodies of American soldiers. Abel and the doctor ran from corpse to corpse. 'It must have been a massacre,' screamed Abel in anger, as he heard the retreating fire. The doctor made no comment: he had screamed three years before.

'Don't worry about the dead,' was all he said. 'Just see if you can find anyone who is still alive.'

'Over here,' shouted Abel as he kneeled down beside a sergeant lying in the German mud. Both his eyes were missing.

'He's dead, Colonel,' said the doctor, not giving the man a second glance. Abel ran to the next body and then the next but it was always the same and only the sight of a severed head placed upright in the mud stopped Abel in his tracks. He kept having to look back at it, like the bust of some Greek god that could no longer move. Abel recited like a child words he had learned at the feet of the Baron: ' "Blood and destruction shall be so in use and dreadful objects so familiar that mothers shall but smile when they behold their infants quarter'd with the hands of war." Does nothing change?' said Abel outraged.

'Only the battlefield,' replied the doctor.

When Abel had checked thirty – or was it forty men? – he once again returned to the doctor who was trying to save the life of a captain who but for a closed eye and his mouth was already swathed in blood-soaked bandages. Abel stood over the doctor watching helplessly, studying the captain's shoulder patch – the Ninth Armoured – and remembered General Leonard's words, 'God knows how many men we lost today.'

'Fucking Germans,' said Abel.

'Yes, sir,' said the doctor.

'Is he dead?' asked Abel.

'Might as well be,' replied the doctor mechanically. 'He's losing so much blood it can only be a matter of time.' He looked up. 'There's nothing left for you to do here, Colonel, so why don't you try and get the one survivor back to the field hospital before he dies and let the base commander know that I intend to go forward and need every man he can spare.'

'Right,' said Abel as he helped the doctor carefully lift the captain on to a stretcher. Abel and the potato peeler tramped slowly back towards the camp, the doctor having warned him that any sudden movement to the stretcher could only result in an even greater loss of blood. Abel didn't let the potato peeler rest for one moment during the entire two-mile trek to the base camp. He wanted to give the man a chance to live and then return to the doctor in the forest.

For over an hour they trudged through the mud and the rain, and Abel felt certain the captain had died. When they finally reached the field hospital both men were exhausted, and Abel handed the stretcher over to a medical team.

As the captain was wheeled slowly away he opened his unbandaged eye which focused on Abel. He tried to raise his arm. Abel saluted and could have leapt with joy at the sight of the open eye and the moving hand. How he prayed that man would live.

He ran out of the hospital, eager to return to the forest with his little band of men when he was stopped by the duty officer.

'Colonel,' he said, 'I have been looking for you everywhere. There are over three hundred men who need feeding. Christ, man, where have you been?'

'Doing something worthwhile for a change.'

Abel thought about the young captain as he headed slowly back to the field kitchen.

For both men the war was over.

25

The stretcher bearers took the captain into a tent and laid him gently on an operating table. Captain William Kane could see a nurse looking sadly down at him, but he was unable to hear anything she was saying. He wasn't sure if it was because his head was swathed in bandages or because he was now deaf. He watched her lips move, but learned nothing. He shut his eye and thought. He thought a lot about the past; he thought a little about the future; he thought quickly in case he died. He knew if he lived, there would be a long time for thinking. His mind turned to Kate in New York. She had refused to accept his determination to enlist. He knew she would never understand, and that he would not be able to justify his reasons to her so he had stopped trying. The memory of her desperate face now haunted him. He never really considered death – no man does – and now he wanted only to live and return to his old life.

William had left Lester's under the joint control of Ted Leach and Tony Simmons until he returned ... until he returned. He had given no instructions for them to follow if he did not return. Both of them had begged him not to go. Two more men who couldn't understand. When he signed up a few days later, he couldn't face the children. Richard, aged ten, had found his own way to the station; he had held back the tears until his father told him he could not go along with him to fight the Germans.

They sent him first to an Officers' Candidate School in Vermont. Last time he had seen Vermont, he had been skiing with Matthew, slowly up the hills and quickly down. Now the journey was slow both ways. The course lasted for three months and made him fit again for the first time since he had left Harvard.

His first assignment was in a London full of Yanks, where he acted as a liaison officer between the Americans and the British. He was billeted at the Dorchester, which the British War Office had taken over and seconded for use by the American army. William had read somewhere that Abel Rosnovski had done the same thing with the Baron in New York and he had thoroughly approved at the time. The blackouts, the doodle-bugs, and the air raid warnings all made him believe that he was involved in a war, but he felt strangely detached from what was going on only a few hundred miles from Hyde Park Corner. Throughout his life he had taken the initiative, and had never been an onlooker. Moving between Eisenhower's staff headquarters in St. James and Churchill's War Operations room in Storey's Gate wasn't William's idea of initiative. It didn't look as if he was going to meet a German face-to-face for the entire duration of the war unless Hitler invaded Trafalgar Square.

When part of the First Army was posted to Scotland for training exercises with the Black Watch, William was sent along as an observer and told to report back with his findings. The long, slow journey to Scotland and back in a train that never stopped stopping made him realise that he was fast becoming a glorified messenger boy and he was beginning to wonder why he had ever signed up. Scotland, William found, was different. There at least they had the air of preparing for war and when he returned to London, he put in a request for an immediate transfer to join the First Army. His colonel, who never believed in keeping a man who wanted to see action behind a desk, released him.

Three days later William returned to Scotland to join his new regiment and begin his training with the American troops at Inveraray for the invasion they all knew had to come soon. Training was hard and intense. Nights spent in the Scottish hills fighting mock battles with the Black Watch made more than a slight contrast to evenings at the Dorchester writing reports.

Three months later they were parachuted into northern France to join Omar N. Bradley's army, moving across Europe. The scent of victory was in the air and William wanted to be the first soldier in Berlin.

The First Army advanced towards the Rhine, determined to cross any bridge they could find. Captain Kane received orders that morning that his division was to advance over the Ludendorff bridge and engage the enemy a mile northeast of Remagen in a forest on the far side of the river. He stood on the crest of a hill and watched the Ninth Division cross the bridge, expecting it to be blown sky high at any moment.

His colonel led his own division in behind them. He followed with the hundred and twenty men under his command, most of them, like William, going into action for the first time. No more exercises with wily Scots pretending to kill him, with blank cartridges and then a meal together afterwards. Germans, with real bullets, death – and perhaps no afterwards.

When William reached the edge of the forest, he and his men met with no resistance, so they decided to press further on into the woods. The going was slow and dull and William was beginning to think the Ninth must have done such a thorough job that his division would only have to follow them through, when from nowhere they were suddenly ambushed by a hail of bullets and mortars. Everything seemed to be coming at them at once. William's men went down, trying to protect themselves among the trees, but he lost over half of the platoon in a matter of seconds. The battle, if that's what it could be called, had lasted for less than a minute, and he hadn't even seen a German. William crouched in the wet undergrowth for a few more seconds and then saw, to his horror, the next Division coming through the forest. He ran from his shelter behind a tree to warn them of the ambush. The first bullet hit him in the head, and, as he sank to his knees in the German mud and continued to wave a frantic warning to his advancing comrades, the second hit him in the neck and a third in the chest. He lay still in the mud and waited to die, not having even seen the enemy – a dirty, unheroic death.

The next thing William knew, he was being carried on a stretcher, but he couldn't hear or see anything and he wondered if it was night or whether he was blind.

It seemed a long journey. When his eye opened, it focused on a short fat colonel limping out of a tent. There was something familiar about him, but he couldn't think what. The stretcher bearers took him into the operating tent and placed him on the table. He tried to fight off sleep for fear it might be death. He slept.

William woke. He was conscious of two people trying to move him. They were turning him over as gently as they could, and then they stuck a needle into him. William dreamed of seeing Kate, and then his mother, and then Matthew playing with his son Richard. He slept.

He woke. He knew they had moved him to another bed; slight hope replaced the thought of inevitable death. He lay motionless, his one eye fixed on the canvas roof of the tent, unable to move his head. A nurse came over to study a chart and then him. He slept.

He woke. How much time had passed? Another nurse. This time he could see a little more and – joy, oh joy – he could move his head, if only with great pain. He lay awake as long as he possibly could; he wanted to live. He slept.

He woke. Four doctors were studying him, deciding what? He could not hear them and so learnt nothing.

They moved him once again. This time he was able to watch them put him in an army ambulance. The doors closed behind him, the engine started, and the ambulance began to move over rough ground while a new nurse sat by his side holding him steady. The journey felt like an hour, but he no longer could be sure of time. The ambulance reached smoother ground and then came to a halt. Once again they moved him. This time they were walking on a flat surface and then up some stairs into a dark room. They waited again and then the room began to move, another car perhaps. The room took off. The nurse stuck another needle into him, and he remembered nothing until he felt a plane landing and taxiing to a halt. They moved him yet again. Another ambulance, another nurse, another smell, another city. New York, or at least America, he thought, no other smell like that in the world. The new ambulance took him over another smooth surface, continually stopping and starting, until it finally arrived at where it wanted to be. They carried him out once again and up some more steps into a small white-walled room. They placed him in a comfortable bed. He felt his head touch the pillow, and when next he woke, thought he was totally alone. Then his eye focused and he saw Kate standing in front of him. He tried to lift his hand and touch her, to speak, but no words came. She smiled, but he knew she could not see his smile, and when he woke again Kate was still there but wearing a different dress. Or had she come and gone many times? She smiled again. How long had it been? He tried to move his head a little, and saw his son Richard, so tall, so good-looking. He wanted to see his daughters, but couldn't move his head any further. They moved into his line of vision, Virginia – she couldn't be that old, and Lucy, it wasn't possible. Where had the years gone? He slept.

He woke. No one was there, but now he could move his head. Some bandages had been removed and he could see more clearly; he tried to say something, but no words came. He slept.

He woke. Less bandages than before. Kate was there again, her fair hair longer, now falling to her shoulders, her soft grown eyes and unforgettable smile, looking beautiful, so beautiful. He said her name. She smiled. He slept.

He woke. Even fewer bandages than before. This time his son spoke.

Richard said, 'Hello, Daddy.'

He heard him and replied, 'Hello, Richard,' but didn't recognise the sound of his own voice. The nurse helped him to sit up ready to greet his family. He thanked her. A doctor touched his shoulder.

'The worst is over, Mr. Kane. You'll soon be well, and then you can return home.'

He smiled as Kate came into the room, followed by Virginia and Lucy. So many questions to ask them. Where should he begin? There were gaps in his memory that demanded satisfaction. Kate told him that he had nearly died.

He knew that but had not realised that over a year had passed since his division had been ambushed in the forest at Remagen.

Where had the months of being unaware gone, life lost resembling death? Richard was almost twelve, already hoping to go to Havard, Virginia was nine, and Lucy nearly seven. Their dresses seemed rather short. He would have to get to know them all over again.

Kate was somehow more beautiful than William even remembered her. She told William how she never learned to face the fact that he might have died, how well Richard was doing at Buckley and how Virginia and Lucy needed a father. She braced herself to tell him of the scars on his face and chest that would never heal and thanked God that the doctors felt certain there would be nothing wrong with his mind and his sight would be restored. Now all she wanted to do was help him recover. Kate slowly, William quickly.

Each member of the family played their part in the process. First sound, then sight, then speech. Richard helped his father to walk, until he no longer needed the crutches. Lucy helped him with his food, until he could feed himself once more and Virginia read Mark Twain to him. William was not sure if the reading was for her benefit or his, they both enjoyed it so much. And then at last, after Christmas had passed, they allowed him to return to his own home.

Once William was back in East Sixty-eighth Street, he recovered more quickly, and his doctors were predicting that he would be able to return to work at the bank within six months. A little scarred, but very much alive, he was allowed to see visitors.

The first was Ted Leach, somewhat taken aback at William's appearance. Something else he would have to learn to live with for the time being. From Ted Leach, William learned news that brought him satisfaction. Lester's had progressed in his absence and his colleagues looked forward to welcoming him back as their chairman. A visit from Tony Simmons brought him news that made him sad. Alan Lloyd and Rupert Cork-Smith had both died. He would miss their prudent wisdom. And then Thomas Cohen called to say how glad he was to learn of his recovery and to prove, as if it were still necessary, that time had moved on by informing William he was now semi-retired and had turned over many of his clients to his son Thaddeus who had opened an office in New York. William remarked on both of them being named after apostles. Thomas Cohen laughed and expressed the hope that Mr. Kane would continue to use the firm. William assured him he would.

'By the way, I do have one piece of information you ought to know about.'

William listened to the old lawyer in silence and became angry, very angry.

Book Five

26

General Alfred Jodl signed the unconditional surrender at Rheims on 7 May 1945 as Abel arrived back into a New York preparing for victory celebrations and an end to the war. Once again, the streets were filled with young people in uniform, but this time their faces showed elation, not fear. Abel was saddened by the sight of so many men with one leg, one arm, blind or badly scarred. For them the war would never be over, whatever piece of paper had been signed four thousand miles away.

When Abel walked into the Baron in his colonel's uniform, no one recognised him. Why should they? When they had last seen him in civilian clothes two years before, there were no lines on his still youthful face. The face they now saw was older than its thirty-nine years and the deep, worn ridges on his forehead showed that the war had left its mark on him. He took the lift to his forty-second floor office, and a security guard told him firmly he was on the wrong floor.

'Where's George Novak?' asked Abel.

'He's in Chicago, Colonel,' the guard replied.

'Well, get him on the phone,' said Abel.

'Who shall I say is calling him?'

'Abel Rosnovski.'

The guard moved quickly.

George's familiar voice crackled down the line with welcome. At once Abel realised just how good it felt to be back home. He decided not to stay in New York that night but to fly the eight hundred miles on to Chicago. He took with him George's up-to-date reports to study on the plane. He read every detail of the Baron Group's progress during the war, and it became obvious that George had done well in keeping the group on an even keel during Abel's absence. His cautious stewardship left Abel with no complaints; the profits were still high because so many staff had been called up to fight in the war, while the hotels had remained full because of the continual movement of personnel across America. Abel decided that he would have to start employing new staff immediately, before other hotels picked up the best of those returning from the Front.

When he arrived at Midway Airport, Terminal 11C, George was standing by the gate waiting to greet him. He'd hardly changed, a little more weight, a little less hair perhaps, and within an hour of swapping stories and bringing each other up to date on the past three years, it was almost as though Abel had never been away. Abel would always be thankful to the *Black Arrow* for the introduction to his senior vice-president.

George, however, was uncharitable about Abel's limp which seemed more pronounced since he'd gone off to the war.

'The Hopalong Cassidy of the hotel business,' he said mockingly. 'Now you don't have a leg to stand on.'

'Only a Pole would make such a dumb crack,' replied Abel.

George stared at Abel, looking slightly hurt, as a puppy does when scolded by its master.

'Thank God I had a dumb Polack to take care of everything while I was away looking for Germans,' Abel added reassuringly.

Abel couldn't resist checking once around the Chicago Baron before he drove home. The veneer of luxury had worn rather thin during the wartime shortages. He could see several things that needed renovation, but they would have to wait, because now all he wanted to do was see his wife and daughter. That was when the first shock came. In George he had seen little change in three years, but Florentyna was now eleven and had blossomed into a beautiful young girl, while Zaphia, although only thirty-eight, had become plump, dowdy and distinctly middle-aged.

To begin with, the two of them were not sure quite how to treat one another, and after only a few weeks Abel began to realise that their relationship was never going to be the same again. Zaphia made little effort to excite Abel or take any pride in his achievements. It saddened Abel to observe her lack of interest and he tried to get her involved in his life once again but she did not respond to any of his suggestions. She only seemed contented when staying at home and having as little to do with the Baron Group as possible. He resigned himself to the fact that she could never change and wondered how long he could remain faithful to her. While he was enchanted with Florentyna, Zaphia, without her looks and with her figure gone, left him cold. When they slept together he avoided making love, and, on the rare occasions when they did, he thought of other women. Soon he began to find any excuse to be away from Chicago and Zaphia's despondent and silently accusing face.

He began by making long trips to his other hotels, taking Florentyna along with him during her school holidays. He spent the first six months after his return to America visiting every hotel in the Baron Group in the same way he had done when he had taken over the company after Davis Leroy's death. Within the year, they were all back to the high standard he expected of them, but Abel wanted to move forward again. He informed Curtis Fenton at the group's next quarterly meeting that his market research team was now advising him to build a hotel in Mexico and another in Brazil, and they were also searching for new lands on which to erect a Baron.

'The Mexico City Baron and the Rio de Janeiro Baron,' said Abel. He liked the ring of those names.

'Well, you have adequate funds to cover the building costs,' said Curtis Fenton. 'The cash has certainly been accumulating in your absence. You could build a Baron almost anywhere you choose. Heaven knows where you'll stop, Mr. Rosnovski.'

'One day, Mr. Fenton, I'll put a Baron in Warsaw, and then I'll think about stopping,' replied Abel. 'I may have licked the Germans, but I still have a little score to settle with the Russians.'

Curtis Fenton laughed. Only later that evening when he repeated the story to his wife did he decide that Abel Rosnovski had meant exactly what he had said ... a Baron in Warsaw.

'Now where do I stand with Kane's bank?'

The sudden change in Abel's tone bothered Curtis Fenton. It worried him that Abel Rosnovski still clearly held Kane responsible for Davis Leroy's premature death. He opened the special file and started reading.

'Lester, Kane and Company's shares are divided among fourteen members of the Lester family and six past and present employees while Mr. Kane himself is the largest stockholder, holding eight per cent.'

'Are any of the Lester family willing to sell their shares?' enquired Abel.

'Perhaps if we can offer the right price. Miss Susan Lester, the late Charles Lester's daughter, has given us reason to believe she might consider parting with her shares, and Mr. Peter Parfitt, a former vice-chairman of Lester's, has also showed some interest in our approaches.'

'What percentage do they both hold?'

'Susan Lester holds six per cent. While Peter Parfitt has only two per cent.'

'How much do they want for their shares?'

Curtis Fenton looked down at his file again while Abel glanced at Lester's latest annual report. His eyes came to a halt on Article Seven.

'Miss Susan Lester wants two million dollars for her six per cent and Mr. Parfitt one million dollars for his two per cent.'

'Mr. Parfitt is greedy,' said Abel. 'We will therefore wait until he is hungry. Buy Miss Susan Lester's shares immediately without revealing whom you represent and keep me briefed on any change of heart by Mr. Parfitt.'

Curtis Fenton coughed.

'Is something bothering you, Mr. Fenton?' asked Abel.

Curtis Fenton hesitated. 'No, nothing,' he said unconvincingly.

'From now on I am putting someone in overall charge of the account whom you will know or certainly know of – Henry Osborne.'

'Congressman Osborne?' asked Curtis Fenton.

'Yes – are you acquainted with him?'

'Only by reputation,' said Fenton, with a faint note of disapproval, his head bowed.

Abel ignored the implied comment. He was only too aware of Henry's reputation, but while he had the ability to cut out all the middle men of bureaucracy and could ensure quick political decisions, he considered the risk was worthwhile. Not to mention the bond of common loathing of Kane. 'I'm also inviting Mr. Osborne to be a director of the Baron Group with special responsibility for the Kane account. This information must, as always, be treated in the strictest confidence.'

'As you wish,' said Fenton unhappily, wondering if he should express his personal misgivings to Abel Rosnovski.

'Brief me as soon as you have closed the deal with Miss Susan Lester.'

'Yes, Mr. Rosnovski,' said Curtis Fenton without raising his head.

Abel returned to the Baron for lunch, where Henry Osborne was waiting to join him.

'Congressman,' said Abel as they met in the foyer.

'Baron,' said Henry, and they laughed and went, arm-in-arm into the dining room and sat at the corner table.

Abel chastised a waiter for serving at table when a button was missing from his tunic.

'How's your wife, Abel?'

'Swell. And yours Henry?'

'Just great.'

They were both lying.

'Any news to report?'

'Yes. That concession you needed in Atlanta has been

taken care of,' said Henry in a conspiratorial voice. 'The necessary documents will be pushed through some time in the next few days. You'll be able to start building the Atlanta Baron round the first of the month.'

'We're not doing anything too illegal, are we?'

'Nothing your competitors aren't up to – that I can promise you, Abel.' Henry Osborne laughed.

'I'm glad to hear that, Henry. I don't want any trouble with the law.'

'No, no,' said Henry. 'Only you and I know all the facts.'

'Good,' said Abel. 'You've made yourself very useful to me over the years, Henry, and I have a little reward for your past services. How would you like to become a director of the Baron Group?'

'I'd be flattered, Abel.'

'Don't give me that. You know you've been invaluable with these state and city permits. I'd never have had the time to deal with all those politicians and bureaucrats. In any case, Henry, they prefer to deal with a Harvard man even if he doesn't so much open doors, as simply kick them down.'

'You've been very generous in return, Abel.'

'It's no more than you have earned. Now, I want you to take on an even bigger job which is close to my heart. This exercise will also require complete secrecy, but it shouldn't take too much of your time and it will give us a little revenge on our mutual friend from Boston, Mr. William Kane.'

The *maître d'hotel* arrived with two large rump steaks, medium rare. Henry listened intently as Abel unfolded his plans for William Kane.

A few days later on 8 May 1946, Abel travelled to New York to celebrate the first anniversary of V-E day. He had laid on a dinner for over a thousand Polish veterans at the Baron Hotel and had invited General Kazimierz Sosnkowski, commander-in-chief of the Polish Forces in France after 1943, to be the guest of honour. Abel had looked forward impatiently to the event for weeks and took Florentyna with him to New York while leaving Zaphia behind in Chicago.

On the night of the celebration, the banqueting room of the New York Baron looked magnificent, each of the one hundred and twenty tables decorated with the stars and stripes of America and the white and red of the Polish national flag. Huge photographs of Eisenhower, Patton, Bradley, Hodges, Paderewski and Sikorski festooned the walls. Abe' sat at the centre of the head table with the general on his right and Florentyna on his left.

When General Sosnkowski rose to address the gathering, he announced that Lieutenant Colonel Rosnovski had been made a life president of the Polish Veterans' Society, in acknowledgment of the personal sacrifices he had made for the Polish-American cause, and in particular for his generous gift of the New York Baron throughout the entire duration of the war. Someone who had drunk a little too much shouted from the back of the room.

'Those of us who survived the Germans had to survive Abel's food as well.'

The thousand veterans laughed and cheered, toasted Abel in Danzig vodka and then fell silent as the general talked of the plight of post-war Poland, in the grip of Stalinist Russia, urging his fellow expatriates to be tireless in their campaign to secure the ultimate sovereignty of their native land. Abel wanted to believe that Poland would one day be free again and that he might even live to see his castle restored to him, but doubted if that was realistic after Stalin's success at the Yalta agreement.

The general went on to remind the guests that Polish-Americans had, per capita, sacrificed more lives and given more money for the war than any other single ethnic group in the United States. '... How many Americans would believe that Poland lost six million of her countrymen while Czechoslovakia only lost one hundred thousand. Some observers declare we were stupid not to surrender when we must have known we were beaten. How could a nation that staged a cavalry charge against the might of the Nazi tanks ever believe they were beaten and my friends I tell you we are not beaten now.' Every Pole in the room applauded the general loudly.

Abel felt sad to think that most Americans would still laugh at the thought of the Polish war effort – or, funnier still, a Polish war hero. The general then waited for complete silence to tell an intent audience the story of how Abel had led a band of men to recover troops who had been killed or wounded at the battle of Remagen. When the general had finished his speech and sat down, the veterans stood and cheered the two men resoundingly. Florentyna felt very proud of her father.

Abel was surprised when the story hit the papers the next morning, as Polish achievements were rarely reported in any medium other than *Dziennik Zwiazkiwy*. He doubted that the press would have bothered on this occasion had he not been the Chicago Baron. Abel basked in his new-found glory as an un-sung American hero and spent most of the day having his photograph taken and giving interviews to newsmen.

By the evening Abel felt a sense of anti-climax. The general had flown on to Los Angeles and another function, Florentyna had returned to school in Lake Forest, George was in Chicago, and Henry Osborne in Washington. The hotel seemed rather large and empty, and he felt no desire to return to Zaphia in Chicago.

He decided to have an early dinner and go over the weekly reports from the other hotels in the group before returning to the penthouse adjoining his office. He seldom ate alone in his private suite as he welcomed the opportunity of being served in one of the dining rooms whenever possible; it was one of the sure ways to keep in constant touch with hotel life. The more hotels he acquired and built, the more he feared losing touch with his staff on the ground.

He took the lift, downstairs and stopped at the reception desk to ask how many people were booked into the hotel that night, but he was distracted by a striking woman signing a registration form. He could have sworn he recognised the profile, but it was difficult to be certain from the side.

Mid-thirties, he thought. When she had finished writing, she turned and looked at him.

'Abel,' she said. 'How marvellous to see you.'

'Good God, Melanie. I hardly recognised you.'

'No one could fail to recognise you, Abel.'

'I didn't know you were in New York.'

'Only overnight. I'm here on some business for my magazine.'

'You're a journalist?' asked Abel with a hint of disbelief.

'No, I'm the economic advisor to a group of magazines whose headquarters are in Dallas, and they've sent me to New York on a market research project.'

'Sounds very impressive.'

'I can assure you it isn't,' said Melanie, 'but it keeps me out of mischief.'

'Are you free for dinner, by any chance?'

'What a nice idea, Abel, but I need a bath and a change of clothes if you don't mind waiting?'

'Sure, I can wait. I'll meet you in the main dining room whenever you're ready. Come to my table, say in about an hour.'

She smiled in agreement and followed a bellhop to the lift. He noticed her perfume as she passed him.

Abel spent the hour checking the dining room to be sure that his table had fresh flowers, and the kitchen to select the dishes he would order for Melanie. Finally, by lack of anything better to do, he was compelled to sit down. He found himself glancing at his watch and looking at the dining room door every few moments to see if Melanie would walk in. She took a little over an hour but it turned out to be worth the wait. When at last she appeared at the doorway, in a long clinging dress that shimmered and sparkled in the dining room lights in an unmistakably expensive way, she looked ravishing. The *maître d'* ushered her to Abel's table. He rose to greet her as a waiter opened a bottle of vintage Krug and poured them both a glass.

'Welcome, Melanie,' said Abel as he raised his goblet. 'It's good to see you in the Baron.'

'It's good to see the Baron,' she replied, 'especially on his day of celebration.'

'What do you mean?' asked Abel.

'I read all about your big dinner in the *New York Post* tonight, how you risked your own life to save those who had been wounded at Remagen. It kept me glued to the page all the way over here from the station. They made you sound like a cross between Audie Murphy and the Unknown Soldier.'

'It's all exaggerated,' said Abel.

'I've never known you to be modest about anything before, Abel, so I can only believe every word must be true.'

He poured her a second glass of champagne.

'The truth is, I've always been a little frightened of you, Melanie.'

'The Baron is frightened of someone? I don't believe it.'

'Well, I'm no Southern gentleman, as you once made very clear, my dear.'

'And you have never stopped reminding me.' She smiled, teasingly. 'Did you marry your nice Polish girl?'

'Yes, I did.'

'How did that work out?'

'Not so well. She's now fat and forty and no longer has any appeal for me.'

'You'll be telling me next that she doesn't understand you,' said Melanie, the tone of her voice betraying her pleasure at his reply.

'And did you find yourself a husband?' asked Abel.

'Oh, yes,' replied Melanie. 'I married a real Southern gentleman with all the right credentials.'

'Many congratulations,' said Abel.

'I divorced him last year ... with a large settlement.'

'Oh, I'm sorry,' said Abel, sounding pleased. 'More champagne?'

'Are you by any chance trying to seduce me, Abel?'

'Not before you've finished your soup, Melanie. Even first-generation Polish immigrants have some standards, although I must admit it's my turn to do the seducing.'

'Then I must warn you, Abel, I haven't slept with another man since my divorce came through. No lack of offers, but no one's been quite right. Too many groping hands and not enough affection.'

After smoked salmon, young lamb, crême brulée and a pre-war Mouton Rothschild, they had both thoroughly reviewed their lives since their last meeting.

'Coffee in the penthouse, Melanie?'

'Do I have any choice, after such an excellent meal?' she enquired.

Abel laughed and escorted her out of the dining room and into the lift. She was teetering very slightly on her high heels as she entered. Abel touched the button marked 'forty-two'. Melanie looked up at the numbers as they ticked by.

'Why no twelfth floor?' she asked innocently. Abel could not find the words to reply.

'The last time I had coffee in your room ...' Melanie tried again.

'Don't remind me,' said Abel, remembering his own vulnerability. As they stepped out of the lift on the forty-second floor, the bellhop opened the door of his suite.

'Good God,' said Melanie, as her eyes swept round the inside of the penthouse for the first time. 'I must say, Abel, you've learned how to adjust to the style of a multi-millionaire. I've never seen anything more extravagant in my life.'

A knock at the door stopped Abel as he was about to reach out for her. A young waiter appeared with a pot of coffee and a bottle of Rémy Martin.

'Thank you Mike,' said Abel. 'That will be all for tonight.'

'Will it?' She smiled.

The waiter would have turned red if he hadn't been black and left quickly.

Abel poured her coffee and brandy. She sipped slowly, sitting cross-legged on the floor. Abel would have sat cross-legged as well, but he couldn't quite manage the position, so instead he lay down beside her. She stroked his hair, and tentatively he began to move his hand up her leg. God, how well he remembered those legs. As they kissed for the first time, Melanie kicked a shoe off and knocked her coffee all over the Persian carpet.

'Oh, hell,' she said. 'I've ruined your beautiful carpet.'

'Forget it,' said Abel, as he pulled her back into his arms and started to unzip her dress. Melanie unbuttoned his shirt, and Abel tried to get it off while he was still kissing her, but his cufflinks stopped him, so he helped her out of her dress instead. Her figure had lost none of its beauty and was exactly as he remembered it, except that it was enticingly fuller. Those firm breasts and long graceful legs. He gave up the one-handed battle with the cufflinks and released her from his grasp to undress himself, aware what an abrupt physical contrast he must have appeared compared to her beautiful body. He hoped all he had read about women being fascinated by powerful men was true. She didn't seem to grimace as she once had at the sight of him. Gently, he caressed her breasts and began to part her legs. The Persian carpet was proving better than any bed. It was her turn to try to undress completely while they were kissing. She too gave up and finally took off everything except for – at Abel's request – her garter belt and nylon stockings.

When he heard her moan, he was aware how long it had been since he had experienced such ecstasy – and then – how quickly the sensation was past. Neither of them spoke for several moments, both breathing heavily.

Then Abel chuckled.

'What are you laughing at?' Melanie enquired.

'Nothing,' said Abel, recalling Dr. Johnson's observation about the position being ridiculous and the pleasure momentary.

Abel rolled over, and Melanie rested her head on his shoulder. Abel was surprised to find that he no longer wanted to be near Melanie, and as he lay there wondering how to get rid of her without actually being rude, she said, 'I'm afraid I can't stay all night, Abel, I have an early appointment tomorrow and I must get *some* sleep. I don't want to look as if I spent the night on your Persian carpet.'

'Must you go?' said Abel, sounding desperate, but not too desperate.

'I'm sorry, darling, yes.' She stood up and walked to the bathroom.

Abel watched her dress, and helped her with her zipper. How much easier the garment was to fasten at leisure than it had been to unfasten in haste. He kissed her gallantly on the hand as she left.

'I hope we'll see each other again soon,' he said, lying.

'I hope so, too,' she said, aware that he did not mean it.

He closed the door behind her and walked over to the phone by his bed.

'Which room was Miss Melanie Leroy booked into?' he asked.

There was a moment's pause; he could hear the flicking of the registration cards.

Abel tapped impatiently on the table.

'There's no one registered under that name, sir,' came the eventual reply. 'We have a Mrs. Melanie Seaton from Dallas, Texas, who arrived this evening, sir, and checks out tomorrow morning?'

'Yes, that will be the lady,' said Abel. 'See that her bill is charged to me.'

'Yes, sir.'

Abel replaced the phone and took a long cold shower before preparing for bed. He felt relaxed as he walked over to the fire to turn out the lamp that had illuminated his first adulterous act and noticed that the large coffee stain had now dried on his Persian carpet.

'Silly bitch,' he said out loud and switched off the light.

After that night, Abel found that several more coffee stains appeared on the Persian carpet during the next few months, some caused by waitresses, some by other nocturnal visitors, as he and Zaphia grew further apart. What he hadn't anticipated was that she would hire a private detective to check on him and then sue for a divorce. Divorce was almost unknown in Abel's circle of Polish friends, separation or desertion being far more common. Abel even tried to talk Zaphia out of her desired course, only too aware it would do nothing to enhance his standing in the Polish community, and certain it would not advance any social or political ambitions he had started to hanker after. But Zaphia was determined to carry the divorce proceedings to their bitter conclusion. Abel was surprised to find that the woman who had been so unsophisticated in his triumph was, to use George's words, a little demon in her revenge.

When Abel consulted his own lawyer, he found out for the second time just how many waitresses and non-paying guests there had been during the last year. He gave in and the only thing he fought for was the custody of Florentyna, now thirteen, and the first true love of his life. Zaphia agreed after a long struggle, accepting a settlement of five hundred thousand dollars, the deed to the house in Chicago, and the right to see Florentyna on the last weekend in every month.

Abel moved his headquarters and permanent home to New York and George dubbed him the Chicago Baron-in-exile, as he roamed America north and south building new hotels, only returning to Chicago when he had to see Curtis Fenton.

27

The letter lay open on a table by William's chair in the living room. He sat in his dressing gown reading it for the third time, trying to figure out why Abel Rosnovski would want to buy so heavily into Lester's Bank, and why he had appointed Henry Osborne as a director of the Baron Group. William felt he could no longer take the risk of guessing and picked up the phone.

The new Mr. Cohen turned out to be a younger version of his father. When he arrived at East 68th Street, he had no need to introduce himself; the hair was beginning to go grey and thin in exactly the same places and the round body was encased in an exactly similar suit. Perhaps, it was in fact the same suit. William stared at him, but not simply because he looked so like his father.

'You don't remember me, Mr. Kane,' said the lawyer.

'Good God,' said William. 'The great debate at Harvard. Nineteen twenty...'

'Twenty-eight. You won the debate and sacrificed your membership of the Porcellian.'

William burst out laughing. 'Maybe we'll do better on the same team, if your brand of socialism will allow you to act for an unabashed capitalist.'

He rose to shake hands with Thaddeus Cohen. For a moment, they both might have been undergraduates again.

William smiled. 'You never did get that drink at the Porcellian. What would you like?'

Thaddeus Cohen declined the offer. 'I don't drink,' he said, blinking in the same disarming way that William recalled so well. '... and I'm afraid I'm now an unabashed capitalist, too.'

He turned out to have his father's head on his shoulders mentally as well as physically, and had clearly briefed himself on the Rosnovski-Osborne file to the finest detail before he faced William. William explained exactly what he now required.

'An immediate report and a further updated one every three months as in the past. Secrecy is still of paramount importance,' he said, 'but I want every fact you can lay your hands on. Why is Abel Rosnovski buying the bank's shares? Does he still feel I am responsible for Davis Leroy's death? Is he continuing his battle with Kane and Cabot even now that they are part of Lester's? What role does Henry Osborne play in all of this? Would a meeting between myself and Rosnovski help, especially if I tell him that it was the bank, not I who refused to support the Richmond Group?'

Thaddeus Cohen's pen was scratching away as furiously as his father's had before him.

'All these questions must be answered as quickly as possible so that I can decide if it's necessary to brief my board.'

Thaddeus Cohen gave his father's shy smile as he shut his briefcase. 'I'm sorry that you should be troubled in this way while you are still convalescing. I'll be back to you as soon as I can ascertain the facts.' He paused at the door. 'I admire greatly what you did at Remagen.'

William recovered his sense of well-being and vigour rapidly in the following months, and the scars on his face and chest faded into relative insignificance. At night Kate would sit up with him until he fell asleep and whisper, 'Thank God you were spared.' The terrible headaches and periods of amnesia grew to be things of the past, and the strength returned to his right arm. Kate would not allow him to return to work until they had taken a long and relaxing cruise in the West Indies. William relaxed with Kate more than at any time since their two weeks together in London. She revelled in the fact that there were no banks on the ship for him to do business with, although she feared if they stayed on board another week William would have acquired the floating vessel as one of Lester's latest assets, reorganising the crew, routes, timings and even the way they sailed 'the boat', as William insisted on called the great liner. He was tanned and restless once the ship docked in New York Harbour, and Kate could not dissuade him from returning immediately to the bank.

He soon became deeply involved again in Lester's problems. A new breed of men, toughened by war, enterprising and fast-moving, seemed to be running America's modern banks, under the watchful eye of President Truman, the man who had won a surprise victory for a second term in the White House after the world had been informed that Dewey was certain to win the election. As if not satisfied with their prediction, the *Chicago Tribune* went on to announce that Dewey had actually won the election, but it was

Harry S. Truman who remained in the White House. William knew very little about the diminutive ex-senator from Missouri, except what he read in the newspapers, and as a staunch Republican, he hoped that his party would find the right man to lead them into the 1952 campaign.

The first report came in from Thaddeus Cohen; Abel Rosnovski was still looking for shares in Lester's bank and had approached all the other benefactors of the will but only one agreement had been concluded. Susan Lester had refused to see William's lawyer when he approached her, so he was unable to discover why she had sold her six per cent. All he could ascertain was that she had no financial reason for doing so. 'Hell hath no fury,' mumbled William.

The document was admirably comprehensive.

Henry Osborne, it seemed, had been appointed a director of the Baron Group in May of 1947, with special responsibility for the Lester's account. More importantly, Abel Rosnovski secured Susan Lester's shares without it being possible to trace the acquisition back to either him or to Osborne. Rosnovski now owned six per cent of Lester's Bank and appeared to be willing to pay at least another $750,000 to obtain Peter Parfitt's two per cent. William was only too aware of the actions Abel Rosnovski could carry out once he was in possession of eight per cent. Even more worrying to William was the fact that the growth rate of Lester's compared unfavourably with that of the Baron Group, which was already catching up its main rivals, the Hilton and the Sheraton Groups. William began to wonder if it would now be wise to brief his board of directors on this newly obtained information, and even whether he ought not to contact Abel Rosnovski direct. After some sleepless nights, he turned to Kate for advice.

'Do nothing,' was Kate's reaction, 'until you can be absolutely certain that his intentions are as disruptive as you fear. The whole affair may turn out to be a tempest in a teapot.'

'With Henry Osborne as his hatchet man you can be sure

that the tempest will pour far beyond the teacup: nothing can be totally innocent. I don't have to sit around and wait to find out what he is planning for me.'

'He might have changed, William. It must be twenty years since you've had any personal dealings with him.'

'Al Capone might have changed, if he had been allowed to complete his jail sentence. We'll never know for certain, but I would not be willing to put a bet on it.'

Kate added nothing more, but William let himself be persuaded by her and did little except to keep a close eye on Thaddeus Cohen's quarterly reports and hope that Kate's intuition would turn out to be right.

28

The Baron Group profited greatly from the post-war explosion in the American economy. Not since the twenties had it been so easy to make so much money so quickly – and by the early fifties, people were beginning to believe that this time it was going to last. But Abel was not content with financial success alone; as he grew older, he began to worry about Poland's place in the post-war world and to feel that his success did not allow him to be a bystander four thousand miles away. What had Pawel Zaleski, the Polish consul in Turkey said? 'Perhaps in your lifetime you will see Poland rise again.' Abel did everything he could to influence and persuade the United States Congress to take a more militant attitude towards Russian control of its Eastern European satellites. It seemed to Abel, as he watched one puppet socialist government after another come into being, that he had risked his life for nothing. He began to lobby Washington politicians, brief journalists and organise dinners in Chicago and New York and other centres of the Polish-American community, until the Polish cause itself became synonymous with the Chicago Baron.

Dr. Teodor Szymanowski, formerly professor of history at the university of Cracow, wrote a glowing editorial about Abel's 'Fight To Be Recognised' in the journal *Freedom*, which prompted Abel to contact him and see what else he could do to help. The professor was now an old man, and when Abel was ushered into his study, he was surprised by the frailty of his appearance, knowing the vigour of his opinions. He greeted Abel warmly and poured him a Danzig vodka. 'Baron Rosnovski,' he said handing him the glass, 'I have long admired the way you work on and on for our cause and although we make such little headway, you never seem to lose faith.'

'Why should I? I have always believed anything is possible in America.'

'But I fear, Baron, the very men you are now trying to influence are the same ones who had allowed these things to take place. They will never do anything positive to free our people.'

'I do not understand what you mean, Professor,' said Abel. 'Why will they not help us?'

The professor leaned his back in his chair. 'You are surely aware, Baron, that the American armies were given specific orders to slow down their advance east to allow the Russians to take as much of central Europe as they could lay their hands on. Patton could have been in Berlin long before the Russians but Eisenhower told him to hold back. It was our leaders in Washington – the same men you are trying to persuade to put American guns and troops back into Europe – who gave those orders to Eisenhower.'

'But they couldn't have known then what the U.S.S.R. would eventually become. The Russians were then our allies. I accept that we were too weak and conciliatory with them in 1945, but it was not the Americans who directly betrayed the Polish people.'

Before Szymanowski spoke, he leaned back again and closed his eyes wearily.

'I wish you could have known my brother, Baron Rosnovski. I had word only last week that he died six months ago, in a Soviet camp not unlike the one from which you escaped.'

Abel moved forward as if to offer sympathy, but Szymanowski raised his hand.

'No, don't say anything. You have known the camps yourself. You would be the first to realise that sympathy is no longer important. We must change the world, Baron, while others sleep.' Szymanowski paused. 'My brother was sent to Russia by the Americans.'

Abel looked at him in astonishment.

'By the Americans? How is that possible? If your brother was captured in Poland by Russian troops ...'

'My brother was never taken prisoner in Poland. He was liberated from a German war camp near Frankfurt. The Americans kept him in a D.P. camp for a month and then they handed him over to the Russians.'

'It can't be true. Why would they do that?'

'The Russians wanted all Slavs repatriated. Repatriated so that they could then be exterminated or enslaved. The ones that Hitler didn't get, Stalin did. And I can prove my brother was in the American Sector for over a month.'

'But,' Abel began, 'was he an exception or were there many others like him?'

'He was no exception: there were many others,' said Szymanowski without apparent emotion. 'Hundreds of thousands. Perhaps as many as a million. I don't think we will ever know the true figures. It's most unlikely the American authorities ever kept careful records of Operation Kee Chanl.'

'Operation Kee Chanl? Why don't people ever mention this? Surely if others realised that we, the Americans, had been sending liberated prisoners back to die in Russia, they would be horrified.'

'There is no proof, no known documentation of Operation Kee Chanl. Mark Clark, God bless him, disobeyed his orders and a few of the prisoners were warned in advance by some kindly disposed G.I.s, and they managed to escape before the Americans could send them to the camps. But they are now lying low and would never admit as much. One of the unlucky ones was with my brother. Anyway, it's too late now.'

'But the American people must be told. I'll form a committee, print pamphlets, make speeches. Surely Congress will listen to us if we tell them the truth.'

'Baron Rosnovski, I think this one is too big even for you.'

Abel rose from his seat.

'No, no, I do not underestimate you, my friend. But you do not yet understand the mentality of world leaders. America agreed to hand over those poor devils because Stalin demanded as much. I am sure they never thought that there would be trials, labour camps and executions to follow. But now, as we approach the fifties, no one is going to admit they were indirectly responsible? No, they will never do that. Not for a hundred years. And then, all but a few historians will have forgotten that Poland lost more lives in the war than any other single nation on earth, including Germany.'

'I had hoped the one conclusion you might come to was that you must play a more direct role in politics.'

'I have already been considering the idea but cannot decide what form it should take.'

'I have my own views on that subject, Baron, so keep in touch.'

The old man raised himself slowly to his feet and embraced Abel. 'In the meantime do what you can for our cause, but don't be surprised when you meet closed doors.'

The moment Abel returned to The Baron, he picked up the phone and told the hotel operator to get him Senator Douglas' office. Paul Douglas was Illinois' liberal Democratic senator, elected with the help of the Chicago machine, and he had always been helpful and responsive to any of Abel's past requests, mindful of the fact that his constituency contained the largest Polish community in the country. His assistant, Adam Tomaszewicz always dealt with his Polish constituents.

'Hello, Adam. It's Abel Rosnovski. I have something very disturbing to discuss with the senator. Could you arrange an early meeting with him?'

'I'm afraid he's out of town today, Mr. Rosnovski. I know he'll be glad to speak with you as soon as he returns on Thursday. I'll ask him to call you direct. Can I tell him what it's all about?'

'Yes. As a Pole you will be interested. I've heard reports from reliable sources that the U.S. authorities in Germany assisted in the return of displaced Polish citizens to territories occupied by the Soviet Union, and that many of these Polish citizens were then sent on to Russian labour camps and have never been heard of since.'

There was a moment's silence from the other end of the line.

'I'll brief the senator on his return, Mr. Rosnovski,' said Adam Tomaszewicz. 'Thank you for calling.'

The senator did not get in touch with Abel on Thursday. Nor did he try on Friday or over the weekend. On Monday morning, Abel put through another call to his office. Again, Adam Tomaszewicz answered the telephone.

'Oh, yes, Mr. Rosnovski.' Abel could almost hear him blushing. 'The senator did leave a message for you. He's been very busy, you know, what with all the emergency bills that have to be acted on before Congress recesses. He asked me to let you know that he'll call back just as soon as he has a spare moment.'

'Did you give him my message?'

'Yes, of course. He asked me to assure you that he felt certain the rumour you heard was nothing more than a piece of anti-American propaganda. He added that he'd been told personally by one of the Joint Chiefs that American troops had orders not to release any of the D.P.s under their supervision.'

Tomaszewicz sounded as if he was reading a carefully prepared statement, and Abel sensed that he had encountered the first of those closed doors. Senator Douglas had never evaded him in the past.

Abel put down the phone and dialed the number of another senator who did make news and didn't evade sitting in judgment on anybody.

Senator Joseph McCarthy's office came on the line asking who was calling. 'I'll try and find the senator,' said a young voice when she heard who it was and his reason for wanting to speak to her boss. McCarthy was approaching the peak of his power, and Abel realised he would be lucky to have more than a few moments on the phone with him.

'Mr. Rosenevski,' were McCarthy's first words.

Abel wondered if he had mangled his name on purpose, or if it was a bad connection. 'What is it you wanted to discuss with me and no one else, this matter of grave urgency?' the senator asked. Abel hesitated; actually speaking to McCarthy directly had slightly taken him aback.

'Your secrets are safe with me,' he heard the senator say, sensing his hesitation.

'If you say so,' said Abel and paused for a moment to collect his thoughts. 'You, Senator, have been a forthright spokesman for those of us who would like to see the Eastern European nations freed from the yoke of communism.'

'So I have. So I have. And I'm glad to see you appreciate the fact, Mr. Rosenevski.'

This time Abel was sure he had mispronounced his name on purpose, but resolved not to comment on it.

'As for Eastern Europe,' the senator continued, 'you must realise that only after the traitors have been driven from within our own government can any real action be taken to free your captive country.'

'That is exactly what I want to speak to you about, Senator. You have had a brilliant success in exposing treachery within our own government. But to date, one of the communists' greatest crimes has as yet gone unpublicised.'

'Just what great crime did you have in mind, Mr. Rosenevski? I have found so many since I came to Washington.'

'I am referring' – Abel drew himself up a little straighter in his chair – 'to the forced repatriation of thousands of displaced Polish citizens by the American authorities after the war ended. Innocent enemies of communism who were sent back to Poland, and then on to the U.S.S.R., to be enslaved and sometimes murdered.'

Abel waited for a response, but none was forthcoming. He heard a click and wondered if someone else was listening to the conversation.

'Now, Rosenevski, listen to me, you simpleton. You dare to phone me to say that Americans – loyal United States soldiers – sent thousands of Poles back to Russia and nobody heard a word about it? Are you asking me to believe that? Even a Polack couldn't be that stupid. And I wonder what kind of person accepts a lie like that without any proof? Do you want me also to believe that American soldiers are disloyal? Is that what you want? Tell me, Rosenevski, tell me what it is with you people? Are you too stupid to recognise communist propaganda even when it hits you right in the face? Do you have to waste the time of an overworked United States senator because of a rumour cooked up by the *Pravda* slime to create unrest in America's immigrant communities?'

Abel sat motionless, stunned by the outburst. Before half of his tirade was over, Abel felt that any counter-argument was going to be pointless. He waited for the histrionic speech to come to an end, and was glad the senator couldn't see his startled face.

'Senator, I'm sure you're right and I'm sorry to have wasted your time,' Abel said quietly. 'I hadn't thought of it in quite that light before.'

'Well, it just goes so show how tricky those commie bastards can be,' said McCarthy, his tone softening. 'You have to keep an eye on them all the time. Anyway, I hope you're more alert now to the continual danger the American people face.'

'I am indeed, Senator. Thank you once again for taking the trouble to speak to me personally. Goodbye, Senator.'

'Goodbye, Rosenovski.'

Abel heard the phone click and realised it was the same sound as a closing door.

29

William became aware of feeling older when Kate teased him about his greying hair, hairs which he used to be able to count and now no longer could, and Richard started to bring girls home whom he found attractive. William almost always approved of Richard's choice of young ladies, as he called them, perhaps because they were all rather like Kate who, he considered, was more beautiful in middle-age than she had ever been. His daughters, Virginia and Lucy, now also becoming young ladies, brought him great happiness as they grew in the image of their mother. Virginia was becoming quite an artist and the kitchen and children's bedrooms were always covered in her latest works of genius, as Richard described them mockingly. Virginia's revenge came the day Richard started cello lessons when even the servants were heard to murmur unsavoury comments whenever the bow came in contact with the strings. Lucy adored them both and considered Virginia with uncritical prejudice the new Picasso and Richard the new Casals. William began to wonder what the future would hold for all three of them when he was no longer around. In Kate's eyes all three children advanced satisfactorily. Richard, now at St. Paul's, had improved enough at the cello to be chosen to play in a school concert, while Virginia was painting well enough for one of her pictures to be hung in the front room. But it became obvious to all the family that Lucy was going to be the beauty when, aged only eleven, she started receiving little love notes from boys who until then had only shown an interest in baseball.

In 1951, Richard, was accepted at Harvard and although he did not win the top mathematics scholarship, Kate was quick to point out to William that he had played baseball and the cello for St. Paul's, two accomplishments William had never so much as attempted to master. William was secretly proud of Richard's achievements but mumbled to Kate something about not knowing many bankers who played baseball or the cello.

Banking was moving into an expansionist period as Americans began to believe in a lasting peace. William soon found himself overworked, and for a short time, the threat of Abel Rosnovski and the problems associated with him had to be pushed into the background.

The flow of quarterly reports from Thaddeus Cohen indicated that Rosnovski had embarked on a course which he had no intention of abandoning – through a third party he had let every stockholder other than William know of his interest in Lester's shares. William wondered if that course was heading towards a direct confrontation between himself and the Pole. He began to feel that the time was fast approaching when he would have to inform the Lester's board of Rosnovski's actions and perhaps even to offer his resignation if the bank looked to be under siege, a move that would result in a complete victory for Abel Rosnovski, which was the one reason William did not seriously contemplate such a move. He decided that if he had to fight for his life, fight he would, and if one of the two had to go under, he would do everything in his power to ensure that it wasn't William Kane.

The problem of what to do about Abel Rosnovski's investment programme was finally taken out of William's hands.

Early in 1951, the bank had been invited to represent one of America's new airline companies, Interstate Airways, when the Federal Aviation Agency granted them a franchise for flights between the East and West coasts. The airline approached Lester's bank when they needed to raise the thirty million dollars to provide them with the financial backing required by governmental regulations.

William considered the airline and the whole project to be well worth supporting, and he spent virtually his entire time setting up a public offering to raise the necessary thirty million. The bank, acting as the sponsor for the project, put all their resources behind the new venture. The project became William's biggest since he had returned to Lester's, and he realised that his personal reputation was at stake when he went to the market for the thirty million dollars. In July, when the details of the offering were announced the stock was snapped up in a matter of days. William received lavish praise from all quarters for the way he had handled the project and carried it through to such a successful conclusion. He could not have been happier about the outcome himself, until he read in Thaddeus Cohen's next report that ten per cent of the airline's stock had been obtained by one of Abel Rosnovski's dummy corporations.

William knew then that the time had come to acquaint Ted Leach and Tony Simmons with his worst fears. He asked Tony to come to New York where he called both of the vice-chairmen to his office and related to them the saga of Abel Rosnovski and Henry Osborne.

'Why didn't you let us know about all this before?' was Tony Simmons' first reaction.

'I dealt with a hundred companies like the Richmond Group when I was at Kane and Cabot, Tony, and I couldn't know at the time that he was that serious about revenge. I was only finally convinced of his obsession when Rosnovski purchased ten per cent of Interstate Airways.'

'I suppose it's possible you may be over-reacting,' said Ted Leach. 'Of one thing I am certain: it would be unwise to inform the rest of the board of this information. The last thing we want a few days after launching a new company is a panic on our hands.'

'That's for sure,' said Tony Simmons. 'Why don't you see this fellow Rosnovski and have it out with him?'

'I expect that's exactly what he'd like me to do,' replied William. 'It would leave him in no doubt that the bank feels it's under siege.'

'Don't you think his attitude might change if you told

him how hard you tried to talk the bank into backing the Richmond Group, but they wouldn't support you and ...'

'I've no reason to believe he doesn't know that already,' said William. 'He seems to know everything else.'

'Well what do you feel the bank should do about Rosnovski?' asked Ted Leach. 'We certainly can't stop him from purchasing our stock if he can find a willing seller. If we went in for buying our own stock, far from stopping him, we would play right into his hands by raising the value of his holding and jeopardising our own financial position. I think you can be certain he would enjoy watching us sweat that one out. We are about the perfect size to be taken on by Harry Truman, and there's nothing the Democrats would enjoy more than a banking scandal with an election in the offing.'

'I realise there's little I can do about it,' said William, 'but I had to let you know what Rosnovski was up to in case he springs another surprise on us.'

'I suppose there's still an outside chance,' said Tony Simmons, 'that the whole thing is innocent, and he simply respects your talent as an investor.'

'How can you say that, Tony, when you know my stepfather is involved? Do you think Rosnovski employed Henry Osborne to further my career in banking? You obviously don't understand Rosnovski as I do. I've watched him operating now for over twenty years. He's not used to losing; he simply goes on throwing the dice until he wins. I couldn't know him much better if he was one of my own family. He will ...'

'Now don't become paranoid, William, I expect ...'

'Don't become paranoid you say, Tony. Remember the power our Articles of Incorporation give to anyone who gets his hands on eight per cent of the bank's stock. An article I had originally inserted to protect myself from being removed. The man already has six per cent and if that's not a bad enough prospect for the future, remember that Rosnovski could wipe out Interstate Airways overnight just by placing his entire stock on the market at once.'

'But he would gain nothing from that,' said Ted Leach. 'On the contrary, he would stand to lose a great deal of money.'

'Believe me, you don't understand how Abel Rosnovski's mind works,' said William. 'He has the courage of a lion, and the loss would mean nothing to him. I'm fast becoming convinced his only interest is in getting even with me. Yes, of course he'd lose money on those shares if he dumped them, but he always has his hotels to fall back on. There are twenty-one of them now, you know, and he must realise that if Interstate stock collapses overnight, we will also be knocked backwards. As bankers, our credibility depends on the fickle confidence of the public, confidence Abel Rosnovski can now shatter as and when it suits him.'

'Calm down William,' said Tony Simmons. 'It hasn't come to that yet. Now we know what Rosnovski is up to, we can keep a closer watch on his activities and counter them as and when we need to. The first thing we must be sure of is that no one else sells their shares in Lester's before first offering them to you. The bank is always going to support any action you take. My own feeling is still that you should speak to Rosnovski personally and have it out in the open with him. At least that way we will know how serious his intentions are, and we can prepare ourselves accordingly.'

'Is that also your opinion, Ted?' asked William.

'Yes, it is. I agree with Tony. I think you should contact the man directly. It can only be in the bank's interests to discover how innocent or otherwise his intentions really are.'

William sat silently for a few moments. 'If you both feel that way, I'll give it a try,' he eventually said. 'I must add that I don't agree with you, but I may be too personally involved to make a dispassionate judgment. Give me a few days to think about how I should best approach him, and I'll let you know the outcome.'

After the two vice-chairmen had left his office, William sat alone, thinking about the action he had agreed to take, certain there could be little hope of success with Abel Rosnovski if Henry Osborne was involved.

Four days later, William sat alone in his office, having given instructions that he was not to be interrupted under any circumstances. He knew that Abel Rosnovski was also sitting in his office in the New York Baron: he had had a man posted at the hotel all morning whose only task had been to report the moment Rosnovski showed up. The waiting man had phoned; Abel Rosnovski had arrived that morning at eight twenty-seven, had gone straight up to his office on the forty-second floor and had not been seen since. William picked up his telephone and asked the operator to get him the Baron Hotel.

'New York Baron.'

'Mr. Rosnovski, please,' said William nervously. He was put through to a secretary.

'Mr. Rosnovski, please,' he repeated. This time his voice was a little steadier.

'May I ask who is calling?' she said.

'My name is William Kane.'

There was a long silence – or did it simply seem long to William?

'I'm not sure if he's in, Mr. Kane. I'll find out for you.'

Another long silence.

'Mr. Kane?'

'Mr. Rosnovski?'

'What can I do for you, Mr. Kane?' asked a very calm lightly accented voice.

Although William had prepared his opening remarks carefully, he was aware that he sounded anxious.

'I'm a little worried about your holdings in Lester's Bank, Mr. Rosnovski,' he said, 'and indeed in the strong position you have built up in one of the companies we represent. I thought perhaps the time had come for us to meet and discuss your full intentions. There is also a private matter I should like to make known to you.'

Another long silence. Had he been cut off?

'There are no conditions which would ever make a meeting with you possible, Kane. I know enough about you already without wanting to hear your excuses about the past. You keep your eyes open all the time, and you'll find out only too clearly what my intentions are, and they differ greatly from those you will find in the Book of Genesis, Mr. Kane. One day you're going to want to jump out of the twelfth floor window of one of my hotels, because you'll be in deep trouble with Lester's Bank over your own holdings. I only need two more per cent to invoke Article Seven, and we both know what that means, don't we? Then perhaps you'll appreciate for the first time what it felt like for Davis Leroy, wondering for months what the bank might do with his life. Now you can sit and wonder for years what I am going to do with yours once I obtain that eight per cent.'

Abel Rosnovski's words chilled William, but somehow he forced himself to carry on calmly, while at the same time banging his fist angrily on the table. 'I can understand how you feel, Mr. Rosnovski, but I still think it would be wise for us to get together and talk this whole thing out. There are one or two aspects of the affair I know you can't be aware of.'

'Like the way you swindled Henry Osborne out of five hundred thousand dollars, Mr. Kane?'

William was momentarily speechless and wanted to explode, but once again managed to control his temper.

'No, Mr. Rosnovski, what I wanted to talk to you about has nothing to do with Mr. Osborne. It's a personal matter and it involves only you. However, I most emphatically assure you that I have never swindled Henry Osborne out of one red cent.'

'That's not Henry's version. He says you were responsible for the death of your own mother, to make sure that you didn't have to honour a debt to him. After your treatment of Davis Leroy, I find that only too easy to believe.'

William had never had to fight harder to control his emotions, and it took him several seconds to muster a reply. 'May I suggest we clear this whole misunderstanding up once and for all by meeting at a neutral place of your choice where no one would recognise us?'

'There's only one place left where no one would recognise you, Mr. Kane.'

'Where's that?' asked William.

'Heaven,' said Abel, and placed the phone back on the hook.

'Get me Henry Osborne at once,' he said to his secretary.

He drummed his fingers on the desk while the girl took nearly fifteen minutes to find Congressman Osborne who, it turned out, had been showing some of his constituents around the Capitol building.

'Abel, is that you?'

'Yes, Henry, I thought you'd want to be the first to hear that Kane knows everything, so now the battle is out in the open.'

'What do you mean, he knows everything? Do you think he knows I'm involved?' asked Henry anxiously.

'He sure does, and he also seems to be aware of the special company accounts, my holdings in Lester's Bank and Interstate Airways.'

'How could he possibly know everything in such detail? Only you and I know about the special accounts.'

'And Curtis Fenton,' said Abel, interrupting him.

'Right. But he would never inform Kane.'

'He must have. There's no one else. Don't forget that Kane dealt directly with Curtis Fenton when I brought the Richmond Group from his bank. I suppose they must have maintained some sort of contact all along.'

'Jesus.'

'You sound worried, Henry.'

'If William Kane knows everything, it's a different ball game. I'm warning you, Abel, he's not in the habit of losing.'

'Nor am I,' replied Abel. 'And William Kane doesn't frighten me; not while I'm holding all the aces in my hand. What is our latest holding in Kane's stock?'

'Off the top of my head, you own six per cent of Lester's

Bank, and ten per cent of Interstate Airways, and odd bits of other companies they're involved with. You only need another two per cent of Lester's to invoke Article Seven and Peter Parfitt is still biting.'

'Excellent,' said Abel. 'I don't see how the situation could be better. Continue talking to Parfitt, remembering that I'm in no hurry while Kane can't even approach him. For the time being we'll let Kane wonder what we're up to. And be sure you do nothing until I return from Europe. After my phone conversation with Mr. Kane this morning, I can assure you that, to use a gentleman's expression, he's perspiring but I'll let you into a secret, Henry. I'm not sweating. He can go on that way because I have no intention of making a move until I'm good and ready.'

'Fine,' said Henry. 'I'll keep you informed if anything comes up at this end that we should worry about.'

'You must get it through your head, Henry, there's nothing for *us* to worry about. We have your friend, Mr. Kane, by the balls, and I now intend to squeeze them very slowly.'

'I shall enjoy watching that,' said Henry, sounding a little happier.

'Sometimes I think you hate Kane more than I do.'

Henry laughed nervously. 'Have a good trip to Europe.'

Abel put the phone back on the hook and sat staring into space as he considered his next move, his fingers still tapping noisily on the desk. His secretary came in.

'Get Mr. Curtis Fenton at the Continental Trust Bank,' he said, without looking at her. His fingers continued to tap. His eyes continued to stare. A few moments later the phone rang.

'Fenton?'

'Good morning, Mr. Rosnovski, how are you?'

'I want you to close all my accounts with your bank.'

There was no reply from the other end.

'Did you hear me, Fenton?'

'Yes,' said the stupefied banker. 'May I ask why, Mr. Rosnovski?'

'Because Judas never was my favourite apostle, Fenton,

that's why. As of this moment, you are no longer on the board of the Baron Group. You will shortly receive written instructions confirming this conversation and telling you to which bank the accounts should be transferred.'

'But I don't understand why, Mr. Rosnovski. What have I done . . . ?'

Abel hung up as his daughter walked into the office.

'That didn't sound very pleasant, Daddy.'

'It wasn't meant to be pleasant, but it's nothing to concern yourself with, darling,' said Abel, his tone changing immediately. 'Did you manage to find all the clothes you need for Europe?'

'Yes, thank you, Daddy, but I'm not absolutely sure what they're wearing in London and Paris. I can only hope that I've got it right. I don't want to stick out like a sore thumb.'

'You'll stick out all right, my darling, by being the most beautiful thing the British have seen in years. They'll know your clothes didn't come out of a ration book with your natural flair and sense of colour. Those young Europeans will be falling all over themselves to get alongside you, but I'll be there to stop them. Now let's go and have some lunch and discuss what we are going to do while we're in London.'

Ten days later, after Florentyna had spent a long weekend with her mother – Abel never enquired after her – the two of them flew from New York's Idlewild Airport to London's Heathrow. The flight in a Boeing 377 took nearly fourteen hours, and although they had private berths, when they arrived at Claridges in Brook Street, the only thing they both wanted to do was have another long sleep.

Abel was making the trip to Europe for three reasons: first to confirm building contracts for new Baron hotels in London, Paris and possibly Rome; second, to give Florentyna her first view of Europe before she went to Radcliffe to study modern languages; and third, and most important to him, to revisit his castle in Poland to see if there was even an outside chance of proving his ownership.

London turned out to be a success for both of them.

Abel's advisors had found a site on Hyde Park corner, and he instructed solicitors to proceed immediately with all the negotiations for the land and the permits that would be needed before England's capital could boast a Baron. Florentyna found the austerity of post-war London forbidding after the excess of her own home, but the Londoners seemed to be undaunted by their war-damaged city, still believing themselves to be a world power. She was invited to lunches, dinners and balls, and her father was proved right about her taste in clothes and the reaction of young European men. She returned each night with sparkling eyes and stories of new conquests made – and forgotten by the following morning. She couldn't make up her mind whether she wanted to marry an Etonian from the Grenadier Guards who saluted her all the time or a member of the House of Lords who was in waiting to the King. She wasn't quite sure what 'in waiting' meant, but he certainly knew exactly how to treat a lady.

In Paris, the pace never slackened and because they both spoke good French, they both managed as well with the Parisians as they had with the English. Abel was normally bored by the end of the second week of any holiday, and would start counting the days until he could return home to work. But not while he had Florentyna as his companion. She had, since his separation from Zaphia, become the centre of his life and the sole heir to his fortune.

When the time came for Abel to leave Paris, neither of them wanted to go, so they stayed on a few more days claiming as an excuse that Abel was still negotiating to buy a famous but now run-down hotel on the Boulevard Raspail. He did not inform the owner, a Monsieur Neuffe, who looked, if it were possible, even more run-down than the hotel, that he planned to demolish the building and start again from scratch. When Monsieur Neuffe signed the papers a few days later, Abel ordered the building razed to the ground while he and Florentyna, with no more excuses left for remaining in Paris, departed reluctantly for Rome.

After the friendliness of the British and the gaiety of the

French capital, the sullen and dilapidated Eternal City immediately dampened their spirits, for the Romans felt they had nothing behind them. In London, they had strolled through the magnificent Royal parks together, admired historic buildings, and Florentyna had danced until the small hours. In Paris, they had been to the Opera, lunched on the banks of the Seine, and taken a boat down the river past Notre Dame and on to supper in the Latin Quarter. In Rome, Abel found only an overpowering sense of financial instability and decided that he would have to shelve his plans to build a Baron in the Italian capital. Florentyna sensed her father's anxiety to once again see his castle in Poland, so she suggested they leave Italy a day early.

Abel had found bureaucracy more reluctant to grant a visa for Florentyna and himself to enter an Iron Curtain country than it had been to issue a permit to build a new five-hundred-room hotel in London. A less persistent visitor would probably have given up, but with the appropriate visas firmly stamped in their passports, Abel and Florentyna set off in a hired car for Slonim. The two travellers were kept waiting for hours at the Polish border, helped along only by the fact that Abel was fluent in the language. Had the border guards known why his Polish was so good, they would doubtless have taken an entirely different attitude to allowing him to return. Abel changed five hundred dollars into zlotys – that at least seemed to please the Poles – and motored on. The nearer they came to Slonim, the more Florentyna was aware of how much the journey meant to her father.

'Daddy, I can never remember you being so excited about anything.'

'This is where I was born,' Abel explained. 'After such a long time in America, where things change every day, it's almost unreal to be back where it looks as if nothing has changed since I left.'

They drove on towards Slonim, Abel's senses heightened in anticipation, while horrified and angry at the devastation of the once trim countryside and small, neat cottages.

Across a time span of nearly forty years he heard his childish voice ask the Baron whether the hour of the submerged peoples of Europe had arrived and would he be able to play his part, and tears came to his eyes to think how short that hour had been, and what a little part he had played.

When they rounded the final corner before approaching the Baron's estate and saw the great iron gates that led to the castle, Abel laughed aloud in excitement as he brought the car to a halt.

'It's all just as I remember it. Nothing's changed. Come on, let's start by visiting the cottage where I spent the first five years of my life – I don't expect anyone is living there now – and then we'll go and see my castle.'

Florentyna followed her father as he marched confidently down a small track into the forest of moss-covered birches and oaks, which was not going to change in a hundred years. After they had walked for about twenty minutes, the two of them came out into a small clearing, and there in front of them was the trapper's cottage. Abel stood and stared. He had forgotten how tiny his first home was: could nine people really have lived there? The thatched roof was now in disrepair, and the building left the impression of being uninhabited with its eroded stone and broken windows. The once tidy vegetable garden was indistinguishable in the matted undergrowth.

Had the cottage been deserted? Florentyna took her father by the arm and led him slowly to the front door. Abel stood there, motionless, so Florentyna knocked gently. They waited in silence. Florentyna knocked again, this time a little more loudly, and they heard someone moving within.

'All right, all right,' said a querulous voice in Polish, and a few moments later, the door inched open. They were being studied by an old woman, bent and thin, dressed entirely in black. Wisps of untidy snow-white hair escaped from her handerchief and her grey eyes looked vacantly at the visitors.

'It's not possible,' said Abel softly in English.

'What do you want?' asked the old woman suspiciously. She had no teeth and the line of her nose, mouth and chin formed a perfect concave arc.

Abel answered in Polish, 'May we come in and talk to you?'

Her eyes looked from one to the other fearfully. 'Old Helena hasn't done anything wrong,' she said in a whine.

'I know,' said Abel gently. 'I have brought good news for you.'

With some reluctance, she allowed them to enter the bare, cold room but she didn't offer them a seat. The room hadn't changed: two chairs, one table and the memory that until he had left the cottage, he hadn't known what a carpet was. Florentyna shuddered.

'I can't get the fire going,' wheezed the old woman, prodding the grate with her stick. The faintly glowing log refused to rekindle, and she scrabbled ineffectually in her pocket. 'I need paper.' She looked at Abel, showing a spark of interest for the first time. 'Do you have any paper?'

Abel looked at her steadily. 'Don't you remember me?' he said.

'No, I don't know you.'

'You do, Helena. My name is ... Wladek.'

'You knew my little Wladek?'

'I am Wladek.'

'Oh, no,' she said with sad and distant finality. 'He was too good for me, the mark of God was upon him. The Baron took him away to be an angel, yes, he took away Matka's littlest one ...'

Her old voice cracked and died away. She sat down, but the ancient, lined hands were busy in her lap.

'I have returned,' said Abel, more insistently, but the old woman paid him no attention, and her old voice quavered on as though she were quite alone in the room.

'They killed my husband, my Jasio, and all my lovely children were taken to the camps, except little Sophia. I hid her, and they went away.' Her voice was even and resigned.

'What happened to little Sophia?' asked Abel.

'The Russians took her away in the other war,' she said dully.

Abel shuddered.

The old woman roused herself from her memories. 'What do you want? Why are you asking me these questions?' she demanded.

'I wanted you to meet my daughter, Florentyna.'

'I had a daughter called Florentyna once, but now there's only me.'

'But I ...' began Abel, starting to unbutton his shirt.

Florentyna stopped him. 'We know,' she said, smiling at the old lady.

'How can you possibly know? It was all so long before you were even born.'

'They told us in the village,' said Florentyna.

'Have you any paper with you?' the old lady asked, 'I need paper for the fire.'

Abel looked at Florentyna helplessly. 'No,' he replied, 'I'm sorry, we didn't bring any with us.'

'What do you want?' reiterated the old woman, once again hostile.

'Nothing,' said Abel, now resigned to the fact that she would not remember him. 'We just wanted to say hello.' He took out his wallet, removed all the new zloty notes he had acquired at the border and handed them over to her.

'Thank you, thank you,' she said as she took each note, her old eyes watering with pleasure.

Abel bent over to kiss his foster-mother, but she backed away.

Florentyna took her father's arm and led Abel out of the cottage and back down the forest track in the direction of their car.

The old woman watched from her window until she was sure they were out of sight. Then she took the new bank notes, crumpled each one into a little ball and placed them all carefully in the grate. They kindled immediately. She placed twigs and small logs on top of the blazing zlotys and sat slowly down by her fire, the best in weeks, rubbing her hands together at the comfort of the warmth.

Abel did not speak on the walk back to the car until the iron gates were once again in sight. Then he promised Florentyna, trying his best to forget the little cottage, 'You are about to see the most beautiful castle in the world.'

'You must stop exaggerating, Daddy.'

'In the world,' Abel repeated quietly.

Florentyna laughed. 'I'll let you know how it compares with Versailles.'

They climbed back into the car and Abel drove through the gates, remembering the vehicles he had been in when he last passed through them, and up the mile-long drive to the castle. Memories came flooding back to him. Happy days as a child with the Baron and Leon, unhappy days of his life when he was taken away from his beloved castle by the Russians, imagining he would never see the building again. But now he, Wladek Koskiewicz, was returning, returning in triumph to reclaim what was his.

The car bumped up the winding road and both remained silent in anticipation as they rounded the final bend to the first sight of Baron Rosnovski's home. Abel brought the car to a halt and gazed at his castle. Neither of them spoke, but simply stared in disbelief at the devastation of the bombed-out remains of his dream.

He and Florentyna climbed slowly out of the car. Still neither spoke. Florentyna held her father's hand very, very tightly as the tears rolled down his cheeks. Only one wall remained precariously standing in a semblance of its former glory; the rest was nothing more than a neglected pile of rubble and red stone. He could not bear to tell her of the great halls, the wings, the kitchens, the bedrooms. Abel walked over to the three mounds, now smooth with thick green grass, that were the graves of the Baron and his son Leon and the other of beloved Florentyna. He paused at each one and could not help but think that Leon and Florentyna could still be alive today. He knelt at their heads, the dreadful visions of their final moments returning to him vividly. His daughter stood by his side, her hand resting on his shoulder, saying nothing. A long time passed before Abel rose slowly and then they tramped over the ruins together. Stone slabs marked the places where once magnificent rooms had been filled with laughter. Abel still said nothing. Holding hands, they reached the dungeons. There Abel sat down on the floor of the damp little room near the grille, or the half of the grille that was still left. He twisted the silver band round and round.

'This is where your father spent four years of his life.'

'It can't be possible,' said Florentyna, who did not sit down.

'It's better now than it was then,' said Abel. 'At least now there is fresh air, birds, the sun and a feeling of freedom. Then there was nothing, only darkness, death, the stench of death, and worst of all, the hope of death.'

'Come on, Daddy, let's leave. Staying here can only make you feel worse.'

Florentyna led her reluctant father to the car and drove him slowly down the long avenue. Abel didn't look back towards the ruined castle as they passed for the last time through its iron gates.

On the journey back to Warsaw he hardly spoke and Florentyna abandoned her attempts at vivacity. When her father said 'There is now only one thing left that I must achieve in this life,' Florentyna wondered what he could mean but did not press him to explain. She did, however, manage to coax him into spending another weekend in London on the return journey, which she convinced herself would cheer her father up a little and perhaps even help him to forget the memory of his demented old foster-mother and the remains of his castle in Poland.

They flew to London the next day. Abel was glad to be back in a country where he could communicate quickly with America. Once they had booked into Claridges, Florentyna went off to reunite with old friends and make new ones. Abel spent his time reading all the papers he could lay his hands on, in the hope of bringing himself up to date with what had happened in America while he had been abroad. He didn't like to feel things *could* happen while he was away; it reminded him only too clearly that the world could get along very well without him.

A little item on an inside page of Saturday's *Times* caught his eye. Things had happened while he was away. A Vickers Viscount of Interstate Airways had crashed immediately after take-off at the Mexico City airport the previous morning. The seventeen passengers and crew had all been killed. The Mexican authorities had been quick to place the blame on Interstate's bad servicing of their aircraft. Abel picked up the phone and asked the girl for the overseas operator.

Saturday, he's probably back in Chicago, thought Abel. He thumbed through his little phone book to find the home number.

'There'll be a delay of about thirty minutes,' said a precise, not unattractive, English voice.

'Thank you,' said Abel, and he lay down on the bed with the phone by his side, thinking. It rang twenty minutes later.

'Your overseas call is on the line, sir,' said the same precise voice.

'Abel, is that you? Where are you?'

'Sure is, Henry. I'm in London.'

'Are you through?' said the girl, who was back on the line.

'I haven't even started,' said Abel.

'I'm sorry, sir. I mean are you speaking to America?'

'Oh yes, sure. Thank you. Jesus, Henry, they speak a different language over here.'

Henry Osborne laughed.

'Now listen. Did you read that item in the press about an Interstate Airways' Vickers Viscount crashing at the Mexico City airport?'

'Yes, I did,' said Henry, 'but there's nothing for you to worry about. The plane was properly insured and the company is completely covered, so they incurred no loss and the stock has remained steady.'

'The insurance is the last thing I'm interested in,' said Abel. 'This could be our best chance yet for a little trial run to discover just how strong Mr. Kane's constitution is.'

'I don't think I understand, Abel. What do you mean?'

'Listen carefully, and I'll explain exactly what I want you to do when the Stock Exchange opens on Monday morning. I'll be back in New York by Tuesday to orchestrate the final crescendo myself.'

Henry Osborne listened attentively to Abel Rosnovski's instructions. Twenty minutes later, Abel replaced the phone on the hook.

He was through.

30

William realised he could expect more trouble from Abel Rosnovski the morning that Curtis Fenton phoned to let him know that the Chicago Baron was closing all the group's bank accounts with Continental Trust and was accusing Fenton himself of disloyalty and unethical conduct.

'I thought I did the correct thing in writing to you about Mr. Rosnovski's acquisitions in Lester's,' said the banker unhappily, 'and it has ended with me losing one of my biggest customers. I don't know what my board of directors will say.'

William formulated an inadequate apology, and calmed Fenton down a little by promising him he would speak to his superiors. He was, however, more preoccupied with wondering what Abel Rosnovski's next move would be.

Nearly a month later, he found out. He was going through the bank's Monday morning mail when a call came through from his broker, telling him that someone had placed a million dollars worth of Interstate Airways' stock on the market. William had to make the instant decision that his personal trust should pick up the shares, and he issued an immediate buy order for them. At two o'clock that afternoon, another million dollars' worth was put on the market. Before William had a chance to pick them up, the price had started falling. By the time the New York Stock Exchange closed at three o'clock, the price of Interstate Airways had fallen by a third.

At ten minutes past ten the next morning, William received a call from his now agitated broker. Another million dollars worth of shares had been placed on the market at the opening bell. The broker reported that the latest dumping had had an avalanche effect: Interstate sell orders were coming on to the floor from every quarter, the bottom had fallen out, and the stock was now trading at only a few cents a share. Only twenty-four hours previously, Interstate had been quoted at four and a half.

William instructed Alfred Rodgers, the company secretary, to call a board meeting for the following Monday. He needed the time to confirm who was responsible for the dumping. By Wednesday, he had abandoned any attempt at shoring up Interstate by buying all the shares that came on the market himself. At the close of business that day, the Securities and Exchange Commission announced that they would be conducting an enquiry into all Interstate transactions. William knew that Lester's board would now have to decide whether to support the airline for the three to six months it would take the S.E.C. to complete their investigation or whether to let the company go under. The alternatives looked extremely damaging, both to William's pocket and to the bank's reputation.

It came as no surprise to William to discover from Thaddeus Cohen the next day that the company that had dumped the original three million dollars worth of Interstate shares was one of those fronting for Abel Rosnovski, Guaranty Investment Corporation by name. A corporation spokesman had issued a plausible little press release explaining their reasons for selling, they had been concerned for the future of the Company after the Mexican government's responsible statement about Interstate Airways' inadequate servicing facilities.

'Responsible statement,' said William, outraged. 'The Mexican government hasn't made a responsible statement since they claimed Speedy Gonzales would win the one hundred metres at the Helsinki Olympics.'

The media made the most of Guaranty Investment's press release, and on Friday, the Federal Aviation Agency grounded the airline until it could conduct an in-depth investigation of its servicing facilities.

William was confident Interstate had nothing to fear from such an inspection, but the action proved disastrous for the short-term passenger bookings. No aviation company can afford to leave aircraft on the ground; they can only make money when they are in the air.

To compound William's problems, other major companies represented by Lester's were reconsidering future commitments. The press had been quick to point out that Lester's was Interstate Airways' underwriters. Surprisingly, Interstate's shares began to pick up again late Friday afternoon, and it did not take William long to guess why, a guess that was later confirmed by Thaddeus Cohen: the buyer was Abel Rosnovski. He had sold his Interstate shares at the top and was now buying them back in small amounts while they were at the bottom. William shook his head in begrudging admiration. Rosnovski was making a small fortune for himself while bankrupting William both in reputation and financial terms.

William worked out that although the Baron Group must have risked over three million dollars, they might well end up making a huge profit. Moreover, it was evident that Rosnovski was unconcerned about a temporary loss, which he could in any case use as a tax write-off; his only interest was in the total destruction of Lester's reputation.

When the board met on Monday, William explained the entire history of his clash with Rosnovski and offered his resignation. It was not accepted, nor was a vote taken, but there were murmurings, and William knew that if Rosnovski attacked again, his colleagues might not take the same tolerant attitude a second time.

The board went on to consider whether they should continue the support for Interstate Airways. Tony Simmons convinced them that the F.A.A.'s enquiry would come out in the bank's favour, and that Interstate would in time recover all their money. Tony had to admit to William after the meeting that their decision could only help Rosnovski in the long run, but the bank had no choice if it wished to protect its reputation.

He proved right on both counts. When the S.E.C. finally published its findings, they declared Lester's 'reproach-proof' although they had some stern words for Guaranty Investment Corporation. When the market started trading in Interstate shares that morning, William was surprised to find the stock rising steadily. It was soon back up to its original four and a half.

Thaddeus Cohen informed William that the principal purchaser was once again Abel Rosnovski.

'That's all I need at the moment,' said William. 'Not only does he make a large profit on the whole transaction, but now he can repeat the same exercise again whenever the time suits him.'

'In fact,' said Thaddeus Cohen, 'that is exactly what you do need.'

'Whatever do you mean, Thaddeus?' said William. 'I've never known you speak in riddles.'

'Mr. Abel Rosnovski has made his first error in judgment, because he's breaking the law and now it's your turn to go after him. He probably doesn't even realise that what he was involved in was illegal, becaues he was doing it for all the wrong reasons.'

'What are you talking about?' asked William.

'Simple,' said Thaddeus Cohen. 'Because of your obsession with Rosnovski – and his with you – it seems that both of you have overlooked the obvious: if you sell shares with the sole intention of causing the market to drop in order to pick up those same shares at the bottom and therefore be certain of a profit, you're breaking Rule 10b-5 of the Securities and Exchange Commission and you are committing the crime of fraud. There's no doubt in my mind that making a quick profit was not Mr. Rosnovski's original intention; in fact, we know very well he only wanted to embarrass you personally. But who is going to believe Rosnovski if he gives as an explanation that he dumped the stock because he thought the company was unreliable, when he has bought all the same shares back when they reached rock bottom? Answer: nobody – and certainly not the S.E.C. I'll have a full written report sent around to you by tomorrow, William, explaining the legal implications.'

'Thank you,' said William, jubilant over the news.

Thaddeus Cohen's report was on William's desk at nine the next morning and after William had read over the contents very carefully, he called another board meeting. The directors agreed with the course of action William wanted to take. Thaddeus Cohen was instructed to draft a carefully written press release to be issued that evening. The *Wall Street Journal* ran a piece on their front page the following morning.

Mr. William Kane, the chairman of Lester's Bank has reason to believe that the sell orders placed by Guaranty Investment Corporation in November 1952 on Interstate Airways shares, a company underwritten by Lester's Bank, were issued for the sole purpose of making an illegal profit.

It has been established that Guaranty Investment Corporation was responsible for placing a million dollars worth of Interstate stock on the market when the exchange opened on Monday, 12 May 1952. A further million dollars worth was on the market six hours later. A third million dollars worth was placed on a sell order by Guaranty Investment Corporation when the exchange reopened on Tuesday, 13 May 1952. This caused the stock to fall to a record low. After an S.E.C. enquiry showed there had been no illegal dealing within either Lester's Bank or Interstate Airways, the market picked up again with the stock trading at the depressed price. Guaranty Investment was quickly back in the market to purchase the shares at as low a price as possible. They continued to buy until they had replaced the three million dollars worth of stock they had originally released on to the market.

The chairman and directors of Lester's Bank have sent a copy of all the relevant documents to the Fraud Division of the Securities and Exchange Commission, and have asked them to proceed with a full enquiry.

The story below the statement gave S.E.C. Rule 10b-5 in full and commented that this was exactly the sort of test case that President Truman had been looking for; a cartoon below the article showed Harry S. Truman catching a businessman with his hands in the cookie jar.

William smiled as he read through the item, confident that that would be the last he would hear of Abel Rosnovski.

Abel Rosnovski frowned and said nothing as Henry Osborne read the statement over to him. Abel looked up, his fingers tapping in irritation on the desk.

'The boys in Washington,' said Osborne, 'are determined to get to the bottom of this one.'

'But Henry, you know very well I didn't sell Interstate shares to make a quick killing on the stock market,' said Abel. 'The profit I made was of no interest to me at all.'

'I know that,' said Henry, 'but you try and convince the Senate Finance Committee that the Chicago Baron had no interest in financial gain, that all he really wanted to do was settle a personal grudge against one William Kane, and they'll laugh you right out of court – or out of the Senate, to be more exact.'

'Damn,' said Abel. 'Now what the hell do I do?'

'Well, first you'll have to lie very low until this has had time to blow over. Start praying that some bigger scandal comes along for Truman to get himself worked up about, or that the politicians become so involved in the election that they haven't time to press for an enquiry. With luck, a new administration may even drop the whole thing. Whatever you do, Abel, don't buy any more shares that are connected with Lester's Bank, or the least you're going to end up with is a very large fine. Leave me to swing what I can with the Democrats in Washington.'

'Remind Harry Truman's office that I gave fifty thousand dollars to his campaign fund during the last election and I intend to do the same for Adlai.'

'I've already done that,' said Henry. 'In fact I would advise you to give fifty thousand to the Republicans as well.'

'They're making a mountain out of a molehill,' said Abel.

'A molehill that Kane will turn into a mountain if we give him the chance.' His fingers continued to tap on the table.

31

Thaddeus Cohen's next quarterly report revealed that Abel Rosnovski had stopped buying or selling stock in any of Lester's companies. It seemed he was now concentrating all his energy on building more hotels in Europe. Cohen's opinion was that Rosnovski was lying low, until a decision had been made by the S.E.C. on the Interstate affair.

Representatives of the S.E.C. had visited William at the bank on several occasions. He had spoken to them with complete frankness, but they never revealed how their enquiries were progressing. The S.E.C. finally finished their investigation and thanked William for his co-operation. He heard nothing more from them.

As the Presidential election grew nearer and Truman seemed to be concentrating his own efforts on the dissolution on the Du Pont industrial combine, William began to fear that Abel Rosnovski might have been let off the hook. He couldn't help feeling that Henry Osborne must have been able to pull a few strings in Congress. He remembered that Cohen had once underlined a note about a fifty thousand dollar donation from the Baron Group to Harry

Truman's campaign fund and was surprised to read in Cohen's latest report that Rosnovski had repeated the donation for Adlai Stevenson, the Democrats' choice for President, along with another fifty thousand for the Eisenhower campaign fund. Cohen had underlined the item again.

William, who had never considered supporting anyone for public office who was not a Republican, wanted General Eisenhower, the candidate who had emerged on the first ballot at the convention in Chicago, to defeat Adlai Stevenson, although he was aware that a Republican administration was less likely to press for a share manipulation enquiry than the Democrats.

When General Dwight D. Eisenhower – it appeared that the nation did like Ike – was elected as the thirty-fourth President of the United States on 4 November 1952, William assumed that Abel Rosnovski had escaped any charge and could only hope that the experience would persuade him to leave Lester's affairs well enough alone in the future. The one small compensation to come out of the election for William was that Congressman Henry Osborne lost his Congressional seat to a Republican candidate. The Eisenhower jacket had turned out to have coat-tails, and Osborne's rival had clung to them. Thaddeus Cohen was inclined to think that Henry Osborne no longer exerted quite the same influence over Abel Rosnovski that he had in the past. The rumour in Chicago was that, since divorcing his rich wife, Osborne owed large sums of money to Rosnovski and was gambling heavily again.

William was happier and more relaxed than he had been for some time and looked forward to joining the prosperous and peaceful era that Eisenhower had promised in his Inauguration speech.

As the first years of the new President's administration went by, William began to put Rosnovski's threats at the back of his mind and to think of them as a thing of the past. He informed Thaddeus Cohen that he believed they had heard the last of Abel Rosnovski. The lawyer made no comment. He wasn't asked to.

William put all his efforts into building Lester's, both in size and reputation, increasingly aware that he was now doing it as much for his son as for himself. Some of his staff at the bank had already started referring to him as the 'old man'.

'It had to happen,' said Kate.

'Then why hasn't it happened to you?' replied William.

Kate looked up at William and smiled. 'Now I know the secret of how you have closed so many deals with vain men.'

William laughed. 'And one beautiful woman,' he added.

With Richard's twenty-first birthday only a year away, William revised the provisions of his will. He set aside five million dollars for Kate and two million for each of the girls, and left the rest of the family fortune to Richard, noting ruefully the bite that would go in estate tax. He also left one million dollars to Harvard.

Richard had been making good use of his four years at Harvard. At the start of his senior year, not only did he look set for a *Summa Cum Laude*, but he was also playing the cello in the university orchestra, and was a pitcher with the varsity baseball team, which even William had to admire. As Kate liked rhetorically to ask, how many students spent Saturday afternoon playing baseball for Harvard against Yale and Sunday evening playing the cello in the Lowell concert hall for the university string quartet?

The final year passed quickly and when Richard left Harvard, armed with a Bachelor of Arts degree in mathematics, a cello and a baseball bat, all he required before reporting to the business school on the other side of the Charles River was a good holiday. He flew to Barbados with a girl called Mary Bigelow of whose existence Richard's parents were blissfully unaware. Miss Bigelow had studied music, among other things, at Vasser, and when they returned two months later almost the same colour as the natives, Richard took her home to meet his parents. William approved of Miss Bigelow; after all, she was Alan Lloyd's great niece.

Richard returned to the Harvard Business School on 1

October 1955 to start his graduate work. He took up residence in the Red House, threw out all William's cane furniture and removed the paisley wallpaper that Matthew Lester had once found so modern, and installed a wall-to-wall carpet in the living room, an oak table in the dining room, a dishwasher in the kitchen and, more than occasionally, Miss Bigelow in the bedroom.

32

Abel returned from a trip to Istanbul in October 1952, immediately upon hearing the news of David Maxton's fatal heart attack. He attended the funeral in Chicago with George and Florentyna and later told Mrs. Maxton that she could be a guest at any Baron in the world whenever she so pleased for the rest of her life. She could not understand why Abel had made such a generous gesture.

When Abel returned to New York the next day, he was delighted to find on the desk of his forty-second floor office a report from Henry Osborne indicating that the heat was now off. In Henry's opinion, the new Eisenhower administration was unlikely to pursue an enquiry into the Interstate Airways fiasco, especially as the stock had now held steady for nearly a year. There had, therefore, been no further incidents to renew any interest in the scandal. Eisenhower's Vice-President, Richard M. Nixon, seemed more involved in chasing the spectral communists whom Joe McCarthy missed.

Abel spent the next two years concentrating on building his hotels in Europe. He opened the Paris Baron in 1953 and the London Baron at the end of 1954. Barons were also in various stages of development for Brussels, Rome, Amsterdam, Geneva, Bonn, Edinburgh, Cannes and Stockholm in a ten-year expansion programme.

Abel became so overworked that he had little time to

consider William Kane's continued prosperity. He had not made any attempt to buy shares in Lester's Bank or its subsidiary companies, although he held on to those he already possessed in the hope that another opportunity might be forthcoming to deal a blow against William Kane from which he would not recover so easily. The next time, Abel promised himself, he'd make sure he didn't unwittingly break the law.

During Abel's increasingly frequent absences abroad George ran the Baron Group and Abel was hoping that Florentyna would join the board as soon as she left Radcliffe in June of 1955. He had already decided that she should take over responsibility for all the shops in the hotels and consolidate their buying, as they were fast becoming an empire in themselves.

Florentyna was very excited by the prospect but was insistent that she wanted some outside experience before joining her father's group. She did not consider her natural gifts for design, colour, and organisation were any substitute for experience. Abel suggested that she train in Switzerland under Monsieur Maurice at the famed *École Hôtelière* in Lausanne. Florentyna baulked at the idea, explaining that she wanted to work for two years in a New York store before she would consider taking over the shops. She was determined to be worth employing, '... and not just as my father's daughter,' she informed him. Abel thoroughly approved.

'A New York store, that's done easily enough,' he said. 'I'll ring up Walter Hoving at Tiffany's and you can start at the top.'

'No,' said Florentyna, revealing that she'd inherited her father's streak of stubbornness. 'What's the equivalent of a junior waiter at the Plaza Hotel?'

'A sales girl at a department store,' said Abel, laughing.

'Then that's exactly what I'm going to be,' she said.

Abel stopped laughing. 'Are you serious? With a degree from Radcliffe and all the experience and knowledge you've gained from your European trips, you want to be an anonymous sales girl?'

'Being an anonymous waiter at the Plaza didn't do you any harm when the time came to set up one of the most successful hotel groups in the world,' replied Florentyna.

Abel knew when he was beaten. He had only to look into the steel grey eyes of his beautiful daughter to realise she had made up her mind, and that no amount of persuasion, gentle or otherwise, was going to change her views.

After Florentyna had graduated from Radcliffe, she spent a month in Europe with her father, watching the progress of the latest Baron hotels. She officially opened the Brussels Baron where she made a conquest of the handsome young French-speaking managing director, whom Abel accused of smelling of garlic. She had to give him up three days later when it reached the kissing stage, but she never admitted to her father that garlic had been the reason.

Florentyna returned to New York with her father and immediately applied for the vacant position (the words used in the classified advertisement) of 'junior sales assistant' at Bloomingdale's. When she filled in the application form, she gave her name as Jessie Kovats, well aware that no one would leave her in peace if they ever thought she was the daughter of the Chicago Baron.

Despite protests from her father, she also left her suite in the Baron Hotel and started looking for her own place to live. Once again Abel gave in and presented Florentyna with a small but elegant co-operative flat on Fifty-seventh Street near the East River as a twenty-second birthday present.

Florentyna already knew her way around New York and enjoyed a full social life, but she had long ago resolved not to let her friends know that she was going to work at Bloomingdale's. She feared that they would want to come and visit her and, in days, her cleverly constructed cover would be blown, making it impossible to be treated as a normal trainee.

When her friends did inquire, she merely told them that she was helping to run the shops in her father's hotels. None of them gave her reply a second thought.

Jessie Kovats – it took her some time to get used to the

name – started in cosmetics. After six months, she was ready to run her own beauty shop. The girls in Bloomingdale's worked in pairs, which Florentyna immediately turned to her advantage by choosing to work with the laziest girl in the department. This arrangement suited both girls as Florentyna's choice was a gorgeous, unenlightened blonde called Maisie who had only two interests in life: the clock pointing to the hour of six p.m. and men. The former happened once a day, the latter all the time.

The two girls soon became comrades without exactly being friends. Florentyna learned a lot from her partner about how to avoid work without being spotted by the floor manager, and also how to get picked up by a man.

The cosmetic counter's profits were well up after their first six months together, despite the fact that Maisie spent most of her time trying out the products rather than selling them. She could take two hours repainting her finger nails alone. Florentyna, in contrast, had a natural gift for selling that could not have been picked up at night school. That combined with an ability to learn quickly made it seem to her employers, after only a few weeks, as if she had been around for years.

The partnership with Maisie suited Florentyna ideally, and when they moved her to Better Dresses, by mutual agreement Maisie went along and passed her time by trying on new dresses all day while Florentyna sold them. Maisie could attract men – in tow with their wives or sweethearts – irrespective of the merchandise, simply by looking at them. Once they were ensnared, Florentyna could move in and sell something to them. It seemed hardly possible that the combination could work in Better Dresses, but Florentyna made Maisie's victims buy something, few escaping with untouched wallets.

The profits for that six months were up again, and the floor supervisor decided that the two girls obviously worked well together. Florentyna said nothing to contradict that impression. While other assistants in the shop were always complaining about how little work their partners did,

Florentyna continually praised Maisie as the ideal workmate, who had taught her so much about how a big store operated. She didn't mention the useful advice that Maisie also imparted on how to deal with over-amorous men.

The greatest compliment an assistant can receive at Bloomingdale's is to be put on one of the counters facing the Lexington Avenue entrance, the first person to be seen by customers coming in through the main doors. To work on that counter was considered as a small promotion and it was rare for a girl to be invited to sell there until she had been with the store at least five years. Maisie had been with Bloomingdale's since she was seventeen, a full five years, while Florentyna had only just completed her first twelve months. But as their results had been so impressive, the manager decided to try the two girls out on the ground floor in the stationery department. Maisie was unable to derive any personal advantage from the stationery department, as she didn't care too much for reading and even less for writing. Florentyna wasn't sure after a year with her that she could read or write. Nevertheless, her new position pleased Maisie greatly because she adored being the centre of attention. So the girls continued their perfect partnership.

Abel admitted to George that he had once sneaked into Bloomingdale's to watch Florentyna at work, and he had to confess that she was damned good. He assured his vice-president that he was looking forward to her finishing the two-years training, so that he could employ the girl himself. They had both agreed that when Florentyna left Bloomingdale's, she would be made a vice-president of the group, with special responsibility for the hotel stores. As Bloomingdale's was finding out, she was a chip off a formidable old block, and Abel had no doubt that Florentyna would have few problems taking on the responsibilities he was planning for her.

Florentyna spent her last six months at Bloomingdale's on the ground floor in charge of six counters with the new title of junior supervisor. Her duties now included stock checking, the cash desks and overall supervision of eighteen sales clerks. Bloomingdale's had already decided that Jessie Kovats was the ideal candidate to be a future buyer.

Florentyna had not yet informed her employers that she would be leaving shortly to join her father as a vice-president of the Baron Group. As the six months was drawing to its conclusion, she began to wonder what would happen to poor Maisie after she had left, Maisie assumed Jessie was at Bloomingdale's for life – wasn't everybody? – and never gave the question a second thought. Florentyna thought she might even offer her a job in one of the shops in the New York Baron. As long as it was behind a counter at which men spent money, Maisie was a valuable asset.

One afternoon when Maisie was waiting on a customer – she was now in gloves, scarves and woolly hats – she pulled Florentyna aside and pointed to a young man who was loitering over the mittens.

'What do you think of him?' she asked, giggling.

Florentyna glanced up at Maisie's latest desire with her customary disinterest, but on this occasion she had to admit to herself that he was rather attractive, and for once she was almost envious of Maisie.

'They only want one thing, Maisie.'

'I know,' said Maisie, 'and he can have it.'

'I'm sure he'll be pleased to hear that,' said Florentyna, laughing as she turned to wait on a customer who was becoming impatient at Maisie's indifference to her presence. Maisie took advantage of Florentyna's move and rushed off to serve the gloveless young man. Florentyna watched them both out of the corner of her eye. She was amused that he kept glancing nervously towards her, checking that Maisie wasn't being spied on by her supervisor. Maisie giggled away and the young man departed with a pair of dark blue leather gloves.

'Well, how did he measure up to your hopes?' asked Florentyna, conscious she felt a little jealous of Maisie's new conquest.

'He didn't,' replied Maisie. 'But I'm sure he'll be back again,' she added, grinning.

Maisies prediction turned out to be correct, for the next day there he was, thumbing among the gloves and looking even more embarrassed.

'I suppose you had better go and wait on him,' said Florentyna.

Maisie hurried obediently away. Florentyna nearly laughed out loud when, a few minutes later, the young man departed with another pair of dark blue gloves.

'Two pairs,' declared Florentyna. 'I think I can say on behalf of Bloomingdale's, he deserves you.'

'But he still didn't ask me out,' said Maisie.

'What?' said Florentyna in mock disbelief. 'He must have a glove fetish.'

'It's very disappointing,' said Maisie, 'because I think he's neat.'

'Yes, he's not bad,' said Florentyna.

The next day when the young man arrived in the shop Maisie leapt forward, leaving an old lady in mid-sentence. Florentyna quickly took her place, once again watching Maisie out of the corner of her eye. This time the two of them appeared to be in deep conversation and the young man finally departed with yet another pair of dark blue leather gloves.

'It must be the real thing,' ventured Florentyna.

'Yes, I think it is,' replied Maisie, 'but he still hasn't suggested a date.'

Florentyna was flabbergasted.

'Listen,' said Maisie desperately, 'if he comes in tomorrow could you serve him? I think he is scared to ask me directly. He might find it easier to make a date through you.'

Florentyna laughed. 'A Viola to your Orsino.'

'What?' said Maisie.

'It doesn't matter,' said Florentyna. 'I wonder if I will be able to sell him a pair of gloves?'

If the man was anything he was consistent, thought Florentyna, as he pushed his way through the doors at exactly the same time the next day and immediately headed towards the glove counter. Maisie dug Florentyna in the ribs, and Florentyna decided the time had come to enjoy herself.

'Good afternoon, sir.'

'Oh, good afternoon,' said the young man looking surprised – or was it disappointment?

'Can I help you?' offered Florentyna.

'No – I mean, yes, I would like a pair of gloves,' he added unconvincingly.

'Yes, sir. Have you considered a dark blue pair? In leather? I'm sure we have your size – unless we're all sold out.'

The young man looked at her suspiciously as she handed him the gloves. He tried them on. They were a little too big. Florentyna offered him another pair but they were slightly too tight. He looked towards Maisie for inspiration but she was surrounded by a sea of male customers but she wasn't sinking because she even found the time to glance towards the young man and grin. He grinned back nervously. Florentyna handed him another pair of gloves. They fitted perfectly.

'I think that's what you're looking for,' said Florentyna.

'No, it's not really,' replied the embarrassed customer.

Florentyna decided the time had come to let the poor man off the hook and lowering her voice, she said, 'I'll go and rescue Maisie. Why don't you ask her out? I'm sure she will say yes.'

'Oh no,' said the young man. 'You don't understand. It's not her I want to take out – it's you.'

Florentyna was speechless. The young man seemed to muster courage.

'Will you have dinner with me tonight?'

She heard herself saying, 'Yes.'

'Shall I pick you up at your home?'

'No,' said Florentyna a little too firmly. The last thing she wanted was to be met at her apartment where it would be obvious to anyone that she was not a salesgirl. 'Let's meet at a restaurant,' she added quickly.

'Where would you like to go? . . .'

Florentyna tried to think quickly of a place that would not be too ostentatious.

'Allen's at Seventy-third and Third?' he ventured.

'Yes, fine,' said Florentyna, thinking how much better Maisie would have been at handling the whole situation.

'Around eight o'clock suit you?'

'Around eight,' replied Florentyna.

The young man left with a smile on his face. Florentyna watched him disappear on to the street, and suddenly realised that he had left without buying a pair of gloves.

Florentyna took a long time choosing which dress she should wear for her evening out. She wanted to be certain that the outfit didn't scream of Bergdorf Goodman. She had acquired a small wardrobe especially for Bloomingdale's, but the clothes were strictly for daytime use, and she had never worn anything from that selection in the evening. If her date – heavens, she didn't even know his name – thought she was a salesgirl she mustn't disillusion him. She couldn't help feeling that she was actually looking forward to the evening more than she ought to be.

She left her flat on East Fifty-seventh Street a little before eight and had to wait for several minutes before she managed to hail an empty taxi.

'Allen's, please,' she said to the taxi driver.

'On Third Avenue.'

'Yes.'

'Sure thing, miss,' he replied.

When Florentyna arrived at the restaurant, she was a few minutes late. Her eyes began to search for the young man. He was standing at the bar, waving. He had changed into a pair of grey flannel slacks and a blue blazer. Very Ivy League, thought Florentyna, but very good looking.

'I'm sorry to be late,' she began.

'It's not important. What's important is that you came.'

'You thought I wouldn't?' said Florentyna.

'I wasn't sure.' He smiled. 'I'm sorry, I don't know your name.'

'Jessie Kovats,' said Florentyna, determined not to give away her alias. 'And yours?'

'Richard Kane,' said the young man, thrusting out his hand.

She took it and he held on to her a little longer than she had expected.

'And what do you do when you're not buying gloves at Bloomingdale's?' she teased.

'I'm at Harvard Business School.'

'I'm surprised they didn't teach you that most people only have two hands.'

He laughed and smiled in such a relaxed and friendly way that she wished she could start again and tell him they might have met in Cambridge when she was at Radcliffe.

'Shall we order?' he said, taking her arm and leading her to a table.

Florentyna looked up at the menu on the blackboard.

'Salisbury steak?' she queried.

'A hamburger by any other name,' said Richard.

They both laughed, in the way two people do when they don't know each other, but want to. She could see he was surprised that she might have known his out-of-context quotation.

Florentyna had rarely enjoyed anyone's company more. Richard chatted about New York, the theatre and music – so obviously his first love – with such grace and charm that she was fully at ease. He may have thought she was a salesgirl but he was treating her as if she'd come from one of the oldest Brahmin families. He hoped he wasn't too surprised by her passion for the same things because, when he inquired, she told him nothing more than that she was Polish and lived in New York with her parents. As the evening progressed the deception became increasingly intolerable. Still, she thought, we may never see each other again after tonight, and then it will all be irrelevant.

When the evening did come to an end and neither of them could drink any more coffee, they left Allen's and

Richard looked for a taxi, the only ones they saw were all full.

'Where do you live?' he asked.

'Fifty-seventh Street,' she said, not thinking about her reply.

'Then's let's walk,' said Richard, taking Florentyna's hand.

She smiled her agreement. They started walking, stopping and looking at shop windows, laughing and smiling. Neither of them noticed the empty taxis that now rushed past them. It took them almost an hour to cover the sixteen blocks and Florentyna nearly told him the truth. When they reached Fifty-seventh Street she stopped outside a small old apartment house, some hundred yards from her own home.

'This is where my parents live,' she said.

He seemed to hesitate and then let go of her hand.

'I hope you will see me again,' said Richard.

'I'd like that,' replied Florentyna in a polite, dismissive way.

'Tomorrow?' asked Richard diffidently.

'Tomorrow?'

'Yes, why don't we go to the Blue Angel and see Bobby Short?' He took her hand again. 'It's a little more romantic than Allen's.'

Florentyna was momentarily taken aback. Her plans for Richard had not included any provisions for tomorrows.

'Not if you don't want to,' he added before she could recover.

'I'd love to,' she said quietly.

'I'm having dinner with my father, so why don't I pick you up at ten o'clock?'

'No, no,' said Florentyna, 'I'll meet you there. It's only two blocks away.'

'Ten o'clock then,' he bent forward and kissed her gently on the cheek. 'Good night, Jessie,' he said, and disappeared into the night.

Florentyna walked slowly back to her apartment, wishing she hadn't told so many lies about herself. Still, it might be over in a few days. She couldn't help feeling that she hoped it wouldn't.

Maisie, who hadn't yet forgiven her, spent a considerable part of the next day asking all about Richard. Florentyna kept trying unsuccessfully to change the subject.

Florentyna left Bloomingdale's the moment the store closed, the first time in nearly two years that she had left before Maisie. She had a long bath, put on the prettiest dress she thought she could get away with, and walked to the Blue Angel. When she arrived Richard was already waiting for her outside the cloakroom. He held her hand as they walked into the lounge where the words of Bobby Short came floating through the air.

Are you telling me the truth, or am I just another lie?

As Florentyna walked in, Short raised his arm in acknowledgment. Florentyna pretended not to notice. Mr. Short had been a guest performer at The Baron on two or three occasions and it never occurred to Florentyna that he would remember her. Richard looked puzzled and then assumed he had been greeting someone else. When they took a table in the dimly-lit room, Florentyna sat with her back to the piano to be certain it wouldn't happen again.

Richard ordered a bottle of wine without letting go of her hand and then asked about her day. She didn't want to tell him; she wanted to tell him the truth – 'Richard, there is something I must...'

'Hi, Richard.' A tall, handsome man stood at Richard's side.

'Hi, Steve. Can I introduce Jessie Kovats – Steve Mellon. Steven and I were at Harvard together.'

Florentyna listened to them chat about the New York Yankees, Eisenhower's handicap – his golf, and why Yale was going from bad to worse. Steve eventually left with a gracious, 'Nice to have met you, Jessie.'

The moment had passed.

Richard began to tell her of his plans once he had left business school, how he hoped to come to New York and join his father's bank, Lester's. She had heard the name before but couldn't remember in what connection. For some reason it worried her. They spent a long evening together, laughing, eating, talking, and just sitting, holding hands, listening to Bobby Short. When they walked home, Richard stopped on the corner of Fifty-seventh and kissed her for the first time. She couldn't recall any other occasion when she was so aware of a first kiss. When he returned her to the shadows of Fifty-seventh Street, she left him and her white lies, aware that this time he had not mentioned tomorrow. She felt slightly wistful about the whole non-affair.

She was take aback by how pleased she felt when Richard phoned her at Bloomingdale's on Monday, asking if she would go out with him on Friday evening.

They wound up spending most of that weekend together: a concert, a film – even the New York Knicks did not escape them. When the weekend was over Florentyna found she had told so many innocent lies about her background that she became inconsistent in her fabrication and puzzled Richard more than once by contradicting herself. It seemed to make it all the more impossible to tell him another entirely different, albeit true, story. When Richard returned to Harvard on the Sunday night, she persuaded herself that the deception would seem unimportant once the relationship had ended. But Richard phoned every day during the week and spent the next few weekends in her company: she began to realise it wasn't going to end that easily. She was falling in love with him. Once she had admitted that to herself, she realised that she had to tell him the truth the following weekend.

33

Richard sat through his morning lecture, daydreaming. He was so much in love with that girl, he could not even concentrate on the 'Twenty-nine crash'. He wished he could work out how to tell his father that he intended to marry a Polish girl who worked behind the scarf, glove and woolly hats counter at Bloomingdale's. Richard was unable to fathom why she was so unambitious for herself when she was obviously very bright: he was certain that if she had had the chances he had been given, she would not have ended up in Bloomingdale's. Richard decided that his parents would have to learn to live with his choice, because that weekend he was going to ask Jessie to be his wife.

Whenever Richard returned to his parent's home in New York on a Friday evening, he would always leave the house on East Sixty-eighth Street to go and pick up something from Bloomingdale's, normally a useless and unwanted item, simply so that he could let Jessie know that he was back in town; he had already given a pair of gloves to every relation he possessed. That Friday, he told his mother that he was going out to buy some razor blades.

'Don't bother, darling, you can use your father's,' she said.

'No, no, it's all right,' he said. 'I'll go and get some of my own. We don't use the same brand in any case,' he added feebly. 'I'll only be a few minutes.'

He almost ran the eight blocks to Bloomingdale's and managed to rush in just as they were closing the doors. He knew he would be seeing Jessie at seven thirty, but he could never resist a chance to chat with her. Steve had told him once that love was for suckers. He had written on his steamed-up shaving mirror that morning 'I am a sucker'. But when he reached Jessie's counter, she was nowhere to be seen. Maisie was standing in a corner filing her finger nails, and he asked her if Jessie was still around. Maisie looked up as if she had been interrupted from her one important task of the day.

'No, she's already gone home, Richard. Left a few seconds ago. She can't have gone far. I thought you were meeting her later.'

Richard ran out on to Lexington Avenue without replying. He searched for Jessie among the faces hurrying home, then spotted her on the other side of the street, heading towards Fifth Avenue. Since she obviously wasn't going home, he somewhat guiltily decided to follow her. As she reached Scribner's at Forty-eighth Street, he stopped and watched her go into the bookshop. If she wanted something to read, surely she could find what she wanted from Bloomingdale's. He was puzzled. He peered through the window as Jessie talked to a sales clerk who left her for a few moments and then returned with two books. He could just make out their titles: *The Affluent Society* by John Kenneth Galbraith and *Inside Russia Today* by John Gunther. Jessie signed for them – that surprised Richard – and left as he ducked around the corner.

'Who *is* she?' said Richard out loud as he watched her enter Bendel's. The doorman saluted respectfully, leaving a distinct impression of recognition. Once again Richard peered through the window as assistants fluttered around Florentyna with more than casual respect. An older lady appeared with a package which she had obviously been expecting. She opened it to reveal a simple, stunning, evening dress. Florentyna smiled and nodded as the assistant placed the dress in a brown and white box. Florentyna mouthed the words 'Thank you' and turned towards the door without even signing for her purchase. Richard was mesmerised by the scene and barely managed to avoid colliding with her as she ran out of the shop and jumped into a cab. He grabbed one himself, telling the driver to follow her. When the cab passed the small building outside of which they normally parted, he began to feel queasy. No wonder she had never asked him in. The cab in front continued for another hundred yards and stopped outside a spanking new block of flats complete with a uniformed hall porter who opened the door for her. With mingled anger and astonishment, he jumped out of the cab and started to march up to the door through which she had disappeared.

'That'll be ninety-five cents, fella,' said a voice behind him.

'Oh, sorry,' said Richard and thrust five dollars at him, showing no interest in his change.

'Thank you,' said the driver. 'Someone sure is happy today.'

Richard ran to the door of the building and managed to catch Florentyna at the lift. Florentyna watched the door slide open and stared at him speechlessly.

'Who are you?' demanded Richard.

'Richard,' she stammered. 'I was going to tell you everything this evening. I never seemed to find the right opportunity.'

'Like hell you were going to tell me,' he said, following Florentyna into her apartment. 'Stringing me along with a pack of lies for nearly three months. Now the time has come for the truth.'

Florentyna had never seen Richard angry before and suspected that it was very rare. He pushed his way past her brusquely and inspected the flat. At the end of the entrance hall, there was a large living room with a fine oriental rug. A superb grandfather clock stood opposite a side table on which there was a bowl of fresh flowers. The room was beautiful, even by the standards of Richard's own home.

'Nice place you've got yourself for a sales girl,' said Richard. 'I wonder which of your lovers pays for this.'

Florentyna slapped him so hard that her own palm stung. 'How dare you?' she said. 'Get out of my home.'

As she heard herself saying the words, she started to cry. She didn't want him to leave – ever. Richard took her in his arms.

'Oh, God, I'm sorry,' he said. 'That was a terrible thing to say. Please forgive me. It's just that I love you so much and thought I knew you so well; and now I find I don't know anything about you.'

'Richard, I love you too, and I'm sorry I slapped you. I didn't want to deceive you, but there's no one else – I promise you that.' Her voice cracked.

'I deserved it,' he said as he kissed her.

Clasped tightly in one another's arms, they sank on to the couch and remained almost motionless for some moments. Gently, he stroked her hair until her tears subsided. Help me to take my clothes off, she wanted to say, but remained silent, slipping her fingers through the gap between his two top shirt buttons. Richard seemed unwilling to make the next move.

'Do you want to sleep with me?' she asked quietly.

'No,' he replied. 'I want to stay awake with you all night.'

Without speaking, they undressed and made love, gently and shyly, frightened to hurt each other, desperately trying to please. Finally, with her head on his shoulder, they talked.

'I love you,' said Richard. 'I have since the first moment we met. Will you marry me? Because I don't give a damn who you are, Jessie, or what you do, but I know I must spend the rest of my life with you.'

'I want to marry you too, Richard, but first I have to tell you the truth.'

Florentyna pulled Richard's jacket over their naked bodies and told him all about herself, ending by explaining how she had come to be working at Bloomingdale's. When she had completed her story, Richard did not speak.

'Have you stopped loving me already?' she said. 'Now you know who I really am?'

'Darling,' said Richard, very quietly, 'my father hates your father.'

'What do you mean?'

'Just that, the only time I ever heard your father's name mentioned in his presence, he flew completely off the handle saying your father's sole purpose in life seemed to be a desire to ruin the Kane family.'

'What? Why?' said Florentyna, shocked. 'I've never heard of your father. How do they even know each other?'

It was Richard's turn to tell Florentyna everything his

mother had told him about the quarrel with her father.

'Oh, my God,' she said. 'That must have been the "disloyalty" my father referred to when he changed banks after twenty-five years. What shall we do?'

'Tell them the truth,' said Richard, 'that we met innocently, fell in love and now we're going to be married, and nothing they can do will stop us.'

'Let's wait a few weeks,' said Florentyna.

'Why?' asked Richard. 'Do you think your father can talk you out of marrying me?'

'No, Richard,' she said, touching him gently as she placed her head back on his shoulder. 'Never, my darling, but let's find out if we can do anything to break it gently, before we present them both with a *fait accompli*. Anyway, maybe they won't feel as strongly as you imagine. After all, you said the affair with the airlines company was nearly five years ago.'

'They still feel strongly, I promise you that. My father would be outraged if he saw us together, let alone thought we were considering marriage.'

'All the more reason to leave it for a little before we break the news to them. That will give us time to think about the best way to go about it.'

He kissed her again. 'I love you, Jessie.'

'Florentyna.'

'That's something else I'm going to have to get used to,' he said. 'I love you, Florentyna.'

During the next four weeks, Florentyna and Richard found out as much as they could about their parents' feud, Florentyna by asking her mother and George Novak a set of carefully worded questions, Richard from his father's filing cabinet. The extent of the mutual hatred appalled them. It became more obvious with each discovery that there was no gentle way to break the news of their love. During the next four weeks they spent every free moment they could find together. Richard was always attentive and kind, and nothing was too much trouble. He went to extremes to take her mind off the problem that they knew they would eventually have to face. They went to the theatre, skating, and on Sundays took long walks through Central Park, always ending up in bed long before it was dark. Florentyna even accompanied Richard to watch the New York Yankees which she 'couldn't understand' and the New York Philharmonic which she 'adored'. She refused to believe Richard could play the cello until he gave her a private recital. She applauded enthusiastically when he had finished his favourite Brahms sonata without noticing that he was staring into her grey eyes.

'We have got to tell them,' he said, placing his bow on the stand and taking her into his arms.

'I know we must. I just don't want to hurt my father.'

It was his turn to say, 'I know.'

She avoided his eyes. 'Next Friday Daddy will be back from Washington.'

'Then it's next Friday,' said Richard, holding her so close she could hardly breathe.

Richard returned to Harvard on Monday morning and they spoke to each other on the phone every night, never weakening, determined that nothing would stop them.

On Friday Richard arrived in New York earlier than usual and spent an hour alone with Florentyna who had asked for a half-day off. As they walked to the corner of Fifty-seventh and Park, they stopped at the flashing red 'Don't Walk' sign, and Richard turned to Florentyna and asked her once again to marry him. He took a small red leather box out of his pocket, opened it and placed a ring on the third finger of her left hand, a sapphire set in diamonds, so beautiful that tears came to Florentyna's eyes; it was a perfect fit. Passers-by looked at them strangely as they stood on the corner, clinging to each other, ignoring the green light flashing 'Walk'. When eventually they did obey its command, they kissed before parting and walked in opposite directions to confront their parents. They had agreed to meet again at Florentyna's flat as soon as the ordeal was over. She tried to smile through her tears.

Florentyna walked towards the Baron Hotel, occasionally looking at her ring. It felt new and strange on her finger and she imagined that the eyes of all who passed by would be drawn to the magnificent sapphire and to her, it looked so beautiful next to the antique ring, her favourite of the past. She had been astonished when Richard had placed it on her finger. The problem of their parents' rivalry had made her forget rings or any of the other trappings that attend a happy engagement. She touched the diamond-encircled sapphire and found that it gave her courage, although she was aware that she was walking more and more slowly as the hotel drew nearer and nearer.

When she reached the reception desk, the clerk told her that her father was in the penthouse with George Novak. He called to say that Florentyna was on her way up. The lift reached the forty-second floor far too quickly for Florentyna, and she hesitated before leaving its safety. She stepped out on to the green carpet and heard the lift door slide closed behind her. She stood alone in the corridor for a moment before knocking quietly at her father's door. Abel opened it immediately.

'Florentyna, what a pleasant surprise. Come on in, my darling. I wasn't expecting to see you today.'

George Novak was standing by the window, looking down at Park Avenue. He turned to greet his goddaughter. Florentyna's eyes pleaded with him to leave. If he stayed, she knew she would lose her nerve. Go, go, go, she said inside her brain. George sensed her anxiety immediately.

'I must get back to work, Abel. There's a goddamn maharajah checking in tonight.'

'Tell him to park his elephants at the Plaza,' said Abel genially. 'Now Florentyna's here, stay and have another drink.'

George looked at Florentyna. 'No, Abel, I have to go. The man's taken the whole of the thirty-third floor. The least he'll expect is the vice-president to greet him. Goodnight, Florentyna,' he said, kissing her on the cheek and briefly clasping her arm, almost as though he knew that she needed strength. He left them alone and suddenly Florentyna wished he had not gone.

'How's Bloomingdale's?' said Abel, ruffling his daughter's hair affectionately. 'Have you told them yet they're going to lose the best floor manager they've had in years? They're sure going to be surprised when they hear that Jessie Kovats' next job will be to open the Cannes Baron.' He laughed out loud.

'I'm going to be married,' said Florentyna, shyly extending her left hand. She could think of nothing to add so she simply waited for his reaction.

'This is a bit sudden, isn't it?' said Abel, more than a little taken aback.

'Not really, Daddy. I've known him for some time.'

'Do I know the boy? Have I ever met him?'

'No, Daddy, you haven't.'

'Where does he come from? What's his background? Is he Polish? Why have you been so secretive about him, Florentyna?'

'He's not Polish, Daddy. He's the son of a banker.'

Abel went white and picked up his drink, swallowing the liquor in one gulp. Florentyna knew exactly what must be going through his mind as he poured himself another drink, so she got the truth out quickly.

'His name is Richard Kane, Daddy.'

Abel swung round to face her. 'Is he William Kane's son?' he demanded.

'Yes, he is,' said Florentyna.

'You could consider marrying William Kane's son? Do you know what that man did to me? He's the man who was responsible for the death of my closest friend. Yes, he's the man who made Davis Leroy commit suicide and, not satisfied with that, he tried to bankrupt me. If David Maxton hadn't rescued me in time, Kane would have taken away my hotels and sold them without a second thought. And where would I be now if William Kane had had his way? You'd have been lucky to have ended up as a shop girl at Bloomingdale's. Have you thought about that, Florentyna?'

'Yes, Daddy, I've thought of little else these past few weeks. Richard and I are horrified about the hatred that exists between you and his father. He's facing him now.'

'Well, I can tell you how he'll react,' said Abel. 'He'll go berserk. That man would never allow that precious wasp son of his to marry you so you might as well forget the whole crazy idea, young lady.'

His voice had risen to a shout.

'I can't forget it, Father,' she said evenly. 'We love each other, and we both need your blessing, not your anger.'

'Now you listen to me, Florentyna,' said Abel, his face now red with fury. 'I forbid you to see the Kane boy ever again. Do you hear me?'

'Yes, I hear you. But I will see him. I'll not be parted from Richard because you hate his father.'

She found herself clutching her ring finger and trembling slightly.

'It will not happen,' said Abel. 'I will never allow the marriage. My own daughter deserting me for the son of that bastard Kane. I say you will not marry him.'

'I am not deserting you. I would have run away with him if that was true, but I couldn't do that behind your back. I'm over twenty-one, and I will marry Richard. I intend to spend the rest of my life with him. Please help us, Daddy. Won't you meet him, and then you'll begin to understand why I feel the way I do about him?'

'He will never be allowed to enter my home. I do not want to meet any child of William Kane. Never, do you hear me?'

'Then I must leave you.'

'Florentyna, if you leave me, to marry the Kane boy, I'll cut you off without a penny. Without a penny, do you hear me?' Abel's voice softened. 'Now use your common sense, girl, you'll get over him. You're still young, and there are lots of other men who'd give their right arms to marry you.'

'I don't want lots of other men,' said Florentyna. 'I've met the man I'm going to marry, and it's not his fault that he is his father's son. Neither of us chose our fathers.'

'If my family isn't good enough for you, then get out,' said Abel. 'And I swear I won't have your name mentioned in my presence again.' He turned away and stared out of the window. 'For the last time, I warn you, Florentyna – do not marry that boy.'

'Daddy, we are going to be married. Although we're both past the stage of needing your consent, we do ask for your approval.'

Abel looked away from the window and walked towards her. 'Are you pregnant? Is that the reason? Do you have to get married?'

'No, Father.'

'Have you ever slept with him?' Abel demanded.

The question shook Florentyna but she didn't hesitate. 'Yes,' she replied. 'Many times.'

Abel raised his arm and hit her full across the face. The silver band caught the corner of her lip and she nearly fell. Blood started to trickle down her chin. She turned, ran out of the room crying, and leaned on the lift button, holding her bloody face. The door slid open and George stepped out. She had a fleeting glimpse of his shocked expression as she stepped quickly in to the car and jabbed at the button continuously. As George stood and watched her crying, the lift doors closed slowly.

Once Florentyna had reached the street, she took a cab straight to her own apartment. On the way, she dabbed at her cut lip with a Kleenex. Richard was already there, standing under the marquee, head bowed and looking miserable.

She jumped out of the cab and ran to him. Once they were upstairs, she opened the door and quickly closed it behind them, feeling blessedly safe.

'I love you, Richard.'

'I love you, too,' said Richard, as he threw his arms around her.

'I don't have to ask how your father reacted,' said Florentyna, clinging to him desperately.

'I've never seen him so angry,' said Richard. 'Called your father a liar and a crook, nothing more than a jumped-up Polish immigrant. He asked me why I didn't marry somebody from my own background.'

'What did you say to that?'

'I told him someone as wonderful as you couldn't be replaced by a suitably Brahmin family friend, and he completely lost his temper.'

Florentyna didn't let go of Richard as he spoke.

'Then he threatened to cut me off without a penny if I married you,' he continued. 'When will they understand we don't care a damn about their money? I tried appealing to my mother for support, but even she could not control his temper. He insisted that she leave the room. I have never seen him treat my mother that way before. She was weeping, which only made my resolve stronger. I left him in mid-sentence. God knows, I hope he doesn't take it out on Virginia and Lucy. What happened when you left?'

'My father hit me,' said Florentyna very quietly. 'For the first time in my life. I think he'll kill you if he finds us together. Richard darling, we must get out of here, before he finds out where you are, and he's bound to try here first. I'm so frightened.'

'No need for you to be frightened, Florentyna. We'll leave tonight and go as far away as possible and to hell with them both.'

'How quickly can you pack?' asked Florentyna.

'I can't,' said Richard. 'I can never return home now. You pack your things and then we'll go. I've got about a hundred dollars on me. How do you feel about marrying a hundred-dollar man?'

'As much as a shop girl can hope for, I suppose – and to think I'd dreamed of being a kept woman. Next you'll be wanting a dowry,' Florentyna added while rummaging in her bag. 'Well, I've got two hundred and twelve dollars and an American Express card, so you owe me fifty-six dollars, Richard Kane, but I'll consider repayment at a dollar a year.'

In thirty minutes Florentyna was packed. Then she sat down at her desk, scrawled a note and left the envelope on the table by the side of her bed.

Richard hailed a cab. Florentyna was delighted to find how capable Richard was in a crisis and it made her feel more relaxed. 'Idlewild,' he said, placing Florentyna's three cases in the boot.

At the airport he booked a flight to San Francisco; they chose the Golden Gate City simply because it seemed the most distant point on the map of America.

At seven thirty, the American Airlines Super Constellation 1049 taxied out on to the runway to start its seven-hour flight.

Richard helped Florentyna with her seat belt. She smiled at him.

'Do you know how much I love you, Mr. Kane?'

'Yes, I think so – Mrs. Kane,' he replied.

34

Abel and George arrived at Florentyna's flat on East Fifty-seventh Street a few minutes after she and Richard had left for the airport. Abel was already remorseful and regretting the blow he had struck his daughter. He did not care to conjecture about what his life would be like without his only child. He thought if he could only reach her before it was too late, he might, with gentle persuasion, still talk her out of marrying the Kane boy. He was willing to offer her anything to stop the marriage.

George rang the door bell as he and Abel stood outside her door. No one answered. George pressed the bell again, and they waited for some time before Abel used the key Florentyna had always left with him for emergencies. They searched the place, neither really expecting to find her.

'She must have left already,' said George, as he joined Abel in the bedroom.

'Yes, but where?' said Abel, and then he saw an envelope addressed to him on the table. He remembered the last letter left for him by the side of a bed that had not been slept in. He ripped it open.

Dear Daddy,

Please forgive me for running away but I do love Richard and will not give him up because of your hatred for his father. We will be married right away and nothing you can do will prevent it. If you ever try to harm him in any way, you will be harming me. Neither of us intend to return to New York until you have ended the senseless feud between our family and the Kane's. I love you more than you will ever realise and I shall always be thankful for everything you have done for me. I pray that this is not the end of our relationship but until you can change your mind, 'Never seek the wind in the field – it is useless to try and find what is gone.'

Your loving daughter,
Florentyna

Abel collapsed on to the bed, and passed the letter to George, who read the handwritten note and asked helplessly, 'Is there anything I can do?'

'Yes, George. I want my daughter back, even if it means dealing direct with that bastard Kane. There's only one thing I feel certain of : he will want this marriage stopped whatever sacrifice he has to make. Get him on the phone.'

It took George some time to locate William Kane's unlisted number. The night security officer at Lester's Bank finally gave it to him when George insisted that it was a family emergency. Abel sat silently on the bed, Florentyna's letter in his hand, remembering how when she was a little girl, he had taught her the old Polish proverb that she had now quoted back to him. When George was put through to the Kane residence, a male voice answered the phone.

'May I speak to Mr. William Kane?' asked George.

'Whom shall I say is calling?' asked the imperturbable voice.

'Mr. Abel Rosnovski,' said George.

'I'll see if he is in, sir.'

'I think that was Kane's butler. He's gone to look for him,' said George, as he passed the receiver over to Abel. Abel waited, his fingers tapping on the bedside table.

'William Kane speaking.'

'This is Abel Rosnovski.'

'Indeed?' William's tone was icy. 'And when exactly did you think of setting up your daughter with my son? At the time, no doubt, when you failed so conspicuously to cause the downfall of my bank?'

'Don't be such a damn...' Abel checked himself. 'I want this marriage stopped every bit as much as you do. I never tried to take away your son. I only learned of his existence today. I love my daughter even more than I hate you, and I don't want to lose her. Can't we get together and work something out between us?'

'No,' said William. 'I asked you that same question once in the past, Mr. Rosnovski, and you made it very clear when and where you would meet me. I can wait until then, because I am confident you will find it is you who are there, not I.'

'What's the good of raking over the past now, Kane? If you know where they are, perhaps we can stop them. That's what you want, too. Or are you so goddamn proud that you'll stand by and watch your son marry my girl rather than help...?'

The telephone clicked as he spoke the word 'help'. Abel buried his face in his hands and wept. George took him back to the Baron.

Through that night and the following day, Abel tried every way he could think of to find Florentyna. He even rang her mother, who admitted that their daughter had told her all about Richard Kane.

'He sounded rather nice,' she added spitefully.

'Do you know where they are right now?' asked Abel impatiently.

'Yes.'

'Where?'

'Find out for yourself.' Another telephone click.

Abel placed advertisements in newspapers and even bought radio time. He tried to get the police involved, but they could only put out a general call since she was over twenty-one. No word came from her. Finally, he had to admit to himself that by the time he found her she would undoubtedly be married to the Kane boy.

He re-read her letter many times, and resolved that he would never attempt to harm the boy in any way. But the father, that was a different matter. He, Abel Rosnovski, had gone down on his knees and pleaded, and the bastard hadn't even listened. Abel vowed that when the chance presented itself, he would finish William Kane off once and for all. George became fearful at the intensity of his old friend's passion.

'Shall I cancel your European trip?' he asked.

Abel had completely forgotten that he was meant to accompany Florentyna to Europe after she had finished her two years with Bloomingdale's at the end of the month. She was going to open the Edinburgh Baron and the Cannes Baron. Now he didn't care who opened what, or whether the hotels were opened at all.

'I can't cancel,' replied Abel. 'I'll have to go and open the hotels myself, but while I'm away, George, you find out exactly where Florentyna is without letting her know. She mustn't think I'm spying on her; she would never forgive me if she found out. Your best bet may well be Zaphia, but be careful because you can be sure she will want to take every advantage of what has happened. It was obvious she had already briefed Florentyna on everything she knew about Kane.'

'Do you want Osborne to do anything about the Kane shares?'

'No, nothing for the moment. Now is not the appropriate time for finishing Kane off. When I do, I want to be certain that it's once and for all. Leave Kane alone for the time being. I can always come back to him. For now, concentrate on finding Florentyna.'

George promised that he would have found her by the time Abel returned.

Abel opened the Edinburgh Baron three weeks later. The hotel looked quite magnificent as it stood on the hill dominating the Athens of the north. It was always little things that annoyed Abel most when he opened a new hotel and he would always check them on arrival. A small electric shock when you touched a light switch caused by nylon carpets. Room service that took forty minutes to materialise or a bed that was too small for anyone who was either fat or tall. The press was quick to point out that it had been expected that Florentyna Rosnovski, daughter of the Chicago Baron, would perform the opening ceremony. One of the gossip columnists, from the *Sunday Express*, hinted at a family rift and reported that Abel had not been his usual exuberant, bouncy self. Abel denied the suggestion unconvincingly, retorting that he was over fifty – not an age for bouncing, his public relations man had told him to say. The press remained unconvinced and the following day the *Daily Mail* printed a photograph of a discarded engraved bronze plaque, discovered on a rubbish heap, which read:

The Edinburgh Baron
opened by
Florentyna Rosnovski
October 17, 1957

Abel flew on to Cannes. Another splendid hotel, this time overlooking the Mediterranean but it didn't help him to get Florentyna out of his mind. Another discarded plaque, this one in French. The openings were ashes without her.

Abel was beginning to dread that he might spend the rest of his life without seeing his daughter again. To kill the loneliness, he slept with some very expensive and some rather cheap women. None of them helped. William Kane's son now possessed the one person he truly loved. France no longer held any excitement for him, and once he had finished his business there, Abel flew on to Bonn where he completed negotiations for the site on which he would build the first Baron in Germany. He kept in constant touch with George by phone, but Florentyna had not been found, and there was some very disturbing news concerning Henry Osborne.

'He's got himself in heavy debt with the bookmakers again,' said George.

'I warned him last time that I was through bailing him out,' said Abel. 'He's been no damn use to anyone since he lost his seat in Congress. I suppose I'll have to deal with the problem when I get back.'

'He's making threats,' said George.

'There's nothing new about that. I've never let them worry me in the past,' said Abel. 'Tell him whatever it is he wants, it will have to wait until my return.'

'When do you expect to be back?' asked George.

'Three weeks, four at the most. I want to look at some sites in Turkey and Egypt. Hilton's already started building there, so I'm going to find out why. Which reminds me, George, the experts tell me you'll never be able to reach me once the plane has landed in the Middle East. Those damned Arabs haven't worked out how to find each other, let alone visitors from foreign countries, so I'll leave you to run everything as usual until you hear from me.'

Abel spent over three weeks looking at sites for new hotels all over the Arab states. His advisors were legion, most of them claiming the title of Prince, each assuring Abel that they had the real influence as a very close personal friend of the key minister, a distant cousin in fact. However, it always turned out to be the wrong minister or too distant a cousin. The only solid conclusion Abel reached, after twenty-three days in the dust, sand, and heat with soda but no whisky, was that if his advisors' forecasts on the Middle East oil reserves were accurate, the Gulf States were going to need a lot of hotels in the long term and the Baron Group had to start planning carefully if they were not to be left behind.

Abel managed to find several sites on which to build

hotels, through his several princes, but he did not have the time to discover which of them had the real power to fix the officials. He objected to bribery only when the money reached the wrong hands. At least in America, Henry Osborne had always known which officials needed to be taken care of. Abel set up a small office in Bahrain, leaving his local representative in no doubt that the Baron Group was looking for sites throughout the Arab world, but not for princes or the cousins of ministers.

He flew on to Istanbul, where he almost immediately found the perfect place to build a hotel, overlooking the Bosphorus, only a hundred yards from the old British embassy. He mused as he stood on the barren ground of his latest acquisition, recalling when he had last been here. He clenched his fist and held the wrist of his right hand. He could hear again the cries of the mob – it still made him feel frightened and sick although more than thirty years had passed.

Exhausted from his travels, Abel flew home to New York. During the interminable journey he thought of little but Florentyna, and whether George had found her. As always, George was standing, waiting outside the customs gate to meet him. His expression indicated nothing.

'What news?' asked Abel as he climbed into the back of the Cadillac while the chauffeur put his bags in the trunk.

'Some good, some bad,' said George, as he pressed a button by the side window. A sheet of glass glided up between the front and rear sections of the car. 'Florentyna has been in touch with her mother. She's living in a small apartment in San Francisco.'

'Married?' said Abel.

'Yes,' said George.

Neither spoke for some moments.

'And the Kane boy?' asked Abel.

'He's found a job in a bank. It seems a lot of people turned him down because word got around that he didn't finish at the Harvard Business School, and his father wouldn't supply a reference. Not many people will consider employing him if as a consequence they might lose his father's business. He finally was hired as a teller with the Bank of America. Way below what he might have expected with his qualifications.'

'And Florentyna?'

'She's working as the assistant manager in a fashion shop called "Wayout Columbus" near Golden Gate Park. She's also been trying to borrow money from several banks.'

'Why? Is she in any sort of trouble?' asked Abel anxiously.

'No, she's looking for capital to open her own shop.'

'How much is she looking for?'

'Only thirty-four thousand dollars which she needs for the lease on a small building on Nob Hill.'

Abel sat back thinking about what George had said, his short fingers tapping on the car window. 'See that she gets the money, George. Make it look as if the transaction is an ordinary bank loan and be sure that it's not traceable back to me.' He continued tapping. 'This must always remain simply between the two of us, George.'

'Anything you say, Abel.'

'And keep me informed of every move she makes, however trivial.'

'What about him?'

'I'm not interested in him,' said Abel. 'Now what's the bad news?'

'Trouble with Henry Osborne again. It seems he owes money everywhere. I'm also fairly certain his only source of income is now you. He's started making veiled threats about you condoning bribes in the early days when we were setting up the group. Says he's kept all the papers from the first day he met you when he claims he fixed an extra payment after the fire at the old Richmond in Chicago, and he now has a file three inches thick.'

'I'll deal with Henry in the morning,' said Abel.

George spent the remainder of the drive into Manhattan bringing Abel up to date on the rest of the group's affairs which were all satisfactory, except for a takeover of the Baron in Lagos after yet another coup. That never worried Abel.

The next morning Abel saw Henry Osborne. He looked old and tired, and the once smooth handsome face was now heavily lined. He made no mention of the three-inch thick file.

'I need a little money to get me through a tricky period,' said Henry. 'I've been a bit unlucky.'

'Again, Henry? You should know better at your age. You're a born loser with horses and women. How much do you need this time?'

'Ten thousand would see me through,' said Henry.

'Ten thousand,' said Abel, spitting out the words. 'What do you think I am, a gold mine? It was only five thousand last time.'

'Inflation,' said Henry, trying to laugh.

'This is the last time, do you understand me?' said Abel as he took out his cheque book. 'Come begging once more, Henry, and I'll remove you from the board as a director and turn you out without a penny.'

'You're a real friend, Abel. I swear I'll never come back again, I promise you that, never again.' Henry plucked a Romeo y Julliyta from the humidor on the table in front of Abel and lit it. 'Thanks, Abel, you'll never regret your decision.'

Henry left, puffing away at the cigar, as George came in. George waited for the door to be closed.

'What happened with Henry?'

'I gave in for the last time,' said Abel. 'I don't know why – it cost me ten thousand.'

'Jesus, I feel like the brother of the prodigal son,' said George. 'Because he'll be back again. I'd be willing to put money on that.'

'He'd better not,' said Abel, 'because I'm through with him. Whatever he has done for me in the past, it's now quits. What's the latest news on Florentyna?'

'Florentyna's fine, but you were right about Zaphia : she's been making regular monthly trips to the coast to see them both.'

'Bloody woman,' said Abel.

'Mrs. Kane has been out a couple of times as well.' added George.

'And Kane?'

'No sign of him relenting.'

'That's one thing we have in common,' said Abel.

'I've set up a facility for her with the Crocker National Bank of San Francisco,' continued George. 'She made an approach to the loan officer there less than a week ago. The agreement will appear to her as if it's one of the bank's ordinary loan transactions, with no special favours. In fact, they're charging her half a per cent more than usual so there can be no reason for her to be suspicious. What she will never know is that the loan is covered by your guarantee.'

'Thanks, George, that's perfect. I'll bet you ten dollars she pays off the loan within two years and never needs to go back for another.'

'I'd want odds of five to one on that,' said George. 'Why don't you try Henry; he's more of a sucker.'

Abel laughed. 'Keep me briefed, George, on everything she's up to, everything.'

35

William felt he had been briefed on everything as he studied Thaddeus Cohen's quarterly report, and only one thing now worried him. Why was Abel Rosnovski still doing nothing with his vast shareholding in Lester's? William couldn't help remembering that he still owned six per cent of the bank and with two more per cent he could invoke Article Seven of Lester's by-laws. It was hard to believe that Rosnovski still feared S.E.C. regulations, especially as the Eisenhower administration was settled into its second term in the White House and had never shown any interest in pursuing the original enquiry.

William was fascinated to read that Henry Osborne was

once again in financial trouble, and that Rosnovski still kept bailing him out. William wondered for how much longer that would go on, and what Henry had on Rosnovski. Was it possible that Rosnovski had enough problems of his own without adding William Kane to them? Cohen's report reviewed progress on the eight new hotels Rosnovski was building across the world. The London Baron was losing money and the Lagos Baron was out of commission; otherwise he continued to grow in strength. William re-read the attached clipping from the *Sunday Express*, reporting that Florentyna Rosnovski had not opened the Edinburgh Baron, and he thought about his son. Then he closed the report and locked the file in his safe, convinced there was nothing in it of importance to concern himself with. His chauffeur drove him home.

William regretted his early loss of temper with Richard. Although he did not want the Rosnovski girl in his life, he wished he had not turned his back so irrevocably on his only son. Kate had pleaded on Richard's behalf, and she and William had had a long and bitter argument – so rare in their married life – which they had been unable to resolve. Kate tried every tactic from gentle persuasion to tears, but nothing seemed to move William. Virginia and Lucy also missed their brother. 'There's no one who will be critical of my paintings,' said Virginia.

'Don't you mean rude?' asked Kate.

Virginia tried to smile.

Lucy used to lock herself in the bathroom, turn on the water, and write secret letters to Richard, who could never figure out why they always seemed damp. No one dared to mention Richard's name in the house in front of William, but it was causing a sad rift within the family.

He had tried spending more time at the bank, even working round the clock in the hope that it might help. It didn't. The bank was once again making heavy demands on his energy at the very time when he most felt like a rest. He had appointed six new vice-presidents over the previous two years, hoping they would take some of the load off his shoulders. The reverse had turned out to be the case. They had created more work and more decisions from him to make and the brightest of them, Jake Thomas, already looked the most likely candidate to take William's place as chairman if Richard did not give up the Rosnovski girl. Although the profits of the bank continued to rise each year, William found he was no longer interested in making money for money's sake. Perhaps he now faced the same problem that Charles Lester had encountered: he had no son to leave his fortune and the chairmanship to now that he had cut Richard out of his life, rewritten his will and dismantled his trust.

In the year of their silver wedding anniversary, William decided to take Kate and the girls for a long holiday to Europe in the hope that it might help to put Richard out of their minds. They flew to London on a Boeing 707 and stayed at the Ritz. The hotel brought back many happy memories of William's first trip to Europe with Kate. They made a sentimental journey to Oxford and showed Virginia and Lucy the university city, and then went on to Stratford-on-Avon to see some Shakespeare: *Richard the Third* with Laurence Olivier. They could have wished for a king with another name.

On the return journey from Stratford they stopped at the church in Henley-on-Thames where William and Kate had been married. They would have stayed at the Bell Inn again, but they still had only one vacant room. An argument started between William and Kate in the car on the way back to London as to whether it had been the Reverend Tukesbury or the Reverend Dukesbury who had married them. They came to no satisfactory conclusion before reaching the Ritz. On one thing they were able to agree; the new roof on the parish church had worn well.

William kissed Kate gently when he climbed into bed that night. 'Best five hundred pounds I ever invested,' he said.

They flew on to Italy a week later, having seen every English sight any self-respecting American tourist is meant to visit and many they usually miss. In Rome, the girls drank too much bad Italian wine and made themselves ill on the night of Virginia's birthday, while William ate too much good pasta and put on seven pounds. All of them would have been so much happier if they could have talked of the forbidden topic of Richard. Virginia cried that night and Kate tried to comfort her.

'Why doesn't someone tell Daddy that some things are more important than pride?' Virginia kept asking.

Kate had no reply.

When they returned to New York, William was refreshed and eager once again to plunge back into his work at the bank. He lost the seven pounds in seven days.

As the months passed by, he felt things were becoming quite routine again. Routine disappeared from his mind when Virginia, just out of Sweetbriar, announced she was going to marry a student from the University of Virginia Law School. The news shook William.

'She's not old enough,' he said.

'Virginia's twenty-two,' said Kate. 'She's not a child any longer, William. How do you feel about becoming a grandfather?' she added, regretting the sequence of her words immediately she had spoken them.

'What do you mean?' said William, horrified. 'Virginia isn't pregnant, is she?'

'Good gracious, no,' said Kate, and then she spoke more softly as if she had been found out. 'Richard and Florentyna have had a baby.'

'How do you know?'

'Richard wrote to tell me the good news,' replied Kate. 'Hasn't the time come for you to forgive him, William?'

'Never,' said William and marched out of the room in anger.

Kate sighed wearily: he had not even asked if his grandchild was a boy or a girl.

Virginia's wedding took place in Trinity Church, Boston, on a beautiful spring afternoon in late March of the following year. William thoroughly approved of David Telford, the young lawyer with whom Virginia had chosen to spend the rest of her life.

Virginia had wanted Richard to be an usher and Kate had begged William to invite him to the wedding, but he had steadfastly refused. He had wanted to say yes, but he knew that Richard would never agree to coming without the Rosnovski girl. On the day of the wedding Richard sent a present and a telegram to his sister. William would not allow the telegram to be read at the reception afterwards.

Book Six

36

Abel was sitting alone in his office on the forty-second floor of the New York Baron waiting to see a fund raiser from the Kennedy campaign. The man was already twenty minutes late. Abel was tapping his fingers impatiently on his desk when his secretary came in.

'Mr. Vincent Hogan to see you, sir.'

Abel sprang out of his chair. 'Come in, Mr. Hogan,' he said, slapping the good-looking young man on the back. 'How are you?'

'I'm fine, Mr. Rosnovski. I'm sorry I'm a little late,' said the unmistakably Bostonian voice.

'I didn't notice,' said Abel. 'Would you care for a drink, Mr. Hogan?'

'No, thank you, Mr. Rosnovski. I try not to drink when I have to see so many people in one day.'

'Absolutely right. I hope you won't mind if I have one,' said Abel. 'I'm not planning on seeing many people today.'

Hogan laughed like a man who knew he was in for a day of other people's jokes. Abel poured a whisky.

'Now, what can I do for you, Mr. Hogan?'

'Well, Mr. Rosnovski, we were hoping the party could once again count on your support.'

'I've always been a Democrat, as you know, Mr. Hogan. I supported Franklin D. Roosevelt, Harry Truman, and Adlai Stevenson, although I couldn't understand what Adlai was talking about half the time.'

Both men laughed falsely.

'I also helped my old friend, Dick Daley, in Chicago and I've been backing young Ed Muskie – the son of a Polish immigrant, you know – since his campaign for governor of Maine back in '54.'

'You've been a loyal supporter of the party in the past, there's no denying that, Mr. Rosnovski,' said Vincent Hogan, in a tone that indicated that the statutory time for small talk had run out. 'We also know the Democrats, not least of all former Congressman Osborne, have done the odd favour for you in return. I don't think it's necessary for me to go into any details of that unpleasant little incident.'

'That's long since past,' said Abel, 'and well behind me.'

'I agree,' said Mr. Hogan, 'and although most self-made multi-millionaires couldn't face having their affairs looked into too closely, you will be the first to appreciate that we have to be especially careful. The candidate, as you will understand, cannot afford to take any personal risks so near the election. Nixon would love a scandal at this stage of the race.'

'We understand each other clearly, Mr. Hogan. Now that's out of the way, how much were you expecting from me for the election campaign?'

'I need every penny I can lay my hands on.' Hogan's words came across clipped and slow. 'Nixon is gathering a lot of support across the country, and it's going to be a very close thing getting our man into the White House.'

'Well, I'll support Kennedy,' said Abel, 'if he supports me. It's as simple as that.'

'He's delighted to support you, Mr. Rosnovski. We all realise that you're now a pillar of the Polish community, and Senator Kennedy is personally aware of the brave stand you took on behalf of your countrymen who are still in slave labour camps behind the Iron Curtain, not to mention the service you gave in the war. I have been authorised to let you know that the candidate has already agreed to open your new hotel in Los Angeles during his campaign trip.'

'That's good news,' said Abel.

'The candidate is also fully aware of your desire to grant Poland most favoured nation status in foreign trade with the United States.'

'No more than we deserve after our service in the last war,' said Abel, and paused briefly. 'What about the other little matter?' he asked.

'Senator Kennedy is canvassing Polish-American opinion at the moment, and we haven't met with any objections. He naturally cannot come to a final decision until after he is elected.'

'Naturally. Would two hundred and fifty thousand dollars help him make that decision?' asked Abel.

Vincent Hogan didn't speak.

'Two hundred and fifty thousand dollars it is then,' said Abel. 'The money will be in your campaign fund headquarters by the end of the week, Mr. Hogan. You have my word on it.'

The business was over, the bargain struck. Abel rose. 'Please give Senator Kennedy my best wishes, and add that of course I hope he'll be the next President of the United States. I always loathed Richard Nixon after his despicable treatment of Helen Gahagan Douglas, and in any case, there are personal reasons why I don't want Henry Cabot Lodge as Vice-President.'

'I shall be delighted to pass on your message,' said Mr. Hogan, 'and thank you for your continued support of the Democratic party, and in particular, of the candidate.' The Bostonian thrust out his hand. Abel grasped it.

'Keep in touch, Mr. Hogan. I don't part with that sort of money without expecting a return on my investment.'

'I fully understand,' replied Vincent Hogan.

Abel showed his guest to the lift and returned smiling to his office. His fingers started to tap on the desk again. His secretary reappeared.

'Ask Mr. Novak to come in,' said Abel.

George came through from his office a few moments later.

'I think I've pulled it off, George.'

'Congratulations, Abel, I'm delighted. If Kennedy becomes the next President, then one of your biggest dreams will be fulfilled. How proud Florentyna will be of you.'

Abel smiled when he heard her name. 'Do you know what

that little minx has been up to?' he said, laughing. 'Did you see the *Los Angeles Times* last week, George?'

George shook his head, and Abel passed him a copy of the paper. One of the items was circled in red ink. George read the article aloud: 'Florentyna Kane opens her third shop in Los Angeles. She already owns two in San Francisco and is hoping to open another in San Diego before the end of the year. "Florentyna's", as they are known, are fast becoming to California what Balenciaga is to Paris.'

George laughed as he put the paper down.

'She must have written the piece herself,' said Abel. 'I can't wait for her to open a Florentyna's in New York. I'll bet she achieves that within five years, ten at the most. Do you want to take another bet on that, George?'

'I didn't take the first one, if you remember, Abel, otherwise I would already have been out ten dollars.'

Abel looked up, his voice quieter. 'Do you think she'd come and see Senator Kennedy open the new Baron in Los Angeles, George? Do you think she might?'

'Not unless the Kane boy is invited along as well.'

'Never,' said Abel. 'That Kane boy is nothing. I read all the facts in your last report, George. He's left the Bank of America to work with Florentyna; couldn't even hold down a good job, had to fall back on her success.'

'You're becoming a selective reader, Abel. You know very well that's not the way it was. I made the circumstances very clear. The Kane boy is in charge of the finances while Florentyna runs the shops, and it's proving to be an ideal partnership. Don't ever forget that a major bank offered Kane the chance to head up its European department but Florentyna begged him to join her when she no longer found it possible to control the finances herself. Abel, you'll have to face the fact that their marriage is a success. I know it's hard for you to stomach, but why don't you climb down off your high horse and meet the boy?'

'You're my closest friend, George. No one else in the world would dare to speak to me like that. So no one knows better than you why I can't climb down, not until that bastard Kane shows he is willing to meet me half way, but until then, I won't crawl again while he's still alive to watch me.'

'What if you were to die first, Abel? You're exactly the same age.'

'Then I'd lose and Florentyna inherits everything.'

'You told me she wouldn't get a thing. You were going to change your will in favour of your grandson.'

'I couldn't do it, George. When the time came to sign the documents, I just couldn't do it. What the hell, that damned grandson is going to end up with both our fortunes in the end.'

Abel removed a wallet from his inside pocket, shuffled through several old pictures of Florentyna and took out a new one of his grandson, which he proffered to George.

'Good-looking little boy.' said George.

'Sure is,' said Abel. 'The spitting image of his mother.'

George laughed. 'You never give up, do you, Abel?'

'What do you think they call him?'

'What do you mean?' said George. 'You know very well what his name is.'

'I mean what do you think they actually call him?'

'How should I know?' said George.

'Find out,' said Abel. 'I care.'

'How am I meant to do that?' said George. 'Have someone follow them while they're pushing the pram around Golden Gate Park? You left clear instructions that Florentyna must never find out that you're still taking an interest in her or the Kane boy.'

'That reminds me, I still have a little matter to settle with his father,' said Abel.

'What are you going to do about the Lester shares?' asked George. 'Because Peter Parfitt has been showing more interest in selling his two per cent lately, and I wouldn't trust Henry with the negotiations. With those two working on the sale, everybody will be in on the deal except you.'

'I'm doing nothing. Much as I hate Kane, I don't want any trouble with him until we know if Kennedy has won the election. So I'm leaving the whole situation dormant for the moment. If Kennedy fails, I'll buy Parfitt's two per cent and go ahead with the plan that we've already discussed. And don't worry yourself about Henry; I've already taken him off the Kane file. From now on I'm handling that myself.'

'I do worry, Abel. I know he's in debt again to half the bookmakers in Chicago, and I wouldn't be surprised if he arrived in New York on the scrounge any minute now.'

'Henry won't be coming here. I made the situation very clear last time I saw him that he wouldn't get another dime out of me. If he does come begging, he'll only lose his seat on the board and with it his only source of income.'

'That worries me even more,' said George. 'Let's say he took it on himself to go to Kane direct for the money.'

'Not possible, George. Henry is the one man alive who hates Kane even more than I do, and not without reason.'

'How can you be so sure of that?'

'William Kane's mother was Henry's second wife,' said Abel, 'and young William, aged only sixteen, threw him out of his own home.'

'Good God, how did you come across that piece of information?'

'There's nothing I don't know about William Kane,' said Abel. 'Or Henry for that matter. Absolutely nothing – from the fact that we started life on the same day, and I'd be willing to bet my good leg there's nothing he doesn't know about me so we have to be circumspect for the time being, but you need have no fear of Henry turning stool pigeon. He'd die before he had to admit his real name was Vittorio Tosna and he once served a jail sentence.'

'Good God – does Henry realise you know all this?'

'No, he doesn't. I've kept it to myself for years always believing, George, that if you think a man might threaten you at some time then you should keep a little more up your sleeve than your arm. I've never trusted Henry since the days he suggested swindling Great Western Casualty while he was still actually working for them, although I'd be the first to admit he's been very useful to me in the past and I am confident he isn't going to cause me any trouble in the future, because without his director's salary, he becomes penniless overnight. So forget Henry and let's be a little more positive. What's the latest date for the completion of the Los Angeles Baron?'

'Middle of September,' replied George.

'Perfect. That will be six weeks before the election. When Kennedy opens that hotel, the news will hit every front page in America.'

37

When William returned to New York, after a bankers' conference in Washington, he found a message awaiting him, requesting that he contact Thaddeus Cohen immediately. He hadn't spoken to Cohen for a considerable time, as Abel Rosnovski had caused no direct trouble since the abortive telephone conversation on the eve of Richard and Florentyna's marriage, nearly three years before. The successive quarterly reports had merely confirmed that Rosnovski was neither trying to buy or sell any of the bank's shares. Nevertheless, William called Thaddeus Cohen immediately and somewhat apprehensively. The lawyer told William that he had stumbled across some information which he did not wish to divulge over the phone. William asked him to come over to the bank as soon as it was convenient.

Thaddeus Cohen arrived forty minutes later. William heard him out in attentive silence.

When Cohen had finished his revelation, William said, 'Your father would never have approved of such underhand methods.'

'Neither would yours,' replied Thaddeus Cohen, 'but they didn't have to deal with the likes of Abel Rosnovski.'

'What makes you think your plan will work?'

'Look at the Bernard Goldfine and Sherman Adams case, only one thousand six hundred and forty-two dollars involved in hotel bills and a vicuna coat, but it sure embarrassed the hell out of the President when Adams was accused of preferred treatment because he was a Presidential assistant. We know Mr. Rosnovski is aiming a lot higher than that. It should, therefore, be easier to bring him down.'

'Game, set and match. How much is it going to cost me?'

'Twenty-five thousand at the outside, but I may be able to pull the whole deal off for less.'

'How can you be sure that Rosnovski doesn't realise that I am personally involved?'

'I'd use a third person who won't even know your name to act as an intermediary.'

'And if you pull it off, what would you recommend we do then?'

'You send all the details to Senator John Kennedy's office, and I guarantee that will finish off Abel Rosnovski's ambitious plans once and for all because the moment his credibility has been shattered he will be a spent force and find it quite impossible to invoke Article Seven of the bank's by-laws – even if he did get hold of eight per cent of Lester's.'

'Maybe – if Kennedy becomes the President,' said William. 'But what happens if Nixon wins the election? He's way ahead in the opinion polls and I'd certainly back his chances against Kennedy. Can you really imagine that America would ever send a Roman Catholic to the White House? I can't, but then on the other hand I admit that an investment of twenty-five thousand is small enough if there's better than an outside chance the move will finish Abel Rosnovski off once and for all and leave me secure at the bank.'

'If Kennedy becomes President . . .'

William opened the drawer of his desk, took out a large cheque book marked 'private account' and wrote out the figures. Two, five, zero, zero, zero.

38

Abel's prediction that Kennedy's opening of the Baron would hit every front page did not turn out to be wholly accurate. Although the candidate did indeed open the hotel, he had to appear at dozens of other events in Los Angeles that day and face Nixon for a televised debate the following evening. Nevertheless, the opening of the newest Baron gained fairly wide coverage in the national press, and Vincent Hogan assured Abel privately that Kennedy had not forgotten the other little matter. Florentyna's shop was only a few hundred yards away, but father and daughter never did meet.

After the Illinois returns came in, and John F. Kennedy looked certain to be the thirty-fifth President of the United States, Abel drank Mayor Daley's health and celebrated at the Democratic National Headquarters on Times Square. He did not return home to his bed until nearly five the next morning.

'Hell, I have a lot to celebrate,' he told George. 'I'm going to be the next ...' He fell asleep before he finished the sentence. George smiled and put him to bed.

William watched the results of the election in the peace of his study on East Sixty-eighth Street. After the Illinois returns which were not confirmed until ten o'clock the next morning (William never had trusted Mayor Daley), Walter Cronkite declared it was all over bar the shouting, and William picked up his phone and dialled Thaddeus Cohen's home number.

All he said was, 'The twenty-five thousand dollars has turned out to be a wise investment, Thaddeus. Now let us be sure that there is no honeymoon period for Mr. Rosnovski.

But don't do anything until he makes his trip to Turkey.'

William placed the phone back on the hook and went to bed. He was disappointed that Richard Nixon had failed to beat Kennedy and that his distant cousin Henry Cabot Lodge would not be the Vice-President but it is an ill wind...

When Abel received his invitation to be a guest at one of President Kennedy's inauguration balls in Washington, D.C., there was only one person he wanted to share the honour with. He talked the idea over with George and had to agree that Florentyna would never be willing to accompany him unless she was convinced that the feud with Richard's father could be finally resolved. So he knew he would have to go alone.

In order to be in Washington to attend the celebrations, Abel had had to postpone his latest trip to Europe and the Middle East for a few days. He could not afford to miss the inauguration, whereas he could always put back the date for the opening of the Istanbul Baron.

Abel had a new, rather conservative dark blue suit made specially for the occasion, and took over the Presidential Suite at the Washington Baron for the day of the inauguration. He enjoyed watching the vital young President deliver his inaugural speech, full of hope and promise for the future.

'A new generation of Americans, born in this century' – Abel only just qualified – 'tempered by war' – Abel certainly qualified – 'disciplined by a hard and bitter peace' – Abel made it again. 'Ask not what your country can do for you. Ask what you can do for your country.'

The crowd rose to a man and everyone ignored the snow that had failed to dampen the impact of John F. Kennedy's brilliant oratory.

Abel returned to the Washington Baron exhilarated. He showered before changing for dinner into white tie and tails, also made especially for the occasion. When he studied his ample frame in the mirror, Abel had to admit to himself that he was not the last word in sartorial elegance. His tailor had done the best he could in the circumstances and did not complain that he had had to make three new and ever larger evening suits for Abel in the past three years. Florentyna would have chastised him for those unnecessary inches, as she used to call them, and for her he would have done something about it. Why did his thoughts always return to Florentyna? He checked his medals. First The Polish Veterans' Medal, next the decorations for his service in the desert and in Europe, and then his cutlery medals, as Abel called them, for distinguished service with knives and forks.

In all, seven inaugural balls were held in Washington that evening, and Abel's invitation directed him to the D.C. Armoury. He was placed at a table of Polish Democrats from New York and Chicago. They had a lot to celebrate. Edmund Muskie was in the Senate and ten more Polish Democrats had been elected to Congress. No one mentioned the two newly elected Polish Republicans. Abel spent a happy evening with two old friends, who along with him were founding members of the Polish-American Congress. They both asked after Florentyna.

The dinner was interrupted by the entrance of John F. Kennedy and his beautiful wife, Jacqueline. They stayed about fifteen minutes, chatted with a few carefully selected people and then moved on. Although Abel didn't actually speak to the President, despite leaving his table and placing himself strategically in his path, he did manage to have a word with Vincent Hogan as he was leaving with the Kennedy entourage.

'Mr. Rosnovski, what a fortuitous meeting.'

Abel would like to have explained to the boy that with him nothing was fortuitous, but now was neither the time nor the place. Hogan took Abel's arm and guided him quickly behind a large marble pillar.

'I can't say too much at the moment, Mr. Rosnovski, as I must stick with the President, but I think you can expect a call from us in the near future. Naturally, the President has rather a lot of appointments to deal with at the moment.'

'Naturally,' said Abel.

'But I am hoping,' continued Vincent Hogan, 'that in

your case everything will be confirmed by late March or early April. May I be the first to offer my congratulations, Mr. Rosnovski? I am confident you will serve the President well.'

Abel watched Vincent Hogan literally run off to be sure he caught up with the Kennedy party, who were already climbing into a fleet of open-doored limousines.

'You look pleased with yourself,' said one of his Polish friends as Abel returned to his table and sat down to attack a tough steak, which would not have been allowed inside a Baron. 'Did Kennedy invite you to be his new Secretary of State?'

They all laughed.

'Not yet,' said Abel. 'But he did tell me the accommodation in the White House was not in the same class as the Baron.'

Abel flew back to New York the next morning after first visiting the Polish Chapel of Our Lady of Czestochowa in the National Shrine. It made him think of both Florentynas. Washington National airport was chaos and Abel eventually arrived at the New York Baron three hours later than planned. George joined him for dinner, and knew that all had gone well when Abel ordered a magnum of Dom Perignon.

'Tonight we celebrate,' said Abel. 'I saw Hogan at the ball and my appointment will be confirmed in the next few weeks. The official announcement will be made soon after I return from the Middle East.'

'Congratulations, Abel. I know of no one who deserves the honour more.'

'Thank you, George. I can assure you that your reward will not be in heaven, because when it's all official, I'm going to appoint you acting president of the Baron Group in my absence.'

George drank another glass of champagne. They were already halfway through the bottle.

'How long do you think you'll be away this time, Abel?'

'Only three weeks. I want to check that those Arabs aren't

robbing me blind and then go on to Turkey to open the Istanbul Baron. I think I'll take in London and Paris on the way.'

George poured some more champagne.

Abel had to spend three more days in London than he had originally anticipated, trying to sort out the hotel's problems, with a manager who kept blaming everything on the British unions. The London Baron had turned out to be one of Abel's few failures, although he never could put his finger on why the hotel continually lost money. He would have considered closing it, but the Baron Group had to have a presence in England's capital city, so once again he fired the manager and made a new appointment.

Paris presented a striking contrast. The hotel was one of his most successful in Europe, and he'd once admitted to Florentyna, as reluctantly as a parent admits to having a favourite child, that the Paris Baron was his favourite hotel. Abel found everything on the Boulevard Raspail well organised and spent only two days in Paris before flying on to the Middle East.

Abel now had sites in five of the Persian Gulf States, but only the Riyadh Baron had actually started construction. If he'd been a younger man, Abel would have stayed in the Middle East for a couple of years himself and sorted the Arabs out. But he couldn't abide the sand, the heat, and never being certain when he could order a whisky. He thought he must be getting older, because he couldn't stand the natives either. He left them to one of his young assistant vice-presidents, who had been told that he would only be allowed to return and manage the infidels in America once Abel was sure he had proved a success with the holy and blessed ones from the Middle East.

He left the poor assistant vice-president in the richest private hell in the world and flew on to Turkey.

Abel had visited Turkey several times during the past few years to watch the progress of the Istanbul Baron. For Abel, there would always be something special about

Constantinople, as he remembered the city. He was looking forward to opening a Baron in the country he had left to start a new life in America.

While he was unpacking his suitcase in yet another Presidential Suite, Abel found fifteen invitations awaiting his reply. There were always several invitations about the time of a hotel opening; a galaxy of freeloaders who wanted to be invited to any opening night party appeared on the scene as if by magic. On this occasion, however, two of the dinner invitations came as an agreeable surprise to Abel from men who certainly could not be classified as freeloaders : namely the ambassadors of America and Britain. The invitation to the old British embassy was particularly irresistible as he had not been inside the building for nearly forty years.

That evening, Abel dined as the guest of Sir Bernard Burrows, Her Majesty's Ambassador to Turkey. To his surprise he found that he had been placed at the right of the ambassador's wife, a privilege Abel had never been afforded in any other embassy in the past. When the dinner was over, he observed the quaint English tradition of the ladies leaving the room while the gentlemen sat alone to smoke cigars and drink port or brandy. Abel was invited to join the American ambassador, Fletcher Warren, for port in Sir Bernard's study. Sir Bernard was taking the American ambassador to task for allowing him to have the Chicago Baron to dinner before he had.

'The British have always been a presumptuous race,' said the American ambassador, lighting a large Cuban cigar.

'I'll say one thing for the Americans,' said Sir Bernard. 'They don't know when they're fairly beaten.'

Abel listened to the two diplomats' banter, wondering why he had been included in such a private gathering. Sir Bernard offered Abel some vintage port, and the American ambassador raised his glass.

'To Abel Rosnovski,' he said.

Sir Bernard also raised his glass. 'I understand that congratulations are in order,' he said.

Abel reddened and looked hastily towards Fletcher Warren, hoping he would help him out.

'Oh, have I let the cat out of the bag, Fletcher?' said Sir Bernard, turning to the American ambassador. 'You told me the appointment was common knowledge, old chap.'

'Fairly common,' said Fletcher Warren. 'Not that the British could ever keep a secret for very long.'

'Is that why your lot took such a devil of a time to discover we were at war with Germany?' replied Sir Bernard.

'And then moved in to make sure of the victory?'

'And the glory,' said Sir Bernard.

The American ambassador laughed. 'I'm told the official announcement will be made in the next few days.'

Both men looked at Abel, who remained silent.

'Well, then may I be the first to congratulate you, Your Excellency,' said Sir Bernard. 'I wish you every happiness in your new appointment.'

Abel flushed to hear aloud the appellation he had whispered so often to his shaving mirror during the past few months. 'You'll have to get used to being called Your Excellency, you know,' continued the British ambassador, 'and a whole lot of worse things than that, particularly all these damned functions you'll be made to attend one after another. If you have a weight problem now, it will be nothing compared to the one you'll have when you finish your term of office. You may yet live to be grateful for the Cold War. It's the one thing that might keep your social life within bounds.'

The American ambassador smiled. 'Well done, Abel, and may I add my best wishes for your continued success. When were you last in Poland?' he enquired.

'I've only been back home once for a short visit a few years ago,' said Abel. 'I've wanted to return ever since.'

'Well, you will be returning in triumph,' said Fletcher Warren. 'Are you familiar with our embassy in Warsaw?'

'No, I'm not,' admitted Abel.

'Not a bad building,' said Sir Bernard. 'Remembering you colonials couldn't get a foothold in Europe until after the

Second World War. But the food is appalling. I shall expect you to do something about that, Mr. Rosnovski. I'm afraid the only thing for it is that you'll have to build a Baron Hotel in Warsaw. As ambassador, that's the least they'll expect from an old Pole.'

Abel sat in a state of euphoria, laughing and enjoying Sir Bernard's feeble jokes. He found he was drinking a little more port than usual and felt at ease with himself and the world. He couldn't wait to return to America and tell Florentyna his news, now that the appointment seemed to be official. She would be so proud of him. He decided then and there that the moment he arrived back in New York he would go straight to San Francisco and make everything up with her. It was what he had wanted to do all along and now he had an excuse. Somehow he'd force himself to like the Kane boy. He must stop referring to him as 'the Kane boy'. What was his name – Richard? Yes, Richard. Abel felt a sudden rush of relief at having made the decision.

After the three men had returned to the main reception room and the ladies, Abel reached up and touched the British ambassador on the shoulder. 'I should be getting back, Your Excellency.'

'Back to the Baron,' said Sir Bernard. 'Allow me to accompany you to your car, my dear fellow.'

The ambassador's wife bade him goodnight at the door.

'Goodnight, Lady Burrows, and thank you for a memorable evening.'

She smiled. 'I know I'm not meant to know, Mr. Rosnovski, but many congratulations on your appointment. You must be so proud to be returning to the land of your birth as your country's senior representative.'

'I am,' replied Abel simply.

Sir Bernard accompanied him down the marble steps of the British embassy to the waiting car. The chauffeur opened the door.

'Goodnight, Rosnovski,' said Sir Bernard, 'and good luck in Warsaw. By the way, I hope you enjoyed your first meal in the British embassy.'

'My second actually, Sir Bernard.'

'You've been before, old boy? When we checked through the guest book we couldn't find your name.'

'No,' said Abel. 'Last time I had dinner in the British embassy, I ate in the kitchen. I don't think they keep a guest book down there, but the meal was the best I'd had in years.'

Abel smiled as he climbed into the back of the car. He could see that Sir Bernard wasn't sure whether to believe him or not. As Abel was driven back to the Baron, his fingers tapped on the side windows, and he hummed to himself. He would have liked to have returned to America the next morning, but he couldn't cancel the invitation to dine with Fletcher Warren at the American embassy the following evening. Hardly the sort of thing a future ambassador does, old fellow, he could hear Sir Bernard saying.

Dinner with the American ambassador turned out to be another pleasant occasion. Abel was made to explain to the assembled guests how he had come to eat in the kitchens of the British embassy. When he told them the truth, they looked on in surprised admiration. He wasn't sure if many of them believed the story of how he nearly lost his hand, but they all admired the silver band, and that night, everyone called him 'Your Excellency'.

The next day, Abel was up early, ready for his flight to America. The D.C.8 flew into Belgrade, where he was grounded for sixteen hours, waiting for the plane to be serviced. Something wrong with the landing gear, they told him. He sat in the airport lounge, sipping undrinkable Yugoslavian coffee. The contrast between the British embassy and the snack bar in a communist-controlled country was not entirely lost on Abel. At last the plane took off, only to be delayed again in Amsterdam. This time they made him change planes.

When he finally arrived at Idlewild, Abel had been travelling for nearly thirty-six hours. He was so tired he could hardly walk. As he left the customs area, he suddenly found himself surrounded by newsmen, and the cameras started flashing and clicking. Immediately he smiled. The announcement must have been made, he thought. Now it's official. He stood as straight as he could and walked slowly and with dignity, disguising his limp. There was no sign of George, as the cameramen jostled each other unceremoniously to be sure of a picture.

Then he saw George standing at the edge of the crowd, looking like death. Abel's heart lurched as he passed the barrier and a journalist, far from asking him what it felt like to be the first Polish-American to be appointed ambassador to Warsaw, shouted: 'Do you have any answers to the charges?'

The cameras went on flashing and so did the questions.

'Are the accusations true, Mr. Rosnovski?'

'How much did you actually pay Congressman Osborne?'

'Do you deny the charges?'

'Have you returned to America to face trial?'

They wrote down Abel's replies although he never spoke.

'Get me out of here,' shouted Abel above the crowd.

George squeezed forward and managed to reach Abel and then pushed his way back through the crowd and bundled him into the waiting Cadillac. Abel bent down and hid his head in his hands, as the cameras' flashbulbs kept popping, and George shouted at the chauffeur to get moving.

'To the Baron, sir?' he asked.

'No, to Miss Rosnovski's flat on Fifty-seventh Street.'

'Why?' said Abel.

'Because the press is crawling all over the Baron.'

'I don't understand,' said Abel. 'In Istanbul they treat me as if I was the ambassador's elect, and I return home to find I'm a criminal. What the hell is going on, George?'

'Do you want to hear it all from me, or wait until you've seen your lawyer?' asked George.

'Who have you got to represent me?' asked Abel.

'H. Trafford Jilks, the best defence attorney in America.'

'And the most expensive.'

'I didn't think you would be worrying about money at a time like this, Abel.'

'You're right, George. I'm sorry. Where is he now?'

'I left him at the courthouse, but he said he'd come to the flat as soon as he was through.'

'I can't wait that long, George. For God's sake put me in the picture. Tell me the worst.'

George drew a deep breath. 'There's a warrant out for your arrest,' he said.

'What the hell's the charge?'

'Bribery of government officials.'

'I've never been directly involved with a government official in my whole life,' protested Abel.

'I know, but it turns out that Henry Osborne has been all along, and everything he did seems to have been in your name or on your behalf.'

'Oh my God,' said Abel. 'I should never have employed the man. I let the fact that we both hated Kane cloud my judgment. But I still find it hard to believe Henry has given anyone the dirt, because he would only end up implicating himself.'

'But Henry has disappeared,' said George, 'and suddenly, mysteriously, all his debts have been cleared up.'

'William Kane,' said Abel, hissing the words out.

'We've found nothing that points in that direction,' said George. 'There's no proof he's involved in this at all.'

'Who needs proof? You tell me how the authorities got hold of all the details.'

'We do know that much,' said George. 'It seems an anonymous package containing a file was sent direct to the Justice Department in Washington.'

'Postmarked New York, no doubt,' said Abel.

'No. Chicago.'

Abel was silent for a few moments. 'It couldn't have been Henry who sent the evidence to them,' he said finally. 'That doesn't make any sense.'

'How can you be so sure?' asked George.

'Because you said all his debts have been cleared up, and the Justice Department wouldn't pay out that sort of money unless they thought they were going to catch Al Capone.

Henry must have sold his file to someone else. But who? The one thing we can be certain of is that he would never have released any information directly to Kane.'

'Directly?' said George.

'Directly,' repeated Abel. 'Perhaps he didn't sell it directly. Kane could have arranged for an intermediary to deal with the whole thing if he already knew that Henry was heavily in debt, and the bookmakers were threatening him.'

'That might be right, Abel, and it certainly wouldn't have taken an ace detective to discover the extent of Henry's financial problems. They were common knowledge to anyone sitting on a bar stool in Chicago, but don't jump to hasty conclusions just yet. Let's find out what your lawyer has to say.'

The Cadillac came to a halt outside Florentyna's former home, which Abel had retained and kept spotless in the hope that his daughter would one day return. George opened the door, and they walked through to join H. Trafford Jilks. Once they had settled down, George poured Abel a large whisky. He drank the malt in one gulp, and gave the empty glass back to George who re-filled it.

'Tell me the worst, Mr. Jilks. Let's get it over with.'

'I am sorry, Mr. Rosnovski,' he began. 'Mr. Novak told me about Warsaw.'

'That's all over now, so we may as well forget "Your Excellency". You can be sure if Vincent Hogan were asked, he wouldn't even remember my name. Come on, Mr. Jilks, what am I facing?'

'You've been indicted on seventeen charges of bribery and corruption of officials in fourteen different states. I've made provisional arrangements with the Justice Department for you to be arrested here at the flat tomorrow morning, and they will make no objection to bail being granted.'

'Very cosy,' said Abel, 'but what if they can prove the charges?'

'Oh, they should be able to prove some of the charges,' said H. Trafford Jilks matter of factly, 'but as long as Henry Osborne stays tucked away, they're going to find it very difficult to nail you on most of them. But you're going to have to live with the fact, Mr. Rosnovski, that most of the real damage has already been done whether you're convicted or not.'

'I can see that only too well,' said Abel, glancing across at a picture of himself on the front page of the *Daily News*. 'So you find out, Mr. Jilks, who the hell bought that file from Henry Osborne. Put as many people to work on the case as you need. I don't care about the cost. But you find out and find out quickly, because if it turns out to be William Kane, I'm going to finish that man off once and for all.'

'Don't get yourself into any more trouble than you are already,' said H. Trafford Jilks. 'You're knee deep in as it is.'

'Don't worry,' said Abel. 'When I finish Kane, it'll be legal and way above board.'

'Now listen carefully, Mr. Rosnovski. You forget about William Kane for the time being and start worrying about your impending trial, because it will be the most important event ever to take place in your life unless you don't mind spending the next ten years in jail. Now there's not much more we can do tonight, so go to bed and catch some sleep. In the meantime, I'll issue a short press statement denying the charges and saying that we have a full explanation which will exonerate you completely.'

'Do we?' asked George hopefully.

'No,' said Jilks, 'but it will give me some much needed time to think. When Mr. Rosnovski has had a chance to check through that file of names, it wouldn't surprise me to discover that he's never had direct contact with any of them. It's possible that Henry Osborne always acted as an intermediary without ever putting Mr. Rosnovski fully in the picture. Then my job will be to prove that Osborne exceeded his authority as a director of the group. Mind you, Mr. Rosnovski, if you did meet any of the people mentioned in that file, for God's sake let me know, because you can be sure the Justice Department will put them on the stand as witnesses to testify against us. But we'll start worrying about that tomorrow. You go to bed and get some sleep. You must be exhausted after your trip. I will see you first thing in the morning.'

Abel was arrested quietly in his daughter's apartment at eight thirty a.m. and driven away by a U.S. marshal to the Federal District Court for the Southern District of New York. The brightly coloured St. Valentine's Day decorations in store windows heightened Abel's sense of loneliness. Jilks had hoped that his arrangements had been so discreet that the press would not have picked them up, but when Abel reached the courthouse, he was once again surrounded by photographers and reporters. He ran the gauntlet into the courtroom with George in front of him and Mr. Jilks behind. They sat silently in an anteroom waiting for their case to be called.

When they were called, the indictment hearing lasted only a few minutes and was a strange anti-climax. The clerk read the charges, H. Trafford Jilks answered 'Not Guilty' to each one on behalf of his client and requested bail. The government, as agreed, made no objection. Jilks asked Judge Prescott for at least three months to prepare his defence. The judge set a trial date of 17 May and, seemingly uninterested, moved on to the next case.

Abel was free again, free to face the press and more flashing bulbs of their cameras. George had the car waiting for him at the bottom of the steps with the door open. The engine was already running and Abel's chauffeur had to do some very skilful driving to free himself from the determined reporters who were still pursuing their story. He did not head back to the flat on East Fifty-seventh Street until he was certain he had shaken them all off. Abel said nothing during the entire chase. When they reached their destination, he turned to George and put his arm on his shoulder.

'Now listen, George, you're going to have to run the group for at least three months while I get my defence sorted out with Mr. Jilks. Let's hope you don't have to run it alone after that,' said Abel, trying to laugh.

'Of course I won't have to, Abel. Mr. Jilks will get you off, you'll see.' George picked up his briefcase and touched Abel on the arm. 'Keep smiling,' he said and left.

'I don't know what I'd do without George,' Abel told his lawyer as they settled down in the front room. 'We came over on the boat together nearly forty years ago, and we've been through a hell of a lot since then. Now it looks as if there's a whole lot more ahead of us, so let's get on with it, Mr. Jilks. Any sign of Henry Osborne yet?'

'No, but I have six men working on it, and I understand the Justice Department have at least another six so we can be pretty sure he'll turn up, not that we want them to find him first.'

'What about the man Osborne sold the file to?' asked Abel.

'I have some people I trust in Chicago detailed to run that down.'

'Good,' said Abel. 'Now the time has come to go over that file of names you left with me last night.'

Trafford Jilks began by reading the indictment and then he went over each of the charges in detail with Abel.

After nearly three weeks of constant meetings, when Jilks was finally convinced there was nothing else Abel could tell him, he left his client to rest. The three weeks had failed to turn up any leads as to the whereabouts of Henry Osborne, either from Trafford Jilks' men or the Justice Department. Jilks' men had also had no breakthrough on finding the person to whom Henry had sold his information and were beginning to wonder if Abel had guessed right.

As the trial date drew nearer, Abel started to face the possibility of actually going to jail. He was now fifty-five and afraid and ashamed at the prospect of spending the last few years of his life the same way as he had spent the first few. As H. Trafford Jilks had pointed out, if the government could prove they had a case, there was enough in Osborne's file to send him to the pen for a very long time. The injustice – as it seemed to him – of his predicament angered Abel. The malfeasances that Henry Osborne had committed in his name had been substantial but not exceptional; Abel doubted that any new business could have grown or any new money made without the sort of handouts and bribes documented with sickening accuracy in Trafford Jilks' file. He thought bitterly of the smooth, impassive face of the young William Kane, sitting in his Boston office all those years ago on a pile of inherited money whose probably disreputable origins were safely buried under generations of respectability. Then Florentyna wrote, a touching letter enclosing some photographs of her son, saying that she still loved and respected Abel, and believed in his innocence.

Three days before the trial was due to open, the Justice Department found Henry Osborne in New Orleans. They undoubtedly would have missed him completely if he hadn't ended up in a local hospital with two broken legs. A zealous policeman discovered Henry had received his injuries for welching on gambling debts. They don't like that in New Orleans. The policeman put two and two together and later that night, after the hospital had put plaster casts on both Osborne's legs, the Justice Department wheeled him on an Eastern Airlines flight to New York.

Henry Osborne was charged the next day with conspiracy to defraud, and he was denied bail. H. Trafford Jilks asked the court's permission to be allowed to question him. The court granted his request, but Jilks gained very little satisfaction from the interview. It became obvious that Osborne had already made his deal with the government, promising to turn state's evidence against Abel in return for lesser charges against him.

'No doubt Mr. Osborne will find the charges against him are surprisingly minor,' commented the lawyer drily.

'So that's his game,' said Abel. 'I take the rap while he escapes. Now we'll never find out who he sold that goddamn file to.'

'No, there you are wrong, Mr. Rosnovski. That was the one thing he was willing to talk about,' said Jilks. 'He said it wasn't William Kane. He would never have sold the file to Kane under any circumstances. A man from Chicago called Harry Smith paid Mr. Osborne cash for the evidence, and, would you believe it, Harry Smith turns out to be an alias because there are dozens of Harry Smiths in the Chicago area and not a single one of them fits the description.'

'Find him,' said Abel. 'And find him before the trial starts.'

'We're already working on that,' said Jilks. 'If the man is still in Chicago we'll pin him down within the week. Osborne also added that this so-called Smith assured him he only wanted the file for private purposes. He had no intention of revealing the contents to anyone in authority.'

'Then why did "Smith" want the details in the first place?' asked Abel.

'The inference was blackmail. That's why Henry Osborne disappeared, to avoid you. If you think about that, Mr. Rosnovski, he could be telling the truth. After all, the disclosures are extremely damaging to him, and he must have been as distressed as you when he heard the file was in the hands of the Justice Department. It's no wonder he decided to stay out of sight and turned state's evidence when he was eventually caught.'

'Do you know,' said Abel, 'the only reason I ever employed that man was because he hated William Kane as much as I did, and now Kane has done us both.'

'There's no proof that Mr. Kane was in any way involved,' said Jilks.

'I don't need proof.'

The trial was delayed at the request of the government. They claimed they needed more time to question Henry Osborne before presenting their case, as he was now their principal witness. Trafford Jilks objected strongly and informed the court that the health of his client, who was no longer a young man, was failing under the strain of false accusations. The plea did not move Judge Prescott, who agreed to the government's request and postponed the trial for a further four weeks.

The month dragged on for Abel and two days before the trial was due to open, he resigned himself to being found guilty and facing a long jail sentence. Then H. Trafford Jilks' investigator in Chicago found the man called Harry

Smith, who turned out to be a local private detective, who had used an alias under strict instructions from his client, a firm of lawyers in New York. It cost Jilks one thousand dollars and another twenty-four hours before Harry Smith revealed that the firm concerned had been Cohen, Cohen and Yablons.

'Kane's lawyer,' said Abel immediately on being told.

'Are you sure?' asked Jilks. 'I would have thought from all we know about William Kane that he would be the last person to use a Jewish firm.'

'Way back, when I bought the hotels from Kane's bank, some of the paperwork was covered by a man called Thomas Cohen. For some reason, the bank used two lawyers for the transaction.'

'What do you want me to do about it?' George asked Abel.

'Nothing,' said Trafford Jilks. 'I don't want any more trouble before the trial. Do you understand me, Mr. Rosnovski?'

'Yes, sir,' said Abel. 'I'll deal with Kane when the trial's over. Now, Mr. Jilks, listen and listen carefully. You must go back to Osborne immediately and tell him the file was sold by Harry Smith to William Kane, and that Kane used the contents to gain revenge on both of us, and stress the "both of us". I promise you when Osborne hears that, he's not going to open his mouth in the witness box, no matter what promises he's made to the Justice Department. Henry Osborne's the one man alive who may hate Kane more than I do.'

'Anything you say,' said Jilks, who clearly wasn't convinced, 'but I feel I must warn you, Mr. Rosnovski, he's still putting the blame firmly on your shoulders, and to date he's been no help to our side at all.'

'You take my word for this, Mr. Jilks. His attitude will change the moment he knows about Kane's involvement.'

H. Trafford Jilks obtained permission to spend ten minutes that night with Henry Osborne in his cell before going on home. Osborne listened but said nothing. Jilks was sure that his news had made no impression on the government's star witness and he decided he would wait until the next morning before telling Abel Rosnovski. He preferred that his client try to get a good night's sleep before the trial opened the next morning.

Four hours before the trial was due to start, Henry Osborne was found hanging in his cell by the guard bringing in his breakfast. He'd used a Harvard tie.

The trial opened for the government without their star witness and they appealed for a further extension. After hearing another impassioned plea by H. Trafford Jilks on the state of his client's health, Judge Prescott refused their request. The public followed every word of the 'Chicago Baron Trial' on television and in the newspapers and to Abel's horror, Zaphia sat in the public gallery seeming to enjoy every moment of his discomfort. After nine days in court, the prosecution knew that their case was not standing up too well and offered to make a deal with H. Trafford Jilks. During an adjournment, Jilks briefed Abel on their offer.

'They will drop all the main indictments of bribery if you will plead guilty to the misdemeanours on two of the minor counts of attempting to improperly influence a public official.'

'What do you estimate are my chances of getting off completely if I turn them down?'

'Fifty-fifty, I would say,' said Jilks.

'And if I don't get off?'

'Judge Prescott is tough. The sentence wouldn't be a day under six years.'

'And if I agree to the deal and plead guilty to the two minor charges, what then?'

'A heavy fine. I would be surprised if it came to anything more than that,' said Jilks.

Abel sat and considered the alternatives for a few moments.

'I'll plead guilty. Let's get the damn thing over with.'

The government lawyers informed the judge that they were dropping fifteen of the charges against Abel Rosnovski.

H. Trafford Jilks rose from his place and told the court that his client wished to change his plea to guilty on the two remaining misdemeanour charges. The jury was dismissed and Judge Prescott was very hard on Abel in his summing-up, reminding him that the right to do business did not include the right to suborn public officials. Bribery was a crime and a worse crime when condoned by an intelligent and competent man, who should not need to stoop to such levels. In other countries, the judge added pointedly, making Abel feel like a raw immigrant once again, bribery might be an accepted way of going about one's daily life, but that was not the case in the United States of America. Judge Prescott gave Abel a six months' suspended sentence and a twenty-five thousand dollar fine plus costs.

George took Abel back to the Baron and they sat in the penthouse drinking whisky for over an hour before Abel spoke.

'George, I want you to contact Peter Parfitt and pay him the one million dollars he asked for his two per cent of Lester's, because once I have my hands on eight per cent of that bank I am going to invoke Article Seven of their by-laws and kill William Kane in his own board room.'

George nodded sadly in agreement.

A few days later the State Department announced that Poland had been granted most favoured nation status in foreign trade with the United States, and that the next American ambassador to Warsaw would be John Moors Cabot.

39

On a bitter February evening, William sat back and re-read Thaddeus Cohen's report. Henry Osborne had released all the information he had needed to finish Abel Rosnovski and had taken his twenty-five thousand dollars and disappeared. Very much in character, thought William as he replaced the well-worn copy of the Rosnovski file back in his safe. The original had been sent to the Justice Department in Washington D.C. some days before by Thaddeus Cohen.

When Abel Rosnovski had returned from Turkey and was subsequently arrested, William had waited for him to retaliate, expecting him to dump all his Interstate stock on the market immediately. This time, William was prepared. He had already warned his broker that Interstate might come on to the open market in large amounts with little warning. His instructions were clear. They were to be bought immediately so that the price did not drop. He was prepared to put up the money from his trust as a short-term measure, to avoid any unpleasantness at the bank. William had also circulated a memo among all the stockholders of Lester's asking them not to sell any Interstate stock without consulting him.

As the weeks passed and Abel Rosnovski made no move, William began to believe that Thaddeus Cohen had been correct in assuming that nothing had been traceable back to him. Rosnovski must surely be placing the blame firmly on Henry Osborne's shoulders.

Thaddeus Cohen was certain that with Osborne's evidence, Abel Rosnovski would end up behind bars for a very long time, which would prevent him from ever finding it possible to invoke Article Seven and be a threat to the bank or William Kane. William hoped that the verdict might also make Richard come to his senses and return home. Surely these latest revelations about that family could only make him detest the Rosnovski girl and realise that his father had been right all along.

William would have welcomed Richard back. There was now a gap on the board of Lester's created by the retirement of Tony Simmons and the death of Ted Leach. Richard would have to return to New York before William's sixty-fifth birthday in ten years, or it would be the first time in over a century that a Kane had not sat in a bank's board room. Cohen had reported that Richard had made a series of brilliant takeover bids for shops that Florentyna needed: but surely the opportunity to become the next chairman of Lester's Bank would mean more to Richard than living with that Rosnovski girl.

Another factor that worried William was that he did not care too much for the new breed of directors now working at the bank. Jake Thomas, the new vice-chairman was the firm favourite to succeed him as chairman. He might have been educated at Princeton and graduated Phi Beta Kappa, but he was flashy – too flashy – thought William and far too ambitious, not at all the right sort to be the next chairman of Lester's. He would have to hang on until his sixty-fifth birthday and try to convince Richard that he should join Lester's before then. William was only too aware that Kate would have had Richard back on any terms, but as the years passed, he had found it harder to give way to his better judgment. Thank heaven Virginia's marriage was going well, and now she was pregnant. If Richard refused to return home and give up that Rosnovski girl, he could still leave everything to Virginia – if only she produced a grandson.

William was at his desk in the bank when he had his first heart attack. Not a very serious one. The doctors told him he should rest a little and he would still live another twenty years. He told his doctor, another bright young man – how he missed Andrew MacKenzie – that he only wanted to survive for ten years to see out his term of office as chairman of the bank.

For the few weeks that he had to convalesce at home, William reluctantly allowed Jake Thomas the overall responsibility for the bank's decisions, but as soon as he returned, he quickly re-established his position as chairman for fear that Thomas might have taken on too much authority in his absence. From time to time, Kate plucked up the courage to beg him to let her make some direct approach to Richard, but William remained obstinate, saying, 'The boy knows he can come home whenever he wants to.

All he has to do is end his relationship with that scheming girl.'

The day Henry Osborne killed himself, William had a second heart attack. Kate sat by his bedside all through the night, fearing he would die, but Abel Rosnovski's trial kept him alive. William followed the trial devoutly every day, and he knew Osborne's suicide could only put Rosnovski in a far stronger position. When Rosnovski was finally released with nothing more than a six month's suspended sentence and a twenty-five thousand dollar fine, the lightness of the penalty did not come as a surprise to William. It wasn't hard to figure out that the government must have agreed to a deal with Rosnovski's brilliant lawyer.

William was, however, surprised to find himself feeling slightly guilty and somewhat relieved that Abel Rosnovski had not been sent to prison.

Once the trial was over William didn't care if Rosnovski dumped his Interstate Airways stock or not. He was still ready for him. But nothing happened, and as the weeks passed, William began to lose interest in the Chicago Baron and could only think of Richard, whom he now desperately wanted to see again. 'Old age and fear of death allows for sudden changes of the heart,' he had once read. One morning in September, he informed Kate of his wish. She didn't ask why he had changed his mind; it was enough for her that William wanted to see his only son.

'I'll call Richard in San Francisco immediately and invite them both,' she told him, and was pleasantly surprised that the word 'both' didn't seem to shock her husband.

'That will be fine,' said William quietly. 'Please tell Richard that I want to see him again before I die.'

'Don't be silly, darling. The doctor said that if you take it easy you'll live for another twenty years.'

'I only want to complete my term as chairman at the bank and see Richard take my place on the board. That will be enough. Why don't you fly to the coast again and tell Richard of my request, Kate?'

'What do you mean, again?' asked Kate nervously.

William smiled. 'I know you've been to San Francisco several times already, my darling. For the last few years whenever I go away on a business trip, you've always used the excuse to visit your mother, but when she died last year, your excuses became increasingly improbable. We've been married for twenty-eight years and by now I think I'm aware of all your habits. You're still as lovely as the day I met you, my darling, but I do believe that at fifty-four you're unlikely to have a lover. So it wasn't all that hard for me to work out that you had been visiting Richard.'

'Yes, I have been seeing him,' said Kate. 'Why didn't you mention that you knew before?'

'In my heart I was glad,' said William. 'I hated the thought of his losing contact with us both. How is he?'

'Both of them are well, and you have a granddaughter now as well as a grandson.'

'A granddaughter as well as a grandson,' William repeated.

'Yes, she's called Annabel,' said Kate.

'And my grandson?' said William, enquiring for the first time.

When Kate told him his name he had to smile. It was only half a lie.

'Good,' said William. 'Well, you fly to San Francisco and see what can be done. Tell him I love him.' He had once heard another old man say that who was going to lose his son.

Kate was more content that night than she had been in years. She called Richard to say she would be flying out to stay with them the following week, bringing good news with her.

When Kate returned to New York three weeks later, William was pleased to learn that Richard and Florentyna could visit them at the end of November, which was the first opportunity for them to get away from San Francisco together. Kate was full of stories of how successful they both were, how young William Kane was the image of his grandfather and how they were all so much looking forward to coming back to New York for a visit.

William listened intently and found he was happy too, and at peace with himself. He had begun to fear that if Richard did not return home soon, he never would, and then the chairmanship of the bank would fall into Jake Thomas's lap. William did not care to think about that.

William returned to work the following Monday in high spirits after his lengthy absence, having made a good recovery from his second heart attack and now feeling he had something worth living for.

'You must pace yourself a little more carefully,' the clever young doctor had told him, but he was determined to re-establish himself as chairman and president of the bank so he could make way for his only son. On his arrival at the bank he was greeted by the doorman, who told him that Jake Thomas was looking for him and had tried to reach him at home earlier. William thanked the senior member of the bank, the only person who had served Lester's more years than the chairman himself.

'Nothing's so important that it can't wait,' he said.

'No, sir.'

William walked slowly to the chairman's office. When he opened his door, he found three of his directors already in conference and Jake Thomas sitting firmly in William's chair.

'Have I been away that long,' said William, laughing. 'Am I no longer chairman of the board?'

'Yes, of course you are. Welcome back, William,' said Jake Thomas, moving quickly out of the Chairman's seat.

William had found it impossible to get used to Jake Thomas calling him by his first name. The new generation were all too familiar. They had only known each other a few years, and the man couldn't have been a day over forty.

'What's the problem?' he asked.

'Abel Rosnovski,' said Jake Thomas without expression.

William felt a sick feeling in the pit of his stomach and sat down in the nearest leather seat.

'What does he want this time?' he said wearily. 'Won't he let me finish my days in peace?'

Jake Thomas stood up and walked towards William.

'He intends to invoke Article Seven and hold a proxy meeting with the sole purpose of removing you from the chair.'

'He can't. He doesn't have the necessary eight per cent and the bank's by-laws state clearly that the chairman must be informed immediately if any outside person comes into possession of eight per cent of the stock.'

'He says he'll have the eight per cent by tomorrow morning.'

'No, no,' said William. 'I've kept a careful check on all the stock. No one would sell to Rosnovski. No one.'

'Peter Parfitt,' said Jake Thomas.

'No,' said William smiling triumphantly. 'I bought his shares a year ago through a third party.'

Jake Thomas looked shocked, and no one spoke for sometime. William realised for the first time just how much Thomas wanted to be the next chairman of Lester's.

'Well.' said Jake Thomas. 'We must face the fact he claims he'll have eight per cent by tomorrow which would entitle him to elect three directors to the board and hold up any major policy decision for three months. The very provisions you put into the articles of incorporation to protect your long term position. He also intends to announce his decision in advertisements placed all across the country. For good measure, he's threatening to make a reverse takeover bid for Lester's using the Baron Group as the vehicle if he receives any opposition to his plans. He has made it clear that there is only one way he will drop the whole plan.'

'What's that?' said William.

'If you submit your resignation as chairman of the bank,' replied Jake Thomas.

'That's blackmail,' said William, nearly shouting.

'Maybe, but if you do not resign by noon next Monday,

he intends to make his announcement to all shareholders. He has already booked space in forty newspapers and magazines.'

'The man's gone mad,' said William. He took his handkerchief from his breast pocket and mopped his brow.

'That's not all he said,' Jake Thomas added. 'He has also demanded that no Kane replace you on the board during the next ten years and that your resignation should not give ill health or, indeed, any reason for your sudden departure.'

He held out a lengthy document bearing 'The Baron Group's' letterhead.

'Mad,' repeated William, when he had scanned the letter rapidly.

'Nevertheless, I've called a board meeting for tomorrow,' said Jake Thomas. 'At ten o'clock. I think we should discuss his demands in detail then, William.'

The three directors left William alone in his office and no one visited him during the day. He sat at his desk trying to contact some of the other directors, but he only managed to have a word with one or two of them and couldn't feel certain of their support. He realised the meeting was going to be a close run thing but as long as no one else had eight per cent he was safe, and he began to prepare his strategy to retain control of his own board room. He checked the list of stockholders: as far as he could tell, not one of them intended to release his stock. He laughed to himself. Abel Rosnovski had failed with his coup. He went home early that night, only telling Kate to cancel Richard's proposed visit, and then retired to his study to consider his tactics for defeating Abel Rosnovski for the last time. He didn't go to bed until three a.m., but by then he had decided what had to be done. Jake Thomas must be removed from the board so that Richard could take his place.

William arrived early for the board meeting the next morning and sat waiting in his office looking over his notes, confident of victory. He felt his plan had taken everything into account. At five to ten his secretary buzzed. 'A Mr. Rosnovski is on the phone for you,' she said.

'What?' said William.

'Mr. Rosnovski.'

'Mr. Rosnovski.' William repeated the name in disbelief. 'Put him through,' he said, his voice quavering.

'Yes, sir.'

'Mr. Kane?'

The slight accent that William could never forget. 'Yes, what do you want this time?'

'Under the by-laws of the bank I have to inform you that I now own eight per cent of Lester's shares and intend to invoke Article Seven unless my earlier demands are met by noon on Monday.'

'How did you get the final two per cent?' stammered William. The phone clicked. He quickly studied the list of shareholders trying to work out who had betrayed him. William was still trembling when it rang again.

'The board meeting is just about to begin, sir.'

As ten o'clock struck William entered the board room. Looking round the table, he suddenly realised how few of the younger directors he knew well. Last time he'd had a fight in this same room, he hadn't known any of the directors and he'd won. He smiled to himself, reasonably confident he could still beat Abel Rosnovski, and rose to address the board.

'Gentlemen, this meeting, has been called because the bank has received a demand from Mr. Abel Rosnovski of the Baron Group; a convicted criminal who has had the effrontery to issue a direct threat to me, namely that he will use his eight per cent holding in my bank to embarrass us and if this tactic fails he will attempt a reverse takeover bid, unless I resign from the presidency and chairmanship of this board without explanation. You all know that I have only nine years left to serve this bank until my retirement and, if I were to leave before then, my resignation would be totally misinterpreted in the financial world.'

William looked down at his notes, deciding to lead with his ace.

'I am willing, gentlemen, to pledge my entire shareholding and a further ten million dollars from my private trust to be placed at the disposal of the bank in order that you can counter any move Mr. Rosnovski makes while still insuring Lester's against any financial loss. I hope, gentlemen, in those circumstances, I can expect your full support in my battle against Abel Rosnovski. I am sure you are not men to give in to vulgar blackmail.'

The room went silent. William felt certain he had won, but then Jake Thomas asked if the board might question him about his relationship with Abel Rosnovski. The request took William by surprise, but he agreed without hesitation. Jake Thomas didn't frighten him.

'This vendetta between you and Abel Rosnovski,' said Jake Thomas, 'has been going on for over thirty years. Do you believe if we followed your plan that would be the end of the matter?'

'What else can the man do? What else can he do?' stuttered William, looking around the room for support.

'We can't be sure until he does it, but with an eight per cent holding in the bank he has powers every bit as great as yours,' said the new company secretary – not William's choice, he talked too much. 'And all we know is that neither of you seems able to give up this personal feud. Although you have offered ten million to protect our financial position, if Rosnovski were continually to hold up policy decisions, call proxy meetings, arrange takeover bids with no interest in the goodwill of the bank, it would undoubtedly cause panic. The bank and its subsidiary companies, to whom we have a duty as directors, would at best, be highly embarrassed and at worst, might eventually collapse.'

'No, no,' said William. 'With my personal backing we could meet him head on.'

'The decision we have to make today,' continued the company secretary, 'is whether there are any circumstances in which this board wants to meet Mr. Rosnovski head on. Perhaps we are bound to be the losers in the long run.'

'Not if I cover the cost from my private trust,' said William.

'That you could do,' said Jake Thomas, 'but it's not just money we're discussing; much bigger problems arise for the bank. Now that Rosnovski can invoke Article Seven, he can play with us when and as he pleases. The bank could be spending its entire time doing nothing but trying to anticipate Abel Rosnovski's every move.'

Jake Thomas waited for the effect of what he had said to sink in. William remained silent. Then Thomas looked at William and continued: 'Now I must ask you a very serious personal question, Mr. Chairman, which worries every one of us around this table, and I hope you'll be nothing less than frank with us when answering it, however unpleasant that may be for you.'

William looked up, wondering what the question could be. What had they been discussing behind his back? Who the hell did Jake Thomas think he was? William felt he was losing the initiative.

'I will answer anything that the board requires,' said William. 'I have nothing and no one to fear,' he said, looking pointedly at Jake Thomas.

'Thank you,' said Jake Thomas. 'Mr. Chairman, were you in any way involved with sending a file to the Justice Department in Washington which caused Abel Rosnovski to be arrested and charged with fraud when at the same time you knew he was a major shareholder of the bank's?'

'Did he tell you that?' demanded William.

'Yes, he claims you were the sole reason for his arrest.'

William stayed silent for a few moments, considering his reply, while he looked down at his notes. They didn't help. He had not thought that question would arise but he had never lied to the board in over twenty-three years. He couldn't start now.

'Yes, I did,' he said, breaking the silence. 'The information came into my hands, and I considered that it was nothing less than my duty to pass it on to the Justice Department.'

'How did the information come into your hands?'

William did not reply.

'I think we all know the answer to that question, Mr. Chairman,' said Jake Thomas. 'Moreover, you let the authorities know without briefing the board of your action and by so doing you put all of us in jeopardy. Our reputations, our careers, everything this bank stands for over a personal vendetta.'

'But Rosnovski was trying to ruin me,' said William, aware he was now shouting.

'So in order to ruin him you risked the bank's stability and reputation.'

'It is my bank,' said William.

'It is not,' said Jake Thomas. 'You own eight per cent of the stock, as does Mr. Rosnovski, and at the moment you are president and chairman of Lester's, but the bank is not yours to use for your own personal whim without consulting the other directors.'

'Then I will have to ask the board for a vote of confidence,' said William. 'I'll ask you to support me against Abel Rosnovski.'

'That is not what a vote of confidence would be about,' said the company secretary. 'The vote would be about whether you are the right man to run this bank in the present circumstances. Can't you see that, Mr. Chairman?'

'So be it,' said William, turning his eyes away. 'This board must decide whether it wishes to end my career in disgrace now, after nearly a quarter of a century's service, or to yield to the threats of a convicted criminal.'

Jake Thomas nodded to the company secretary and voting slips were passed around to every board member. It looked to William as if everything had been decided before the meeting. He glanced around the crowded table at the twenty-nine men. Many of them he had chosen himself, but some of them he didn't know at all well. He had once heard that a small group of young directors openly supported the Democratic Party and John Kennedy. Some of them were looking at him; some were not. Surely they'd back him; they wouldn't let Rosnovski beat him. Not now. Please let me finish my term as chairman, he said to himself, then

I'll go quietly and without any fuss – but not this way.

He watched the members of the board as they passed their voting slips back to the secretary. He was opening them slowly. The room was silent and all eyes were turned towards the secretary as he began opening the last few slips, noting down each aye and nay meticulously on a piece of paper placed in front of him that revealed two columns. William could see that one list of names was considerably longer than the other, but his failing eyesight did not permit him to decipher which was which. He could not accept that the day could have come when there would be a vote in his own board room between himself and Abel Rosnovski.

The secretary was saying something. William couldn't believe what he heard. By seventeen votes to twelve he had lost the confidence of the board. He managed to stand up. Abel Rosnovski had beaten him in the final battle. No one spoke as William left the board room. He returned to the Chairman's office and picked up his coat, stopping only to look at the portrait of Charles Lester for the last time, and then walked slowly down the long corridor and out of the front entrance.

The doorman said, 'Nice to have you back again, Mr. Chairman. See you tomorrow, sir.'

William realised he would never see him again. He turned around and shook hands with the man who had directed him to the board room twenty-three years before.

The rather surprised doorman said, 'Goodnight, sir,' as he watched William climb into the back of his car for the last time.

His chauffeur took him home and when he reached East Sixty-eighth Street, William collapsed on his front door step. The chauffeur and Kate helped him into the house. Kate could see he was crying, and she put her arms round him.

'What is it, William? What's happened?'

'I've been thrown out of my own bank,' he wept. 'My own board no longer have confidence in me. When it mattered, they supported Abel Rosnovski.'

Kate managed to get him up to bed and sat with him through the night. He never spoke. Nor did he sleep.

The announcement in the *Wall Street Journal* the following Monday morning said simply: 'William Lowell Kane, the president and chairman of Lester's Bank resigned after yesterday's board meeting.'

No mention of illness or any explanation was given for his sudden departure, and there was no suggestion that his son would take his place on the board. William knew that rumour would sweep through Wall Street and that the worst would be assumed. He sat in bed alone, caring no longer for this world.

Abel read the announcement of William Kane's resignation in the *Wall Street Journal* the same day. He picked up the phone, dialled Lester's Bank and asked to speak to the new chairman. A few seconds later Jake Thomas came on the line. 'Good morning, Mr. Rosnovski.'

'Good morning, Mr. Thomas. I'm just phoning to confirm that I shall release all my Interstate Airways shares to the bank at the market price this morning and my eight per cent holding in Lester's to you personally for two million dollars.'

'Thank you, Mr. Rosnovski, that's most generous of you.'

'No need to thank me, Mr. Chairman, it's no more than we agreed on when you sold me your two per cent of Lester's,' said Abel Rosnovski.

Book Seven

40

Abel was surprised to find how little satisfaction his final triumph had given him.

George tried to persuade him that he should go to Warsaw to look over sites for the new Baron but Abel didn't want to. As he grew older he became fearful of dying abroad and never seeing Florentyna again, and for months Abel showed no interest in the group's activities. When John F. Kennedy was assassinated on 22 November 1963, Abel became even more depressed and feared for America. Eventually George did convince him that a trip abroad could do no harm, and that things would perhaps seem a little easier for him when he returned.

Abel travelled to Warsaw where he obtained a highly confidential agreement to build the first Baron in the communist world. His command of the language impressed Warsawians, and he was proud to beat Holiday Inns and Intercontinental behind the Iron Curtain. He couldn't help thinking ... and it didn't help when Lyndon Johnson appointed John Gronowski to be the first Polish-American ambassador to Warsaw. But now nothing seemed to give any satisfaction. He had defeated Kane and lost his own daughter, and he wondered if the man felt the same way about his son. After Warsaw, he roamed the world, staying in his hotels, watching the construction of new ones. He opened the first Baron in Cape Town, South Africa, and flew back to Germany to open one in Düsseldorf.

Abel then spent six months in his favourite Baron in Paris, roaming the streets by day, and attending the opera at night, hoping it might revive happy memories of Florentyna.

He eventually left Paris and returned to America, after his long exile. As he descended the metal steps of an Air France 707 at Kennedy International Airport, his back hunched and his bald head covered with a black hat, nobody recognised him. George was there to greet him, loyal, honest George, looking quite a bit older. On the ride to the New York Baron, George, as always, brought him up to date on group news. The profits, it seemed, were even higher as his keen young executives thrust forward in every major country in the world. Seventy-two hotels run by twenty-two thousand staff. Abel didn't seem to be listening. He only wanted news of Florentyna.

'She's well,' said George, 'and coming to New York early next year.'

'Why?' said Abel, suddenly excited.

'She's opening one of her shops on Fifth Avenue.'

'Fifth Avenue?'

'The eleventh Florentyna,' said George.

'Have you seen her?'

'Yes,' he admitted.

'Is she well, is she happy?'

'Both of them are very well and happy, and so successful. Abel, you should be very proud of them. Your grandson is quite a boy, and your granddaughter's beautiful. The image of Florentyna when she was that age.'

'Will she see me?' said Abel.

'Will you see her husband?'

'No, George. I can never meet that boy, not while his father is still alive.'

'What if you die first?'

'You mustn't believe everything you read in the Bible.'

Abel and George drove in silence back to the hotel, and Abel dined alone in his room that night.

For the next six months, he never left the penthouse.

41

When Florentyna Kane opened her new boutique on Fifth Avenue in March 1967, everyone in New York seemed to be there, except William Kane and Abel Rosnovski.

Kate and Lucy had left William in bed muttering to himself while they went off to the opening of 'Florentyna's'.

George left Abel alone in his suite so that he could attend the celebrations. He had tried to talk Abel into going along with him. Abel grunted that his daughter had opened ten shops without him, and one more wouldn't make any difference. George told him he was a stubborn old fool and left for Fifth Avenue on his own. When he arrived at the shop, a magnificent modern boutique with thick carpets and the latest Swedish furniture – it reminded him of the way Abel used to do things – he found Florentyna, wearing a long blue gown with the now famous F on the high collar. She gave George a glass of champagne and introduced him to Kate and Lucy Kane who were chatting with Zaphia. Kate and Lucy were clearly happy and they surprised George by enquiring after Abel Rosnovski.

'I told him he was a stubborn old fool to miss such a good party. Is Mr. Kane here?' he asked.

George was delighted by Kate Kane's happy reply.

William was still muttering angrily at the *New York Times*, something about Johnson's pulling his punches in Vietnam, when he folded the newspaper and got himself out of bed. He started to dress slowly, staring at himself in the mirror when he had finished. He looked like a banker. He scowled. How else should he look? He put on a heavy black overcoat and his old Homburg hat, picked up his black walking stick with the silver handle, the one Rupert Cork-Smith had left him, and somehow got himself out on to the street. The first time he had been out on his own, he thought, for the best part of three years, since that last serious heart attack. The maid was surprised to see him leaving the house unaccompanied.

It was an unusually warm spring evening, but William felt the cold after being in the house so long. It took him a considerable time to reach Fifth Avenue and Fifty-sixth Street, and when he eventually did arrive, the crowd was so large outside Florentyna's that he felt he didn't have the strength to fight his way through it. He stood at the kerb, watching the people enjoying themselves. Young people, happy and excited, thrusting their way into Florentyna's beautiful shop. Some of the girls were wearing the new mini skirts from London. What next? thought William, and then he saw his son talking to Kate. He had grown into such a fine looking man – tall, confident, and relaxed, he had an air of authority about him that reminded William of his own father. But in the bustle and continual movement, he couldn't quite work out which one was Florentyna. He stood there for nearly an hour enjoying the comings and goings, regretting the stubborn years he had thrown away.

The wind was beginning to race down Fifth Avenue. He'd forgotten how cold that March wind could be. He turned his collar up. He must get home, because they were all coming to dinner that night, and he was going to meet Florentyna and the grandchildren for the first time. His grandson and little Annabel and their father, his beloved son. He had told Kate what a fool he'd been and begged her forgiveness. All he remembered her saying was 'I'll always love you.' Florentyna had written to him. Such a generous letter. She had been so understanding and kind about the past. She had ended with 'I can't wait to meet you.'

He must get home. Kate would be cross with him if she ever discovered he'd been out on his own in that cold wind. But he had to see the opening of the shop and in any case tonight he would be with them all. He must leave now and let them enjoy their celebrations. They could tell him all about the opening over dinner. He wouldn't tell them he'd been there, that would always be his secret.

He turned to go home and saw an old man standing a few yards away in a black coat, with a hat pulled way down on his head, and a scarf around his neck. He, too, was cold. Not a night for old men, thought William, as he walked towards him. And then he saw the silver band on his wrist, just below his sleeve. In a flash it all came back to him, fitting into place for the first time. First the Plaza, then Boston, then Germany, and now Fifth Avenue. The man turned and started to walk towards him. He must have been standing there for a long time because his face was red from the wind. He stared at William out of those unmistakable blue eyes. They were now only a few yards apart. As they passed, William raised his hat to the old man. He returned the compliment, and they continued on their separate ways without a word.

I must get home, thought William, before they do. The joy of seeing Richard and his two grandchildren would make everything worthwhile again. He must come to know Florentyna, ask for her forgiveness, and trust that she would understand what he could scarcely understand himself now. Such a fine girl, they all told him.

When he reached East Sixty-eighth Street, he fumbled for his key and opened the front door. Must turn on all the lights, he told the maid, and build the fire up to make them feel welcome. He was very contented and very, very tired.

'Draw the curtains,' he said, 'and light the candles on the dining room table. There's so much to celebrate.'

William couldn't wait for them all to return. He sat in the old crimson leather chair by a blazing fire and thought happily of the evening that lay ahead of him. Grandchildren around him, the years he had missed. When had his little grandson first said three? A chance to bury the past and earn forgiveness in the future. The room was so nice and warm after that cold wind, but the journey had been well worthwhile.

A few minutes later there was an excited bustle downstairs and the maid came in to tell William that his son had arrived. He was in the hall with his mother, and his wife and two of the loveliest children the maid had ever seen. And then she ran off to be sure that dinner would be ready for Mr. Kane on time. He would want everything to be perfect for them that night.

When Richard came into the room, Florentyna was by his side. She looked quite radiant.

'Father,' he said. 'I would like you to meet my wife.'

William Lowell Kane would have turned to greet them but he could not. He was dead.

42

Abel placed the envelope on the table by the side of his bed. He hadn't dressed yet. Nowadays he rarely rose before noon. He tried to remove his breakfast tray from his knees on to the floor. A bending movement that demanded too much dexterity for his stiff body to accomplish. He inevitably ended by dropping the tray with a bang. It was no different today. He no longer cared. He picked up the envelope once more, and read the covering note for second time.

'We were instructed by the late Mr. Curtis Fenton, sometime manager of the Continental Trust Bank, La Salle Street, Chicago, to send you the enclosed letter, when certain circumstances have come about. Please acknowledge receipt of this letter by signing the enclosed copy, returning it to us in the stamped addressed envelope supplied herewith.'

'Goddamn lawyers,' said Abel, and tore open the letter.

Dear Mr. Rosnovski:

This letter has been in the keeping of my lawyers until today for reasons which will become apparent to you as you read on.

When in 1951 you closed your accounts at the Continental Trust after over twenty years with the bank, I was naturally very unhappy and very concerned. My concern was engendered not by losing one of the bank's most valued customers, sad though that was, but because I know you felt that I had acted in a dishonourable fashion. What you were not aware of at the time was that I had specific instructions from your backer not to reveal certain facts to you.

When you first visited me at the bank in 1929, you requested financial help to clear the debt incurred by Mr. Davis Leroy, in order that you might take possession of the hotels which then formed the Richmond Group. I was unable to find a backer, despite approaching several leading financiers myself. I took a personal interest, as I believed that you had an exceptional flair for your chosen career. It has given me a great deal of satisfaction to observe in old age that my confidence was not misplaced. I might add at this point that I also felt some responsibility, having advised you to buy twenty-five per cent of the Richmond Group from my client, Miss Amy Leroy, when I did not know the financial predicament that was facing Mr. Leroy at that time. I digress.

I did not succeed in finding a backer for you and had given up all hope when you came to visit me on that Monday morning. I wonder if you remember that day. Only thirty minutes before your appointment I had a call from a financier who was willing to put up the necessary money, who, like me, had a great confidence in you personally. His only stipulation was, as I advised you at the time, that he insisted on remaining anonymous because of a potential conflict between his professional and private interests. The terms he offered, allowing you to gain eventual control of the Richmond Group, I considered at the time to be extremely generous and you rightly took full advantage of them. Indeed your backer was delighted when you found it possible, through your own diligence, to repay his original investment.

I lost contact with you both after 1951, but after I retired from the bank, I read a distressing story in the newspapers concerning your backer, which prompted me to write this letter, in case I died before either of you.

I write not to prove my good intentions in this whole affair, but so that you should not continue to live under the illusion that your backer and benefactor was Mr. David Maxton of the Stevens Hotel. Mr. Maxton was a great admirer of yours, but he never approached the bank in that capacity. The gentleman who made the Baron Group possible, by his foresight and personal generosity was William Lowell Kane, the chairman of Lester's Bank, New York.

I begged Mr. Kane to inform you of his personal involvement, but he refused to break the clause in his trust deed that stipulated that no benefactor should be privy to the investments of the family trust. After you had paid off the loan and he later learned of Henry Osborne's personal involvement with the Baron Group he became even more adamant that you should never be informed.

I have left instructions that this letter is to be destroyed if you die before Mr. Kane. In those circumstances, he will receive a letter, explaining your total lack of knowledge of his personal generosity.

Whichever one of you receives a letter from me, it was a privilege to have served you both.

  As ever,
   your faithful servant,
    Curtis Fenton.

Abel picked up the phone by the side of his bed. 'Find George for me,' he said. 'I need to get dressed.'

43

William Lowell Kane's funeral was well attended. Richard and Florentyna stood on one side of Kate; Virginia and Lucy were on the other. Grandmother Kane would have approved of the turn-out. Three senators, five congressmen, two bishops, most of the leading banks' chairmen, and the publisher of the *Wall Street Journal* were all there. Jake Thomas and every director of the Lester's board was also present, their heads bowed in prayer to the God in whom William had never really believed.

No one noticed two old men, standing at the back of the gathering, their heads also bowed, looking as if they were not attached to the main party. They had arrived a few minutes late and left quickly at the end of the service. Florentyna thought she recognised the limp as the shorter old man hurried away. She told Richard. They didn't mention their suspicion to Kate Kane.

A few days later, the taller of the two old men went to see Florentyna in her shop on Fifth Avenue. He had heard she was returning to San Francisco and needed to seek her help before she left. She listened carefully to what he had to say and agreed to his request with joy.

Richard and Florentyna Kane arrived at the Baron Hotel the next afternoon. George Novak was there to meet and escort them to the forty-second floor. After ten years, Florentyna hardly recognised her father, now propped up in bed, half-moon glasses on the end of his nose, still no pillows, but smiling defiantly. They talked of happier days and both laughed a little and cried a lot.

'You must forgive us, Richard,' said Abel. 'The Polish are a sentimental race.'

'I know, my children are half Polish,' said Richard.

Later that evening they dined together, magnificent roast

veal, appropriate for the return of the prodigal daughter, said Abel.

He talked of the future and how he saw the progress of his group.

'We ought to have a Florentyna's in every hotel,' he said.

She laughed and agreed.

He told Richard of his sadness concerning his father, revealing in detail the mistakes he had made for so many years, and how it had never crossed his mind even for a moment that he could have been his benefactor, and how he would have liked one chance to thank him personally.

'He would have understood,' said Richard.

'We met, you know, the day he died,' said Abel.

Florentyna and Richard stared at him in surprise.

'Oh yes,' said Abel. 'We passed each other on Fifth Avenue, he had come to watch the opening of your shop. He raised his hat to me. It was enough, quite enough.'

Abel had only one request of Florentyna. That she and Richard would accompany him on his journey to Warsaw in nine months' time for the opening of the latest Baron.

'Can you imagine,' he said, again excited, his fingers tapping the side table. 'The Warsaw Baron. Now there is a hotel that could only be opened by the president of the Baron Group.'

During the following months the Kanes visited Abel regularly and Florentyna grew very close to her father again. Abel came to admire Richard and the common sense that tempered all his daughter's ambitions. He adored his grandson. And little Annabel was – what was that awful modern expression? – she was something else. Abel had rarely been happier in his life and began elaborate plans for his triumphant return to Poland to open the Warsaw Baron.

The president of the Baron Group opened the Warsaw Baron six months later than had been originally scheduled. Building contracts run late in Warsaw just as they do in every other part of the world.

In her first speech, as president of the group, she told her guests that her pride in the magnificent hotel was mingled with a feeling of sadness that her late father could not have been present to open the Warsaw Baron himself.

In his will, Abel left everything to Florentyna, with the single exception of a small bequest. The testament described the gift as a heavy engraved silver bracelet, rare, but of unknown value, and bearing the legend 'Baron Abel Rosnovski'.

The beneficiary was his grandson, William Abel Kane.

The End

Here are the opening pages of Jeffrey Archer's new novel, A MATTER OF HONOUR, available now in hardback from Hodder and Stoughton, and available in paperback from Coronet in 1987.

A Matter of Honour

Jeffrey Archer

1

The Kremlin   May 1966

"It's a fake," said the Russian leader, staring down at the small exquisite painting he held in his hands.

"That isn't possible," replied his Politburo colleague. "The Tsar's icon of St George and the Dragon has been in the Winter Palace at Leningrad under heavy guard for over fifty years."

"True, Comrade Zaborski," said the old man, "but for fifty years we've been guarding a fake. The Tsar must have removed the original some time before the Red Army entered St Petersburg and overran the Winter Palace."

The head of State Security moved restlessly in his chair as the cat and mouse game continued. Efimovich Zaborski knew, after years of running the KGB, who had been cast as the mouse the moment his phone had rung at four that morning to say that the General Secretary required him to report to the Kremlin – immediately.

"How can you be so sure it's a fake, Leonid Ilyich?" the diminutive figure enquired.

"Because, my dear Zaborski, during the past eighteen months, the age of all the treasures in the Winter Palace has been tested by carbon-dating, the modern scientific process that does not call for a second opinion," said Brezhnev, displaying his new-found knowledge. "And what we have always thought to be one of the nation's masterpieces," he continued, "turns out to have been painted five hundred years after Rublev's original."

"But by whom and for what purpose?" asked the Chairman of State Security, incredulous.

"The experts tell me it was probably a court painter," replied the Russian leader, "who must have been commissioned to execute the copy only months before the Revolution took place. It has always worried the curator at the Winter Palace that the Czar's traditional silver crown was not attached to the back of the frame, as it was to all his other masterpieces," added Brezhnev.

"But I always thought that the silver crown had been removed by a souvenir hunter before we even entered St Petersburg."

"No," said the General Secretary drily, his bushy eyebrows rising every time he had completed a statement. "It wasn't the Tsar's silver crown that had been removed, but the painting itself."

"Then what can the Tsar have done with the original?" the Chairman said, almost as if he were asking himself the question.

"That is exactly what I want to know, Comrade," said Brezhnev, splaying his hands and dwarfing the little painting that remained in front of him. "And you are the one who has been chosen to come up with the answer," he added.

For the first time the Chairman of the KGB looked unsure of himself.

"But do you have anything for me to go on?"

"Very little," admitted the General Secretary, flicking open a file on the desk in front of him. He stared down at the closely-typed notes headed 'The Significance of the Icon in Russian History'. Someone had been up all through the night preparing a ten-page report that the leader had only found time to scan. Brezhnev's real interest began on page four. He quickly turned over the first three pages before reading aloud: "'At the time of the Revolution, Tsar Nicholas II obviously saw Rublev's masterpiece as his passport to freedom in the West. He must have had a copy made which he then left on his study wall where the original had previously hung.'" The Russian leader looked up. "Beyond that we have little to go on."

The head of the KGB looked perplexed. He remained puzzled as to why Brezhnev should want State Security involved in the theft of a minor masterpiece. "And how important is it that we find the original?" he asked, trying to pick up a further clue.

Leonid Brezhnev stared down at his Kremlin colleague.

"Nothing could be more important, Comrade," came back the unexpected reply. "And I shall grant you any resources you may consider necessary in terms of people and finance to discover the whereabouts of the Tsar's icon."

"But if I were to take you at your word, Comrade General Secretary," said the head of the KGB, trying to disguise his disbelief, "I could end up spending far more than the painting is worth."

"That would not be possible," said Brezhnev, pausing for effect, "because it's not the icon itself that I'm after." He turned his back on the Chairman of State Security and stared out of the window. He had always disliked not being able to see over the Kremlin wall and into Red Square. He waited for some moments before he proclaimed, "The money the Tsar might have raised from selling such a masterpiece, would only have kept Nicholas in his accustomed lifestyle for a matter of months, perhaps a year at the most. No, it's what we feel certain the Tsar had secreted *inside* the icon that would have guaranteed security for himself and his family for the rest of their days."

A little circle of condensation formed on the window pane in front of the General Secretary.

"What could possibly be that valuable?" asked the Chairman.

"Do you remember, Comrade, what the Tsar promised Lenin in exchange for his life?"

"Yes, but it turned out to be a bluff because no such document was hidden . . ." He stopped himself just in time before saying "in the icon".

Zaborski was unable to witness Brezhnev's triumphant smile.

"You have caught up with me at last. You see, Comrade, it was hidden in the icon all the time. We just had the wrong icon."

The Russian leader waited for some time before he turned back and passed over a single sheet of paper to his colleague. "This is the Tsar's testimony indicating what we would find in the icon of St George and the Dragon. At the time, nothing was discovered in the icon which only convinced Lenin that it had been a bluff by the Tsar to save his family from execution."

Yuri Efnimovich Zaborski slowly read the hand-written testimony that had been signed by the Tsar hours before his execution. Zaborski's hands began to tremble and a bead of sweat appeared on his forehead long before he had reached the last paragraph. He looked up towards the tiny painting, no larger than a book, that remained in the centre of the Chairman's desk.

"Not since the death of Lenin," continued Brezhnev, "has anyone believed the Tsar's claim. But now, there can be little doubt that if we are able to locate the genuine masterpiece, we will undoubtedly also be in possession of the promised document."

"And with the authority of those who signed that document, no one could question our legal claim," said Zaborski.

"That would undoubtedly prove to be the case, Comrade Chairman," replied the Russian leader. "And I also feel confident that we would receive the backing of the United Nations and the World Court if the Americans tried to deny us our right. But I fear time is now against us."

"Why?" asked the Chairman of State Security.

"Look at the date in the Tsar's testimony and you will see how much time we have left to honour our part of the agreement," said Brezhnev.

Zaborski stared at the date scrawled in the hand of the Tsar – June 20, 1966. He handed back the testimony as he considered the enormity of the task with which his leader had entrusted him. Leonid Ilyich Brezhnev continued his monologue.

"So, as you can see, Comrade Zaborski, we have only one month left before the deadline, but if you can discover the whereabouts of the original icon, President Johnson's defence strategy would be rendered virtually useless, and the United States would then become a pawn on the Russian chessboard."

2

Appleshaw, Hampshire, England   June 1966

"And to my dearly beloved and only son, Captain Adam Scott, MC, I bequeath the sum of five hundred pounds."

Although Adam had anticipated the amount would be pitiful, he nevertheless remained bolt upright in his chair as the solicitor glanced over his half-moon spectacles.

The old lawyer who was seated behind the large partner's desk raised his head and blinked at the handsome young man before him. Adam put a hand nervously through his thick black hair, suddenly conscious of the lawyer's stare. Then Mr Holbrooke's eyes returned to the papers in front of him.

"And to my dearly beloved daughter, Margaret Scott, I bequeath the sum of four hundred pounds." Adam was unable to prevent a small grin spreading across his face. Even in the minutiae of his final act, father had remained a chauvinist.

"To the Hampshire County Cricket Club," droned on Mr Holbrooke unperturbed by Miss Scott's relative misfortunes, "twenty-five pounds, life membership." Finally paid up, thought Adam. "To the Old Contemptibles, fifteen pounds. And to the Appleshaw Parish Church, ten pounds." Death membership, Adam mused. "To Wilf Proudfoot, our loyal gardener part time, ten pounds, and to Mrs Mavis Cox, our daily help, five pounds."

"And finally, to my dearly beloved wife Susan, our marital home, and the remainder of my estate."

This pronouncement made Adam want to laugh out loud because he doubted if the remainder of Pa's estate, even if they sold his premium bonds and the pre-war golf clubs, amounted to more than another thousand pounds.

But Mother was a daughter of the Regiment and wouldn't complain, she never did. If God ever announced the saints, as opposed to some Pope in Rome, Saint Susan of Appleshaw would be up there with Mary and Elizabeth. All through his life 'Pa', as Adam always thought of him, had set such high standards for the family to live up to. Perhaps that was why Adam continued to admire him above all men. He only hoped that if he ever had a son those standards would be passed on to another generation. Sometimes the very thought made him feel strangely out of place in the swinging sixties.

Adam began to move restlessly in his chair, assuming that the proceedings were now drawing to a close. The sooner they were all out of this cold, drab little office the better.

Mr Holbrooke looked up once more and cleared his throat, as if he were about to announce who was to be left the Goya or the Hapsburg diamonds. He pushed his half-moon spectacles further up the bridge of his nose and stared back down at the last paragraphs of his late client's testament. The three surviving members of the Scott family sat in silence. What could he have to add? thought Adam.

Whatever it was, the solicitor had obviously pondered the final bequest several times, because he delivered the words like a well-versed actor, his eyes returning to the script only once.

"And I also leave to my son," Mr Holbrooke paused, "the enclosed envelope," he said, holding it up, "which I can only hope will bring him greater happiness than it did me. Should he decide to open the envelope it must be on the condition that he will never divulge its contents to any other living person." Adam caught his sister's eye but she only shook her head slightly, obviously as puzzled as he was. He glanced towards his mother who looked shocked. Was it fear or was it distress? Adam couldn't decide. Mr Holbrooke passed the yellowed envelope over to the Colonel's only son.

Everyone in the room remained seated, not quite sure what to do next. Mr Holbrooke finally closed the thin file marked Colonel Gerald Scott, DSO, OBE, MC, pushed back his chair and walked slowly over to the widow. They shook hands and she said, "Thank you", a faintly ridiculous courtesy, Adam felt, as the only person in the room who had made any sort of profit on this particular transaction had been Mr Holbrooke, and that on behalf of Holbrooke, Holbrooke and Gascoine.

He rose and went quickly by his mother's side.

"You'll join us for tea, Mr Holbrooke?" she was asking.

"I fear not, dear lady," the lawyer began, but Adam didn't bother to listen further. Obviously the fee hadn't been large enough to cover Holbrooke taking time off for tea.

Once they had left the office and Adam had ensured his mother and sister were seated comfortably in the back of the family Morris Minor, he took his place behind the steering wheel. He had parked outside the solicitor's office in the middle of the High Street. No yellow lines in the streets of Appleshaw – yet, he thought. Even before he had switched on the ignition she had offered matter-of-factly, "We'll have to get rid of this, you know. I can't afford to run it now, not with petrol at six shillings a gallon."

"Don't let's worry about that today," said Margaret consolingly, but in a voice that accepted that her mother was right. "I wonder what can be in that envelope, though," she added, wanting to change the subject.

"Detailed instructions on how to invest my five hundred pounds, no doubt," said Adam, attempting to lighten their mood.

"Don't be disrespectful of the dead," said his mother, the same look of fear returning to her face. "I begged your father to destroy that envelope," she added, in a voice that was barely a whisper.

Adam's lips pursed when he realised this must be *the* envelope his father had referred to all those years ago when he had witnessed the one row between his parents that he had ever experienced. Adam still remembered his father's raised voice and angry words just a few days after he had returned from Germany.

"I have to open it, don't you understand?" Pa had insisted.

"Never," his mother had replied. "After all the sacrifices I have made, you at least owe me that."

Over twenty years had passed since that confrontation and he had never heard the subject referred to again. The only time Adam ever mentioned it to his sister she could throw no light on what the dispute might have been over.

Adam put his foot on the brake as they reached a T-junction at the end of the High Street.

He turned right and continued to drive out of the village and a mile or so down a winding country lane before bringing the old Morris Minor to a halt outside a trellised gate whose path led through a neat lawn to a little thatched cottage.

"I'm sure you have to get back to London," were his mother's first words as she entered the drawing room.

"I'm in no hurry, mother. There's nothing that can't wait until tomorrow."

"Just as you wish, my dear, but you don't have to worry yourself over me," his mother continued. She stared up at the tall young man who reminded her so much of Gerald. He would have been as good looking as her husband if it wasn't for the broken nose. The same dark hair and deep brown eyes, the same open, honest face, even the same gentle approach to everyone he came across. But most of all the same high standards of morality that had brought them to their present sad state. "And in any case I've always got Margaret to take care of me," she added. Adam looked across at his sister and wondered how she would now cope with Saint Susan of Appleshaw.

Margaret had recently become engaged to a City stockbroker, and although the marriage had been postponed, she would soon be wanting to start a life of her own. Thank God her fiancé had already put a down-payment on a little house only fourteen miles away.

After tea and a sad uninterrupted monologue from his mother on the virtues and misfortunes of their father, Margaret cleared away and left Adam alone with his mother. They had both loved him in such different ways Adam felt but he had never let 'Pa' really know how much he respected him.

"Now that you're no longer in the army, my dear, I do hope you'll be able to find a worthwhile job," his mother said uneasily, as she recalled how difficult that had proved to be for his father.

"I'm sure everything will be just fine, Mother," he replied, "the Foreign Office have asked to see me again," he added, hoping to reassure her.

"Still, now that you've got five hundred pounds of your own," she said, "that should make things a little easier for you." Adam smiled fondly at his mother, wondering when she had last spent a day in London. His share of the Chelsea flat alone was four pounds a week and he still had to eat occasionally. She raised her eyes and, looking up at the clock on the mantelpiece, said, "You'd better be getting along, my dear, I don't like the thought of you on that motorbike after dark."

Adam bent down to kiss her on the cheek. "I'll give you a call tomorrow," he said, and left her. He stuck his head around the kitchen door and shouted "I'm off," to his sister. "I'll be sending you a cheque for fifty pounds," he added.

"Why?" asked Margaret, looking up from the sink.

"Let's just say it's my blow for women's rights." He shut the kitchen door smartly to avoid the dish-cloth that was hurled in his direction. Adam revved up his BSA and drove down the A303 through Andover and on towards London. As most of the traffic was coming west out of the city, he was able to make good time on his way back to the flat in the Ifield Road.

Adam had decided to wait until he had reached the privacy of his own room before he opened the envelope. Lately the excitement in his life had not been such that he felt he could be blasé about the little ceremony. After all, in a way, he had waited most of his life to discover what was in the envelope he had now inherited.

Adam had been told the story of the family tragedy by his father a thousand times – "It's all a matter of honour, old chap," his father would repeat, lifting his chin and squaring his shoulders. Adam had spent a lifetime overhearing the snide comments of lesser men and suffering the side-long glances from other officers who had made sure they were not seen too regularly in his company. Petty men with petty minds. Adam knew his father too well to believe, even for a moment, that he could have been involved in such treachery as was whispered. Adam took one hand off the handle bars and fingered the envelope in his inside pocket like a schoolboy the day before his birthday feeling the shape of a present in the hope of discovering some clue as to its contents. He felt certain that whatever it contained would not be to anyone's advantage now his father was dead, but it did not lessen his curiosity.

He tried to piece together the few facts he had been told over the years. In 1946, within a year of his fiftieth birthday, his father had resigned his commission from the army. *The Times* had described 'Pa' as a brilliant tactical officer with a courageous war record. His resignation had been a decision that had surprised *The Times* correspondent, astonished his immediate family and shocked his regiment, as it had been assumed by all that it was only a matter of months before crossed swords and a baton would have been sewn on to his epaulette.

Because of the Colonel's sudden and unexplained departure from the regiment, fact was augmented by fiction. When asked, all the Colonel would offer was that he had had enough of war, and felt the time had come to make a little money on which Susan and he could retire before it was too late. Even at the time, few people found his story credible, and that credibility was not helped when the only job the Colonel managed to secure for himself was as secretary of the local golf club.

It was only through the generosity of Adam's late grandfather, General Sir Pelham Westlake, that Adam had been able to remain at Wellington College, and thereby be given the opportunity to continue the family tradition and pursue a military career.

After leaving school, Adam was offered a place at the Royal Military Academy, Sandhurst. During his days at the RMA, Adam was to be found diligently studying military history, tactics, and battle procedure while at weekends he concentrated on rugby and squash although his greatest success came whenever he completed the different cross country courses he encountered. For two years, panting cadets from Cranwell and Dartmouth only saw his mud-spattered back as Adam went on to become the Inter-Services champion. He also became the middleweight boxing champion despite a Nigerian cadet breaking his nose in the first round of the final. The Nigerian made the mistake of assuming the fight was already over.

When Adam passed out of Sandhurst in August 1956, he managed to come seventh in the academic order of merit, but his leadership and example outside the classroom was such that no one was surprised when he was awarded the Sword of Honour. Adam never doubted he would therefore follow his father and command the Regiment.

The Royal Wessex Regiment accepted the Colonel's son soon after he had been awarded his regular commission. Adam quickly gained the respect of the soldiers and was also popular with those officers whose currency was not to deal in rumour. As a tactical officer in the field he had no equal, and when it came to combat duty it was clear he had inherited his father's courage. Yet, when six years later, the War Office published in the *London Gazette* the names of those subalterns who had been promoted to captain, Lieutenant Adam Scott was not to be found on the list. His contemporaries were genuinely surprised, while senior officers of the regiment remained tight-lipped. To Adam it was becoming clear that he was not to be allowed to atone for whatever it was his father was thought to have done.

Eventually Adam was made up to captain, but not before he had distinguished himself in the Malayan jungle in hand-to-hand fighting against the never-ending waves of Chinese soldiers. Having been captured and held prisoner by the Communists, he endured solitude and torture such that no amount of training could have prepared him for. He escaped eight months after his incarceration only to discover on returning to the front line that he had been awarded a posthumous Military Cross. When, at the age of twenty-nine, Captain Scott passed his staff exam but still failed to be offered a regimental place at the staff college, he finally accepted he could never hope to command the regiment. He resigned his commission a few weeks later; there was no need to suggest that the reason he had done so was because he needed to earn more money.

While he was serving out his last few months with the regiment, Adam learned from his mother that Pa only had weeks to live. Adam therefore decided not to inform his father of the decision to leave the army. He knew Pa would only blame himself and he was at least thankful that he had died without realising the stigma that had become part of his son's daily life.

When Adam reached the outskirts of London his mind returned, as it had so often lately, to the pressing problem of finding himself gainful employment. In the seven weeks he had been out of work Adam had already had more interviews with his bank manager than with prospective employers. It was true that he had another meeting lined up with the Foreign Office, but he had been impressed by the standard of the other candidates he had encountered on the way, and was only too aware of his lack of a university qualification. However, he felt the first interview had gone well and he quickly became aware of how many ex-officers had joined the service. When he discovered that the chairman of the selection board had a Military Cross, Adam assumed he wasn't being considered for desk work.

As he swung the motorbike into Chelsea Adam once again fingered the envelope in his inside jacket pocket hoping, uncharitably, that Lawrence would not yet have returned from the bank. Not that he could complain: his old school friend had been extremely generous in offering him such a pleasant room in his spacious flat for only four pounds a week.

"You can start paying more when they make you an ambassador," Lawrence had told him.

"You're beginning to sound like Rachmann," Adam had replied as he grinned at the man he had so admired during their days at Wellington. For Lawrence – in direct contrast to Adam – everything seemed to come easily – exams, jobs, sport and women, especially women. When he had gone up to Baliol and then taken a first in PPE, no one was surprised. When Lawrence chose banking as a profession, his contemporaries could not hide their disbelief. It seemed to be the first step down on a ladder that previously had had no limits.

Adam parked his motorbike just off Ifield Road, aware that, like his mother's old Morris Minor, it would have to be sold if the Foreign Office job didn't materialise. As he strolled towards the flat a girl who passed gave him a second look: he didn't notice. He took the stairs by three's and had reached the fifth floor, and was pushing his Yale key into the lock when a voice from inside shouted, "It's on the latch."

"Damn," said Adam under his breath as he turned the handle.

"How did it go?" were Lawrence's first words as Adam entered the drawing room.

"Very well, considering," Adam replied, not quite sure what else he could be expected to say to his flatmate. Lawrence had already changed from his City clothes into a blazer and grey flannels. He was slightly shorter and stockier than Adam with a head of wiry fair hair and grey thoughtful eyes that always seemed to be enquiring.

"I admired your father so much," he continued. "He always assumed one had the same standard as he did." Adam could still remember nervously introducing Lawrence to his father one Speech Day. They had become friends immediately. But then Lawrence was not a man who dealt in rumours.

"Able to retire on the family fortune, are we?" asked Lawrence in a lighter vein.

"Only if that dubious bank you work for has found a way of converting five hundred pounds into five thousand in a matter of days."

"Can't manage it at the present time, old chum – not now Harold Wilson has announced a standstill in wages and prices."

Adam smiled as he looked across at his friend. Although taller than him now, he could still remember those days when Lawrence seemed to him like a giant.

"Late again, Scott," he would say as Adam scampered past him in the corridor. Adam had looked forward to the day when he could do everything in the same relaxed, superior style. Or was it just that Lawrence was superior? His suits always seemed to be well-pressed, his shoes always shone and he never had a hair out of place. Adam still hadn't fathomed out how he did it all so effortlessly.

Adam heard the bathroom door open. He glanced interrogatively toward Lawrence.

"It's Carolyn," whispered Lawrence. "She'll be staying the night . . . I think."

When Carolyn entered the room Adam smiled at the tall, elegant woman. Her long, blonde hair bounced on her shoulders as she walked towards them, but it was the faultless figure that most men couldn't take their eyes off. How did Lawrence manage it?

"Care to join us for a meal?" asked Lawrence, putting his arm round Carolyn's shoulder, his voice suddenly sounding a little *too* enthusiastic. "I've discovered this Italian restaurant that's just opened in the Fulham Road."

"I might join you later," said Adam, "but I still have one or two papers left over from this afternoon that I ought to check through."

"Forget the finer details of your inheritance, Adam. Why not join us and spend the entire windfall in one wild spaghetti fling?"

"Oh, have you been left lots of lovely lolly?" asked Carolyn, in a voice so shrill and high-pitched nobody would have been surprised to learn that she had recently been Deb of the Year.

"Not," said Adam, "when considered against my present overdraft."

Lawrence laughed. "Well, come along later if you still feel you can afford it." He winked at Adam – his customary sign for "Be sure you're out of the flat by the time we get back. Or at least stay in your own room and pretend to be asleep."

"Yes, do come," cooed Carolyn, sounding as if she meant it – her hazel eyes remained fixed on Adam as Lawrence guided her firmly towards the door.

Adam didn't move until he was sure he could no longer hear her penetrating little voice echoing on the staircase. Satisfied, he retreated to his bedroom and locked himself in. Adam sat down on the one comfortable chair he possessed and pulled his father's envelope out of his inside pocket. It was the heavy, expensive type of stationery 'Pa' had always used, purchasing it at Smythson of Bond Street at almost twice the price of the local W. H. Smith's. 'Captain Adam Scott, MC' was written in his father's neat copperplate hand.

Adam opened the envelope carefully and extracted the contents: a letter in his father's unmistakable hand and a smaller envelope which was clearly old as it was faded with time. Written on the old envelope in an unfamiliar hand were the words 'Colonel Gerald Scott' in faded ink of indeterminate colour. Adam placed the faded envelope on the little table by his side and, unfolding his father's letter, began to read. It was undated.

My dear Adam,

Over the years, you will have heard many explanations for my sudden departure from the Regiment. Most of them will have been farcical, and a few of them libellous, but I always considered it better for all concerned to keep my own counsel. I feel, however, that I owe you a fuller explanation, and that is what this letter will set out to do.

As you know, my last posting before I resigned my commission was at Nuremberg from February 1945 to October 1946. After four years of almost continuous action in the field, I was given the task of commanding the British section which had responsibility for those senior ranking Nazis who were awaiting trial for war crimes. Although the Americans had overall responsibility, I came to know those officers quite well and after a year or so I had even grown to tolerate some of them – Hess, Doenitz and Speer in particular – and I often wondered how the Germans would have treated us had the situation been reversed. Such views were considered disloyal at the time. 'Fraternisation' was often on the lips of men who are never given to second thoughts.

Among the senior Nazis with whom I came into daily contact was Reichsmarshal Hermann Goering, but unlike the three other officers I have previously mentioned, here was a man I detested from the first moment I came across him. I found him arrogant, overbearing and totally without shame about the barbaric role he had played in the war. And I never once found any reason to change my opinion of him. In fact, I sometimes wondered how I didn't end up on several occasions hitting him.

The night before Goering was due to be executed, he requested a private interview with me. It was a Monday, and I can still remember every detail of that encounter as if it were only yesterday. I received the request when I took over the Russian watch from Major Vladimir Kosky. In fact Kosky personally handed me the written request. As soon as I inspected the guard and dealt with the usual paperwork, I went along with the duty corporal to see the Reichsmarshal in his cell. Goering stood to attention by his small low bed and saluted as I entered the room. The sparse, grey-painted, brick cell always made me shudder.

"You asked to see me?" I said. I never could get myself to address him by his name or rank.

"Yes," he replied. "It was kind of you to come in person, Colonel. I simply wish to make the last request of a man condemned to death. Would it be possible for the corporal to leave us?"

Imagining it was something highly personal I asked the corporal to wait outside. I confess I had no idea what could be so private when the man only had hours to live but as the door closed he saluted again and then passed over the envelope you now have in your possession. As I took it, all he said was, "Would you be good enough to open this after my execution the following day." He then added, "I can only hope this will compensate for any blame that might later be placed on your shoulders." I did not understand what he was alluding to at the time and presumed some form of mental instability had overtaken him. Many of the prisoners confided in me during their last few days, and towards the end, some of them were undoubtedly on the verge of madness.

Adam stopped to consider what he would have done in the same circumstances, and decided to read on to discover if father and son would have taken the same course.

However, Goering's final words to me as I left his cell seemed hardly those of a madman. He said quite simply: "Be assured. It is a masterpiece, do not underestimate its value." Then he lit up a cigar as if he was relaxing at his club after a rather good dinner. We all had different theories as to who smuggled the cigars in for him, and equally wondered what might also have been smuggled out from time to time.

I placed the envelope in my jacket pocket and left him to join the corporal in the corridor. We then inspected the other cells to see that all the prisoners were locked up for the night. The inspection completed, I returned to my office. As I was satisfied that there were no immediate duties I settled down to make out my report. I left the envelope in the jacket pocket of my uniform with every intention of opening it immediately after Goering's execution had been carried out the following morning. I was checking over the orders of the day when the corporal rushed into my office without knocking. "It's Goering, sir, it's Goering," he said, frantically. From the panic on the man's face, I didn't need to ask any details. We both ran all the way back to the Reichsmarshal's cell.

I found Goering lying face downwards on his bunk. I turned him over to find he was already dead. In the commotion that followed I quite forgot Goering's letter. An autopsy a few days later showed that he had died from poisoning, the court came to the conclusion that the cyanide capsule that had been found in his body must have been implanted in one of his cigars.

As I had been the last to see him alone and privately, it took only a few whispers before my name was linked with his death. There was, of course, no truth in the accusation. Indeed I never doubted for one moment that the court had delivered the correct verdict and that he justly deserved to be hanged for the part he had played in the war.

So stung was I by the continual behind-the-back accusations that I might have helped Goering to an easy death by smuggling in the cigars that I felt the only honourable thing to do in the circumstances was to resign my commission immediately for fear of bringing further dishonour to the regiment. When I returned to England later that year, and finally decided to throw out my old uniform, I came across the envelope again. When I explained to your mother the details of the incident she begged me to destroy the envelope as she considered it had brought enough dishonour to our family already, and even if it did point to whom had been responsible for helping Goering to an easy death, in her opinion such knowledge could no longer do anyone any good. I agreed to comply with her wishes and although I never opened the envelope I could never get myself to destroy it remembering the last sentence Goering had uttered. And so finally I hid it among my personal papers.

However, since the imagined sins of the father are inevitably visited upon the next generation, I feel no such qualms should influence you. If there is therefore anything to be gained from the contents of this envelope I make only one request, namely that your mother should be the first to benefit from it without ever being allowed to know how such good fortune came about.

Over the years, I have watched you grow up with considerable pride and feel confident that I can leave you to make the correct decision.

If you are left with any doubts about opening the envelope yourself, destroy it without further consideration. But if you open it only to discover its purpose is to involve you in some dishonourable enterprise, be rid of it without a second thought.

May God be with you.
Your loving father,

Gerald Scott

Adam read the letter over once again realising how much trust his father had placed in him. His heart thumped in his chest as he considered how 'Pa''s life had been wasted by the murmurings and innuendoes of lesser men – the same men who had also succeeded in bringing his own career to a premature halt. When he had finished reading the missive for a third time he folded it up neatly and slipped it back into the envelope.

He then picked up the second envelope from the side table. The words 'Colonel Gerald Scott' were written in a faded Germanic script across it.

Adam removed a comb from his inside pocket and wedged it into the corner of the envelope. Slowly he began to slit it open. He hesitated for a moment before extracting two pieces of paper, both yellowed with age. One appeared to be a letter while the other was a document of some sort. The crest of the Third Reich was embossed at the head of the letterpaper above the printed name of Reichsmarshal Hermann Goering. Adam's hands began to tremble as he read the first line.

It began, *Sehr geehrter Herr Oberst Scott:*

You have just been reading an exclusive extract from Jeffrey Archer's new novel A MATTER OF HONOUR, available now in hardback from Hodder and Stoughton, and available in paperback from Coronet in 1987.